NATIVE TONGUE
AND
STRIP TEASE

Carl Hiaasen was born and raised in Florida. His other novels are *Tourist Season*, *Double Whammy*, *Skin Tight*, *Strip Tease*, *Stormy Weather*, *Lucky You* and *Sick Puppy*, which together have been translated into twenty languages. Since 1979 he has worked at the *Miami Herald* as a magazine writer, investigative reporter and metropolitan columnist.

CARL HIAASEN

NATIVE TONGUE

AND

STRIP TEASE

PAN BOOKS

Native Tongue first published 1991 by Alfred A. Knopf, Inc., New York.
First published in Great Britain 1992 by Macmillan.
First published in paperback 1992 by Pan Books.
Strip Tease first published in Great Britain 1993 by Macmillan.
First published in paperback 1994 by Pan Books.

This omnibus edition published 2003 by Pan Books
an imprint of Pan Macmillan Ltd
Pan Macmillan, 20 New Wharf Road, London N1 9RR
Basingstoke and Oxford
Associated companies throughout the world
www.panmacmillan.com

ISBN 0 330 43678 3

A CIP catalogue record for this book is available from
the British Library.

Printed and bound in Great Britain by
Mackays of Chatham plc, Chatham, Kent

NATIVE TONGUE

For my brother Rob

This is a work of fiction. The events described are imaginary.

However, the depiction of aberrant sexual behaviour by bottle-nosed dolphins is based on true cases on file with the Florida state marine laboratory in St. Petersburg.

ONE

On July 16, in the aching torpid heat of the South Florida summer, Terry Whelper stood at the Avis counter at Miami International Airport and rented a bright red Chrysler LeBaron convertible. He had originally signed up for a Dodge Colt, a sensible low-mileage compact, but his wife had told him go on, be sporty for once in your life. So Terry Whelper got the red LeBaron plus the extra collision coverage, in anticipation of Miami drivers. Into the convertible he inserted the family—his wife Gerri, his son Jason, his daughter Jennifer—and bravely set out for the turnpike.

The children, who liked to play car games, began counting all the other LeBarons on the highway. By the time the Whelpers got to Snapper Creek, the total was up to seventeen. 'And they're all rentals,' Terry muttered. He felt like a fool; every tourist in Miami was driving a red LeBaron convertible.

'But look at all this legroom,' said his wife.

From the back seat came Jennifer's voice: 'Like, what if it rains?'

'Like, we put up the top,' Terry said.

His wife scolded him for being sarcastic with their daughter. 'She's only eleven, for heaven's sake.'

1

'Sorry,' said Terry Whelper. Then louder, over his shoulder: 'Jenny, I'm sorry.'

'For what?'

Terry shook his head. 'Nothing, hon.'

It started raining near Florida City, and of course the convertible top wouldn't go up; something was stuck, or maybe Terry wasn't pushing the right button on the dash. The Whelpers sought shelter at an Amoco station, parked near the full-service pumps and waited for the cloudburst to stop. Terry was dying to tell his wife I-told-you-so, sporty my ass, but she wouldn't look up from the paperback that she was pretending to read.

Jennifer asked, 'Like, what if it rains all day and all night?'

'It won't,' said Terry, trying hard to be civil.

The shower stopped in less than an hour, and the Whelpers were off again. While the kids used beach towels to dry off the interior of the convertible, Gerri passed around cans of Pepsi-Cola and snacks from the gas station vending machine. In vain Terry fiddled with the buttons on the car radio, trying to find a station that played soft rock.

The Whelpers were halfway down Card Sound Road when a blue pickup truck passed them the other way doing at least eighty. Without warning, something flew out of the truck driver's window and landed in the back seat of the LeBaron. Terry heard Jason yell; then Jennifer started to wail.

'Pull over!' Gerri cried.

'Easy does it,' said her husband.

The convertible skidded to a halt in a spray of grass and gravel. The Whelpers scrambled from the car,

2

checked themselves for injuries and reassembled by the side of the road.

'It was two guys,' Jason declared, pointing down the road. 'White guys, too.'

'Are you sure?' asked his mother. The family had been on guard for possible trouble from blacks and Hispanics; a neighbor in Dearborn had given them the scoop on South Florida.

'They looked white to me,' Jason said of the assailants.

Terry Whelper frowned. 'I don't care if they were purple. Just tell me, what did they throw?'

Jennifer stopped crying long enough to say: 'I dunno, but it's alive.'

Terry said, 'For Christ's sake.' He walked over to the convertible and leaned inside for a look. 'I don't see anything.'

Jennifer cried even harder, a grating subhuman bray. 'You ... don't ... believe ... me!' she said, sobbing emphatically with each word.

'Of course we believe you,' said her mother.

'I saw it, too,' said Jason, who rarely took his sister's side on anything. 'Try down on the floor, Dad.'

Terry Whelper got into the back of the LeBaron, squeezed down to his knees and peered beneath the seat. The children heard him say, 'Holy shit,' then he leapt out of the car.

'What is it?' asked his wife.

'It's a rat,' said Terry Whelper. 'The ugliest goddamn rat I ever saw.'

'They threw a rat in our car?'

'Apparently.'

Jason said, 'Too bad we didn't bring Grandpa's gun.'

Gerri Whelper looked shaken and confused. 'Why would they throw a rat in our car? Is it alive?'

'Very much so,' Terry reported. 'It's eating from a bag of Raisinets.'

'Those are mine!' Jennifer cried.

The Whelpers stood there discussing the situation for fifteen minutes before a highway patrol car pulled up, and a young state trooper asked what was the matter. He listened sympathetically to the story about the rat in the rented LeBaron.

'You want me to call the Avis people?' he asked. 'Maybe they'll send another car.'

'Actually, we're on a pretty tight schedule,' explained Gerri Whelper. 'We've got reservations at a motor lodge in Key Largo. They said we had to be there by five or else we lose the rooms.'

Jennifer, who had almost stopped crying, said: 'I don't care about the motel, I want a different car.'

Terry Whelper said to the trooper, 'If you could just help me get rid of it.'

'The rat?'

'It's a big one,' Terry said.

'Well, I can probably shoot it.'

'Could you?' Gerri said. 'Please?'

The trooper said, 'Technically, it's against regulations. But since you're from out of town . . .'

He stepped out of the patrol car and unsnapped the holster strap on his .357.

'Wow!' said Jason.

Jennifer put her arms around her mother's waist. Terry Whelper manfully directed his brood to move safely out of the line of fire. The state trooper

4

approached the LeBaron with the calm air of a seasoned lawman.

'He's under the seat,' Terry advised.

'Yeah, I see him.'

The trooper fired three times. Then he holstered the gun, reached into the convertible and picked up what remained of the creature by what remained of its tail. He tossed the misshapen brown lump into some holly bushes.

'Thank you so much,' said Gerri Whelper.

'You say it was a blue pickup. You didn't happen to see the license plate?'

'No,' said Terry. He was wondering what to tell Avis about the bullet holes in the floorboard. When the kids climbed back in the rental car, their mother said, 'Don't touch any of those raisins! We'll get more candy when we get to the Amazing Kingdom.'

'Good, I want a Petey Possum Popsicle,' Jennifer said, nearly recovered from the trauma. Jason asked if he could keep one of the empty shell casings out of the state trooper's revolver, and the trooper said sure.

Terry Whelper grimly contemplated the upcoming journey in the red, rat-befouled LeBaron. He felt fog-headed and emotionally drained. To think, just that morning he'd been safe and sound in his bed back in Michigan.

'Don't forget to buckle up,' said the trooper, holding the door open.

Terry said, 'This ever happen before?'

'What do you mean?'

'This rat business.'

'I'm sure it has. We don't hear about everything.'

The trooper smiled as he closed Terry Whelper's door. 'Now, you all have a nice vacation.'

In the blue pickup truck, still heading north, Danny Pogue said, 'That was the damnedest thing I ever saw.'

Bud Schwartz, who was driving, said, 'Yeah, that was some shot. If I do say so.'

'There was kids in that car.'

'It was just a mouse, for Chrissakes.'

'It wasn't a mouse, it was a rat.' Danny Pogue poked his partner in the shoulder. 'What if those was your kids? You like it, somebody throws a fucking rat in their laps?'

Bud Schwartz glanced at the place on his shoulder where Danny Pogue had touched him. Then he looked back at the highway. His bare bony arms got rigid on the steering wheel. 'I wasn't exactly aiming for the kids.'

'Were too.'

After a few strained moments, Bud Schwartz said, 'You don't see that many convertibles anymore.'

'So when you finally see one, you throw a rat in it? Is that the deal?' Danny Pogue picked at a pair of ripe pimples on the peak of his Adam's apple.

'Let's just drop it,' said Bud Schwartz.

But Danny Pogue remained agitated all the way to Florida City. He told Bud Schwartz to let him off in front of the Long John Silver's.

'No way,' said Bud Schwartz.

'Then I'll jump outta the goddamn truck.'

Danny Pogue would damn sure try it, too, Bud thought. Jump out of the damn truck purely on principles.

Bud Schwartz said, 'Hey, you don't want to do that. We've gotta go get your money.'

'I'll find my own ride.'

'It'll look hinky, we don't show up together.'

Danny Pogue said, 'I'm not riding nowhere with a guy that throws rats on little kids. Understand?'

'What if I said I was sorry,' Bud Schwartz said. 'I'm sorry, all right? It was a shitty thing to do. I feel terrible, Danny, honest to God. I feel like a shit.'

Danny Pogue gave him a sideways look.

'I mean it,' said Bud Schwartz. 'You got me feeling so bad I got half a mind to cry. Swear to God, look here—my eyes are all watered up. For a second I was thinking of Bud, Jr., about what I'd do, some asshole throwed a rat or any other damn animal at my boy. Probably kill him, that's what I'd do.'

As he spun through this routine, Bud Schwartz was thinking: The things I do to keep him steady.

And it seemed to work. In no time Danny Pogue said, 'It's all right, Bud. Least nobody got hurt.'

'That's true.'

'But don't scare no more little kids, understand?'

Bud Schwartz said, 'I won't, Danny. That's a promise.'

Ten minutes later, stopped at a traffic light in Cutler Ridge, Danny Pogue turned in the passenger seat and said, 'Hey, it just hit me.'

He was grinning so wide that you could count all the spaces where teeth used to be.

'What?' said Bud Schwartz.

'I remember you told me that Bud Schwartz wasn't your real name. You said your real name was Mickey Reilly.'

'Mike. Mike Reilly,' said Bud Schwartz, thinking, Here we go.

'Okay, then how could you have a kid named Bud, Jr.?'

'Well—'

'If your name's Mike.'

'Simple. I changed the boy's name when I changed mine.'

Danny Pogue looked skeptical. Bud Schwartz said, 'A boy oughta have the same name as his daddy, don't you agree?'

'So his real name was—'

'Mike, Jr. Now it's Bud, Jr.'

'You say so,' said Danny Pogue, grinning again, a jack-o'-lantern with volcanic acne.

'What, you don't believe me?'

'No, I don't believe you,' said Danny Pogue, 'but it was a damn good story. Whatever your fucking name is.'

'Bud is just fine. Bud Schwartz. And let's not fight no more, we're gonna be rich.'

Danny Pogue got two beers out of the Styrofoam cooler in the back of the cab. He popped one of the cans for his partner and handed it to him. 'I still can't believe they're payin' us ten grand apiece to steal a boxful of rats.'

'This is Miami,' said Bud Schwartz. 'Maybe they're voodoo rats. Or maybe they're fulla dope. I heard where they smuggle coke in French rubbers, so why not rats.'

Danny Pogue lifted the box from behind the front seat and placed it carefully on his lap. He leaned down and put his ear to the lid. 'Wonder how many's in there,' he said.

8

Bud Schwartz shrugged. 'Didn't ask.'

The den box was eighteen inches deep, and twice the size of a briefcase. It was made of plywood, painted dark green, with small hinged doors on each end. Air holes had been drilled through the side panels; the holes were no bigger than a dime, but somehow one of the animals had managed to squeeze out. Then it had scaled the front seat and perched on Danny Pogue's headrest, where it had balanced on its hind legs and wiggled its velvety snout in the air. Laughing, Bud Schwartz had deftly snatched it by the tail and dangled it in his partner's face. Over Danny Pogue's objections, Bud Schwartz had toyed with the rodent for six or seven miles, until he'd spotted the red convertible coming the other way down the road. Then he had said, 'Watch this,' and had tossed the animal out the window, into the passing car.

Now Danny Pogue lifted the green box off his lap and said, 'Sure don't weigh much.'

Bud Schwartz chuckled. 'You want a turn, is that it? Well, go ahead then, grab one.'

'But I don't wanna get bit.'

'You got to do it real fast, way I did. Hurry now, here comes one of them Winnebagos. I'll slow down when we go by.'

Danny Pogue said, 'The top of this box ain't even locked.'

'So what're you waiting for?' said his partner. 'Pop goes the weasel.'

After the rat attack, the Whelper family rode in edgy silence until they arrived at the Amazing Kingdom of

Thrills. They parked the red LeBaron in the Mr. Bump-a-Rump lot, Section Jellybean, and took the tram to the main gate. There they came upon a chaotic scene: police cars, an ambulance, TV trucks, news photographers. The ticket turnstiles were all blocked.

'Swell,' said Terry Whelper. 'Beautiful.'

'Maybe they're filming a movie,' his wife suggested. 'Maybe it's not real.'

But it was. The center of attention was a supremely tanned young man in a blue oxford shirt with a dark red club tie, loosened fashionably at the throat. Once all the TV lights were on, the man started to read from a typed sheet of paper. He said he was a spokesperson for the company.

'This is a message for all our friends and visitors to the Amazing Kingdom of Thrills,' the man began. 'We deeply regret the incident that disturbed today's Summerfest celebration. We are proud of our security arrangements here at the park, and proud of our safety record. Up until today, there had been—and I say this unequivocally—no serious crimes committed within our friendly gates.'

In the swell of the crowd, Terry Whelper felt his wife's chin digging into his shoulder blade. 'What do you suppose he's talking about?' she said.

The man in the oxford shirt continued: 'We believe there was no way to anticipate, much less prevent, what happened this afternoon in the Rare Animal Pavilion.'

Terry Whelper said, 'This oughta be good.' A large woman wearing a damp cotton blouse and a Nikkormat around her neck turned and shot him a dirty look.

The man at the TV microphones was saying, 'At approximately 2.15 p.m., two men entered the compound and attacked one of the wildlife exhibits with a sledgehammer, breaking the glass. One of our park employees courageously tried to stop the intruders, but was overpowered and beaten. The two men then grabbed a box of specimens from the exhibit arena and ran. In the confusion, the suspects managed to escape from the park, apparently by mingling with ordinary tourists aboard the Jungle Jerry Amazon Boat Cruise.'

Jason Whelper said, 'Specimens? What kinda specimens?'

Jennifer announced, 'I don't want to go on the Jungle Jerry anymore.'

Terry Whelper told the children to be quiet and listen. The tanned man in the blue shirt was saying that the park employee who had so bravely tried to stop the crime was being rushed to the hospital for X-rays.

'Hey, look!' said Jason, pointing.

Somebody in an oversized polyester animal outfit was being loaded into the ambulance.

'That's Robbie Raccoon!' cried Jennifer Whelper. 'He must be the one who got hurt.'

All around them in the crowd, other tourist children began to whimper and sniffle at the sight of Robbie Raccoon on the stretcher. Jason swore he saw some blood on Robbie Raccoon's nose.

'No, he's going to be fine,' said Gerri Whelper. 'See there, he's waving at us!'

And, indeed, whoever was inside the Robbie Raccoon costume managed a weak salute to the crowd before the ambulance doors swung closed.

'It's gotta be ninety-eight degrees out here,' marveled Terry Whelper. 'You'd think they'd get the poor guy out of that raccoon getup.'

11

Terry Whelper's wife whispered urgently to the nape of his neck, 'Not in front of Jennifer. She thinks he's real.'

'Oh, you're kidding,' Terry said.

Under the TV lights, the tan young spokesperson finally was revealing what had been stolen in the daring robbery.

'As many of you know,' he said, 'the Amazing Kingdom of Thrills is home to several endangered varieties of wildlife. Unfortunately, the animals that were stolen this afternoon are among the rarest, and most treasured, in our live-animal collection. In fact, they were believed to be the last two surviving specimens of the blue-tongued mango vole.' Here the handsome spokesman paused dramatically. Then: 'The animals were being kept here in a specially climatized habitat, in the hope that they might breed and keep the species alive. Tragically, that dream came to an end this afternoon.'

'Mango voles!' exclaimed Jason Whelper. 'Dad, did you hear? Maybe that's what landed in our car. Maybe those guys in the pickup truck were the crooks!'

Terry Whelper took his son by the arm and led him back toward the tram, away from the tourist crowd. Gerri and Jennifer followed steadfastly.

Gerri whispered to her husband: 'What do you think? Maybe Jason is right.'

'I don't know what to think. You were the one who wanted to come to Florida.'

Jason cut in: 'Dad, there was only two of those mangos left in the whole-wide world. And we shot one!'

'No, we didn't. The policeman did.'

'But we told him to!'

Terry Whelper said, 'Be quiet, son. We didn't know.'

'Your father's right,' added Gerri. 'How were we to know?'

Jennifer hugged her mother fiercely around the waist. 'I'm so scared—can we drive to Epcot instead?'

'Excellent idea,' said Terry Whelper. Like a cavalry commander, he raised his right arm and cocked two fingers toward the parking lot. 'Everybody back to the car.'

TWO

As soon as Charles Chelsea got back to the Publicity Department, he took a poll of the secretaries. 'How was I?' he asked. 'How'd I do? What about the necktie?'

The secretaries told Chelsea that he looked terrific on television, that loosening the necktie was a nifty touch, that overall it was quite a solid performance. Chelsea asked if Mr. Kingsbury had called, but the secretaries said he hadn't.

'Wonder why not,' said Chelsea.

'He's playing golf up at Ocean Reef.'

'Yeah, but he's got a cellular. He could've called.' Chelsea told one of the secretaries to get Joe Winder, and then went into his private office and closed the door.

Ten minutes later, when Joe Winder got there, Charles Chelsea was watching himself on the VCR, reliving the press conference.

'Whadja think?' he asked, motioning at the television screen in the cabinet.

'I missed it,' said Joe Winder.

'You missed it? It was your bloody speech—how'd you miss it?'

'I heard you were dynamite.'

Charles Chelsea broke into a grin. 'Yeah? Who said?'

14

'Everybody,' lied Joe Winder. 'They said you're another Mario Cuomo.'

'Well, your speech had something to do with it.'

It wasn't a speech, Winder thought; it was a *statement*. Forty lines, big deal.

'It was a great speech, Joe,' Chelsea went on, 'except for one part. *Specially climatized habitat*. That's a mouthful. Maybe we should've tried something else.' With pursed lips he repeated the culprit phrase: 'Climatized habitat—when I was trying to say it, I accidentally spit on that girl from Channel 10. The cute one. Next time be more careful, okay? Don't sneak in any zingers without me knowing.'

Joe Winder said, 'I was in a hurry.' The backs of his eyeballs were starting to throb. Sinus headache: Chelsea always gave him one. But Winder had to admit, the guy looked like a million bucks in an oxford shirt. He looked like a vice president in charge of public relations, which he was.

Chelsea was saying, 'I don't even know what it means, climatized habitat.'

'That's the beauty of it,' Winder said.

'Now, now.' Chelsea wagged a well-tanned finger. 'None of that, Joey. There's no place for cynics here at the Amazing Kingdom. You know what Kingsbury says.'

'Yeah. We're all little kids.' Winder kneaded his skull with both hands, trying to squeeze out the pain.

'Children,' Charles Chelsea said. He turned off the VCR and spun his chair to face Joe Winder. 'The moment we walk through that gate, we're all children. We see the world through children's eyes; we cry children's tears, we laugh children's laughter. We're all innocent again, Joe, and where there's innocence there can't be cynicism. Not here in the Amazing Kingdom.'

Joe Winder said, 'You're giving me a fucking headache. I hope you're happy.'

Charles Chelsea's blue eyes narrowed and darkened. 'Look, we hired you because you're good and you're fast. But this isn't a big-city newsroom, you can't use that type of coarse language. Children don't talk like that, Joe. That's gutter language.'

'Sorry,' said Winder, concealing his amusement. Gutter language, that was a good one.

'When's the last time you heard a child say that word?'

'Which word, Charlie?'

'You know. The 'F' word.'

'I've heard children say it. Plenty of times.'

'Not here, you haven't.' Charles Chelsea sat up straight, trying to radiate authority. 'This is a major event for us, Joey. We've had a robbery on the premises. Felons invaded the theme park. Somebody could've been hurt.'

'Rat-nappers,' Winder remarked. 'Not exactly Ted Bundy.'

'Hey,' Chelsea said, tapping a lacquered fingernail on the desk. 'Hey, this is serious. Mr. X is watching very closely to see how we do. All of us, Joe, all of us in Publicity are on red alert until this thing blows over. We mishandle it, and it blows up into a story about crime at the Amazing Kingdom. If we can spin it around, it's a story about a crime against Nature. Nature with a capital 'N.' The annihilation of an entire species. Where's your notebook?'

'Downstairs, on my desk.'

'Listen, you're my ace in the hole. Whatever gets dumped in my lap gets dumped in yours.'

Joe Winder's sinuses hurt so much he thought his eyeballs must be leaking from the inside. He didn't want to be Chelsea's ace in the hole.

Chelsea said, 'And, Joe, while we're at it, what'd I tell you about the hair? No braids.'

'But it's all the rage,' Winder said.

'Get it cut before Kingsbury sees you. Please, Joe, you look like a Navajo nightmare.'

'Nice talk, Charlie.'

'Sit down,' said Chelsea, 'and put on your writing cap.'

'I'd love to look as spiffy as you, but you bought up all the oxford shirts in Miami. Either that or you wear the same one every day.'

Chelsea wasn't listening. 'Before we begin, there's some stuff you need to know.'

'Like what?'

'Like their names.'

'Whose names?'

'The voles,' Charles Chelsea said. 'Vance and Violet—two helpless, adorable, fuzzy little furballs. Mated for life. The last of their species, Joey.'

With a straight face, Winder repeated the names of the missing creatures. 'Vance and Violet Vole. That's lovely.' He glanced at his wristwatch, and saw that it was half past five. 'Charlie,' he said, 'you don't happen to have any Darvons?'

Chelsea said, 'I wish you were writing this stuff down.'

'What the hell for?'

'For the story. The story of how Francis X. Kingsbury

tried everything in his power to save the blue-tongued mango voles from extinction.'

'Only to be thwarted by robbers?'

'You got it,' said Charles Chelsea. 'Stay late if necessary and take a comp day next week—I need a thousand words by tomorrow morning. I promised Corporate a press kit.' He stood up and waited for Joe Winder to do the same. 'Get with Koocher for more background on the missing animals. He's got reams of pictures, too, in case you need inspiration. By the way, did you ever get to see them?'

Winder felt oddly detached. 'The voles? No, not in person,' he said. 'I wasn't even aware they had actual names.'

'They do now.'

At the door, Charles Chelsea winked and shook Joe Winder's hand. 'You know, Joe, some people in the organization weren't too thrilled when we brought you aboard. I mean, after what happened up at Disney.'

Winder nodded politely. Chelsea's hand felt moist and lifeless, like a slab of cold grouper.

'But, by God, I knew you'd be fine. That speech today was masterful, Joey, a classic.'

'A classic.'

'I need you on this one. The other kids are fine, they can turn a phrase. But they're right out of school, most of them, and they're not ready for something so big. For this I need somebody with scars. Combat experience.'

With effort, Joe Winder said, 'Guess I'm your man.'

Charles Chelsea chucked him on the arm and opened the door.

'What about a reward?' Winder asked. 'In the press release, should I say we're offering a reward?'

Thinking about it, Chelsea nearly rubbed the tan off his chin. 'I guess it couldn't hurt,' he said finally. 'What do you think?'

'For two rats? Ten grand is good.'

'Voles, Joe. Don't ever say rats. And five grand is plenty.'

Winder shrugged. 'The park netted forty-two million dollars last year. I know a few reporters who'd be happy to remind us.'

'All right, go for ten,' said Charles Chelsea. 'But don't overplay it. Otherwise every geek in Miami is going to show up at the gate with shoe boxes full of God knows what.'

The thought of it made Joe Winder smile for the first time all day.

One of the few things Winder liked about his new job was the golf cart he got to drive around the Amazing Kingdom of Thrills. It was a souped-up Cushman with an extra set of twelve-volts, and headlights scavenged off a real Jeep. It was the closest thing to a company car that Joe Winder had ever had, and sometimes (especially on that long downhill stretch between Magic Mansion and the Wet Willy) he could stomp on the tiny accelerator and forget what exactly he did for a living.

At night Joe Winder tried to drive more carefully, because it was harder to watch out for the tourists. The tourists at the Amazing Kingdom seldom paid attention to where they were going; they wandered and weaved, peered and pointed. And who could blame them? There were so many colorful and entertaining distractions. Before Charles Chelsea had given Joe Winder the keys to the Cushman, he had warned him to be wary when driving near the tourists. 'Whatever you do, don't hit one,' Chelsea had said. 'If you're going to crash, aim for a building,' he had advised, 'or even a park employee. Anything but a paying customer.'

So Joe Winder drove with extra caution in the golf cart at night. He arrived at the Rare Animal Pavilion shortly after eight, and parked in the back. Dr. Will Koocher, the vole man, was waiting inside with hand-outs and glossy photographs. Winder sat on a lab stool and skimmed the material.

Koocher said, 'We kept the information fairly general. They tell me the pictures usually go over big.'

As Winder studied the photographs, he said, 'Cute little buggers.'

'They're just rodents,' the doctor noted, without malice.

'You don't understand,' Winder said, 'Cuteness is vital for a story like this.' He explained how newspapers and television stations got much more excited about animal stories when the animal came across as cuddly and lovable. 'I'm not saying it's good or bad, but that's the way it is.'

Will Koocher nodded. 'Like with the manatees—everybody wants to save the manatees, but nobody gives a hoot about the poor crocodiles.'

'Because they're not particularly cute,' Winder said. 'Who wants to hug a reptile?'

'I see your point.' Will Koocher was a gaunt young man with the longest neck that Joe Winder had ever seen. He seemed painfully earnest and shy, and Winder liked him immediately.

'I'll tell you what I can,' Koocher said, 'but I've only been here a month.'

Like everything else at the Amazing Kingdom, the Vole Project had begun as a scheme to compete with Walt Disney World. Years earlier, Disney had tried to save the dusky seaside sparrow, a small marsh bird whose habitat was being wiped out by overdevelopment along Florida's coastline. With much fanfare, Disney had unveiled a captive-breeding program for the last two surviving specimens of the dusky. Unfortunately, the last two surviving specimens were both males, and even the wizards of Disney could not induce the scientific miracle of homosexual procreation. Eventually the sparrow fell to extinction, but the Disney organization won gobs of fawning publicity for its conservation efforts.

Not to be outdone (although he invariably was), Francis X. Kingsbury had selected another endangered species and commanded that his staff save it, ASAP. And so the Vole Project was born.

Koocher had gotten the phone call while finishing his thesis at Cornell. 'I'd published two field studies on the genus *Microtus*, so I suppose that's where they got my name. Anyway, this guy Chelsea calls and asks if I'd heard of *Microtus mango*, and I said no, all my work was on the northern species. He sent me a scientific paper that had been published, and offered me a job. Forty grand a year.'

'That's good money right out of school.'

'Tell me about it. I burned up the interstate getting down here.'

'And that's when you met Violet and Vance.'

'Who's that?'

'The voles,' Winder said. 'They've got names now.'

'Really?' Will Koocher looked doubtful. 'I always called them Male One and Female One.'

'Not anymore. Kingsbury's got big plans, PR-wise. The little mango cuties are going to be famous—don't be surprised if the networks show up tomorrow.'

'Is that so,' Koocher said, with not the wildest enthusiasm. Winder sensed that the scientist disapproved of anthropomorphizing rodents, so he decided to lay off the Vance-and-Violet routine. Instead he asked about the tongue.

'Well, it really is blue,' Koocher said stiffly. 'Remarkably blue.'

'Could I say indigo?' Joe Winder was taking notes.

'Yeah,' said Koocher, 'that's about right.' He started to say something more, but caught himself.

Joe Winder asked: 'So what killed off the rest of them? Was it disease?'

'No, same old story. The encroachment of mankind.' Koocher unfolded a map that illustrated how the mango vole had once ranged from the Middle Keys up to Palm Beach. As the coastline surrendered to hotels, subdivisions and condominiums, the voles' territory shrank. 'They tell me the last known colony was here, on North Key Largo. One of Kingsbury's foremen found it in 1988, but so did a hungry barn owl. They were lucky to save the two that they did.'

'And they mated for life?' said Winder.

Koocher seemed amused. 'Who told you that?'

'Chelsea.'

'That figures. Voles don't mate for life. They mate for fun, and they mate with just about anything that resembles another vole.'

Winder said, 'Then here's another dumb question: Why were there only two in our exhibit? They'd been together, what, a year? So where're all the bouncing baby voles?'

Edgily, Koocher said, 'That's been our biggest disappointment.'

'I did some reading up on it,' Winder said. 'With your typical *Microtus*, the female gives birth every two months. Each litter's got eight or nine babies—at that rate, you could replenish the whole species in a year.'

Will Koocher shifted uncomfortably. 'Female One was not receptive,' he said. 'Do you understand what that means?'

'Do I ever.'

'This was an extreme case. The female nearly killed the male on several occasions. We had to hire a Wackenhut to watch the cage.'

'A guard?' said Joe Winder.

'To make sure she didn't hurt him.'

Winder swallowed a laugh. Apparently, Koocher saw no humor in the story. He said, 'I felt sorry for the little guy. The female was much larger, and extremely hostile. Every time the male would attempt to mount her, she would attack.'

Joe Winder put his notebook away. He'd think of a way to write around the reproduction question.

Koocher said: 'The female vole wasn't quite right.'

'In what way?'

But Koocher was staring past him. Winder turned and saw Charles Chelsea on the other side of the glass door. Chelsea gave a chipper, three-fingered salute and disappeared.

The doctor said, 'Now's not a terrific time to get into all this. Can we talk later?'

'You bet. I'll be in the publicity office.'

'No, not here. Can I call you at home in a day or two?'

Winder said sure. 'But I've got to write the press release tonight. If there's something I ought to know, please tell me before I make an ass of myself.'

Koocher stood up and smoothed the breast of his lab coat. 'That business about the networks coming—were you serious?'

'Cute sells,' Winder said. 'You take an offbeat animal story on a slow news day, we're talking front page.'

'Christ.' Koocher sighed.

'Hey, I'm sorry,' Winder said. He hadn't meant to come off as such a coldhearted prick. 'I know what these little critters meant to you.'

Will Koocher smiled ruefully. He folded the habitat map and put it away. He looked tired and sad, and Winder felt bad for him. 'It's all right,' the young scientist said. 'They were doomed, no matter what.'

'We're all doomed,' said Joe Winder, 'if you really think about it.' Which he tried not to.

Bud Schwartz parked the pickup truck under an immense ficus tree. He told Danny Pogue not to open the doors right away, because of all the mosquitoes. The insects had descended in a sibilant cloud, bouncing off the windows and the hood and the headlights.

'I bet we don't have no bug spray,' said Danny Pogue.

Bud Schwartz pointed at the house. 'On the count of three, make a run for it.'

Danny Pogue remarked that the old place was dark. 'She saving on the electricity, or what? I bet she's not even home. I bet she was hoping we got caught, so she wouldn't have to pay us.'

'You got no faith,' said Bud Schwartz. 'You're the most negative fucking person I ever met. That's why your skin's broke out all the time—all those negative thoughts is like a poison in your bloodstream.'

'Wait a minute, now. Everybody gets pimples.'

Bud Schwartz said, 'You're thirty-one years old. Tell me that's normal.'

'Do we got bug spray or not?'

'No.' Bud Schwartz unlocked his door. 'Now let's go—one, two, three!'

They burst out of the pickup and bolted for the house, flailing at mosquitoes as they ran. When they got inside the screened porch, the two men took turns swatting the insects off each other. A light came on, and Molly McNamara poked out of the door. Her white hair was up in curlers, her cheeks were slathered in oily yellow cream and her broad, pointy-shouldered frame was draped in a blue terry-cloth bathrobe.

'Get inside,' she said to the two men.

Immediately Bud Schwartz noticed how grim the woman looked. The curlers, cream and bathrobe didn't help.

The house was all mustiness and shadows, made darker and damper by the ubiquitous wood paneling. The living room smelled of jasmine, or some other old-woman scent. It reminded Bud Schwartz of his grandmother's sewing room.

Molly McNamara sat down in a rocker. Bud

Schwartz and Danny Pogue just stood there like the hired help they were.

'Where are they?' Molly demanded. 'Where's the box?'

Danny Pogue looked at Bud Schwartz, who said, 'They got away.'

Molly folded her hands across her lap. She said, 'You're lying to me.'

'No, ma'am.'

'Then tell me what happened.'

Before Bud Schwartz could stop him, Danny Pogue said, 'There was holes in the box. That's how they got out.'

Molly McNamara's right hand slipped beneath her bathrobe and came out holding a small black pistol. Without saying a word she shot Danny Pogue twice in the left foot. He fell down, screaming, on the smooth pine floor. Bud Schwartz couldn't believe it; he tried to speak, but there was no air in his lungs.

'You boys are lying,' Molly said. She got up from the rocker and left the room. She came back with a towel, chipped ice, bandages and a roll of medical adhesive tape. She told Bud Schwartz to patch up his partner before the blood got all over everything. Bud Schwartz knelt on the floor next to Danny Pogue and tried to calm him. Molly sat down and started rocking.

'The towel is for his mouth,' she said, 'so I don't have to listen to all that yammering.'

And it was true, Danny Pogue's wailing was unbearable, even allowing for the pain. It reminded Bud Schwartz of the way his first wife had sounded during the thrashings of childbirth.

Molly said, 'It's been all over the news, so at least I

know that you went ahead and did it. I suppose I'm obliged to pay up.'

Bud Schwartz was greatly relieved; she wouldn't pay somebody she was about to kill. The thought of being murdered by a seventy-year-old woman in pink curlers was harrowing on many levels.

'Tell me if I'm wrong,' Molly said. 'Curiosity got the best of you, right? You opened the box, the animals escaped.'

'That's about the size of it,' said Bud Schwartz, wrapping a bandage around Danny Pogue's foot. He had removed the sneaker and the sock, and examined the wounds. Miraculously (or maybe by design) both bullets had missed the bones, so Danny Pogue was able to wiggle all his toes. When he stopped whimpering, Bud Schwartz removed the towel from his mouth.

'So you think they're still alive,' Molly said.

'Why not? Who'd be mean enough to hurt 'em?'

'This is important,' said Molly. The pistol lay loose on her lap, looking as harmless as a macramé.

Danny Pogue said, 'We didn't kill them things, I swear to God. They just scooted out of the damn truck.'

'They're awful fast,' added Bud Schwartz.

'Oh, please,' said Molly McNamara, shaking her head. Even Danny Pogue picked up on the sarcasm.

'We didn't know there was only two,' he said. 'We thought there must be a whole bunch in a box that size. That's how come we wasn't so worried when they got away—see, we thought there was more.'

Molly started rocking a little faster. The rocking chair didn't squeak a bit on the varnished pine. She said, 'I'm very disappointed in the both of you.'

Bud Schwartz helped his partner limp to an ottoman.

All he wanted was to get the money and get the hell out of this spooky old house, away from this crazy witch.

'Here's the really bad news,' said Molly McNamara. 'It's your truck—only about a thousand people saw you drive away. Now, I don't know if they got the license tag, but they sure as hell got a good description. It's all over the TV.'

'Shit,' said Bud Schwartz.

'So you're going to have to keep a low profile for a while.'

Still breathing heavily, Danny Pogue said, 'What's that mean?'

Molly stopped rocking and sat forward. 'For starters, say goodbye to the pickup truck. Also, you can forget about going home. If the police got your tag, they'll be waiting.'

'I'll take my chances,' said Bud Schwartz.

'No, you won't,' said Molly. 'I'll give you a thousand dollars each. You'll get the rest in two weeks, if things die down. Meanwhile, I've arranged a place for you boys to stay.'

'Here?' asked Danny Pogue in a fretful, pain-racked voice.

'No, not here,' Molly said. 'Not on your life.'

She stood up from the rocker. The pistol disappeared again into a fuzzy pocket of the blue robe. 'Your foot's going to be fine,' she announced to Danny Pogue. 'I hope I made my point.'

The bafflement on the two men's faces suggested otherwise.

Molly McNamara said, 'I chose you for a reason.'

'Come on,' said Bud Schwartz, 'we're just burglars.'

'And don't you ever forget it,' Molly said.

Danny Pogue couldn't believe she was talking to them this way. He couldn't believe he was being terrorized by an old lady in a rocking chair.

'There's something else you should know,' said Molly McNamara. 'There are others.'

Momentarily Bud Schwartz's mind had stuck on that thousand dollars she'd mentioned. He had been thinking: Screw the other nine, just grab the grand and get lost. Now she was saying something about others— what others?

'Anything happens to me,' Molly said, 'there's others that know who you are. Where you live. Where you hang out. Everything.'

'I don't get it,' muttered Danny Pogue.

'Burglars get shot sometimes,' Molly McNamara said. 'Nobody says boo about it, either. Nobody gets arrested or investigated or anything else. In this country, you kill a burglar and the Kiwanis gives you a plaque. That's the point I was trying to make.'

Danny Pogue turned to Bud Schwartz, who was staring down at his partner's swollen foot and wondering if it was too late to make a run for it. Finally he said, 'Lady, we're very sorry about your animals.'

'They're not my animals,' said Molly, 'any more than you are.'

THREE

At half past ten Joe Winder went down to The Catacombs, the underground network of service roads that ran beneath the Amazing Kingdom of Thrills. It was along these winding cart paths, discreetly out of view from visitors, that the food, merchandise, money and garbage were moved throughout the sprawling amusement park. It was also along these secret subterranean passageways that the kiddie characters traveled, popping up suddenly at strategic locations throughout the Amazing Kingdom and imploring tourists to snap their picture. No customers ('guests' was the designated term) ever were allowed to venture into The Catacombs, lest they catch a glimpse of something that might tarnish their image of the Amazing Kingdom—a dog rooting through a dumpster, for example. Or one of Uncle Ely's Elves smoking a joint.

Which is what Joe Winder saw when he got to the bottom of the stairs.

'I'm looking for Robbie Raccoon,' he said to the elf, who wasn't particularly jolly or gnomelike.

The elf belched blue smoke and asked which Robbie Raccoon he was looking for, since there were three.

'The one who was on duty this afternoon,' Winder said. 'The one who fought with the rat robbers.'

The big elf pointed with the smoldering end of the joint. 'Okay, there's a locker room on the west side. Just follow the orange signs.' He took another drag. 'I'd offer you a hit, but I got this nasty chest virus. Hate to pass it along.'

'Sure,' said Joe Winder. 'No problem.'

The lockers were at the end of a damp concrete tunnel that smelled of stale laundry and ammonia. Robbie Raccoon was straddling the bench, trying to unzip his head. Winder introduced himself, and explained that he was from the Publicity Department.

'I'm writing a press release about what happened earlier today,' he said. 'A few quick questions is all.'

'Fire away,' said Robbie Raccoon. The words came out muffled, from a small opening in the neck of the costume.

Winder said, 'I can barely hear you.'

With a grunt Robbie Raccoon removed his head, which was as large as a beach ball. Joe Winder was startled by what he saw beneath it: long shimmering blond hair, green eyes and mascara. Robbie Raccoon was a woman.

She said, 'If you're going to make a joke, get it over with.'

'No, I wasn't.'

'Don't think this is my life ambition or anything.'

'Of course not,' said Joe Winder.

The woman said her name was Carrie Lanier. 'And I got my SAG card,' she said, still somewhat defensive. 'That's the only reason I took this stupid job. I'm going to be an actress.'

Mindlessly Winder said, 'You've got to start somewhere.'

'Darn right.'

He waited for Carrie Lanier to remove the rest of the raccoon outfit, but she didn't. He took out his notebook and asked her to describe what had happened at the Rare Animal Pavilion.

Carrie shrugged in an exaggerated way, as if she were still in character. 'It was two men, we're talking white trash. One of them has a sledgehammer, and they're both walking real fast. I start to follow, don't ask me why—I just had a hunch. All of a sudden the one with the hammer smashes out the glass in one of the exhibits.'

'And you tried to stop him?'

'Yeah, I jumped the guy. Climbed on his back. He turned around and clobbered me pretty solid. Thank God for this.' Carrie knocked on the crown of the raccoon head, which was propped face-up on the bench. Her fist made a sharp hollow sound. 'Chicken wire, plaster and Kevlar,' she explained. 'They say it's bulletproof.'

Joe Winder wrote this down, even though Charles Chelsea would never let him use it in the press release. At the Amazing Kingdom, each publicity announcement was carefully purged of all intriguing details. Winder was having a tough time kicking the habit of taking good notes.

Carrie Lanier said, 'He knocked me down pretty hard, but that's about it. There was a tour group from Taiwan, Korea, someplace like that. They helped me off the ground, but by then the two dirtbags were long gone. I could've done without the ambulance ride, but Risk Management said I had to.'

'Can I say you suffered a slight head injury?' Joe Winder asked, pen poised.

'No,' said Carrie Lanier. 'As soon as the X-rays came out negative, they hauled me back to work. I'm fine.'

That wouldn't go over well with Charles Chelsea; the vole story was infinitely more dramatic if a park employee had been wounded in the rescue attempt.

'Not even a headache?' Winder persisted.

'Yeah, I've got a headache,' Carrie said. 'I've always got a headache. Take a whiff of this place.' She stood up and yanked on the fluffy striped raccoon tail, which was attached to the rump of the costume by a Velcro patch. The tail made a ripping sound when Carrie took it off. She tossed it in her locker and said, 'Why would anyone steal rats?'

'Voles,' said Joe Winder.

'The guys who did it, boy, what a pair. Scum of the earth.'

Again Winder didn't bother to write this down.

'It's crazy,' said Carrie Lanier. She reached beneath her left armpit and found, deep in the fur, another zipper. Carefully she unzipped the costume lengthwise down to her ankle. She did the same on the other side. As she stepped out of the animal outfit, Winder saw that she was wearing only a bra and panties. He tried not to stare.

Carrie hung the costume on a pair of hooks in the locker. She said, 'This damn thing weighs a ton, I wish you'd write that down. It's about a hundred twenty degrees inside, too. OSHA made them put in air conditioners, but they're always broken.'

Winder stepped closer to examine the raccoon costume, not Carrie Lanier in her bra (which was the type that unhooked in the front; pink with lacy cups).

Winder held up the animal suit and said, 'Where's the AC?'

'In the back. Here, look.' Carrie showed him. 'The batteries last about two hours max, then forget about it. We tried to call the feds and complain—what a joke. They haven't been out here since the day Petey Possum died.'

'Do I want to hear this story?'

'Heart attack,' Carrie Lanier went on. 'This was Sessums. Billy Sessums. The very first Petey Possum. He'd been twenty-two years with Disneyland—Goofy, Pluto, you name it. Billy was a pro. He taught me plenty.'

'So what happened?'

'One of those days. Ninety-two in the shade, one twelve inside the possum suit. The AC went out, and so did Billy.' Carrie Lanier paused reflectively. 'He was an older fella but still . . .'

'I'm sorry,' said Joe Winder. He put his notebook away. He was starting to feel prickly and claustrophobic.

Carrie said, 'You're gonna put my name in the press release?'

'I'm afraid not. It's company policy not to identify the actors who portray the animal characters. Mr. Kingsbury says it would spoil the illusion for the children.'

Carrie laughed. 'Some illusion. I've had kids grab my boobs, right through the costume. One time there was a Shriner, tried to goose me in the Magic Mansion.'

Winder said, 'How'd they know you were a woman?'

'That's the scary part.' Her eyes flashed mischievously. 'What if they didn't know I was a woman? What if they thought I was a real raccoon? What would Mr. Francis X. Kingsbury say about that?' She took a pair of blue jeans out of the locker and squirmed into them. 'Anyhow, I don't want my name in any stupid press release,' she said. 'Not for this place.'

'Maybe not, but you did a brave thing,' said Winder.

As Carrie buttoned her blouse, she said, 'I don't want my folks knowing what I do. You blame me?'

'You make lots of little children happy. What's wrong with that?'

She looked at him evenly. 'You're new here, aren't you?'

'Yeah,' Joe Winder said.

'My job's crummy, but you know what? I think your job is worse.'

Joe Winder wrote the press release in forty minutes. 'Theft of Rare Animals Stuns Amazing Kingdom.' Ten paragraphs on the crime itself, with a nod to the heroics of Robbie Raccoon ('who barely escaped serious injury'). Three paragraphs of official reaction ('a sad and shocking event') from Francis X. Kingsbury, chairman and president of the park. Three grafs more of scientific background on the blue-tongued mango vole, with a suitable quote from Dr. Will Koocher. A hundred words about the $10,000 reward, and a hundred more announcing new beefed-up security precautions at the park.

Winder put the press release on Charles Chelsea's desk and went home. By the time he called Nina, it was nearly one in the morning. He dialed the number and hoped she would be the one to answer.

'Hello, sugar,' Nina said.

'It's me.'

'God, I need to talk to a real man,' she said. 'I had a fantasy that got me so hot. We were on the bow of a sailboat. Making love in the sun. I was on top. Suddenly a terrible storm came—'

'Nina, it's me!'

'—but instead of hiding in the cabin, we lashed each other to the deck and kept on doing it in the lightning and thunder. Afterwards the warm rain washed the salt off our bodies. . . .'

'For Christ's sake.'

'Joe?'

'Yeah, it's me. Why don't you ever listen?'

'Because they don't pay me to listen,' Nina said. 'They pay me to talk.'

'I wish you'd get a normal job.'

'Joe, don't start.'

Nina was a voice for one of those live dial-a-fantasy telephone services. She worked nights, which put a strain on her personal relationships. Also, every time Joe Winder called, it cost him four bucks. At least the number was easy to remember: 976-COME.

Nina said, 'What do you think about the lightning-and-thunder business? I added it to the script myself.'

'What was it before—something about whales, right?'

'Porpoises, Joe. *A school of friendly porpoises leaped and frolicked in the water while we made love. Our animal cries only seemed to arouse them.*'

Nina had a wonderful voice, Winder had to admit. 'I like the new stuff better,' he agreed. 'The storm idea is good—you wrote that yourself?'

'Don't sound so surprised.' She asked him how

his day had gone, and he told her about the stolen
voles.

Nina said, 'See? And you thought you were going to
be bored.'

'I am bored. Most of the time.'

'Joe, it's never going to be like the old days.'

He wasn't in the mood to hear it. He said, 'How's it
going with you?'

'Slow,' Nina said. 'Beverly went home early. It's just
me and Miriam.'

'Any creeps call in?' Of course creeps had called—
who else would bother?

'The usual jack-off artists,' Nina reported. 'They're
harmless, Joe, don't worry. I just give a straight read,
no moans or groans, and still they get off in about thirty
seconds. I had one guy fall asleep afterwards. Snoring
like a baby.'

Sometimes she talked about her job as if it were a
social service, like UNICEF or Meals on Wheels.

'When will you be home?' Winder asked.

The usual, Nina said, meaning four in the morning.
'Want me to wake you up?'

'Sure.' She had loads of energy, this girl. Winder
needed somebody with energy, to help him use up his
own. One of the drawbacks of his high-paying bullshit
PR job was that it took absolutely nothing out of him,
except his pride.

Hurriedly Nina said, 'Joe, I got another call waiting.'

'Make it short and sweet.'

'I'll deal with you later, sailor boy.'

And then she hung up.

*

Winder couldn't sleep, so he put a Warren Zevon tape in the stereo and made himself a runny cheese omelet. He ate in the living room, near the speakers, and sat on a box because there were no chairs in the apartment. The box was filled with old newspaper clippings, his own, as well as plaques and certificates from various journalism awards that he had received over the years. The only important journalism award that wasn't in the box was the single one that impressed anybody—the Pulitzer Prize, which Joe Winder had never won.

When he was first interviewed for the publicity-writing job at the Amazing Kingdom of Thrills, Joe Winder had been asked if he'd ever gotten a Pulitzer. When he answered no, Charles Chelsea had threatened to put him on the polygraph machine.

'I never won,' Winder insisted. 'You can look it up.'

And Charles Chelsea did. A Pulitzer on the wall would have disqualified Joe Winder from the PR job just as surely as flunking a urinalysis for drugs.

'We're not in the market for aggressive, hard-bitten newshounds,' Chelsea had warned him. 'We're looking for writers with a pleasing, easygoing style. We're looking for a certain attitude.'

'I'm flexible,' Joe Winder had said. 'Especially my attitude.'

Chelsea had grilled him about the other journalism awards, then about the length of his hair, then about the thin pink scar along his jawline.

Eyeing Winder's face at close range, the publicity man had said, 'You look like a bar fighter. Did you get that scar in a fight?'

'Car accident,' Joe Winder had lied, figuring what the hell, Chelsea must've known the truth. One phone call to the newspaper, and any number of people would've been happy to drop the dime.

But Chelsea never said another word about the scar, never gave a hint that he'd even picked up the rumor. It was Joe Winder's journalism achievements that seemed to disturb the publicity man, although these concerns were ultimately outweighed by the discovery that Winder had been born and raised in Florida. The Publicity Department at the Amazing Kingdom was desperate for native talent, somebody who understood the mentality of tourists and crackers alike.

The Disney stint hadn't hurt Joe Winder's chances, either; he had worked among the enemy, and learned many of their professional secrets. So Charles Chelsea had set aside his doubts and hired him.

That was two weeks ago. It was still too early for Winder to compare the new job with the one at Disney World. Certainly Disney was slicker and more efficient than the Amazing Kingdom, but it was also more regimented and impersonal. The Disney bureaucracy, and its reach, was awesome. In retrospect Joe Winder wasn't sure how he had lasted as long as he did, six months, before he was caught having sex on Mr. Toad's Wild Ride and fired for not wearing his ID card. Winder felt especially bad that the young woman with whom he'd been dallying, a promising understudy to Cinderella, had also been dismissed over the incident; she for leaving Main Street during Mickey's Birthday Parade.

During the job interview at the Amazing Kingdom, Charles Chelsea had told him: 'You work for us, you'd better keep it in your pants, understand?'

'I've got a girlfriend now,' Joe Winder had said.

'Don't think you won't be tempted around here.'

Winder hadn't been tempted once, until today. Now he was thinking about Carrie Lanier, the fearless beauty inside a seven-foot raccoon suit.

This is what happens when you turn thirty-seven, Winder thought; the libido goes blind with fever. What else could explain his attraction to Nina? Or her attraction to him?

Being a newspaper reporter had left Joe Winder no time for such reckless attachments. Being a flack left him all the time in the world. Now that he was forbidden to write about trouble, he seemed determined to experience it.

He finished his omelet and opened a beer and slumped down on the floor, between the stereo speakers. Something had been nagging at him all afternoon, ever since the insufferable Chelsea had drafted him to help with the robbery crisis. In the push toward his deadline, it was clear to Joe Winder that none of his writing skills had eroded—his speed at the keyboard, his facile vocabulary, his smooth sense of pacing and transition. Yet something from the old days was missing.

Curiosity. The most essential and feral of reporters' instincts, the urge to pursue. It was dead. Or dying.

Two strangers had invaded a family theme park in broad daylight and kidnapped a couple of obscure rodents from an animal exhibit. Winder had thoroughly and competently reported the incident, but had made no effort to explore the fascinating possibilities. Having established the *what*, he had simply ignored the *why*.

Even by South Florida standards the crime was perverse, and the old Joe Winder would have reveled energetically in its mysteries. The new Joe Winder had merely typed up his thousand words, and gone home.

Just as he was supposed to do.

So this is how it feels, he thought. This is how it feels to sell out. On the stereo, Warren Zevon was singing about going to the Louvre museum and throwing himself against the wall. To Joe Winder it sounded like a pretty good idea.

He closed his eyes tightly and thought: Don't tell me I'm getting used to this goddamn zombie job. Then he thought: Don't tell me I'm getting drunk on one lousy beer.

He crawled across the carpet to the phone, and tried to call Nina at the service. The woman named Miriam answered instead, and launched into a complicated fantasy involving trampolines and silver ankle bracelets. Miriam was struggling so valiantly in broken English ('Ooooh, bebee, chew make me comb so many time!') that Joe Winder didn't have the heart to interrupt.

What the hell, it was only four bucks. He could certainly afford it.

FOUR

On the morning of July 17, Danny Pogue awoke in a cold sweat, his T-shirt soaked from neck to navel. He kicked the covers off the bed and saw the lump of gauze around his foot. It wasn't a dream. He limped to the window and from there he could see everything: the Olympic-sized swimming pool, the freshly painted tennis courts, the shady shuffleboard gazebo. Everywhere he looked there were old people with snowy heads and pale legs and fruit-colored Bermuda shorts. All the men wore socks with their sandals, and all the women wore golf visors and oversized sunglasses.

'Mother of Christ,' said Danny Pogue. He hollered for his partner to come quick.

Bud Schwartz ambled in, looking settled and well rested. He was spooning out half a grapefruit, cupped in the palm of one hand. 'Do you believe this fucking place?' he said to Danny Pogue. 'What a gas.'

'We gotta get out.'

'How come?'

'Just look.' Danny Pogue pointed out the window.

'So now you got a problem with senior citizens? What—they don't have the right to have fun? Besides, there's some young people that live here, too. I saw a couple a hot ones out by the swimming pool. Major titties.'

'I don't care,' mumbled Danny Pogue.

'Hey,' Bud Schwartz said. 'She shot your foot, not your weenie.'

'Where is she?'

'Long gone. You want some lunch? She loaded up at the Publix, you should see. Steaks, chops, beer—we're set for a couple a weeks, easy.'

Danny Pogue hopped back to the bed and peeled off the damp shirt. He spotted a brand-new pair of crutches propped in the corner. He said, 'Bud, I'm gonna split. Seriously, I'm taking off.'

'I can give you ten thousand reasons not to.'

'Speaking of which.'

'She's bringing a grand for each of us, just like she promised,' said Bud Schwartz. 'Good faith money is what she called it.'

'Invisible is what I call it.'

'Hey, lighten the fuck up. She's an old lady, Danny. Old ladies never lie.' Bud Schwartz lobbed the grapefruit skin into some kind of designer wastebasket. 'What's wrong with you, man? This is like a vacation, all expenses paid. Look at this freaking condo—two bedrooms, two bathrooms. Microwave in the kitchen, Cinemax on the cable. Say what you will, the old geezer knows how to live.'

'Who is she?' Danny Pogue asked.

'Who cares?'

'I care. She shot me.'

Bud Schwartz said, 'Just some crazy, rich old broad. Don't worry about it.'

'It's not you that got shot.'

43

'She won't do it again, Danny. She got it out of her system.' Bud Schwartz wiped his hands on the butt of his jeans to get the grapefruit juice off. He said, 'She was pissed, that's all. On account of us losing the rats.'

Danny Pogue said, 'Well, screw that deal. I'm leaving.' He made a move for the crutches but faltered, hot and dizzy. Molly McNamara had fed him some pain pills late last night; that much he remembered.

'I don't know where you think you're going,' said Bud Schwartz. 'The truck's history.'

'I'll hitch,' said Danny Pogue woozily.

'Look in the mirror. Your own mother wouldn't pick you up. The Hell's Fucking Angels wouldn't pick you up.'

'Somebody'll stop,' Danny Pogue said. 'Especially with me on them crutches.'

'Oh, sure.'

'Maybe even some girls.' Danny Pogue eased himself back on the pillow. He took deep breaths and tried to blink away the haze in his brain.

'Have another codeine,' said Bud Schwartz. 'Here, she got a whole bottle.' He went to the kitchen and came back with a cold Busch.

Danny Pogue swallowed two more pills and slurped at the beer can noisily. He closed his eyes and said, 'She ain't never gonna pay us, Bud.'

'Sure she is,' said his partner. 'She's loaded, just look at this place. You should see the size of the TV.'

'We better get away while we can.'

'Go back to sleep,' said Bud Schwartz. 'I'll be down at the pool.'

*

The Mothers of Wilderness met every other Tuesday at a public library in Cutler Ridge. This week the main item on the agenda was the proposed bulldozing of seventy-three acres of mangroves to make room for the back nine of a championship golf course on the shore of North Key Largo. The Mothers of Wilderness strenuously opposed the project, and had begun to map a political strategy to obstruct it. They pursued such crusades with unflagging optimism, despite the fact that they had never succeeded in stopping a single development. Not one. The builders ignored them. Zoning boards ignored them. County commissioners listened politely, nodded intently, then ignored them, too. Of all the environmental groups fighting to preserve what little remained of Florida, the Mothers of Wilderness was regarded as the most radical and shrill and intractable. It was also, unfortunately, the smallest of the groups and thus the easiest to brush off.

Still, the members were nothing if not committed. Molly McNamara steadfastly had refused all offers to merge her organization with the Audubon Society or the Sierra Club or the Friends of the Everglades. She wanted no part of coalitions because coalitions compromised. She enjoyed being alone on the fringe, enjoyed being the loose cannon that establishment environmentalists feared. The fact that the Mothers of Wilderness was politically impotent did not diminish Molly McNamara's passion, though occasionally it ate at her pride.

She ran the meetings with brusque efficiency, presiding over a membership that tended to be retired and liberal and well-to-do. For its size, the Mothers of Wilderness was exceedingly well financed; Molly knew this was why the other environmental groups wooed her, in hopes of a merger. The Mothers had bucks.

They had hired a hotshot Miami land-use lawyer to fight the golf course project, which was called Falcon Trace. The lawyer, whose name was Spacci, stood up at the meeting to update the Mothers on the progress of the lawsuit, which, typically, was about to be thrown out of court. The case was being heard in Monroe County—specifically, Key West—where many of the judges were linked by conspiracy or simple inbreeding to the crookedest politicians. Moreover, the zoning lawyer admitted he was having a terrible time ascertaining the true owners of the Falcon Trace property; he had gotten as far as a blind trust in Dallas, then stalled.

Molly McNamara thanked Spacci for his report and made a motion to authorize another twenty thousand dollars for legal fees and investigative expenses. It passed unanimously.

After the meeting, Molly took the lawyer aside and said, 'Next time I want to see some results. I want the names of these bastards.'

'What about the lawsuit?'

'File a new one,' Molly said. 'You ever considered going federal?'

'How?' asked Spacci. 'On what grounds?'

Pinching his elbow, Molly led him to an easel behind the rostrum. Propped on the easel was an aerial map of North Key Largo. Molly pointed and said, 'See? There's where they want the golf course. And right here is a national wildlife refuge. That's your federal jurisdiction, Counselor.'

The lawyer plucked a gold pen from his breast pocket

and did some pointing of his own. 'And right here, Ms. McNamara, is a two-thousand-acre amusement park that draws three million tourists every year. We'd be hard pressed to argue that one lousy golf course would be more disruptive to the habitat than what's already there—a major vacation resort.'

Molly snapped, 'You're the damn attorney. Think of something.'

Bitterly she remembered the years she had fought the Kingsbury project; the Mothers of Wilderness had been the only group that had never given up. Audubon and the others had realized immediately that protest was futile; the prospect of a major theme park to compete with Disney World carried an orgasmic musk to local chambers of commerce. The most powerful of powerful civic leaders clung to the myth that Mickey Mouse was responsible for killing the family tourist trade in South Florida, strangling the peninsula so that all southbound station wagons stopped in Orlando. What did Miami have to offer as competition? Porpoises that could pitch a baseball with their blow-holes? Wisecracking parrots on unicycles? Enjoyable diversions, but scarcely in the same high-tech league with Disney. The Mouse's sprawling self-contained empire sucked tourists' pockets inside out; they came, they spent until there was nothing left to spend; then they went home *happy*. To lifelong Floridians it was a dream concept: fleecing a snowbird in such a way that he came back for more. Astounding! So when Francis X. Kingsbury unveiled his impressive miniature replica of the Amazing Kingdom of Thrills— the Wet Willy water flume, the Magic Mansion, Orky the Killer Whale, Jungle Jerry, and so on—roars of exultation were heard from Palm Beach to Big Pine.

The only cry of dismay came from the Mothers of Wilderness, who were (as usual) ignored.

'No golf course,' Molly told Spacci the lawyer, 'and no more chickenshit excuses from you.' She sent him away with the wave of a blue-veined hand.

After the rank and file had gone home, Molly gathered the board of directors in the back of the library. Five women and two men, all nearly as gray as Molly, they sat in molded plastic chairs and sipped herbal tea while Molly told them what had happened.

It was a bizarre and impossible scheme, but no one asked Molly why she had done it. They knew why. In a fussy tone, one of the Mothers said: 'This time you went too far.'

'It's under control,' Molly insisted.

'Except for the voles. They're not under control.'

Another Mother asked: 'Any chance of finding them?'

'You never know,' said Molly.

'Horseshit,' said the first Mother. 'They're gone for good. Dead, alive, it doesn't matter if we can't locate the damn things.'

Molly said, 'Please. Keep your voice down.'

The second Mother: 'What about these two men? Where are they now?'

'My condo,' Molly replied. 'Up at Eagle Ridge.'

'Lord have mercy.'

'That's enough,' said Molly sharply. 'I said it's under control, and it's under control.'

A silence fell over the small group. No one wished to challenge her authority, but this time things had really gotten out of hand. This time there was a chance they could all go to jail. 'I'll have some more tea,' the first

Mother said finally, 'and then I'd love to hear your new plan. You do have one?'

'Of course I do,' said Molly McNamara. 'For heaven's sake.'

When Joe Winder got to work, Charles Chelsea was waiting in yet another blue oxford shirt. He was sitting on the edge of Winder's desk in a pose of casual superiority. A newspaper was freshly folded under one arm. 'Fine job on the press release,' Chelsea said. 'I changed a word or two, but otherwise it went out just like you wrote it.'

Calmly Joe Winder said, 'Which word or two did you change?'

'Oh, I improved Mr. Kingsbury's comments. Couple of adverbs here and there.'

'Fine.' Winder wasn't so surprised. It was well known that Chelsea invented all of Francis X. Kingsbury's quotes. Kingsbury was one of those men who rarely spoke in complete sentences. Didn't have to. For publicity purposes this made him perfectly useless and unquotable.

Chelsea said, 'I also updated the info on Robbie Raccoon. Turns out he got a mild concussion from that blow to the head.'

Winder forced a smile and set his briefcase on the desk. 'It's a she, Charlie. And she was fine when I spoke to her last night. Not even a bruise.'

Chelsea's voice took on a scolding tone. 'Joey, you know the gender rule. If it's a male character, we always refer to it with masculine pronouns—regardless of who's inside the costume. I explained all this the day you were hired. It comes straight from Mr. X. Speaking of which, weren't you supposed to get a haircut?'

'Don't be a dork, Charlie.'

'What's a dork?'

'You're not serious.'

Charles Chelsea said, 'Really, tell me. You called me a dork, I'd like to know what exactly that is.'

'It's a Disney character,' said Joe Winder. 'Daffy Dork.' He opened the briefcase and fumbled urgently for his sinus medicine. 'Anyway, Charlie, the lady in the coon suit didn't have a concussion. That's a lie, and it's a stupid lie because it's so easy to check. Some newspaper reporter is going to make a few calls and we're going to look sleazy and dishonest, all because you had to exaggerate.'

'No exaggeration,' Charles Chelsea said, stiffening. 'I spoke with Robbie Raccoon myself, first thing this morning. He said he got dizzy and sick overnight. Doctor said it's probably a concussion.'

Winder popped two pills into his mouth and said, 'You're amazing.'

'We'll have a neurologist's report this afternoon, in case anybody wants to see. Notarized, too.' Chelsea looked pleased with himself. 'Mild concussion, Joe. Don't believe me, just ask Robbie.'

'What'd you do, threaten to fire her? Bust her down to the elf patrol?'

Charles Chelsea stood up, shot his cuffs, gave Joe Winder his coldest, hardest look. 'I came down here to thank you for doing such outstanding work, and look what I get. More of your cynicism. Just because you had a rotten night, Joey, it's no reason to rain on everyone else's parade.'

Did the man really say that? Winder wondered. Did he really accuse me of raining on his parade? 'That's the only reason you're here?' Winder said. 'To thank me?'

'Well, not entirely.' Charles Chelsea removed the newspaper from under his arm, unfolded it and handed it to Joe Winder. 'Check the last three paragraphs.'

It was the story about the theft of the blue-tongued mango voles. The *Herald* had stripped it across the top of the Local News page, a feature play. 'Hey,' Winder said brightly, 'they even used one of our pictures.'

'Never mind that, just read the last three grafs.'

The newspaper story ended like this:

An anonymous caller identifying himself as an animal-rights activist telephoned the Miami office of the Associated Press late Monday and took credit for the incident at the popular theme park. The caller claimed to be a member of the radical Wildlife Rescue Corps.

'We freed the voles because they were being exploited,' he said. 'Francis Kingsbury doesn't care about saving the species, he just wanted another stupid tourist attraction.'

Officials at the Amazing Kingdom of Thrills were unavailable for comment late Monday night.

Joe Winder gave the newspaper back to Charles Chelsea and said, 'What a kick in the nuts. I'll bet the boss man is going batshit.'

'You find this amusing?'

'Don't you?' Winder asked. 'I guess not.'

'No,' said Chelsea. He refolded the newspaper and

returned it to his armpit. 'What do you suggest in the way of a response?'

'I suggest we forget the fucking voles and get on with our lives.'

'This is serious.'

Winder said, 'So I was right, Kingsbury's on a tear. Then I would suggest you tell him that we're waiting to see if there's any truth to this claim. Tell him that if we say anything now, it might turn around and bite us in the rat hole.'

Chelsea started rubbing his chin, a sign of possible cognition. 'Go on,' he told Winder. 'I'm listening.'

'For instance, suppose the real Wildlife Rescue Corps calls up and denies any involvement. Hell, Charlie, there's a good chance the caller was a crank. Had nothing to do with the group. To play it safe, we don't respond for now. We say absolutely nothing.'

'But if it turns out to be true?'

'Then,' said Joe Winder, 'we express outrage that any organization, no matter how worthy its cause, would commit a violent felony and endanger the lives of innocent bystanders.'

Chelsea nodded enthusiastically; he liked what he was hearing. 'Not just any bystanders,' he said. 'Tourists.'

Winder went on: 'We would also recount Mr. Kingsbury's many philanthropic gifts to the ASPCA, the World Wildlife Fund, Save the Beavers, whatever. And we would supply plenty of testimonial quotes from eminent naturalists supporting our efforts on behalf of the endangered mango vole.'

'Excellent,' Charles Chelsea said. 'Joe, that's perfect.'

'Pure unalloyed genius,' Winder said.

'Let's hope it doesn't come to that,' Chelsea said. 'You don't want to spend the rest of the week writing about rodents. Too much like covering City Hall, right?'

Joe Winder chuckled politely. He could tell Chelsea was worried about pitching it to Kingsbury.

In a hopeful voice, Chelsea said, 'You think the guy was really just a nut? This guy who called the AP?'

'Who knows,' Winder said. 'We've certainly got our share.'

Charles Chelsea nodded hopefully. A simple nut would be fine with him, PR-wise; it's the zealots you had to worry about.

'The only thing to do is wait,' said Joe Winder. Already he could feel his sinuses drying up. He felt suddenly clearheaded, chipper, even optimistic. Maybe it was the medicine flushing his head, or maybe it was something else.

Like having a real honest-to-God story, for a change. A story getting good and hot.

Just like the old days.

FIVE

Chelsea had a stark, irrational fear of Francis X. Kingsbury. It was not Kingsbury's physical appearance (for he was gnomish and flabby) but his volcanically profane temper that caused Chelsea so much anxiety. Kingsbury long ago had practically ceased speaking in complete sentences, but his broken exclamations could be daunting and acerbic. The words struck venomously at Charles Chelsea's insecurities, and made him tremble.

On the afternoon of July 17, Chelsea finished his lunch, threw up, flossed his teeth and walked briskly to Kingsbury's office. Kingsbury was leaning over the desk; the great man's sleeves were rolled up to reveal the famous lewd tattoo on his doughy left forearm. The other arm sparkled with a gold Robbie Raccoon wristwatch, with emerald insets. Today's surfer-blond hairpiece was longish and curly.

Kingsbury grunted at Charles Chelsea and said: 'Wildlife Rescue Corps?' He raised his hands. 'Well?'

Chelsea said, 'The group exists, but the phone call could be a crank. We're checking it out.'

'What's this exploitation—shit, we're talking about, what, some kind of rodent or such goddamn thing.'

Not even close to a quotable sentence, Chelsea thought. It was astounding—the man spoke in overtorqued, expletive-laden fragments that somehow made perfect sense. At all times, Charles Chelsea knew exactly what Francis X. Kingsbury was talking about.

The publicity man said, 'Don't worry, sir, the situation is being contained. We're ready for any contingency.'

Kingsbury made a small fist. 'Damage control,' he said.

'Our top gun,' Chelsea said. 'His name is Joe Winder, and he's a real pro. Offering the reward money was his idea, sir. The AP led with it this morning, too.'

Kingsbury sat down. He fingered the florid tip of his bulbous nose. 'These animals, there's still a chance maybe?'

Chelsea could feel a chilly dampness spreading in deadly crescents from his armpits. 'It's unlikely, sir. One of them is dead for sure. Shot by the highway patrol. Some tourists apparently mistook it for a rat.'

'Terrific,' said Kingsbury.

'The other one, likewise. The bandits threw it in the window of a Winnebago camper.'

Kingsbury peered from beneath dromedary lids. 'Don't,' he said, exhaling noisily. 'This is like . . . no, don't bother.'

'You might as well know,' said Chelsea. 'It was a church group from Boca Raton in the Winnebago. They beat the poor thing to death with a golf umbrella. Then they threw it off the Card Sound Bridge.'

There, Chelsea thought. He had done it. Stood up and delivered the bad news. Stood up like a man.

Francis X. Kingsbury entwined his hands and said: 'Who knows about this? Knows that *we* know? Anybody?'

'You mean anybody on the outside? No.' Charles

Chelsea paused. 'Well, except the highway patrol. And I took care of them with some free passes to the Kingdom.'

'But civilians?'

'No, sir. Nobody knows that we know the voles are dead.'

'Fine,' said Francis X. Kingsbury. 'Good time to up the reward.'

'Sir?'

'Make it a million bucks. Six zeros, if I'm not mistaken.'

Chelsea took out a notebook and a Cross pen, and began to write. 'That's one million dollars for the safe return of the missing voles.'

'Which are dead.'

'Yes, sir.'

'Simple, hell. Very simple.'

'It's a most generous offer,' said Charles Chelsea.

'Bullshit,' Kingsbury said. 'It's PR, whatever. Stuff for the fucking AP.'

'But your heart's in the right place.'

Impatiently Kingsbury pointed toward the door. 'Fast,' he said. 'Before I get sick.'

Chelsea was startled. Backing away from Kingsbury's desk, he said, 'I'm sorry, sir. Is it something I said?'

'No, something you are.' Kingsbury spoke flatly, with just a trace of disgust.

On the way back to his office, Charles Chelsea stopped in the executive washroom and threw up again.

Like many wildly successful Floridians, Francis X. Kingsbury was a transplant. He had moved to the Sunshine State in balding middle age, alone and uprooted, never expecting that he would become a multi-millionaire.

And, like so many new Floridians, Kingsbury was a felon on the run. Before arriving in Miami, he was known by his real name of Frankie King. Not Frank, but Frankie; his mother had named him after the singer Frankie Laine. All his life Frankie King had yearned to change his name to something more distinguished, something with weight and social bearing. A racketeering indictment (twenty-seven counts) out of Brooklyn was as good an excuse as any.

Once he was arrested, Frankie King exuberantly began ratting on his co-conspirators, which included numerous high-ranking members of the John Gotti crime organization. Frankie's testimony conveniently glossed the fact that it was he, not the surly Zuboni brothers, who had personally flown to San Juan and picked up the twenty-seven crate-loads of bootleg 'educational' videotapes that were eventually sold to the New York City school system for $119.95 apiece. Under oath, Frankie King indignantly blamed the Zubonis and, indirectly, John Gotti himself for failing to inspect the shipment once it had arrived at JFK. On the witness stand, Frankie expressed tearful remorse that, in TV classrooms from Queens to Staten Island, students expecting to see 'Kermit's Wild West Adventure' were instead exposed to a mattress-level montage of Latin porn star Pina Kolada deepthroating a semi-pro soccer team.

The Zuboni brothers and a cluster of dull-eyed knee-cappers were swiftly convicted by a horrified jury. The

57

reward for Frankie King's cooperation was a suspended sentence, ten years' probation and a new identity of his choosing: Francis X. Kingsbury. Frankie felt the 'X' was a classy touch; he decided it should stand for Xavier.

When the man from the Witness Relocation Program told him that Miami would be his new home, Frankie King thought he had died and gone to heaven. *Miami!* Frankie couldn't believe his good fortune; he had no idea the U.S. government could be so generous. What Frankie did not know was that Miami was the prime relocation site for scores of scuzzy federal snitches (on the theory that South Florida was a place where just about any dirtbag would blend in smoothly with the existing riffraff). Frankie King continued to entertain the false notion that he was somebody special in the witness program, a regular Joe Valachi, until he saw the accommodations provided by his government benefactors: a one-bedroom apartment near the railroad tracks in beautiful downtown Naranja.

When Frankie complained about the place, FBI agents reminded him that the alternative was to return to New York and take his chances that John Gotti was a compassionate and forgiving fellow. With this on his mind, Francis X. Kingsbury began a new life.

Like all Floridians with time on their hands, he went to night school and got his real-estate license. It was an entirely new racket, and Frankie worked at it tirelessly; first he specialized in small commercial properties, then citrus groves and farmlands. Doggedly he worked his way east toward the good stuff—oceanfront, the Big O. He went from condos to prime residential estates in no time flat.

Francis X. Kingsbury had found a new niche. He

was, undeniably, a whiz at selling Florida real estate. In five short years he had accumulated more money than in an entire lifetime of mob bunko, jukebox skimming and mail fraud. He had a home down on Old Cutler, a beautiful young wife and a closetful of mustard blazers. But he wanted more.

One day he walked into the boardroom of Kingsbury Realty and announced that he was selling the business. 'I'm ready to move up in the world,' he told his startled partners. 'I'm ready to become a developer.'

Six months later, Kingsbury stood before a luncheon meeting of the Greater Miami Chamber of Commerce and unveiled his model of the Amazing Kingdom of Thrills. It was the first time in his life that Frankie had gotten a standing ovation. He blushed and said: 'Florida is truly the land of opportunity.'

His probation officer, standing near the salad bar, had to bite back tears.

'This is a very bad idea, Charlie.' Joe Winder was talking about the phony million-dollar reward. 'A very bad idea. And cynical, I might add.'

Over the phone, Chelsea said: 'Don't give me any lectures. I need five hundred words by tomorrow morning.'

'This is nuts.'

'And don't overdo it.'

'This is not just dumb,' continued Joe Winder, 'it's dishonest. The blue-tongued mango voles are dead, Charlie. Everybody at the park is talking about it.'

Chelsea said, 'Mr. X is adamant. He considers the

money a symbolic gesture of his commitment to preserving the environment.'

'Did you write that yourself?' Winder asked. 'That's
fucking awful, Charlie. *Symbolic gesture!* You ought to
be shot.'

'Joey, don't talk to me that way. This thing was your
idea, offering a reward.'

'I was wrong,' Winder said. 'It was a big mistake.'

'No, it was genius. The AP had it all over the wires.'

'Look, I'm trying to save your ass,' Winder said.
'And mine, too. Listen to me. This morning, a man with
a cardboard box showed up at the front gate of the
Amazing Kingdom. Said he'd found the missing voles.
Said he'd come to collect his ten-thousand-dollar
reward. Listen to me, Charlie. Know what was in the
box? Rabbits. Two baby rabbits.'

'So what? They don't look anything like a vole.'

'They do when you cut their ears off, Charlie. That's
what the sonofabitch had done. Cut the ears off a couple
of little tiny bunny rabbits.'

Charles Chelsea gasped.

'I know, I know,' Winder said, 'Think about what's
going to happen we dangle a million bucks out there.
Think of the freaks and sadists and degenerates stampeding this place.'

'Holy Christ,' said Chelsea.

'Now,' said Joe Winder, 'think of the headlines.'

'I'll talk to Kingsbury.'

'Good.'

'Maybe I'll bring you along.'

'No thank you.'

'You owe me,' said Chelsea. 'Please. I've been good
to you, Joe. Remember who hired you in the first place.'

Thanks for reminding me, Winder thought, for the two-thousandth time. 'I'm not the right man to deal with Mr. X,' he said. 'I make a lousy first impression.'

'You're right,' said Chelsea, rethinking his plan. 'Tell me one thing—that sicko with the bunny rabbits . . . what happened?'

'Don't worry,' said Winder. 'We paid him to go away.'

'How much? Not the whole ten grand?'

'No, not ten grand.' Winder sighed. 'Try fifty bucks. And he was delighted, Charlie. Positively thrilled.'

'Thank God for that.' There was a brittle pause on Chelsea's end. 'Joe?'

'What?'

'This is turning into something real bad, isn't it?'

Late in the afternoon, Joe Winder decided to drive down to the Rare Animal Pavilion and find out more about the voles. He needed someone to take his mind off the rabbit episode, which made him heartsick. He should've seen it coming—naturally some greedy psychopath would mutilate helpless bunny rabbits for ten lousy thousand fucking dollars. It's South Florida, isn't it? Winter should've anticipated the worst. That's why Chelsea had hired him, for his native instinct.

The door to the vole lab was locked but the lights were on. Winder knocked twice and got no answer. He could hear a telephone ringing on the other side of the door. It stopped briefly, then began ringing again. He used his car keys to rap sharply on the glass, but there was no sign of Koocher. Winder figured the doctor was taking a late lunch.

He strolled out to the pavilion, where he found a

group of tourists milling around the empty mango-vole exhibit. A tarpaulin had been hung to cover the mess, but somebody had lifted a corner to peek inside the enclosure, which was littered with glass and smudged with fingerprint dust. A yellow police ribbon lay crumpled like a dead snake on the porch of the vole hutch. Some of the tourists were snapping pictures of the scene of the crime.

A voice behind Joe Winder said, 'You work here?'

It was an old woman wearing a floppy pink Easter hat and a purse the size of a saddlebag. She eyed Joe Winder's ID badge, which was clipped to his belt.

'You a security man?' the woman asked.

Winder tried to remember what Chelsea had told him about speaking to park visitors; some gooey greeting that all employees were supposed to say. *Welcome to the Amazing Kingdom. How can I help you?* Or was it: *How may I help you?* No, that wasn't it. *How can we help you?*

Eventually Joe Winder said, 'I work in Publicity. Is something wrong?'

The old lady made a clucking noise and foraged in her enormous purse. 'I've got a little something for you.'

In a helpful tone Winder said, 'The Lost and Found is down by the killer-whale tank.'

'This isn't lost and it isn't found.' The old lady produced an envelope. 'Here,' she said, pressing it into Joe Winder's midsection. 'And don't try to follow me.'

She turned and scuttled off, one hand atop her head, holding the Easter hat in place. Winder stuffed the envelope into his pocket and started after her. 'Hey! Wait a second.'

He had taken only three steps when a fist came out

NATIVE TONGUE

of somewhere and smashed him behind the right ear. He pitched forward on the walkway, skidding briefly on his face. When he awoke, Joe Winder was staring at shoes: Reeboks, loafers, sandals, Keds, orthopedics, Hush Puppies, flip-flops. The tourists had gathered in a murmuring semicircle around him. A young man knelt at his side, asking questions in German.

Winder sat up. 'Did anybody see who hit me?' His cheek stung, and he tasted blood on his lower lip.

'Beeg orange!' sputtered a woman wearing two cameras around her neck. 'Beeg orange man!'

'Swell,' Winder said. 'Did he have a cape? A ray gun?'

The young German tourist patted him on the shoulder and said: 'You okay, *ja?*'

'Yah,' Winder muttered. 'Fall down go boom.'

He picked himself up, waved idiotically at his audience and retreated to the men's room. There he tore open the old lady's envelope and studied the message, which was typed double-spaced on ordinary notebook paper. It said: 'WE DID IT. WE'RE GLAD. LONG LIVE THE VOLES.'

It was signed by the Wildlife Rescue Corps.

With copies, Joe Winder noted glumly, to every major news organization on the planet.

Bud Schwartz shook Danny Pogue awake and said, 'Look who's here. I told you not to worry.'

Molly McNamara was in the kitchen, fussing around. Danny Pogue was on the sofa in the living room. He had fallen asleep watching *Lady Chatterley IV* on Cinemax.

Bud Schwartz sat down, grinning. 'She brought the money, too,' he said.

'All of it?'

'No, just the grand. Like she said before.'

'You mean the two grand,' Danny Pogue said. 'One for each of us.' He didn't entirely trust his partner.

Bud Schwartz said, 'Yeah, that's what I meant. A thousand bucks each.'

'Then let's see it.'

Molly came in, drying her hands on a flowered towel. She looked at Danny Pogue as if he were a dog that was supposed to stay off the good furniture. She said, 'How's that foot?'

'Hurts.' Danny Pogue frowned. 'Hurts like a bitch.'

'He's all out of them pills,' added Bud Schwartz.

'Already?' Molly sounded concerned. 'You finished the whole bottle?'

'Danny's got what you call a high resistance to pharmaceuticals,' Bud Schwartz said. 'We had to double the dose.'

'Bull,' said Danny Pogue. 'Bud here just helped hisself.'

'Is that true?' asked Molly McNamara. 'Did you take some of your friend's pills?'

'Aw, come on,' said Bud Schwartz. 'Jesus Christ, there's nothing else to do around here. I was bored stiff.'

'That was prescription medicine,' Molly said sternly.

She went back to the kitchen and got her handbag. It was the largest handbag that Bud Schwartz or Danny Pogue had ever seen. Molly took out another plastic bottle of codeine pills and handed them to Danny

Pogue. Then she took out her gun and shot Bud Schwartz once in the left hand.

He fell down, shaking his arm as if it were on fire.

In a whisper Danny Pogue said, 'Oh Lord Jesus.' He felt the blood flooding out of his brain, and saw the corners of the room get fuzzy.

Molly said, 'Am I getting through to you fellows?' She returned the gun to her purse. 'There will be no illegal drug activity in this condominium, is that clear? The owners' association has very strict rules. Here, take this.' She handed Danny Pogue two packets of cash. Each packet was held together with a fresh bank wrapper.

'That's one thousand each, just like I promised,' she said. Then, turning to Bud Schwartz: 'Does it hurt?'

'The fuck do you think?' He was squeezing the wounded purple hand between his knees. 'Damn right it hurts!'

'In that case, you may borrow your friend's pills. But only as needed.' Then Molly McNamara put on her floppy pink Easter hat and said good night.

Nina was naked, kneeling on Joe Winder's back and rubbing his shoulders. 'See, isn't this better than sex?'

'No,' he said, into the pillow. 'Good, but not better.'

'It's my night off,' Nina said. 'All week long, all I do is talk about it.'

'We don't have to talk,' Joe Winder mumbled. 'Let's just do.'

'Joe, I need a break from it.' She kneaded his neck so ferociously that he let out a cry. 'You understand, don't you?'

'Sure,' he said. It was the second time in a week that they'd had this conversation. Winder had a feeling that Nina was burning out on her job; practically nothing aroused her lately. All she wanted to do was sleep, and of course she talked in her sleep, said the most tantalizing things.

It was driving Joe Winder crazy. 'I had a particularly lousy day,' he said. 'I was counting on you to wear me out.'

Nina climbed off his back. 'I love you,' she said, slipping her long legs under the sheets, 'but at this moment I don't have a single muscle that's the least bit interested.'

This, from the same wonderful woman who once left fingernail grooves in the blades of a ceiling fan. Winder groaned in self-pity.

From the other side of the bed came Nina's delicious voice: 'Tell me the weirdest thing that happened to you today.'

It was a bedtime ritual, exchanging anecdotes about work. Joe Winder said: 'Some creep claimed he found the missing voles, except they weren't voles. They were baby rabbits. He was trying to con us.' Winder left out the grisly details.

'That's a tough one to beat,' Nina remarked.

'Also, I got slugged in the head.'

'Really?' she said. 'Last night I had a caller jerk himself off in eleven seconds flat. Miriam said it might be a new world's record.'

'You timed it?'

'Sort of.' Playfully she reached between his legs and tweaked him. 'Miriam has an official Olympic stopwatch.'

'Nina, I want you to get another job. I'm serious.'

She said, 'That reminds me—some strange guy phoned for you this afternoon. A doctor from the park. He called twice.'

'Koocher?'

'Yeah,' said Nina. 'Interesting name. Anyway, he made it sound important. I told him to try you at the office, but he said no. He wouldn't leave a message, either, just said he'd call back. The second time he said to tell you a man from Security was in the lab.'

Joe Winder lifted his head off the pillow. 'A man from Security?'

'That's what he said.'

'Anything else?' Winder was thinking about the empty laboratory: lights on, phone ringing. Maybe he should've tried the back door.

'I told him you'd be home soon, but he said he couldn't call back. He said he was leaving with the guy from Security.' Nina propped herself on one elbow. 'Joe, what's going on over there?'

'I thought I knew,' said Winder, 'but obviously I don't.'

With a fingertip she traced a feathery line down his cheek. 'Do me a favor,' she said.

'I know what you're going to say.'

She scooted closer, under the covers, and pressed against him. 'But things are going so great.'

Winder kissed her on the tip of the nose, and started to roll out of bed.

'Joe, don't go crazy on me,' Nina said. 'Please.'

He rolled back, into her arms. 'All right,' he said. 'Not just yet.'

SIX

The next morning, in the hallway by the water fountain, Charles Chelsea seized Joe Winder by the sleeve and tugged him into the office. Two men shared opposite ends of Chelsea's leather sofa—one was the immense Pedro Luz, chief of Security for the Amazing Kingdom, and the other was a serious-looking fellow with a square haircut and a charcoal suit.

'Joe,' Chelsea said, 'this gentleman is from the FBI.'

'I can see that.'

Chelsea cleared his throat. 'This is Agent Hawkins.'

Joe Winder stuck out his hand. 'Billy, isn't it? You worked a Coral Gables Savings job about four years back.'

The agent smiled cautiously. 'And you were with the *Herald.*'

'Right.'

'Dated one of the tellers.'

'Right again.'

Charles Chelsea was trying to set some sort of record for clearing his throat. 'What a coincidence that you two guys know each other.'

Joe Winder sat down and stretched his legs. 'Bank robbery. Billy here was the lead agent. Funny story, too—it was the Groucho guy.'

'Yeah,' said Hawkins, loosening up. 'Wore the big nose and the eyebrows, even carried a cigar. We finally caught up with him in Clearwater.'

'No kidding?' Winder said, knowing that it was driving Chelsea crazy, all this friendly conversation with a real FBI man. 'All the way up in Clearwater?'

'Gentlemen,' Chelsea cut in, 'if you don't mind.'

'What is it, Charlie?'

'Agent Hawkins is here at Mr. Kingsbury's personal request.' Chelsea lowered his voice. 'Joe, there were three notes delivered to employees in the park. Each was signed by this Wildlife Rescue Corps.'

Winder reached in his pocket. 'You mean like this?' He handed his copy to Billy Hawkins. He told him what had happened at the Rare Animal Pavilion—the old lady in the Easter bonnet, the phantom punch. Hawkins took it all down in a notebook.

Chelsea tried to contain his irritation. 'Why didn't you report this to Security?' he asked Joe Winder.

'Because I didn't want to interrupt Pedro's nap.'

Pedro Luz darkened. Every now and then he dozed off in the security office. 'All you had to do was ring the buzzer,' he snapped at Winder. He glanced at the FBI man, whose expression remained impassive and nonjudgmental. 'I've had a touch of the flu,' Pedro Luz added defensively. 'The medicine makes me sleepy.' For a large man he had a high tinny voice.

'Never mind,' said Charles Chelsea. 'The point is, everybody's calling up for comment. The networks. The wires. We're under siege, Joe.'

Winder felt his headache coming back. Agent Billy Hawkins admitted that the federal government didn't know much about the Wildlife Rescue Corps.

'Most of these groups seem to specialize in rodents,' the agent said. 'Laboratory rats, mostly. Universities, pharmaceutical houses—those are the common targets. What usually happens, they break in at night and free the animals.'

'But we weren't doing experiments.' Chelsea was exasperated. 'We treated Vance and Violet as royalty.'

'Who?' the agent said.

'The voles,' Joe Winder explained cheerfully.

Charles Chelsea continued to whine. 'Why have they singled out the Amazing Kingdom? We didn't abuse these creatures. Quite the opposite.'

'You do any vivisections here?' asked Agent Hawkins. 'These groups are quite vocal against vivisection.'

Chelsea paled. 'Vivisection? Christ, we gave the little bastards fresh corn on the cob every morning. Sometimes even citrus!'

'Well, this is what we've got.' Hawkins flipped backwards in his notebook. 'Two white males ages twenty-five to thirty-five, fleeing the scene in a 1979 blue Ford pickup, license GPP-B06. The registration comes back to a convicted burglar whose current alias is Buddy Michael Schwartz. I might add that Mr. Schwartz's rap sheet shows no history of a social conscience with regard to animal rights, or any other.'

'Somebody hired him,' Joe Winder said.

'Most likely,' agreed the FBI man. 'Anyway, they dragged the truck out of a rock pit this morning. No bodies.'

'Any sign of the voles?'

Billy Hawkins allowed himself a slight frown. 'We believe the animals are dead.' He handed Winder copies of the highway patrol reports, which described the incident with the tourist family in the red LeBaron, as well as the subsequent Winnebago attack. As Winder scanned the reports, Charles Chelsea reminded him to keep the news under his hat.

Agent Hawkins said, 'I heard something on the radio about a million-dollar reward.'

'Right!' Winder said.

'How can you do that,' the FBI man said, 'when you know these animals are dead?'

Joe Winder was having a wonderful time. 'Go ahead,' he said to Charles Chelsea. 'Explain to the gentleman.'

'Where's Koocher?' Chelsea grumbled. 'I left about a dozen messages.'

'Let's ask Pedro,' said Joe Winder. 'He sent one of his boys over to the lab yesterday. Must've had a reason.'

Charles Chelsea folded his hands on the desk, waiting. Agent Billy Hawkins turned slightly on the couch to get a better angle on the security chief. Joe Winder arched his eyebrows and said, 'How about it, Pedro? Something else happen at the Rare Animal Pavilion?'

Pedro Luz scowled, his tiny black eyes receding under the ledge of his forehead. 'I don't know what you're talking about,' he said. 'Nothing happened nowhere.' He fumbled with his clipboard. 'See? There is no report.'

The Security Department at the Amazing Kingdom of Thrills was staffed exclusively by corrupt ex-policemen, of which there was a steady supply in South Florida. The chief of Security, Pedro Luz, was a black-haired pinheaded giant of a young man who had been fired from the Miami Police for stealing cash and cocaine from drug dealers, then pushing them out of a Beechcraft high over the Everglades. Pedro Luz's conviction had been overturned by an appeals court, and the charges ultimately dropped when the government's key witness failed to appear for the new trial. The witness's absence was later explained when bits and pieces of his body were found in a shrimper's net off Key West, although there was no evidence linking this sad turn of events to Pedro Luz himself.

Once the corruption and murder charges had been dismissed, Pedro Luz promptly sued the police department to reclaim his old job, plus back wages and vacation time. Meanwhile, to keep his hand in law enforcement, Pedro Luz went to work at Francis X. Kingsbury's vacation theme park. The pay was only $8.50 an hour, but as a perk Pedro was given free access to the executive gym, where he spent hours of company time lifting weights and taking anabolic steroids. This leisurely regimen was interrupted by the embarrassing daylight theft of the prized voles—and a personal communication of urgency from Francis X. Kingsbury himself. Chief Pedro Luz immediately put the security staff on double shifts, and rented a cot for himself in the office.

Which is where he snoozed at one-thirty in the afternoon when he heard a knock on the bulletproof glass.

Pedro Luz sat up slowly and swung his thick legs off the bed. He stood up, strapped on his gun, straightened the shoulders of his uniform shirt. The knocking continued.

Through the glass, Pedro Luz saw a wiry brown man in a sweaty tank top. The man battled a spastic tic on one side of his face; it looked as if a wasp were loose in one cheek.

Pedro Luz opened the door and said, 'What do you want?'

'I'm here for the money,' the man said, twitching. He clutched a grocery bag to his chest. 'The million dollars.'

'Go away,' said Pedro Luz.

'Don't you even want to see?'

'The voles are dead.'

The wiry man said, 'But I heard on the news—'

'Go away,' said Pedro Luz, 'before I break your fucking legs.'

'But I found the mango voles. I want my money.'

Pedro Luz stepped out of the office and closed the door. He stood a full foot taller than the man with the grocery bag, and outweighed him by a hundred pounds.

'You don't listen so hot,' Pedro Luz said.

The man's face twitched uncontrollably as he tried to open the bag. 'Just one look,' he said, 'please.'

Pedro Luz seized the man by the throat and shook him like a doll. The grocery bag fell to the ground and tore open. Pedro Luz was so involved in assaulting the derelict that he didn't notice what came out of the bag: two half-starved, swaybacked ferrets, eyes glazed and bluish, lips flecked with foam. Instantly they settled in chewing on Pedro Luz's right ankle, and did not stop until he tore them off, bare-handed, and threw them with all his might against the nearest wall.

One hour later, the Publicity Department of the Amazing Kingdom of Thrills faxed the following statement to all media, under the caption 'Rare Voles Now Believed Dead':

> Police authorities reported today that the blue-tongued mango voles stolen this week from the Amazing Kingdom of Thrills are probably dead. According to the Florida Highway Patrol and the Federal Bureau of Investigation, the rare mammals—believed to be the last of the species—were killed while crossing a highway after being abandoned by the robbers who took them.
>
> Francis X. Kingsbury, founder and chairman of the Amazing Kingdom, expressed shock and sorrow at the news. 'This is a tragedy for all of us at the park,' he said Wednesday. 'We had come to love and admire Vance and Violet. They were as much a part of our family as Robbie Raccoon or Petey Possum.'
>
> Mr. Kingsbury, who had offered $1 million for the safe return of the missing animals, said he will use part of the money as a reward for information leading to the arrest and conviction of those responsible for the crime.
>
> A radical outlaw group calling itself the Wildlife Rescue Corps has claimed responsibility for the robbery at the popular amusement resort. Mr. Kingsbury said he was 'shocked and dismayed that anyone claiming to support such a cause would commit crimes of violence—crimes that ultimately led not only to the animals' deaths, but to the extinction of an entire species.'
>
> Charles Chelsea, vice president in charge of public relations, said that the blue-tongued mango voles were provided with the best possible care while in

captivity at the Amazing Kingdom. Only last year, the Florida Audubon Society praised the Vole Project as 'a shining example of private enterprise using its vast financial resources to save a small but precious resource of nature.'

Next week, the Amazing Kingdom of Thrills will present a multi-media retrospective featuring slides and videotapes of the voles during their time at the park. Entitled 'Vance and Violet: The Final Days,' the presentation will be shown three times daily at the Rare Animal Pavilion.

Tickets will be $4 for adults, $2.75 for children and senior citizens.

In the cafeteria, Charles Chelsea handed Joe Winder the fax and said, 'Nice job, big guy.'

Winder stopped on the last sentence. 'You're charging money? For a goddamn slide show?'

'Joey, we're running a business here. We're not the *National Geographic*, okay? We're not a charity.'

'A rodent slide show.' Joe Winder wadded up the press release. 'The amazing thing is not that you'd do it, because I think you'd charge tourists twenty bucks to watch the pelicans fuck, if they'd let you. The amazing thing is, people will actually come and pay.' He clapped his hands once, loudly. 'I love this business, Charlie. Every day I learn something new.'

Chelsea tightened his necktie. 'Christ, here we go again. I try to pay you a compliment, and you twist it into some sort of cynical . . . *commentary*.'

'Sorry,' said Winder. He could feel his sinuses filling up like a bathtub.

'For your information,' said Chelsea, 'I got people

calling all the way from Alaska, wanting to buy Vance-and-Violet T-shirts.' Chelsea sighed, to show how disappointed he was in Joe Winder's attitude. Then he said, with an edge of reluctance, 'You did some nice writing on this piece, Joe. Got us all off the hook.'

'Thanks, boss. And you're right—it was a piece.'

Chelsea sat down, eyeing the fast-food debris on Joe Winder's tray. One of Uncle Ely's Elves, sitting at the other end of the table, belched sonorously. Charles Chelsea pretended not to notice. He said, 'Not to brag, Joey, but I think I did a pretty fair job with this ditty myself. Mr. X loved his quotes. He said I made him sound like a real human being.'

With the tips of his fingers, Joe Winder began to rub both his temples in a ferocious circular motion.

Chelsea asked, 'Now what's the matter?'

'Headache.' Winder squinted as tightly as he could, to wring the pain out of his eyeballs. 'Listen, I called Dr. Koocher's house. He didn't go home last night. His wife is scared out of her mind.'

'Maybe he just got depressed and tied one on. Or maybe he's got a girlfriend.'

Joe Winder decided not to tell Chelsea that Koocher had tried to reach him. 'His wife's eight months pregnant, Charlie. She says he usually calls about nineteen times an hour, but she hasn't heard a word since yesterday.'

'What would you like me to do?'

'Worry like hell,' said Winder. He stood up. 'Also, I'd like your permission to talk to Pedro Luz. I think he's hiding something.'

Charles Chelsea said, 'You can't talk to him, Joe.

He's in the hospital.' He paused wearily and shook his head. 'Don't ask.'

'Come on, Charlie.'

'For rabies shots.'

'I should've guessed,' Winder said. 'My condolences to the dog.'

'It wasn't a dog,' Chelsea said. 'Can't this wait till tomorrow? Pedro's in a lot of pain.'

'No,' said Joe Winder, 'that's perfect.'

Pedro Luz had been taken to the closest emergency room, which was Mariners' Hospital down on Plantation Key. The nurse on duty remembered Pedro Luz very well, and directed Joe Winder to a private room on the second floor.

He didn't bother to knock, just eased the door open. The impressive bulk of Pedro Luz was propped up in bed, watching a Spanish-language soap opera on Channel 23. He was sucking on one end of the plastic IV tube, which he had yanked out of his arm.

'That doesn't go in your mouth,' Winder told him.

'Yeah, well, I'm thirsty.'

'You're bleeding all over the place.'

'What do you care?' said Pedro Luz. With a corner of the sheet he swabbed the blood from his arm. 'You better get out of here. I mean right now.'

Joe Winder pulled a chair close to the bed and sat down. Pedro Luz smelled like a fifty-five-gallon drum of rubbing alcohol. His luxuriant hair stood in oily black spikes, and his massive neck was covered with angry purple acne, a side effect of the fruit-and-steroid body-building diet.

'You like your job?' Winder asked him.

'What do you mean—at the Kingdom? Sure, I guess.' The security man pulled the covers off his legs, so Joe Winder could see the bandages on his ferret-gnawed ankle. 'Except for shit like this,' said Pedro Luz. 'Otherwise, it's an okay job most of the time.'

Winder said, 'So you really wouldn't want to get fired.'

'The hell are you talking about?'

'For lying. I think you're lying.'

'What about?'

Joe Winder said, 'Don't play dumb with me.' As if the guy had a choice. 'Tell me why you sent a man to Koocher's lab yesterday. I know you did, because he called me about it.'

Pedro Luz got red in the cheeks. The cords in his neck stood out like a rutting bull's. 'I already told you,' he said. 'I don't have no report on that guy.'

'He's missing from the park.'

'Then I'll do up a report,' Pedro Luz said. He breathed deeply, as if trying to calm himself. 'Soon as I get outta here, I'll make a report.' He took the IV tube out of his mouth. 'This stuff's not so bad,' he said thoughtfully. 'Tastes like sugar syrup.' He replaced the tube between his lips and sucked on it loudly.

Joe Winder said, 'You're a moron.'

'What did you say?'

'Make that a submoron.'

Pedro Luz shrugged. 'I'd beat the piss out of you, if I didn't feel so bad. They gave me about a million shots.' He leered woozily and opened his gown. 'See, they broke two needles on my stomach.'

Joe Winder couldn't help but admire Pedro Luz's

physique. He could see the bright crimson spots where the hypodermics had bent against the muscle.

'Least I won't get the rabies,' said Pedro Luz, drawing merrily on the tube. 'You oughta take off, before I start feeling better.'

Winder stood up and slid the chair back to its corner. 'Last chance, Hercules. Tell me why you sent a man to the lab yesterday.'

'Or else what?'

'Or we play "*This Is Your Life, Pedro Dipshit.*" I tell Kingsbury's people all about your sterling employment record with the Miami Police Department. I might even give them a copy of the indictment. A spine-chilling saga, Pedro. Not for the meek and mild.'

Pedro Luz removed the tube and wiped his lips on the sleeve of his gown. He looked genuinely puzzled. 'But they know,' he said. 'They know all about it.'

'And they hired you anyway?'

''Course,' said Pedro Luz. 'It was Kingsbury himself. He said every man deserves a second chance.'

'I admire that philosophy,' Joe Winder said, 'most of the time.'

'Yeah, well, Mr. X took a personal liking to me. That's why I'm not too worried about all your bullshit.'

'Yes,' said Joe Winder. 'I'm beginning to understand.'

'Because you couldn't get me fired no matter what,' said Pedro Luz. 'And you know what else? Don't never call me a moron again, if you know what's good for you.'

'I guess I don't,' said Joe Winder. 'Obviously.'

SEVEN

The ticket taker at the Wet Willy attraction was trying to control his temper. *Firm, but friendly.* That's how you deal with difficult customers; that's what they taught in ticket-taker training.

The young man, who was new to the job, said, 'I'm sorry, sir, but you can't cut to the front of the line. These other people have been waiting for a long time.'

'These other people,' the man said; 'tell me, do they own this fucking joint?'

The ticket taker did not recognize Francis X. Kingsbury, who wore thong sandals, baggy pastel swim trunks and no shirt. He also had a stopwatch hanging from a red lanyard around his neck.

'Now, you don't want me to call Security,' the ticket taker said.

'Nothing but idiots,' Kingsbury muttered, pushing his pallid belly through the turnstile. He shuffled up two flights of stairs to the launching ramp, and dropped to all fours.

The Wet Willy ride was one of the Amazing Kingdom's most popular thrill attractions, and one of the cheapest to operate. A marvel of engineering simplicity, it was nothing but a long translucent latex tube. The inside was painted in outrageous psychedelic hues, and kept slippery with drain water diverted at no cost from nearby drinking fountains. The narrow tube descended from a height of approximately six stories, with riders plunging downhill at an average angle of twenty-seven exhilarating degrees.

Francis X. Kingsbury was exceptionally proud of the Wet Willy because the whole contraption had been his idea, his concept. The design engineers at the Amazing Kingdom had wanted something to compete with Disney's hugely successful Space Mountain ride. Kingsbury had collected all the press clippings about Space Mountain and used a bright yellow marker to emphasize his contempt for the project, particularly the development cost. 'Seventeen million bucks,' he had scoffed, 'for a frigging roller ride in the dark.'

The engineers had earnestly presented several options for the Amazing Kingdom—Jungle Coaster, Moon Coaster, Alpine Death Coaster—but Kingsbury rejected each for the obvious reason that roller-coaster cars and roller-coaster tracks cost money. So did the electricity needed to run them.

'Gravity!' Kingsbury had grumped. 'The most underused energy source on the planet.'

'So you're suggesting a slide,' ventured one of the engineers. 'Maybe a water slide.'

Kingsbury had shaken his head disdainfully. Slides *look* cheap, he'd complained, we're not running a goddamn State Fair. A tube would be better, a sleek space-age tube.

'Think condom,' he had advised the engineers. 'A three-hundred-foot condom.'

And so the Wet Willy was erected. Instantly it had become a sensation among tourists at the park, a fact that edified Kingsbury's belief that the illusion of quality is more valuable than quality itself.

Lately, though, ridership figures for the Wet Willy had shown a slight but troubling decline. Francis X. Kingsbury decided to investigate personally, without notifying the engineers, the ticket takers, the Security Department or anyone else at the park. He wanted to test his theory that the ride had become less popular because it had gotten slower. The stopwatch would tell the story.

The way the Wet Willy was designed, a 110-pound teenager would be able to slide headlong from the ramp to the gelatin-filled landing sac in exactly 22.7 seconds. Marketing specialists had calibrated the time down to the decimal point—the ride needed to be long enough to make customers think they were getting their money's worth, yet fast enough to seem dangerous and exciting.

Francis X. Kingsbury weighed considerably more than 110 pounds as he crawled into the slippery chute. Ahead of him, he saw the wrinkled bare soles of a child disappear swiftly into the tube, as if flushed down a rubber commode. Kingsbury pressed the button on the stop-watch, eased to his belly and pushed off. He held his arms at his sides, like an otter going down a river-bank. In this case, an overweight otter in a ridiculous Jack Kemp hairpiece.

Kingsbury grimaced as he swooshed downward, skimming on a thin plane of clammy water. He thought: This is supposed to be fun? The stopwatch felt cold and hard against his breastbone. The bright colors on the walls of the tube did little to lift his spirits; he noticed that some of the reds had faded to pink, and the blues were runny. Not only that, sections of the chute seemed irregular and saggy, as if the latex were giving way.

He took his eyes off the fabric long enough to notice, with alarm, that he was gaining on the youngster who had entered the Wet Willy ahead of him. Being so much heavier, Francis X. Kingsbury was plummeting earthbound at a much faster speed. Suddenly he was close enough to hear the child laughing, oblivious to the danger—no! Close enough to make out the grinning, bewhiskered visage of Petey Possum waving from the rump of the youngster's swimming trunks.

'Shit,' said Kingsbury. Feverishly he tried to brake, digging into the rubber with his toes and fingernails. It was no use: gravity ruled the Wet Willy.

Kingsbury overtook the surprised child and they became one, hurtling down the slick pipe in a clumsy union of tangled torsos.

'Hey!' the kid cried. 'You're smushing me!' It was a boy, maybe nine or ten, with bright red hair and freckless all over his neck. Francis X. Kingsbury now steered the kid as if he were a toboggan.

They hit the gelatin sac at full speed and disengaged. The boy came out of the goo bawling, followed by Kingsbury, who was studying the dial of the stopwatch and frowning. He seemed not to notice the solemn group waiting outside the exit: the earnest young ticket taker, plus three uniformed security men. All were breathing heavily, as if they had run the whole way.

The ticket taker pointed at Kingsbury and said, 'That's him. Except he wasn't bald before.'

The security men, all former crooked cops recruited by Pedro Luz, didn't move. They recognized Mr. X right away.

The ticket taker said, 'Get him, why don't you!'

'Yeah,' said the red-haired tourist kid. 'He hurt me.'

'Mildew,' said Francis X. Kingsbury, still preoccupied. 'Fucking mildew under my fingernails.' He looked up and, to no one in particular, said: 'Call Maintenance and have them Lysol the Willy, A-S-A-P.'

The tourist kid raised the pitch of his whining so that it was impossible to ignore. 'That's the man who tried to smush me. On my bottom!'

'Give the little turd a free pass to the Will Bill Hiccup,' said Francis X. Kingsbury. 'And *him*,' pointing at the ticket taker, 'throw his ass, I mean it, off the property.'

The boy with the Petey Possum swimsuit ran off, sniffling melodramatically. As the security men surrounded the ticket taker, Kingsbury said, 'What, like it takes three of you monkeys?'

The men hesitated. All were reluctant to speak.

'You,' Kingsbury said, nodding at the smallest of the guards. 'Go back up and slide this goddamn tube. Yeah, you heard me. See if you can beat twenty-seven-point-two.'

The security man nodded doubtfully. 'All right, sir.'

'Yeah, and my hair,' said Kingsbury, 'it's up there somewhere. Grab it on the way down.'

Bud Schwartz paused at the door and looked back. 'It don't seem right,' he said. 'Maybe just the VCR.'

'Forget it.' Danny Pogue was rocking on his crutches down by the elevator. 'Where we gonna hide anything? Come on, Bud, let's just go.'

The elevator came and Danny Pogue clumped in.

With one crutch he held the elevator door and waited for his partner. Bud Schwartz was trying to tear himself away from Molly McNamara's fancy condo. 'Look at all this shit we're leaving behind,' he said longingly. 'We could probably get five hundred easy for the Dolbys.'

Danny Pogue leaned out of the elevator. 'And how the fuck we supposed to carry 'em? Me with these toothpicks and you with one good arm. Would you get your ass moving, please, before the bitch comes back?'

As they rode to the first floor, Danny Pogue said, 'Besides, we got no car.'

Bud Schwartz grunted sourly, wondering what became of the blue pickup. 'I feel like she owes us.'

'She does owe us. She owes us nine grand, to be exact. But we agreed it wasn't worth waiting, right?'

'I mean, owes us for this.' Bud Schwartz brandished a gauze-wrapped hand. 'Shooting us, for no good reason.'

'She's a nut case. She don't need a reason.' They got off the elevator and for once Danny Pogue led the way, swinging on his crutches.

They could see the gatehouse at the main entrance, on the other side of the condominium complex. Rather than follow the sidewalks, they decided to shorten the trip by cutting across the grounds, which were sparsely landscaped and dimly lit. In the still of the evening, the high-rise community of Eagle Ridge was at rest, except for a noisy bridge tournament being held in the rec room. On the screened porches of ground-floor apartments, couples could be seen watering their plants or feeding their cats.

As the two outsiders made their way across the darkened, shuffle-board courts, Danny Pogue's left crutch gave out and he went down with a cry.

'Goddamn,' he said, splayed on the concrete. 'Look here, somebody left a puck on the court.'

Bud Schwartz said, 'It's not a puck. Pucks are for hockey.'

Danny Pogue held the plastic disk like a Danish. 'Then what do you call it?'

'I don't know what you call it,' said Bud Schwartz, 'but people are staring, so why don't you get up before some fucking Good Samaritan calls 911.'

'I ought to sue the assholes for leaving this damn thing lying around.'

'Good idea, Danny. We'll go see a lawyer first thing in the morning. We'll sue the bastards for a jillion trillion dollars. Then we'll retire down to Club Med.' With great effort, Bud Schwartz helped Danny Pogue off the cement and steadied him on the crutches.

'So who's watching us?'

'There.' Bud Schwartz raised his eyes toward a third-floor balcony, where three women stood and peered, arms on their hips, like cranky old cormorants drying their wings.

'Hey!' Danny Pogue yelled. 'Get a life!'

The women retreated into the apartment, and Danny Pogue laughed. Bud Schwartz didn't think it was all that funny; he'd been in a rotten frame of mind ever since Molly McNamara had shot him in the hand.

As they approached the gatehouse, Danny Pogue said, 'So where's the taxi?'

'First things first,' said Bud Schwartz. Then, in a whisper: 'Remember what we talked about. The girl's name is Annie. Annie Lefkowitz.'

He had met her that afternoon by the swimming pool and gotten nowhere—but that's who they were visiting, if anybody asked. No way would they mention Molly McNamara; never heard of her.

A rent-a-cop came out of the gatehouse and nodded neutrally at the two men. He was a young muscular black with a freshly pressed uniform and shiny shoes. Over his left breast pocket was a patch that said, in navy-blue stitching: 'Eagle Ridge Security.' Danny Pogue and Bud Schwartz were surprised to see what appeared to be a real Smith & Wesson on his hip.

The rent-a-cop said: 'Looks like you guys had a rough night.'

'Barbecue blew up,' said Bud Schwartz. 'Ribs all over the place.'

Danny Pogue extended his wounded foot, as if offering it for examination. 'Burns is all,' he said. 'We'll be okay.'

The rent-a-cop didn't seem in a hurry to move out of the way. He asked for their names, and Bud Schwartz made up a couple of beauts. Ron Smith and Dick Jones.

'Where are you staying?' the rent-a-cop said. 'Which building?'

'With Amy Leibowitz,' answered Danny Pogue.

'Lefkowitz,' said Bud Schwartz, grinding his molars. 'Annie *Lefkowitz*. Building K.'

'Which unit?' asked the rent-a-cop.

'We're visiting from up North,' said Bud Schwartz. 'We're not related or anything. She's just a friend, if you know what I mean.'

'But which unit?'

Bud Schwartz made a sheepish face. 'You know, I don't even remember. But her last name's Lefkowitz, you can look it up.'

The rent-a-cop said: 'There are four different Lef-kowitzes that live here. Hold tight, I'll be right back.'

The guard went back inside, and Danny Pogue leaned closer to his partner. The gatehouse cast just enough light to reveal a change in Bud Schwartz's expression.

'So help me God,' said Danny Pogue, 'if you leave me here, I'll go to the cops.'

'What're you talking about?'

'You're gonna run, goddamn you.'

'No, I'm not,' said Bud Schwartz, although that was precisely what he was considering. He had spotted the yellow taxi, parked near a mailbox across the street.

'Don't even think about it,' said Danny Pogue. 'You're still on probation.'

'And you're on parole,' Bud Schwartz snapped. Then he thought: Hell, what are we worried about? We're not even arrested. And this jerk-off's not even a real cop.

'This guy, he can't stop us from leaving,' said Bud Schwartz. 'He can stop us from trying to get in, but he can't stop us from getting out.'

Danny Pogue thought about this. 'You're right,' he said. 'Why don't we just take off?'

'Taking off is not how I'd describe it, considering the shape we're in. Limping off is more like it.'

'I wonder if that gun's loaded,' said Danny Pogue. 'Or if he's allowed to use it.'

Bud Schwartz told him not to worry, they could still talk their way out of it. When the rent-a-cop came out of the gatehouse, he held a clipboard in one hand and a big ugly Maglite in the other.

'Miss Lefkowitz says she's had no visitors.'

Bud Schwartz looked stunned. 'Annie? Are you sure you got the right one?' He stuck with it, digging them in even deeper. 'She's probably just pissed off 'cause we're leaving, that's all. Got a good taste and doesn't want to let go.'

The rent-a-cop pointed the white beam of the Maglite at Bud Schwartz's face and said, 'Why don't you fuckheads come with me.'

Danny Pogue retreated a couple of steps. 'We didn't do nothin' wrong.'

'You lied,' said the rent-a-cop. 'That's wrong.'

Half-blind from the flashlight, Bud Schwartz shielded his eyes and said, 'Look, I can explain about Annie.' He was ummming and awwwwing, trying to come up with something, when he heard a shuffling noise off to his left. The rent-a-cop aimed the flashlight toward Danny Pogue, but Danny Pogue was gone.

Bud Schwartz said, 'I'm not believing this.'

The rent-a-cop seemed mildly annoyed. They could hear the frantic thwuck-thwuck of the crutches, heading down the unlit road.

'Bastard,' said Bud Schwartz. He felt sharp fingers—impressively strong—seize the loose span of flesh where his neck met his shoulder.

'Before I go get the gimper,' said the rent-a-cop, pinching harder, 'how about you telling me some portion of the truth.'

'Really I can't,' said Bud Schwartz. 'I'd like to, but it's just not possible.'

Then the Maglite came down against the top of his forehead, and the shutters of his brain slammed all at once, leaving the interior of his skull very cool, black, empty.

*

Joe Winder parked at the end of the gravel road and changed out of his work clothes. The necktie was the first thing to come off. He put on a pair of cutoffs, slipped into some toeless sneakers, slathered on some Cutter's and grabbed his spinning rod out of the car. He found the path through the mangroves—his path, to the water's edge. He came here almost every day after work, depending on how badly the wind was blowing. Sometimes he fished, sometimes he sat and watched.

Today he made his way quickly, worried about missing the best of the tide. When he got to the shoreline, he put on the Polaroids and swept the shallow flats with his eyes. He spotted a school of small bonefish working against the current, puffing mud about forty yards out. He grinned and waded out purposefully, sliding his feet silently across the marly bottom. A small plane flew over and the rumble of the engine flushed the fish. Joe Winder cursed, but kept his gaze on the nervous wake, just in case. Sure enough, the bonefish settled down and started feeding again. As he edged closer, he counted five in all, small black torpedoes.

As Joe Winder lifted his arm to cast, he heard a woman call out his name. The distraction was sufficient to ruin his aim; the small pink jig landed smack in the middle of the school, causing the fish to depart at breakneck speed for Andros Island and beyond. An absolutely terrible cast.

He turned and saw Nina waving from the shore. She was climbing out of her blue jeans, which was no easy task.

'I'm coming out,' she called.

'I can see that.'

And out she came, in an aqua T-shirt, an orange Dolphins cap, black panties and white Keds. Under these circumstances, it was impossible for Joe Winder to stay angry about the bonefish.

Nina was laughing like a child when she reached him. 'The water's so warm,' she said. 'Makes me want to dive in.'

He gave her a left-handed hug. 'Did you put on some bug spray?' he asked.

'Designer goo,' said Nina. 'Some sort of weird enzyme. The bugs gag on it.'

Joe Winder pointed with the tip of the fishing rod. 'See that? They're mocking me.' Another school of bonefish cavorted, tails flashing, far out of human casting range.

'I'll take your word for it,' said Nina, squinting. 'Joe, what'd you do to your hair?'

'Cut it.'

'With what?'

'A steak knife. I couldn't find the scissors.'

Nina reached up and touched what was left. 'For God's sake, why?'

'Chelsea said I looked like one of the Manson family.'

Nina frowned. 'Since when do you give a hoot what Charlie Chelsea thinks?'

'It's part of the damn dress code. Kingsbury's cracking down, or so Charlie says. I was trying to be a team player, like you wanted.' Joe Winder spotted a small bonnet shark cruising the shallows, and cast the jig for the hell of it. The shark took one look and swam away arrogantly.

Joe Winder said, 'So now I look like a Nazi.'

'No,' said Nina, 'the Nazis had combs.'

'How's the new routine coming? I assume that's why you're here.' It was the time of the week when the girls on the sex-phone line had to update their shtick.

'Tell me what you think.' Nina reached into the breast pocket of the T-shirt and pulled out a folded piece of notebook paper. Carefully she unfolded it. 'Now, be honest,' she said to Winder.

'Always.'

''Kay, here goes.' She cleared her throat. 'You say "Hello."'

'Hello!' Joe Winder sang out.

'*Hi, there*,' said Nina, reading. '*I was just thinking about you. I was thinking it would be so nice to go on a train, just you and me. A long, romantic train ride. I love the way trains rock back and forth. At first they start out so slow and hard, but then*'—here Nina had scripted a pause—'*but then they get faster and stronger. I love the motion of a big locomotive, it gets me so hot.*'

'Gets me going,' suggested Joe Winder. 'Hot is a cliché.'

Nina nodded in agreement. 'That's better, yeah. *I love the motion of a big locomotive, it really gets me going.*'

Joe Winder noticed that the tide was slowing. These fish would be gone soon.

But there was Nina in her black panties. Knee deep in the Atlantic. Blond hair tied back under her cap with a pink ribbon. Reading some damn nonsense about sex on the Amtrak, in that killer voice of hers. The words didn't matter, it was all music to Joe Winder; he was stirred by the sight of her in the water with the sun dropping behind the Keys. At times like this he sure loved Florida.

Nina told him to quit staring at her all sappy and listen, so he did.

'*Sometimes, late at night, I dream that you're a loco-motive. And I'm riding you on top, stretched out with my legs around your middle. First we go uphill, real slow and hard and rough. Then all of a sudden I'm riding the engine down, faster and harder and hotter until . . .*'

'Until what?' Joe Winder said.

'Until whatever,' said Nina with a shrug. 'I figure I'd just leave the rest to their imagination.'

'No,' said Winder. 'A metaphor like that, you need a big ending.' He slapped a mosquito that had pene-trated the sheen of Cutter's on his neck. 'How about: *We're going downhill, out of control, faster and hotter. I scream for you to stop but you keep pumping and pumping until I explode, melting against you.*'

From someplace—her bra?—Nina produced a ballpoint pen and began to scribble. 'The pumping busi-ness is a bit much,' she said, 'but I like the melting part. That's good imagery, Joe, thanks.'

'Any time.'

'Miriam's writing up another hot-tub blowjob.'

'Not again,' said Joe Winder.

'She says it's going to be a series.' Nina folded up the notebook paper and slipped it back in the pocket of her shirt. 'I'm going to be late to work if I don't get a move on. You coming in?'

'No, there's another school working that deep edge. I'm gonna try not to brain 'em with this feather.'

Nina said good luck and sloshed back toward shore.

Halfway there, she turned and said, 'My God, I almost forgot. I got one of those phone calls at home.'

Winder stopped tracking the fish. He closed the bail on his spinning reel, and tucked the rod in the crook of an elbow. 'Was it Koocher?' he asked, across the flat.

Nina shook her head. 'It was a different voice from last time.' She took a half-dozen splashy steps toward him, so she wouldn't have to yell so far. 'But that's what I wanted to tell you. The guy today said he was Dr. Koocher, only he wasn't. It was the wrong voice from before.'

Joe Winder said, 'You're sure?'

'It's my business, Joe. It's what I do all night, listen to grown men lie.'

'What exactly did he say, Nina? The guy who called. Besides that he was Koocher.'

'He said all hell was breaking loose at the park.'

'All hell,' repeated Winder.

'And he said he wanted to meet you tonight at the Card Sound Bridge.'

'When?'

'Midnight sharp.' Nina shifted her weight from one leg to the other, rippling the water. 'You're not going,' she said. 'Please?'

Joe Winder looked back across the flats, lifeless in the empty auburn dusk. 'No sign of those fish,' he said. 'I believe this tide is officially dead.'

EIGHT

Bud Schwartz didn't have to open his eyes to know where
he was; the scent of jasmine room freshener assailed
his nostrils. He was in Molly McNamara's place, lying
on the living-room sofa. He could feel her stare,
unblinking, like a stuffed owl.

'I know you're awake,' she said.

He elected not to open his eyes right away.

'Son, I know you're there.'

It was the same tone she had used the first time they
met, at one of the low points in Bud Schwartz's burglary
career; he had been arrested after his 1979 Chrysler
Cordoba stalled in the middle of 163rd Street, less than
a block from the duplex apartment he had just burglarized with his new partner, Danny Pogue. The victim of
the crime had been driving home when he saw the
stalled car, stopped to help and immediately recognized
the Sony television, Panasonic clock radio, Amana
microwave and Tandy laptop computer stacked neatly
in the Cordoba's back seat. The reason the stuff was
lying in the back seat was because the trunk was full of
stolen Neil Diamond cassettes that the burglars could
not, literally, give away.

Bud Schwartz had been smoking in a holding cell of
the Dade County Jail when Molly McNamara arrived.

At the time, she was a volunteer worker for Jackson Memorial Hospital and the University of Miami Medical School; her job was recruiting jail inmates as subjects for medical testing, a task that suited her talent for maternal prodding. She had entered the holding cell wearing white rubber-soled shoes, a polyester nurse's uniform and latex gloves.

'I'm insulted,' Bud Schwartz had said.

Molly McNamara had eyed him over the top of her glasses and said, 'I understand you're looking at eighteen months.'

'Twelve, tops,' Bud Schwartz had said.

'Well, I'm here to offer you a splendid opportunity.'

'And I'm here to listen.'

Molly had asked if Bud Schwartz was interested in testing a new ulcer drug for the medical school.

'I don't have no ulcers.'

'It doesn't matter,' Molly had said. 'You'd be in the control group.' A pill a day for three months, she had explained. Sign up now, the prosecutor asks the judge to chop your time in half.

'Your friend's already agreed to it.'

'That figures,' Bud Schwartz had said. 'I end up with ulcers, he'll be the cause of it.'

When he'd asked about possible side effects, Molly read from a printed page: headaches, high blood pressure, urinary-tract infections.

'Run that last one by me again.'

'It's unlikely you'll experience any problems,' Molly had assured him. 'They've been testing this medication for almost two years.'

'Thanks, just the same.'

'I know you're smarter than this,' Molly had told him in a chiding tone.

'If I was really smart,' Bud Schwartz had said, 'I'd a put new plugs in the car.'

A week later she had returned, this time without the rubber gloves. Pulled his rap sheet out of her purse, held it up like the Dead Sea Scrolls.

'I've been looking for a burglar,' she had said.

'What for?'

'Ten thousand dollars.'

'Very funny,' Bud Schwartz had said.

'Call me when you get out. You and your friend.'

'You serious?'

'It's not what you think,' Molly had said.

'I can't think of anything. Except maybe you're some kinda snitch for the cops.'

'Be serious, young man.' Again with the needle in her voice, worse than his mother. 'Don't mention this to anyone.'

'Who the hell would believe it? Ten grand, I swear.'

'Call me when you get out.'

'Be a while,' he said. 'Hey, is it too late to get me in on that ulcer deal?'

That was six months ago.

Bud Schwartz touched the place on his brow where the rent-a-cop's flashlight had clobbered him. He could feel a scabby eruption the size of a golf ball. 'Damn,' he said, opening his eyes slowly.

Molly McNamara moved closer and stood over him. She was wearing her reading glasses with the pink roses on the frames. She said, 'Your friend is in the bedroom.'

'Danny's back?'

'I was on my way here when I spotted him at the Farm Stores. He tried to get away, but—'

'You didn't shoot him again?' Bud Schwartz was asking more out of curiosity than concern.

'No need to,' said Molly. 'I had the Cadillac. I think your friend realized there's no point in getting run over.'

With a wheeze, Bud Schwartz sat up. His ears pounded and stomach juices bubbled up sourly in his throat. As always, Molly was prompt with the first aid. She handed him a towel filled with chipped ice and told him to pack it against his wound.

Danny Pogue clumped into the living room and sat on the other end of the sofa. 'You look like shit,' he said to Bud Schwartz.

'Thank you, Tom Selleck.' From under the towel Bud Schwartz glared with one crimson eye.

Molly McNamara said, 'That's enough, the both of you. I can't begin to tell you how much trouble you've caused.'

'We was trying to get out of your hair is all,' said Danny Pogue. 'Why're you keeping us prisoners?'

Molly said, 'Aren't we being a bit melodramatic? You are not prisoners. You're simply two young men in my employ until I decide otherwise.'

'In case you didn't hear,' said Bud Schwartz, 'Lincoln freed the slaves a long time ago.'

Molly McNamara ignored the remark. 'At the gatehouse I had to tell Officer Andrews a lie. I told him you were my nephews visiting from Georgia. I told him we'd had a fight and that's why you were trying to sneak out of Eagle Ridge. I told him your parents died in a plane crash when you were little, and I was left responsible for taking care of you.'

'Pitiful,' said Bud Schwartz.

'I told him you both had emotional problems.'

'We're heading that direction,' Bud Schwartz said.

'I don't like to lie,' Molly added sternly. 'Normally I don't believe in it.'

'But shooting people is okay?' Danny Pogue cackled bitterly. 'Lady, pardon me for saying, but I think you're goddamn fucking nutso.'

Molly's eyes flickered. In a frozen voice she said, 'Please don't use that word in my presence.'

Danny Pogue mumbled that he was sorry. He wasn't sure which word she meant.

'I'm not certain Officer Andrews believed any of it,' Molly went on. 'I wouldn't be surprised if he reported the entire episode to the condominium association. You think you've got problems now! Oh, brother, just wait.'

Bud Schwartz removed the towel from his forehead and examined it for bloodstains. Molly said, 'Are you listening to me?'

'Hanging on every word.'

'Because I've got some very bad news. For all of us.'

Bud Schwartz grunted wearily. What now? What the hell now?

'It was on the television tonight,' Molly McNamara said. 'The mango voles are dead. Killed on the highway.'

Nervously Danny Pogue glanced at his partner, whose eyes were fixed hard on the old woman. Waiting, no doubt, to see if she pulled that damn pistol from her sweater.

Molly said, 'I don't know all the details, but I suppose it's not important. I feel absolutely sick about this.'

Good, thought Bud Schwartz, maybe she's not blaming us.

But she was. 'If only I'd known how careless and irresponsible you were, I would never have recruited you for this job.' Molly took off her rose-framed glasses and folded them meticulously. Her gray eyes were misting.

'The blue-tongued mango voles are extinct because of me,' she said, blinking, 'and because of you.'

Bud Schwartz said, 'We're real sorry.'

'Yeah,' agreed Danny Pogue. 'It's too bad they died.'

Molly was downcast. 'This is an unspeakable sin against Nature. The death of these dear animals, I can't tell you—it goes against everything I've worked for, everything I believe in. I was so stupid to entrust this project to a couple of reckless, clumsy criminals.'

'That's us,' said Bud Schwartz.

Danny Pogue didn't like his partner's casual tone. He said to Molly, 'We didn't know they was so important. They looked like regular old rats.'

The old woman absently fondled the buttons of her sweater. 'There's no point belaboring it. The damage is done. Now we've got to atone.'

'Atone,' said Bud Schwartz suspiciously.

'What does that mean?' asked Danny Pogue. 'I don't know that word.'

Molly said, 'Tell him, Bud.'

'It means we gotta do something to make up for all this.'

Molly nodded. 'That's right. Somehow we must redeem ourselves.'

Bud Schwartz sighed. He wondered what crazy lie she'd told the rent-a-cop about their gunshot wounds.

And this condo association—what's she so worried about?

'Have you ever heard of the Mothers of Wilderness?' asked Molly McNamara.

'No,' said Bud Schwartz, 'can't say that I have.' Danny Pogue said he'd never heard of them, either.

'No matter,' said Molly, brightening, 'because as of tonight, you're our newest members. Congratulations, gentlemen!'

Restlessly Danny Pogue squeezed a pimple on his neck. 'Is it like a nature club?' he said. 'Do we get T-shirts and stuff?'

'Oh, you'll enjoy it,' said Molly. 'I've got some pamphlets in my briefcase.'

Bud Schwartz clutched at the damp towel. This time he pressed it against his face. 'Cut to the chase,' he muttered irritably. 'What the hell is it you want us to do?'

'I'm coming to that,' said Molly McNamara. 'By the way, did I mention that Mr. Kingsbury is offering a reward to anyone who turns in the vole robbers?'

'Oh, no,' said Danny Pogue.

'Quite an enormous reward, according to the papers.'

'How nice,' said Bud Schwartz, his voice cold.

'Oh, don't worry,' Molly said. 'I wouldn't dream of saying anything to the authorities.'

'How could you?' Danny Pogue exclaimed. 'You're the one asked us to rob the place!'

Molly's face crinkled in thought. 'That'd be awfully hard to swallow, that an old retired woman like myself would get involved in such a distasteful crime. I suppose the FBI would have to decide whom to believe—two young fellows with your extensive criminal pasts, or an older woman like myself who's never even had a parking ticket.'

Danny Pogue angrily pounded the floor with one of his crutches. 'For someone who don't like to lie, you sure do make a sport of it.'

Bud Schwartz stretched out on the sofa, closed his eyes and smiled in resignation. 'You're a piece a work,' he said to Molly McNamara. 'I gotta admit.'

The Card Sound Bridge is a steep two-lane span that connects the northern tip of Key Largo with the South Florida mainland. Joe Winder got there two hours early, at ten o'clock. He parked half a mile down the road and walked the rest of the way. He staked out a spot on some limestone boulders, which formed a jetty under the eastern incline of the bridge. From there Winder could watch for the car that would bring the mystery caller to this meeting.

He knew it wouldn't be Dr. Will Koocher; Nina was never wrong about phone voices. Joe Winder had no intention of confronting the impostor, but at least he wanted to get a good look, maybe even a tag number.

Not much was biting under the bridge. Effortlessly Winder cast the same pink wiggle-jig he'd been using on the bonefish flats. He let it sink into the fringe of the sea grass, then reeled in slowly, bouncing the lure with the tip of his rod. In this fashion he picked up a couple of blue runners and a large spiny pinfish, which he tossed back. The other fishermen were using dead shrimp with similar unexciting results. By eleven most of them had packed up their buckets and rods and gone home, leaving the jetty deserted except for Joe Winder and two other diehards.

The other men stood side by side, conversing quietly in Spanish. As Joe Winder watched them more closely, it seemed that the men were doing more serious talking than fishing. They were using Cuban yo-yo rigs, twirling the lines overhead and launching the baits with a loud plop into the water. Once in a while they'd pull in the lines and cast out again, usually without even checking the hooks.

One of the men was a husky no-neck in long canvas pants. The other was short and wiry, and as dark as coffee. Both wore baseball caps and light jackets, which was odd, considering the heat. Every few minutes a pair of headlights would appear down Card Sound Road, and Joe Winder would check to see if the car stopped at the foot of the bridge. After a while, he noticed that the two other fishermen were doing the same. This was not a good sign.

As midnight approached, the other men stopped pretending to fish and concentrated on the road. Joe Winder realized that he was stranded on the jetty with two goons who probably were waiting to ambush him. Worse, they stood squarely between Winder and the relative safety of the island. The most obvious means of escape would be jumping into Card Sound; while exceptionally dramatic, such a dive would prove both stupid and futile. The bay was shallow and provided no cover; if the goons had guns, they could simply shoot him like a turtle.

Joe Winder's only hope was that they wouldn't recognize him in the dark with his hair hacked off. It was a gray overcast night, and he was doing a creditable impersonation of a preoccupied angler. Most likely the goons would be expecting him at twelve sharp, some dumb shmuck hollering Koocher's name under the bridge.

The strategy of staying invisible might have worked if only a powerful fish had not seized Joe Winder's lure. The strike jolted his arms, and reflexively he yanked back hard to set the hook. The fish streaked toward the rock, then back out again toward open water. The buzz of Winder's reel cut like a saw through the stillness of the bay. The two goons stopped talking and looked up to see what was happening.

Joe Winder knew. It was a snook, a damn big one. Any other night he would have been thrilled to hook such a fish, but not now. From the corner of his eye he could see the goons rock-hopping down the jetty so they could better view the battle. Near a piling the fish broke to the surface, shaking its gills furiously before diving in a frothy silver gash. The goons pointed excitedly at the commotion, and Winder couldn't blame them; it was a grand fish.

Joe Winder knew what to do, but he couldn't bring himself to do it. Palm the spool. Break the damn thing off, before the two guys got any closer. Instead Joe Winder was playing the fish like a pro, horsing it away from the rocks and pilings, letting it spend itself in short hard bursts. What am I, crazy? Winder thought. From up here I could never land this fish alone. The goons would want to help, sure they would, and then they'd see who I was and that would be it. One dead snook and one dead flack.

Again the fish thrust its underslung snout from the water and splashed. Even in the tea-colored water the black lateral stripe was visible along its side. Twelve pounds easy, thought Winder. A fine one.

One of the goons clapped his hands and Joe Winder looked up. 'Nize goying,' the man said. 'Dat's some fugging fish.' It was the short wiry one.

'Thanks,' said Winder. Maybe he was wrong. Maybe these weren't the bad guys, after all. Or maybe they hadn't come to hurt him; maybe they just wanted to talk. Maybe they had Koocher and were scheming for a ransom.

After five minutes of back-and-forth, the snook was tiring. Twenty yards from the jetty it glided to the surface and flopped its tail once, twice. Not yet, Winder thought; don't give up yet, you marvelous bastard.

He heard their heavy footsteps on the rocks. Now they were behind him. He heard their breathing. One of them was chewing gum. Joe Winder smelled hot spearmint and beer.

'What're you waiting for?' asked the big one.

'He's not ready,' Winder said, afraid to turn and give them a look at his face. 'He's still got some gas.'

'No, look at the fugging thin,' said the little one. 'He juice about dead, mang.'

The snook was dogging it on top, barely putting a bend in Joe Winder's fishing rod.

'That's some good eating,' the big no-neck goon remarked.

Winder swallowed dryly and said, 'Too bad they're out of season.'

He heard both of the men laugh. 'Hey, you don't want him, we'll take it off your hands. Fry his ass up in a minute. Right, Angel?'

The little one, Angel, said, 'Yeah, I go down and

grab hole the fugging thin.' He took off his baseball cap and scrabbled noisily down the rocks.

Joe Winder got a mental picture of these two submorons in yellowed undershirts—swilling beer, watching 'Wheel' on the tube—cooking up the snook on a cheap gas stove in some rathole Hialeah duplex. The thought of it was more than he could stand. He placed his hand on the spool of the reel and pulled once, savagely.

The snook had one good powerful surge left in its heart, and the fishing line snapped like a rifle shot. Joe Winder fell back, then steadied himself. 'Goddammit,' he said, trying to sound disappointed.

'That was really stupid,' said the big goon. 'You don't know shit about fighting a fish.'

'I guess not.'

The wiry one had been waiting by the water when the fish got off. Cursing in Spanish, he monkeyed back up the rocks. To guide himself, he held a small flashlight in one hand. The beam caught Joe Winder flush in the face; there was nothing he could do.

Instantly the big goon grabbed him by the shoulder. 'Hey! You work at the park.'

'What park?'

The wiry one said, 'Doan tell me he's the guy.'

'Yup,' said the big one, tightening his grip.

The men edged closer. Joe Winder could sense they were angry about not recognizing him sooner.

'Mr. Fisherman,' said the big one acidly.

'That's me,' said Winder. 'You must be the one who wanted to talk about Dr. Koocher.'

The goon named Angel turned off the flashlight and buried it in his jacket. 'Two hours with these damn mosquitoes and you standing right here, the whole fugging tine!' He punched Joe Winder ferociously in the kidney.

As Winder fell, he thought: So they're not here to chat.

His head bounced against limestone and he began to lose consciousness. Then he felt himself being lifted by the armpits, which hurt like hell. They were carrying him somewhere in a hurry.

The husky one, Spearmint Breath, was talking in Joe Winder's ear. 'What'd he say on the phone?'

'Who?'

'The rat doctor.'

'Nothing.' Winder was panting.

'Aw, bullshit.'

'I swear. He left a message, that's all.' Winder tried to walk but felt his legs pedaling air, being swept along. 'Just a message was all,' he said again. 'He wanted to see me but he didn't say why.'

In his other ear, Joe Winder heard the wiry one call him a stinken fugging liar.

'No, I swear.'

They had him up against the side of a truck. Bronco. White. Rusty as hell. Ford Bronco, Winder thought. In case I live through this.

In case anybody might be interested.

The big goon spun Joe Winder around and pinned his arms while the one named Angel slugged him on the point of the jaw. Then he hit him once in each eye. Winder felt his face start to bloat and soften, like a melon going bad. With any luck, total numbness would soon follow.

Angel was working up a sweat. Every time he threw

a punch, he let out a sharp yip, like a poodle. It would have been hilarious except for the pain that went with it.

Finally, Spearmint Breath said, 'I don't think he knows jack shit.' Then he said something in Spanish.

Angel said, 'Chur he does, the cokesucker.' This time he hit Joe Winder in the gut.

Perfect. Can't breathe. Can't see. Can't talk.

The big goon let go, and Winder fell limp across the hood of the truck.

The man named Angel said, 'Hey, what the fug.' There was something new in his voice; he sounded very confused. Even in a fog, Joe Winder could tell that the little creep wasn't talking to him—or to Spearmint Breath, either.

Suddenly a great turmoil erupted around the truck, and the man named Angel gave out a scream that didn't sound anything like a little dog. The scream made Joe Winder raise his head off the fender and open what was left of his eyelids.

Through misty slits he saw the husky no-neck goon running toward the bridge. Running away as fast as he could.

Where was Angel?

Something lifted Joe Winder off the truck and laid him on the gravel. He struggled to focus on the face. Face? Naw, had to be a mask. A silvery beard of biblical proportions. Mismatched eyes: one as green as mountain pines, the other brown and dead. Above that, a halo of pink flowers. Weird. The mask leaned closer and whispered in Joe Winder's ear.

The words tumbled around like dice in his brainpan. Made no damn sense. The stranger bent down and said it again.

'I'll get the other one later.'

Joe Winder tried to speak but all that came out was a gulping noise. He heard a car coming down the old road and turned his head to see. Soon he became mesmerized by the twin beams of yellow light, growing larger and larger; lasers shooting out of the mangroves. Or was it a spaceship?

When Winder turned back, he was alone. The man who had saved his life was gone.

The car went by in a rush of noise. Joe Winder watched the taillights vanish over the crest of the bridge. It was an hour before he could get to his feet, another twenty minutes before he could make them move in any sensible way.

As he staggered along the pavement, he counted the cars to keep his mind off the pain. Seven sped past without stopping to help. Winder was thinking, Maybe I feel worse than I look. Maybe the blood doesn't show up so well in the dark. Two or three drivers actually touched the brakes. One honked and hurled a Heineken bottle at him.

The eighth car went by doing seventy at least, heading eastbound to the island. Joe Winder saw the brake lights wink and heard the tires squeal. Slowly the car backed up. The door on the passenger side swung open.

A voice said: 'My God, are you all right?'

'Not really,' said Joe Winder. Half-blind, he was trying to fit himself into the car when he encountered something large and fuzzy on the upholstery.

It was an animal head. He hoped it was not real.

Carrie Lanier picked it up by the snout and tossed it into the back seat. She took Joe Winder's elbow and helped him sit down. Reaching across his lap, she slammed the car door and locked it. 'I can't believe this,' she said, and stepped on the accelerator.

To Joe Winder it felt as if they were going five hundred miles an hour, straight for the ocean.

Carrie Lanier kept glancing over at him, probably to make sure he was still breathing. After a while she said, 'I'm sorry, what was your name again?'

'Joe. Joe Winder.'

'Joe, I can't believe they did this to you.'

Winder raised his head. 'Who?' he said. 'Who did this to me?'

NINE

Carrie Lanier pulled off Joe Winder's shoes and said, 'You want me to call your girlfriend?'

Winder said no, don't bother. 'She'll be home in a couple hours.'

'What does she do? What kind of work?'

'She talks dirty,' said Joe Winder, 'on the phone.'

Carrie sat on the edge of the bed. She put a hand on his forehead and felt for fever.

He said, 'Thanks for cleaning me up.'

'It's all right. You want more ginger ale?'

'No, but there's some Darvocets in the medicine cabinet.'

'I think Advils will do just fine.'

Winder grunted unhappily. 'Look at me. You ever see a face like this on an Advil commercial?'

She brought him one lousy Darvocet and he swallowed it dry. He felt worse than he could remember ever feeling, and it wasn't only the pain. It was anger, too.

'So who beat me up?' he said.

'I don't know,' said Carrie Lanier. 'I imagine it was somebody from the park. I imagine you stuck your nose where it doesn't belong.'

'I didn't,' Joe Winder said, 'not yet.'

He felt her rise from the bed, and soon heard her moving around the apartment. He called her name and she came back to the bedroom, sitting in the same indentation on the mattress.

'I was looking for something to bandage those ribs.'

'That's okay,' said Winder. 'It only hurts when I breathe.'

Carrie said, 'Maybe I don't need to tell you this, but the Amazing Kingdom is not what it seems. It's not fun and games, there's a ton of money at stake.'

'You mean it's a scam?'

'Hey, everything's a scam when you get down to it.' Her voice softened. 'All I'm saying is, stick to your job. I know it's boring as hell, but stick to it anyway. You shouldn't go poking around.'

Joe Winder said, 'My poking days are over.'

'Then what were you doing out there tonight?'

'Meeting someone at the bridge. What about you?'

'I had a free-lance gig,' Carrie said. 'A birthday party up in South Miami. Mummy and Daddy wanted Junior to meet Robbie Raccoon in person. What the heck, it was an easy five hundred. And you should've seen the house. Or should I say mansion.'

Floating, Joe Winder said: 'What do you have to do at these parties?'

'Dance with the kiddies. Waggle my coon tail. Juggle marshmallows, whatever. And pose for pictures, of course. Everybody wants a picture.'

She touched his brow again. 'You're still hot. Maybe I ought to call your girlfriend at work.'

'Don't do that,' said Joe Winder, 'please.' He didn't want Carrie to hook up with Miriam by accident. Miriam and her hot-tub 'blow-yobs.'

'This is important,' he said. 'Did you see anyone else on the road out there? Like maybe a circus-type person.'

'You're not well,' said Carrie Lanier.

'No, I mean it. Big guy with a beard. Flowers on his head.' It sounded so ridiculous, maybe he'd hallucinated the whole thing.

'That's not a circus person you're describing. That's Jesus. Or maybe Jerry García.'

'Whatever,' Joe Winder said. 'Did you see anybody on the road? That's all I'm asking.'

'Nope,' Carrie said. 'I really ought to be on my way. What'd you decide about calling the cops?'

'Not a good idea,' said Winder. 'Especially with Dr. Koocher still missing. Maybe the bad guys'll call back.'

'The creeps who did this to you?' Carrie sounded incredulous. 'I don't think so, Joe.'

She didn't say anything for several moments. Joe Winder tried to read her expression but she had turned away.

'How much does she make, your girlfriend, talking sexy on the phone?'

'Not much. Two hundred a week, sometimes two fifty. They get a bonus for selling videos. And panties, too. Twenty bucks a pair. They buy 'em wholesale from Zayre's.'

'Two fifty, that stinks,' said Carrie Lanier. 'But, hey, I've been there. You do what you have to.'

'Nina's got no complaints,' said Joe Winder. 'She says there's a creative component to every job; the trick is finding it.'

Carrie turned around, glowing. 'She's absolutely right, your girlfriend is. You know what I did before I got my SAG card? I worked in a cough-drop factory.

Wrapping the lozenges in foil, one at a time. The only way I kept from going crazy—each cough drop, I'd make a point to wrap it differently from the others. One I'd do in squares, the next I'd do in a triangle, the one after that I'd fold into a rhombus or something. Believe me, it got to be a challenge, especially at thirty lozenges per minute. That was our quota, or else we got docked.'

Joe Winder said the first dumb thing that popped into his brain. 'I wonder if Nina has a quota.'

'She sounds like she's doing just fine,' Carrie said. 'Listen, Joe, I think you ought to know. There's a rumor going around about the rat doctor. Supposedly they found a note.'

'Yeah?'

'You know what kind of note I mean. The bad kind. Good-bye, cruel world, and all that. Supposedly they found it in his desk at the lab.'

Joe Winder said, 'What exactly did it say, this supposed note?'

'I don't know all the details.' Carrie Lanier stood up to go. 'Get some rest. It's just a rumor.'

'Give me another pill, and sit down for a second.'

'Nope, I can't.'

'Get me another goddamn pill!'

'Go to sleep, Joe.'

By eight the next morning, a crowd had gathered beneath the Card Sound Bridge to see the dead man hanging from the center span. From a distance it looked like a wax dummy with an elongated neck. Up close it looked much different.

The crowd was made up mostly of tourist families on their way down to the Florida Keys. They parked haphazardly on the shoulder of the road and clambered down to where the police cars and marine patrols were positioned, blue lights flashing in that insistent syncopation of emergency. A few of the tourist husbands took out portable video cameras to record the excitement, but the best vantage was from the decks of the yachts and sleek sailboats that had dropped anchor in the channel near the bridge. The mast of one of the sloops had snagged on the hanging dead man and torn off his trousers as the vessel had passed through the bridge at dawn. By now everyone had noticed that the corpse wore no underwear.

A man from the Dade County Medical Examiner's Office stood on the jetty and looked up at the dead body swinging in the breeze, forty feet over the water. Standing next to the man from the medical examiner's was FBI Agent Billy Hawkins, who was asking lots of questions that the man from the medical examiner's didn't answer. He was keenly aware that the FBI held absolutely no authority in this matter.

'I was on my way to the park,' Agent Hawkins was saying, 'and I couldn't help but notice.'

With cool politeness, the man from the medical examiner's office said: 'Not much we can tell you at the moment. Except he's definitely dead, that much is obvious.' The coroner knew that most FBI agents went their whole careers without ever setting eyes on an actual corpse. The way Billy Hawkins was staring, he hadn't seen many.

'The poor bastard has no pants,' the agent observed. 'What do you make of that?'

'Sunburned testicles is what I make of that. If we don't haul him down soon.'

Agent Hawkins nodded seriously. He gave the coroner a card. The feds, they loved to hand out cards.

The man from the medical examiner's played along. 'I'll call if anything turns up,' he lied. The FBI man said thanks and headed back toward his car; he was easy to track—a blocky gray suit moving through a bright sea of Hawaiian prints and Day-Glo surfer shorts. A dog in a flower bed.

The amused coroner soon was joined by an equally amused trooper from the Florida Highway Patrol.

'Nice day for a hangin',' drawled the trooper. His name was Jim Tile. He wore the standard mirrored sunglasses with gold wire frames.

'I don't see a rope,' said the coroner, gesturing at the dead man high above them. 'What the hell's he hanging with?'

'That would be fishing line,' Jim Tile said.

The coroner thought about it for several moments. Then he said, 'All right, Jim, what do you think?'

'I think it's a pretty poor excuse for a suicide,' said the trooper.

A tanned young man in a crisp blue shirt and a red necktie worked his way out of the crowd. The man walked up to the coroner and somberly extended his right hand. He wore some kind of plastic ID badge clipped to his belt. The coroner knew that the tanned young man wasn't a cop, because his ID badge was in the shape of an animal head, possibly a raccoon or a small bear.

Charles Chelsea gestured toward the dead man

without looking. In a voice dripping with disgust, he said, 'Can't you guys do something about that?'

'We're working on it,' replied the coroner.

'Well, work a little faster.'

The man from the medical examiner's looked down at Charles Chelsea's animal-head ID and smiled. 'These things can't be hurried,' he said.

A jurisdictional dispute had delayed the removal of the offending body for most of the morning. It was a tricky geographic dilemma. The middle of the Card Sound Bridge marked the boundary line between Dade and Monroe counties. The Monroe County medical examiner's man had arrived first on the scene, and decided that the dead man was hanging in Dade County airspace and therefore was not his responsibility. The Dade County medical examiner's man had argued vigorously that the victim had most certainly plummeted from the Monroe County side of the bridge. Besides which the Dade County morgue was already packed to the rafters with homicides, and it wouldn't kill Monroe County to take just one. Neither coroner would budge, so the dead body just hung there for four hours until the Monroe County medical examiner announced that he was needed at a fatal traffic accident in Marathon, and scurried away, leaving his colleague stuck with the corpse—and now some whiny pain-in-the-ass PR man.

The coroner said to Charles Chelsea: 'We've got to get some pictures. Take some measurements. Preserve the scene, just in case.'

'In case of what? The poor jerk killed himself.' Chelsea sounded annoyed. Preserving the scene was the opposite of what he wanted.

Trooper Jim Tile removed his sunglasses and folded

them into a breast pocket. 'I guess I can go home. Now that we got an expert on the case.'

Charles Chelsea started to rebuke this impertinent flatfoot, but changed his mind when he took a good look. The trooper was very tall and very muscular and very black, all of which made Chelsea edgy. He sensed that Jim Tile was not the sort to be impressed by titles, but nonetheless he introduced himself as a vice president at the Amazing Kingdom of Thrills.

'How nifty,' said the trooper.

'Yes, it is,' Chelsea said pleasantly. Then, lowering his voice: 'But, to be frank, we could do without this kind of spectacle.' His golden chin pointed up at the hapless corpse. Then he jerked a thumb over his shoulder at the chattering throng of onlookers.

'All these people,' Chelsea said urgently, 'were on their way to our theme park.'

'How do you know?' asked Jim Tile.

'Look around here—where else would they be going? What else is there to see?'

'In other words, you would like us to remove the deceased as quickly as possible.'

'Yes, exactly,' said Charles Chelsea.

'Because it's competition.'

The publicity man's eyes narrowed. Frostily he said, 'That's not at all what I meant.' Giving up on the black policeman, he appealed to the coroner's sense of propriety: 'All the young children hanging around—they shouldn't be witness to something like this. Vacations are for fun and fantasy, not for looking at dead bodies.'

Jim Tile said, 'They seem to be enjoying it.'

'We didn't ask for an audience,' the coroner added. He was accustomed to gawkers in Miami. Shopping malls were the worst; drug dealers were always leaving murdered rivals in the trunks of luxury automobiles at shopping malls. The crowds were unbelievable, pushing and shoving, everybody wanting a peek at the stiff.

The coroner told Charles Chelsea: 'This always happens. It's just a sick fact of human nature.'

'Well, can't you hurry up and get him—it—down? The longer it stays up there, the more people will stop.' Chelsea paused to survey the size of the crowd. 'This is horrible,' he said, 'right in the middle of Summerfest. It's giving all these folks the wrong idea.'

Jim Tile couldn't wait to hear more. 'The wrong idea about what?'

'About Florida,' said Charles Chelsea. The indignation in his tone was authentic. 'This is not the image we're trying to promote. Surely you can understand.'

Grimly he turned and disappeared into the gallery of onlookers.

The coroner once again fixed his attention on what was hanging from the Card Sound Bridge. He asked Jim Tile, 'So what do you think about getting him down from there?'

'Easy,' said the trooper. 'I'll go up and cut the line.'

'You really think that's safe?'

Jim Tile looked at him curiously.

'With all these people milling around,' said the coroner. 'What if he hits somebody? Look at all these damn boats.' He frowned and shook his head. 'I think we've got a serious liability risk here. Somebody could be injured or killed.'

'By a falling corpse,' said Jim Tile thoughtfully.

'You betcha. Look at all these damn tourists.'

Jim Tile took out a bullhorn and ordered the boats

to weigh anchor. He also instructed the bystanders to get off the jetty under threat of arrest. Then he went to the top of the bridge and quickly found what he was looking for: a nest of heavy monofilament fishing line tangled around the base of a concrete column. One end of the monofilament was attached to the type of flat plastic spool used by Cuban handline fishermen. The other end of the line led over the side of the bridge, and was attached to the dead man's neck.

The trooper got a 35-millimeter camera out of the patrol car and took pictures of the column and the knot. Then he got down on his belly and extended his head over the side of the bridge and snapped several aerial-type photographs of the hanging corpse.

After Jim Tile put the camera away, he waved twice at the coroner, still standing on the rocks below. Then, when the coroner gave the signal, the trooper unfolded his pocketknife and cut through the monofilament fishing line.

He heard the crowd go *ooooohhhh* before he heard the splash. A marine patrol boat idled up to the dead man and fished him out of the water with a short-handled gaff.

They were loading the body into the van when the coroner told his theory to Jim Tile. 'I don't think it's a suicide,' he said.

'What, somebody was using him for bait?'

'No, this is what I think happened,' said the coroner, demonstrating with his arms. 'You know how these Cuban guys twirl the fishlines over their heads real fast to make a long cast? It looks to me like he messed up and wrapped the damn thing tight around his neck, like a bolo. That's what I think.' He picked up a clipboard and began to write. 'What was the color of his eyes? Brown, I think.'

'I didn't look,' said Jim Tile. He wasn't crazy about dead bodies.

The man from the medical examiner's reached into the van and tugged at the woolen blanket, revealing the dead man's features.

'I was right,' said the coroner, scribbling again. 'Brown they are.'

Jim Tile stared at the rictus face and said, 'Damn, I know that guy.' He wasn't a fisherman.

'A name would be nice,' the coroner said. 'He lost his wallet when he lost his pants.'

Angel, the trooper said. Angel Gaviria. 'Don't ask me how to spell it.'

'Where do you know him from?'

'He used to be a cop.' Jim Tile yanked the blanket up to cover the dead man's face. 'Before he got convicted.'

'Convicted of what?'

'Everything short of first-degree murder.'

'Jesus Christ. And here he is, out of the slammer already.'

'Yeah,' said Jim Tile. 'Modeling neckwear.'

Bud Schwartz had been a two-bit burglar since he was seventeen years old. He was neither proud of it nor ashamed. It was what he did, period. It suited his talents. Whenever his mother gave him a hard time about getting an honest job, Bud Schwartz reminded her that he was the only one of her three children who was not in psychoanalysis. His sister was a lawyer and his brother was a stockbroker, and both of them were miserably fucked up. Bud Schwartz was a crook, sure, but at least he was at peace with himself.

He considered himself a competent burglar who was swift, thorough and usually cautious. The times he'd been caught—five in all—these were flukes. A Rottweiler that wasn't in the yard the night before. A nosy neighbor, watering her begonias at three in the goddamn morning. A getaway car with bad plugs. That sort of thing. Occupational hazards, in Bud Schwartz's opinion—plain old lousy luck.

Normally he was a conservative guy who played the odds and didn't like unnecessary risks. Why he ever accepted the rat-napping job from Molly McNamara, he couldn't figure. Broad daylight, thousands of people, the middle of a fucking theme park. Jesus! Maybe he did it just to break the monotony. Or maybe because ten grand was ten grand.

Definitely a score. In his entire professional burgling career, Bud Schwartz had never stolen anything worth ten thousand dollars. The one time he'd pinched a Rolex Oyster, it turned out to be fake. Another time he got three diamond rings from a hotel room on Key Biscayne—a big-time movie actress, too—and the fence informed him it was all zircon. Fucking paste. Or so said the fence.

Who could blame him for saying yes to Molly McNamara, or at least checking it out? So when he gets out of jail, he rounds up Danny Pogue—Danny, who's really nothing but a pair of hands; somebody you drag along to help carry the shit to the car. But reliable, as far as that goes. Not really smart enough to pull anything.

So together they meet the old lady once, twice. Get directions, instructions. Go over the whole damn thing until they're bored to tears, except for the part about what to do with the voles. Bud Schwartz had assumed the whole point was to free the damn things, the way Molly talked. 'Liberate' was the word she'd used. Of course, if he'd known then what he knew now, he wouldn't have chucked that one little rat into the red convertible. If he'd known there were only two of the damn things left on the whole entire planet, he wouldn't ever have let Danny take a throw at the Winnebago.

Now the voles were gone, and Bud Schwartz and Danny Pogue were nursing their respective gunshot wounds in the old lady's apartment.

Watching a slide show about endangered species.

'This formidable fellow,' Molly McNamara was saying, 'is the North American crocodile.'

Danny Pogue said, 'Looks like a gator.'

'No, it's a different animal entirely,' said Molly. 'There's only a few dozen left in the wild.'

'So what?' said Danny Pogue. 'You got tons of gators. So many they went and opened a hunting season. I can't see gettin' all worked up about crocodiles dyin' off, not when they got a season on gators. It don't make sense.'

Molly said, 'You're missing the point.'

'He can't help it,' said Bud Schwartz. 'Just go on to the next slide.'

Molly clicked the remote. 'This is the Schaus' swallowtail butterfly.'

'Now that's pretty,' said Danny Pogue. 'I can see wanting to save somethin' like that. Isn't that a pretty butterfly, Bud?'

'Beautiful,' said Bud Schwartz. 'Really gorgeous. Next?'

Molly asked why he was in such a hurry.

'No reason,' he replied.

Danny Pogue snickered. 'Maybe 'cause there's a movie he wants to see on cable.'

'Really?' Molly said. 'Bud, you should've told me. We can always continue the orientation tomorrow.'

'That's okay,' Bud Schwartz said. 'Go on with the program.'

'*Amazon Cheerleaders*,' said Danny Pogue. 'We seen the ending the other night.'

Molly said, 'I don't believe I've heard of that one.'

'Get on with the slides,' said Bud Schwartz gloomily. Of all the partners he'd ever had, Danny Pogue was turning out to be the dumbest by a mile.

A picture of something called a Key Largo wood rat appeared on the slide screen, and Danny exclaimed: 'Hey, it looks just like one a them voles!'

'Not really,' said Molly McNamara patiently. 'This hardy little fellow is one of five endangered species native to the North Key Largo habitat.' She went on to explain the uniqueness of the island—hardwood hammocks, brackish lakes and acres of precious mangroves. And, only a few miles offshore, the only living coral reef in North America. 'Truly a tropical paradise,' said Molly McNamara, 'which is why it's worth fighting for.'

As she clicked through the rest of the slides, Bud Schwartz was thinking: How hard would it be to overpower the old bat and escape? Two grown men with six functional limbs, come on. Just grab the frigging purse, take the gun—what could she do?

The trouble was, Bud Schwartz wasn't fond of guns. He didn't mind stealing them, but he'd never pointed one at anybody, never fired one, even at a tin can. Getting shot by Molly McNamara had only reinforced his view that guns were a tool for the deranged. He knew the law, and the law smiled on harmless unarmed house burglars. A burglar with a gun wasn't a burglar anymore, he was a robber. Not only did robbers get harder time, but the accommodations were markedly inferior. Bud Schwartz had never been up to Raiford but he had a feeling he wouldn't like it. He also had a hunch that if push came to shove, Danny Pogue would roll over like a big dumb puppy. Do whatever the cops wanted, including testify.

Bud Schwartz decided he needed more time to think.

A new slide came up on the screen and he told Molly McNamara to wait a second. 'Is that an endangered species, too?' he asked.

'Unfortunately not,' Molly said. 'That's Francis X. Kingsbury, the man who's destroying the island.'

Danny Pogue lifted his chin out of his hands and said, 'Yeah? How?'

'Mr. Kingsbury is the founder and chief executive officer of the Amazing Kingdom of Thrills—the so-called amusement park you boys raided the other day. It's a tourist trap, plain and simple. It brings traffic, garbage, litter, air pollution, effluent—Kingsbury cares nothing about preserving the habitat. He's a developer.'

The word came out as an epithet.

Bud Schwartz studied the jowly middle-aged face on the screen. Kingsbury was smiling, and you could tell it was killing him. His nose was so large that it seemed three-dimensional, a huge mottled tuber of some kind, looming out of the wall.

'Public enemy number one,' said Molly. She glared

at the picture on the screen. 'Yes, indeed. The park is only a smokescreen. We've got reason to believe that Mr. Kingsbury holds the majority interest in a new golfing resort called Falcon Trace, which abuts the Amazing Kingdom. We have reason to believe that Kingsbury's intention is to eventually bulldoze every square inch of ocean waterfront. You know what that means?'

Danny Pogue pursed his lips. Bud Schwartz said nothing; he was trying to guess where the old coot was heading with this.

Molly said, 'It means no more crocodiles, no more wood rats, no more swallowtail butterflies.'

'No more butterflies?' Danny Pogue looked at her with genuine alarm. 'What kinda bastard would do something like that?'

'This kind,' said Molly, aiming a stern papery finger at the screen.

'But we can stop him, right?' Bud Schwartz was smiling.

'You can help, yes.'

'How?' Danny Pogue demanded. 'What do we do?'

Molly said, 'I need to know the full extent of Mr. Kingsbury's financial involvement—you see, there are legal avenues we could pursue, if only we knew.' She flicked off the slide projector and turned on a pair of brass table lamps. 'Unfortunately,' she said, 'Mr. Kingsbury is a very secretive man. Every document we've gotten, we've had to sue for. He is extremely wealthy and hires only the finest attorneys.'

From his expression it was clear that Danny Pogue was struggling to keep up. 'Go on,' he said.

Bud Schwartz inhaled audibly, a reverse sigh. 'Danny, we're burglars, remember? What do burglars do?'

Danny Pogue glanced at Molly McNamara, who said, 'Your partner's got the right idea.'

'Wait a second,' said Danny Pogue. 'More voles?'

'Jesus Christ, no,' Bud Schwartz said. 'No more voles.'

By now he was planning ahead again, feeling better about his prospects. He was wondering about Francis X. Kingsbury's money, and thinking what a shame that a bunch of greedy lawyers should get so much of it, all for themselves.

TEN

Nina didn't believe him, not for a second.

'You were drinking. You opened your big fat mouth and somebody smacked you.'

'No,' Joe Winder said. 'That's not what happened.'

Well, the truth would only frighten her. He sat up and squinted brutally at the sunlight.

'I'm so disappointed in you,' Nina said. She studied the bruises on his face, and not out of concern; she was looking for clues.

'I wasn't drinking,' said Joe Winder. That much he had to assert, out of pride. 'They were muggers, that's all.'

Nina pointed to his wallet, which was on the dresser. 'Muggers, Joe? Some muggers.'

'A car scared them off.'

She rolled her eyes. 'You're only making it worse.'

'What happened to trust?' Winder said. 'What happened to true goddamn love?' He got out of bed and tested his legs. Nina watched reproachfully.

'I smell perfume,' she said. 'Did you bring a woman home last night?'

'No, a woman brought *me*. She saw me on Card Sound Road and wanted to go to the police. I told her to bring me here so I could be with the love of my life.'

'Did you screw her?'

'Only six or seven times.' He went to the bathroom and stuck his face under the shower and screamed at the top of his lungs, it hurt so bad. He screamed until his ears reverberated. Then he came out, dripping, and said: 'Nina, be reasonable. Who'd make love with me, looking like this?'

'Not me.'

'Not anybody. Besides, I was half blind. I probably would've stuck it in her ear by mistake.'

Nina smiled. Finally.

Winder asked her who'd called so damn early. The phone is what woke him up.

'Your employer, Mr. Charles Chelsea. He wanted you to know there was a dead person hanging from the bridge this morning.'

Joe Winder shuffled back to the shower. This time he stepped all the way in and braced his forehead against the tile. He made the water as hot as he could bear. Maybe the dead man was Angel, he thought, or maybe it was the big guy who'd saved him from Angel.

When Winder got out, Nina stood poised with a towel in her hand. She wore a white halter top and no panties. Winder took the towel and draped it over his head.

'Why do you do this to me,' he mumbled.

'Did you hear what I said? About the dead man?' She peeled off the halter and climbed in the shower. 'Did you save me some hot water? I've got to shave my legs.' She turned the faucet handles and cursed the cold.

'Sorry,' said Joe Winder. Raising his voice over the beating of the water: 'So why is Chelsea calling me, just because there's some dead guy? The bridge is five miles from the Kingdom.'

Nina didn't answer; just filed the question away and kept on shaving. Joe Winder sat down on the toilet and watched the fixtures fog up. Plenty of hot water, he thought; no problem.

When she came out, he remarked how beautiful she looked. 'Like a sleek arctic seal.'

'Oh stop it.'

'Don't dry off, please. Don't ever dry off.'

'Get your hand away from there.' Nina slapped him sharply. 'Put your clothes on. Chelsea's waiting at the office.'

Joe Winder said, 'I'm phoning in sick.'

'No, you're not. You can't.' She wrapped the towel around her hair and left the rest bare. 'He wasn't calling about the dead person on the bridge, he was calling about the whale.'

'Orky?'

Nina opened the bathroom door to let out the steamy humidity. Joe Winder impulsively clutched her around the waist. He pressed his cheek against her damp thigh, and began to hum the tune of 'Poor Pitiful Me.' Nina pried him loose and said, 'I'm glad you don't get beat up every day.'

Something was out of alignment in Winder's brain. He blinked three or four times, slowly, but even as the steam cleared it didn't go away. Double vision! The bastards had pounded him that badly. Nina's bare bottom appeared to him as four gleaming porcelain orbs.

Distractedly, he said, 'Go on. Something about the whale?'

'Yes,' said Nina. She stood before the mirror, checking her armpits for stubble. 'Chelsea said the whale is dead.'

'Hmmm,' said Joe Winder. Orky the Killer Whale. 'And?' he said.

'And, I don't know.' Nina stepped into her panties. 'He said for you to come right away. He said it was an emergency.'

'First let's go to bed.' Winder came up behind her. In the mirror he saw two pairs of hands cupping two pairs of nipples. He saw two faces that looked just like his— lumpy, lacerated, empurpled—nuzzling the tan silky slopes of two feminine necks.

'All right, Joe,' Nina said, turning around. 'But I've got to be honest: I'm very disappointed in you—'

'It wasn't what you think.'

'—and I'm only doing this because you're in pain.' Mechanically Nina took his hand and led him toward the bed. She kicked off her underwear and unwrapped the towel from her hair. Winder was grinning like an idiot.

'I'm warning you,' Nina said, 'this isn't an act of passion, it's an act of pity.'

'I'll take it,' said Joe Winder. 'But, please, no more talking for a while.'

'All right,' she said. 'No more talking.'

Orky the Killer Whale had come to the Amazing Kingdom of Thrills under clouded circumstances. His true name (or the name bestowed by his human captors off the coast of British Columbia) was Samson. Delivered in a drugged stupor to a north California marine park, he was measured at twenty-nine feet and seven inches, a robust male example of the species *orca*. Samson was larger than the other tame killer whales in the tank, and proved considerably more recalcitrant and unpredictable. In his first six months of captivity he mauled two trained porpoises and chomped the tail off a popular sea lion named Mr. Mugsy. Trainers worked overtime trying to teach their new star the most rudimentary of whale tricks—leaping through a plastic hoop, or snatching a dead mackerel from the fingers of a pretty model—with minimal success. One day he would perform like a champ, the next he would sink to the bottom of the tank and fart belligerently, launching balloon-sized bubbles of fishy gas to the surface. The audience seldom found this entertaining. Eventually most of the seasoned whale trainers refused to enter the water with Samson. Those who tried to ride his immense black dorsal were either whiplashed or pretzeled or corkscrewed into semiconsciousness.

Quite by accident, it was discovered that Samson was enraged by the color green. This became evident on the day that the human trainers switched to vivid Kelly-green tank suits without telling the other performing mammals. Samson was supposed to open the first show by fetching an inflatable topless mermaid and gaily delivering it to a young man on a ladder, in exchange for a fistful of smelts. On this particular morning, Samson retrieved the toy, carried it across the water on his snout, flipped it into the bleachers, snatched the green-clad trainer off the ladder, flipped *him* into the bleachers, then dived to the bottom of the tank and began to pass gas relentlessly. Each time somebody tried to lure him up, Samson shot from the depths with his mouth open, the great black-and-white jaws clacking like a truck door. The crowd loved it. They thought it was part of the act.

Reluctantly the curators of the California marine park concluded that this whale was one dangerous rogue. They attempted to peddle him to another marine park, far away on the western coast of Florida, but first they changed his name to Ramu. The transaction took place at a time when ocean-theme parks around the country were reporting various troubles with trained killer whales, and animal-rights groups were seeking legislation to prevent capturing them for exhibit. Word of Samson's behavioral quirks had spread throughout the marine-park industry, which is why it was necessary to change his name before trying to sell him.

The day the deal was done, Samson was tranquilized, lashed to a canvas litter and placed aboard a chartered Sikorsky helicopter. There workers took turns sponging him with salt water during the arduous cross-country flight, which lasted seventeen hours, including stops for refueling. By the time Samson arrived in Sarasota, he was in a vile and vindictive mood. During his first fifteen minutes in the new tank, he savagely foreshortened a pectoral fin on another male *orca* and destroyed the floating basket through which he was supposed to slam-dunk beach balls. Weeks passed with little improvement in the new whale's temperament. One fateful Sunday, the animal abruptly awakened from its funk, tail-walked across the tank and did a dazzling double somer-sault before hundreds of delighted tourists. When a stubby woman in a green plaid sundress leaned too close with her Nikon, the whale seized her in his teeth, dragged her once around the tank, then spit her out like an olive pit.

It was then that Samson's new owners realized that they had been duped; they'd bought themselves a bum whale. Ramu was in fact the infamous and incorrigible Samson. Immediately the beast was quarantined as a repeat offender, while the Sarasota theme park made plans to resell him under the misleadingly gentle name of Orky.

Francis X. Kingsbury was the ideal chump. The soon-to-be-opened Amazing Kingdom of Thrills was shopping for a major ocean attraction to compete with Disney World's 'living reef.' Kingsbury saw the Orky offer as a bargain of a lifetime—a trained killer whale for only nine hundred bucks, plus freight! Kingsbury snapped at it.

Orky was more than a disappointment, he was a dud. No one at the Amazing Kingdom could train the whale to do a single trick on cue; capable of wondrous gymnastic feats, the animal remained oblivious of regimen and performed only when he damn well felt like it. Often he did his best work in the middle of the night, when the stadium was empty. But on those nocturnal occasions, when the park was closed and there was no one to reward him with buckets of dead mullet, Orky furiously would ram the sides of the whale tank until the Plexiglas cracked and the plaster buckled.

Because it was impossible to predict his moods, Orky's shows were not posted in a regular schedule. Tourists paid their money, took their seats and hoped for the best. Once in a great while, the killer whale would explode in exuberant ballet, but more often he just sulked or blew water aimlessly.

One time Francis X. Kingsbury had suggested punishing the mammoth creature by withholding supper. Orky retaliated by breaking into the pelican pool and wolfing down nine of the slow-moving birds. After that, Kingsbury said to hell with the goddamn whale and gave up on training the beast. He knew he'd been scammed but was too proud to admit it. Kingsbury's corporate underlings sensed that Orky was a sore spot with the boss, and avoided mentioning the whale exhibit in his presence.

Until today.

With Orky unexpectedly dead, the subject was bound to come up. Charles Chelsea decided on a pre-emptive strike. He broke the news as Francis Kingsbury was munching his regular breakfast bagel. 'Good,' Kingsbury said, spraying crumbs. 'Hated that fucking load.'

'Sir, it's not good,' said Charles Chelsea, 'publicity-wise.'

'How do you figure,' Kingsbury said. 'I mean, shit, what's a lousy whale to these people. You know who I mean—the media.'

Charles Chelsea said he would try to explain it on the way to the autopsy.

Joe Winder's vision returned to normal after making love to Nina; he regarded this as providential. He took a cab to Card Sound Road and retrieved his car. When he got back to the apartment, he changed to a long-sleeved shirt, charcoal trousers and a navy necktie, in the hope that high fashion would divert attention from his pulverized face. When he got to the Amazing

Kingdom, he saw he had nothing to worry about. Everybody was staring at the dead killer whale.

They had hauled the remains to one of the parking lots, and roped a perimeter to keep out nosy customers. To conceal Orky's corpse, which was as large as a boxcar, Charles Chelsea had rented an immense tent from an auto dealership in Homestead. The tent was brilliantly striped and decorated with the legend 'SOUTH FLORIDA TOYOTA-THON.' A dozen or so electric fans had been requisitioned to circulate the air, which had grown heavy with the tang of dead whale. The staff veterinarian, a man named Kukor, was up to his knees in Orky's abdomen when Joe Winder arrived.

'Joe, thank God,' said Chelsea, with an air of grave urgency. He led Winder to a corner and said, 'Mr. X is here, to give you some idea.'

'Some idea of what?'

'Of how serious this is.'

Joe Winder said, 'Charlie, I don't mean to be disrespectful but I'm not sure why I'm needed.' Over his shoulder, he heard somebody crank up a chain saw.

'Joey, think! First the damn mango voles and now Orky. It's gonna look like we're neglecting the wildlife. And this whole killer-whale thing, it's gotten very controversial. There was a piece in *Newsweek* three weeks ago.' Charles Chelsea was sweating extravagantly, and Winder assumed it had something to do with the presence of Francis X. Kingsbury.

Chelsea went on, 'I know it's unpleasant, Joe, but you can leave as soon as Doc Kukor gives us a cause of death.'

Joe Winder nodded. 'How many words?'

'Three hundred. And I need it for the early news.'

'Fine, Charlie. Later you and I need to talk.'

Chelsea was peering through the flaps in the tent, making sure that no gawkers had sneaked past the security men.

'Listen to me,' Joe Winder said. 'There's some big trouble in this park. I got the shit kicked out of me last night because of it.'

For the first time Chelsea noticed the battered condition of Joe Winder's face. He said, 'What the hell happened? No, wait, not now. Not with Mr. X around. We'll chat later, I promise.'

Winder grabbed his elbow. 'I need to know everything about the dead man at the bridge.'

Chelsea shook free and said, 'Later, Joe, for heaven's sake. Let's tackle the crisis at hand, shall we?'

Together they returned to the autopsy. Instead of concentrating on Orky's entrails, Joe Winder scanned the small group of official observers: a state wildlife officer, taking notes; the tow-truck drivers who had hauled the whale corpse to the tent; three of Uncle Ely's Elves, apparently recruited as extra manpower; and Francis X. Kingsbury himself, mouthing obscenities over the gruesome ceremony.

Nervously Chelsea directed Joe Winder to Kingsbury's side and introduced him. 'This is the fellow I told you about,' said the PR man. 'Our ace in the hole.'

Kingsbury chuckled darkly. 'Blame us for this? Some fucking fish croaks, how can they blame us?'

Joe Winder shrugged. 'Why not?' he said.

Cutting in quickly, Chelsea said: 'Don't worry, sir, it'll die down. It's just the crazy pro-animal types, that's all.' He planted a moist hand on Winder's shoulder. 'Joe's got the perfect touch for this.'

'Hope so,' said Francis X. Kingsbury. 'Meanwhile, the stink, holy Christ! Don't we have some Glade. I mean, this is fucking rank.'

'Right away,' said Chelsea, dashing off in search of air freshener.

Kingsbury gestured at the billowing tent, the murmuring onlookers, the husk of deceased behemoth. 'You believe this shit?' he said to Joe Winder. 'I'm a goddamn real-estate man is all. I don't know from animals.'

'It's a tricky business,' Winder agreed.

'Who'd believe it, I mean, looking at this thing.'

It was quite a strange scene, Joe Winder had to admit. 'I'm sure they can find a new whale for the show.'

'This time mechanical,' Kingsbury said, jabbing a finger at Orky's lifeless form. 'No more real ones. Computerized, that'd be the way to go. That's how Disney would handle it, eh?'

'Either that or a hologram,' said Joe Winder with a wink. 'Think of all the money you'd save on whale food.'

Just then Dr. Kukor, the veterinarian, tripped on something and fell down inside Orky's closet-sized stomach cavity. Two of Uncle Ely's Elves bravely charged forward to help, hoisting the doctor to his feet.

'Oh my,' Kukor said, pointing. The elves ran away frantically, their huge curly-toed shoes slapping noisily on the blood-slickened asphalt.

'What?' barked Francis X. Kingsbury. 'What is it?'

'I don't believe this,' said the veterinarian.

Kingsbury stepped forward to see for himself and Joe Winder followed, though he was sorry he did.

'Call somebody,' wheezed Dr. Kukor.

'Looks like a human,' Kingsbury remarked. He

turned to stare at Winder because Winder was clinging to his arm. 'Don't puke on me or you're fired,' said Kingsbury.

Joe Winder was trying not to pass out. The corpse wasn't in perfect condition, but you could tell who it was.

A wan and shaky Dr. Kukor stepped out of Orky's excavated carcass. 'Asphyxiation,' he declared numbly. 'The whale choked to death.'

'Well, damn,' said Francis X. Kingsbury.

Joe Winder thought: Choked to death on Will Koocher. Koocher, in a mint-green golf shirt.

'Somebody call somebody,' Kukor said. 'This is way out of my field.'

Winder reeled away from the scene. In a croaky voice he said, 'That's the worst thing I ever saw.'

'You?' Kingsbury laughed harshly. 'Three fucking tons of whale meat, talk about a nightmare.'

'Yes,' Joe Winder said, gasping for fresh air.

'I'm thinking South Korea or maybe the Sudan,' Kingsbury was saying. 'Stamp it "Tuna," who the hell would ever know? Those little fuckers are starving.'

'What?' said Winder. 'What did you say?'

'Providing I can get some goddamn ice, pronto.'

ELEVEN

Charles Chelsea decreed that there should be no mention of Dr. Will Koocher in the press release. 'Stick to Orky,' he advised Joe Winder. 'Three hundred words max.'

'You're asking me to lie.'

'No, I'm asking you to omit a few superfluous details. The whale died suddenly overnight, scientists are investigating, blah, blah, blah. Oh, and be sure to include a line that Mr. Francis X. Kingsbury is shocked and saddened.' Chelsea paused, put a finger to his chin. 'Scratch the "shocked," he said. ' "Saddened" is plenty. "Shocked" makes it sound like something, I don't know, something—'

'Out of the ordinary?' said Joe Winder.

'Right. Exactly.'

'Charlie, you are one sorry bucket of puss.'

Chelsea steepled his hands on his chest. Then he unfolded them. Then he folded them once more and said, 'Joe, this is a question of privacy, not censorship. Until Dr. Koocher's wife is officially notified, the least we can do is spare her the agony of hearing about it on the evening news.'

For a moment, Winder saw two Charles Chelseas instead of one. Somewhere in the cacophonous gearbox of his brain, he heard the hiss of a petcock, blowing off steam. 'Charlie,' he said blankly, 'the man was eaten by a fucking thirty-foot leviathan. This isn't going to remain our little secret very long.'

Chelsea's brow wrinkled. 'Eventually, yes, I suppose we'll have to make some sort of public statement. Seeing as it was our whale.'

Joe Winder leaned forward on one elbow. 'Charlie, I'm going to be honest.'

'I appreciate that.'

'Very soon I intend to kick the living shit out of you.'

Chelsea stiffened. He shifted in his chair. 'I don't know what to make of a remark like that.'

Joe Winder imagined his eyeballs pulsating in the sockets, as if jolted by a hot wire.

Charles Chelsea said, 'You mean, punch me? Actually punch me?'

'Repeatedly,' said Winder, 'until you are no longer conscious.'

The publicity man's voice was plaintive, but it held no fear. 'Do you know what kind of day I've had? I've dealt with two dead bodies—first the man on the bridge, and now the vole doctor. Plus I've been up to my knees in whale guts. I'm drained, Joe, physically and emotionally drained. But if it makes you feel better to beat me up, go ahead.'

Joe Winder said he was a reasonable man. He said he would reconsider the beating if Charles Chelsea would show him the suicide note allegedly written by Dr. Will Koocher.

Chelsea unlocked a file drawer and took out a sheet of paper with block printing on it. 'It's only a Xerox,' he said, handing it to Winder, 'but still it breaks your heart.'

It was one of the lamest suicide notes that Joe Winder had ever seen. In large letters it said: 'TO MY FRIENDS AND FAMILY, I SORRY BUT I CAN'T GO ON. NOW THAT MY WORKS IS OVER, SO AM I.'

The name signed at the bottom was '*William Bennett Koocher, PhD.*'

Winder stuffed the Xerox copy in his pocket and said, 'This is a fake.'

'I know what you're thinking, Joey, but it wasn't only the voles that got him down. There were problems at home, if you know what I mean.'

'My goodness.' Winder whistled. 'Problems at home. I had no idea.'

Chelsea continued: 'And I know what else you're thinking. Why would anybody kill himself in this ... *extreme* fashion? Jumping in a whale tank and all.'

'It struck me as a bit unorthodox, yes.'

'Well, me too,' said Chelsea, regaining some of his starch, 'until I remembered that Koocher couldn't swim a lick. More to the point, he was deathly afraid of sharks. It's not so surprising that he chose to drown himself here, indoors, rather than the ocean.'

'And the green shirt?'

'Obviously he wasn't aware of Orky's, ah, problem.'

Joe Winder blinked vigorously in an effort to clear his vision. He said, 'The man's spine was snapped like a twig.'

'I am told,' said Charles Chelsea, 'that it's not as bad as it appears. Very quick, and nearly painless.' He took out a handkerchief and discreetly dried the palms of his hands. 'Not everyone has the stomach for using a gun,' he said. 'Myself, I'd swallow a bottle of roach dust before I'd resort to violence. But, anyway, I was thinking: Maybe this was Koocher's way of joining the lost voles. A symbolic surrender to Nature, if you will. Sacrificing himself to the whale.'

Chelsea squared the corners of the handkerchief and tucked it into a pants pocket. He looked pleased with his theory. Sagely he added, 'In a sense, what happened that night in Orky's tank was a purely natural event: Dr. Koocher became part of the food chain. Who's to say he didn't plan it that way?'

Joe Winder stood up, clutching the corners of Charles Chelsea's desk. 'It wasn't a suicide,' he said, 'and it wasn't an accident.'

'Then what, Joe?'

'I believe Koocher was murdered.'

'Oh, for God's sake. At the Amazing Kingdom?'

Again Winder felt the sibilant whisper from a valve letting off pressure somewhere deep inside his skull. He reached across the desk and got two crisp fistfuls of Chelsea's blue oxford shirt. '*I sorry but I can't go on?*'

Perplexed, Chelsea shook his head.

Joe Winder said, 'The man was a PhD, Charlie. *I sorry but I can't go on?* Tonto might write a suicide note like that, but not Dr. Koocher.'

Chelsea pulled himself free of Winder's grip and said: 'It was probably just a typo, Joe. Hell, the man was terribly depressed and upset. Who proofreads their own damn suicide note?'

Pressing his knuckles to his forehead, Winder said, 'A typo? With a Magic Marker, Charlie? *I sorry* is not a bummed-out scientist making a mistake; it's an illiterate moron trying to fake a suicide note.'

'I've heard just about enough.' Chelsea circled the

desk and made for the door. He stepped around Winder as if he were a rattlesnake.

Chelsea didn't leave the office. He held the door open for Joe Winder, and waited.

'I see,' said Winder. On his way out, he stopped to smooth the shoulders of Chelsea's shirt, where he had grabbed him.

'No more talk of murder,' Charles Chelsea said. 'I want you to promise me.'

'All right, but on the more acceptable subject of suicide—who was the dead guy hanging from the Card Sound Bridge?'

'I've no idea, Joe. It doesn't concern us.'

'It concerns me.'

'Look, I'm starting to worry. First you threaten me with physical harm, now you're blabbing all these crazy theories. It's alarming, Joe. I hope I didn't misjudge your stability.'

'I suspect you did.'

Warily, Chelsea put a hand on Winder's arm. 'We've got a tough week ahead. I'd like to be able to count on you.'

'I'm a pro, Charlie.'

'That's my boy. So you'll give me Orky by four o'clock?'

'No sweat,' Winder said. 'Three hundred words.'

'Max,' reminded Charles Chelsea, 'and keep it low key.'

'My middle name,' said Joe Winder.

In the first draft of the press release, he wrote: *Orky the killer whale, a popular but unpredictable performer at the Amazing Kingdom of Thrills, died suddenly last night after asphyxiating on a foreign object.*

Chelsea sent the press release back, marked energetically in red ink.

In the second draft, Joe Winder wrote: *Orky the whale, one of the most colorful animal stars at the Amazing Kingdom of Thrills, passed away last night of sudden respiratory complications.*

Chelsea returned it with a few editing suggestions in blue ink.

In the third draft, Winder began: *Lovable Orky the whale, one of the most colorful and free-spirited animal stars at the Amazing Kingdom of Thrills, was found dead in his tank this morning.*

While pathologists conducted tests to determine the cause of death, Francis X. Kingsbury, founder of the popular family theme park, expressed deep sorrow over the sudden loss of this majestic creature.

'We had come to love and admire Orky,' Kingsbury said. 'He was as much a part of our family as Robbie Raccoon or Petey Possum.'

Joe Winder sent the press release up to Charles Chelsea's office and decided not to wait for more revisions. He announced that he was going home early to have his testicles reattached.

Before leaving the park, Winder stopped at a pay phone near the Magic Mansion and made a few calls. One of the calls was to an old newspaper source who worked at the Dade County Medical Examiner's Office. Another call was to the home of Mrs. Will Koocher, where a friend said she'd already gone back to Ithaca to await her husband's coffin. A third phone call went to Nina at home, who listened to Joe Winder's sad story of the dead vole doctor, and said: 'So the new job isn't working out, is that what you're saying?'

'In a nutshell, yes.'

'If you ask me, your attitude is contributing to the problem.'

Joe Winder spotted the acne-speckled face of Pedro Luz, peering suspiciously from behind a Snappy-the-Troll photo gazebo, where tourists were lined up to buy Japanese film and cameras. Pedro Luz was again sucking on the business end of an intravenous tube; the tube snaked up to a bottle that hung from a movable metal sling. Whenever Pedro Luz took a step, the IV rig would roll after him. The liquid dripping from the bottle was the color of weak chicken soup.

Joe Winder said to Nina: 'My attitude is not a factor.'

'Joe, you sound . . .'

'Yes?'

'Different. You sound different.'

'Charlie made me lie in the press release.'

'And this comes as a shock? Joe, it's a whole different business from before. We talked about this at length when you took the job.'

'I can fudge the attendance figures and not lose a minute of sleep. Covering up a murder is something else.'

On Nina's end he heard the rustling of paper. 'I want to read you something,' she said.

'Not now, please.'

'Joe, it's the best thing I've ever done.'

Winder glanced over toward the Snappy photo gazebo, but Pedro Luz had slipped out of sight.

Nina began to read: *Last night I dreamed I fell asleep on a diving board; the highest one, fifty meters. It was a hot steamy day, so I took my top off and lay down. I was so high up that no one but the sea gulls could see me. The sun felt wonderful. I closed my eyes and drifted off to sleep—*

'Not *"meters,"* ' Winder cut in. ' "Meters" is not a sexy word.'

Nina kept going: *When I awoke, you were standing over me, naked and brown from the sun. I tried to move but I couldn't—you had used the top of my bikini to tie my hands to the board. I was helpless, yet afraid to struggle . . . we were up so high. But then you knelt between my legs and told me not to worry. Before long, I forgot where we were. . . .*

'Not bad.' Joe Winder tried to sound encouraging, but the thought of trying to have sex on a high diving board made his stomach pitch.

Nina said: 'I want to leave something to the imagination. Not like Miriam, she's unbelievable. *I took chew in my mouth and sock like a typhoon.*'

Winder conceded that this was truly dreadful.

'I've got to listen to that pulp all night long,' Nina said. 'While she's clipping her toenails!'

'And I thought I had problems.'

She said, 'Was that sarcasm? Because if it was—'

The telephone receiver was getting heavy in Joe Winder's hand. He wedged it in the crook of his shoulder and said, 'Can I tell you what I was thinking just now? I was thinking about the gastric secretions inside a killer whale's stomach. I was thinking how unbelievably powerful the digestive juices must be in order for a whale to be able to eat swordfish beaks and seal bones and giant squid gizzards and the like.'

In a flat voice, Nina said, 'I have to go now, Joe. You're getting morbid again.'

'I guess I am.'

The click on the other end seemed an appropriate punctuation.

On the way home he decided to stop and try some bonefishing at his secret spot. He turned off County Road 905 and came to the familiar gravel path that led through the hardwoods to the mangrove shore.

Except the woods were gone. The buttonwoods, the mahogany, the gumbo-limbos—all obliterated. So were the mangroves.

Joe Winder got out of his car and stared. The hammock had been flattened; he could see all the way to the water. It looked as if a twenty-megaton bomb had gone off. Bulldozers had piled the dead trees in mountainous tangles at each corner of the property.

Several hundred yards from Joe Winder's car, in the center of what was now a vast tundra of scrabbled dirt, a plywood stage had been erected. The stage was filled with men and women, all dressed up in the dead of summer. A small crowd sat in folding chairs laid out in rows in front of the stage. Joe Winder could hear the brassy strains of 'America the Beautiful' being played by a high-school band, its lone tuba glinting in the afternoon sun. The song was followed by uneven applause. Then a man stood up at a microphone and began to speak, but Joe Winder was too far away to hear what was being said.

In a daze, Winder kicked out of his trousers and changed into his cutoffs. He got his fly rod out of the trunk of the car and assembled it. To the end of the monofilament leader he attached a small brown epoxy fly that was intended to resemble a crustacean. The tail of the fly was made from deer hair; Winder examined it to make sure it was bushy enough to attract fish.

Then he tucked the fly rod under his left arm, put on his Polaroid sunglasses and marched across the freshly flattened field toward the stage. Absolutely nothing of logic went through his mind.

The man at the microphone turned out to be the mayor of Monroe County, Florida. It was largely a ceremonial title that was passed in odd-numbered years from one county commissioner to another, a tradition interrupted only by death or indictment. The current mayor was a compact fellow with silvery hair, olive skin and the lean fissured face of a chain-smoker.

'This is a grand day for the Florida Keys,' the mayor was saying. 'Nine months from today, this will be a gorgeous fairway.' A burst of masculine clapping. 'The sixteenth fairway, if I'm not mistaken. A four-hundred-and-twenty-yard par-four dogleg toward the ocean. Is that about right, Jake?'

A heavyset man sitting behind the mayor grinned enormously in acknowledgment. He had squinty eyes and a face as brown as burned walnut. He waved at the audience; the hearty and well-practiced wave of a sports celebrity. Joe Winder recognized the squinty-eyed man as Jake Harp, the famous professional golfer. He looked indefensibly ridiculous in a bright lemon blazer, brown beltless slacks, shiny white loafers and no socks.

At the microphone, the mayor was going on about the championship golf course, the lighted tennis courts, the his-and-her spas, the posh clubhouse with its ocean view and, of course, the exclusive luxury waterfront homesites. The mayor was effervescent in his presentation, and the small overdressed audience seemed to share his enthusiasm. The new development was to be called Falcon Trace.

'And the first phase,' said the mayor, 'is already sold out. We're talking two hundred and two units!'

Joe Winder found an empty chair and sat down. He propped the fly rod in his lap so that it rose like a nine-foot CB antenna out of his crotch. He wondered why he hadn't heard about this project, considering that the property abutted the southern boundary of the Amazing Kingdom of Thrills. He didn't remember seeing anything in the newspapers about a new country club. He felt a homicidal churning in his belly.

Not again, he thought. Not again, not again, not again.

The mayor introduced Jake Harp—'one of the greatest cross-handed putters of all time'—and the audience actually rose to its feet and cheered.

Jake Harp stood at the podium and waved ebulliently. Waved and waved, as if he were the bloody pope.

'Welcome to Falcon Trace,' he began, reading off an index card. 'Welcome to my new home.'

More clapping as everyone settled back in their chairs.

'You know, I've won the PGA three times,' said Jake Harp, 'and finished third in the Masters twice. But I can honestly say that I was never so honored as when y'all selected me as the touring pro for beautiful Falcon Trace.'

A voice piped up near the stage: 'You rot in hell!'

A strong empassioned voice—a woman. The crowd murmured uncomfortably. Jake Harp nervously cleared his throat, a tubercular grunt into the microphone.

Again the woman's voice rose: 'We don't need another damn golf course. Why don't you go back to Palm Springs with the rest of the gangsters!'

Now she was standing. Joe Winder craned to get a good look.

The famous golfer tried to make a joke. Painfully he said, 'I guess we got ourselves a golf widow in the audience.'

'No,' the woman called back, 'a real widow.'

On stage, Jake Harp bent over and whispered something to the mayor, who was smoking fiercely. Someone signaled to the conductor of the high-school band, which adroitly struck up a Michael Jackson dance number. Meanwhile three uniformed sheriff's deputies materialized and edged toward the rude protester. The woman stood up, shook a fist above the silvery puff that was her head and said something that Joe Winder couldn't quite hear, except for the word 'bastard.'

Then she put on a floppy pink Easter bonnet and permitted herself to be arrested.

Well, hello, thought Winder. The lady from the Wildlife Rescue Corps, the one who'd slipped him the note at the Amazing Kingdom.

Joe Winder watched the deputies lead the old woman away. He wanted to follow and ask what in the hell was going on, but she was quickly deposited in the back of a squad car, which sped off toward Key Largo. As Jake Harp resumed his speech, Winder got up and walked past the stage toward the ocean. In a few minutes he found the familiar stretch of shoreline where he usually searched for bonefish, but the water was too milky to see over the tops of his own sneakers. As he waded into the flats, he could hear the high-school band begin to play 'The Star Spangled Banner,' signaling the climax of the groundbreaking ceremony.

As he slid his feet across the rocks and sea grass, Joe Winder started false-casting his fly, stripping out the line as he moved forward. The water was murky, roiled, just a mess. There would be no fish here, Winder knew, but still he drove the meat of the line seventy feet hard into the wind, and watched the tiny plop of the fly when it landed.

Joe Winder fished in manic motion because he knew time was running out. Before long, this fine little bay would be a stagnant ruin and the only fish worth catching would be gone, spooked by jet skis, sailboarders, motorboats and plumes of rank sewage blossoming from submerged drainage pipes.

Welcome to Falcon Trace.

He took another step and felt something seize his right ankle. When he tried to pull free, he lost his balance and fell down noisily in the water. He landed on his ass but quickly rolled to his knees, careful to hold the expensive Seamaster fly reel high and dry. Irritably Winder groped beneath the surface for the thing that had tripped him.

His fingers closed around the slick branch of a freshly cut tree. He lifted it out of the water, examined it, then let it drop again. A red mangrove, bulldozed, ripped out by the roots and dumped on the flats. Illegal as hell, but who besides the fish would ever know?

Joe Winder knelt in the shallows and thought about what to do next. Back on the soon-to-be-sixteenth hole, the band played on. After a while, the music stopped and voices could be heard, collegial chamber-of-commerce good-old-boy voices, dissipating in the afternoon breeze. Not long afterward came the sounds of luxury cars being started.

Eventually the place got quiet, and Joe Winder knew he was alone again in his favorite fishing spot. He stayed on his knees in the water until the sun went down.

In the evening he drove out to the Card Sound Bridge and parked. He got a flashlight from the trunk and began to walk along the road, keeping close to the fringe of the trees and playing the light along the ground. Soon he found the place where he had been beaten by the two goons, Angel and Spearmint Breath. Here Joe Winder slowed his pace and forced himself to concentrate.

He knew what he was looking for: a trail.

He'd spent most of his childhood outdoors, cutting paths to secret hideaways in the hammocks, glades and swamps. At a young age he had become an expert woodsman, a master of disappearing into impenetrable pockets where no one else wanted to go. Every time his father bought a new piece of property, Joe Winder set out to explore each acre. If there was a big pine, he would climb it; if there was a lake or a creek, he'd fish it. If there was a bobcat, he'd track it; a snake, he'd catch it.

He would pursue these solitary adventures relentlessly until the inevitable day when the heavy machinery appeared, and the guys in the hard hats would tell him to beat it, not knowing he was the boss's kid.

On those nights, lying in his bed at home, he would

wait for his mother to come in and console him. Often she would suggest a new place for his expeditions, a mossy parcel off Old Cutler Road, or twenty acres in the Gables, right on the bay. Pieces his father's company had bought, or was buying, or was considering.

Raw, tangled, hushed, pungent with animals, buzzing with insects, glistening with extravagant webs, pulsing, rustling and doomed. And always the portal to these mysterious places was a trail.

Which is what Winder needed on this night.

Soon he found it: an ancient path of scavengers, flattened by raccoons and opossums but widened recently by something much larger. As Winder slipped into the woods, he felt ten years old again. He followed the trail methodically but not too fast, though his heart was pounding absurdly in his ears. He tried to travel quietly, meticulously ducking boughs and stepping over rotted branches. Every thirty or so steps, he would turn off the flashlight, hold his breath and wait. Before long, he could no longer hear the cars passing on Card Sound Road. He was so deep in the wetlands that a shout or a scream would be swallowed at once, eternally.

He walked for fifteen minutes before he came upon the remains of a small campfire. Joe Winder knelt and sniffed at the half-burned wood; somebody had doused it with coffee. He poked at the acrid remains of something wild that had been cooked in a small rusty pan. He swung the flashlight in a semicircle and spotted a dirty cooler, some lobster traps and a large cardboard box with the letters 'EDTIAR' stamped on the side. On the ground, crumpled into a bright pile, was a fluorescent orange rainsuit. Winder unfolded it, held it up to gauge the size. Then he put it back the way he found it.

Behind him, a branch snapped and a voice said, 'How do you like the new pants?'

Winder wheeled around and pointed the flashlight as if it were a pistol.

The man was eating—and there was no mistaking it—a fried snake on a stick.

'Cottonmouth,' he said, crunching off a piece. 'Want some?'

'No thanks.'

'Then we've got nothing to talk about.'

Joe Winder politely took a bite of snake. 'Like chicken,' he said.

The man was cleaning his teeth with a fishhook. He looked almost exactly as Joe Winder remembered, except that the beard was now braided into numerous silvery sprouts that drooped here and there from the man's jaw. He was probably in his early fifties, although it was impossible to tell. The mismatched eyes unbalanced his face and made his expression difficult to read; the snarled eyebrows sat at an angle of permanent scowl. He wore a flowered pink shower cap, sunglasses on a lanyard, a heavy red plastic collar and no shirt. At first Joe Winder thought that the man's chest was grossly freckled, but in the flashlight's trembling beam the freckles began to hover and dance: mosquitoes, hundreds of them, feasting on his blood.

In a strained voice Joe Winder said, 'I can't help but notice that thing on your neck.'

'Radio collar.' The man lifted his chin so Winder could see it. 'Made by Telonics. A hundred fifty megahertz. I got it off a dead panther.'

'Does it work?' Winder asked.

'Like a charm.' The man snorted. 'Why else would I be wearing it?'

Joe Winder decided this was something they could chat about later. He said, 'I didn't mean to bother you. I just wanted to thank you for what you did the other night.'

The stranger nodded. 'No problem. Like I said, I got a pair of pants out of the deal.' He slapped himself on the thigh. 'Canvas, too.'

'Listen, that little guy—Angel Gaviria was his name. They found him hanging under the bridge.' Winder's friend at the medical examiner's office had confirmed the identity.

'What do you know,' the stranger said absently.

'I was wondering about the other one, too,' said Winder, 'since they were trying to kill me.'

'Don't blame you for being curious. By the way, they call me Skink. And I already know who you are. And your daddy, too, goddamn his soul.'

He motioned for Joe Winder to follow, and crashed down a trail that led away from the campfire. 'I went through your wallet the other night,' Skink was saying, 'to make sure you were worth saving.'

'These days I'm not so sure.'

'Shit,' said Skink. 'Don't start with that.'

After five minutes they broke out of the hardwoods into a substantial clearing. A dump, Joe Winder noticed.

'Yeah, it's lovely,' muttered Skink. He led Winder to the oxidized husk of an abandoned Cadillac, and lifted the trunk hatch off its hinges. The nude body of Spearmint Breath had been fitted inside, folded as neatly as a beach chair.

'Left over from the other night,' Skink explained. 'He ran out of steam halfway up the big bridge. Then we had ourselves a talk.'

'Oh Jesus.'

'A bad person,' Skink said. 'He would've brought more trouble.'

An invisible cloud of foul air rose from the trunk. Joe Winder attempted to breathe through his mouth.

Skink played the beam of the flashlight along the dead goon's swollen limbs. 'Notice the skeeters don't go near him,' he said, 'so in one sense, he's better off.'

Joe Winder backed away, speechless. Skink handed him the light and said, 'Don't worry, this is only temporary.' Winder hoped he wasn't talking to the corpse.

Skink replaced the trunk hatch on the junked Cadillac. 'Asshole used to work Security at the Kingdom. He and Angel baby. But I suppose you already knew that.'

'All I know,' said Winder, 'is that everything's going bad and I'm not sure what to do.'

'Tell me about it. I still can't believe they shot John Lennon and it's been—what, ten years?' He sat down heavily on the trunk of the car. 'You ever been to the Dakota?'

'Once,' Joe Winder said.

'What's it like?'

'Sad.'

Skink twirled the fishhook in his mouth, bit off the barb, and spit it out savagely. 'Some crazy shithead with a .38—it's the story of America, isn't it?'

'We live in violent times. That's what they say.'

'Guys like that, they give violence a bad name.' Skink stretched out on the trunk, and stared at the stars.

'Sometimes I think about that bastard in jail, how he loves all the publicity. Went from being nobody to The Man Who Shot John Lennon. I think some pretty ugly thoughts about that.'

'It was a bad day,' Joe Winder agreed. He couldn't tell if the man was about to sleep or explode.

Suddenly Skink sat up. With a blackened fingernail he tapped the radio collar on his neck. 'See, it's best to keep moving. If you don't move every so often, a special signal goes out. Then they think the panther's dead and they all come searching.'

'Who's they?'

'Rangers,' Skink replied. 'Game and Fish.'

'But the panther *is* dead.'

'You're missing the whole damn point.'

As usual. Joe Winder wondered which way to take it, and decided he had nothing to lose. 'What exactly are you doing out here?' he asked.

Skink grinned, a stunning, luminous movie-star grin.

'Waiting,' he said.

TWELVE

On the morning of July 21, a Saturday, Molly McNamara drove Bud Schwartz and Danny Pogue to the Amazing Kingdom of Thrills for the purpose of burglarizing the office of Francis X. Kingsbury.

'All you want is files?' asked Bud Schwartz.

'As many as you can fit in the camera bag,' Molly said. 'Anything to do with Falcon Trace.'

Danny Pogue, who was sitting in the back seat of the El Dorado, leaned forward and said, 'Suppose there's some other good stuff. A tape deck or a VCR, maybe some crystal. Is it okay we grab it?'

'No, it is not,' Molly replied. 'Not on my time.'

She parked in the Cindy-the-Sun-Queen lot and left the engine running. The radio was tuned to the classical station, and Bud Schwartz asked if Molly could turn it down a notch or two. She went searching through her immense handbag and came out with a Polaroid camera. Without saying a word, she snapped a photograph of Bud Schwartz, turned halfway in the seat and snapped one of Danny Pogue. The flashbulb caused him to flinch and make a face. Molly plucked the moist negatives from the slot in the bottom of the camera and slipped them into the handbag.

'What's that all about?' said Danny Pogue.

'In case you get the itch to run away,' Molly McNamara said, 'I'd feel compelled to send your photographs to the authorities. They are still, I understand, quite actively investigating the theft of the mango voles.'

'Pictures,' said Bud Schwartz. 'That's cute.'

Molly smiled pleasantly and told both men to listen closely. 'I rented you a blue Cutlass. It's parked over by the tram station. Here are the keys.'

Bud Schwartz put them in his pocket. 'Something tells me we won't be cruising down to Key West.'

'Not if you know what's good for you,' Molly said.

Danny Pogue began to whine again. 'Ma'am, I don't know nothin' about stealing files,' he said. 'Now I'm a regular bear for tape decks and Camcorders and shit like that, but frankly I don't do much in the way of, like, *reading*. It's just not my area.'

Molly said, 'You'll do fine. Get in, grab what you can and get out.'

'And hope that nobody recognizes us from before.' Bud Schwartz arched his eyebrows. 'What happens then? Or didn't you think of that.'

Molly chuckled lightly. 'Don't be silly. No one will recognize you dressed the way you are.'

She had bought them complete golfing outfits, polyester down to the matching socks. Danny Pogue's ensemble was raspberry red and Bud Schwartz's was baby blue. The pants were thin and baggy; the shirts had short sleeves and loud horizontal stripes and a tiny fox stitched on the left breast.

Bud Schwartz said, 'You realize we look like total dipshits.'

'No, you look like tourists.'

'It's not that bad,' agreed Danny Pogue.

'Listen,' Molly said again. 'When you're done with the job, get in the Cutlass and come straight back to my place. The phone will ring at one sharp. If you're not there, I'm going directly to the post office and mail these snapshots to the police, along with your names. Do you believe me?'

'Yeah, sure,' said Bud Schwartz.

She got out of the Cadillac and opened the doors for the burglars. 'How is your hand?' she asked Bud Schwartz. 'Better let your friend carry the camera bag.'

She held Danny Pogue's crutch (mending quickly, he was down to one) while he slipped the camera bag over his right shoulder. 'The tram's coming,' she announced. 'Better get moving.'

As the men hobbled away, Molly called out cheerfully and waved good-bye, as if she were their mother, or a loving old aunt.

With a trace of fondness, Danny Pogue said, 'Look at her.'

'Look at *us*,' said Bud Schwartz. 'Real fucking pros.'

'Well, at least it's for a good cause. You know, saving them butterflies.'

Bud Schwartz eyed his partner in a clinical way. 'Danny, you ever had a CAT scan?'

'A what?'

'Nothing.'

The burglars were huffing pretty heavily by the time they made it to the tram. They climbed on the last car, along with a family of nine from Minneapolis. Every one of them had sandy hair and Nordic-blue eyes and eyebrows so blond they looked white in the sunlight.

A little girl of about seven turned to Danny Pogue and asked what had happened to his foot.

'I got shot,' he said candidly.

The little girl flashed a glance at her mother, whose eyes widened.

'A tetanus shot,' said Bud Schwartz. 'He stepped on a rusty nail.'

The mother's eyes softened with relief. 'Where are you from?' she asked the men.

'Portugal,' said Danny Pogue, trying to live up to the tourist act.

'Portugal, Ohio,' Bud Schwartz said, thinking: There is no hope for this guy; he simply can't be allowed to speak.

The tiny blond girl piped up: 'We heard on the radio that the whale died yesterday. Orky the whale.'

'Oh no,' said Danny Pogue. 'You sure?'

The tram rolled to a stop in front of the main gate, where the burglars got off. Nodding good-bye to the blond Minneapolitans, Bud Schwartz and Danny Pogue slipped into the throng and located the shortest line at the ticket turnstiles.

In a gruff tone, Bud Schwartz said, '*Portugal*? What kind of fuckhead answer is that?'

'I don't know, Bud. I don't know a damn thing about tourists or where they come from.'

'Then don't say anything, you understand?' Bud Schwartz got out the money that Molly had given them to buy the admission tickets. He counted out thirty-six dollars and handed the cash to his partner.

'Just hold up one finger, that's all you gotta do,' said Bud Schwartz. 'One finger means one ticket. Don't say a goddamn thing.'

'All right,' Danny Pogue said. 'Man, I can't believe the whale croaked, can you?'

'Shut up,' said Bud Schwartz. 'I'm not kidding.'

Danny Pogue didn't seem the least bit nervous about returning to the scene of their crime. To him the Amazing Kingdom of Thrills was a terrific place, and he strutted around with a permanent grin. Bud Schwartz thought: He's worse than these damn kids.

Outside the Magic Mansion, Danny Pogue stopped to shake hands with Petey Possum. A tourist lady from Atlanta took a photograph, and Danny Pogue begged her to send him a copy. At this point Bud Schwartz considered ditching the dumb shit altogether and pulling the job alone.

Golf duds and all, Bud Schwartz was antsy about being back on the premises so soon after the rat-napping; it went against his long-standing aversion to dumb risk. He wanted to hurry up and get the hell out.

It wasn't easy locating Francis X. Kingsbury's office because it didn't appear on any of the colorful maps or diagrams posted throughout the amusement park. Bud Schwartz and Danny Pogue checked closely; there was the Cimarron Trail Ride, Orky's Undersea Paradise, the Wet Willy, the Jungle Jerry Amazon Boat Cruise, Bigfoot Mountain, Excitement Boulevard, and so on, with no mention of the administration building. Bud Schwartz decided Kingsbury's headquarters must be somewhere in the geographic center of the Amazing Kingdom of Thrills, and for security reasons probably wasn't marked.

'Why don't we ask somebody?' Danny Pogue suggested.

'Very smart,' said Bud Schwartz. 'I got a better idea. Why don't we just paint the word "thief" in big red letters on our goddamn foreheads?'

Danny Pogue wasn't sure why his partner was in such a lousy mood. The Kingdom was awesome, fantastic, sensational. Everywhere they went, elves and fairy princesses and happy animal characters waved or shook hands or gave a hug.

'I never seen so much friendliness,' he remarked.

'It's the crutch,' said Bud Schwartz.

'No way.'

'It's the damn crutch, I'm tellin' you. They're only being nice because they got to, Danny. Anytime there's a customer on crutches, they make a special point. You know, in case he's dying a some fatal disease.'

Danny Pogue said, 'You go to hell.'

'Ten bucks says it's right in the training manual.'

'Bud, I swear to God.'

'Gimme the crutch and I'll prove it.'

Danny Pogue said, 'You're the one's always on my ass about attitude. And now just listen to yourself—all because people're actin' nice to me and not to you.'

'That's not it,' said Bud Schwartz, but when he turned around his partner was gone. He found him on line at the Wild Bill Hiccup rodeo ride; Danny Pogue had stashed his crutch in the men's room and was determined to give Wild Bill Hiccup a go. Bud Schwartz was tired of bickering.

The ride was set up in an indoor corral that had been laboriously fabricated, from the brown-dyed dirt to the balsa fence posts to the polyethylene cowshit that lay in neat regular mounds, free of flies. Twenty-five mechanical bulls (only the horns were real) jumped and bucked on hidden tracks while a phony rodeo announcer described the action through a realistically tinny megaphone.

During this particular session, the twenty-five bulls were mounted by twenty-three tourists and two professional crooks. Before the ride began, Bud Schwartz leaned over to Danny Pogue and told him to be sure and fall off.

'What?'

'You heard me. And make it look good.'

When the bell rang, Bud Schwartz hung on with his good hand and bounced back and forth for maybe a minute without feeling anything close to excitement. Danny Pogue, however, was launched almost instantly from the sponge hump of his motorized Brahma—a tumble so spectacular that it brought three Company Cowpokes out of the bronco chute at a dead run. They surrounded Danny Pogue, measured his blood pressure, palpated his ribs and abdomen, listened to his heart, shined a light in his eyeballs and finally shoved a piece of paper under his nose.

'Why don't you put your name on this, li'l pardner?' said one of the Cowpokes.

Danny Pogue examined the document, shook his head and handed it to Bud Schwartz for interpretation.

'Release of liability,' Bud Schwartz said. He looked up with a dry smile. 'This means we can't sue, right?'

'Naw,' said the solicitous Cowpoke. 'All it means is your buddy's not hurt.'

'Says who?' said Bud Schwartz. 'Bunch a dumb cowboy shit-kickers. Thanks, but I think we'll try our luck with an actual doctor.'

The Cowpokes didn't look so amiable anymore, or

so Western. In fact, they were starting to look like pissed-off Miami insurance men. Danny Pogue got to his feet, dusted off his butt and said, 'Hell, Bud, it's my fault anyhow—'

'Not another word.' Bud Schwartz seized his partner by the elbow, as if to prop him up. Then he announced to the Cowpokes: 'We'd like to file a complaint about this ride. Where exactly is the administration office?'

The Cowpoke in charge of the blood-pressure cuff said, 'It's closed today.'

'Then we'll come back Monday,' said Bud Schwartz. 'Where is the office, please?'

'Over Sally's Saloon,' the Cowpoke answered. 'Upstairs, ask for Mr. Dexter in Risk Management.'

'And he'll be in Monday?'

'Nine sharp,' muttered the Cowpoke.

The other tourists watched curiously as Bud Schwartz led Danny Pogue haltingly out of the corral. By this time the Wild Bill Hiccup attraction had come to a complete and embarrassing stop (a man with a sprocket wrench had beheaded Danny Pogue's bull), and Bud Schwartz wanted to depart the arena before his partner spoiled the plan by saying something irretrievably stupid.

Into Danny Pogue's ear he said, 'You're doing fine.'

'It wasn't on purpose.'

'Yeah, I had a feeling.'

As they watched Danny Pogue's genuine hobble, the three Cowpokes from Risk Management began to worry that they might have missed something during their quickie medical exam.

One of them called out: 'Hey, how about a wheelchair?'

Without turning around, Bud Schwartz declined the offer with the wave of an arm.

'No thanks, li'l pardner,' he called back.

The same tool that picked the lock on Francis X. Kingsbury's office did the job on the rosewood file cabinet.

'So now what?' Danny Pogue said.

'We read.' Bud Schwartz divided the files into two stacks. He showed his partner how to save time by checking the index labels.

'Anything to do with banks and property, put it in the bag. Also, anything that looks personal.'

'What about Falcon Trace?' asked Danny Pogue. 'That's what Mrs. McNamara said to get.'

'That, too.'

They used pocket flashlights to examine the files because Bud Schwartz didn't want to turn on the lights in Kingsbury's office. They were on the third floor of the administration building, above Sally's Cimarron Saloon. Through the curtains Bud Schwartz could watch the Wild West show on the dusty street below. Tourists shrieked as two scruffy bank robbers suddenly opened fire on the sheriff; bloodied, the sheriff managed to shoot both bandits off their horses as they tried to escape. The tourists cheered wildly. Bud Schwartz grunted and said, 'Now there's a job for you. Fallin' off horses.'

Sitting on the floor amid Kingsbury's files, Danny Pogue looked orphaned. He said, 'I know lawyers that couldn't make sense a this shit.' He couldn't take his eyes off a portable Canon photocopier: seventy-five bucks, staring him in the face.

'We'll give it an hour,' said Bud Schwartz, but it didn't take him that long to realize that his partner was right. The files were impenetrable, stuffed with graphs and pie charts and computer printouts that meant nothing to your average break-in artist. The index tabs were marked with hopelessly stilted titles like 'Bermuda Intercontinental Services, Inc.,' and 'Ramex Global Trust, N.A.,' and 'Jersey Premium Market Research.'

Bud Schwartz arbitrarily selected the three thickest files and stuffed them in the camera bag. This would keep the old bat busy for a while.

'Look here,' said Danny Pogue, holding up a thin file. 'Credit cards.'

The index tab was marked 'Personal Miscellany.' Inside was a folder from the American Express Company that listed all the activity on Francis X. Kingsbury's Platinum Card for the previous twelve months. Bud Schwartz's expression warmed as he skimmed the entries.

Reading over his shoulder, Danny Pogue said. 'The guy sure knows how to eat.'

'He knows how to buy jewelry, too.' Bud Schwartz pointed at some large numbers. 'Look here.'

'Yeah,' said Danny Pogue, catching on. 'I wonder where he keeps it, all that jewelry.'

Bud Schwartz slipped Kingsbury's American Express folder into the camera bag. 'This one's for us,' he told his partner. 'Don't show the old lady unless I say so.'

Danny Pogue said, 'I heard a that place in New York. Cartier's.' He pronounced it 'Car-teer's.' 'That's some expensive shit they sell.'

'You bet,' said Bud Schwartz. Another thin file had caught his attention. He opened it on his lap, using his good hand to hold the flashlight while he read. The file contained Xeroxed copies of numerous old newspaper clippings, and three or four letters from somebody at the U.S. Department of Justice. The letterhead was embossed, and it felt important.

'Jesus,' said Bud Schwartz, sizing things up.

'What is it?'

He thrust the file at Danny Pogue. 'Put this in the damn bag, and let's get going.'

Danny Pogue peered at the index tab and said, 'So what does it mean?'

'It means we're gonna be rich, li'l pardner.'

Danny Pogue contemplated the name on the file folder. 'So how do you pronounce it anyway?'

'Gotti,' said Bud Schwartz. 'Rhymes with body.'

THIRTEEN

Rummaging through a dead man's belongings at midnight was not Joe Winder's idea of fun. The lab was as cold and quiet as a morgue. Intimate traces of the late Will Koocher were everywhere: a wrinkled lab coat hung on the back of a door; a wedding picture in a brass frame on a corner of his desk; a half-eaten roll of cherry-flavored Tums in the drawer; Koocher's final paycheck, endorsed but never cashed.

Winder shivered and went to work. Methodically he pored through the vole file, and quickly learned to decipher Koocher's daily charts: size, weight, feeding patterns, sleeping patterns, stool patterns. Some days there was blood work, some days there were urine samples. The doctor's notes were clinical, brief and altogether unenlightening. Whatever had bothered Koocher about the mango-vole program, he hadn't put it in the charts.

It was an hour before Joe Winder found something that caught his eyes: a series of color photographs of the voles. These were different from the glossy publicity pictures—these were extreme close-ups taken from various angles to highlight anatomical characteristics. Typed labels identified the animals as either 'Male One' or 'Female One.' Several pictures of the female had been marked up in red wax pencil, presumably by Will Koocher. In one photograph, an arrow had been drawn to the rump of the mango vole, accompanied by the notation 'CK. TAIL LENGTH.' On another, Koocher had written: 'CK. MICROTUS FUR COLOR—IS THERE BLOND PHASE?' In a third photograph, the animal's mouth had carefully been propped open with a Popsicle stick, which allowed a splendid frontal view of two large yellow incisors and a tiny indigo tongue.

Obviously the female vole had troubled Koocher, but why? Winder slipped the photos into his briefcase, and turned to the next file. It contained a muddy Xerox of a research paper titled, 'Habitat Loss and the Decline of *Microtus mango* in Southeastern Florida.' The author of the article was listed as Dr. Sarah Hunt, PhD, of Rollins College. In red ink Koocher had circled the woman's name, and put a question mark next to it. The research paper was only five pages long, but the margins were full of Koocher's scribbles. Winder was trying to make sense of them when he heard a squeaking noise behind him.

In the doorway stood Pedro Luz—pocked, bloated, puffy-eyed Pedro. 'The fuck are you doing?' he said.

Joe Winder explained that a janitor had been kind enough to loan him a key to the lab.

'What for?' Pedro Luz demanded.

'I need some more information on the voles.'

'Haw,' said Pedro Luz, and stepped inside the lab. The squeaking came from the wheels of his mobile steroid dispenser, the IV rig he had swiped from the hospital. A clear tube curled from a hanging plastic bag to a scabby junction in the crook of Pedro Luz's left arm; the needle was held in place by several cross-wraps of cellophane tape.

The idea had come to him while he was hospitalized with the ferret bites. He had been so impressed with the wonders of intravenous refueling that he'd decided to try it with his anabolic steroids. Whether this method was effective, or even safe, were questions that Pedro Luz hadn't considered because the basic theory seemed unassailable: straight from bottle to vein, just like a gasoline pump. No sooner had he hung the first bag than he had felt the surge, the heat, the tingling glory of muscles in rapture. Even at ease, his prodigious biceps twitched and rippled as if prodded by invisible electrodes.

Joe Winder wondered why Pedro Luz kept staring down at himself, smiling as he admired the dimensions of his own broad chest and log-sized arms.

'Are you feeling all right?' Winder asked.

Pedro Luz looked up from his reverie and blinked, toadlike.

Affably, Winder remarked, 'You're working mighty late tonight.'

Pedro Luz grunted: 'I feel fine.' He walked up to the desk and grabbed the briefcase. 'You got no authorization to be here after hours.'

'Mr. Chelsea won't mind.'

Invoking Charlie's name made no impression on Pedro Luz, who plucked a leaf out of Joe Winder's hair. 'Look at this shit on your head!'

'I spent some time in the mangroves,' Winder said. 'Ate snake-on-a-stick.'

Pedro Luz announced: 'I'm keeping your damn briefcase.' He tucked it under his right arm. 'Until I see some fucking authorization.'

'What's in the IV bag?' Joe Winder asked.

'Vitamins,' said Pedro Luz. 'Now get the hell out.'

'You know what I think? I think Will Koocher was murdered.'

Pedro Luz scrunched his face as if something toxic were burning his eyes. His jaw was set so rigidly that Joe Winder expected to hear the teeth start exploding one by one, like popcorn.

Winder said, 'Well, I guess I'll be going.'

Pedro Luz followed him out the door, the IV rig squeaking behind them. To the back of Winder's neck, he growled, 'You dumb little shit, now I gotta do a whole report.'

'Pedro, you need some rest.'

'The doctor wasn't murdered. He killed hisself.'

'I don't think so.'

'Man, I used to be a cop. I know the difference between murder and suicide.'

Pedro Luz turned around to lock the laboratory door. Joe Winder thought it would be an excellent moment to snatch his briefcase from the security man and make a run for it. He figured Pedro Luz could never catch him as long as he was attached to the cumbersome IV rig.

Winder pondered the daring maneuver too long. Pedro Luz glanced over his shoulder and caught him staring at the briefcase.

'Go ahead,' the big man taunted. 'Just go ahead and try.'

*

Francis X. Kingsbury and Jake Harp had an early starting time at the Ocean Reef Club, up the road a few miles from the Amazing Kingdom of Thrills. Kingsbury played golf two or three times a week at Ocean Reef, even though he was not a member and would never be a member. A most exclusive outfit, the Ocean Reef board had voted consistently to blackball Kingsbury because it could not verify several important details of his biography, beginning with his name. Infuriated by the rejection, Kingsbury made himself an unwelcome presence by wheedling regular golf invitations from all acquaintances who happened to be members, including the famous Jake Harp.

Reluctantly Jake Harp had agreed to play nine holes. He didn't like golf with rich duffers but it was part of the deal; playing with Francis X. Kingsbury, though, was a special form of torture. All he talked about was Disney this and Disney that. If the stock had dropped a point or two, Kingsbury was euphoric; if the stock was up, he was bellicose and depressed. He referred to the Disney mascot as Mickey Ratface, or sometimes simply The Rat. 'The Rat's updating his pathetic excuse for a jungle cruise,' Kingsbury would report with a sneer. 'The fake hippos must be rusting out.' Another time, while Jake Harp was lining up a long putt for an eagle, Kingsbury began to cackle. 'The Rat's got a major problem at the Hall of the Presidents! Heard they had to yank the Nixon robot because his jowls were molting!'

Jake Harp, a lifelong Republican, had suppressed the urge to take a Ping putter and clobber Francis X. Kingsbury into a deep coma. Jake Harp had to remain civil because of the Falcon Trace gig. It was his second chance at designing a golf course and he didn't want to screw up again; over on Sanibel they were still searching for that mysterious fourteenth tee, the one Jake Harp's architects had mistakenly located in the middle of San Carlos Bay.

As for his title of Falcon Trace 'touring pro,' it was spending money, that's all—tape a couple of television spots, get your face on a billboard, play a couple of charity tournaments in the winter. Hell, no one seriously expected you to actually show up and give golf lessons. Not the great Jake Harp.

In the coffee shop Francis X. Kingsbury announced that he was in a hurry because he was leaving town later in the day. The sooner the better, thought Jake Harp.

Standing on the first tee, Kingsbury spotted two of the Ocean Reef board members waiting in a foursome behind them. The men smiled thinly and nodded at him. Kingsbury placidly flipped them the finger. Jake Harp grimaced and reached for his driver.

'Love it,' said Kingsbury. 'Think they're such hot snots.'

Jake Harp knocked the ball two hundred and sixty yards down the left side of the fairway. Kingsbury hit it about half as far and shrugged as if he didn't care. Once he got in the golf cart, he drove like a maniac and cursed bitterly.

'Our club'll make this place look like a buffalo latrine.' The cart jounced heedlessly along the asphalt path. 'Like fucking Goony Golf—I can't wait.'

Jake Harp, who was badly hung over, said: 'Let's take it easy, Frank.'

'They're dying to know how I did it,' Kingsbury went on, full tilt. 'This island, it's practically a goddamn nature preserve. I mean, you can't mow your lawn without a permit from the fucking EPA.'

He stomped the brake, got out and lined up his second shot. Jake Harp asked: 'You gonna use the driver again?'

Kingsbury swung like a canecutter, topping the ball noisily. It skidded maybe eighty yards, cutting a bluish vector through the dew-covered grass.

'Keep your head down,' advised Jake Harp.

Kingsbury hopped back in the cart and said: 'Grandfathering, that's how I did it. The guy I bought from, he'd had his permits since '74. I'm talking Army Corps, Fish and Wildlife, even Interior. The state—well, yeah, that was a problem. For that I had to spread a little here and there. And Monroe County, forget it.'

He shut up long enough to get out and hit again. This time he switched to a four-wood, which he skied into a liver-shaped bunker. 'Fuck me,' muttered Francis Kingsbury. He remained silent as Jake Harp casually knocked his second shot thirty feet from the pin.

'What was that, a five-iron? A six?'

'A six,' replied Jake Harp, pinching the bridge of his nose. He figured if he could just cut off circulation, it would starve the pain behind his eyeballs and make his hangover go away.

Kingsbury punched the accelerator and they were off again. 'You know how I got the county boys? The ones giving me a bad time, I promised 'em units. Not raw lots, no fucking way—town houses is all, the one-bedrooms with no garage.'

'Oh,' said Jake Harp, feeling privileged. He'd been given a double lot, oceanfront, plus first option on one of the spec homes.

'Townhouses,' Kingsbury repeated with a laugh. 'And they were happy as clams. All I got to do, it's easy, is sit on the titles until Phase One is built. You know, keep it off the tax rolls for a few months. 'Case some damn reporter shows up at the courthouse and starts looking up names.'

Jake Harp didn't understand the nuances of Francis Kingsbury's scheme. The man was proud of himself, that much was obvious.

When they pulled up to the sand trap, they saw that Kingsbury's golf ball was practically buried under the lip. It appeared to have landed at the approximate speed and trajectory of a mortar round.

Kingsbury stood over the ball for a long time, as if waiting for it to make a move. Finally he said to Jake Harp: 'You're the pro. What the hell now, a wedge? A nine, maybe?'

'Your only prayer,' said Jake Harp, forcing a rheumy chuckle, 'is a stick of dynamite.' Miraculously, Kingsbury needed only three swings to blast out of the bunker, and two putts to get down.

While waiting on the next tee, Jake Harp said he thought it would be better if he didn't do any more speaking engagements on behalf of Falcon Trace.

Kingsbury scowled. 'Yeah, I heard what happened, some broad.'

'I'm not comfortable in those situations, Frank.'

'Well, who the hell is? We got her name, the old bitch.' Kingsbury took out a wood and started whisking the air with violent practice swings. Jake Harp could scarcely stand to look.

'One of those damn bunny huggers,' Kingsbury was

saying. 'Anti this and anti that. Got some group, the Mothers of some fucking thing.'

'It doesn't really matter,' said Jake Harp.

'The hell it doesn't.' Francis X. Kingsbury stopped swinging and pointed the polished head of the driver at Jake Harp's chest. 'Now that we know who she is, don't you worry. This shit'll stop—it's been taken care of. You'll be fine from now on.'

'I'm a golfer is all. I don't do speeches.'

Kingsbury wasn't listening. 'Maybe these assholes'll let us play through.' He hollered down the fairway toward the other golfers, but they seemed not to hear. Kingsbury teed up a ball. He said, 'Fine, they want to be snots.'

'Don't,' pleaded Jake Harp. The slow-playing foursome was well within the limited range of Kingsbury's driver. 'Frank, what's the hurry?'

Kingsbury had already coiled into his backswing. 'Yuppie snots,' he said, following through with a ferocious grunt. The ball took off like a missile, low and true.

Terrific, thought Jake Harp. The one time he keeps his left arm straight.

The other golfers scattered and watched the ball streak past. They reassembled in the middle of the fairway, shook their fists at Kingsbury and began a swift march back toward the tee.

'Shit,' said Jake Harp. He didn't have the energy for a fistfight; he didn't even have the energy to watch.

Francis X. Kingsbury put the wood in his bag, and sat down behind the steering wheel of the golf cart. The angry players were advancing in an infantry line that was the color of lollipops. Where Kingsbury came from, it would be hard to regard such men as dangerous.

'Aw, let's go,' said Jake Harp.

Kingsbury nodded and turned the golf cart around. 'Trying to make a point is all,' he said. 'Etiquette, am I right? Have some fucking common courtesy for other players.'

Jake Harp said, 'I think they got the message.' He could hear the golfers shouting and cursing as they drove away. He hoped none of them had recognized him.

On the drive back to the clubhouse, Francis Kingsbury asked Jake Harp for the name of the restaurant manager at Ocean Reef.

'I've got no idea,' Jake Harp said.

'But you're a member here.'

'Frank, I'm a member of seventy-four country clubs all over the damn country. Some I've never even played.'

Kingsbury went on: 'The reason I asked, I got a line on a big shipment of fish. Maybe they'd want to buy some.'

'I'll ask around. What kind of fish?'

'Tuna, I think. Maybe king mackerel.'

'You don't know?'

'Hell, Jake, I'm a real-estate man, not a goddamn chef. It's a trailer full of fish is all I know. Maybe six thousand pounds.'

Jake Harp said, 'Holy Jesus.'

Francis Kingsbury wasn't about to get into the whole messy story. He'd been having a devil of a time penetrating the Sudanese bureaucracy; UNICEF was no better. *Yes, of course we'd welcome any famine relief, but first you'll have to fill out some forms and answer some questions.* . . . Meanwhile, no one at the Amazing Kingdom seemed to know how long whale meat would stay fresh.

From the back of the golf cart came a high-pitched electronic beeping. Kingsbury quickly pulled off the path and parked in a stand of Australian pines. He unzipped his golf bag and removed a cellular telephone.

When he heard who was on the other end, he lowered his voice and turned away. Jake Harp took the hint; he slipped into the trees to get rid of the two Bloody Marys he'd had for breakfast. It was several seconds before he realized he was pissing all over somebody's brand-new Titleist. He carefully wiped it dry with a handkerchief and dropped it in his pocket.

Francis X. Kingsbury was punching a new number into the phone when Jake Harp returned to the golf cart.

'Get me that dildo Chelsea,' he was saying. 'No . . . who? I don't care—where did you say he is? Twenty minutes, he's not in my office and that's it. And get that fucking Pedro, he's in his car. Keep him on the line till— right—I get back.'

He touched a button and the cellular phone made a burp. Kingsbury put it away. He was steaming mad.

Jake Harp said, 'More problems?'

'Yeah, a major goddamn problem,' said Kingsbury. 'Only this one works for me.'

'So fire him.'

'Oh, I am,' Kingsbury said, 'and that's just for starters.'

FOURTEEN

Molly McNamara came out of the kitchen carrying a silver teapot on a silver tray.

'No thank you,' said Agent Billy Hawkins.

'It's herbal,' Molly said, pouring a cup. 'Now I want you to try this.'

Hawkins politely took a drink. It tasted like cider.

'There now,' said Molly. 'Isn't that good?'

Hiding behind the door of the guest bedroom, Bud Schwartz and Danny Pogue strained to hear what was going on. They couldn't believe she was serving tea to an FBI man.

'I'd like to ask you a few questions,' Billy Hawkins was saying.

Molly cocked her head pleasantly. 'Of course. Fire away.'

'Let's begin with the Mothers of Wilderness. You're the president?'

'And founder, yes. We're just a small group of older folks who are deeply concerned about the future of the environment.' She held her teacup steady. 'I'm sure you know all this.'

Agent Hawkins went on: 'What about the Wildlife Rescue Corps? What can you tell me about it?'

Molly McNamara was impressed by the FBI man's

grammar; most people would have used 'them' instead of 'it.'

'Just what I've read in the papers,' she said, sipping. 'That's the organization that is taking credit for freeing the mango voles, is that correct?'

'Right.'

'I'm assuming this is what gives you jurisdiction in this matter—the fact that the voles are a federally protected endangered species.'

'Right again,' said Hawkins. She was a sharp one.

Behind the bedroom door, Bud Schwartz was ready to yank his hair out. The crazy old twat was screwing with the FBI, and enjoying it!

Danny Pogue looked as confused as ever. He leaned close and whispered: 'I thought sure he was after you and me.'

'Shut up,' Bud Schwartz said. He was having a hard enough time hearing the conversation in the living room.

The FBI man was saying: 'We have reason to suspect a connection between the Wildlife Rescue Corps and the Mothers of Wilderness—'

'That's outlandish,' said Molly McNamara.

Agent Hawkins let the idea hang. He just sat there with his square shoulders and his square haircut, looking impassive and not the least bit accusatory.

Molly asked: 'What evidence do you have?'

'No evidence, just indications.'

'I see.' Her tone was one of pleasant curiosity.

Billy Hawkins opened his briefcase and took out two shiny pieces of paper. Xeroxes. 'Last month the Mothers of Wilderness put out a press release. Do you remember?'

'Certainly,' said Molly. 'I wrote it myself. We were calling for an investigation of zoning irregularities at Falcon Trace. We thought the grand jury should call a few witnesses.'

The FBI agent handed her the papers. 'That one's a copy of your press release. The other is a note delivered to the Amazing Kingdom of Thrills soon after the theft of the blue-tongued mango voles.'

Molly held both documents in her lap. 'It looks like they were done on the same typewriter,' she remarked.

In the bedroom, Bud Schwartz slumped to his knees when he heard what Molly said. He thought: She's insane. She's crazy as a goddamn bedbug. *We're all going to jail!*

Back in the living room, Molly was saying, 'I'm no expert, but the typing looks very similar.'

If Agent Billy Hawkins was caught off guard, he masked it well.

'You're right,' he said without expression. 'Both of these papers were typed on a Smith-Corona model XD 5500 electronic. We don't know yet if they came out of the same machine, but they were definitely done on the same model.'

Molly cheerfully took the half-empty teapot back to the kitchen. Hawkins heard a faucet running, the sound of silverware clanking in the sink. In the bedroom, Danny Pogue put his mouth to Bud Schwartz's ear and said: 'What if she shoots him?'

Bud Schwartz hadn't thought of that. Christ, she couldn't be that loony, to kill an FBI man in her own apartment! Unless she planned to pin it on a couple of dirtbag burglars in the bedroom. . . .

When Molly came bustling out again, Billy Hawkins

said: 'We've sent the originals to Washington. Hopefully they'll be able to say conclusively if it was the same typewriter.'

Molly sat down. 'It's quite difficult to tell, isn't it? With these new electronic typewriters, I mean. The key strokes are not as distinct. I read that someplace.'

The FBI man smiled confidently. 'Our lab is very, very good. Probably the best in the world.'

Molly McNamara took out a pale blue tissue and began to clean her eyeglasses: neat, circular swipes. 'I suppose it's possible,' she said, 'that somebody in our little group has gotten carried away.'

'It's an emotional issue,' agreed Billy Hawkins, 'this animal-rights thing.'

'Still, I cannot believe any of the Mothers would commit a crime. I simply cannot believe they would steal those creatures.'

'Perhaps they hired somebody to do it.'

Hawkins went into the briefcase again and came out with a standard police mug shot. He handed it to Molly and said: 'Buddy Michael Schwartz, a convicted felon. His pickup truck was seen leaving the Amazing Kingdom shortly after the theft. Two white males inside.'

Behind the bedroom door, Bud Schwartz steadied himself. His gut churned, his throat turned to chalk. Danny Pogue looked frozen and glassy-eyed, like a rabbit trapped in the diamond lane of I-95. 'Bud,' he said. 'Oh shit.' Bud Schwartz clapped a hand over his partner's mouth.

They could hear Molly saying, 'He looks familiar, but I just can't be sure.'

The hair prickled on Bud Schwartz's arms. The old witch was going to drop the dime. Unbelievable.

Agent Hawkins was saying, 'Do you know him personally?'

There was a pause that seemed to last five minutes. Molly nudged her eyeglasses up the bridge of her nose. She held the photograph near a lamp, and examined it from several angles.

'No,' she said finally. 'He looks vaguely familiar, but I really can't place the face.'

'Do me a favor. Think about it.'

'Certainly,' she said. 'May I keep the picture?'

'Sure. And think about the Wildlife Rescue Corps, too.'

Molly liked the way this fellow conducted an interview. He knew precisely how much to say without giving away the good stuff—and he certainly knew how to listen. He was a pro.

'Talk to your friends,' said Billy Hawkins. 'See if they have any ideas.'

'You're putting me in a difficult position. These are fine people.'

'I'm sure they are.' The FBI man stood up, straight as a flagpole. He said, 'It would be helpful if I could borrow that Smith-Corona—the one that was used for your press announcements. And the ribbon cartridge as well.'

Molly said, 'Oh dear.'

'I can get a warrant, Mrs. McNamara.'

'That's not it,' she said. 'You see, the typewriter's been stolen.'

Billy Hawkins didn't say anything.

'Out of my car.'

'That's too bad,' the agent said.

'The trunk of my car,' Molly added. 'While I was grocery-shopping.'

She walked the FBI man to the front door. 'Can I ask you something, Agent Hawkins? Are you fellows investigating the death of the killer whale, as well?'

'Should we?'

'I think so. It looks like a pattern, doesn't it? Terrible things are happening at that park.' Molly looked at him over the tops of her glasses. He felt as if he were back in elementary school. She said, 'I know the mango voles are important, but if I may make a suggestion?'

'Sure,' said Hawkins.

'Your valuable time and talents would be better spent on a thorough investigation of the Falcon Trace resort. It's a cesspool down there, and Mr. Francis X. Kingsbury is the root of the cess. I trust the FBI is still interested in bribery and public corruption.'

'We consider it a priority.'

'Then you'll keep this in mind.' Molly's eyes lost some of their sparkle. 'They've up and bulldozed the whole place,' she said. 'The trees, everything. It's a crime what they did. I drove by it this morning.'

For the first time Billy Hawkins heard a trembling in her voice. He handed her a card. 'Anything solid, we'll look into it. And thank you very much for the tea.'

She held the door open. 'You're a very polite young man,' she said. 'You renew my faith in authority.'

'We'll be talking soon,' said Agent Hawkins.

As soon as he was gone, Molly McNamara heard a whoop from the bedroom. She found Danny Pogue dancing a one-legged jig, ecstatic that he was not in federal custody. Bud Schwartz sat on the edge of the bed, nervously pounding his fist in a pillow.

Danny Pogue took Molly by the arms and said: 'You did good. You stayed cool!'

Bud Schwartz said, 'Cool's not the word for it.'

Molly handed him the mug shot. 'Next time comb your hair,' she said. 'Now then—let's have a look at those files you boys borrowed from Mr. Kingsbury.'

Joe Winder took Nina's hand and led her down the trail. 'You're gonna love this guy,' he said.

'What happened to the movie?'

'Later,' Winder said. 'There's a ten-o'clock show.' He hated going to the movies. Hated driving all the way up to Homestead.

Nina said, 'Don't you have a flashlight?'

'We've got a good hour till dusk. Come on.'

'It's my night off,' she said. 'I wanted to go someplace.'

Winder pulled her along through the trees. 'Just you wait,' he said.

They found Skink shirtless, skinning a raccoon at the campsite. He grunted when Joe Winder said hello. Nina wondered if the plastic collar around his neck was from a prison or some other institution. She stepped closer to get a look at the dead raccoon.

'Import got him,' Skink said, feeling her stare. 'Up on 905 about two hours ago. Little guy's still warm.'

Winder cleared a spot for Nina to sit down. 'How do you know it was a foreign car?' he asked. He truly was curious.

'Low bumper broke his neck, that's how I know.

Usually it's the tires that do the trick. That's because the rental companies prefer mid-sized American models. Fords and Chevys. We get a ton of rentals up and down this stretch.'

He stripped the skin off the animal and laid it to one side. To Nina he said: 'They call me Skink.'

She took a small breath. 'I'm Nina. Joe said you were the governor of Florida.'

'Long time ago.' Skink frowned at Winder. 'No need to bring it up.'

The man's voice was a deep, gentle rumble. Nina wondered why the guys who phoned the sex line never sounded like that. She shivered and said: 'Joe told me you just vanished. Got up and walked away from the job. It was in all the papers.'

'I'm sure. Did he also tell you that I knew his daddy?'

'Ancient history,' Winder cut in. 'Nina, I wanted you to meet this guy because he saved my life the other night.'

Skink sliced the hindquarters off the dead raccoon and placed them side by side in a large fry pan. He said to Nina: 'Don't believe a word of it, darling. The only reason he wanted you to meet me was so you'd understand.'

'Understand what?'

'What's about to happen.'

Nina looked uncomfortable. With one hand she began twisting the ends of her hair into tiny braids.

'Don't be nervous,' Joe Winder said, touching her knee.

'Well, what's he talking about?'

Skink finished with the raccoon carcass and slopped the innards into a grocery bag, which he buried. After he got the fire going, he wiped his palms on the seat of his new canvas trousers, the ones he'd taken off Spearmint Breath. He watched, satisfied as the gray meat began to sizzle and darken in the fry pan.

'I don't suppose you're hungry,' Skink said.

'We've got other plans.' Nina was cordial but firm.

Skink foraged through a rubble of old crates and lobster traps, mumbled, stomped into the woods. He came back carrying a dirty blue Igloo cooler. He took out three beers, opened one and gave the other two to Nina and Joe Winder.

Before taking a drink, Nina wiped the top of the can on the sleeve of Winder's shirt. She touched a hand to her neck and said, 'So what's with the collar?'

'Telemetry.' Skink pointed a finger at the sky. 'Every week or so, a plane comes around.'

'They think he's a panther,' Joe Winder explained. 'See, it's a radio collar. He took it off a dead panther.'

Skink quickly added: 'But I'm not the one who killed it. It was a liquor truck out of Marathon. Didn't even stop.'

Nina wasn't plugging in. After a pause she said, 'Joe, don't forget about our movie.'

Winder nodded. Sometimes he felt they were oceans apart. 'The panther's all but extinct,' he said. 'Maybe two dozen left alive. The Game and Fish Department uses radio collars to keep track of where they are.'

Skink drained his beer. 'Two nights later, here comes the liquor truck again. Only this time he blows a tire on some barbed wire.'

'In the middle of the road?' Nina said.

'Don't ask me how it got there. Anyway, I had a good long talk with the boy.'

Winder said, 'Jesus, don't tell me.'

'Cat's blood was still on the headlights. Fur, too.' Skink spat into the fire. 'Cracker bastard didn't seem to care.'

'You didn't . . .'

'No, nothing permanent. Nothing his insurance wouldn't cover.'

In her smoothest voice Nina asked, 'Did you eat the panther, too?'

'No, ma'am,' said Skink. 'I did not.'

The big cat was buried a half-mile up the trail, under brilliant bougainvilleas that Skink himself had planted. Joe Winder thought about showing Nina the place, but she didn't act interested. Darkness was settling in, and the mosquitoes had arrived by the billions. Nina slapped furiously at her bare arms and legs, while Joe Winder shook his head to keep the little bloodsuckers out of his ears.

Skink said, 'I got some goop if you want it. Great stuff.' He held his arms out in the firelight. The left one was engulfed by black mosquitoes; the right one was untouched.

'It's called EDTIAR,' Skink said. 'Extended Duration Topical Insect/Arthropod Repellent. I'm a field tester for the U.S. Marines; they pay me and everything.' Studiously he began counting the bites on his left arm.

Nina, on the shrill edge of misery, whacked a big fat arthropod on Joe Winder's cheek. 'We've got to get going,' she said.

'They're nasty tonight,' Skink said sympathetically. 'I just took seventeen hits in thirty seconds.'

Winder himself was getting devoured. He stood up,

flailing his own torso. The bugs were humming in his eyes, his mouth, his nostrils.

'Joe, what's the point of all this?' Nina asked.

'I'm waiting for him to tell me who killed Will Koocher.'

'Oh, for God's sake.'

Skink said, 'We're in dangerous territory now.'

'I don't care,' Winder said. 'Tell me what happened. It had something to do with the mango voles, I'm sure.'

'Yes,' said Skink.

Nina announced that she was leaving. 'I'm getting eaten alive, and we're going to miss the movie.'

'Screw the movie,' said Joe Winder, perhaps too curtly.

For Nina was suddenly gone—down the trail, through the woods. Snapping twigs and muffled imprecations divulged her path.

'Call me Mr. Charm,' Winder said.

Skink chuckled. 'You'd better go. This can wait.'

'I want to know more.'

'It's the voles, like you said.' He reached into his secondhand trousers and took out a bottle so small it couldn't have held more than four ounces. He pressed it into the palm of Joe Winder's right hand.

'Ah, the magic bug goop!'

'No,' Skink said. 'Now take off, before Snow White gets lost in the big bad forest.'

Blindly Winder jogged down the trail after his girl-friend. He held one arm across his face to block the branches from slashing him, and weaved through the low viny trees like a halfback slipping tacklers.

Nina had given up her solo expedition forty yards from Skink's campsite, and that's where Winder found her, leaning against the slick red trunk of a gumbo-limbo.

'Get us out of here,' she said, brushing a squadron of plump mosquitoes from her forehead.

Out of breath, Winder gave her a hug. She didn't exactly melt in his arms. 'You were doing fine,' he said. 'You stayed right on the trail.'

They were in the car, halfway to Homestead, when she spoke again: 'Why can't you leave it alone? The guy's nothing but trouble.'

'He's not crazy, Nina.'

'Oh right.'

'A man was murdered. I can't let it slide.'

She picked a buttonwood leaf from her sleeve, rolled down the window and flicked the leaf away. She said, 'If he's not crazy, then how come he lives the way he does? How come he wears that electric collar?'

'He says it keeps him on his toes.' Joe Winder plugged a Zevon tape in the stereo. 'Look, I'm not saying he's normal. I'm just saying he's not crazy.'

'Like you would know,' Nina said.

FIFTEEN

On Sunday, July 22, Charles Chelsea got up at eight-thirty, showered, shaved, dressed (navy slacks, Cordovan loafers, blue oxford shirt, burgundy necktie), trimmed his nose hairs, splashed on about three gallons of Aramis and drove off to work in his red Mazda Miata, for which he had paid thirty-five hundred dollars over dealer invoice.

Chelsea had two important appointments at the Amazing Kingdom of Thrills. One of them would be routine, and one promised to be unpleasant. He had not slept well, but he didn't feel exceptionally tired. In fact, he felt surprisingly confident, composed, tough; if only he could remain that way until his meeting with Joe Winder.

A crew from Channel 7 was waiting outside the main gate. The reporter was an attractive young Latin woman wearing oversized sunglasses. Chelsea greeted her warmly and told her she was right on time. They all got in a van, which was driven by a man wearing a costume of bright neoprene plumes. The man introduced himself as Baldy the Eagle, and said he was happy to be their host. He began a long spiel about the Amazing Kingdom of Thrills until Charles Chelsea flashed his ID badge, at which point the bird man shrugged and shut up. Chelsea slapped his arm when he tried to bum a Marlboro off the Channel 7 cameraman.

When they arrived at the killer-whale tank, Chelsea stepped from the van and held the door for the reporter, whose first name was Maria. Chelsea led the way inside the marine stadium, where the TV crew unpacked and began to set up the equipment. Chelsea sat next to Maria in the front row, facing the empty blue pool. Above them, men on scaffolds were sandblasting the word 'Orky' from the coral-colored wall.

Chelsea said, 'I guess the others will be along soon.'

Maria removed her sunglasses and brushed her hair. She took out a spiral notebook and flipped to a blank page.

'The other stations,' Chelsea said, 'they must be running a little late.'

Five others had received the same fax as Channel 7 had. Surely more crews would show up—it was Sunday, after all, the slowest news day of the week.

Maria said, 'Before we go on the air—'

'You want some background,' Chelsea said helpfully. 'Well, to be perfectly frank, Orky's death left us with a rather large vacancy. Here we have this beautiful salt-water tank, as you see, and a scenic outdoor stadium. A facility like this is too special to waste. We thought about getting another whale, but Mr. Kingsbury felt it would be inappropriate. He felt Orky was irre-placeable.'

Charles Chelsea glanced over Maria's shoulder to see the Minicam pointed at him. Its red light winked innocuously as the tape rolled. The cameraman was on his knees. Squinting through the viewfinder, he signaled for Chelsea to keep talking.

'Are we on?' the PR man said. 'What about the mike? I don't have a mike.'

The cameraman pointed straight up. Chelsea raised his eyes. A gray boom microphone, the size of a fungo bat, hung over his head. The boom was controlled by a sound man standing to Chelsea's right. The man wore earphones and a Miami Dolphins warm-up jacket.

Maria said, 'You mentioned Orky. Could you tell us what your staff has learned about the whale's death? What exactly killed it?'

Chelsea fought to keep his Adam's apple from bobbing spasmodically, as it often did when he lied. 'The tests,' he said, 'are still incomplete.'

Maria's warm brown eyes blinked inquisitively. 'There's a rumor that the whale died during an encounter with an employee of the Amazing Kingdom.'

'Oh, that's a good one.' Chelsea laughed stiffly. 'Where did you hear that?'

'Is it true?'

The camera's blinking red light no longer seemed harmless. Charles Chelsea said, 'I'm not going to dignify such a question by responding.'

The reporter said nothing, just let the tape roll. Let him choke on the silence. It worked.

'We did have a death that night,' Chelsea admitted, toying with his cuffs. 'An employee of the park apparently took his own life. It was very, very tragic—'

'What was the name of this employee?'

Chelsea's tone became cold, reproachful. 'It is our strict policy not to discuss such matters publicly. There is an issue of privacy, and respect for the family.'

Maria said, 'The rumor is—'

'We don't respond to rumors, Ms. Rodríguez.' Now

Chelsea was leaning forward, lecturing. The boom mike followed him. 'Would you like to hear about our newest attraction, or not?'

She smiled like a moray eel. 'That's why we're here.'

Oh no it isn't, thought Chelsea, trying not to glare, trying not to perspire, trying not to look like the unvarnished shill he was.

'I brought a bathing suit,' Maria said, 'as you suggested.'

'Maybe we should wait for the others.'

'I think we're it, Mr. Chelsea. I don't think any of the other stations are coming.'

'Fine.' He tried not to sound disappointed.

The cameraman stopped taping. Chelsea dabbed his forehead in relief; he needed to collect himself, recover from the ambush. Everybody wants to be Mike Wallace, he thought bitterly. Everybody's a hardass.

Maria picked up a tote bag and asked directions to the lady's room. When she returned, she was wearing a tight melon-colored tonga that required continual adjustment. At the sight of her, Charles Chelsea inadvertently licked the corners of his mouth. It wasn't so bad after all, coming to work on a Sunday.

'Should I get in?' Maria asked.

'Sure.' Chelsea signaled across the pool to a young man dressed in khaki shorts. This was one of the trainers.

Maria slipped into the whale pool, dipped her head underwater, and smoothed her hair straight back. The tape was rolling again.

Eyes twinkling, she smiled up at the camera. The guy with the boom mike leaned over the wall of the tank to capture her words.

'Hi, this is Maria Rodríguez. Today we're visiting the Amazing Kingdom of Thrills in North Key Largo. As you can see, it's a gorgeous summer day—'

Chelsea was thinking: Good girl, stick to the fluff.

'—and we're about to meet the newest star of the Kingdom's outdoor marine show. His name is Dickie the Dolphin . . . cut! Hold it, Jimmy.'

The cameraman stopped the tape. Bobbing in the whale pool, Maria groped beneath the surface, frowned and spun away. Chelsea could see that she was struggling to realign the bathing suit.

'Damn thing's riding up my crack.'

'Take your time,' said the cameraman. 'We got plenty of light.'

Moments later, Maria was ready again; fresh, sleek, languid. She splashed herself lightly in the face so that droplets glistened in her eyelashes; Charles Chelsea was transfixed.

'Hi, this is Maria Rodríguez reporting from the Amazing Kingdom of Thrills in North Key Largo. As you can see, it's a gorgeous summer day in South Florida—perfect for a swim with the newest star of the Amazing Kingdom's marine show. His name is Dickie the Dolphin and, starting tomorrow, you can swim with him, too!'

Chelsea cued the trainer, who pulled the pin on the gate to the whale pool. Pushing a V-shaped wake, the dolphin charged from the holding tank and sounded.

The TV reporter continued: 'It's the latest concept in marine theme parks—customer participation. Instead of sitting in the bleachers and watching these remarkable mammals do tricks, you can actually get in the water and play with them. It costs a little more, but—believe me—it's worth it.'

A few yards behind her, Dickie the Dolphin rolled, blowing air noisily. Maria kept her poise, glancing over one shoulder with a breezy, affectionate smile. Chelsea was impressed; she had the whole script memorized.

Turning back to the camera, Maria said: 'To be in the water with these gentle, intelligent creatures is an experience you'll never forget. Scientists say the dolphin's brain is actually larger than ours, and much of their complex social behavior remains a mystery. . . .'

Dickie the Dolphin surfaced lazily near Maria, who grabbed its dorsal fin with both hands. Chelsea stood up quickly and waved a warning, but it was too late. The dolphin carried the TV reporter across the top of the water; she closed her eyes and squealed with child-like excitement.

'Great fucking video,' remarked Jimmy the cameraman, panning expertly with the action.

The boom man said, 'She's getting out of range.'

Charles Chelsea cupped his hands and shouted. 'Let go! No rides allowed!'

Maria couldn't hear a word. She was holding her breath underwater while the dolphin imitated a torpedo. Every few seconds her long brown legs would slice the surface as she was dragged along, like the tail of a kite. Chelsea bit his lip and watched in queasy silence. Finally Maria splashed to the surface—and she was laughing, thank God! She thought it was all in fun, and maybe it was.

The sound man scurried along the rim of the tank and repositioned the boom. Giggling, short of breath, Maria's eyes found the camera. She said, 'Folks, this is unbelievable. Bring the family, you're gonna love it!' Dickie the Dolphin appeared at her side, and she stroked its sleek flank. Wondrously, it seemed to nuzzle her bosom with its snout.

'He's so *adorable*!' Maria exclaimed.

From the feeding platform on the side of the tank, the trainer called out, 'Hey, be careful!' Then he started peeling off his khakis.

'Such friendly animals,' Maria was saying. 'Notice how they always look like they're smiling!'

Dickie the Dolphin slapped its tail on the surface and pushed even closer. Maria threw both arms around the slippery mammal, which obligingly rolled on its back.

Chelsea saw the trainer dive in. He saw Maria's expression change from tenderness to awe. Then he saw the dolphin hook her with its flippers and drag her down.

When she broke to the top, Maria's giggle had become a low fearful moan. As the dolphin's dark form appeared beneath her, she seemed to rise from the water. Then, just as slowly, the creature drew her under.

The cameraman muttered that he was running out of tape. A voice behind him said: 'You'll miss the best part.'

It was Joe Winder. He stood next to Charles Chelsea, who was clutching the rail with knuckles as pink as shrimp. In the water, the trainer was trying without much success to separate the dolphin from the TV reporter.

Chelsea said to Winder: 'Maybe it's a new trick—'

'It's no trick. He's trying to boink her.'

'That's not funny, Joe.'

Winder pointed. 'What do you think *that* is? See?'

'I—I don't know.'

'It's a dolphin shlong, Charlie. One of Nature's marvels.'

Chelsea began to stammer.

'They get in moods,' Joe explained. 'Same as dogs.'

'My God.'

'Don't worry, Charlie, it'll pass.'

With the trainer's help, Maria Rodríguez finally broke free from Dickie the Dolphin's embrace. Cursing, tugging at her tonga, she paddled furiously toward the ladder on the wall of the tank.

'Faster!' Charles Chelsea hollered. 'Here he comes again!'

Two hours later, he was still trying to apologize without admitting the truth. 'Sometimes they play too rough, that's all.'

'Playing?' Maria sniffed sarcastically. 'Excuse me, Mr. Chelsea, but I know a dick when I see one.' She had changed back to TV clothes, although her hair was still wrapped in a towel. 'I ought to sue your ass,' she said.

They were sitting in Chelsea's office—the reporter, Charles Chelsea, and Joe Winder. The crew had returned to the truck to put the dish up, just in case.

'Come on,' Winder said to Maria, 'be a sport.'

'What?' She gave him an acid glare. 'What did you say?' She whipped the towel off her head and tossed it on the floor.

Very impolite, Winder thought, and unprofessional. 'Take it easy,' he said. 'Nothing unspeakable happened.'

Maria pointed a finger in his face and said, 'Someone could get killed out there.'

Charles Chelsea was miserable. 'How can we make it up to you?' he asked Maria Rodríguez. 'How about we comp you some passes to the Wild Bill Hiccup show?'

She was gone before he could come up with something better. On her way out, she kicked at the towel.

Joe Winder said, 'Don't worry, she won't sue.'

'How do you know?'

'It's too embarrassing. Hell, she'll probably destroy the tape on the way back to Miami.'

Defensively Chelsea said, 'She wasn't supposed to grab the dolphin. No touching is allowed—swimming only.'

'This was a terrible idea, Charlie. Who thought of it?'

'Fifty bucks a head. They've got a bunch of these places in the Keys.'

Joe Winder asked where Kingsbury had purchased the new dolphin.

'How should I know?' Chelsea snapped. 'A dolphin's a dolphin, for Christ's sake. They don't come with a pedigree.'

'This one needs a female,' Winder said, 'before you let tourists in the water.'

'Thank you, Doctor Cousteau.' The publicity man got up and closed the door. He looked gravely serious when he returned to the desk.

Joe Winder said, 'I hope you're not going to make me write a press release about this. I've got more important things to do.'

'Me, too.' To steel himself, Charles Chelsea tightened

his stomach muscles. 'Joe, we're going to have to let you go.'

'I see.'

Chelsea studied his fingernails, trying not to make eye contact with Winder. 'It's a combination of things.'

'My attitude, I suppose.'

'That's a factor, yes. I tried to give some latitude. The hair. The casual clothing.'

Winder said, 'Anything else?'

'I understand you broke into the vole lab.'

'Would you like to hear what I found?'

'Not particularly,' Chelsea said.

'A paper written about the blue-tongued mango voles. The one you sent to Will Koocher when you were recruiting him.'

Chelsea gave Winder a so-what look. 'That it?'

'Funny thing, Charlie. The person who supposedly wrote that paper, this Dr. Sarah Hunt? Rollins College never heard of her.' Winder raised his palms in mock puzzlement. 'Never on the faculty, never graduated, never even attended—what do you make of that, Charlie?'

'Pedro told me of your ridiculous theory.' Chelsea's lips barely moved when he spoke; he looked like a goldfish burping. 'Dr. Koocher wasn't murdered, Joe, but in your twisted brain I'm sure you've made some connection between his unfortunate death and this . . . this typographical error.'

Winder laughed. 'A typo? You're beautiful, Charlie. The paper's a goddamn fake.'

Chelsea rolled his eyes. 'And I suppose a simpler explanation is impossible—that perhaps the author's name was misspelled by the publisher, or that the university was misidentified. . . .'

'No way.'

'You're not a well person,' Chelsea said. 'And now I learn that you've telephoned Koocher's widow in New York. That's simply inexcusable.' The way he spit out the word was meant to have a lacerating effect.

'What's inexcusable,' said Winder, 'is the way you lied.'

'It was a judgment call.' Chelsea's cheek twitched. 'We were trying to spare the woman some grief.'

'I told her to get a lawyer.'

Chelsea's tan seemed to fade.

Joe Winder went on: 'The newspapers are bound to find out the truth. 'Man Gobbled by Whale. Modern-Day Jonah Perishes in Freak Theme Park Mishap.' Think about it, Charlie.'

'The coroner said he drowned. We've never denied it.'

'But they didn't say *how* he drowned. Or why.'

Charles Chelsea began to rock back and forth. 'This is all academic, Joey. As of this moment, you no longer work here.'

'And here I thought I was your ace in the hole.'

Chelsea extended a hand, palm up. 'The keys to the Cushman, please.'

Winder obliged. He said, 'Charlie, even though you're an obsequious dork, I'd like to believe you're not a part of this. I'd like to believe that you're just incredibly dim.'

'Go clean out your desk.'

'I don't have to. There's nothing in it.'

Chelsea looked momentarily confused.

Winder waved his arms. 'Desks are places to keep

facts, Charlie. Who needs a desk when the words simply fly off the tops of our heads! Hell, I've done my finest work for you while sitting on the toilet.'

'If you're trying to insult me, it won't work.' Chelsea lowered his eyelids in lizardly disinterest. 'We all fudge the truth when it suits our purposes, don't we? Like when you told me you got that scar in a car accident.'

So he knew all along, just as Joe Winder had suspected.

'I heard it was a fight in the newsroom,' Chelsea said, 'a fistfight with one of your editors.'

'He had it coming,' said Winder. 'He screwed up a perfectly good news story.'

The story concerned Joe Winder's father bribing a county commissioner in exchange for a favorable vote on a zoning variance. Winder had written the story himself after digging through a stack of his father's canceled checks and finding five made out to the commissioner's favorite bagman.

Though admiring of Winder's resourcefulness, the editor had said it created an ethical dilemma; he decided that someone else would have to write the piece. You're too emotionally involved, the editor had told him.

So Winder had gotten a firm grip on the editor's head and rammed it through the screen of the word processor, cutting himself spectacularly in the struggle that followed.

'I'm sorry, Charlie,' he said. 'Maybe you shouldn't have hired me.'

'The understatement of the year.'

'Before I go, may I show you something?' He took out the small bottle that Skink had given him and placed it in the center of Chelsea's desk blotter.

The publicity man examined it and said, 'It's food coloring, so what?'

'Look closer.'

'Betty Crocker food coloring. What's the point, Joe?'

'And what color?'

'Blue.' Chelsea was impatient. 'The label says blue.'

Winder twisted the cap off the bottle. He said, 'I believe this came from the vole lab, too. You might ask Pedro about it.'

Baffled, Charles Chelsea watched Joe Winder toss back his head and empty the contents of the bottle into his mouth. He sloshed the liquid from cheek to cheek, then swallowed.

'Ready?' Winder said. He stuck out his tongue, which now was the color of indigo dye.

'That's a very cute trick.' Chelsea sounded nervous.

Joe Winder climbed onto the desk on his hands and knees. 'The voles were phony, Charlie. Did you know that?' He extended his tongue two inches from Chelsea's nose, then sucked it back in. He said, 'There's no such thing as a blue-tongued mango vole. Kingsbury faked the whole deal. Invented an entire species!'

'You're cracking up,' Chelsea said thinly.

Winder grabbed him by the collar. 'You fucker, did you know all along?'

'Get out, or I'm calling Security.'

'That's why Will Koocher was killed. He'd figured out everything. He was going to rat, so to speak, on the upstanding Mr. Kingsbury.'

Chelsea's upper lip was a constellation of tiny droplets. He tried to pull away. 'Let me go, Joe. If you know what's good for you.'

'They painted their tongues, Charlie. Think of it.

They took these itty-bitty animals and dyed their tongues blue, all in the name of tourism.'

Straining against Winder's grasp, Chelsea said, 'You're talking crazy.'

Joe Winder licked him across the face.

'Stop it!'

Winder slurped him again. 'It's your color, Charlie. Very snappy.'

His tongue waggled in mockery; Chelsea eyed the fat blue thing as if it were a poisonous slug.

'You can fire me,' Winder announced, 'but I won't go away.'

He climbed off the desk, careful not to drop the bottle of food coloring. Chelsea swiftly began plucking tissues from a silver box and wiping his face, examining each crumpled remnant for traces of the dye. His fingers were shaking.

'I should have you arrested,' he hissed.

'But you won't,' Winder said. 'Think of the headlines.'

He was halfway to the door when Chelsea said, 'Wait a minute, Joey. What is it you want?'

Winder kept walking, and began to laugh. He laughed all the way down the hall, a creepy melodic warble that made Charles Chelsea shudder and curse.

SIXTEEN

As a reward for the successful theft of Francis X. Kingsbury's files, Molly McNamara allowed Bud Schwartz and Danny Pogue to keep the rented Cutlass for a few days.

On the evening of July 22, they drove down Old Cutler Road, where many of Miami's wealthiest citizens lived. The homes were large and comfortable-looking, and set back impressively from the tree-shaded road. Danny Pogue couldn't get over the size of the yards, the tall old pines and colorful tropical shrubbery; it was beautiful, yet intimidating.

'They got those Spanish bayonets under the windows,' he reported. 'God, I hate them things.' Wicked needles on the end of every stalk—absolute murder, even with gloves.

Bud Schwartz said, 'Don't sweat it, we'll find us a back door.'

'For sure they got alarms.'

'Yeah.'

'And a goddamn dog, too.'

'Probably so,' said Bud Schwartz, thinking: Already the guy's a nervous wreck.

'You ever done a house like this?'

'Sure.' Bud Schwartz was lying. Mansions, that's

what these were, just like the ones on 'Miami Vice.' The bandage on his bad hand was damp with perspiration. Hunched over the steering wheel, he thought: Thank God for the rental—at least we got a car that'll move.

To cut the tension, he said: 'Ten bucks it's a Dobie.'

'No way,' said Danny Pogue. 'I say Rottweiler, that's the dog nowadays.'

'For the Yuppies, sure, but not this guy. I'm betting on a Dobie.'

Danny Pogue fingered a pimple on his neck. 'Okay, but give me ten on the side.'

'For what?'

'Give me ten on the color.' Danny Pogue slugged him softly on the shoulder. 'Black or brown?'

Bud Schwartz said, 'I'll give you ten if it's brown.'

'Deal.'

'You're a sucker. Nobody in this neighborhood's got a brown Doberman.'

'We'll see,' said Danny Pogue. He pointed as they passed a crimson Porsche convertible parked on a cobbler drive. A beautiful dark-haired girl, all of seventeen, was washing the sports car under a quartet of halogen spotlights. The girl wore a dazzling green bikini and round reflector sunglasses. The sun had been down for two hours.

Danny Pogue clapped his hands. 'Jesus, you see that?'

'Yeah, hosing down her Targa. And here we are in the middle of a drought.' Bud Schwartz braked softly to peer at the name on a cypress mailbox. 'Danny, what's that house number? I can't see it from here.'

'Four-oh-seven.'

'Good. We're almost there.'

'I was wondering,' said Danny Pogue.

'Yeah, what else is new.'

'Do I get twenty bucks if it's a brown Rottweiler?'

'They don't come in brown,' said Bud Schwartz. 'I thought you knew.'

It wasn't a Doberman pinscher or a Rottweiler.

'Maybe some type of weasel,' whispered Danny Pogue. 'Except it's got a collar on it.'

They were kneeling in the shadow of a sea-grape tree. 'One of them beady-eyed dogs from Asia,' said Bud Schwartz, 'or maybe it's Africa.' Dozing under the electric bug lamp, the animal showed no reaction to the sizzle and zap of dying moths.

Carefully Bud Schwartz inserted four Tylenol No. 3 tablets into a ten-ounce patty of prime ground sirloin. With his good hand he lobbed the meat over the fence. It landed with a wet slap on the patio near the pool. The weasel-dog lifted its head, barked once sharply and got up.

Danny Pogue said, 'That's the ugliest goddamn thing I ever saw.'

'Like you're Mel Gibson, right?'

'No, but just look.'

The dog found the hamburger and gulped it in two bites. When its front legs began to wobble, Danny Pogue said, 'Jesus, what'd you use?'

'About a hundred milligrams of codeine.'

Soon the animal lay down, snuffling into a stupor. Bud Schwartz hopped the fence and helped his crutch-less partner across. The two burglars crab-walked along a low cherry hedge until they reached the house. Through a glass door they saw that all the kitchen lights were on; in fact, lamps glowed in every window. Bud Schwartz heard himself take a short breath; he was acting against every instinct, every fundamental rule of the trade. Never *ever* break into an occupied dwelling— especially an occupied dwelling protected by four thousand dollars' worth of electronic burglar alarm.

Bud Schwartz knew the screens would be wired, so busting the windows was out of the question. He knew he couldn't jimmy the sliding door because that would trip the contact, also setting off the alarm. The best hope was cutting the glass door in such a way that it wouldn't trigger the noise detectors; he could see one of the matchbook-sized boxes mounted on a roof beam in the kitchen. Its tiny blue eye winked insidiously at him.

'What's the plan?' asked Danny Pogue.

Bud Schwartz took the glass cutter out of his pocket and showed it to his partner, who hadn't the faintest idea what it was. Bud Schwartz got to his knees. 'I'm going to cut a square,' he said, 'big enough to crawl through.'

'Like hell.' Danny Pogue was quite certain they would be arrested any moment.

Bud Schwartz dug the blades of the glass cutter into the door and pressed with the full strength of his good arm. The door began to slide on its rollers. 'Damn,' said Bud Schwartz. Cold air rushed from the house and put goose bumps on his arms.

Danny Pogue said: 'Must not be locked.'

The door coasted open. No bells or sirens went off. The only sound came from a television, probably upstairs.

They slipped into the house. Bud Schwartz's sneakers

squeaked on the kitchen tile; hopping on one leg, Danny Pogue followed his partner through the living room, which was decorated hideously in black and red. The furniture was leather, the carpeting a deep stringy shag. On a phony brick wall over the fireplace hung a painting that was, by Bud Schwartz's astonished calculation, larger than life-sized. The subject of the painting was a nude blond with a Pepsodent smile and breasts the size of soccer balls. She wore a yellow visored cap, and held a flagstick over her shoulder. A small brass plate announced the title of the work: 'My Nineteenth Hole.'

It was unspeakably crude, even to two men who had spent most of their adult lives in redneck bars and minimum-security prisons. Bud Schwartz gazed at the painting and said: 'I'll bet it's the wife.'

'No way,' said Danny Pogue. He couldn't imagine being married to somebody who would do such a thing.

As they moved cautiously through the house, Bud Schwartz couldn't help but notice there wasn't much worth stealing, even if they'd wanted to. Oh, the stuff was expensive enough, but tacky as hell. A Waterford armadillo—how could millionaires have such lousy taste?

The burglars followed the sound of the television down a hallway toward a bedroom. Bud Schwartz had never been so jittery. *What if the asshole has a gun?* This had been Danny Pogue's question, and for once Bud Schwartz couldn't answer. The asshole probably *did* have a gun; it was Miami, after all. Probably something in a semi-automatic, a Mini-14 or a MAC-11. Christ, there's a pleasant thought. Ten, fifteen rounds a second. Hardly time to piss in your pants.

Danny Pogue's whiny breathing seemed to fill the

hallway. Bud Schwartz glared, held a finger to his lips. The door to the bedroom was wide open; somebody was switching the channels on the television. Momentously, Bud Schwartz smoothed his hair; Danny Pogue did the same. Bud Schwartz nodded and motioned with an index finger; Danny Pogue gave a constipated nod in return.

When they stepped into the room, they saw the blond woman from the golf painting. She was lying naked on the bed; two peach-colored pillows were tucked under her head, and the remote control was propped on her golden belly. At the sight of the burglars, the woman covered her chest. Excitedly she tried to speak—no sounds emerged, though her jaws moved vigorously, as if she were chewing a wad of bubble gum.

Inanely, Bud Schwartz said, 'Don't be afraid.'

The woman forced out a low guttural cry that lasted several seconds. She sounded like a wildcat in labor.

'Enough a that,' said Danny Pogue tensely.

Suddenly a door opened and a porky man in powder-blue boxer shorts stepped out of the bathroom. He was short and jowly, with skin like yellow lard. Tattooed on his left forearm was a striking tableau: Minnie Mouse performing oral sex on Mickey Mouse. At least that's what it looked like to Danny Pogue and Bud Schwartz, who couldn't help but stare. Mickey was wearing his sorcerer's hat from *Fantasia*, and appeared to be whistling a happy tune.

Danny Pogue said, 'That'd make a great T-shirt.'

With fierce reddish eyes, the man in the boxer shorts studied the two intruders.

'Honey!' cried the woman on the bed.

The man scowled impatiently. 'Well, shit, get it over with. Take, you know, whatever the hell.'

Bud Schwartz said, 'We didn't mean to scare you, Mr. Kingsbury.'

'Don't fucking flatter yourself. And, Penny, watch it with that goddamn thing!'

Still recumbent, the naked Mrs. Kingsbury now was aiming a small chrome-plated pistol at Danny Pogue's midsection.

'I knew it,' muttered Bud Schwartz. He hated the thought of getting shot twice in the same week, especially by women. This one must've had it under the damn pillows, or maybe in the sheets.

Danny Pogue's lips were quivering, as if he were about to cry. He held out his arms beseechingly.

Quickly Bud Schwartz said: 'We're not here to rob you. We're here to talk business.'

Kingsbury hooked his nubby thumbs into the elastic waistband of his underpants. 'Make me laugh,' he said. 'Break into my house like a couple of putzes.'

'We're pros,' said Bud Schwartz.

Kingsbury cackled, snapping the elastic. 'Two hands, babe,' he reminded his wife.

Danny Pogue said, 'Bud, make her drop it!'

'It's only a .25,' said Kingsbury. 'She's been out to the range—what?—a half-dozen times. Got the nerves for it, apparently.'

Bud Schwartz tried to keep his voice level and calm. He said to Kingsbury: 'Your office got hit yesterday, right?'

'As a matter of fact, yeah.'

'You're missing some files.'

The naked Mrs. Kingsbury said, 'Frankie, you didn't

tell me.' Her arms were impressively steady with the gun.

Kingsbury took his hands out of his underwear and folded them in a superior way across his breasts, which were larger than those of a few women whom Danny Pogue had known.

'Not exactly the Brink's job,' Kingsbury remarked.

'Well, we got your damn files,' said Bud Schwartz.

'That was you? Bullshit.'

'Maybe you need some proof. Maybe you need to see some credit-card slips.'

Kingsbury hesitated. 'Selling them back, is that the idea?'

Some genius businessman, thought Bud Schwartz. The guy was a bum, a con. You could tell right away.

'Tell your wife to drop the piece.'

'Penny, you heard the man.'

'And tell her to go lock herself in the john.'

'What?'

The wife said, 'Frankie, I don't like this.' Carefully she placed the gun on the nightstand next to a bottle of Lavoris mouthwash. A tremor of relief passed through Danny Pogue, starting at the shoulders. He hopped across the room and sat down on the corner of the bed.

'It's better if she's in the john,' Bud Schwartz said to Francis X. Kingsbury. 'Or maybe you don't care.'

Kingsbury gnawed his upper lip. He was thinking about the files, and what was in them.

His wife wrapped herself in a sheet. 'Frank?'

'Do what he said,' Kingsbury told her. 'Take a magazine, something. A book if you can find one.'

'Fuck you,' said Penny Kingsbury. On her way to the bathroom, she waved a copy of GQ in his face.

'At Doral is where I met her. Selling golf shoes.'

'How nice,' said Bud Schwartz.

'Fuzzy Zoeller, Tom Kite, I'm not kidding. Penny's customers.' Kingsbury had put on a red bathrobe and turned up the television, in case his wife was at the door trying to eavesdrop. Bud Schwartz lifted the handgun from the nightstand and slipped it into his pocket; the cold weight of the thing in his pants, so close to his privates, made him shudder. God, how he hated guns.

Kingsbury said, 'The painting in the big room—you guys get a look at it?'

'Yeah, boy,' answered Danny Pogue.

'We did that up on the Biltmore. Number seven or ten, I can't remember. Some par three. Anyway, I had to lease the whole fucking course for a day, that's how long it took. Must've been two hundred guys standing around, staring at her boobs. Penny didn't mind, she's proud of 'em.'

'And who wouldn't be,' said Bud Schwartz, tight as a knot. 'Can we get to it, please? We got plenty to talk about.'

Francis X. Kingsbury said, 'I'm trying to remember. You got the Ramex Global file. Jersey Premium. What else?'

'You know what else.'

Kingsbury nodded. 'Start with the American Express. Give me a number.'

Bud Schwartz sat down in a high-backed colonial chair. From memory he gave Kingsbury an inventory: 'We got a diamond tennis necklace in New York, earrings in Chicago. Yeah, and an emerald stickpin in Nassau of all places, for like three grand.' He motioned to Danny Pogue, who hobbled over to Mrs. Kingsbury's dresser and began to look through the boxes.

Dispiritedly, Kingsbury said, 'Forget it, you won't find it there.'

'So who got it all?'

'Friends. It's not important.'

'Not to us, maybe.' Bud Schwartz nodded toward the bathroom. 'I got a feeling your old lady might be interested.'

Kingsbury lowered his voice. 'The reason I use the credit card, hell, who carries that much cash?'

'Plus the insurance,' said Danny Pogue, pawing through Mrs. Kingsbury's jewelry. 'Stuff gets broke or stolen, they replace it, no questions. It's a new thing.'

Great, Bud Schwartz thought; now he's doing commercials.

'There's some excellent shit here. Very nice.' Danny Pogue held up a diamond solitaire and played it off the light. 'I'm guessin' two carats.'

'Try one-point-five,' said Kingsbury.

'There were some dinners on your card,' Bud Schwartz said. 'And plane tickets, too. It's handy how they put it all together at the end of the year where you can check it.'

Kingsbury asked him how much.

'Five grand,' Bud Schwartz said, 'and we won't say a word to the wife.'

'The file, Jesus, I need it back.'

'No problem. Now let's talk about serious money.'

Kingsbury frowned. He pulled on the tip of his nose with a thumb and forefinger, as if he were straightening it.

Bud Schwartz said, 'The Gotti file, Mr. King.'

'Mother of Christ.'

"Frankie, The Ferret, King.' That's what the indictment said.'

'You got me by surprise,' Kingsbury said.

Danny Pogue looked up from an opal bracelet he was admiring. 'So who's this Gotti dude again? Some kinda gangster is what Bud said.'

'How much?' said Kingsbury. He leaned forward and put his hands on his bare knees. 'Don't make it, like . . . a game.'

Bud Schwartz detected visceral fear in the man's voice; it gave him an unfamiliar feeling of power. On the other side of the bathroom door, Francis Kingsbury's wife shouted something about wanting to get out. Kingsbury ignored her.

'The banks that made the loans on Falcon Trace, do they know who you are?' Bud Schwartz affected a curious tone. 'Do they know you're a government witness? A mob guy?'

Kingsbury didn't bother to reply.

'I imagine they gave you shitloads a money,' Bud Schwartz went on, 'and I imagine they could call it back.'

Francis Kingsbury went to the bathroom door and told Penny to shut up and sit her sweet ass on the can. He turned back to the burglars and said: 'So what's the number, the grand total? For Gotti, I mean.'

Danny Pogue resisted the urge to enter the negotiation; expectantly he looked at his partner. Bud Schwartz smoothed his hair, pursed his mouth. He wanted to hear what kind of bullshit offer Kingsbury would make on his own.

'I'm trying to think what's fair.'

'Give me a fucking number,' said Kingsbury, 'and I'll goddamn tell you if it's fair.'

What the hell, thought Bud Schwartz. 'Fifty grand,' he said calmly. 'And we toss in Ramex and the rest for free.'

Excitedly Danny Pogue began excavating a new pimple.

Kingsbury eyed the men suspiciously. 'Fifty, you said? As in five-oh?'

'Right.' Bud Schwartz gave half a grin. 'That's fifty to give back the Gotti file . . .'

'And?'

'Two hundred more to forget what was in it.'

Kingsbury chuckled bitterly. 'So I was wrong,' he said. 'You're not such a putz.'

Danny Pogue was so overjoyed that he could barely control himself on the ride back to Molly's condominium. 'We're gonna be rich,' he said, pounding both hands on the upholstery. 'You're a genius, man, that's what you are.'

'It went good,' Bud Schwartz agreed. Better than he had ever imagined. As he drove, he did the arithmetic in his head. Five thousand for the American Express file, fifty for the Gotti stuff, another two hundred in hush money . . . rich was the word for it. 'Early retirement,' he said to Danny Pogue. 'No more damn b-and-e's.'

'You don't think he'll call the cops?'

'That's the last place he'd call. Guy's a scammer, Danny.'

They stopped at a U-Tote-Em and bought two six-packs of Coors and a box of jelly doughnuts. In the parking lot they rolled down the windows and turned up the radio and stuffed themselves in jubilation. It was an hour until curfew; if they weren't back by midnight, Molly had said, she would call the FBI and say her memory had returned.

'I bet she'll cut us some slack,' said Danny Pogue, 'if we're a little late.'

'Maybe.' Bud Schwartz opened the door and rolled an empty beer can under the car. He said, 'I'm sure gettin' tired of being her pet burglar.'

'Well, then, let's go to a tittie bar and celebrate.' Danny Pogue said he knew of a place where the girls danced naked on the tables, and let you grab their ankles for five bucks.

Bud Schwartz said not tonight. There would be no celebration until they broke free from the old lady. Tonight he would make a pitch for the rest of the ten grand that she'd promised. Surely they were square by now; Molly had been so thrilled by the contents of the Ramex file that she'd given him a hug. Then she'd gone out and had eight copies made. What more could she want of them?

Back on the road, Bud Schwartz said: 'Remember, don't say a damn thing about what we done tonight.'

'You told me a hundred times.'

'Well, it'll screw up everything. I mean it, don't tell her where we been.'

'No reason,' said Danny Pogue. 'It's got nothin' to do with the butterflies, right?'

'No, it sure does not.'

Danny Pogue said he was hungry again, so they stopped to pick up some chicken nuggets. Again they ate in the parking lot, listening to a country station. Bud Schwartz had never before driven an automobile with a working clock, so he was surprised to glance at the dashboard of the Cutlass and find that it was half past twelve, and counting.

'Better roll,' Danny Pogue said, 'just in case.'

'I got a better idea—gimme a quarter.' Bud Schwartz got out and walked to a pay telephone under a street-light. He dialed the number of Molly McNamara's condominium and let it ring five minutes. He hung up, retrieved the quarter and dialed again. This time he let it ring twice as long.

In the car, speeding down U.S. 1, Danny Pogue said, 'I can't believe she'd do it—maybe she went someplace else. Maybe she left us a note.'

Bud Schwartz gripped the wheel with both hands; the bullet wound was numb because he had forgotten about it. Escape was on his mind—what if the old bitch had run to the feds? Worse, what if she'd found the Gotti file? What if she'd gone snooping through the bedroom and found it hidden between the mattress and the box spring, which in retrospect was probably not the cleverest place of concealment.

'Shit,' he said, thinking of the bleak possibilities.

'Don't jump the gun,' said Danny Pogue, for once the optimist.

They made it back to the condo in twenty-two minutes, parked the rental car and went upstairs. The door to Molly's apartment was unlocked. Bud Schwartz knocked twice anyway. 'It's just us,' he announced lightly, 'Butch and Sundance.'

When he went in, he saw that the place had been torn apart. 'Oh Jesus,' he said.

Danny Pogue pushed him with the crutch. 'I can't fucking believe it,' he said. 'Somebody hit the place.'

'No,' said Bud Schwartz, 'it's more than that.'

The sofas had been slit, chairs broken, mirrors shattered. A ceramic Siamese cat had been smashed face-first through the big-screen television. While Danny Pogue hopscotched through the rubble, Bud Schwartz went directly to the bedroom, which also had been ransacked and vandalized. He reached under the mattress and found the Kingsbury files exactly where he had left them. Whoever did the place hadn't been looking very hard, if it all.

A hoarse shout came from the kitchen.

Bud Schwartz found Danny Pogue on his knees next to Molly McNamara. She lay on her back, with one leg folded crookedly under the other. Her housecoat, torn and stained with something dark, was bunched around her hips. Her face had been beaten to pulp; beads of blood glistened like holly berries in her snowy hair. Her eyes were closed and her lips were gray, but she was breathing—raspy, irregular gulps.

Danny Pogue took Molly's wrist. 'God Almighty,' he said, voice quavering. 'What—who do we call?'

'Nobody.' Bud Schwartz shook his head ruefully. 'Don't you understand, we can't call nobody.' He bent down and put his bandaged hand on Molly's forehead. 'Who the hell would do this to an old lady?'

'I hope she don't die.'

'Me, too,' said Bud Schwartz. 'Honest to God, this ain't right.'

SEVENTEEN

Joe Winder's trousers were soaked from the thighs down. Nina took a long look and said: 'You've been fishing.'

'Yes.'

'In the middle of the day.'

'The fish are all gone,' Winder said dismally. 'Ever since they bulldozed the place.'

Nina sat cross-legged on the floor. She wore blue-jean shorts and a pink cotton halter; the same outfit she'd been wearing the day he'd met her, calling out numbers at the Seminole bingo hall. Joe Winder had gone there to meet an Indian named Sammy Deer, who purportedly was selling an airboat, but Sammy Deer had hopped over to Freeport for the weekend, leaving Joe Winder stuck with three hundred chain-smoking white women in the bingo hall. Halfway out the door, he'd heard Nina's voice ('Q 34; Q, as in "quicksilver," 34!'), spun around and went back to see if she looked as lovely as she sounded, and she had. Nina informed him that she was part-timing as a bingo caller until the telephone gig came through, and he confided to her that he was buying an airboat so he could disappear into the Everglades at will. He changed his plans after their first date.

Now, analyzing her body language, Joe Winder knew

that he was in danger of losing Nina's affections. A yellow legal pad was propped on her lap. She tapped on a bare knee with her felt-tipped pen, which she held as a drummer would.

'What happened to your big meeting?' she said. 'Why aren't you at the Kingdom?'

He pretended not to hear. He said, 'They dumped a ton of fill in the cove. The bottom's mucky and full of cut trees.' He removed his trousers and arranged them crookedly on a wire hanger. 'All against the law, of course. Dumping in a marine sanctuary.'

Nina said, 'You got canned, is that it?'

'A mutual parting of the ways, and not a particularly amicable one.' Joe Winder sat down beside her. He sensed a lecture coming on.

'Put on some pants,' she said.

'What's the point?'

Nina asked why his tongue was blue, and he told her the story of the bogus mango voles. She said she didn't believe a word.

'Charlie practically admitted everything.'

'I don't really care,' Nina said. She stopped drumming on her kneecap and turned away.

'What is it?'

'Look, I can't afford to support you.' When she looked back at him, her eyes were moist and angry. 'Things were going so well,' she said.

Winder was stunned. Was she seriously worried about the money? 'Nina, there's a man dead. Don't you understand? I can't work for a murderer.'

'Stop it!' She shook the legal pad in front of his nose. 'You know what I've been working on? Extra scripts. The other girls like my stuff so much they offered to buy, like, two or three a week. Twenty-five bucks each, it could really add up.'

'That's great.' He was proud of her, that was the hell of it. She'd never believe that he could be proud of her.

Pen in mouth, Nina said: 'I wrote about an out-of-body experience. Like when you're about to die and you can actually see yourself lying there—but then you get saved at the very last minute. Only my script was about making love, about floating out of yourself just as you're about to come. *Suspended in air, I looked down at the bed and saw myself shudder violently, my fingernails raking across your broad tan shoulders.* I gave it to the new girl, Addie, and she tried it Friday night. One guy, she said, he called back eleven times.'

'Is that a new record?'

'It just so happens, yes. But the point is, I'm looking at a major opportunity. If I start selling enough scripts, maybe I can get off the phones. Just stay home and write—wouldn't that be better?'

'Sure would.' Winder put his arm around her. 'You can still do that, honey. It would be great.'

'Not with you sitting here every day. Playing your damn Warren Zevon.'

'I'll get another job.'

'No, Joe, it'll be the same old shit.' She pulled away and got up from the floor. 'I can't write when my life is in turmoil. I need a stabilizer. Peacefulness. Quiet.'

Winder felt wounded. 'For God's sake, Nina, I know a little something about writing. This place is plenty quiet.'

'There is tension,' she said grimly, 'and don't deny it.'

'Writers thrive on domestic tension. Look at Poe, Hemingway—and Mailer in his younger days, you talk about tense.' He hoped Nina would appreciate being included on such an eminent roster, but she didn't. Impatiently he said, 'It isn't exactly epic literature, anyway. It's phone porn.'

Her expression clouded. 'Phone porn? Thanks, Joe.'

'Well, Christ, that's what it is.'

Coldly she folded her arms and leaned against one of the tall speakers. 'It's still writing, and writing is hard work. If I'm going to make a go of it, I need some space. And some security.'

'If you're talking about groceries, don't worry. I intend to pull my own weight.'

Nina raised her hands in exasperation. 'Where can you find another job that pays so much?'

Joe Winder couldn't believe what he was hearing. Why the sudden anxiety? The laying on of guilt? If he'd known he was in for a full-blown argument, he indeed would have put on some pants.

Nina said, 'It's not just the money. I need someone reliable, someone who will be here for me.'

'Have I ever let you down?'

'No, but you will.'

Winder didn't say anything because she was absolutely correct; nothing in his immediate plans would please her.

'I know you,' Nina added, in a sad voice. 'You aren't going to let go of this thing.'

'Probably not.'

'Then I think we're definitely heading in different directions. I think you're going to end up in jail, or maybe dead.'

'Have some faith,' Joe Winder said.

'It's not that easy.' Nina stalked to the closet, flung

open the door and stared at the clutter. 'Where'd you put my suitcase?'

In the mid-1970s, Florida elected a crusading young governor named Clinton Tyree, an ex-football star and Vietnam War veteran. At six feet six, he was the tallest chief executive in the history of the state. In all likelihood he was also the most honest. When a ravenous and politically connected land-development company attempted to bribe Clinton Tyree, he tape-recorded their offers, turned the evidence over to the FBI and volunteered to testify at the trial. By taking a public stand against such omnipotent forces, Clinton Tyree became something of a folk hero in the Sunshine State and beyond. The faint scent of integrity attracted the national media, which roared into Florida and anointed the young governor a star of the new political vanguard.

It was, unfortunately, a vanguard of one. Clinton Tyree spoke with a blistering candor that terrified his fellow politicians. While others reveled in Florida's boom times, Clinton Tyree warned that the state was on the brink of an environmental cataclysm. The Everglades were drying up, the coral reefs were dying, Lake Okeechobee was choking on man-made poisons and the bluegills were loaded with mercury. While other officeholders touted Florida as a tropical dreamland, the governor called it a toxic dump with palm trees. On a popular call-in radio show, he asked visitors to stay away for a couple of years. He spoke not of managing the state's breakneck growth, but of halting it altogether. This, he declared, was the only way to save the place.

The day Clinton Tyree got his picture on the cover

of a national newsmagazine, some of the most powerful special interests in Florida—bankers, builders, highway contractors, sugar barons, phosphate-mining executives—congealed in an informal conspiracy to thwart the new governor's reforms by stepping around him, as if he were a small lump of dogshit on an otherwise luxuriant carpet.

Bypassing Clinton Tyree was relatively easy to do; all it took was money. In a matter of months, everyone who could be compromised, intimidated or bought off was. The governor found himself isolated from even his own political party, which had no stake in his radical bluster because it was alienating all the big campaign contributors. Save Florida? Why? And from what? The support that Clinton Tyree enjoyed among voters didn't help him one bit in the back rooms of Tallahassee; every bill he wanted passed got gutted, buried or rebuffed. The fact that he was popular with the media didn't deter his enemies; it merely softened their strategy. Rather than attack the governor's agenda, they did something worse—they ignored it. Only the most gentlemanly words were publicly spoken about young Clint, the handsome war hero, and about his idealism and courage to speak out. Any reporter who came to town could fill two or three notebooks with admiring quotes—so many (and so effusive) that someone new to the state might have assumed that Clinton Tyree had already died, which he had, in a way.

On the morning the Florida Cabinet decided to shut down a coastal wildlife preserve and sell it dirt cheap to a powerful land-sales firm, the lone dissenting vote trudged from the Capitol Building in disgust and vanished from the political landscape in the back of a limousine.

At first authorities presumed that the governor was the victim of a kidnapping or other foul play. A nation-wide manhunt was suspended only after a notarized resignation letter was analyzed by the FBI and found to be authentic. It was true; the crazy bastard had up and quit.

Journalists, authors and screenwriters flocked to Florida with hopes of securing exclusive rights to the renegade governor's story, but none could find him. Consequently, nothing was written that even bordered on the truth.

Which was this: Clinton Tyree now went by the name of Skink, and lived in those steamy clawing places where he was least likely to be bothered by human life-forms. For fifteen years the governor had been submerged in an expatriation that was deliberately remote and anony-mous, if not entirely tranquil.

Joe Winder wanted to talk about what happened in Tallahassee. 'I read all the stories,' he said. 'I went back and looked up the microfiche.'

'Then you know all there is to know.' Skink was on his haunches, poking the embers with a stick. Winder refused to look at what was frying in the pan.

He said, 'All this time and they never found you.'

'They quit searching,' Skink said. A hot ash caught in a wisp of his beard. He snuffed it with two fingers. 'I don't normally eat soft-shell turtle,' he allowed.

'Me neither,' said Joe Winder.

'The flavor makes up for the texture.'

'I bet.' Winder knelt on the other side of the fire.

Out of the blue Skink said, 'Your old man wasn't a bad guy, but he was in a bad business.'

Winder heard himself agree. 'He never understood what was so wrong about it. Or why I was so goddamn mad. He died not having a clue.'

Skink lifted the turtle by the tail and stuck a fork in it. 'Ten more minutes,' he said, 'at least.'

It wasn't easy trying to talk with him this way, but Winder wouldn't give up: 'It's been an interesting day. In the space of two hours I lost my job and my girlfriend.'

'Christ, you sound like Dobie Gillis.'

'The job was shit, I admit. But I was hoping Nina would stay strong. She's one in a million.'

'Love,' said Skink, 'it's just a kiss away.'

Dejectedly, Winder thought: I'm wasting my time. The man couldn't care less. 'I came to ask about a plan,' Winder said. 'I've been racking my brain.'

'Come on, I want to show you something.' Skink rose slowly and stretched, and the blaze-orange rainsuit made a crackling noise. He pulled the shower cap tight on his skull and, in high steps, marched off through the trees. To the west, the sky boiled with fierce purple thunderheads.

'Keep it moving,' Skink advised, over his shoulder.

Joe Winder followed him to the same dumpsite where the corpse of Spearmint Breath had been hidden. When they walked past the junker Cadillac, Winder noted that the trunk was open, and empty. He didn't ask about the body. He didn't want to know.

Skink led him through a hazardous obstacle course of discarded household junk—shells of refrigerators, ripped sofas, punctured mattresses, crippled Barca-loungers, rusty barbecue grills, disemboweled air conditioners—until they came to a very old Plymouth station wagon, an immense egg-colored barge with no wheels and no windshield. A yellow beach umbrella sprouted like a giant marigold from the dashboard, and offered minimal protection from blowing rain or the noonday sun. Skink got in the car and ordered Joe Winder to do the same.

The Plymouth was full of books—hundreds of volumes arranged lovingly from the tailgate to the front. With considerable effort, Skink turned completely in the front seat; he propped his rear end on the warped steering wheel. 'This is where I come to read,' he said. 'Believe it or not, the dome light in this heap still works.'

Joe Winder ran a finger along the spines of the books, and found himself smiling at the exhilarating variety of writers: Churchill, Hesse, Sandburg, Steinbeck, Camus, Paine, Wilde, Vonnegut, de Tocqueville, Salinger, García Márquez, even Harry Crews.

'I put a new battery in this thing,' Skink was saying. 'This time of year I've got to run the AC at least two, three hours a day. To stop the damn mildew.'

'So there's gas in this car?' Winder asked.

'Sure.'

'But no wheels.'

Skink shrugged. 'Where the hell would I be driving?'

A cool stream of wind rushed through the open wind-shield, and overhead the yellow beach umbrella began to flap noisily. A fat drop of rain splatted on the hood, followed by another and another.

'Damn,' said Skink. He put a shoulder to the door

and launched himself out of the station wagon, 'Hey, Flack, you coming or not?'

The storm came hard and they sat through it, huddled like Sherpas. The campfire washed out, but the soft-shelled turtle was cooked to perfection. Skink chewed intently on its tail and blinked the raindrops from his good eye; the other one fogged up like a broken headlight. Water trickled down his bronze cheeks, drenching his beard. Lightning cracked so close they could smell it—Winder ducked, but Skink showed no reaction, even when thunder rattled the coffeepot.

He adjusted the blaze weather suit to cover the electronic panther collar on his neck. 'They say it's waterproof, but I don't know.'

Winder could scarcely hear him over the drum of the rain against the trees. Lightning flashed again, and reflexively he shut his eyes.

Skink raised his voice: 'You know about that new golf resort?'

'I saw where they're putting it.'

'No!' Skink was shouting now. 'You know who's behind it? That fucking Kingsbury!'

The wind was getting worse, if that was possible. With his free hand, Skink wrung out the tendrils of his beard. 'Goddammit, man, are you listening? It all ties together.'

'What—with Koocher's death?'

'Everything—' Skink paused for another white sizzle of lightning. 'Every damn thing.'

It made sense to Winder. A scandal at the Amazing Kingdom would not only be bad for business, it might jeopardize Francis Kingsbury's plans for developing Falcon Trace. If anyone revealed that he'd lied about the 'endangered' voles, the feds might roll in and halt the whole show. The EPA, the Army Corps of Engineers, the Department of Interior—they could jerk Kingsbury around until he died of old age.

'Look at the big picture,' Skink said. With a tin fork he cleaned out the insides of the turtle shell. The wind was dying quickly, and the rain was turning soft on the leaves. The clouds broke out west, revealing raspberry patches of summer sunset. The coolness disappeared and the air turned muggy again.

Skink put down the fry pan and wiped his mouth on the sleeve of his rainsuit. 'It's beautiful out here,' he remarked. 'That squall felt damn good.'

'It might be too late,' Joe Winder said. 'Hell, they've started clearing the place.'

'I know.' The muscles in Skink's neck tightened. 'They tore down an eagle nest the other day. Two little ones, dead. That's the kind of bastards we're talking about.'

'Did you see—'

'I got there after the fact,' Skink said. 'Believe me, if I could've stopped them . . .'

'What if we're too late?'

'Are you in or not? That's all I need to know.'

'I'm in,' said Winder. 'Of course I am. I'm just not terribly optimistic.'

Skink smiled his matinee smile, the one that had gotten him elected so many years before. 'Lower your sights, boy,' he said to Joe Winder. 'I agree, justice is probably out of the question. But we can damn sure ruin their day.'

He reached under the flap of his rainsuit, grunted, fumbled inside his clothing. Finally his hand came out holding a steel-blue semi-automatic pistol.

'Don't worry,' he said. 'I've got an extra one for you.'

The woman who called herself Rachel Lark was receiving a vigorous massage when Francis X. Kingsbury phoned. She'd been expecting to hear from him ever since she'd read in the *Washington Post* about the theft of the blue-tongued mango voles in Florida. Her first thought, a natural one, was that Kingsbury would try to talk her into giving some of the money back. Rachel Lark braced for the worst as she sat up, naked, and told the masseur to give her the damn telephone.

On the other end, Kingsbury said: 'Is this my favorite redhead?'

'Forget it,' said the woman who called herself Rachel Lark, though it was not her true name.

Kingsbury said, 'Can you believe it, babe? My luck, the goddamn things get swiped.'

'I've already spent the money,' Rachel Lark said, 'and even if I didn't, a deal's a deal.'

Instead of protesting, Kingsbury said, 'Same here. I spent mine, too.'

'Then it's a social call, is it?'

'Not exactly. Are you alone, babe?'

'Me and a nice young man named Sven.'

The image gave Kingsbury a tingle. Rachel was an attractive woman, a bit on the heavy side, but a very hot dresser. They had met years before in the lobby of a prosecutor's office in Camden, where both of them were waiting to cut deals allowing them to avert unpleasant prison terms. Frankie King had chosen to drop the dime on the Zubonis, while the woman who now called herself Rachel Lark (it was Sarah Hunt at that time) was preparing to squeal on an ex-boyfriend who had illegally imported four hundred pounds of . elephant ivory. In the lobby that day, the two informants had amiably traded tales about life on the lam. Later they'd exchanged phone numbers and a complete list of aliases, and promised to keep in touch.

Rachel's specialty was wildlife, and Kingsbury phoned her soon after opening the Amazing Kingdom of Thrills. Before then, he had never heard of the Endangered Species Act, never dreamed that an obscure agency of the federal government would casually fork over two hundred thousand dollars in grant money for the purpose of preserving a couple of lousy rodents. Rachel Lark had offered to provide the animals and the documentation, and Kingsbury was so intrigued by the plan—not just the dough, but the radiant publicity for the Amazing Kingdom—that he didn't bother to inquire if the blue-tongued mango voles were real.

The government check had arrived on time, they'd split it fifty-fifty and that was that. Francis Kingsbury paid no further attention to the creatures until customers started noticing that the voles' tongues were no longer very blue. Once children openly began grilling the Amazing Kingdom tour guides about how the animals got their name, Kingsbury ordered Pedro Luz to get some food coloring and touch the damn things up. Unfortunately, Pedro had neither the patience nor the gentle touch required to be an animal handler, and one of the voles—the female—was crushed accidentally during a tongue-painting session. Afraid for his job,

Pedro Luz had told no one of the mishap. To replace the deceased vole, he had purchased a dwarf hamster for nine dollars from a pet store in Perrine. After minor modifications, the hamster had fooled both the customers and the male vole, which repeatedly attempted to mount its chubby new companion. Not only had the hamster rejected these advances, it had counterattacked with such ferocity that Pedro Luz had been forced to hire a night security guard to prevent a bloodbath.

Matters were further complicated by the appearance of an ill-mannered pinhead from U.S. Fish and Wildlife, who had barged into the theme park and demanded follow-up data from the 'project manager.' Of course there was no such person because there was no project to manage; research consisted basically of making sure that the rodents were still breathing every morning before the gates were opened. With the feds suddenly asking questions, Charles Chelsea had quietly put out an all-points bulletin for a legitimate biologist—a recruiting effort that eventually induced Dr. Will Koocher to come to the Amazing Kingdom of Thrills.

Kingsbury decided not to burden Rachel Lark with the details of the doctor's grisly demise; it was irrelevant to the purpose of his call.

'Forget the money,' Kingsbury told her.

'I must be hearing things.'

'No, I mean it.'

'Then what do you want?'

'More voles.'

'You're joking.'

'My customers, hell, they go nuts for the damn things. Now I got spin-offs, merchandise—a major warehouse situation, if you follow me.'

'Sorry,' Rachel Lark said, 'it was a one-time deal.' She'd pulled off the endangered-species racket on two other occasions—once for a small Midwestern zoo, and once for a disreputable reptile farm in South Carolina. Neither deal made as much money as the mango-vole scam, but neither had wound up in the headlines of the *Washington Post*, either.

Kingsbury said, 'Look, I know there's no more mango voles—'

'Hey, sport, there never *were* any mango voles.'

'So what you're saying, we defrauded the government.'

'God, you're quick.'

'I'm wondering,' said Kingsbury, 'those fucking furballs I paid for—what were they? Just out of curiosity.'

Rachel Lark said, 'Give me some credit, Frankie. They were voles. *Microtus pitymys*. Common pine voles.'

'Not endangered?'

'There's billions of the darn things.'

It figures, Kingsbury thought. The blue tongues were a neat touch. 'So get me some more,' he said. 'We'll call 'em something else, banana voles or whatever. The name's not important, long as they're cute.'

The woman who called herself Rachel Lark said: 'Look, I can get you other animals—rare, not endangered—but my advice is to stay away from the feds for a while. You put in for another big grant, it's a swell way to get audited.'

Again Kingsbury agreed without objection. 'So what else have you got, I mean, in the way of a species?'

'Lizards are your best bet.' Rachel Lark stretched on

her belly and motioned the masseur, whose real name was Ray, to do her spine.

'Christ on a Harley, who wants goddamn lizards!' Kingsbury cringed at the idea; he had been thinking more along the lines of a panda or a koala bear. 'I need something, you know, soft and furry and all that. Something the kiddies'll want to take home.'

Rachel Lark explained that the Florida Keys were home to a very limited number of native mammals, and the sudden discovery of a new species (so soon after the mango-vole announcement) would attract more scientific scrutiny than the Amazing Kingdom could withstand.

'You're saying, I take it, forget about pandas.'

'Frank, they'd die of heatstroke in about five minutes.'

Exasperated, Kingsbury said, 'I got problems down here you wouldn't believe.' He nearly told her about the blackmailing burglars.

'A new lizard you can get away with,' she said, 'especially in the tropics.'

'Rachel, what'd I just say? Fuck the lizards. I can't market lizards.'

Rachel Lark moaned blissfully as the masseur kneaded the muscles of her neck. 'My advice,' she said into the phone, 'is stay away from mammals and birds—it's too risky. Insects are another story. Dozens of species of insects are discovered every year. Grasshoppers, doodlebugs, you name it.'

There was a grumpy pause on the other end. Finally, Francis X. Kingsbury said, 'Getting back to the lizards. I mean, for the sake of argument . . .'

'They're very colorful,' said the woman who called herself Rachel Lark.

'Ugly is out of the question,' Kingsbury stated firmly. 'Ugly scares the kiddies.'

'Not all reptiles are ugly, Frankie. In fact, some are very beautiful.'

'All right,' he said. 'See what you can do.'

The woman who called herself Rachel Lark hung up the phone and closed her eyes. When she awoke, the masseur was gone and the man from Singapore was knocking on the door. In one hand was a small bouquet of yellow roses, and in the other was a tan briefcase holding a large down payment for a shipment of rare albino scorpions. Real ones.

EIGHTEEN

On the morning of July 23, a semi-tractor truck leaving North Key Largo lost its brakes on the Card Sound Bridge. The truck plowed through the tollbooth, jack-knifed and overturned, blocking both lanes of traffic and effectively severing the northern arm of the island from the Florida mainland. The gelatinous contents of the container were strewn for ninety-five yards along the road, and within minutes the milky-blue sky filled with turkey buzzards—hundreds of them, wheeling counter-clockwise lower and lower; only the noisy throng of gawkers kept the hungry scavengers from landing on the crash site. The first policeman to arrive was Highway Patrol Trooper Jim Tile, who nearly flipped his Crown Victoria cruiser when he tried to stop on the freshly slickened pavement. The trooper tugged the truck driver from the wreckage and, while splinting the man's arm, demanded to know what godforsaken cargo he'd been hauling.

'A dead whale,' moaned the driver, 'and that's all I'm saying.'

Charles Chelsea was summoned to Francis X. Kingsbury's office at the unholy hour of seven in the morning.

Kingsbury looked as if he hadn't slept since Easter. He asked Chelsea how long it would take to get the TV stations out to the Amazing Kingdom of Thrills.

'Two hours,' Chelsea said confidently.

'Do it.' Kingsbury blew his nose. 'On the horn, now.'

'What's the occasion, if I might ask?'

Kingsbury held up five fingers. 'Today's the big day. Our five-millionth visitor. Arrange something, a fucking parade, I don't care.'

Charles Chelsea felt his stomach yaw. 'Five million visitors,' he said. 'Sir, I didn't realize we'd reached that milestone.'

'We haven't.' Kingsbury hacked ferociously into a monogrammed handkerchief. 'Damn my hay fever, I think it's the mangroves. Every morning my whole head's fulla snot.' He pushed a copy of the *Wall Street Journal* at Chelsea. A column on the front page announced that Walt Disney World was expanding its empire to build a mammoth retail shopping center, one of the largest in the Southeastern United States.

'See, we can't just sit here,' Kingsbury said. 'Got to come back strong. Big media counterpunch.'

Chelsea skimmed the *Journal* article and laid it on his lap. Tentatively he said, 'It's hard to compete with something like this. I mean, it goes so far beyond the realm of a family theme park—'

'Bullshit,' said Kingsbury. 'The Miami-Lauderdale TV market is—what, three times the size of Orlando. Plus CNN, don't they have a bureau down here?' Kingsbury spun his chair and gazed out the window. 'Hell, that new dolphin I bought—can't you work him into the piece? Say he rescued somebody who fell in the tank. A pregnant lady or maybe an orphan. Rescued them from drowning—that's your story! "Miracle Dolphin Saves Drowning Orphan." '

'I don't know if that's such a good plan,' said Chelsea, though inwardly he had to admit it would have been one helluva headline.

'This celebration, make it for noon,' Kingsbury said. 'Whoever comes through the turnstiles, strike up the band. But make sure it's a tourist, no goddamn locals. Number five million, okay? In giant letters.'

His gut tightening, Chelsea said, 'Sir, it might be wiser to go with two million. It's closer to the real number . . . just in case somebody makes an issue of it.'

'No, two is—chickenshit, really. Five's better. And the parade, too, I'm serious.' Kingsbury stood up. He was dressed for golf. 'A parade, that's good video,' he said. 'Plenty of time to get it for the six-o'clock news. That's our best demographic, am I right? Fucking kids, they don't watch the eleven.'

Chelsea nodded. 'What do we give the winner? Mr. Five Million, I mean.'

'A car, Jesus Christ.' Kingsbury looked at him as if he were an idiot. A few years earlier, Disney World had given away an automobile every day for an entire summer. Kingsbury had never gotten over it. 'Make it a Corvette,' he told Chelsea.

'All right, but you're looking at forty thousand dollars. Maybe more.'

Kingsbury extended his lower lip so far that it seemed to touch his nose; for a moment he wore the pensive look of a caged orangutan. 'Forty grand,' he repeated quietly. 'That's brand new, I suppose.'

'When you give one away, yes. Ordinarily the cars should be new.'

CARL HIAASEN

'Unless they're classics.' Kingsbury winked. 'Make it a classic. Say, a 1964 Ford Falcon. You don't see many of those babies.'

'Sure don't.'

'A Falcon convertible, geez, we could probably pick one up for twenty-five hundred.'

'Probably,' agreed Chelsea, not even pretending enthusiasm.

'Well, move on it.' Francis X. Kingsbury thumbed him out of the office. 'And tell Pedro, get his ass in here.'

Pedro Luz was in the executive gym, bench-pressing a bottle of stanozolol tablets. He was letting the tiny pink pills drop one by one into his mouth.

A man named Churrito, lounging on a Nautilus, said: 'Hiss very bad for liver.'

'Very good for muscles,' said Pedro Luz, mimicking the accent.

Churrito was his latest hire to the security squad at the Amazing Kingdom of Thrills. He had accompanied Pedro Luz on his mission to Miami, but had declined to participate in the beating. Pedro Luz was still miffed about what had happened—the old lady chomping off the top joint of his right index finger.

'You're useless,' he had told Churrito afterward.

'I am a soldier,' Churrito had replied. 'I dun hit no wooman.'

Unlike the other security guards hired by Pedro Luz, Churrito had not been a crooked cop. He was a Nicaraguan *contra* who had moved to Florida when things were bleak, and had not gotten around to moving back.

While Churrito was pleased at the prospect of democracy taking seed in his homeland, he suspected that true economic prosperity was many years away. Elections notwithstanding, Churrito's buddies were still stuck in the border hills, frying green bananas and dynamiting the rivers for fish. Meanwhile his uncle, formerly a sergeant in Somoza's National Guard, now lived with a twenty-two-year-old stewardess in a high-rise condo on Key Biscayne. To Churrito, this seemed like a pretty good advertisement for staying right where he was.

Pedro Luz had hired him because he looked mean, and because he'd said he had killed people.

'*Comunistas*,' Churrito had specified, that night at the old lady's apartment. 'I only kill commoonists. And I dun hit no wooman.'

And now here he was, lecturing Pedro Luz about the perils of anabolic steroids.

'Make you face like balloon.'

'Shut up,' said Pedro Luz. He was wondering if the hospital in Key Largo would sell him extra bags of dextrose water for the IV. Grind up the stanozolols, drop them in the mix and everything would be fine again.

'Make you bulls shrink, too.'

'That's enough,' Pedro Luz said.

Churrito held up two fingers. 'Dis big. Like BBs.'

'Quiet,' said Pedro Luz, 'or I call a friend a mine at INS.' He couldn't decide whether to fire the guy or beat him up. He knew which would give more pleasure.

'They got, like, three flights a day to Managua,' he said to Churrito. 'You getting homesick?'

The Nicaraguan grimaced.

'I didn't think so,' said Pedro Luz. 'So shut up about my medicines.'

Charles Chelsea appeared at the foot of the weight bench. He had never seen Pedro Luz without a shirt, and couldn't conceal his awe at the freakish physique—the hairless bronze trunk of a chest, cantaloupe biceps, veins as thick as a garden hose. Chelsea didn't recognize the other fellow—shorter and sinewy, with skin the color of nutmeg.

'I'm working out,' said Pedro Luz.

'Mr. Kingsbury needs to see you.'

'Who ees that?' Churrito said.

Pedro Luz sat up. 'That be the boss.'

'Right away,' said Charles Chelsea.

'Can I go?' asked Churrito. He didn't want to miss an opportunity to meet the boss; according to his uncle, that's what success in America was all about. Kissing ass.

'I'm sorry,' Chelsea said, 'but Mr. Kingsbury wants to see Chief Luz alone.'

'Yeah,' said Pedro Luz. As he rolled off the bench, he made a point of clipping Churrito with a casual forearm. Churrito didn't move, didn't make a sound. His eyes grew very small and he stared at Pedro Luz until Pedro Luz spun away, pretending to hunt for his sweatshirt.

Churrito pointed at the scarlet blemishes on Pedro Luz's shoulder blades and said: 'You all broke out, man.'

'Shut up before I yank your nuts off.'

Backing away, Charles Chelsea thought: Where do they get these guys?

*

Francis X. Kingsbury offered a Bloody Mary to Pedro Luz, who guzzled it like Gatorade.

'So, Pedro, the job's going all right?'

The security chief was startled at Kingsbury's genial tone. A ration of shit was what he'd expected; the old fart had been livid since the burglary of his private office. The crime had utterly baffled Pedro Luz, who hadn't the first notion of how to solve it. He had hoped that the mission to Eagle Ridge would absolve him.

'I took care of that other problem,' he announced to Kingsbury.

'Fine. Excellent.' Kingsbury was swiveling back and forth in his chair. He didn't look so good: nervous, ragged, droopy-eyed, his fancy golf shirt all wrinkled. Pedro Luz wondered if the old fart was doing coke. The very idea was downright hilarious.

'She won't bother you no more,' he said to Kingsbury.

'You made it look, what—like muggers? Crack fiends?'

'Sure, that's what the cops would think. If she calls them, which I don't think she will. I made it clear what could happen.'

'Fine. Excellent.' Kingsbury propped his elbows on the desk in a way that offered Pedro Luz an unobstructed view of the lurid mouse tattoo.

'Two things—' Kingsbury paused when he spotted the bandage on Pedro Luz's finger.

'Hangnail,' said the security chief.

'Whatever,' Kingsbury said. 'Two things—some assholes, the guys who stole my files, they're blackmailing me. You know, shaking me down.'

Pedro Luz asked how much money he had promised them.

'Never mind,' Kingsbury replied. 'Five grand so far is what I paid. But the files, see, I can't just blow 'em off. I need the files.'

'Who are these men?'

Francis Kingsbury threw up his hands. 'That's the thing—just ordinary shitheads. White trash. I can't fucking believe it.'

Pedro Luz had never understood the concept of white trash, or how it differed from black trash or Hispanic trash or any other kind of criminal dirtbag. He said, 'You want the files but you don't want to pay.'

'Exacto!' said Kingsbury. 'In fact, the five grand—I wouldn't mind getting it back.'

Pedro Luz laughed sharply. Months go by and the job's a snooze—now suddenly all this dirty work. Oh well, Pedro thought, it beats painting rat tongues. He hadn't shed a tear when the mango voles were stolen.

Kingsbury was saying, 'The other thing, I fired a guy from Publicity.'

'Yeah?' Watching that damn tattoo, it was driving Pedro silly. Minnie on her knees, polishing Mickey's knob—whoever did the drawing was damn good, almost Disney caliber.

'You need to go see this guy I fired,' Kingsbury was saying. 'Find out some things.'

Pedro Luz asked what kind of things.

Kingsbury moved his lips around, like a camel getting ready to spit. Eventually he said, 'The problem we had before? This is worse, okay. The guy I mentioned, we're talking major pain in the rectum.'

'Okay.'

'As long as he worked for us, we had some control. On the outside, hell, he's a major pain. I just got a feeling.'

Pedro Luz gave him a thumbs-up. 'Don't worry.'

'Carefully,' Kingsbury added. 'Same as before would be excellent. Except no dead whales this time.'

God, thought Pedro Luz, what a fuckup *that* was.

'Do I know him?' he asked Kingsbury.

'From Publicity. Joe Winder's his name.'

'Oh.' Pedro Luz perked up. Winder was the smartass who'd been hassling him about Dr. Koocher. The same guy he'd sent Angel and Big Paulie to teach a lesson, only something went sour and Angel ended up dead and Paulie must've took off. Next thing Pedro knows, here's this smartass Winder snooping around the animal lab in the middle of the night.

Mr. X was right about the guy. Now that he was fired, he might go hog-wild. Start talking crazy shit all over the place.

'You look inspired,' Kingsbury said.

Pedro Luz smiled crookedly. 'Let's just say I got some ideas.'

When Molly McNamara opened her eyes, she was surprised to see Bud Schwartz and Danny Pogue at her bedside.

'I thought you boys would be long gone.'

'No way,' said Danny Pogue. His eyes were large and intent, like a retriever's. His chin was in his hands, and he was sitting very close to the bed. He patted Molly's brow with a damp washcloth.

'Thank you,' she said. 'I'm very thirsty.'

Danny Pogue bolted to the kitchen to get her a glass of ginger ale. Bud Schwartz took a step closer. He said, 'What happened? Can you remember anything?'

'My glasses,' she said, pointing to the nightstand.

'They got busted,' said Bud Schwartz. 'I used some Scotch tape on the nose part.'

Molly McNamara put them on, and said, 'Two men. Only one did the hitting.'

'Why? What'd they want—money?'

Molly shook her head slowly. Danny Pogue came back with the ginger ale, and she took two small sips. 'Thank you,' she said. 'No, they didn't want money.'

Danny Pogue said, 'Who?'

'The men who came. They said it was a warning.'

'Oh Christ.'

'It's none of your concern,' said Molly.

Grimly Bud Schwartz said, 'They were after the files.'

'No. They never mentioned that.'

Bud Schwartz was relieved; he had worried that Francis X. Kingsbury had somehow identified them, connected them to Molly and sent goons to avenge the burglary. It was an irrational fear, he knew, because even the powerful Kingsbury couldn't have done it so quickly after their blackmail visit.

Still, it was discouraging to see how they had battered Molly McNamara. These were extremely bad men, and Bud Schwartz doubted they would have allowed him and Danny Pogue to survive the encounter.

'I think we ought to get out of here,' he said to Molly. 'Take you back to the big house.'

'That's a sensible plan,' Molly agreed, 'but you boys don't have to stay.'

'Like hell,' Danny Pogue declared. 'Look at you, all busted up. You'll be needing some help.'

'You got some bad bruises,' agreed Bud Schwartz. 'Your right knee's twisted, too, but I don't think it's broke. Plus they knocked out a couple teeth.'

Molly ran her tongue around her gums and said, 'I was the only one in this building who still had their own.'

Danny Pogue paced with a limp. 'I wanted to call an ambulance or somebody, only Bud decided we better not.'

Molly said that was a smart decision, considering what the three of them had been up to lately. She removed the damp cloth from her forehead and folded it on the nightstand.

Danny Pogue wanted to know all about the attackers—how big they were, what they looked like. 'I bet they was niggers,' he said.

Molly raised herself off the pillow, cocked her arm and slapped him across the face. Incredulous, Danny Pogue rubbed his cheek.

She said, 'Don't you ever again use that word in my presence.'

'Christ, I didn't mean nothin'.'

'Well, it just so happens these men were white. White Hispanic males. The one who beat me up was very large and muscular.'

'My question,' said Bud Schwartz, 'is how they slipped past that crack security guard. What's his name, Andrews, the ace with the flashlight.'

Molly said: 'You won't believe it. The big one had a badge. A police badge, City of Miami.'

'Wonderful,' Bud Schwartz said.

'I saw it myself,' Molly said. 'Why do you think I even opened the door? He said they were plainclothes detectives. Once they had me down, I couldn't get to my purse.'

Danny Pogue looked at his partner with the usual mix of confusion and concern. Bud Schwartz said, 'It sounds like some serious shitkickers. You say they were Cubans?'

'Hispanics,' Molly said.

'Did they speak American?' asked Danny Pogue.

'The big one did all the talking, and his English was quite competent. Especially his use of four-letter slang.'

Danny Pogue rocked on his good leg, and slammed a fist against the wall. 'I'll murder the sumbitch!'

'Sure you will,' said his partner. 'You're a killer and I'm the next quarterback for the Dolphins.'

'I mean it, Bud. Look what he done to her.'

'I see, believe me.' Bud Schwartz gave Molly McNamara two Percodans and said it would help her sleep. She swallowed the pills in one gulp and thanked the burglars once again. 'It's very kind of you to look after me,' she said.

'Only till you're feeling better,' said Bud Schwartz. 'We got some business that requires our full attention.'

'Of course, I understand.'

'We made five grand tonight!' said Danny Pogue. Quickly he withered under his partner's glare.

'Five thousand is very good,' Molly said. 'Add the money I still owe you, and that's quite a handsome nest egg.' She slid deeper into the sheets, and pulled the blanket to her chin.

'Get some rest,' Bud Schwartz said. 'We'll take you to the house in the morning.'

'Yeah, get some sleep.' Danny Pogue gazed at her dolorously. Bud Schwartz wondered if he was about to cry.

'Bud?' Molly spoke in a fog.

'Yeah.'

'Did you boys happen to find a piece of finger on the floor?'

'No,' said Bud Schwartz. 'Why?'

'Would you check in the kitchen, please?'

'No problem.' He wondered how the pills could mess her up so quickly. 'You mean, like a human finger?'

But Molly's eyes were already closed.

NINETEEN

Charles Chelsea worked feverishly all morning. By half past eleven the parade was organized. The gateway to the Amazing Kingdom of Thrills was festooned with multi-colored streamers and hundreds of Mylar balloons. Cheerleaders practiced cartwheels over the turnstiles while the Tavernier High School band rehearsed the theme from *Exodus*. Several of the most popular animal characters—Robbie Raccoon, Petey Possum and Barney the Bison—were summoned from desultory lunch breaks in The Catacombs to greet and be photographed with the big winner. Above a hastily constructed stage, a billowy hand-painted banner welcomed 'OUR FIVE-MILLIONTH SPECIAL GUEST!!!'

And there, parked in the courtyard, was a newly restored 1966 Chevrolet Corvair, one of Detroit's most venerated deathtraps. Charles Chelsea had been unable to locate a mint-condition Falcon, and the vintage Mustangs were beyond Francis Kingsbury's budget. The Corvair was Chelsea's next choice as the giveaway car because it was a genuine curiosity, and because it was cheap. The one purchased by Chelsea had been rear-ended by a dairy tanker in 1972, and the resulting explosion had wiped out a quartet of home-appliance salesmen. The rebuilt Corvair was seven inches shorter from bumper to bumper than the day it had rolled off the assembly line, but Charles Chelsea was certain no one would notice. Two extra coats of cherry paint and the Corvair shouted classic. It was exactly the sort of campy junk-mobile that some dumb Yuppie would love.

The scene was set for the coronation of the alleged five-millionth visitor to the Amazing Kingdom. The only thing missing from the festive tableau, Chelsea noted lugubriously, was customers. The park had opened more than two hours ago, yet not a single carload of tourists had arrived. The trams were empty, the cash registers mute; no one had passed through the ticket gates. Chelsea couldn't understand it—the place had not experienced such a catastrophic attendance drop since salmonella had felled a visiting contingent of Rotarians at Sally's Cimarron Saloon.

Chelsea prayed with all his heart that some tourists would show up before the television vans. He did not know, and could not have envisioned, that an eighteen-wheeler loaded with the decomposing remains of Orky the Whale had flipped on Card Sound Road and paralyzed all traffic heading toward the Amazing Kingdom. The highway patrol diligently had set up a roadblock at the junction near Florida City, where troopers were advising all buses, campers and rental cars filled with Francis X. Kingsbury's customers to turn around and return to Miami. The beleaguered troopers did not consider it their sworn duty to educate the tourists about an alternate route to the Amazing Kingdom—taking Highway 1 south past Jewfish Creek, then backtracking up County Road 905 to the park. The feeling among the troopers (based on years of experience) was that no matter how simple and explicit they made the directions, many of the tourists would manage to get lost, run out of gas and become the victims of some nasty roadside crime. A more sensible option was simply to tell them to go back, there'd been a bad accident.

Consequently Charles Chelsea stood in eery solitude on the makeshift stage, the cheery banner flapping over his head as he stared at the empty parking lot and wondered how in the hell he would break the news to Francis X. Kingsbury. Today there would be no celebration, no parade, no five-millionth visitor. There were no visitors at all.

Joe Winder felt like a damn redneck—he hadn't been to a firing range in ten or twelve years, and that was to shoot his father's revolver, an old Smith. The gun Skink had given him was a thin foreign-made semi-automatic. It didn't have much weight, but Skink promised it would do the job, whatever job needed doing. Winder had decided to keep it for ornamental purposes. It lay under the front seat as he drove south on County Road 905.

He stopped at a pay phone, dialed the sex-talk number and billed it to his home. Miriam answered and started in with a new routine, something about riding bareback on a pony. When Winder broke in and asked for Nina, Miriam told him she wasn't there.

'Tell her to call me, please.'

'Hokay, Joe.'

'On second thought, never mind.'

'Whatever chew say. You like the horsey business?'

'Yes, Miriam, it's very good.'

'Nina wrote it. Want me do the end?'

'No thank you.'

'Is hot stuff, Joe. Cheese got some mansionation.'

'She sure does.'

Joe Winder drove until he reached the Falcon Trace construction site. He parked on the side of the road and watched a pair of mustard-colored bulldozers plow a fresh section of hammock, creating a tangled knoll of uprooted tamarinds, buttonwoods, pigeon plums and rouge-berry. Each day a few more acres were being destroyed in the name of championship golf.

A team of surveyors worked the distant end of the property, near Winder's fishing spot. He assumed they were marking off the lots where the most expensive homes would be built—the more ocean frontage, the higher the price. This was how Francis X. Kingsbury would make his money—the golf course itself was never meant to profit; it was a real-estate tease, plain and simple. The links would be pieced together in the middle of the development on whatever parcels couldn't be peddled as residential waterfront. Soon, Winder knew, they'd start blasting with dynamite to dig fairway lakes in the ancient reef rock.

He saw that both bulldozers had stopped, and that the drivers had gotten down from the cabs to look at something in the trees. Joe Winder stepped out of the car and started running. He remembered what Skink had told him about the baby eagles. He shouted at the men and saw them turn. One folded his arms and slouched against his dozer.

Winder covered the two hundred yards in a minute. When he reached the men, he was panting too hard to speak.

One of them said: 'What's your problem?'

Winder flashed his Amazing Kingdom identification

badge, which he had purposely neglected to turn in upon termination of employment. The lazy bulldozer driver, the one leaning against his machine, studied the badge and began to laugh. 'What the hell is this?'

When Joe Winder caught his breath, he said: 'I work for Mr. Kingsbury. He owns this land.'

'Ain't the name on the permit. The permit says Ramex Global.'

The other driver spoke up: 'Anyway, who gives a shit about some goddamn wolves?'

'Yeah,' the first driver said. 'Bury 'em.'

'No,' said Joe Winder. They weren't wolves, they were gray foxes—six of them, no larger than kittens. The bulldozers had uprooted the den tree. Half-blind, the little ones were crawling all over each other, squeaking and yapping in toothless panic.

Winder said, 'If we leave them alone, the mother will probably come back.'

'What is this, "Wild Kingdom"?'

'At least help me move them out of the way.'

'Forget it,' the smartass driver said. 'I ain't in the mood for rabies. Come on, Bobby, let's roll it.'

The men climbed back in the dozers and seized the gear sticks. Instinctively Joe Winder positioned himself between the large machines and the baby foxes. The drivers began to holler and curse. The smartass lowered the blade of his bulldozer and inched forward, pushing a ridge of moist dirt over the tops of Joe Winder's shoes. The driver grinned and whooped at his own cleverness until he noticed the gun pointed up at his head.

He quickly turned off the engine and raised his hands. The other driver did the same. In a scratchy whine he said, 'Geez, what's your problem?'

Winder held the semi-automatic steady. He was surprised at how natural it felt. He said, 'Is this what it takes to have a civilized conversation with you shit-heads?'

Quickly he checked over his shoulder to make sure the kits hadn't crawled from the den. The outlandishness of the situation was apparent, but he'd committed himself to melodrama. With the gun on display, he was already deep into felony territory.

The smartass driver apologized profusely for burying Winder's shoes. 'I'll buy you some new ones,' he offered.

'Oh, that's not necessary.' Winder yearned to shoot the bulldozers but he didn't know where to begin; the heavy steel thoraxes looked impervious to cannon fire.

The lazy driver said: 'You want us to get down?'

'Not just yet,' said Joe Winder, 'I'm thinking.'

'Hey, there's no need to shoot. Just tell us what the hell you want.'

'I want you to help me fuck up these machines.'

It was nine o'clock when the knock came. Joe Winder was sitting in the dark on the floor of the apartment. He had the clip out of the gun, and the bullets out of the clip. A full load, too, sixteen rounds; he had lined up the little rascals side by side on a windowsill, a neat row of identical copper-headed soldiers.

The knocking wouldn't go away. Winder picked up the empty gun. He went to the door and peeked out of the peephole. He saw an orb of glistening blond; not Nina-style blond, this was lighter. When the woman turned around, Winder flung open the door and pulled her inside.

In the darkness Carrie Lanier took a deep breath and said: 'I hope that's you.'

'It's me,' Joe Winder said.

'Was that a gun I saw?'

'I'm afraid so. My situation has taken a turn for the worse.'

Carrie said, 'That's why I came.'

Winder led her back to the living room, where they sat between two large cardboard boxes. The only light was the amber glow from the stereo receiver; Carrie Lanier could barely hear the music from the speakers.

'Where's your girlfriend?' she asked.

'Moved out.'

'I'm sorry.' She paused; then, peering at him: 'Is that a beret?'

'Panties,' Joe Winder said. 'Can you believe it—that's all she left me. Cheap ones, too. The mail-order crap she sold over the phone.' He pulled the underwear off his head to show her the shoddy stitching.

'You've had a rough time,' said Carrie Lanier. 'I didn't know she'd moved out.'

'Yeah, well, I'm doing just fine. Adjusting beautifully to the single life. Sitting here in a dark apartment with a gun in my lap and underpants on my head.'

Carrie squeezed his arm. 'Joe, are you on drugs?'

'Nope,' he said. 'Pretty amazing, isn't it?'

'I think you should come home with me.'

'Why?'

'Because bad things will happen if you stay here.'

'Ah.' Winder scooped the bullets off the windowsill and fed them into the gun clip. 'You must be talking about Pedro Luz.'

'It's all over the Magic Kingdom,' Carrie said, 'about the reasons you were fired.'

'Mr. X doesn't kill his former employees, does he?'

She leaned closer. 'It's no joke. The word is, you're number one on Pedro's list.'

'So that's the word.'

'Joe, I get around. Spend the day in a raccoon suit, people forget there's a real person inside. I might as well be invisible—the stuff I pick up, you wouldn't believe.'

'The spy wore a tail! And now you hear Pedro's irritated.'

'I got it from two of the other guards on lunch break. They were doing blow behind the Magic Mansion.'

Winder was struck by how wonderful Carrie looked, her eyes all serious in the amber light. Impulsively he kissed her on the cheek. 'Don't worry about me,' he said. 'You can go home.'

'You aren't listening.'

'Yes, I—'

'No, you aren't.' Her tone was one of motherly disapproval. 'I warned you about this before. About sticking your nose where it doesn't belong.'

'You did, yes.'

'Last time you were lucky. You truly were.'

'I suppose so.' Joe Winder felt oppressively tired. Suddenly the handgun weighed a ton. He slid it across the carpet so forcefully that it banged into the baseboard of the opposite wall.

Carrie Lanier told him to hurry and pack some clothes.

'I can't leave,' he said. 'Nina might call.'

'Joe, it's not just Pedro you've got to worry about. It's the police.'

Winder's chin dropped to his chest. 'Already?'

'Mr. X swore out a warrant this afternoon,' Carrie said. 'I heard it from his secretary.'

Francis Kingsbury's secretary was a regular visitor to The Catacombs, where she was conducting an athletic love affair with the actor who portrayed Bartholomew, the most shy and bookish of Uncle Ely's Elves.

Carrie said, 'She mentioned something about destruction of private property.'

'There was an incident,' Joe Winder acknowledged, 'but no shots were fired.'

Under his supervision, the two bulldozers had torn down the three-dimensional billboard that proclaimed the future home of the Falcon Trace Golf and Country Club. The bulldozers also had demolished the air-conditioned double-wide trailer (complete with beer cooler and billiard table) that served as an on-site office for the construction company. They had even wrecked the Port-O-Lets, trapping one of the foremen with his anniversary issue of *Hustler* magazine.

Afterwards Joe Winder had encouraged the bulldozer operators to remove their clothing, which he'd wadded in the neck of the gas tanks. Then—after borrowing the smartass driver's cigarette lighter—Joe Winder had suggested that the men aim their powerful machines toward the Atlantic Ocean, engage the forward gear and swiftly exit the cabs. Later he had proposed a friendly wager on which of the dozers would blow first.

'They spotted the flames all the way from Homestead Air Base,' Carrie Lanier reported. 'Channel 7 showed up in a helicopter, so Kingsbury made Chelsea write up a press release.'

'A freak construction accident, no doubt.'

'Good guess. I've got a Xerox in my purse.'

'No thanks.' Joe Winder wasn't in the mood for Chelsea's golden lies. He stood up and stretched; joints and sockets popped in protest. Lights began to flash blue, green and red on the bare wall, and Winder assumed it was fatigue playing tricks with his vision.

He squinted strenuously, and the lights disappeared. When he opened his eyes, the lights were still strobing. 'Shit, here we go.' Winder went to the window and peeked through the curtain.

'How many?' Carrie asked.

'Two cops, one car.'

'Is there another way out?'

'Sure,' he said.

They heard the tired footsteps on the front walk, the deep murmur of conversation, the crinkle of paper. In the crack beneath the door they saw the yellow flicker of flashlight as the policemen examined the warrant one more time, probably double-checking the address.

Winder picked up the semi-automatic and arranged it in his waistband. Carrie Lanier followed him to the kitchen, where they slipped out the back door just as the cops got serious with their knocking. Once outside, in the pale blue moonlight, she deftly grabbed the gun from Joe Winder's trousers and put it in her handbag.

'In case you go stupid on me,' she whispered.

'No chance of that,' he said. 'None at all.'

TWENTY

A thin coil of copper dangled by a string from Carrie Lanier's rearview mirror. Joe Winder asked if it was some type of hieroglyphic emblem.

'It's an IUD,' said Carrie, without taking her eyes off the road. 'A reminder of my ex-husband.'

'I like it.' Winder tried to beef up the compliment. 'It's better than fuzzy dice.'

'He wanted to have babies,' Carrie explained, shooting into the left lane and passing a cement truck. 'A baby boy and a baby girl. House with a white picket fence and big backyard. Snapper riding mower. Golden retriever named Champ. He had it all planned.'

Joe Winder said, 'Sounds pretty good, except for the golden. Give me a Lab any day.'

'Well, he wanted to get me pregnant,' Carrie went on. 'Every night, it was like a big routine. So I'd say sure, Roddy, whatever you want, let's make a baby. I never told him about wearing the loop. And every month he'd want to know. "Did we do it, sweetie? Is there a zygote?" And I'd say "Sorry, honey, guess we'd better try harder."'

'Roddy was his name? That's a bad sign right there.'

'He was a screamer, all right.'

'What happened?' Winder asked. 'Is he still around?'

'No, he's not.' Carrie hit the intersection at Highway 1 without touching the brakes, and merged neatly into the northbound traffic. She said, 'Roddy's up at Eglin doing a little time.'

'Which means he's either a drug dealer or a crooked lawyer.'

'Both,' she said. 'Last month he sent a Polaroid of him with a tennis trophy. He said he can't wait to get out and start trying for a family again.'

'The boy's not well.'

'It's all Oedipal, that's my theory.' Carrie nodded at the IUD and said, 'I keep it there to remind myself that you can't be too careful when it comes to men. Here's Roddy with his Stanford diploma and his fancy European car and his heavy downtown law firm, everything in the whole world going for him. Turns out he's nothing but a dipshit, and a dumb dipshit to boot.'

Winder said she'd been smart to take precautions.

'Yeah, well, I had my career to consider.' Carrie turned a corner into a trailer park, and coasted the car to the end of a narrow gravel lane. 'Home sweet home,' she said. 'Be sure to lock your door. This is not a wonderful neighborhood.'

Joe Winder said, 'Why are you doing this for me?'

'I'm not sure. I'm really not.' She tossed him the keys and asked him to get the raccoon costume from the trunk of the car.

Bud Schwartz and Danny Pogue helped Molly McNamara up the steps of the old house in South Miami. They eased her into the rocker in the living room, and opened the front windows to air the place out. Bud

Schwartz's hand still throbbed from the gunshot wound, but his fingers seemed to be functioning.

Danny Pogue said, 'Ain't it good to be home?'

'Indeed it is,' said Molly. 'Could you boys fix me some tea?'

Bud Schwartz looked hard at his partner. 'I'll do it,' said Danny Pogue. 'It don't bother me.' Cheerfully he hobbled toward the kitchen.

'He's not a bad young man,' Molly McNamara said. 'Neither of you are.'

'Model citizens,' said Bud Schwartz. 'That's us.'

He lowered himself into a walnut captain's chair but stood again quickly, as if the seat were hot. He'd forgotten about the damn thing in his pocket until it touched him in the right testicle. Irritably he removed it from his pants and placed it on an end table. He had wrapped it in a blue lace doily.

He said, 'Can we do something with this, please?'

'There's a Mason jar in the cupboard over the stove,' Molly said, 'and some pickle juice in the refrigerator.'

'You're kidding.'

'This is important, Bud. It's evidence.'

In the hall he passed Danny Pogue carrying a teapot on a silver tray. 'You believe this shit?' Bud Schwartz said. He held up the doily.

'What now?'

'She wants me to pickle the goddamn thing!'

Danny Pogue made a squeamish face. 'What for?' When he returned to the living room, Molly was rocking tranquilly in the chair. He poured the tea and said, 'You must be feeling better.'

'Better than I look.' She drank carefully, watching Danny Pogue over the rim of the cup. In a tender voice she said: 'You don't know what this means to me, the fact that you stayed to help.'

'It wasn't just me. It was Bud, too.'

'He's not a bad person,' Molly McNamara allowed. 'I suspect he's a man of principle, deep down.'

Danny Pogue had never thought of his partner as a man of principle, but maybe Molly had spotted something. While Bud was an incorrigible thief, he played by a strict set of rules. No guns, no violence, no hard drugs—Danny Pogue supposed that these could be called principles. He hoped that Molly recognized that he, too, had his limits—moral borders he would not cross. Later on, when she was asleep, he would make a list.

He said, 'So what are you gonna do now? Stay at it?'

'To tell the truth, I'm not certain.' She put down the teacup and dabbed her swollen lips with a napkin. 'I've had some experts go over Kingsbury's files. Lawyers, accountants, people sympathetic to the cause. They made up a cash-flow chart, ran the numbers up and down and sideways. They say it's all very interesting, these foreign companies, but it would probably take months for the IRS and Customs to sort it out; another year for an indictment. We simply don't have that kind of time.'

'Shoot,' said Danny Pogue. He hadn't said 'shoot' since the third grade, but he'd been trying to clean up his language in Molly's presence.

'I'm a little discouraged,' she went on. 'I guess I'd gotten my hopes up prematurely.'

Danny Pogue felt so lousy that he almost told her about the other files, about the blackmail scam that he and Bud Schwartz were running on the great Francis X. Kingsbury.

He said, 'There's nothing we can do? Just let him go ahead and murder off them butterflies and snails?' Molly had given him a magazine clipping about the rare tropical snails of Key Largo.

She said, 'I didn't say we're giving up—'

'Because we should talk to Bud. He'll think a something.'

'Every day we lose precious time,' Molly said. 'Every day they're that much closer to pouring the concrete.'

Danny Pogue nodded. 'Let's talk to Bud. Bud's sharp as a tack about stuff like this—'

Molly stopped rocking and raised a hand. 'I heard something, didn't you?'

From the kitchen came muffled percussions of a struggle—men grunting, something heavy hitting a wall, a jar breaking.

Danny Pogue was shaking when he stood up. The bum foot made him think twice about running.

'Hand me the purse,' Molly said. 'I'll need my gun.'

But Danny Pogue was frozen to the pine floor. His eyelids fluttered and his arms stiffened at his side. All he could think was: *Somebody's killing Bud!*

'Danny, did you hear me? Get me my purse!'

A block of orange appeared in the hallway. It was a tall man in a bright rainsuit and a moldy-looking shower cap. He had a damp silvery beard and black wraparound sunglasses and something red fastened to his neck. The man carried Bud Schwartz in a casual way, one arm around the midsection. Bud Schwartz was limp, gasping, flushed in the face.

Danny Pogue's tongue was as dry as plaster when the stranger stepped out of the shadow.

'Oh, it's you,' Molly McNamara said. 'Now be careful, don't hurt that young man.'

The stranger dropped Bud Schwartz butt-first on the pine and said, 'I caught him putting somebody's fingertip in a Mason jar.'

'I'm the one who told him to,' said Molly. 'Now, Governor, you just settle down.'

'What happened to you?' the stranger demanded. 'Who did this to you, Miss McNamara?'

He took off the sunglasses and glared accusingly at Danny Pogue, who emitted a pitiful hissing noise as he shook his head. Bud Schwartz, struggling to his feet, said: 'It wasn't us, it was some damn Cuban.'

'Tell me a name,' said the stranger.

'I don't know,' said Molly McNamara, 'but I got a good bite out of him.'

'The finger,' Bud Schwartz explained, still gathering his breath.

The stranger knelt beside the rocking chair and gently examined the raw-looking cuts and bruises on Molly's face. 'This is ... intolerable.' He was whispering to himself and no one else. 'This is barbarism.'

Molly touched the visitor's arm and said, 'I'll be all right. Really.'

Bud Schwartz and Danny Pogue had seen men like this only in prison, and not many. Wild was the only way to describe the face ... wild and driven and fearless, but not necessarily insane. It would be foolish, perhaps even fatal, to assume the guy was spaced.

He turned to Bud Schwartz and said, 'How about giving me that Cuban's nub.'

'I dropped it on the floor.' Bud Schwartz thought: Christ, he's *not* going to make me go pick it up, is he?

Danny Pogue said, 'No sweat, I'll find it.'

'No,' said the man in the orange rainsuit. 'I'll grab it on the way out.' He squeezed Molly's hands and stood up. 'Will you be all right?'

'Yes, they're taking good care of me.'

The stranger nodded at Bud Schwartz, who couldn't help but notice that one of the man's eyes was slipping out of the socket. The man calmly reinserted it.

'I didn't mean to hurt you,' he said to Bud Schwartz. 'Well, actually, I *did* mean to hurt you.'

Molly explained: 'He didn't know you fellows were my guests, that's all.'

'I'll be in touch,' said the stranger. He kissed Molly on the cheek and said he would check on her in a day or two. Then he was gone.

Bud Schwartz waited until he heard the door slam. Then he said: 'What the hell was that?'

'A friend,' Molly replied. They had known each other a long time. She had worked as a volunteer in his gubernatorial campaign, whipping up both the senior-citizen vote and the environmental coalitions. Later, when he quit office and vanished, Molly was one of the few who knew what happened, and one of the few who understood. Over the years he had kept in touch in his own peculiar way—sometimes a spectral glimpse, sometimes a sensational entrance; jarring cameos that were as hair-raising as they were poignant.

'Guy's big,' said Danny Pogue. 'Geez, he looks like— did he do time? What's his story?'

'We don't want to know,' Bud Schwartz said. 'Am I right?'

'You're absolutely right,' said Molly McNamara.

*

Shortly before midnight on July 23, Jim Tile received a radio call that an unknown individual was shooting at automobiles on Card Sound Road. The trooper told the dispatcher he was en route, and that he'd notify the Monroe County Sheriff's Office if he needed back-ups—which he knew he wouldn't.

The cars were lined up on the shoulder of the road a half-mile east of the big bridge. Jim Tile took inventory from the stickers on the bumpers: two Alamos, a Hertz, a National and an Avis. The rental firms had started putting bumper plates on all their automobiles, which served not only as advertisement but as a warning to local drivers that a disoriented tourist was nearby. On this night, though, the bright stickers had betrayed their unsuspecting drivers. Each of the vehicles bore a single .45-caliber bullet hole in the left-front fender panel.

Jim Tile knew exactly what had happened. He took brief statements from the motorists, who seemed agitated by the suggestion that anyone would fire at them simply because they were tourists. Jim Tile assured them that this sort of thing didn't happen every day. Then he called Homestead for tow trucks to get the three rental cars whose engine blocks had been mortally wounded by the sniper in the mangroves.

One of the drivers, a French-Canadian textile executive, used a cellular phone to call the Alamo desk at Miami International Airport and explain the situation. Soon new cars were on the way.

It took Jim Tile several hours to clear the scene. A pair of Monroe County deputies stopped by and helped search for shell casings until the mosquitoes drove them away. After the officers had fled, and after the tourists had motored north in a wary caravan of Thunderbirds, Skylarks and Zephyrs, Jim Tile got in his patrol car and mashed on the horn with both fists. Then he rolled up the windows, turned up the air conditioner and waited for his sad old friend to come out of the swamp.

'I'm sorry.' Skink offered the trooper a stick of EDTIAR insect repellent.

'You promised to behave,' said Jim Tile. 'Now you've put me in a tough position.'

'Had to blow off some steam,' Skink said. 'Anyway, I didn't hurt anybody.' He took off his sunglasses and tinkered unabashedly with the fake eyeball. 'Haven't you ever had days like this? Days where you just had to go out and shoot the shit out of something, didn't matter what?'

Jim Tile sighed. 'Rental cars?'

'Why the hell not.'

The tension dissolved into weary silence. The men had talked of such things before. When Clinton Tyree was the governor of Florida, Jim Tile had been his chief bodyguard—an unusually prestigious assignment for a black state trooper. After Clinton Tyree resigned, Jim Tile immediately lost his job on the elite security detail. The new governor, it was explained, felt more comfortable around peckerwoods. By the end of that fateful week, Jim Tile had found himself back on road patrol, Harney County, night shifts.

Over the years he had stayed close to Clinton Tyree, partly out of friendship, partly out of admiration and partly out of certitude that the man would need police assistance now and then, which he had. Whenever Skink got restless and moved his hermitage to deeper wilderness, Jim Tile would quietly put in for a transfer and move, too. This meant more rural two-lanes, more night duty and more ignorant mean-eyed crackers—but the trooper knew that his friend would have done the same for him, had fortunes been reversed. Besides, Jim Tile was confident of his own abilities and believed that one day he'd be in charge of the entire highway patrol—dishing out a few special night shifts himself.

Usually Skink kept to himself, except for the occasional public sighting when he dashed out of the pines to retrieve a fresh opossum or squirrel off the road. Once in a while, though, something triggered him in a tumultuous way and the results were highly visible. Standing on the crowded Fort Lauderdale beach, he'd once put four rounds into the belly of an inbound Eastern 727. Another time he'd crashed the Miss Florida pageant and tearfully heaved a dead baby manatee on stage to dramatize the results of waterfront development. It was fortunate, in such instances, that no one had recognized the hoary cyclopic madman as Clinton Tyree; it was even more fortunate that Jim Tile had been around to help the ex-governor slip away safely and collect what was left of his senses.

Now, sitting in the trooper's patrol car, Skink polished his glass eye with a bandanna and apologized for causing his friend so much inconvenience. 'If you've got to arrest me,' he said, 'I'll understand.'

'Wouldn't do a damn bit of good,' said Jim Tile. 'But I tell you what—I'd appreciate if you'd let me know what's going on down here.'

'The usual,' Skink said. 'The bad guys are kicking our collective ass.'

'We got a dead body off the bridge, a guy named Angel Gaviria. You know about that, right?' The trooper didn't wait for an answer. 'The coroner is saying suicide or accident, but I was there and I don't think it's either one. The deceased was a well-known scumbucket and they don't usually have the decency to kill themselves. Usually someone else does the honor.'

'Jim, we live in troubled times.'

'The other day I pull over a blue Ford sedan doing eighty-six down the bridge. Turns out to be a Feeb.'

'FBI?' Skink perked up. 'All the way down here?'

'Hawkins was his name. He badges me, we get to chatting. Turns out he's working a case at the Amazing Kingdom. Something to do with militant bunny huggers and missing blue-tongued rats.' Jim Tile gave a lazy laugh. 'Now this is the FBI, interviewing elves and cowboys and fairy princesses. I don't suppose you can fill me in.'

Skink was pleased that the feds had taken notice of events in North Key Largo. He said, 'All I know is bits and pieces.'

'Speaking of which, what can you tell me about killer whales? This morning a semi rolls over and I got stinking gobs of dead whale all over my nice clean blacktop. I'm talking tonnage.'

Skink said, 'That would explain the buzzard shit on this state vehicle.' Secretly he wished he could have been there to witness the spectacle.

'You think it's funny?'

'I think,' said Skink, 'you should prepare for the worst.'

Jim Tile took off his Stetson and lowered his face in front of the dashboard vents; the cool air felt good on his cheeks. A gumdrop-shaped sports car blew by doing ninety-plus, and the trooper barely glanced up. He radioed the dispatcher in Miami and announced he was going off duty. 'I'm tired,' he said to Skink.

'Me, too. You haven't seen anybody from Game and Fish, have you?'

'The panther patrol? No, I haven't.' Jim Tile sat up. 'I haven't seen the plane in at least a month.'

Skink said, 'Must've broken down. Else they're working the Fokahatchee.'

'Listen,' the trooper said, 'I won't ask about the dead guy on the bridge, and I won't ask about the whale—'

'I had nothing whatsoever to do with the whale.'

'Fair enough,' said Jim Tile, 'but what about torching those bulldozers up on 905? Were you in on that?'

Skink looked at him blankly. The trooper described what had happened that very afternoon at the Falcon Trace construction project. 'They're looking for a guy who used to work at the Kingdom. They say he's gone nuts. They say he's got a gun.'

'Is that right?' Skink tugged pensively at his beard.

'Do you know this person?'

'Possibly.'

'Then could you *possibly* get him a message to stop this shit before it gets out of hand?'

'It's already out of hand,' Skink said. 'The sons-of-bitches are beating up little old ladies.'

'Damn.' The trooper stared out the window of the car. A trio of mosquitoes bounced off the glass and circled his head. Skink reached over and snatched the insects out of the air. Then he opened the window and let them buzz away into the thick fragrant night.

Jim Tile said, 'I'm worried about you.'

Skink grinned. 'That's a good one.'

'Maybe I should haul you in after all.'

'Wouldn't stick. No one saw me do it, and no one found the gun. Hell, they wouldn't even hold me overnight.'

'Yeah, they would,' Jim Tile said, 'on my word.'

Skink's smile went away.

The trooper said, 'The charge wouldn't stick, that's true. But I could take you out of circulation for a month or two. Let the situation simmer down.'

'Why?' Skink demanded. 'You know I'm right. You know what I'm doing is right.'

'Not shooting rental cars.'

'A lapse of judgment,' Skink admitted. 'I said I was sorry, for God's sake.'

Jim Tile put a hand on his friend's shoulder. 'I know you think it's the right thing, and the cause is good. But I'm afraid you're gonna lose.'

'Maybe not,' Skink said. 'I think the Mojo's rising.'

The trooper always got lost when Skink started quoting old rock-and-roll songs; someday he was going to sit Skink's shiny ass down and make him listen to Aretha. Put some soul in his system. Jim Tile said, 'I've got a life, too. Can't spend the rest of it looking out for you.'

Skink sagged against the car door. 'Jim, they're paving the goddamn island.'

'Not the whole thing—'

'But this is how it begins,' Skink said. 'Jesus Christ, you ought to know. This is how it begins!'

There was no point in pushing it. The state had bought up nearly all North Key Largo for preservation; the Amazing Kingdom and the Falcon Trace property were essentially all that remained in private hands. Still, Skink was not celebrating.

Jim Tile said, 'This guy you recruited—'

'I didn't recruit him.'

'Whatever. He's in it, that's the main thing.'

'Apparently so,' Skink said. 'Apparently he's serious.'

'So locking you up won't do any good, will it? Not with him still out there.' The trooper put on his hat and adjusted it out of habit. In the darkness of the car, Skink couldn't read the expression on his friend's face. Jim Tile said, 'Promise me one thing, all right? Talk some sense to the boy. He's new at it, Governor, and he could get hurt. That stunt with the bulldozers, it's not cool.'

'I know,' said Skink, 'but it's got a certain flair.'

'Listen to me,' Jim Tile said sternly. 'Already he's got some serious people after his ass, you understand? There's things I can help with and things I can't.'

Skink nodded. 'I'll talk to him, I promise. And thanks.'

Then he was gone. Jim Tile reached across to shut the door and his arm instantly was enveloped by an influx of mosquitoes. Frenzied humming filled the car.

He stomped the accelerator and the big Crown Victoria sprayed a fusillade of gravel into the mangroves. Westbound at a hundred fifteen miles an hour, the trooper rolled down the windows to let the wind suck the bugs from the car.

'Two of them.' His words were swallowed in the roar of the open night. 'Now I got two of the crazy bastards.'

TWENTY-ONE

Carrie Lanier's place was furnished as exquisitely as any mobile home. It had a microwave, an electric can opener, a stove, a nineteen-inch color TV, two paddle fans and a Naugahyde convertible sofa where Joe Winder slept. But there was no music, so on his third day as a fugitive Winder borrowed Carrie's car and went back to the apartment to retrieve his stereo system and rock tapes. He was not totally surprised to find that his place had been broken, entered and ransacked; judging by the viciousness of the search, Pedro Luz was the likely intruder. The inventory of losses included the portable television, three champagne glasses, a tape recorder, the plumbing fixtures, the mattress, a small Matisse print and the toaster. One of Nina's pink bras, which she had forgotten, had been desecrated ominously with cigarette burns, and hung from a Tiffany lamp. Also, the freshwater aquarium had been shattered, and the twin Siamese fighting fish had been killed. It appeared to Joe Winder that their heads were pinched off.

The stereo tuner and tape deck escaped harm, though the turntable was in pieces. A pair of hedge clippers protruded from one of the speakers; the other, fortunately, was undamaged.

'It's better than nothing,' Joe Winder said when he got back to the trailer. 'Low fidelity is better than no fidelity.'

While he reassembled the components, Carrie Lanier explored the box of cassettes. Every now and then she would smile or go 'Hmmm' in an amused tone.

Finally Winder looked up from the nest of colored wires and said, 'You don't like my music?'

'I like it just fine,' she said. 'I'm learning a lot about you. We've got The Kinks. Seeger live at Cobo Hall. Mick and the boys.'

'Living in the past, I know.'

'Oh, baloney.' She began to stack the tapes alphabetically on a shelf made from raw plywood and cinder blocks.

'Do you have a typewriter?' he asked.

'In the closet,' Carrie said. 'Are you going to start writing again?'

'I wouldn't call it writing.'

She got out the typewriter, an old Olivetti manual, and made a place for it on the dinette. 'This is a good idea,' she said to Joe Winder. 'You'll feel much better. No more shooting at heavy machinery.'

He reminded her that he hadn't actually pulled the trigger on the bulldozers. Then he said, 'I stopped writing a long time ago. Stopped being a journalist, anyway.'

'But you didn't burn out, you sold out.'

'Thanks,' Winder said, 'for the reminder.'

It was his fault for staggering down memory lane in the first place. Two nights earlier, Carrie had quizzed him about the newspaper business, wanted to know what kind of stories he'd written. So he'd told her about

CARL HIAASEN

the ones that had stuck with him. The murder trial of a thirteen-year-old boy who'd shot his little sister because she had borrowed his Aerosmith album without asking. The marijuana-smuggling ring led by a fugitive former justice of the Florida Supreme Court. The bribery scandal in which dim-witted Dade County building inspectors were caught soliciting Lotto tickets as payoffs. The construction of a $47 million super-highway by a Mafia contractor whose formula for high-grade asphalt included human body parts.

Joe Winder did not mention the story that had ended his career. He offered nothing about his father. When Carrie Lanier had asked why he'd left the newspaper for public relations, he simply said, 'Because of the money.' She had seemed only mildly interested in his short time as a Disney World flack, but was impressed by the reckless sexual behavior that had gotten him fired. She said it was a healthy sign that he had not become a corporate drone, that the spark of rebellion still glowed in his soul.

'Maybe in my pants,' Winder said, 'not in my soul.'

Carrie repeated what she had told him the first night: 'You could always go back to being a reporter.'

'No, I'm afraid not.'

'So what is it you want to type—love letters? Maybe a confession?' Mischievously she tapped the keys of the Olivetti; two at a time, as if she were playing 'Chopsticks.'

The trailer was getting smaller and smaller. Joe Winder felt the heat lick at his eardrums. He said, 'There's a reason you've hidden that gun.'

'Because it's not your style.' Carrie slapped the carriage and made the typewriter ring. 'God gave you a talent for expression, a gift with the language.'

Winder moaned desolately. 'Have you ever read a single word I've written?'

'No,' she admitted.

'So my alleged talent for expression, this gift—'

'I'm giving you the benefit of the doubt,' she said. 'The fact is, I don't trust you with a firearm. Now come help me open the wine.'

Every evening at nine sharp, visitors to the Amazing Kingdom of Thrills gathered on both sides of Kingsbury Lane, the park's main thoroughfare, to buy overpriced junk food and await the rollicking pageant that was the climax of the day's festivities. All the characters in the Kingdom were expected to participate, from the gunslingers to the porpoise trainers to the elves. Sometimes a real marching band would accompany the procession, but in the slow months of summer the music was usually canned, piped in through the garbage chutes. Ten brightly colored floats comprised the heart of the parade, although mechanical problems frequently reduced the number of entries by half. These were organized in a story line based loosely on the settlement of Florida, going back to the days of the Spaniards. The plundering, genocide, defoliation and gang rape that typified the peninsula's past had been toned down for the sake of Francis X. Kingsbury's younger, more impressionable customers; also, it would have been difficult to find a musical score suitable to accompany a mass disemboweling of French Huguenots.

For the feel-good purposes of the Amazing

Kingdom's nightly pageant, the sordid history of Florida was compressed into a series of amiable and bloodless encounters. Floats celebrated such fabricated milestones as the first beachfront Thanksgiving, when friendly settlers and gentle Tequesta Indians shared wild turkey and fresh coconut milk under the palms. It was a testament to Charles Chelsea's imagination (and mortal fear of Kingsbury) that even the most shameful episodes were reinterpreted with a positive commercial spin. A float titled 'Migrants on a Mission' depicted a dozen cheery, healthful farm workers singing Jamaican folk songs and swinging their machetes in a precisely choreographed break-dance through the cane fields. Tourists loved it. So did the Okeechobee Sugar Federation, which had bankrolled the production in order to improve its image.

One of the highlights of the pageant was the arrival of 'the legendary Seminole maiden' known as Princess Golden Sun. No such woman and no such lore ever existed; Charles Chelsea had invented her basically as an excuse to show tits and ass, and pass it off as ethnic culture. Traditional Seminole garb was deemed too dowdy for the parade, so Princess Golden Sun appeared in a micro-bikini made of simulated deerskin. The authentic Green Corn Dance, a sacred Seminole rite, was politely discarded as too solemn and repetitious; instead Golden Sun danced the *lambada*, a pelvic-intensive Latin step. Surrounded by ersatz Indian warriors wearing bright Brazilian slingshots, the princess proclaimed in song and mime her passionate love for the famous Seminole chieftain Osceola. At the news of his death, she broke into tears and vowed to haunt the Everglades forever in search of his spirit. The peak of

the drama, and the parade, was the moment when
Golden Sun mounted a wild panther (in this case, a
heavily drugged African lioness) and disappeared from
sight in a rising fog of dry ice.

It was the role most coveted among the female actors
employed at the Amazing Kingdom, and for six months
it had belonged to Annette Fury, a dancer of mountainous dimensions whose previous job was as a
waitress at a topless doughnut shop in Fort Lauderdale.
A competent singer, Miss Fury had done so well with
the role of Princess Golden Sun that the newspaper
in Key Largo had done a nice write-up, including a
photograph of Miss Fury straddling the bleary-eyed cat.
The reporter had been careful to explain that the spav-
ined animal was not actually a Florida panther, since
real panthers were all but extinct. Given Princess
Golden Sun's appearance, it was doubtful that a single
reader even noticed the lion in the picture. Miss Fury's
pose—head flung back, eyes closed, tongue between
the teeth—was suggestive enough to provoke indignant
outcries from a fundamentalist church in Big Pine Key,
as well as the entire Seminole Nation, or what was left
of it. At the first whiff of controversy, Charles Chelsea
swiftly purchased the negatives from the newspaper and
converted the most provocative one to a color postcard,
which went on sale for $1.95 in all gift shops in the
Amazing Kingdom of Thrills. As far as Chelsea was
concerned, a star had been born.

On the night of July 25, however, Annette Fury's
stint as Princess Golden Sun ended abruptly in a scandal
that defied even Chelsea's talents for cosmetic counter-
publicity. Shortly before the pageant, the dancer had
ingested what were probably the last three Quaalude

tablets in the entire continental United States. She had scrounged the dusty pills from the stale linty recesses of her purse, and washed them down with a warm bottle of Squirt. They had kicked in just as the float made the wide horseshoe turn onto Kingsbury Lane. By the time it rolled past the Cimarron Saloon, Annette Fury was bottomless, having surrendered her deerskin costume to a retired postal worker who had brought his wife and family all the way from Providence, Rhode Island. By the time the float reached the Wet Willy, the stone-faced Indian entourage of Princess Golden Sun had been augmented by nine rowdy Florida State fraternity men, who were taking turns balancing the drowsy young maiden on their noses, or so it must have appeared to the children in the audience. Afterwards, several parents threatened to file criminal obscenity charges against the park. They were appeased by a prompt written apology signed by Francis X. Kingsbury, and a gift of laminated lifetime passes to the Amazing Kingdom. Reluctantly, Charles Chelsea advised the Talent Manager to inform Annette Fury that her services were no longer required. The following day, Carrie Lanier was told that the role of Princess Golden Sun was hers if she wanted it. This was after they'd asked for her measurements.

So tonight she'd splurged on a bottle of Mondavi.

'To the late Robbie Raccoon,' Carrie said, raising her glass.

'No one did him better,' said Joe Winder.

He put on a tape of Dire Straits and they both agreed that it sounded pretty darn good, even with only one speaker. The wine was tolerable, as well.

Carrie said, 'I told them I want a new costume.'

'Something in beads and grass would be authentic.'

'Also, no lip-synching,' she said. 'I don't care if the music's canned, but I want to do my own singing.'

'What about the lion?' Joe Winder asked.

'They swear she's harmless.'

'Tranked out of her mind is more like it. I'd be concerned, if I were you.'

'If she didn't maul Annette, I can't imagine why she'd go after me.'

A police siren penetrated the aluminium husk of the trailer; Joe Winder could hear it even over the guitar music and the tubercular groan of the ancient air conditioner. Parting the drapes, he watched one Metro squad car, and then another, enter the trailer park at high speed. Throwing dust, they sped past the turnoff to Carrie's place.

'Another domestic,' Winder surmised.

'We average about four a week.' Carrie refilled the wineglasses. 'People who take love too damn seriously.'

'Which reminds me.' He opened his wallet and removed twelve dollars and placed it on a wicker table. 'I was a very bad boy. I called her three times.'

'You shmuck.'

The Nina Situation. Every time he picked up the phone, it added four bucks to Carrie Lanier's bill. Worse, Nina pretended not to recognize his voice— stuck to the script to the bitter end, no matter how much he pleaded for her to shut up and listen.

'It is pathetic,' Winder conceded.

'No other word for it.'

'Haven't you ever been like this?' Obsessed is what he meant.

'Nope.' Carrie shrugged. 'I've got to be honest.'

'So what's the matter with me?'

'You're just having a bad week.'

She went to the bedroom and changed to a lavender nightshirt that came down to the knees—actually, a good four inches above the knees. Her hair was pulled back in a loose, sandy-colored ponytail.

Winder said, 'You look sixteen years old.' Only about three dozen other guys must have told her the same thing. His heart was pounding a little harder than he expected. 'Tomorrow I'll get a motel room,' he said.

'No, you're staying here.'

'I appreciate it but—'

'Please,' Carrie said. 'Please stay.'

'I've got serious plans. You won't approve.'

'How do you know? Besides, I'm a little nervous about this new job. It's nice to have someone here at the end of the day, someone to talk with.'

Gazing at her, Winder thought: God, don't do this to me. Don't make me say it.

But he did: 'You just want to keep an eye on me. You're afraid I'll screw everything up.'

'You're off to a pretty good start.'

'It's only fair to warn you: I'm going after Kingsbury.'

'That's what I figured, Joe. Call it a wild hunch.' She took his hand and led him toward the bedroom.

I'm not ready for this, Winder thought. Sweat broke out in a linear pattern on the nape of his neck. He felt as if he were back in high school, the day the prettiest cheerleader winked at him in biology class; at the time, he'd been examining frog sperm under a microscope, and the wink from Pamela Shaughnessy had fractured his concentration. It had taken a month or two for Joe Winder to recover, and by then Pamela was knocked up by the co-captain of the junior wrestling squad. The teacher said that's what she got for not paying attention in class.

The sheets in Carrie Lanier's bedroom were rose, the blanket was plum. A novel by Anne Tyler was open on the bedstand, next to a bottle of nose drops.

A fuzzy stuffed animal sat propped on the pillow: shoe-button eyes, round ears and short whiskers. Protruding slightly from its upturned, bucktoothed mouth was a patch of turquoise cotton that could only be a tongue.

'Violet the Vole,' Carrie explained. 'Note the sexy eyelashes.'

'For Christ's sake,' Joe Winder said.

'The Vance model comes with a tiny cigar.'

'How much?' Winder asked.

'Eighteen ninety-five, plus tax. Mr. X ordered a shipment of three thousand.' Carrie stroked his arm. 'Come on, I feel like cuddling.'

Wordlessly, Winder moved the toy mango vole off the bed. The tag said it was manufactured in the People's Republic of China. What must they think of us on the assembly line? Winder wondered. Stuffed rats with cigars!

Carrie Lanier said, 'I've got the jitters about singing in the parade. I don't look much like a Seminole.'

Winder assured her she would do just fine. 'Listen, I need to ask a favor. If you say no, I'll understand.'

'Shoot.'

'I need you to steal something for me,' he said.

'Sure.'

'Just like that?'

Carrie said, 'I trust you. I want to help.'

'Do you see the possibilities?'

'Surprise me,' she said.

'Don't worry, it won't be dangerous. A very modest effort, as larcenies go.'

'Sure. First thing tomorrow.'

'Why are you doing this?' he asked.

'Because it's a fraud, the whole damn place. But mainly because an innocent man is dead. I liked Will Koocher.' She paused. 'I like his wife, too.'

She didn't have to add the last part, but Winder was glad she did. He said, 'You might lose your job.'

Carrie smiled. 'There's always dinner theater.'

It seemed a good time to break the ice, so he tried— a brotherly peck on the cheek.

'Joe,' she murmured, 'you kiss like a parakeet.'

'I'm slightly nervous myself.'

Slowly she levered him to the bed, pinning his arms. 'Why,' she said, giggling, 'why are you so nervous, little boy?'

'I really don't know.' Her breasts pressed against his ribs, a truly wonderful sensation. Winder decided he could spend the remainder of his life in that position.

Carrie said, 'Lesson Number One: How to smooch an Indian maiden.'

'Go ahead,' said Winder. 'I'm all lips.'

'Now do as I say.'

'Anything,' he agreed. 'Anything at all.'

As they kissed, an unrelated thought sprouted like a mushroom in the only dim crevice of Joe Winder's brain that was not fogged with lust.

The thought was: If I play this right, we won't need the gun after all.

TWENTY-TWO

Pedro Luz was in Francis Kingsbury's den when the blackmailers called. He listened to Kingsbury's half of the conversation, a series of impatient grunts, and said to Churrito, 'Looks like we're in business.'

Kingsbury put down the phone and said, 'All set. Monkey Mountain at four sharp. In front of the baboons.'

Monkey Mountain was a small animal park off Krome Avenue, a cut-rate imitation of the venerable Monkey Jungle. To Pedro Luz, it didn't sound like an ideal place to kill a couple of burglars.

With a snort, Kingsbury said, 'These assholes, who knows where they get these cute ideas. Watching television, maybe.'

'What is this monkey place?' Churrito asked.

'For Christ's sake, like the name says, it's basically monkeys. Two thousand of the damn things running all over creation.' Kingsbury disliked monkeys and had summarily vetoed plans for a Primate Pavilion at the Amazing Kingdom of Thrills. He felt that apes had limited commercial appeal; Disney had steered clear of them, too, for what that was worth.

'For one thing, they bite. And, two, they shit like a sewer pipe.' Kingsbury put the issue to rest. 'If they're so damn smart, how come they don't hold it. Like people.'

'They tasty good,' Churrito remarked, licking his lips. 'Squirrel monkey is best, where I come from.'

Pedro Luz sucked noisily on the open end of the IV tube. He had purchased a dozen clear bags of five-percent dextrose solution from a wholesale medical shop in Perrine. The steroid pills he pulverized with the butt of his Colt, and funneled the powder into the bags. No one at the gym had ever heard of getting stoked by this method; Pedro Luz boasted that it was all his idea, he'd never even checked with a doctor. The only part that bothered him was using the needle—a problematic endeavor, since anabolic steroids were usually injected into muscle, not veins. Whenever Pedro Luz was having second thoughts, he'd yank out the tube and insert it directly in his mouth.

Sitting in Kingsbury's house, it gave him great comfort to feel again these magnificent potent chemicals flooding his system. With nourishment came strength, and with strength came confidence. Pedro Luz was afraid of nothing. He felt like stepping in front of a speeding bus, just to prove it.

Churrito pointed at the intravenous rig and said: 'Even monkeys aren't that stupid.'

'Put a lid on it,' Pedro growled. He thought: No wonder these dorks lost the war.

'Stuff make you bulls shrink up. Dick get leetle tiny.' Churrito seemed unconcerned by the volcanic mood changes that swept over Pedro Luz every few hours. To Francis Kingsbury he said, 'Should see the zits on his cholders.'

'Some other time,' Kingsbury said. 'You guys, now,

don't get into it. There's work to do—I want these
assholes off my back, these fucking burglars, and I want
the files. So don't start up with each other, I mean, save
your energy for the job.'

Pedro Luz said, 'Don't worry.'

The phone rang and Kingsbury snatched it. The call
obviously was long-distance because Kingsbury began
to shout. Something about a truck accident ruining an
important shipment of fish. The caller kept cutting in
on Kingsbury, and Kingsbury kept making half-assed
excuses, meaning some serious money already had
changed hands.

When Kingsbury hung up, he said, 'That was Hong
Kong. Some cat-food outfit, I set up this deal and it
didn't work out. What the hell, they'll get their dough
back.'

'My uncle had a fish market,' remarked Pedro Luz.
'It's a very hard business.'

Without warning Mrs. Kingsbury came into the
room. She wore terry-cloth tennis shorts and the top
half of a lime-colored bikini. She nodded at Churrito,
who emitted a low tomcat rumble. Pedro Luz glowered
at him.

She said, 'Frankie, I need some money for my
lessons.'

Under his breath, Churrito said, 'I give her some
lessons. Chew bet I will.'

Kingsbury said, 'I just gave you—was it yesterday?—
like two hundred bucks.'

'That was yesterday.' Mrs. Kingsbury's eyes shifted
to Pedro Luz, and the bottle of fluid on the hanger.
'What's the matter with him?' she asked.

'One of them crash diets,' said her husband.

Churrito said, 'Yeah, make your muscles get big and your dick shrivel up like a noodle.'

Pedro Luz reddened. 'It's vitamins, that's all.' He gnawed anxiously on the end of the tube, as if it were a piece of beef jerky.

'What kind of vitamins?' asked Kingsbury's wife.

'For men,' said Pedro Luz. 'Men-only vitamins.'

As always, it was a test to be in the same room with Mrs. Kingsbury and her phenomenal breasts. Pedro Luz had given up sex three years earlier in the misinformed belief that ejaculation was a waste of precious hormones. Somehow, Pedro Luz had acquired the false notion that semen was one-hundred-percent pure testosterone, and consequently he was distraught when a popular weightlifter magazine reported that the average sexually active male would squirt approximately 19.6 gallons in a lifetime. For a fitness fiend such as Pedro Luz, the jism statistic was a shocker. To expend a single pearly drop of masculine fuel on a recreational pleasure was frivolous and harmful and plainly against God's plan; how could it do anything but weaken the body?

As it happened, Pedro Luz's fruit-and-steroid diet had taken the edge off his sex drive anyway. Abstinence had not proved to be difficult, except when Mrs. Kingsbury was around.

'I don't like needles,' she announced. 'I don't like the way they prick.'

Again Churrito began to growl lasciviously. Pedro Luz said, 'After a while, you don't even notice.' He showed Mrs. Kingsbury how the IV rig moved on wheels.

'Like a shopping cart,' she said gaily. Her husband

handed her a hundred-dollar bill and she waved goodbye.

'There she goes,' Kingsbury said. 'Pedro, did you show your little buddy the golf painting? The one we did at Biltmore?'

'I saw,' Churrito said. 'In the living room.'

'Those are the real McCoys,' said Kingsbury.

Churrito looked perplexed. 'McCoys?'

'Her tits, I mean. How you say, *hoot-aires*?' Kingsbury cackled. 'Now, about this afternoon, these assholes—I'm not interested in details. Not at all interested.'

That was fine with Pedro Luz. He'd skipped the details the last time, too, when they had roughed up the old lady at the condo. Although Churrito had nagged him to lighten up, the beating had been therapeutic for Pedro, a venting of toxic brain fumes. Like the rush he got while pinching the heads off Joe Winder's goldfish.

'I doubt this monkey place will be crowded,' Kingsbury was saying, 'except for the baboons.'

'We'll be careful,' Pedro Luz assured him.

'You get caught, no offense, but I don't know you. Never seen you bastards before in my life.'

'We won't get caught.'

Kingsbury snapped his fingers. 'The files, I'll give you a list. Don't do anything till you get my files back. After that, it's your call.'

Pedro Luz looked at his wristwatch and said it was time to go. The wheels on the IV rig twittered as it followed him to the door.

'I wanted to ask,' Churrito said, 'is it okay I look at

the pitcher again? The one with your wife and those real McCoys.'

'Be my guest,' said Kingsbury, beaming. 'That's what it's there for.'

One problem, Bud Schwartz realized, was that he and his partner had never done a blackmail before. In fact, he wasn't sure if it was blackmail or extortion, technically speaking.

'Call it a trade,' said Danny Pogue.

Bud Schwartz smiled. Not bad, he thought. A trade it is.

They were waiting in the rented Cutlass in the parking lot of Monkey Mountain. Mrs. Kingsbury's chrome-plated pistol lay on the seat between them. Neither of them wanted to handle it.

'Christ, I hate guns,' said Bud Schwartz.

'How's your hand?'

'Getting there. How's your foot?'

'Pretty good.' Danny Pogue opened a bag of Burger King and the oily smell of hot fries filled the car. Bud Schwartz rolled down the window and was counter-assailed by the overpowering odor of monkeys.

Chewing, Danny Pogue said, 'I can't get over that guy in the house, Molly's friend. Just come right in.'

'Bigfoot,' said Bud Schwartz, 'without the manners.'

'I just hope he don't come back.'

'You and me both.'

Bud Schwartz was watching out for Saabs. Over the phone Kingsbury had told him he'd be driving a navy Saab with tinted windows; so far, no sign of the car.

He asked his partner: 'You ever done a Saab?'

'No, they all got alarms,' said Danny Pogue. 'Like radar is what I heard. Just look at 'em funny, and they go off. Same with the Porsches, I fucking whisper just walkin' by the damn things.'

At two minutes after four, Bud Schwartz said it was time to get ready. Gingerly he put the gun in his pocket. 'Leave the files under the seat,' he said. 'We'll make the trade after we got the money.'

At the ticket window they got a map of Monkey Mountain. It wasn't exactly a sprawling layout.

'Hey, they even got a gorilla,' said Danny Pogue, 'name of Brutus. From the picture it looks like an African silverback.'

'Fascinating,' Bud Schwartz said. He'd had about enough of animal lore. Lately Danny Pogue had been spending too many hours watching wildlife documentaries on the Discovery Channel. It was all he talked about, he and Molly, and it was driving Bud Schwartz up the wall. One night, instead of the Cubs game, he had to sit through ninety minutes of goddamn hummingbirds. To Bud Schwartz they resembled moths with beaks; he got dizzy watching the damn things, even the slow-motion parts. Danny Pogue, on the other hand, had been enthralled. The fact that hummingbirds also inhabited North Key Largo heightened his sense of mission against Francis X. Kingsbury.

As they set out for the Baboon Tree, Danny Pogue said, 'Why'd you pick this place, Bud?'

''Cause it's out in public. That's how you do these things, extortions.'

'Are you sure?'

The visitor paths through Monkey Mountain were enclosed by chicken wire, giving the effect that it was the humans who were encaged while the wild beasts roamed free. Bud Schwartz was uncomfortable with this arrangement. Above his head, screeching monkeys loped along the mesh, begging for peanuts and crackers that Bud Schwartz had neglected to purchase at the concession stand. The impatient animals—howlers, gibbons, rhesus and spider monkeys—got angrier by the second. They bared yellow teeth and spit maliciously and shook the chicken wire. When Danny Pogue reached up to give one of them a shiny dime, it defecated in his hair.

'You happy now?' said Bud Schwartz.

'Damn, I can't believe it.' Danny Pogue stopped to stick his head under a water fountain. 'Don't they ever feed these goddamn things?' he said.

Above them, the gang of furry, shrieking, incontinent beggars had swollen to three dozen. Bud Schwartz and Danny Pogue shielded their heads and jogged the rest of the way to the Baboon Tree, an ancient ficus in the hub of a small plaza. Bud Schwartz was relieved to escape the yammering din and the rain of monkey feces. With a sigh he sat next to a Japanese family on a concrete bench. A moat of filmy brown water separated them from the bustling baboon colony in the big tree.

Danny Pogue said: 'Know why they don't let the other monkeys together with the baboons?'

'Why not?'

'Because the baboons'd eat 'em.'

'What a loss that would be.'

'Let's go see Brutus.'

'Danny, we're here on business. Now shut the fuck up, if you don't mind.'

The Japanese husband apparently understood at least

one word of English, because he gave Bud Schwartz a sharp look. The Japanese wife, who hadn't heard the profane remark, signaled that she would like a photograph of the whole family in front of the moat. Bud Schwartz motioned that his partner would do the honors; Danny Pogue had stolen many Nikons, but he'd never gotten a chance to use one. He arranged the Japanese in a neat row according to height, and snapped several pictures. In the background were many wild-eyed baboons, including a young male gleefully abusing itself.

Bud Schwartz was glad the children weren't watching. After the Japanese had moved on, Danny Pogue said: 'That was two hundred bucks right there, a Nikon with autofocus. I got a guy in Carol City fences nothing but cameras.'

'I told you,' said Bud Schwartz, 'we're through with that. We got a new career.' He didn't sound as confident as he would've liked. Where the hell was Kingsbury?

Danny Pogue joined him on the concrete bench. 'So how much is he gonna bring?'

'Fifty is what I told him.' Bud Schwartz couldn't get the tremor out of his voice. 'Fifty thousand, if he ever shows up.'

In the parking lot, Pedro Luz and Churrito got into a heated discussion about bringing the IV rack. Churrito prevailed on the grounds that it would attract too much attention.

The first thing they noticed about Monkey Mountain was the stink, which Churrito likened to that of a mass grave. Next came the insistent clamor of the creatures themselves, clinging to the chicken wire and extending miniature brown hands in hopes of food. Churrito lit up a Marlboro and handed it to a rhesus, who took a sniff and hurled it back at him. Pedro Luz didn't think it was the least bit funny; he was sinking into one of his spells—every heartbeat sent cymbals crashing against his brainpan. An act of irrational violence was needed to calm the mood. It was fortunate, then, that the monkeys were safely on the other side of the chicken wire. Every time one appeared on the mesh over his head, Pedro Luz would jump up and smash at it savagely with his knuckles. This exercise was repeated every few seconds, all the way to the Baboon Tree.

The burglars—and it *had* to be them, greasy-looking rednecks—were sitting on a bench. Nobody else was around.

Pedro Luz whispered to Churrito: 'Remember to get their car keys. They left the damn files in the car.'

'What if they dint?'

'They did. Now be quiet.'

Danny Pogue wasn't paying attention. He was talking about a TV program that showed a male baboon killing a zebra, that's how strong they were. A monkey that could kill something as big as a horse! Bud Schwartz was tuned out entirely; he was sizing up the two new men. The tall one, God Almighty, he was trouble. Built like a grizzly but that wasn't the worst of it; the worst was the eyes. Bud Schwartz could spot a doper two miles away; this guy was buzzing like a yellow jacket. The other one was no prize, dull-eyed and cold, but at least he was of normal dimensions. What caught Bud Schwartz's eye was the Cordovan briefcase that the smaller man was carrying.

'Get ready,' he said to Danny Pogue.

'But that ain't Kingsbury.'

'You don't miss a trick.'

'Bud, I don't like this.'

'Really? I'm having the time of my life.' Bud Schwartz stood up and approached the two strangers. 'Where's the old man?'

'Where's the files?' asked Pedro Luz.

'Where's the money?'

Churrito held up the briefcase. It was plainly stuffed with something, possibly fifty thousand in cash.

'Now,' said Pedro Luz, 'where's the damn files?'

'We give 'em to the old man and nobody else.'

Pedro Luz checked over both shoulders to make sure there were no tourists around. In the same motion his right hand casually fished into the waistband of his trousers for the Colt. Before he could get to it, something dug into his right ear. It was another gun. *A burglar with a gun*! Pedro Luz was consumed with fury.

Bud Schwartz said, 'Don't move.' The words fluttered out. Danny Pogue gaped painfully.

Churrito laughed. 'Good work,' he said to Pedro Luz. 'Excellent.'

'I'm gonna be straight about this,' said Bud Schwartz, 'I don't know shit about guns.'

The veins in Pedro Luz's neck throbbed like a tangle of snakes. He was seething, percolating in hormones, waiting for the moment. The gun barrel cut into his earlobe but he didn't feel a thing. Trying not to snarl, he said, 'Don't push it, *chico*.'

'I ain't kidding,' Bud Schwartz said in a voice so high he didn't recognize it as his own. 'You even fart, I may blow your brains out. Explain that to your friend.'

Churrito seemed indifferent to the idea. He shrugged and handed the briefcase to Danny Pogue.

'Open it,' Bud Schwartz told him.

Again Pedro Luz asked, 'Where are the files?' He anticipated that the burglars would soon be unable to answer the question, since he intended to kill them. And possibly Churrito while he was in the mood.

Even the baboons sensed trouble, for they had fallen silent in the boughs of the ficus. Danny Pogue opened the Cordovan briefcase and showed Bud Schwartz what was inside: sanitary napkins.

'Too bad,' said Bud Schwartz. And it was too bad. He had no clue what to do next. Danny Pogue took one of the maxi-pads out of the briefcase and examined it, as if searching for insight.

Pedro Luz's steroid-marinated glands were starting to cook. Infused with the strength of a thousand warriors, he announced that he wouldn't let a mere bullet spoil Mr. Kingsbury's plan. He told Bud Schwartz to go ahead and fire, and went so far as to reach up and seize the burglar's arm.

As they struggled, Pedro Luz said, 'Shoot me, you pussy! Shoot me now!'

Out of the corner of his eye, Bud Schwartz spotted Danny Pogue running away in the general direction of the gorilla compound—moving impressively for someone fresh off crutches.

Just as Pedro Luz was preparing to snap Bud Schwartz's arm like a matchstick, Mrs. Kingsbury's chrome-plated pistol shook loose from the burglar's fingers and flew over the moat. The gun landed in a pile of dead leaves at the foot of the ficus tree, where it was retrieved by a laconic baboon with vermilion buttocks. Bud Schwartz wasn't paying attention, what with Pedro Luz hurling him to the ground and kneeling on his neck and trying to twist his head off. Meanwhile the other man was going through Bud Schwartz's trousers in search of the car keys.

When Bud Schwartz tried to shout for help, Pedro Luz slapped a large moist hand over his mouth. It was then that Bud Schwartz spotted the bandaged nub of the right index finger, and assimilated in his dying deoxygenated consciousness the probability that this was the same goon who had brutalized Molly McNamara. The burglar decided, in the hastening gray twilight behind his eyeballs, that the indignity of being found mugged and dead in a monkey park might be mitigated by a final courageous deed, such as disfiguring a murderous steroid freak—which Bud Schwartz attempted to do by sucking Pedro Luz's hand into his jaws and chomping down with heedless ferocity.

The wailing of Pedro Luz brought the baboon colony to life, and a hellish chorus enveloped the three men as they fought on the ground. A gunshot was heard, and the monkeys scattered adroitly to the highest branches of the graceful old tree.

Pedro Luz rolled off Bud Schwartz and groped with his bloody paw for the Colt. It was still in his waistband. Only two things prevented him from shooting the burglar: the sight of fifty chattering children skipping toward him down the monkey trail, and the sight of Churrito lying dead with a grape-sized purple hole beneath his left eye.

Pedro Luz pushed himself to his feet, stepped over the body and ran. Bud Schwartz did the same—much more slowly and in the opposite direction—but not before pausing to contemplate the visage of the dead Nicaraguan. Judging by the ironic expression on Churrito's face, he knew exactly what had happened to him.

Now the killer was halfway up the ficus tree, barking and slobbering and shaking the branches. Mrs. Kingsbury's gun glinted harmlessly in the brackish shallows, where the startled baboon had dropped it.

The oxygen returning to Bud Schwartz's head brought a chilling notion that maybe the monkey had been aiming the damn thing. Maybe he'd even done it before. Stranger things had occurred in Miami.

Bud Schwartz lifted the keys to the Cutlass from the dead man's hand and jogged away just as Miss Juanita Pedrosa's kindergarten class marched into the plaza.

TWENTY-THREE

Francis X. Kingsbury was on the thirteenth green at the Ocean Reef Club when Charles Chelsea caught up with him and related the problem.

'Holy piss,' said Kingsbury as Jake Harp was about to putt. 'If it's not one thing, it's—hell, you deal with it, Charlie. Isn't that what I pay you for, to deal with this shit?'

Jake Harp pushed the putt to the right. He looked up stonily and said, 'Thank you both very much.'

'Sorry,' Chelsea said. 'We've got a little emergency here.'

Kingsbury said, 'If you're gonna be a crybaby, Jake, then do it over. Take another putt. And you, Charlie, what emergency? This is nothing, a goddamn prank.'

Charles Chelsea suggested that it was considerably more serious than a prank. 'Every television station in South Florida received a copy, Mr. Kingsbury. Plus the *Herald* and the *New York Times*. We'll be getting calls all day, I expect.'

He followed Kingsbury and Jake Harp to the four-teenth tee. 'The reason I say it's serious, we've got less than a week until the Summerfest Jubilee.' It was set for August 6, the day Kingsbury had rescheduled the arrival of the phony five-millionth visitor to the

Amazing Kingdom of Thrills. The postponement caused by the truck accident had been a blessing in one way— it had given Charles Chelsea time to scout for a flashy new giveaway car. The 'classic' Corvair had been junked in favor of a jet-black 300-Z, which had been purchased at bargain price from the estate of a murdered amphetamine dealer. Chelsea was further buoyed by the news that NBC weatherman Willard Scott had tentatively agreed to do a live broadcast from the Kingdom on Jubilee morning, as long as Risk Management cleared it with the network.

Overall, the publicity chief had been feeling fairly positive about Summerfest until some worm from the *Herald* called up to bust his hump about the press release.

What press release? Chelsea had asked.

The one about hepatitis, said the guy from the newspaper. The hepatitis epidemic among Uncle Ely's Elves.

In his smoothest, most controlled tone, Chelsea had asked the newspaper guy to please fax him a copy. The sight of it creeping off the machine had sent a prickle down the ridge of his spine.

As Jake Harp prepared to tee off, Chelsea showed the press release to Francis X. Kingsbury and said, 'It's ours.'

'What the hell you—I don't get it. Ours?'

'Meaning it's the real thing. The stationery is authentic.'

Kingsbury frowned at the letterhead. 'Jesus Christ, then we got some kinda mole. That what you're saying? Somebody on the inside trying to screw with our plans?'

'Not necessarily,' Chelsea said.

Jake Harp hooked his drive into a fairway bunker. He said, 'Don't you boys know when to shut up?'

This time Charles Chelsea didn't bother to apologize. He itched to remind Jake Harp that dead silence hadn't helped him one bit in the '78 Masters, when he'd four-putted the third hole at Augusta and let Nicklaus, Floyd, everybody and their mothers blow right past him.

Kingsbury said, 'Probably it's some bastard from Disney. A ringer, hell, I should've known. Somebody they sent just to screw me up for the summer.'

'It's nobody on the inside,' said Chelsea. 'It wasn't done on one of our typewriters.'

'Who then? I mean, why in the name of fuck?'

Jake Harp marveled at the inventive construction of Kingsbury's profanity. He imagined how fine it would feel to take a two-iron and pulverize the man's skull into melon rind. Instead he said, 'You're up, Frank.'

Charles Chelsea stood back while Kingsbury took a practice swing. It was not a thing of beauty. From the safety of the cart path, Chelsea said, 'I think it's Joe Winder. The fellow we fired last week. The one we've had some trouble with.'

'What makes you so sure—wait, Christ, didn't he used to work for The Rat?'

'Yes, briefly. Anyway, there's some stationery missing from Publicity. I thought you ought to know.'

'How much?'

'Two full boxes,' Chelsea replied. Enough to do one fake press release every day for about three years. Or one hundred a day until the Summerfest Jubilee.

Kingsbury knocked his drive down the left side of the fairway and grunted in approval. He plopped his butt in the golf cart and said to Chelsea: 'Let me see it one more time.'

Chelsea gave him the paper and climbed on the back of the cart, wedging himself between the two golf bags. He wondered if this was how the Secret Service rode when the President was playing.

Pointing over Kingsbury's shoulder, Chelsea said, 'It's definitely Winder's style. I recognize some of the dry touches.'

The press release said:

Medical authorities at the Amazing Kingdom of Thrills announced today that the outbreak of viral hepatitis that struck the popular theme park this week is 'practically under control.'

Visitors to the Amazing Kingdom are no longer in immediate danger of infection, according to specialists who flew in from the National Center for Disease Control in Atlanta. So far, five cases of hepatitis have been positively diagnosed. All the victims were actors who portray Uncle Ely's Elves, a troupe of mischievous trolls who frolic and dance in daily performances throughout the park.

Experts say there is no reason to suspect that the highly contagious disease is being transmitted in the food and beverages being served at the Amazing Kingdom. A more likely source is the vending machine located in a dressing room often used by Uncle Ely's Elves and several other performers.

Charles Chelsea, vice president in charge of publicity, said: 'We know that the candy machine down there hadn't been serviced for about seven months. There are serious questions regarding the freshness and edibility of some of the chocolate products, as well as the breath mints. All items have been removed from the machine and are presently being tested for contamination.'

Although no cases of hepatitis have been reported among visitors to the Amazing Kingdom, Monroe County health officials advise testing for anyone who has had recent contact with any of Uncle Ely's Elves—or food products handled by the elves. This advisory applies to all persons who might have posed for photographs or danced with one of the little people during the Nightly Pageant of Tropics.

Moe Strickland, the veteran character actor who popularized the role of Uncle Ely, said the stricken performers are resting quietly at Baptist Hospital in Miami, and are expected to recover. He added, 'I'm worried about what the kids will think when they don't see us around the park for a few weeks. I guess we'll have to tell them that Uncle Ely took the elves on a summer vacation to Ireland, or wherever it is that elves go.'

Chelsea said there are no plans to close the Amazing Kingdom to the public. 'This was a freakish incident, and we are confident that the worst is over,' he said. 'From now on, we get back to the business of having fun.'

Beginning tonight, the Amazing Kingdom of Thrills will present a multi-media tribute to Vance and Violet, the last surviving blue-tongued mango voles. The gentle animals were stolen from the park ten days ago in a daring daylight robbery, and later died tragically.

The show will be presented at 8 p.m. in the Rare

Animal Pavilion, and will feature color slides, video-tapes, rare outdoor film footage and a Claymation exhibit. Admission is $4 for adults, $2.50 for children.

Kingsbury reread the press release as they jolted down the cart path with Jake Harp at the wheel. When they stopped next to his golf ball, Kingsbury shoved the paper back at Chelsea. 'It sounds awfully damn . . . what's the word?'

'Authentic, sir. This is what we're up against.'

'I mean, hell, it sure puts me off the candy machines.'

'It's fooling the reporters, too,' Chelsea said.

'You say this maniac's got—what, two goddamn boxes?'

'That's what's missing.'

Jake Harp said, 'If you're not going to play that lie, pick the damn thing up.'

Kingsbury paid no attention. 'I guess we'll need—obviously, what am I saying!—get a new letterhead for Publicity.'

'I ordered it this morning,' Chelsea reported. 'I'm afraid it won't be ready for two weeks.'

'Don't tell me—God, two weeks. So what do we do if your theory's right? If it's Winder, I mean.' Kingsbury took his stance and rifled a six-iron dead into the heart of a tea-colored pond.

'See what happens when you run your mouth,' said Jake Harp.

'The options are limited,' Chelsea told Kingsbury. 'Do we come right out and admit it's a fake? A dis-gruntled former employee, blah, blah, blah. Or do we roll with it? Take the hit and hope it's over.'

'Is that your advice? Roll with it?'

'For now, yes.'

'Me, too,' Francis Kingsbury said. 'Besides, Pedro's on the case.' A brand-new golf ball appeared in Kingsbury's right hand, and he dropped it with a flourish on the fairway. This time he nailed the six-iron to the center of the green, fifteen feet from the flag.

Jake Harp blinked sullenly and said nothing.

A duel.

That's how Charles Chelsea saw it. The ultimate test of skills.

He warmed up the word processor and began to write:

The outbreak of viral hepatitis among performers at the Amazing Kingdom of Thrills was not as serious as first believed, according to a respected epidemiologist who visited the popular tourist attraction Friday.

The disease was confined to only four persons, none of whom became seriously ill, according to Dr. Neil Shulman, an international expert on liver pathology.

'Visitors to the Amazing Kingdom are in absolutely no danger,' Dr. Shulman declared. 'There's no evidence that the disease originated here. The food and beverages I've sampled are perfectly safe—and tasty, too!'

Initially it was believed that five persons were infected with hepatitis. Later, however, it was determined that one of the ill employees was actually suffering from gallstones, a common and non-transmittable disorder.

The four men who were diagnosed with hepatitis all began showing symptoms on Wednesday morning. Contrary to earlier reports, however, the victims did not contract the virus from contaminated candy purchased at a vending machine in the Amazing Kingdom. It is now believed that the men—all of whom portray members of Uncle Ely's Elves—became infected during a recent promotional trip to the Caribbean aboard a Nassau-based cruise ship.

Moe Strickland, the crusty character actor who immortalized the character of Uncle Ely, recalled how some of his troupe had complained of 'funky-tasting lobster' during the four-day excursion. Viral hepatitis has an incubation period of 15 to 45 days.

Those who were stricken spent only one night in the hospital, and are now resting comfortably at home. Although their conditions are good, they will not return to work until doctors are sure that they are not contagious.

Dr. Shulman, who has written extensively for national medical journals, said he is certain that the disease has been contained, and that no other employees or visitors to the Amazing Kingdom are in jeopardy. 'It's as safe as can be,' he said. 'In fact, I'm staying over the weekend myself so I can ride the new porpoise!'

Skimming the text, Charles Chelsea changed the word 'outbreak' to 'incidence.' Then, with uncharacteristic fire, he punched the Send button.

To an invisible enemy he snarled, 'All right, Joey. It's go time.'

The queasy feeling that always accompanied the prospect of bad publicity had given way to a fresh sense of challenge; Chelsea felt he'd been training his whole professional life for such a test. He was up against an opponent who was talented, ruthless and quite possibly insane.

As much as Chelsea feared and distrusted Winder, he respected his creative skills: the vocabulary, so rich in adjectives; the glib turn of an alliterative phrase—and, of course, the speed. Joe Winder was the fastest writer that Chelsea had ever seen.

Now it was just the two of them: Winder, holed up God knows where, hammering out inflammatory libels as fast as his fingers could fly. And on the other end, Chelsea himself, waiting to catch these malicious grenades and smother them. The alternative—meaning, to tell the truth—was unthinkable. To admit a hoaxster was loose, forging demented fantasies on Amazing Kingdom letterhead . . . what a story *that* would make. In their excitement the media would come all over themselves. Even worse, each publicity announcement from the theme park would be scrutinized severely by reporters and editors, whose careers are seldom enhanced by getting duped into print. One thing that Charles Chelsea (or any PR flack) didn't need was a more toxic level of skepticism and suspicion among the journalists he was supposed to manipulate.

So telling the truth about Joe Winder was out of the question. Whatever revolting fable Winder concocted next, Chelsea would be ready to extinguish it with press

releases that were both calm and plausible. One pack
of lies softening another.

It was going to be one roaring hell of a battle.

As the Publicity Department's fax machines were
launching Chelsea's counterattack against the hepatitis
scare, Moe Strickland arrived to bitch about sick
pay and what the almighty Screen Actors Guild would
say.

He lit up a cigar and said, 'The union would go
nuts.'

'We don't recognize the union,' Chelsea said coolly.
'I really don't understand your objections, Moe. Most
people would kill for two weeks off.'

Moe Strickland protested with a wet cough. 'You're
docking us sick days, that's the objection. Because we're
not really sick.'

'That's something to be taken up with Personnel. It's
simply not my bailiwick.' Charles Chelsea waved his
hands to clear the rancid smoke. The office was starting
to smell like dead mice.

'I don't see why they can't just give us two weeks
paid,' said Moe Strickland, 'and leave us our sick days.
Whatever happened, it's sure not our fault.'

'No, it's not,' Chelsea agreed. 'Listen to me, Moe.
Uncle Ely and the Elves are on vacation, all right? They
went to Ireland. That's the official story.'

'For Christ's sake—Ireland? Does Ely sound like an
Irish name?' Moe Strickland sneered in contempt.

'I'm not here to argue,' Chelsea said. 'But I do wish to
caution you against speaking to the media. All interview
requests are to be routed through me, understand?'

'You mean like the newspapers.'

'Newspapers, television, anybody asking questions

about a cruise. You tell them to call me. And make sure the elves do the same.'

'What, now you don't trust us?'

'No interviews, Moe. The order comes straight from Mr. X.'

'Figures,' said Moe Strickland. 'What's the name of that disease? Tell me again.'

'Viral hepatitis.'

'Sounds terrible.'

'It's a nasty one,' Chelsea conceded.

'Who in hell would make up a story like that?' The actor smacked on the soggy stump of cigar. 'What kind of sick bastard would say such a thing?'

Chelsea did not reply. He was watching a string of brown drool make its way down Moe Strickland's snowy beard.

'I feel like suing the sonofabitch,' Moe Strickland remarked.

Chelsea said, 'Don't take it personally. It's got nothing to do with you.'

'I never had hepatitis. Is it some kind of dick disease? Because if it is, we're definitely suing the bastard. The boys're as clean as a whistle down there and they can sure prove it.'

'Moe,' said Chelsea, 'please settle down.'

'Does this mean we can't march in the Jubilee?'

'Not as Uncle Ely and the Elves. We'll get you some other costumes—gunslingers, how about that?'

'Oh great, midget gunslingers. No thanks.' On his way out the door, Moe Strickland spit something heavy into Charles Chelsea's wastebasket.

*

That night, Channel 7 devoted forty seconds to the hepatitis scare, closing the piece with a sound-bite from Charles Chelsea, cool in a crisp blue oxford shirt and tortoiseshell eyeglasses. The glasses were a new touch.

Not bad, thought Joe Winder, if you like the George Will look.

He was watching the news with a notebook on his lap. He called toward the kitchen: 'He got the number of victims down from five to four. Plus he's planted the idea that the disease was picked up in the Caribbean, not at the Amazing Kingdom. Pretty damn slick on short notice!'

Carrie Lanier was fixing popcorn. 'So they're toughing it out,' she said.

'Looks that way.'

She came out and placed the bowl on the sofa between them. 'They've got to be worried.'

'I hope so.' Joe Winder thanked her again for stealing the letterhead paper from the stockroom in the Publicity Department. 'And for renting the fax,' he added. 'I'll pay you back.'

'Not necessary, sir. Hey, I heard somebody shot up some rental cars on Card Sound Road.'

'Yeah, it was on the news.'

'Did they catch the guy?'

'No,' he said, 'and they won't.' He wondered if Skink's sniper attack was the beginning of a major offensive.

Carrie pointed at the television. 'Hey, look, it's Monkey Mountain!'

A blue body bag was being carried out of the amusement park. A florid middle-aged schoolteacher, a Miss Pedrosa, was being interviewed about what happened.

She said her students thought the man was merely sleeping, not dead. The news reporter said the victim was believed to be a recent immigrant, a Latin male in his mid-thirties. A police detective at the scene of the shooting said it appeared to be a suicide. The detective's voice was nearly drowned out by the jabbering of angry baboons in a tree behind him.

Carrie said, 'Well, Mr. X ought to be happy. Finally someplace else is getting bad press.'

'Strange place for a suicide,' observed Joe Winder.

Carrie Lanier stuffed a handful of popcorn into his mouth. 'They gave me my new costume today. You're gonna die.'

'Let's see.'

It was a white fishnet tank suit. Carrie put it on and struck a Madonna pose. 'Isn't it awful?' she said.

Joe Winder said she looked irresistibly slutty. 'The Indians aren't going to like it, though.'

'I've got a headband, too. And a black wig.'

'The Seminoles didn't wear fishnets; they used them on bass. By the way, are those your nipples?'

'Who else's would they be?'

'What I mean is, isn't there supposed to be something underneath?'

'A tan body stocking,' Carrie said. 'I must've forgot to put it on.'

Winder told her not to bother. Exuberantly she positioned herself on his lap and fastened her bare legs around his waist. 'Before we make love,' Carrie said, 'you've got to hear the song.'

It was a bastardized version of the famous production number in *Evita*. They both burst out laughing when she did the refrain. 'I can't believe it,' Joe Winder said.

Carrie kept singing, 'Don't Cry for Me, Osceola!' Winder buried his face in her breasts. Unconsciously he began nibbling through the fishnet suit.

'Now stop.' Carrie clutched the back of his head. 'I've forgotten the rest of the words.'

Still gnawing, Winder said, 'I feel like a shark.'

'You do indeed.' She pulled him even closer. 'I know a little boy who forgot to shave this morning, didn't he?'

'I was busy writing.' A muffled voice rising out of her cleavage.

Carrie smiled. 'I know you were writing, and I'm proud of you. What's the big news at the Kingdom tomorrow—typhoid? Trichinosis?'

He lifted his head. 'No more diseases. From now on, it's the heavy artillery.'

She kissed him on the nose. 'You're a very sick man. Why do I like you so much?'

'Because I'm full of surprises.'

'Oh, like this?' Carrie grabbed him and gave a little tug. 'Is this for me?'

'If you're not careful.'

'Hold still,' she told him.

'Aren't you going to take off that outfit?'

'What for? Look at all these convenient holes. We've just got to get you lined up.'

'It's a good thing,' Joe Winder said, 'it doesn't have gills.'

He held his breath as Carrie Lanier worked on the delicate alignment. Then she adjusted the Naugahyde sofa cushion behind his head, and braced her hands on the windowsill. The lights from the highway skipped in her eyes, until she closed them. Slowly she started rocking and said, 'Tonight we're shooting for four big ones.'

'Excuse me?'

'I told you, Joe, I'm a very goal-oriented person.'

'I think I'm tangled.'

'You're doing fine,' she said.

He was still hanging on, minutes later, when Carrie stopped moving.

'What is it?'

'Joe, did you go back to the apartment tonight?' She was whispering.

'Just for a minute. I needed some clothes.'

'Oh boy.'

'What's the matter?'

Carrie said, 'Somebody's watching us. Somebody followed you here.' She lowered herself until she was flat against him, so she couldn't be seen from the window. 'It's a man,' she said. 'He's just standing out there.'

'What's he look like?'

'Very large.'

'Guess I'd better do something.'

'Such as?'

'I'm not exactly sure,' Joe Winder said. 'I need to refocus here.'

'In other words, you want me to climb off.'

'Well, I think the mood has been broken.'

'The thing is—'

'I know. We'll need scissors.' His fingers, his chin, everything was tangled in the netting.

Outside the trailer, something moved. A shadow flickering across the windowpane. Footsteps crunching on the gravel. Then a hand on the doorknob, testing the lock.

Carrie's muscles tightened. She put her lips to his ear. 'Joe, are we going to die like this?'

'There are worse ways,' he said.

And then the door buckled.

TWENTY-FOUR

Skink said he was sorry, and turned away. Joe Winder and Carrie Lanier scrambled to disengage, tearing the fishnet suit to strings.

'I heard noises,' said Skink. 'Thought there might be trouble.'

The adrenaline ebbed in a cold tingle from Winder's veins. Breathlessly he said, 'How'd you know I was here?'

'Followed you from the apartment.'

'In what—the bookmobile?'

'I've got friends,' Skink said.

While Joe Winder fastened his trousers, Carrie Lanier dived into a University of Miami football jersey. Skink turned to face them, and Carrie gamely shook his hand. She said, 'I didn't catch your name.'

'Jim Morrison,' said Skink. '*The* Jim Morrison.'

'No, he's not,' Winder said irritably.

Carrie smiled. 'Nice to meet you, Mr. Morrison.' Winder considered her cordiality amazing in view of Skink's menacing appearance.

Skink said, 'I suppose he told you all about me.'

'No,' Carrie replied. 'He didn't say a word.'

Skink seemed impressed by Joe Winder's discretion. To Carrie he said: 'Feel free to stare.'

'I am staring, Mr. Morrison. Is that a snake you're eating?'

'A mud snake, yes. Medium-rare.' He took a crackling bite and moved through the trailer, turning off the television and all the lights. 'A precaution,' he explained, peeking out a window.

In the darkness Carrie found Joe Winder's hand and squeezed it. Winder said, 'This is the man who saved my life a couple weeks ago—the night I got beaten up, and you gave me a lift.'

'I live in the hammocks,' Skink interjected. 'The heavy rains have brought out the snakes.'

Winder wondered when he would get to the point.

Carrie said, 'Can I ask about the red collar? Is it some sort of neck brace?'

'No, it isn't.' Skink crouched on his haunches in front of them, beneath the open window. The highway lights twinkled in his sunglasses.

'Events are moving haphazardly,' he said, gnawing a piece of the cooked reptile. 'There needs to be a meeting. A confluence, if you will.'

'Of whom?' Winder asked.

'There are others,' Skink said. 'They don't know about you, and you don't know about them.' He paused, cocking an ear toward the ceiling. 'Hear that? It's the plane. They've been tracking me all damn day.'

Carrie gave Joe Winder a puzzled look. He said, 'The rangers from Game and Fish—it's a long story.'

'Government,' Skink said. 'A belated pang of conscience, at tax-payer expense. But Nature won't be fooled, the damage is already done.'

Sensing trouble, Winder lurched in to change the subject. 'So who are these mysterious others?'

'Remember that afternoon at the Amazing Kingdom, when a stranger gave you something?'

'Yeah, some old lady at the Rare Animal Pavilion. She handed me a note and then I got my lights punched out.'

Skink said, 'That was me who slugged you.'

'What an odd relationship,' Carrie remarked.

'My specialty,' Joe Winder said. Then to Skink: 'Can I ask why you knocked the door down tonight? Your timing stinks, by the way.'

Skink was at the window again, lurking on the edge of the shadow. 'Do you know anyone who drives a blue Saab?'

'No—'

'Because he was waiting at your apartment this morning. Big Cuban meathead who works at the park. He saw you arrive.' Skink dropped down again. He said to Winder, 'You were driving the young lady's car, right?'

'She loaned it to me. So what?'

'So it's got a parking sticker on the rear bumper.'

'Oh shit, you're right.' Joe Winder had completely forgotten; employees of the Amazing Kingdom were issued Petey Possum parking permits. Each decal bore an identification number. It was a simple matter to trace the car to Carrie Lanier.

'I need to go to fugitive school,' Winder said. 'This was really stupid.'

Carrie asked Skink about the man in the blue Saab. 'Did he follow Joe, too? Is he out there now?'

'He was diverted,' Skink said, 'but I'm sure he'll be here eventually. That's why we're leaving.'

'No,' Winder said, 'I can't.'

Skink asked Carrie Lanier for a paper napkin. Carefully he wrapped the uneaten segment of mud snake and placed it in a pocket of his blaze rainsuit.

He said, 'There'll be trouble if we stay.'

'I can't go,' Winder insisted. 'Look, the fax lines are already set up. Everything's in place right here.'

'So you've got something more in mind?'

'You know I do. In fact, you've given me a splendid inspiration.'

'All right, we'll wait until daybreak. Can you type in the dark?'

'It's been a while, but sure.' Back in the glory days, Winder had once written forty inches in the blackness of a Gulfport motel bathroom—a Royal manual typewriter balanced on his lap. This was during Hurricane Frederic.

Skink said, 'Get busy, genius. I'll watch the window.'

'What can I do to help?' Carrie asked.

'Put on some Stones,' said Skink.

'And some panties,' Winder whispered.

She told him to hush and quit acting like an old prude.

While the tow truck hooked up the Saab, Pedro Luz forced himself to reflect on events.

There he was, waiting for Winder to come out of the apartment when here comes this big spade highway patrolman knocking on the window of the car.

'Hey, there,' he says from behind those damn reflector shades.

'Hey,' says Pedro Luz, giving him the slight macho nod that says, I'm one of you, brother.

But the spade doesn't go for it. Asks for Pedro's driver's license and also for the registration of the Saab. Looks over the papers and says, 'So who's Ramex Global?'

'Oh, you know,' Pedro says, flashing his old Miami PD badge.

Trooper goes 'Hmmm.' Just plain 'Hmmm.' And then the fucker jots down the badge number, like he's going to check it out!

Pedro resists the urge to reach under the seat for his gun. Instead he says, 'Man, you're burning me. I'm sitting on a dude out here.'

'Yeah? What's his name?'

Pedro Luz says, 'Smith. José Smith.' It's the best he can do on short notice, with his brain twitching all crazy inside his skull. 'Man, you and that marked unit are burning me bad.'

Trooper doesn't act too damn concerned. 'So you're a police officer, is that right?'

'Hell,' Pedro says, 'you saw the badge.'

'Yes, I sure did. You're a long way from the city.'

'Hey, *chico*, we're in a war, remember.'

'Narcotics?' The trooper sounds positively intrigued. 'This man Smith, he's some big-time dope smuggler, eh?'

'Was,' Pedro says. 'He sees your car sitting out here, he's back in wholesale footwear.'

'Hmmm,' the spade trooper says again. Meanwhile Pedro's fantasizing about grabbing him around the middle and squeezing his guts out both ends, like a very large tube of licorice toothpaste.

'Don't tell me you're gonna run my tag,' Pedro says.

'Nah.' But the trooper's still leaning his thick black arms against the door of the Saab, his face not a foot from Pedro's, so that Pedro can see himself twice in the mirrored sunglasses. Now the trooper says: 'What happened to your finger?'

'Cat bite.'

'Looks like it took the whole top joint.'

'That's right,' says Pedro, aching all over, wishing he'd brought his intravenous bag of Winstrol-V. Talking high-octane. Same stuff they use on horses. One thousand dollars a vial, and worth every penny.

Trooper says, 'Must've been some cat to give you a bite like that.'

'Yeah, I ought to put the damn thing to sleep.'

'Sounds like a smart idea,' says the trooper, 'before he bites you someplace else.'

And then the sonofabitch touches the brim of his Stetson and says so long. Like John Fucking Wayne.

And here comes Winder, cruising out of the apartment with an armful of clothes. Gets in the car—not his car, somebody else's; somebody with an employee sticker from the Kingdom—and drives off with the radio blasting.

Pedro Luz lays back cool and sly, maybe half a mile, waiting until the cocky bastard reaches that long empty stretch on Card Sound Road, south of the Carysfort Marina. That's where Pedro aims to make the big move.

Until the Saab dies. Grinds to a miserable wheezing halt. A *Saab!*

Pedro Luz is so pissed he yanks the steering wheel off its column and heaves it into a tamarind tree. Only afterwards does it dawn on him that Mr. X isn't going to appreciate having a $35,000 automobile and no way to steer it.

An hour later, here comes Pascual's Wrecker Service.

Guy lifts the hood, can't find a thing. Slides underneath, zero. Then he says maybe Pedro ran out of gas, and Pedro says don't be an asshole. Guy pulls off the gas cap, closes one eye and looks inside, like he can actually *see* something.

Then he sniffs real hard, rubs his nose, sniffs again. Then he starts laughing like a fruit.

'Your friends fucked you up real good,' he says.

'What are you talking about?'

'Come here and take a whiff.'

'No, thanks,' Pedro says.

Guy hoots. 'Now I seen everything.'

Pedro's trying to figure out when it happened. Figures somebody snuck up and did it while he was talking to that hardass trooper. Which means the trooper was in on it.

'Did a number on your engine,' says the tow-truck man, chuckling way too much.

Pedro Luz grabs him by the arm until his fingers lock on bone. He says, 'So tell me. What exactly's in the gas tank?'

'Jack Daniels,' the guy says. 'I know that smell anywhere.'

So now Pedro's watching him put the hook to Mr. Kingsbury's Saab and wondering what else could go wrong. Thinking about the monkeys and shithead burglars and what happened to Churrito. Thinking about the black state trooper busting his balls for no reason, and how somebody managed to pour booze in the tank without Pedro even knowing it.

Pedro thinks he'd better shoot some horse juice in his arms as soon as possible, and get tight on Joe Winder's ass.

In one of his pockets he finds the scrap of paper where he wrote the decal number off the car Winder was driving. It's not much, but it's the only thing he's got to show for a long sorry morning.

So Pedro tells the tow-truck guy he's going to ride in the busted Saab on the way to the shop. Use Kingsbury's car phone to make a few calls.

Guy says no way, it's against company policy. Gotta sit up front in the truck.

Which is not what Pedro wants to hear after such a shitty day. So he tackles the guy and yanks his arms out of the sockets one at a time, pop-pop. Leaves him thrashing in the grass by the side of the road.

Jumps in the tow truck and heads for the Amazing Kingdom of Thrills.

The Mothers of Wilderness listened solemnly as Molly McNamara recounted the brutal assault. They were gathered in the Florida room of Molly's old house, where a potluck supper had been arranged on a calico tablecloth. Normally a hungry bunch, the Mothers scarcely touched the food; a huge bacon-cheese ball lay undisturbed on a sterling platter—a sure sign that the group was distracted.

And no wonder: Molly's story was appalling. No one dreamed that the battle against Falcon Trace would ever come to violence. That Molly had been attacked by thugs in her own apartment was horrifying; equally unsettling was her lurid description of the finger-biting episode. In disbelief, several of the older members fiddled frenetically with the controls to their hearing aids.

'Obviously we've struck a nerve with Kingsbury,' Molly was saying. 'Finally he considers us a serious threat.'

One of the Mothers asked why Molly had not called the police.

'Because I couldn't prove he was behind it,' she replied. 'They'd think I was daffy.'

The members seemed unsatisfied by this explanation. They clucked and whispered among themselves until Molly cut in and asked for order. The lawyer, Spacci, stood up and said it was a mistake not to notify the authorities.

'You're talking about a felony,' he said. 'Aggravated assault, possibly even attempted murder.'

One of the Mothers piped up: 'It's not worth dying for, Molly. They're already clearing the land.'

Molly's gray eyes flashed angrily. 'It is not too late!' She wheeled on Spacci. 'Did you file in federal court?'

'These things take time.'

'Can you get an injunction?'

'No,' said the lawyer. 'You mean, to stop construction? No, I can't.'

Molly drummed her fingers on the portable podium. Spacci was preparing to sit down when she jolted him back to attention: 'Give us a report on the blind trust.'

'Yes, well, I talked to a fellow over in Dallas. He tells me the paperwork comes back to a company called Ramex Global, which is really Francis Kingsbury—'

'We *know*.'

'—but the bulk of the money isn't his. It's from some S & L types. Former S & L types, I should say. Apparently they were in a hurry to invest.'

'I'll bet,' said one of the Mothers in the front row.

'They moved the funds through Nassau,' Spacci said. 'Not very original, but effective.'

Molly folded her arms. 'Perfect,' she said. 'Falcon Trace is being built with stolen savings accounts. And you people are ready to give up!'

'Our options,' the lawyer noted, 'are extremely limited.'

'No, they're not. We're going to kill this project.'

A worried murmuring swept through the Mothers. 'How?' one asked. 'How can we stop it now?'

'Sabotage,' Molly McNamara answered. 'Don't you people have any imagination?'

Immediately Spacci began waving his arms and whining about the ramifications of criminal misconduct.

Molly said: 'If it makes you feel better, Mr. Spacci, get yourself a plate of the chicken Stroganoff and go out on the patio. And take your precious ethics with you.'

Once the lawyer was gone, Molly asked if anyone else was having doubts about the Falcon Trace campaign. One board member, a devout Quaker, fluttered his hand and said yes, he was afraid of more bloodshed. Then he made a motion (quickly seconded) that the Mothers telephone the police to report the two men who had attacked Molly.

'We don't need the police,' she said. 'In fact, I've already retained the services of two experienced security men.' With both hands she motioned to the back of the room, where Bud Schwartz and Danny Pogue stood near an open door. Danny Pogue flushed at the introduction and puffed his chest, trying to look like a tough customer. Bud Schwartz focused sullenly on an invisible tarantula, dangling directly over Molly McNamara's hair.

Eventually the Mothers of Wilderness quit staring at the burglars-turned-bodyguards, and Molly resumed her pep talk. Danny Pogue picked up a spoon and sidled over to the cheese ball. Bud Schwartz slipped out the door.

In a butcher shop near Howard Beach, Queens, a man known as The Salamander picked up the telephone and said: 'Talk.'

'Jimmy gave me the number. Jimmy Noodles.'

'I'm listening,' said The Salamander, whose real name was Salvatore Delicato.

'I got Jimmy's number from Gino Ricci's brother.'

The Salamander said, 'Fine. Didn't I already say I was listening? So talk.'

'In case you wanna check it out—I'm calling from Florida. I did time with Gino's brother.'

'How thrilling for you. Now I'm hangin' up, asshole.'

'Wait,' said the voice. 'You been lookin' for a certain rat. I know where he is. The man who did the Zubonis.'

The Salamander slammed down his cleaver. 'Gimme a number I can call you back,' he said. 'Don't say another word, just tell me a number.'

The caller from Florida repeated it twice. Sal Delicato used a finger to write the numerals in pig blood on a butcher block. Then he untied his apron, washed his hands, combed his hair, snatched a roll of quarters from the cash register and walked three blocks to a pay phone.

'All right, smart guy,' he said when the man answered in Florida. 'First off, I don't know any Zuboni brothers.'

'I never said they was brothers.'

'You didn't?' Shit, thought The Salamander, I gotta pay closer attention. 'Look, never mind. Just hurry up and tell me what's so important.'

'There's this creep in the Witness Relocation Program, you know who I'm talking about. He testified against the Zuboni brothers, the ones you never heard of. Anyway, they gave this creep a new name, new Social Security, the whole nine yards. He's doing real nice for himself. In fact, he's worth a couple million bucks is what I hear.'

Sal Delicato said, 'You're a dreamer.'

'Well, maybe I got the wrong man. Maybe I got some bad information. I was under the impression you people were looking for Frankie King, am I wrong?'

'I don't know no Frankie King.'

'Fine. Nice talkin' with you—'

'Hold on,' said The Salamander. 'I probably know somebody who might be interested. What'd you say your name was?'

'Schwartz. Buddy Schwartz. I was with Gino's brother at Lake Butler, Florida. You can check it out.'

'I will.'

'In the meantime, you oughta talk to Mr. Gotti.'

'I don't know no Gotti,' said The Salamander. 'I definitely don't know no fucking Gotti.'

'Whatever.'

Over the phone Bud Schwartz heard the din of automobile horns and hydraulic bus brakes and jackhammers and police sirens. He felt glad he was in Miami instead of on a street corner in Queens. At the other end, Sal Delicato cleared his throat with a series of porcine grunts. 'You said they gave him a new name, right? This Frankie King.'

'Yep,' said Bud Schwartz.

'Well, what name does he got at the moment?'

'See, this is what I wanna talk about.'

'Sounds like you're playin' games, huh?'

Bud Schwartz said, 'No, sir. This ain't no game.'

'All right, all right. Tell you what to do: First off, you might already got some problems. The phone lines to my shop aren't so clean, understand?'

Bud Schwartz said, 'I'll be gone from here in a few days.'

'Be that as it may,' said The Salamander, 'next time you call me at the shop, do it from a pay booth—they got pay booths in Florida, right? And don't say shit, either. Just say you want five dozen lamb chops, all right? That's how I know it's you—five dozen lamb chops.'

'No problem,' said Bud Schwartz.

'Thirdly, it don't matter what phones we're on, don't ever mention that fucking name.'

'Frankie King?'

'No, the other one. The one starts with "G." '

'The one you never heard of?'

'Right,' said Salvatore (The Salamander) Delicato. 'That's the one.'

Later, drinking a beer on the porch, Danny Pogue said, 'I can't believe you done that.'

'Why not?' said Bud Schwartz. 'The asshole double-crossed us. Tried to rip us off.'

'Plus what he done to Molly.'

'Yeah, there's that.'

Danny Pogue said, 'Do you think they'll kill him?'

'Something like that. Maybe worse.'

'Jesus, Bud, I wouldn't know how to call up the Mafia, my life depended on it. The Mafia!'

'It wasn't easy finding the right people. They're not in the Yellow Pages, that's for sure.'

Danny Pogue laughed uproariously, exposing cheese-spackled teeth. 'You're a piece a work,' he said.

'Yeah, well.' Bud Schwartz had surprised himself with the phone call. He had remained cool and composed even with a surly mob heavyweight on the other end of the line. Bud Schwartz felt he had braved a higher and more serious realm of criminality; what's more, he had single-handedly set in motion a major event.

Danny Pogue said, 'How much'll they give us for turning the bastard in?'

'Don't know,' said Bud Schwartz. 'The man's checking it out.'

Danny Pogue drained his beer and stared at his dirty tennis shoes. In a small voice he said, 'Bud, I'm really sorry I ran away at the monkey place.'

'Yeah, what a surprise. You taking off and leaving me alone to get my brains knocked out. Imagine that.'

'I got scared is all.'

'Obviously.' What the hell could he expect? Like all thieves, Danny Pogue was low on valor and high on self-preservation.

He said, 'It's okay if you killed that guy. I mean, it was definitely self-defense. No jury in the world would send you up on that one.'

Great, Bud Schwartz thought, now he's Perry Mason. 'Danny, I'm gonna tell you one more time: it wasn't me, it was a damn baboon.'

Here was something Danny Pogue admired about his partner; most dirtbags would have lied about what happened so they could take credit for the shooting. Not Bud—even if a monkey was involved. That was Danny Pogue's idea of class.

'I got a feeling they meant to kill us,' Bud Schwartz said. He had replayed the scene a hundred times in his head, and it always added up to a murderous rip-off. It made him furious to think that Francis Kingsbury would try it . . . so furious that he'd tracked down his old cellmate Mario, who steered him to Jimmy Noodles, who gave him the number of the butcher shop in Queens.

Nothing but revenge was on Bud Schwartz's mind. 'I want them to know,' he said to Danny Pogue, 'that they can't screw with us just 'cause we're burglars.'

The screen door squeaked open and Molly McNamara joined the men on the porch. Her eyes looked puffy and tired. She asked Danny Pogue to fix her a glass of lemonade, and he dashed to the kitchen. She adjusted her new dentures and said, 'The meeting went poorly. There's not much support for my ideas.'

One hand moved to her chest, and she took a raspy, labored breath.

Bud Schwartz said, 'You ain't feeling so good, huh?'

'Not tonight, no.' She placed a tiny pill under her tongue and closed her eyes. A flash of distant lightning announced a thunderstorm sweeping in from the Everglades. Bud Schwartz spotted a mosquito on Molly's cheek, and he brushed it away.

She blinked her eyes and said, 'You boys have been up to something, I can tell.'

'It's going to be a surprise.'

'I'm too old for surprises,' said Molly.

'This one you'll like.'

'Be careful, please.' She leaned forward and dropped her voice. 'For Danny's sake, be careful. He's not as sharp as you are.'

Bud Schwartz said, 'We look out for each other.' Unless there's trouble, then the little dork runs for the hills.

'There's a reason I can't spill everything,' Bud Schwartz said to Molly, 'but don't you worry.' She was in a mood, all right. He'd never seen her so worn out and gloomy.

Danny Pogue returned with a pitcher of lemonade. Molly thanked him and held her glass with both hands as she drank. 'I'm afraid we won't be able to count on the Mothers of Wilderness,' she said. 'I sensed an alarming lack of resolve in the meeting tonight.'

'You mean, they wimped out.'

'Oh, they offered to picket Falcon Trace. And sign a petition, of course. They're very big on petitions.' Molly sighed and tilted her head. The oncoming thunder made the pine planks rumble beneath their feet.

'Maybe it's me. Maybe I'm just a batty old woman.'

Danny Pogue said, 'No, you're not!'

Yes, she is, thought Bud Schwartz. But that was all right. She was entitled.

Molly gripped the arms of the chair and pulled herself up. 'We'll probably get a visitor soon,' she said. 'The tall fellow with the collar on his neck.'

'Swell,' Bud Schwartz muttered. His ribs still throbbed from last time.

'He's not to be feared,' Molly McNamara said. 'We should hear what he has to say.'

This ought to be good, thought Bud Schwartz. This ought to be priceless.

TWENTY-FIVE

Early on the morning of July 29, a Sunday, the fax machine in the wire room of the *Miami Herald* received the following transmission:

REPTILE SCARE CLOSES THEME PARK; HIGH WATER BLAMED

The Amazing Kingdom of Thrills will be closed Sunday, July 29, due to an infestation of poisonous snakes caused by heavy summer rains and flooding. Cottonmouth moccasins numbering 'in the low hundreds' swarmed the popular South Florida theme park over the weekend, according to Charles Chelsea, vice president of publicity.

Several workers and visitors were bitten Saturday, but no deaths were reported. 'Our medical-emergency personnel responded to the crisis with heroic efficiency,' Chelsea stated.

Reptile experts say snakes become more active in times of heavy rainfall, and travel great distances to seek higher ground. Even the so-called water moccasin, which thrives in canals and brackish lagoons, becomes uncommonly restless and aggressive during flood-type conditions.

The cottonmouth is a pit viper known for its large curved fangs and whitish mouth. While extremely painful, the bite of the snake is seldom fatal if medical treatment is administered quickly. However, permanent damage to muscle and soft tissue often occurs.

The moccasin is prevalent throughout South Florida, although it is rare to find more than two or three snakes together at a time. Cluster migrations are a rarity in nature. 'They appeared to be hunting for toads,' Chelsea explained.

Officials ordered the theme park to be closed temporarily while teams of armed hunters captured and removed the wild reptiles, some of which were nearly six feet in length.

Chelsea said that the Amazing Kingdom will reopen Tuesday morning with a full schedule of events. He added: 'While we are confident that the grounds will be perfectly safe and secure, we are also suggesting, as a precaution, that our visitors wear heavy rubber boots. These will be available in all sizes, for a nominal rental fee.'

Reporters began calling before eight o'clock. Charles Chelsea was summoned from home; he arrived bleary-eyed and tieless. Clutching a Styrofoam cup of black coffee, he hunched over the desk to examine Joe Winder's newest atrocity.

'Wicked bastard,' he said after reading the last line.

A secretary told him about the TV helicopters. 'We've counted five so far,' she reported. 'They're trying to get an aerial shot of the snakes.'

'The snakes!' Chelsea laughed dismally.

To ignite his competitive spirit, the secretary said, 'I can't believe they'd fall for a dumb story like this.'

'Are you kidding?' Chelsea buried his hands in his hair. 'Snakes are dynamite copy. Anything with a snake, the media eats it up.' A law of journalism of which Joe Winder, the ruthless sonofabitch, was well aware.

Chelsea sucked down the dregs of the coffee and picked up the phone. Francis X. Kingsbury answered on the seventeenth ring.

'I've got some extremely bad news,' Chelsea said.

'Horseshit, Charlie, if you get my drift.' It sounded as if Kingsbury's hay fever was acting up. 'Calling me at home, Christ, what's your job description anyway—*professional pussy?* Is that what I hired you for?'

'No, sir.' The publicity man gritted his teeth and told Kingsbury what had happened. There was a long unpleasant silence, followed by the sound of a toilet being flushed.

'I'm in the can,' Kingsbury said. 'That's what you get for calling me at home.'

'Sir, did you hear what I said? About the snake story that Winder put out?'

'Yes, hell, I'm not deaf. Hold on.' Chelsea heard the toilet flush again. Grimly he motioned for his secretary to get him another cup of coffee.

On the other end, Kingsbury said, 'All right, so on this snake thing, what do you think?'

'Close the park for a day.'

'Don't be an idiot.'

'There's no choice, Mr. Kingsbury. Even if we came clean and admitted the press release was fake, nobody's going to believe it. They'll think we're covering up.' That was the insidious genius of Joe Winder's strategy.

Kingsbury said: 'Close the goddamn park, are you kidding? What about business?'

'Business is shot,' Chelsea replied. 'Nobody but reptile freaks would show up today. We're better off closing the Kingdom and taking our lumps.'

'Un-fucking-real, this is.'

'I forgot to mention, we'll also need to purchase some boots. Several hundred pairs.' Chelsea's fingers began to cramp on the telephone receiver. He said, 'Don't worry, I'll put something out on the wires right away.'

'Everything's under control, blah, blah, blah.'

'Right,' said Chelsea. Now he could hear the water running in Francis Kingsbury's sink.

'I bruffing my teef,' Kingsbury gargled.

Chelsea waited for the sound of spitting. Then he said, 'I'll call a press conference for noon. We'll get somebody, some scientist, to say the snakes are almost gone. Then we'll reopen tomorrow.'

Kingsbury said, 'Four hundred grand is what this fucking clown is costing me, you realize? A whole day's receipts.'

'Sir, it could get worse.'

'Don't say that, Charlie.'

In a monotone Chelsea read the phony press release to Francis Kingsbury, who said: 'Christ Almighty, they get six feet long! These poison cottonheads do?'

'I don't know. I don't know how big they get.' Chelsea wanted to tell Kingsbury that it really didn't matter if the imaginary snakes were two feet or twenty feet, the effect on tourists was the same.

Over the buzz of his electric razor, Kingsbury shouted, 'What does he want—this prick Winder— what's he after?'

'Nothing we can give him,' Chelsea said.

'It's got to stop or he'll kill our business.'

'Yes, I know.'

'And I'll tell you what else,' Francis Kingsbury said. 'I'm very disappointed in that fucking Pedro.'

Molly McNamara was writing a letter to her daughter in Minneapolis when Danny Pogue rushed into the den. Excitedly he said: 'I just saw on the news about all them snakes!' His Adam's apple juked up and down.

'Yes,' Molly said, 'it's very odd.'

'Maybe you could get your people together. The Mothers of Wilderness. Maybe go down to Key Largo and demonstrate.'

'Against what?'

'Well, it said on the news they're killing 'em all. The snakes, I mean. That don't seem right—it ain't their fault about the high water.' Danny Pogue was rigid with indignation, and Molly hated to dampen the fervor.

Gently she said, 'I don't know that they're actually killing the snakes. The radio said something about capture teams.'

'No, unh-uh, I just saw on the TV. A man from the Amazing Kingdom said they were killing the ones they couldn't catch. Especially the preggy ones.' He meant 'pregnant.' 'It's that Kingsbury asshole, pardon my French.'

Molly McNamara capped her fountain pen and turned the chair toward Danny Pogue. She told him she understood how he felt. 'But we've got to choose our battles carefully,' she said, 'if we hope to get the public on our side.'

'So?'

'So there's not much sympathy for poisonous snakes.'

Danny Pogue looked discouraged. Molly said, 'I'm sorry, Danny, but it's true. Nobody's going to care if they use flamethrowers, as long as they get rid of the cottonmouths.'

'But it ain't right.'

Molly patted his knee. 'There's plenty of snakes out there. Not like the mango voles, where there were only two left in the entire world.'

With those words she could have hammered an icepick into Danny Pogue's heart. Morosely he bowed his head. As his environmental consciousness had been awakened, the vole theft had begun to weigh like a bleak ballast on his soul; he'd come to feel personally responsible for the extinction of the voles, and had inwardly promised to avenge his crime.

He said to Molly: 'What's that word you used before—"*atome*"?'

'Atone, Danny. A-t-o-n-e. It means making amends.'

'Yeah, well, that's me.'

Molly smiled and removed her reading glasses. 'Don't worry, we've all made mistakes in our lives. We've all committed errors of judgment.'

'Like when you shot me and Bud. Before you got to know us better.'

'No, Danny, that wasn't a mistake. I'd do the same thing all over again, if it became necessary.'

'You would?'

'Oh, now, don't take it the wrong way. Come here.' Molly reached out and took him by the shoulders. Firmly she pulled his greasy head to her breast. The heavy jasmine scent brought the tickle of a sneeze to Danny Pogue's nostrils.

Molly gave him a hug and said, 'Both you boys mean so much to me.' Danny Pogue might have been moved to tears, except for the familiar bluish glint of the pistol tucked in the folds of Molly's housedress.

He said, 'You want some tea?'

'That would be lovely.'

As soon as Carrie Lanier left for work, Skink curled up in the shower, turned on the cold water and went to sleep.

Joe Winder kept writing for thirty minutes, until his will dissolved and he could no longer concentrate. He dialed Miriam's house and asked for Nina.

'It's six-dirty inna morning,' Miriam complained.

'I know what time it is. May I speak to her, please?'

'What if chee no here?'

'Miriam, I swear to God—'

'All rye, Joe. Chew wait.'

When Nina came on the line, she sounded wide awake. 'This is very rude of you,' she said crossly, 'waking Miriam.'

'What about you?'

'I was writing.'

'Me, too,' Joe Winder said. 'You were working on your phone fantasies?'

'My stories, yes.'

'That's the main reason for the call. I had an idea for you.'

Nina said, 'I've got some good news, Joe. I'm getting syndicated.'

'Hey, that's great.' Syndicated? What the hell was she talking about. Ann Landers was *syndicated*. Ellen Goodman was syndicated. Not women who write about bondage on Olympic diving boards.

'There's a company called Hot Talk,' Nina said. 'They own, like, two hundred of these adult phone services. They're going to buy my scripts and market them all over. Chicago, Denver, even Los Angeles.'

'That's really something.'

'Yeah, in a few months I'll be able to get off the phones and write full-time. It's like a dream come true.'

She asked about Joe's idea for a fantasy and he described it. 'Not bad,' Nina admitted. 'It just might work.'

'Oh, it'll work,' Winder said, but Nina didn't take the bait. She expressed no curiosity. 'Remember,' he added, 'it has to be a fishnet suit with absolutely nothing underneath.'

'Joe, please. I understand the principle.'

He was hoping she would ask how he was doing, what he'd been up to, and so on. Instead she told him she'd better go because she didn't want to keep Miriam awake.

Winder fought for more time. 'Basically, I called to see how you're doing. I admit it.'

'Well, I'm doing fine.'

'Things might get crazy in the next week or so. I didn't want you to worry.'

'I'll try not to.' Her tone was disconcertingly sincere. Winder waited for a follow-up question, but none came.

He blurted: 'Are you seeing anybody?'

'Not exactly.'

'Oh?'

'What I mean is, there's a man.'

'Oh, ho!' A hot stab in the sternum.

'But we're not exactly seeing each other,' Nina said. 'He calls up and we talk.'

'He calls on the 976 number? You mean he's a customer?'

'It's not like the others. We talk about deep things, personal things—I can't describe it, you wouldn't understand.'

'And you've never actually met him?'

'Not face-to-face, no. But you can tell a lot from the way a person talks. I think he must be very special.'

'What if he's a hunchback? What if he's got pubic lice?' Joe Winder was reeling. 'Nina, don't you see how sick this is? You're falling in love with a stranger's voice!'

'He's very sensual, Joe. I can tell.'

'For God's sake, the man's calling on the come line. What does that tell you?'

'I don't want to get into it,' Nina said. 'You asked if I was interested in anyone, and I told you. I should've known you'd react this way.'

'Just tell me, is he paying for the telephone calls?'

'We've agreed to split the cost.'

'Sweet Jesus.'

'And we're meeting for dinner Tuesday up in the Gables.'

'Wonderful,' said Joe Winder. 'What color trench coat did he say he'd be wearing?'

'I hate you,' Nina remarked.

They hung up on each other at precisely the same instant.

*

Pedro Luz slithered beneath Carrie's mobile home. Lying on his back in the cool dirt, he listened to the shower running and laughed giddily. He placed both hands on a wooden floor beam and pushed with all his strength; he was certain that he felt the double-wide rise above him, if only a few millimeters. With a bullish snort, he tried again. To bench-press a mobile home! Pedro Luz grimaced in ecstasy.

He was proud of himself for tracing the car, even if the detective work entailed only the pushing of three lousy buttons on a computer. He was equally proud of himself for locating the address in the dark and remaining invisible to the occupants of the trailer. At dawn he had watched the woman drive off to work, leaving him alone with that crazy doomed bastard, Joe Winder.

Pedro Luz had spent a long time fueling himself for the task. He had strung the intravenous rigs in the storage room of the Security Department at the Amazing Kingdom of Thrills. There, stretched on a cot, he had dripped large quantities of horse steroids into both arms. Afterwards, Pedro Luz had guzzled nine Heinekens and studied himself naked in a full-length mirror.

The mirror examination had become a ritual to make sure that his penis and testicles were not shrinking, as Churrito had warned they would. Pedro Luz had become worried when his security-guard uniform had gotten baggy in the crotch, so every night he took a measuring tape and checked his equipment. Then he would leaf through some pornographic magazines to make sure he could still get a hard-on; on some evenings, when he was particularly anxious, he would even measure the angle of his erection.

On the night he went after Joe Winder, the angle was exactly zero degrees. Pedro Luz blamed it on the beer.

Inside the trailer, Winder finished typing another counterfeit press release, which said:

The widow of a young scientist killed at the Amazing Kingdom of Thrills has been offered a settlement of $2.8 million, officials of the popular amusement park have announced.

The payment would be made in a single installment to Deborah Koocher, age 31, of New York. Her husband, Dr. William Bennett Koocher, was a noted wildlife biologist who helped supervise the Endangered Species Program at the Amazing Kingdom. Dr. Koocher died two weeks ago in a tragic drowning at the park's outdoor whale tank. That incident is still under investigation.

Charles Chelsea, vice president of publicity, said the cash offer to Mrs. Koocher 'demonstrates our sense of loss and sorrow over the untimely death of her husband.'

Added Chelsea: 'Will was instrumental in our rare-animal programs, and his heroic efforts to save the blue-tongued mango vole won international acclaim.'

In a statement released Sunday morning, Francis X. Kingsbury, founder and chairman of the Amazing Kingdom, said that Dr. Koocher's death 'was a tragedy for all of us at the park. We had come to love and admire Will, who was as much a part of our family as Robbie Raccoon or Petey Possum.'

The $2.8 million settlement offer is 'a gesture not only of compassion, but fairness,' Mr. Kingsbury added. 'If Dr. Koocher's family isn't satisfied, we would certainly consider increasing the payment.'

Joe Winder reread the announcement, inserted the word 'completely' before 'satisfied,' and fed the paper into the fax machine. He considered phoning Nina again, but decided it was no use; the woman was groping recklessly for male companionship. What else could explain her irrational attraction to a disembodied masculine voice?

Besides, Joe had Carrie now—or she had him. The dynamics of the relationship had yet to be calibrated.

Winder was in the mood for acoustic guitar, so he put on some Neil Young and fixed himself four eggs, scrambled, and two English muffins with tangerine marmalade. Glancing out the kitchen window, he noticed a tow truck parked crookedly on the shoulder of the dirt lane. He didn't see a driver.

The shower had been running for some time. Winder cracked the door and saw Skink curled in a fetal snooze, cold water slapping on the blaze weather suit. Winder decided not to wake him.

Suddenly he heard a pop like a car backfiring, and a hole the size of a nickel appeared in the tile six inches above Skink's face. Then came another bang, another hole.

Joe Winder yelled and dived out of the doorway.

*

In a way, Carrie Lanier was glad that the Amazing Kingdom was closed. It meant an extra day to work on her singing, which was still rusty, and to design a new costume for Princess Golden Sun.

Driving back toward the mainland, she couldn't wait to tell Joe about all the TV trucks and helicopters at the park's main gate. A reporter from Channel 10 had approached the car and thrust a microphone in her face and asked if she had seen any snakes. Quickly Carrie had improvised a story about a teeming herd—she wasn't sure it was the right term—slithering across County Road 905 near Carysfort. The fellow from Channel 10 had marshaled his camera crew and sprinted off toward the van.

Carrie was impressed by the immediate and dramatic effect of Joe Winder's hoax: everyone was wearing sturdy rubber hip boots.

On the way home, she practiced another song from the show.

> You took our whole Indian nation,
> Stuck us on this reservation.
> Took away our way of life,
> The garfish gig and the gator knife.
> Seminole people! Seminole tribe!

It was a variation of a song called 'Indian Reservation,' which was recorded by Paul Revere and the Raiders, a band not generally remembered for its biting social commentary. Carrie Lanier thought the new lyrics were insipid, but she liked the simple tune and tom-tom rhythms. She was singing the third verse when she turned into the trailer park and spotted a bloated body-builder firing a pistol into the side of her double-wide.

Without hesitating, without even honking the horn, Carrie Lanier took aim.

Pedro Luz was so thoroughly engrossed in assassinating Joe Winder in the shower that he didn't hear the 1979 Buick Electra until it mowed a row of garbage cans ten feet behind him. Pedro Luz started to run but tripped over a garden hose and pitched forward, arms outstretched; it seemed as if he were tumbling in slow motion. When he stopped, the Buick was parked squarely on his left foot.

He lay there for a full minute, bracing for agony that never came: Each of the twenty-six bones in Pedro Luz's foot had been pulverized, yet the only sensation was a mildly annoying throb. Four thousand pounds of ugly Detroit steel on his toes and not even a twinge of pain. Incredible, Pedro thought; the ultimate result of supreme physical conditioning! Or possibly the drugs.

Apparently the driver had abandoned the Buick with the engine running. Steroids and all, Pedro Luz could not budge the sedan by himself. Meanwhile, the gunfire and crash had awakened other denizens of the trailer park; bulldogs yapped, doors slammed, babies wailed, a rooster cackled. Probably somebody had phoned the police.

Pedro Luz probed at the bloody burrito that was now his left foot, protruding beneath a Goodyear white-wall, and made a fateful decision.

What the hell, he mused. Long as I'm feeling no pain.

*

Dr. Richard Rafferty's assistant called him at home to say there was an emergency, he'd better come right away. When he arrived at the office, the doctor sourly observed a tow truck parked in the handicapped zone. Inside the examining room, a husky one-eyed man with a radio collar lay prone on the steel table.

Dr. Rafferty said: 'Is this some kind of joke?'

The couple who had brought the injured man said he had been shot at least twice.

'Then he's got a big problem,' said Dr. Rafferty, 'because I'm a veterinarian.'

The couple seemed to know this already. 'He won't go to a regular doctor,' Joe Winder explained.

Carrie Lanier added, 'We took him to the hospital but he refused to get out of the truck.'

Dr. Rafferty's assistant pulled him aside. 'I believe I saw a gun,' he whispered.

Skink opened his good eye and turned toward the vet. 'Richard, you remember me?'

'I'm not sure.'

'The night that panther got nailed by the liquor truck.'

Dr. Rafferty leaned closer and studied the face. 'Lord, yes,' he said. 'I do remember.' It was the same fellow who'd charged into the office with a hundred-pound wildcat in his bare arms. The doctor remembered how the dying panther had clawed bloody striations on the man's neck and shoulders.

Skink said, 'You did a fine job, even though we lost the animal.'

'We gave it our best.'

'How about another try?'

'Look, I don't work on humans.'

'I won't tell a soul,' Skink said.

'Please,' Joe Winder cut in, 'you're the only one he'll trust.'

Skink's chest heaved, and he let out a groan.

'He's lost some blood,' Carrie said.

Dr. Rafferty slipped out of his jacket and told the assistant to prepare a surgical tray. 'Oh, we've got plenty of blood,' the doctor said, 'but unless you're a schnauzer, it won't do you much good.'

'Whatever,' Skink mumbled, drifting light-headedly. 'If you can't fix me up, then put me to sleep. Like you would any old sick dog.'

TWENTY-SIX

Charles Chelsea decided that 'dapper' was too strong a word for Francis X. Kingsbury's appearance; 'presentable' was more like it.

Kingsbury wore a gray silk necktie, and a long-sleeved shirt to conceal the lewd mouse tattoo. The reason for the sartorial extravagance was an invitation to address the Tri-County Chamber of Commerce luncheon; Kingsbury intended to use the occasion to unveil a model of the Falcon Trace Golf and Country Club Resort Community.

Impatiently he pointed at Charles Chelsea's belly and said: 'So? The damn snake situation—let's hear it.'

'The worst is over,' said Chelsea, with genuine confidence. He had countered Joe Winder's moccasin attack with a publicity blurb announcing that most of the reptiles had turned out to be harmless banded water snakes that only *looked* like deadly cottonmouths. For reinforcement Chelsea had released videotape of a staged capture, peppered with reassuring comments from a local zoologist.

'By the end of the week, we can send back all those boots,' Chelsea said in conclusion.

'All right, that's fine.' Kingsbury swiveled toward the window, then back again. Restlessly he kneaded the folds of his neck. 'Item Number Two,' he said. 'This shit with the doctor's widow, is that cleared up yet?'

Here Chelsea faltered, for Joe Winder had stymied him with the Koocher gambit. The publicity man was at a loss for remedies. There was no clever or graceful way to recant a $2.8 million settlement offer for a wrongful death.

Anxiety manifested itself in a clammy deluge from Chelsea's armpits. 'Sir, this one's a stumper,' he said.

'I don't want to hear it!' Kingsbury clasped his hands in a manner suggesting that he was trying to control a homicidal rage. 'What was it, two-point-eight? There's no fucking way—what, do I look like Onassis?'

Chelsea's jaws ached from nervous clenching. He pushed onward: 'To rescind the offer could have very grave consequences, publicity-wise. The fallout could be ugly.'

'Grave consequences? I'll give you grave, Charlie. Two million simoleons outta my goddamn pocket, how's that for grave?'

'Perhaps you should talk to the insurance company.'

'Ha!' Kingsbury tossed back his head and snorted insanely. 'They just jack the rates, those assholes, every time some putz from Boise stubs his little toe. No way, Charlie, am I talking to those damn insurance people.'

In recent years the insurance company had tripled its liability premium for the Amazing Kingdom of Thrills. This was due to the unusually high incidence of accidents and injuries on the main attractions; the Wet Willy water slide alone had generated seventeen lawsuits, and out-of-court settlements totaling nearly three-quarters of a million dollars. Even more costly was the freakish malfunction of a mechanical bull at the Wild Bill Hiccup

Corral—an elderly British tourist had been hospitalized with a 90-degree crimp in his plastic penile implant. The jury's seven-figure verdict had surprised no one.

There was no point rehashing these sad episodes with Francis Kingsbury, for it would only appear that Charles Chelsea was trying to defend the insurance company.

'I think you should be aware,' he said, 'Mrs. Koocher has retained an attorney.'

'Good for her,' Kingsbury rumbled. 'Let her explain to a judge what the hell her old man was doing, swimming with a damn killer whale in the middle of the night.'

Chelsea was now on the precipice of anger himself. 'If we drag this out, the *Herald* and the TV will be all over us. Do we really want a pack of reporters investigating the doctor's death?'

Kingsbury squinted suspiciously. 'What are you getting at?'

'I'm simply advising you to take time and think about this. Let me stall the media.'

The swiveling started again, back and forth, Kingsbury fidgeting like a hyperactive child. 'Two-point-eight-million dollars! Where the hell did that crazy number come from? I guess he couldn't of made it a hundred grand, something do-able.'

'Winder? No, sir, he tends to think big.'

'He's trying to put me out of business, isn't he?' Francis Kingsbury stopped spinning the chair. He planted his elbows on the desk and dug his polished fingernails into his jowls. 'The fucker, this is my theory, the fucker's trying to put me under.'

'You might be right,' Chelsea admitted.

'What's his—you hired him, Charlie—what's his angle?'

'I couldn't begin to tell you. For now, my advice is to get the insurance company in touch with Mrs. Koocher's lawyer. Before it blows up even worse.'

Kingsbury gave an anguished moan. 'Worse? How is that possible?'

'Anything's possible.' Chelsea was alarmed by the weariness in his own voice. He wondered if the tempest of bad news would ever abate.

The phone buzzed and Kingsbury plucked it off the hook. He listened, grunted affirmatively and hung up. 'Pedro's on his way in,' he said. 'And it better be good news or I'm gonna can his fat ass.'

Pedro Luz did not look like a cheery bundle of good tidings. The wheelchair was one clue. The missing foot was another.

Kingsbury sighed. 'Christ, now what?' He saw a whopper of a worker's comp claim coming down the pike.

'An accident,' Pedro Luz said, wheeling to a stop in front of Kingsbury's desk. 'Hey, it's not so bad.'

Chelsea noticed that the security man's face was swollen and mottled like a rotten melon, and that his massive arms had exploded in fresh acne sores.

Kingsbury drummed on a marble paperweight. 'So? Let's hear it.'

Pedro Luz said, 'I shot the bastard.'

'Yeah?'

'You better believe it.'

Charles Chelsea deftly excused himself, talk of felonies made him uncomfortable. He closed the door softly and nearly sprinted down the hall. He was thinking: Thank God it's finally over. No more dueling flacks.

Kingsbury grilled Pedro Luz on the details of the Joe Winder murder, but the security man edited selectively.

'He was in the shower. I fired eleven times, so I know damn well I hit him. Besides, I heard the shouts.'

Kingsbury asked, 'How do you know he's dead?'

'There was lots of blood,' said Pedro Luz. 'And like I told you, I fired almost a dozen goddamn rounds. Later I set the place on fire.'

'Yeah?' Kingsbury had seen footage of a trailer blaze on Channel 4; there had been no mention of bodies.

Pedro Luz said, 'It went up like a damn torch. One of them cheap mobile homes.'

'You're sure the bastard was inside?'

'Far as I know. And the bitch, too.'

Francis Kingsbury said, 'Which bitch? You're losing me here.'

'The dumb bitch he was staying with. The one who ran me over.'

Pedro Luz gestured at the bandaged stump on the end of his leg. 'That's what she did to me.'

The puffy slits made it difficult to read the expression in Pedro Luz's eyes. Kingsbury said, 'She hit you with a car?'

'More than that, she ran me down. Parked right on top of me.'

'On your foot? Jesus Christ.' Kingsbury winced sympathetically.

Pedro Luz said: 'Good thing I'm in shape.' Self-consciously he folded his bulging arms and spread his hands in a way that covered the pimples.

Kingsbury said, 'So what happened?'

'What do you mean? I told you what happened.'

'No, I mean with the car on your foot. How'd you get free?'

'Oh, I chewed it off,' said Pedro Luz, 'right below the ankle.'

Kingsbury stared at the stump. He couldn't think of anything to say.

'Animals do it all the time,' Pedro Luz explained, 'when they get caught in traps.'

Francis Kingsbury nodded unconsciously. His eyes roamed the office, searching for a convenient place to throw up.

'The hard part wasn't the pain. The hard part was the reach.' Pedro Luz bent down to demonstrate.

'Oh Lord,' Kingsbury muttered.

'Like I said, it's a good thing I'm in shape.'

At the campsite, Joe Winder told Molly McNamara it was nice to see her again. Molly congratulated Joe for blowing up Kingsbury's bulldozers. Skink thanked Molly for the bottle of Jack Daniels, and briefly related how it had been utilized. Carrie Lanier was introduced to the burglars, whom she instantly recognized as the scruffy vole robbers. Bud Schwartz and Danny Pogue were stunned to learn that Robbie Raccoon was a woman, and apologized for knocking Carrie down during the heist.

The heat was throbbing and the hammock steamed. No breeze stirred off the water. A high brown haze of African dust muted the hues of the broad summer sky. Skink handed out cold sodas and tended the fire; he wore cutoff jeans, the panther collar and a thick white vest of tape and bandages.

'You were lucky,' Molly told him.

'Guy was aiming high,' Skink said. 'He assumed I'd be standing up.'

As most people do in the shower, thought Joe Winder. 'He also assumed that you were me,' he said.

'Maybe so.' Skink smeared a stick of EDTIAR bug repellent on both arms. Then he sat down under a buttonwood tree to count the mosquitoes biting his legs.

Carrie Lanier told the others about the breakneck ride to the veterinarian. 'Dr. Rafferty did a great job. We're lucky he knew somebody over at the Red Cross.'

Between insect frenzies, Danny Pogue struggled to follow the conversation. 'You got shot?' he said to Skink. 'So did me and Bud!'

Sharply, Molly cut in: 'It wasn't the same.'

'Like hell,' mumbled Bud Schwartz miserably. The humidity made him dizzy, and his arms bled from scratching the bugs. In addition, he wasn't thrilled about the lunch menu, which included fox, opossum and rabbit— Skink's road-kill bounty from the night before.

Joe Winder was in a lousy mood, too. The sight of Carrie's burned-out trailer haunted him. The fax machine, the Amazing Kingdom stationery, his stereo— all lost. Neil Young, melting in the flames. Helpless, helpless, helpless, helpless.

Skink said, 'It's time to get organized. Those damn John Deeres are back.' He looked at Winder. 'Now they've got cops on the site.'

'What can we blow up next?' Molly asked.

Skink shook his head. 'Let's try to be more imaginative.'

'All the building permits are in Kingsbury's name,' Winder noted. 'If he goes down, the project goes under.'

Carrie wondered what Joe meant by 'goes down.'

'You mean, if he dies?'

'Or gets bankrupt,' Winder said.

'Or lost,' added Skink, glancing up from his mosquito census.

Danny Pogue elbowed Bud Schwartz, who kept his silence. He had spoken again to the butcher in Queens, who had relayed an offer from unnamed friends of the Zubonis: fifty thousand for the whereabouts of Frankie King. Naturally Bud Schwartz had agreed to the deal; now, sitting in the wilderness among these idealistic crusaders, he felt slightly guilty. Maybe he should've ratted on Kingsbury for free.

'Mr. X had a terrible run of luck the last few days,' Carrie was saying, 'thanks to Joe.'

Skink got up to check the campfire. He said, 'It's time for a full-court press.'

'Each day is precious,' agreed Molly McNamara. She dabbed her forehead with a linen handkerchief. 'I think we should move against Mr. Kingsbury as soon as possible.'

Bud Schwartz crumpled a soda can. 'Why don't we hold off a week or so?'

'No.' Skink offered him a shank of opossum on a long-handled fork. He said, 'Every hour that passes, we lose more of the island.'

'Kingsbury's got worse problems than all of us put together,' said Bud Schwartz. 'If we can just lay back a few days.'

Joe Winder urged him to elaborate.

'Tell him, Bud, go on!' Danny Pogue was nearly bursting.

'I wish I could.'

Skink fingered the silvery tendrils of his beard. Towering over the burglar, he said, 'Son, I'm not fond of surprises.'

'This is serious shit.' Bud Schwartz was pleading. 'You gotta understand—heavy people from up North.'

Wiping the condensation from her eyeglasses, Molly said, 'Bud, what on earth are you talking about?'

Winder leaned toward Carrie and whispered: 'This is getting interesting.'

'No damn surprises,' Skink repeated balefully. 'We act in confluence, you understand?'

Reluctantly Bud Schwartz took a bite of fried opossum. He scowled as the warm juices dripped down his chin.

'Is that blood?' asked Danny Pogue.

Skink nodded and said, 'Nature's gravy.'

Suddenly he turned his face to the sky, peered toward the lemon sun and cursed vehemently. Then he was gone, running barefoot into the bright tangles of the hammock.

The others looked at one another in utter puzzlement.

Joe Winder was the first to stand. 'When in Rome,' he said, reaching for Carrie's hand.

Humanity's encroachment had obliterated the Florida panther so thoroughly that numerals were assigned to each of the few surviving specimens. In a desperate attempt to save the species, the Game and Fresh Water

Commission had embarked on a program of monitoring the far-roaming panthers and tracking their movements by radio telemetry. Over a period of years most of the cats were treed, tranquilized and fitted with durable plastic collars that emitted a regular electronic signal on a frequency of 150 megahertz. The signals could be followed by rangers on the ground or, when the animal was deep in the swamp, by air. Using this system, biologists were able to map the territories traveled by individual cats, chart their mating habits and even locate new litters of kittens. Because the battery-operated collars were activated by motion, it was also possible for rangers to know when a numbered panther was sick or even dead; if a radio collar was inert for more than a few hours, it automatically began sending a distress signal.

No such alarm was transmitted if an animal became abnormally active, but the rangers were expected to notice any strange behavior and react accordingly. For instance, a panther that was spending too much time near populated areas was usually captured and relocated for its own safety; the cats had a long and dismal record of careless prowling along busy highways.

Sergeant Mark Dyerson had retrieved too many dead panthers that had been struck by trucks and automobiles. Recently the ranger had become certain that if something wasn't done soon, Panther 17 would end up the same way. The Game and Fish files indicated that the animal was a seven-year-old male whose original range stretched from Homestead south to Everglades National Park, and west all the way to Card Sound. Because this area was crisscrossed by high-speed roads, the rangers paid special attention to the travels of Number 17.

For months the cat had seemed content to hunker in the deep upland hammocks of North Key Largo, which made sense, considering the dicey crossing to the mainland. But Sergeant Dyerson had grown concerned when, two weeks earlier, radio readings on Number 17 began to show extraordinary, almost unbelievable movement. Intermittent flyovers had pinpointed the cat variously at Florida City, North Key Largo, Homestead, Naranja and South Miami—although Sergeant Dyerson believed the latter coordinates were a mistake, probably a malfunction of the radio tracking unit. South Miami was simply an impossible destination; not only was it well out of the panther's range, but the animal would have had to travel at a speed of sixty-five miles an hour to be there when the telemetry said it was. Unlike the cheetah, panthers prefer loping to racing. The only way Number 17 could go that far, Sergeant Dyerson joked to his pilot, is if it took a bus.

Even omitting South Miami from the readings, the cat's travels were inexplicably erratic. The rangers were concerned at the frequency with which Number 17 crossed Card Sound between Key Largo and the mainland. The only two possible routes—by water or the long bridge—were each fraught with hazards. It was Sergeant Dyerson's hope that Number 17 chose to swim the bay rather than risk the run over the steep concrete span, where the animal stood an excellent chance of getting creamed by a speeding car.

On July 29, the ranger took up the twin Piper to search for the wandering panther. The homing signal didn't come to life until the plane passed low over a trailer park on the outskirts of Homestead. It was not a safe place for humans, much less wild animals, and the panther's presence worried Sergeant Dyerson. Though the tawny cats were seldom visible from the Piper, the ranger half-expected to see Number 17 limping down the center lane of U.S. Highway 1.

Later that afternoon, Sergeant Dyerson went up again; this time he marked the strongest signal in thick cover near Steamboat Creek, on North Key Largo. The ranger couldn't believe it—twenty-nine miles in one day! This cat was either manic, or chained to the bumper of a Greyhound.

When Sergeant Dyerson landed in Naples, he asked an electrician to double-check the antenna and receiver of the telemetry unit. Every component tested perfectly.

That night, the ranger phoned his supervisor in Tallahassee and reviewed the recent radio data on Number 17. The supervisor agreed that he'd never heard of a panther moving such a great distance, so fast.

'Send me a capture team as soon as possible,' Sergeant Dyerson said. 'I'm gonna dart this sonofabitch and find out what's what.'

The twin Piper made three dives over the campsite. Joe Winder and Carrie Lanier watched from the bank of Steamboat Creek.

'Game and Fish,' Winder said, 'just what we need.'

'What do we do?' Carrie asked.

'Follow the water.'

They didn't get far. A tall uniformed man materialized at the edge of the tree line. He carried an odd small-bore rifle that looked like a toy. When he motioned to Joe and Carrie, they obediently followed him through the hammock out to the road. Molly

McNamara and the two burglars already had been rounded up; another ranger, with a clipboard, was questioning them. There was no sign of Skink.

Sergeant Mark Dyerson introduced himself and asked to see some identification. Joe Winder and Carrie Lanier showed him their driver's licenses. The ranger was copying down their names when a gaunt old cracker, pulled by three lean hounds, came out of the woods.

'Any luck?' Sergeant Dyerson asked.

'Nope,' said the tracker. 'And I lost me a dog.'

'Maybe the panther got him.'

'They ain't no panther out there.'

'Hell, Jackson, the radio don't lie.' The ranger turned back to Joe Winder and Carrie Lanier. 'And I suppose you're bird-watchers, too. Just like Mrs. McNamara and her friends.'

Beautiful, thought Winder. We're bird-watchers now.

Playing along, Carrie informed the ranger they were following a pair of nesting kestrels.

'No kidding?' Sergeant Dyerson said. 'I've never met a birder who didn't carry binoculars—and here I get five of 'em, all at one time.'

'We're thinking of forming a club,' said Carrie. Joe Winder bit his lip and looked away. Molly's Cadillac took off, eastbound—a crown of white hair behind the wheel, the burglars slouched in the back seat.

'I'll give you this much,' the ranger said, 'you sure don't look like poachers.' A Florida Highway Patrol car pulled up and parked beside Sergeant Dyerson's Jeep. A muscular black trooper got out and tipped his Stetson at the ranger.

'Whatcha know?' the trooper said affably.

'Tracking a panther. These folks got in the way.'

'A panther? You *got* to be kidding.' The trooper's laughter boomed. 'I've been driving this stretch for three years and never saw a bobcat, much less a panther.'

'They're very secretive,' Sergeant Dyerson said. 'You wouldn't necessarily spot them.' He wasn't in the mood for a nature lesson. He turned to the old tracker and told him to run the frigging dogs one more time.

'Ain't no point.'

'Humor me,' said Sergeant Dyerson. 'Come on, let's go find your other hound.'

Once the wildlife officers were gone, the trooper's easygoing smile dissolved. 'You folks need a lift.'

'No, thanks,' Joe Winder said.

'It wasn't a question, friend.' The trooper opened the back door of the cruiser, and motioned them inside.

TWENTY-SEVEN

The trooper took them to lunch at the Ocean Reef Club. The clientele seemed ruffled by the sight of a tall black man with a sidearm.

'You're making the folks nervous,' Joe Winder observed.

'Must be the uniform.'

Carrie popped a shrimp into her mouth. 'Are we under arrest?'

'I'd be doing all three of us a favor,' Jim Tile said, 'but no, unfortunately, you're not under arrest.'

Winder was working on a grouper sandwich. Jim Tile had ordered the fried dolphin and conch fritters. The dining room was populated by rich Republican golfers with florid cheeks and candy-colored Izod shirts. The men shot anxious squinty-eyed glances toward the black trooper's table.

Jim Tile motioned for iced tea. 'I can't imagine why I've never gotten a membership application. Maybe it got lost in the mail.'

'What's the point of all this?' Winder asked.

'To have a friendly chat.'

'About what?'

Jim Tile shrugged. 'Flaming bulldozers. Dead whales. One-eyed woodsmen. You pick the subject.'

'So we've got a mutual friend.'

'Yes, we do.' The trooper was enjoying the fish platter immensely; despite the stares, he seemed in no hurry to finish. He said, 'The plane scared him off, right?'

'It doesn't make sense,' Winder said. 'They're not after him, they're after a cat. Why does he run?'

Jim Tile put down the fork and wiped his mouth. 'My own opinion—he feels a duty to hide because that's what the panther would've done. He wears that damn collar like a sacred obligation.'

'To the extreme.'

'Yeah,' the trooper said. 'I don't expect they'll find that missing dog. You understand?'

Carrie said, 'He's a very interesting person.'

'A man to be admired but not imitated.' Jim Tile paused. 'I say that with no disrespect.'

Winder chose not to acknowledge the warning. 'Where do you think he went?' he asked the trooper.

'I'm not sure, but it's a matter of concern.'

The manager of the restaurant appeared at the table. He was a slender young man with bleached hair and pointy shoulders and brand new teeth. In a chilly tone he asked Jim Tile if he were a member of the club, and the trooper said no, not yet. The manager started to say something else but changed his mind. Jim Tile requested a membership application, and the manager said he'd be back in a jiffy.

'That's the last we'll see of him,' the trooper predicted.

Joe Winder wanted to learn more about Skink. He decided it was safe to tell Jim Tile what the group had been doing in the hammock before the airplane came: 'We were hatching quite a plot.'

'I figured as much,' the trooper said. 'You know much about rock and roll?'

Carrie pointed at Winder and said, 'Hard core.'

'Good,' said Jim Tile. 'Maybe you can tell me what's a Mojo? The other day he was talking about a Mojo flying.'

'*Rising*,' Winder said. 'Mojo rising. It's a line from The Doors—I believe it's got phallic connotations.'

'No,' Carrie jumped in. 'I think it's about drugs.'

The trooper looked exasperated. 'White people's music, I swear to God. Sinatra's all right, but you can keep the rest of it.'

'Shall we discuss rap?' Joe Winder said sharply. 'Shall we examine the lyrical genius of, say, 2 Live Crew?' He could be very defensive when it came to rock. Carrie reached under the table and pinched his thigh. She told him to lighten up.

'Rikers Island,' Jim Tile said. 'Is there a song about Rikers Island?'

Winder couldn't think of one. 'You sure it's not Thunder Island?'

'No.' Jim Tile shook his head firmly. 'Our friend said he'd be leaving Florida one day. Go up to Rikers Island and see to some business.'

'But that's a prison,' Carrie said.

'Yeah. A prison in New York City.'

Joe Winder remembered something Skink had told him the first day at the campsite. If it was a clue, it foreshadowed a crime of undiluted madness.

Winder said, 'Rikers is where they keep that idiot who shot John Lennon.' He cocked an eyebrow at Jim Tile. 'You *do* know who John Lennon was?'

'Yes, I do.' The trooper's shoulders sagged. 'This could be trouble,' he added emptily.

'Our mutual friend never got over it,' Winder said. 'The other night, he asked me about the Dakota.'

'Wait a minute.' Carrie Lanier made a time-out signal with her hands. 'You guys aren't serious.'

Gloomily Jim Tile stirred the ice in his tea. 'The man gets his mind set on things. And these days, I've been noticing he doesn't handle stress all that well.'

Joe Winder said, 'Christ, it was only an airplane. It's gone now, he'll calm down.'

'Let's hope.' The trooper called for the check.

Carrie looked sadly at Winder. 'And here I thought *you* were bonkers,' she said.

Agent Billy Hawkins told Molly McNamara that the house was simply beautiful. Old-time Florida, you don't see pine floors like this anymore. Dade County pine.

Molly said, 'I've got carpenter ants in the attic. All this wet weather's got 'em riled.'

'You'd better get that seen to, and soon. They can be murder on the beams.'

'Yes, I know. How about some more lemonade?'

'No, thank you,' said Agent Hawkins. 'We really need to talk about this telephone call.'

Molly began to rock slowly. 'I'm completely stumped. As I told you before, I don't know a living soul in Queens.'

Hawkins held a notebook on his lap, a blue Flair pen in his right hand. He said, 'Salvatore Delicato is an associate of the John Gotti crime family.'

'Goodness!' Molly exclaimed.

'Prior arrests for racketeering, extortion and income-tax evasion. The phone call to his number was made from here. It lasted less than a minute.'

'There must be some mistake. Did you check with Southern Bell?'

'Miss McNamara,' Hawkins said, 'can we please cut the crap.'

Molly's grandmotherly expression turned glacial. 'Watch your language, young man.'

Flushing slightly, the agent continued: 'Have you ever met a Jimmy Nardoni, otherwise known as Jimmy Noodles? Or a man named Gino Ricci, otherwise known as Gino The Blade?'

'Such colorful names,' Molly remarked. 'No, I've never heard of them. Do you have my telephone bugged, Agent Hawkins?'

He resisted the impulse to tell her that Sal Delicato's telephone was tapped by a squadron of eavesdroppers—not only the FBI, but the New York State Police, the U.S. Drug Enforcement Administration, the Tri-State Task Force on Organized Crime and the Bureau of Alcohol, Tobacco and Firearms. The New York Telephone box on the utility pole behind The Salamander's butcher shop sprouted so many extra wires, it looked like a pigeon's nest.

'Let me give you a scenario,' Agent Hawkins said to Molly. 'A man used your phone to call Sal Delicato for the purpose of revealing the whereabouts of a federally protected witness now living in Monroe County, Florida.'

'That's outlandish,' Molly said. 'Who is this federal witness?'

'I imagine you already know.' Hawkins jotted something in the notebook. 'The man who made the phone call, we believe, was Buddy Michael Schwartz. I showed you his photograph the last time we visited. You said he looked familiar.'

'I vaguely remember.'

'He has other names,' Hawkins said. 'As I told you before, Schwartz is wanted in connection with the animal theft from the Amazing Kingdom.'

'Wanted?'

'For questioning,' the agent said. 'Anyway, we believe the events are connected.' The ominous wiretap conversation had elevated the vole investigation from zero-priority to high-priority. Billy Hawkins had been yanked off a bank-robbery case and ordered to find out why anyone would be setting up Francis X. Kingsbury, aka Frankie King. The Justice Department had pretty much forgotten about Frankie The Ferret until the phone call to Sal Delicato. The renewed interest in Washington was not a concern for Frankie's well-being so much as fear of a potential publicity nightmare; the murder of a protected government informant would not enhance the reputation of the Witness Relocation Program. It could, in fact, have a profoundly discouraging effect on other snitches. Agent Hawkins was told to track down Buddy Michael Schwartz and then call for backup.

Molly McNamara said, 'You think this man might have broken into my house to use the phone!'

'Not exactly,' Hawkins said.

She peered at him skeptically. 'How do you know it was he on the line? Did you use one of those voice-analyzing machines?'

The FBI man chuckled. 'No, we didn't need a machine. The caller identified himself.'

'By name?' The blockhead! Molly thought.

'No, not by name. He told Mr. Delicato that he was an acquaintance of Gino Ricci's brother. It just so happens that Buddy Michael Schwartz served time with Mario Ricci at the Lake Butler Correctional Institute.'

Molly McNamara said, 'Could be a coincidence.'

'They shared a cell. Buddy and Gino's brother.'

'But still—'

'Would you have a problem,' the agent said, 'if I asked you to come downtown and take a polygraph examination?'

Molly stopped rocking and fixed him with an indignant glare. 'Are you saying you don't believe me?'

'Call it a hunch.'

'Agent Hawkins, I'm offended.'

'And I'm tired of this baloney.' He closed the notebook and capped the pen. 'Where is he?'

'I don't know what you're talking about.'

Hawkins stood up, pocketed his notebook, straightened his tie. 'Let's go for a ride,' he said. 'Come on.'

'No!'

'Don't make it worse for yourself.'

'You're not paying attention,' Molly said. 'I thought G-men were trained to be observant.'

Billy Hawkins laughed. 'G-men? I haven't heard that one in a long—'

It was then he noticed the pistol. The old lady held it impassively, with both hands. She was pointing it directly at his crotch.

'This is amazing,' said the agent. 'The stuff of

legends.' Wait till the tough guys at Quantico hear about it.

Molly asked Billy Hawkins to raise his hands.

'No, ma'am.'

'And why not?'

'Because you're going to give me the gun now.'

'No,' said Molly, 'I'm going to shoot you.'

'Lady, gimme the goddamn gun!'

Calmly she shot him in the thigh, two and one-quarter inches below the left hip. The FBI man went down with a howl, clawing at the burning hole in his pants.

'I told you to watch your language,' Molly said.

The pop of the pistol brought Danny Pogue and Buddy Schwartz scrambling down the stairs. From a living-room window they cautiously surveyed the scene on the porch: Molly rocking placidly, a man in a gray suit thrashing on the floor.

Danny Pogue cried, 'She done it again!'

'Christ on a bike,' said Bud Schwartz, 'it's that dick from the FBI.'

The burglars cracked the door and peeked out. Molly assured them the situation was under control.

'Flesh wound,' she reported. 'Keep an eye on this fellow while I get some ice and bandages.' She confiscated Billy Hawkins's Smith & Wesson and gave it to Bud Schwartz, who took it squeamishly, like a dog turd, in his hands.

'It works best when you aim it,' Molly chided.

Danny Pogue reached for the barrel. 'I'll do it!'

'Like hell,' said Bud Schwartz, spinning away. He sat in the rocker and braced the pistol on his knee. The air smelled pungently of gunpowder; it brought back the memory of Monkey Mountain and the trigger-happy baboon.

Watching the gray-suited man squirm in pain, Bud Schwartz fought the urge to get up and run. What was the old bat thinking this time? Nothing good could come of shooting an FBI man. Surely she understood the consequences.

Danny Pogue opened the front door for Molly, who disappeared into the house with a pleasant wave. Danny Pogue sat down, straddling an iron patio chair. 'Take it easy,' he told the agent. 'You ain't hurt so bad.'

Billy Hawkins grunted up at him: 'What's your name?'

'Marcus Welby,' Bud Schwartz cut in. 'Don't he look like a doctor?'

'I know who *you* are,' the agent said. It felt as if a giant wasp were boring into his thigh. Billy Hawkins unbuckled his trousers and grimaced at the sight of his Jockey shorts soaked crimson.

'You assholes are going to jail,' he said, pinching the pale flesh around the bullet wound.

'We're just burglars,' said Danny Pogue.

'Not anymore.' Hawkins attempted to rise to his feet, but Bud Schwartz wiggled the gun and told him to stay where he was. The agent's forehead was sprinkled with sweat, and his lips were gray. 'Hey, Bud,' he said, 'I've seen your jacket, and this isn't your style. Assault on a federal officer, man, you're looking at Atlanta.'

Bud Schwartz was deeply depressed to hear the FBI man call him by name. 'You don't know shit about me,' he snapped.

'Suppose you tell me what the hell's going on out here. What's your beef with Frankie King?'

Bud Schwartz said, 'I don't know who you're talkin' about.'

Miraculously, Danny Pogue caught on before saying something disastrous. He flashed a checkerboard grin and said, 'Yeah, who's Frankie King? We never heard a no Frankie King.'

'Bullshit,' Agent Billy Hawkins growled. 'Go ahead and play it stupid. You're all going to prison, anyhow. You and that crazy old lady.'

'If it makes you feel any better,' said Danny Pogue, 'she shot us, too.'

The campsite was . . . gone.

'I'm not surprised,' Joe Winder said. He took Carrie's hand and kept walking. A light rain was falling, and the woods smelled cool.

Carrie asked, 'What do we do if he's really gone?'

'I don't know.'

Ten minutes later she asked if they were lost.

'I got turned around,' Winder admitted. 'It can't be too far.'

'Joe, where are we going?'

The rain came down harder, and the sky blackened. From the west came a roll of thunder that shook the leaves. The birds fell silent; then the wind began to race across the island, and Joe Winder could taste the storm. He dropped Carrie's hand and started to jog, slapping out a trail with his arms. He called over his shoulder, urging Carrie to keep up.

It took fifteen more minutes to find the junkyard where the ancient Plymouth station wagon sat on rusty bumpers. The yellow beach umbrella—still stuck in the dashboard—fluttered furiously in the gale.

Joe Winder pulled Carrie inside the car, and hugged her so tightly she let out a cry. 'My arms are tingling,' she said. 'The little hairs on my arms.'

He covered her ears. 'Hold on, it's lightning.'

It struck with a white flash and a deafening rip. Twenty yards away, a dead mahogany tree split up the middle and dropped a huge leafless branch. 'God,' Carrie whispered. 'That was close.'

Raindrops hammered on the roof. Joe Winder turned around in the seat and looked in the back of the car. 'They're gone,' he said.

'What, Joe?'

'The books. This is where he kept all his books.'

She turned to see. Except for several dead roaches and a yellowed copy of the *New Republic*, the station wagon had been cleaned out.

Winder was vexed. 'I don't know how he did it. You should've seen—there were hundreds in here. Steinbeck, Hemingway. Jesus, Carrie, he had García Márquez in Spanish. First editions! Some of the greatest books ever written.'

'Then he's actually gone.'

'It would appear to be so.'

'Think we should call somebody?'

'What?'

'Somebody up in New York,' Carrie said, 'at the prison. I mean, just in case.'

'Let me think about this.'

'I can't believe he'd try it.'

The thunderstorm moved quickly over the island and out to sea. Soon the lightning stopped and the downpour softened to a drizzle. Carrie said, 'The breeze felt nice, didn't it?'

Joe Winder wasn't listening. He was trying to decide if they should keep looking or not. Without Skink, new choices lay ahead: bold and serious decisions. Winder suddenly felt responsible for the entire operation.

Carrie turned to kiss him and her knee hit the glove compartment, which popped open. Curiously she poked through the contents—a flashlight, a tire gauge, three D-sized batteries and what appeared to be the dried tail of a squirrel.

And one brown envelope with Joe Winder's name printed in small block letters.

He tore it open. Reading the note, he broke into a broad smile. 'Short and to the point,' he said.

Carrie read it:

> Dear Joe,
> You make one hell of an oracle.
> Don't worry about me, just keep up the fight.
> We all shine on!

Carrie folded the note and returned it to the envelope. 'I assume this means something.'

'Like the moon and the stars and the sun,' Joe Winder said. He felt truly inspired.

TWENTY-EIGHT

The Amazing Kingdom of Thrills reopened with only a minimal drop in attendance, thanks to a three-for-one ticket promotion that included a free ride on Dickie the Dolphin, whose amorous behavior was now inhibited by four trainers armed with electric stun guns. Francis X. Kingsbury was delighted by the crowds, and emboldened by the fact that many customers actually complained about the absence of wild snakes. Kingsbury regarded it as proof that closing the Amazing Kingdom had been unnecessary, a costly overestimation of the average tourist's brainpower. Obviously the yahoos were more curious than afraid of lethal reptiles. A thrill is a thrill, Kingsbury said.

The two persons forced to sit through this speech were Pedro Luz and Special Agent Ron Donner of the U.S. Marshal Service. Agent Donner had come to notify Francis X. Kingsbury of a possible threat against his life.

'Ho! From who?'

'Elements of organized crime,' the marshal said.

'Well, fuck em.'

'Excuse me?'

'This is just, I mean really, the word is horseshit!' Kingsbury flapped his arms like a tangerine-colored buzzard. He was dressed for serious golf; even his cleats were orange.

Agent Donner said: 'We think it would be wise if you left town for a few weeks.'

'Oh, you do? Leave town, like hell I will.'

Pedro Luz spun his wheelchair slightly toward the marshal. 'Organized crime,' he said. 'You mean the Mafia?'

'We're taking it very seriously,' said Agent Donner, thinking: Who's the freak with the IV bag?

With the proud sweep of a hand, Francis Kingsbury introduced his chief of Security. 'He handles everything for the park and so on. Personal affairs, as well. You can say anything in front of him, understand? He's thoroughly reliable.'

Pedro Luz casually adjusted the drip valve on the intravenous tube.

The marshal asked, 'What happened to your foot?'

'Never mind!' blurted Kingsbury.

'Car accident,' Pedro Luz volunteered affably. 'I had to chew the damn thing off.' He pointed with a swathed, foreshortened index finger. 'Right there above the ankle-bone, see?'

'Tough luck,' said Agent Donner, thinking: Psycho City.

'It's what animals do,' Pedro Luz added, 'when they get caught in traps.'

Kingsbury clapped his hands nervously. 'Hey, hey! Can we get back to the issue, please, this Godfather thing. For the record, I'm not going anyplace.'

The marshal said, 'We can have you safely in Bozeman, Montana, by tomorrow afternoon.'

'What, do I look like fucking Grizzly Adams? Listen

to me—*Montana*, don't even joke about something like that.'

Pedro Luz said, 'Why would the Mafia want to kill Mr. Kingsbury? I don't exactly make the connection.' Then his chin dropped, and he appeared to drift off.

Agent Donner said, 'I wish you'd consider the offer.'

'Two words.' Kingsbury held up two fingers as if playing charades. 'Summerfest Jubilee. One of our biggest days, receipt-wise, of the whole damn year. Parades, clowns, prizes. We're giving away . . . I forget, some kinda car.'

'And I suppose you need to be here.'

'Yeah, damn right. It's my park and my show. And know what else? You can't make me go anywhere. I kept my end of the deal. I'm free and clear of you people.'

'You're still on probation,' said the marshal. 'But you're right, we can't force you to go anyplace. This visit is a courtesy—'

'And I appreciate the information. I just don't happen to believe it.' But a part of Francis Kingsbury did believe it. What if the men who stole his files had given up on the idea of blackmail? What if the damn burglars had somehow made touch with the Gotti organization? It strained Kingsbury's imagination because they'd seemed like such jittery putzes that night at the house. Yet perhaps he'd misjudged them.

'Where'd you get the tip?' he demanded.

Agent Donner was briefly distracted by the cartoon depiction of rodent fellatio that adorned Kingsbury's forearm. Eventually the marshal looked up and said, 'It surfaced during another investigation. I can't go into details.'

'But, really, you guys think it's on the level? You think some guineas are coming after me?' Kingsbury struggled to maintain an air of amused skepticism.

Soberly the marshal said, 'The FBI is checking it out.'

'Well, regardless, I'm not going to Montana. Just thinking about it hurts my mucous membranes—I got the world's worst hay fever.'

'So your mind is made up.'

'Yep,' said Kingsbury. 'I'm staying put.'

'Then let us provide you with protection here at the park. A couple of men, at least.'

'Thanks, but no thanks. I got Pedro.'

At the mention of his name, Pedro Luz's swollen eyelids parted. He reached up and squeezed the IV bag. Then he tugged the tube out of the needle in his arm, and fitted the end into the corner of his mouth. The sound of energetic sucking filled Francis Kingsbury's office.

Agent Donner was dumbfounded. In a brittle voice he assured Kingsbury that the marshals would be extremely discreet, and would in no way interfere with the Summerfest Jubilee events. Kingsbury, in a tone approaching politeness, declined the offer of body-guards. The last thing he needed was federal dicks nosing around the Amazing Kingdom.

'Besides, like I mentioned, there's Pedro. He's as tough as they come.'

'All right,' said Agent Donner, casting his eyes once again on the distended, scarified, cataleptic, polyp-headed mass that was Pedro Luz.

Kingsbury said, 'I know what you're thinking but, hell, he's worth ten of yours. Twenty of yours! Any sonofabitch that would bite off his own damn leg—you tell me, is that tough or what?'

The marshal rose stiffly to leave. 'Tough isn't the word for it,' he said.

The trailer fire had left Carrie Lanier with only three possessions: her Buick Electra, the gun she had taken from Joe Winder and the newly retired raccoon suit. The costume and the gun had been stowed in the trunk of the car. Everything else had been destroyed in the blaze.

Molly McNamara offered her a bedroom on the second floor of the old house. 'I'd loan you the condo but the cleaners are in this week,' Molly said. 'It's hard to rent out a place with bloodstains in the carpet.'

'What about Joe?' Carrie said, 'I'd like him to stay with me.'

Molly clucked. 'Young lady, I really can't approve. Two unmarried people—'

'But under the circumstances,' Carrie persisted, 'with all that's happened.'

'Oh . . . I suppose it's all right.' Molly had a sparkle in her eyes. 'I was teasing, darling. Besides, you act as if you're in love.'

Carrie said it was a long shot. 'We're both very goal-oriented, and very stubborn. I'm not sure we're heading in the same direction.' She paused and looked away. 'He doesn't seem to fit anywhere.'

'You wouldn't want him if he did,' Molly said. 'The world is full of nice boring young men. The crazy ones are hard to find and harder to keep, but it's worth it.'

'Your husband was like that?'

'Yes. My lovers, too.'

'But crazy isn't the word for it, is it?'

Molly smiled pensively. 'You're a smart cookie.'

'Did you know that Joe's father built Seashell Estates?'

'Oh dear,' Molly said. A dreadful project: six thousand units on eight hundred acres, plus a golf course. Wiped out an egret rookery. A mangrove estuary. And too late it was discovered that the fairways were leaching fertilizer and pesticides directly into the waters of Biscayne Bay.

Molly McNamara said, 'Those were the bad old days.'

'Joe's still upset.'

'But it certainly wasn't his fault. He must've been barely a teenager when Seashell was developed.'

'He's got a thing about his father,' Carrie said.

'Is that what this is all about?'

'He hears bulldozers in his sleep.'

Molly said, 'It's not as strange as you might imagine. The question is, can you take it? Is this the kind of fellow you want?'

'That's a tough one,' Carrie said. 'He could easily get himself killed this week.'

'Take the blue bedroom at the end of the hall.'

'Thank you, Miss McNamara.'

'Just one favor,' Molly said. 'The headboard—it's an antique. I found it at a shop in Williamsburg.'

'We'll be careful,' Carrie promised.

That night they made love on the bare pine floor. Drenched in sweat, they slid like ice cubes across the slick varnished planks. Eventually they wound up wedged headfirst in a corner, where Carrie fell asleep with Joe Winder's earlobe clenched tenderly in her teeth. He was starting to doze himself when he heard Molly's voice in the adjoining bedroom. She was talking sternly to a man who didn't sound like either Skink or the two redneck burglars.

When Winder heard the other door close, he delicately extricated himself from Carrie's bite and lifted her to the bed. Then he wrapped himself in an old quilt and crept into the hall to see who was in the next room.

The last person he expected to find was Agent Billy Hawkins of the Federal Bureau of Investigation. Trussed to a straight-backed chair, Hawkins wore someone else's boxer shorts and black nylon socks. A bandage was wadded around one bare thigh, and two strips of hurricane tape crisscrossed his mouth. He reeked of antiseptic.

Joe Winder slipped into the room and twisted the lock behind him. Gingerly he peeled the heavy tape from the agent's face.

'Fancy meeting you here.'

'Nice getup,' Billy Hawkins remarked. 'Would you please untie me?'

'First tell me what happened.'

'What does it look like? The old bird shot me.'

'Any particular reason?'

'Just get me loose, goddammit.'

Winder said, 'Not until I hear the story.'

Reluctantly, Hawkins told him about Bud Schwartz and the long-distance phone call to Queens and the possible exposure of a federally protected witness.

'Who's the flip?'

'I can't tell you *that*.'

Joe Winder pressed the hurricane tape over Hawkins's lips—then fiercely yanked it away. Hawkins yelped. Tears of pain sprang to his eyes. In colorful expletives he offered the opinion that Winder had gone insane.

The excruciating procedure was repeated on one of Billy Hawkins's bare nipples and nearly uprooted a cluster of curly black hairs. 'I can do this all night,' Winder said. 'I'm way past the point of caring.'

The agent took a long bitter moment to compose himself. 'You could go to prison,' he mumbled.

'For assaulting you with adhesive tape? I don't think so.' Winder placed one gummy strip along the line of soft hair that trailed southward from Billy Hawkins's navel. The agent gaped helplessly as Winder jerked hard; the tape came off with a sibilant rip.

'You—you're a goddamn lunatic!'

'But I'm your only hope. Who's going to believe you were shot and abducted by an elderly widow? And if they should believe it, what would that do to your career?' Joe Winder spread the quilt on the floor and sat cross-legged in front of the hog-tied agent.

'Blaine, Washington,' Winder said. 'Isn't that the FBI's equivalent of Siberia?'

Hawkins conceded the point silently. The political cost of prosecuting a grandmother and a pair of candyass burglars would be high. The Bureau was hypersensitive to incidents incongruous with the lantern-jawed crime-buster image promoted by J. Edgar Hoover; for an FBI agent to be overpowered by a doddering senior citizen was a disgrace. An immediate transfer to some godforsaken cowtown would be a certainty.

'So what can *you* do?' Hawkins asked Winder sourly.

'Maybe nothing. Maybe save your skin. Did Molly make you call the office?'

The agent nodded. 'At gunpoint. I told them I was taking a couple of sick days.'

'They ask about this Mafia thing?'

'I told them it wasn't panning out. Looked like a bullshit shakedown.' Hawkins sounded embarrassed. 'That's what she made me say. Threatened to shoot me again if I didn't go along with the routine—and it didn't sound like a bluff.'

'You did the right thing,' Joe Winder said. 'No sense chancing it.' He stood up and rewrapped himself in the quilt. 'You'll have to stay like this a while,' he told the agent. 'It's the only way.'

'I don't get it. What's your connection to these crackpots?'

'Long story.'

'Winder, don't be a jackass. This isn't a game.' Hawkins spoke sternly for a man in his ridiculous predicament. 'Somebody could get killed. That's not what you want, is it?'

'Depends. Tell me the name of this precious witness.'

'Frankie King.'

Joe Winder shrugged. 'Never heard of him.'

'Moved down from New York after he snitched on some of Gotti's crowd. This was a few years back.'

'Swift move. What's he calling himself these days?'

'That I can't possibly tell you.'

'Then you're on your own, Billy. Think about it. Your word against Grandma Moses. Picture the headlines: "Sharpshooter Widow Gunned Me Down, Nude G-Man Claims." '

Hawkins sagged dispiritedly. He said, 'The flip's name is Francis Kingsbury. You happy now?'

'Kingsbury?' Joe Winder raised his eyes to the heavens and cackled raucously. 'The Mafia is coming down here to whack Mr. X!'

'Hey,' Billy Hawkins said, 'it's not funny.'

But it was very funny to Joe Winder. 'Francis X. Kingsbury. Millionaire theme-park developer and real-estate mogul, darling of the Chamber of Commerce, 1988 Rotarian Citizen of the Year. And you're telling me he's really a two-bit jizzbag on the run from the mob?'

Ecstatically, Joe Winder hopped from foot to foot, spinning in a circle and twirling Molly's quilt like a calico cape.

'Oh, Billy boy,' he sang, 'isn't this a great country!'

They were thirty minutes late to the airport because Danny Pogue insisted on watching the end of a *National Geographic* television documentary about rhinoceros poachers in Africa.

In the car he couldn't stop talking about the program. 'The only reason they kill 'em, see, what they're after is the horns. Just the horns!' He put his fist on his nose to simulate a rhinoceros snout. 'In some places they use 'em for sex potions.'

'Get off it,' said Bud Schwartz.

'No shit. They grind the horns into powder and put it in their tea.'

'Does it work?'

'I don't know,' Danny Pogue said. 'The TV didn't say.'

'Like, it gives you a super big boner or what?'

'I don't know, Bud, the TV didn't say. They just talked about how much the powder goes for in Hong Kong, stuff like that. Thousands of bucks.'

Bud Schwartz said, 'You ask me, they left out the most important part of the show. Does it work or not?'

He drove into one of the airport garages and snatched a ticket from the machine. He parked on Level M, as always. 'M' for Mother; it was the only way Bud Schwartz could remember how to find his car. He was annoyed that his partner wasn't sharing in the excitement of the moment: they were about to be rich.

'After today, you can retire,' Bud Schwartz said. 'No more b-and-e's. Man, we should throw us a party tonight.'

Danny Pogue said, 'I ain't in the mood.'

They stepped onto the moving sidewalk and rode in silence to the Delta Airlines concourse. The plane had arrived on time, so the visitor already was waiting outside the gate. As promised, he was carrying a blue umbrella; otherwise Bud Schwartz would never have known that he was the hit man. He stood barely five feet tall and weighed at least two hundred pounds. He had thinning brown hair, small black eyes and skin that was the color of day-old lard. Under a herringbone sport coat he wore a striped polyester shirt, open at the neck, with a braided gold chain. The hit man seemed fond of gold; a bracelet rattled on his wrist when he shook Bud Schwartz's hand.

'Hello,' said the burglar.

'You call me Lou.' The hit man spoke in a granite baritone that didn't match the soft roly-polyness of his figure.

'Hi, Lou,' said Danny Pogue. 'I'm Bud's partner.'

'How nice for you. Where's the car?' He pointed to a Macy's shopping bag near his feet. 'That's yours. Now, where's the car?'

On the drive south, Danny Pogue peeked in the Macy's bag and saw that it was full of cash. Lou was up in the front seat next to Bud Schwartz.

'I wanna do this tomorrow,' he was saying. 'I gotta get home for my wife's birthday. She's forty.' Then he farted loudly and pretended not to hear it.

'Forty? No kidding?' said Bud Schwartz. He had been expecting something quite different in the way of a mob assassin. Perhaps it wasn't fair, but Bud Schwartz was disappointed in Lou's appearance. For Francis Kingsbury's killer, he had envisioned someone taut, snake-eyed and menacing—not fat, balding and flatulent.

Just goes to show, thought Bud Schwartz, these days everything's hype. Even the damn Mafia.

From the back seat, Danny Pogue asked: 'How're you gonna do it? What kinda gun?'

Lou puffed out his cheeks and said, 'Brand X. The fuck do you care, what kinda gun?'

'Danny,' Bud Schwartz said, 'let's stay out of the man's private business, okay?'

'I didn't mean nothin'.'

'You usually don't.'

The man named Lou said, 'This the neighborhood?'

'We're almost there,' said Bud Schwartz.

'I can't get over all these trees,' Lou said. 'Parts a Jersey look like this. My wife's mother lives in Jersey, a terrific old lady. Seventy-seven years old, she bowls twice a week! In a league!'

Bud Schwartz smiled weakly. Perfect. A hit man who loves his mother-in-law. What next—he collects for the United Way?

The burglar said to Lou: 'Maybe it's better if you rent a car. For tomorrow, I mean.'

'Sure. Usually I do my own driving.'

Danny Pogue tapped his partner on the shoulder and said, 'Slow down, Bud, it's up here on the right.'

Kingsbury's estate was bathed in pale orange lights. Gray sedans with green bubble lights were parked to block both ends of the driveway. Three men sat in each sedan; two more, in security-guard uniforms, were posted at the front door. It was, essentially, the complete private security force of the Amazing Kingdom of Thrills—except for Pedro Luz, who was inside the house, his wheelchair parked vigilantly at Francis Kingsbury's bedroom door.

Bud Schwartz drove by slowly. 'Look at this shit,' he muttered. Once they had passed the house, he put some muscle into the accelerator.

'An army,' Lou said, 'that's what it was.'

Danny Pogue sank low in the back seat. With both hands he clutched the Macy's bag to his chest. 'Let's just go,' he said. 'Bud, let's just haul ass.'

TWENTY-NINE

On the morning of August 2, Jake Harp crawled into the back of a white limousine and rode in a dismal gin-soaked stupor to the construction site on North Key Largo. There he was met by Charles Chelsea, Francis X. Kingsbury and a phalanx of armed security men whose crisp blue uniforms failed to mitigate their shifty felonious smirks. The entourage moved briskly across a recently bulldozed plateau, barren except for a bright green hillock that was cordoned with rope and ringed by reporters, photographers and television cameramen. Kingsbury took Jake Harp by the elbow and, ascending the grassy knob, waved mechanically; it reminded Charles Chelsea of the rigidly determined way that Richard Nixon had saluted before boarding the presidential chopper for the final time. Except that, compared to Francis Kingsbury, Nixon was about as tense as Pee Wee Herman.

Jake Harp heard himself pleading for coffee, please God, even decaf, but Kingsbury seemed not to hear him. Jake Harp blinked amphibiously and struggled to focus on the scene. It was early. He was outdoors. The sun was intensely bright. The Atlantic Ocean murmured at his back. And somebody had dressed him: Izod shirt, Sansibelt slacks, tasseled Footjoy golf shoes. What could this be! Then he heard the scratchy click of a portable microphone and the oily voice of Charles Chelsea.

'Welcome, everybody. We're standing on what will soon be the first tee of the Falcon Trace Championship Golf Course. As you can see, we've got a little work ahead of us. . . .'

Laughter. These numbnuts are laughing, thought Jake Harp. He squinted at the white upturned faces and recognized one or two as sportswriters.

More from Chelsea: ' . . . and we thought it would be fun to inaugurate the construction of this magnificent golfing layout with a hitting clinic.'

Jake Harp's stomach clenched as somebody folded a three-wood into his fingers. The golf pro stared in disgust: a graphite head. They expect me to hit with metal!

Charles Chelsea's well-tanned paw settled amiably on Jake Harp's shoulder; the stench of Old Spice was overpowering.

'This familiar fellow needs no introduction,' Chelsea was saying. 'He's graciously agreed to christen the new course by hitting a few balls into the ocean—since we don't actually have a fairway yet.'

Laughter again. Mysterious, inexplicable laughter. Jake Harp swayed, bracing himself with the three-wood. What had he been drinking last night? Vodka sours? Tanqueray martinis? Possibly both. He remembered dancing with a banker's wife. He remembered telling her how he'd triple-bogeyed the Road Hole and missed the cut at the British Open; missed the damn cut, all because some fat Scotsman booted the ball. . . .

Jake Harp also remembered the banker's wife whispering something about a blowjob—but did it happen?

He hoped so, but he truly couldn't recall. One thing was certain: today he was physically incapable of swinging a golf club; it was simply out of the question. He wondered how he would break the news to Francis Kingsbury, who was bowing to the photographers in acknowledgment of Charles Chelsea's effusive introduction.

'Frank,' said Jake Harp. 'Where am I?'

With a frozen smile, Kingsbury remarked that Jake Harp looked about as healthy as dog barf.

'A bad night,' the golfer rasped. 'I'd like to go home and lie down.'

Then came an acrid gust of cologne as Chelsea leaned in: 'Hit a few, Jake, okay? No interviews, just a photo op.'

'But I can't use a fucking graphite wood. This is Jap voodoo, Frank, I need my MacGregors.'

Francis Kingsbury gripped Jake Harp by the shoulders and turned him toward the ocean. 'And would you please, for Christ's sake, try not to miss the goddamn ball?'

Chelsea cautioned Kingsbury to keep his voice down. The sportswriters were picking up on the fact that Jake Harp was seriously under the weather.

'Coffee's on the way,' Chelsea chirped lightly.

'You want me to hit it in the ocean?' Jake Harp said. 'This is nuts.'

One of the news photographers shouted for the security officers to get out of the way, they were blocking the picture. Kingsbury commanded the troops of Pedro Luz to move to one side; Pedro Luz himself was not present, having refused with vague mutterings to exit the storage room and join the phony golf clinic at Falcon Trace. His men, however, embraced with

CARL HIAASEN

gusto and amusement the task of guarding Francis X. Kingsbury from assailants unknown.

Having cleared the security force to make an opening for Jake Harp, Kingsbury ordered the golfer to swing away.

'I can't, Frank.'

'What?'

'I'm hung over. I can't lift the bloody club.'

'Assume the position, Jake. You're starting to piss me off.'

Tottering slightly, Jake Harp slowly arranged himself in the familiar stance that *Golf Digest* once hailed as 'part Hogan, part Nicklaus, part Baryshnikov'—chin down, feet apart, shoulders square, left arm straight, hands interlocked loosely on the shaft of the club.

'There,' Jake Harp said gamely.

Charles Chelsea cleared his throat. Francis Kingsbury said, 'A golf ball would help, Jake.'

'Oh Jesus, you're right.'

'You got everything but a goddamn ball.'

Under his breath, Jake Harp said, 'Frank, would you do me a favor? Tee it up?'

'What?'

'I can't bend down. I'm too hung over, Frank. If I try to bend, I'll fall on my face. I swear to God.'

Francis Kingsbury dug in his pocket and pulled out a scuffed Maxfli and a plastic tee that was shaped like a naked woman. 'You're quite an athlete, Jake. A regular Jim Fucking Thorpe.'

Gratefully Jake Harp watched Kingsbury drop to one knee and plant the tee. Then suddenly the sun exploded, and a molten splinter tore a hole in the golfer's belly, spinning him like a tenpin and knocking him flat. A darkening puddle formed as he lay there and floundered, gulping for breath through a mouthful of fresh Bermuda sod. Jake Harp was not too hung over to realize he could be dying, and it bitterly occurred to him that he would rather leave his mortal guts on the fairways of Augusta or Muirfield or Pebble Beach.

Anywhere but here.

Bud Schwartz and Danny Pogue had driven up to Kendall to break into a house. The house belonged to FBI Agent Billy Hawkins, who was still tied up as Molly McNamara's prisoner.

'Think he's got a dog?' said Danny Pogue.

Bud Schwartz said probably not. 'Guys like that, they think dogs are for pussies. It's a cop mentality.'

But Bud Schwartz was wrong. Bill Hawkins owned a German shepherd. The burglars could see the animal prowling the fence in the backyard.

'Guess we gotta do the front-door routine,' said Bud Schwartz. What a way to end a career: breaking into an FBI man's house in broad daylight. 'I thought we retired,' Bud Schwartz complained. 'All that dough we got, tell me what's the point if we're still pullin' these jobs.'

Danny Pogue said, 'Just this one more. And besides, what if Lou takes the money back?'

'No way.'

'If he can't get to the guy, yeah, he might. Already he thinks we tipped Kingsbury off, on account of all those rent-a-cops.'

Bud Schwartz said he wasn't worried about Lou going back on the deal. 'These people are pros, Danny.

Now gimme the scroogie.' They were poised at Billy Hawkins's front door. Danny Pogue checked the street for cars or pedestrians; then he handed Bud Schwartz a nine-inch screwdriver.

Skeptically Danny Pogue said, 'Guy's gotta have a deadbolt. Anybody works for the FBI, probably he's got an alarm, too. Maybe even lasers.'

But there was no alarm system. Bud Schwartz pried the doorjamb easily. He put his shoulder to the wood and pushed it open. 'You believe that?' he said to his partner. 'See what I mean about cop mentality. They think they're immune.'

'Yeah,' said Danny Pogue. 'Immune.' Later he'd ask Molly McNamara what it meant.

They closed the door and entered the empty house. Bud Schwartz would never have guessed that a federal agent lived there. It was a typical suburban Miami home: three bedrooms, two baths, nothing special. Once they got used to the idea, the burglars moved through the rooms with casual confidence—wife at work, kids at school, no sweat.

'Too bad we're not stealin' anything,' Bud Schwartz mused.

'Want to?' said his partner. 'Just for old times' sake.'

'What's the point?'

'I saw one of the kids has a CD player.'

'Wow,' said Bud Schwartz acidly. 'What's that, like, thirty bucks. Maybe forty?'

'No, man, it's a Sony.'

'Forget it. Now gimme the papers.'

In captivity Billy Hawkins had agreed to notify his family that he was out of town on a top-secret assignment. However, the agent had displayed a growing reluctance to call the FBI office and lie about being sick. To motivate him, Molly McNamara had composed a series of cryptic notes and murky correspondence suggesting that Hawkins was not the most loyal of government servants. Prominently included in the odd jottings were the telephone numbers of the Soviet Embassy and the Cuban Special Interest Section in Washington, D.C. For good measure, Molly had included a bank slip showing a suspicious $25,000 deposit to Agent Billy Hawkins's personal savings account—a deposit that Molly herself had made at the South Miami branch of Unity National Savings & Loan. The purpose of these maneuvers was to create a shady portfolio that, despite its sloppiness, Billy Hawkins would not wish to try to explain to his colleagues at the FBI.

Who would definitely come to the house in search of clues, if Agent Hawkins failed to check in.

Molly McNamara had entrusted the bank receipt, phone numbers and other manufactured evidence to Bud Schwartz and Danny Pogue, whose mission was to conceal the material in a semi-obvious location in Billy Hawkins's bedroom.

Bud Schwartz chose the second drawer of the nightstand. He placed the envelope under two unopened boxes of condoms. 'Raspberry-colored,' he marveled. 'FBI man uses raspberry rubbers!' Another stereotype shattered.

Danny Pogue was admiring a twelve-inch portable television as if it were a rare artifact. 'Jesus, Bud, you won't believe this.'

'Don't tell me it's a black-and-white.'

'Yep. You know the last time I saw one?'

'Little Havana,' said Bud Schwartz, 'that duplex off Twelfth Avenue. I remember.'

'Remember what we got for it.'

'Yeah. Thirteen goddamn dollars.' The fence was a man named Fat Jack on Seventy-ninth Street, near the Boulevard. Bud Schwartz couldn't stand Fat Jack not only because he was cheap but because he smelled like dirty socks. One day Bud Schwartz had boosted a case of Ban Extra Dry Roll-on Deodorant sticks from the back of a Publix truck, and given it to Fat Jack as a hint. Fat Jack had handed him eight bucks and said that nobody should ever use roll-ons because they cause cancer of the armpits.

'I don't get it,' said Danny Pogue. 'I thought the FBI paid big bucks—what's a baby Magnavox go for, two hundred retail? You'd think he could spring for color.'

'Who knows, maybe he spends it all on clothes. Come on, let's take off.' Bud Schwartz wanted to be long gone before the mailman arrived and noticed what had happened to the front door.

Danny Pogue turned on the portable TV and said, 'That's not a bad picture.' The noon news was just starting.

'I said let's go, Danny.'

'Wait, look at this!'

A video clip showed a heavyset man in golf shoes being hoisted on a stretcher. The man's shirt was drenched in blood, but his eyelids were half open. A plastic oxygen mask covered the man's face and nose, but the jaw moved as if he were trying to speak. The newscaster reported that the shooting had taken place at a new resort development called Falcon Trace, near Key Largo.

'Lou! He did it!' exclaimed Danny Pogue. 'You were right.'

'Only trouble is, that ain't Mr. Kingsbury.'

'You sure?'

Bud Schwartz sat down in front of the television. The anchorman had tossed the sniper story to a sportscaster, who was somberly recounting the stellar career of Jake Harp. The golfer's photograph, taken in happier times, popped up on a wide green mat behind the sports desk.

Danny Pogue said, 'Who the hell's that?'

'Not Kingsbury,' grunted Bud Schwartz. The mishap confirmed his worst doubts about Lou's qualifications as a hit man. It was unbelievable. The asshole had managed to shoot the wrong guy.

'Know what?' said Danny Pogue. 'There's a Jake Harp Cadillac in Boca Raton where I swiped a bunch of tape decks once. Is that the same guy? This golfer?'

Bud Schwartz said, 'I got no earthly idea.' What was all this crap the TV guy was yakking about—career earnings, number of Top Ten finishes, average strokes per round, percentage of greens hit in regulation. To Bud Schwartz, golf was as foreign as polo. Except you didn't see so many fat guys playing polo.

'The main thing is, did they catch the shooter?'

'Nuh-huh.' Danny Pogue had his nose to the tube. 'They said he got away in a boat. No arrests, no motives is what they said.'

Bud Schwartz was trying to picture Lou from Queens at the helm of a speedboat, racing for the ocean's horizon.

'He's gonna be pissed,' Danny Pogue said.

'Yeah, well, I don't guess his boss up North is gonna be too damn thrilled, either. Whackin' the wrong man.'

'He ain't dead yet. Serious but stable is what they said.'

Bud Schwartz said it didn't really matter. 'Point is, it's still a fuckup. A major *major* fuckup.'

The Mafia had gunned down a life member of the Professional Golfers Association.

Pedro Luz finally emerged from the storage room, where he had been measuring his penis. He rolled the wheelchair out to Kingsbury Lane for the morning rehearsal of the Summerfest Jubilee, a greatly embellished version of the nightly musical pageant. Pedro Luz needed something to lift his spirits. His leg had begun to throb in an excruciating way; no combination of steroids and analgesics put a dent in the pain. To add psychic misery to the physical, Pedro Luz had now documented the fact that his sexual wand was indeed shrinking as a result of prolonged steroid abuse. At first, Pedro Luz had assured himself that it was only an optical illusion; the more swollen his face and limbs became, the smaller everything else appeared to be. But weeks of meticulous calibrations had produced conclusive evidence: His wee-wee had withered from 10.4 centimeters to 7.9 centimeters in its flaccid state. Worse, it seemed to Pedro Luz (although there was no painless way to measure) that his testicles had also become smaller—not yet as tiny as BBs, as Churrito had predicted, but more like gumballs.

These matters weighed heavily on his mind as Pedro Luz sat in the broiling sun and watched the floats rumble by. He was hoping that the sight of Annette Fury's regal bosom would buoy his mood, and was disappointed to see that she had been replaced as Princess Golden Sun. The new actress looked familiar, but

Pedro Luz couldn't place the face. She was a very pretty girl, but the black wig needed some work, as did the costume—buckskin culottes and a fringed halter top. Her singing was quite lovely, much better than Annette's, but Pedro Luz would've preferred larger breasts. The lioness that shared the Seminole float was in no condition to rehearse; panting miserably in the humidity, the animal sprawled half-conscious on one side, thus thwarting the cat-straddling exit that culminated the princess's dramatic performance.

As the parade disbanded, Pedro Luz eased the wheelchair off the curb and approached the Seminole float. The pretty young singer was not to be seen; there was only the driver of the float and Dr. Kukor, the park veterinarian, who had climbed aboard to revive the heatstruck lioness. Dr. Kukor was plainly flabbergasted by the sight of Pedro Luz.

'I lost my foot in an accident,' the security chief explained.

Dr. Kukor hadn't noticed the missing foot. It was the condition of Pedro Luz's face, so grossly inflated, that had generated the horror. The man looked like a blowfish: puffed cheeks, bulging lips, teeny eyes wedged deep under a pimpled, protuberant brow.

To Pedro Luz, Dr. Kukor directed the most inane inquiry of a long and distinguished career: 'Are you all right?'

'Just fine. Where's the young lady?'

Dr. Kukor pointed, and Pedro Luz spun the wheelchair to see: Princess Golden Sun stood behind him. She was zipping a black Miami Heat warm-up jacket over the halter.

Pedro Luz introduced himself and said, 'I've seen you before, right?'

'It's possible,' said Carrie Lanier, who recognized him instantly as the goon who shot up her double-wide, the creep she'd run over with the car. She noticed the bandaged trunk of his leg, and felt a pang of guilt. It passed quickly.

'You sing pretty nice,' Pedro Luz said, 'but you could use a couple three inches up top. If you get my meaning.'

'Thanks for the advice.'

'I know a doctor who specializes in that sort of thing. Maybe I could get you a discount.'

'Actually,' said Carrie, patting her chest, 'I kind of like the little fellas just the way they are.'

'Suit yourself.' Pedro Luz scratched brutally at a raw patch on his scalp. 'I'm trying to figure where I saw you before. Take off the wig for a second, okay?'

Carrie Lanier pressed her hands to her eyes and began to cry—plaintive, racking sobs that attracted the concern of tourists and the other pageant performers.

Pedro Luz said, 'Hey, what's the matter?'

'It's not a wig!' Carrie cried. 'It's my real hair.' She turned and scampered down a stairwell into The Catacombs.

'Geez, I'm sorry,' said Pedro Luz, to no one. Flustered, he rolled full tilt toward the security office. Speeding downhill past the Wet Willy, he chafed his knuckles trying to brake the wheelchair. When he reached the chilled privacy of the storage room, he slammed the door and drove the bolt. In the blackness Pedro Luz probed for the string that turned on the ceiling's bare bulb; he found it and jerked hard.

The white light revealed a shocking scene. Someone

had entered Pedro's sanctuary and destroyed the delicate web of sustenance. Sewing shears had snipped the intravenous tubes into worthless inch-long segments, which littered the floor like plastic rice. The same person had sliced open every one of Pedro's unused IV bags; the wheelchair rested, literally, in a pond of liquid dextrose.

But by far the worst thing to greet Pedro Luz was the desolate sight of brown pill bottles, perhaps a half-dozen, open and empty on the floor. Whoever he was, the sonofabitch had flushed Pedro's anabolic steroids down the john. The ceramic pestle with which he had so lovingly powdered his Winstrols lay shattered beneath the toilet tank.

And, on the wall, a message in coral lipstick. Pedro Luz groaned and backed the wheelchair so he could read it easier. A wild rage heaved through his chest and he began to snatch items from the storage shelves and hurl them against the cinder block: nightsticks, gas masks, flashlights, handcuffs, cans of Mace, pistol grips, boxes of bullets.

Only when there was nothing left to throw did Pedro Luz stop to read the words on the wall again. Written in a loopy flamboyant script, the message said:

Good morning, Dipshit!
Just wanted you to know I'm not dead.
Have a nice day, and don't forget your Wheaties!

It was signed, 'Yours truly, J. Winder.'

Pedro Luz emitted a feral cry and aimed himself toward the executive gym, where he spent the next two hours alone on the bench press, purging the demons and praying for his testicles to grow back.

THIRTY

Somehow Charles Chelsea summoned the creative energy necessary for fabrication:

> Golf legend Jake Harp was accidentally shot Thursday during groundbreaking ceremonies for the new Falcon Trace Golf and Country Club Resort on North Key Largo.
>
> The incident occurred as Mr. Harp was preparing to hit a ball off what will be the first tee of the 6,970-yard championship golf course, which Mr. Harp designed himself. The golfer apparently was struck by a stray bullet from an unidentified boater, who may have been shooting at nearby sea gulls.
>
> Mr. Harp was listed in serious but stable condition after undergoing surgery at South Miami Hospital.
>
> 'This is a tragedy for the entire golfing world, professionals and amateurs alike,' said Francis X. Kingsbury, the developer of Falcon Trace, and a close personal friend of Mr. Harp.
>
> 'We're all praying for Jake to pull through,' added Kingsbury, who is also the founder and chairman of the Amazing Kingdom of Thrills, the popular family theme park adjacent to the sprawling Falcon Trace project.

By mid-afternoon Thursday, police had not yet arrested any suspects in the shooting. Charles Chelsea, vice president of publicity for Falcon Trace Ltd., disputed accounts by some reporters on the scene who claimed that Mr. Harp was the victim of a deliberate sniper attack.

'There's no reason to believe that this terrible event was anything but a freak accident,' Chelsea said.

Kingsbury approved the press release with a disgusted flick of his hand. He drained a third martini and asked Chelsea if he had ever before witnessed a man being shot.

'Not that I can recall, sir.'

'Close up, I mean,' Kingsbury said. 'Dead bodies are one thing—car wrecks, heart attacks—I'm not counting those. What I mean is, *bang*!'

Chelsea said, 'It happened so damn fast.'

'Well, you know who they were aiming at? *Moi*, that's who. How about that!' Kingsbury pursed his lips and drummed his knuckles.

'You?' Chelsea said. 'Who would try to kill you?' He instantly thought of Joe Winder.

But Kingsbury smiled drunkenly and began to hum the theme from *The Godfather*.

Chelsea said, 'There's something you're not telling me.'

'Of course there's something I'm not telling you. There's tons of shit I'm not telling you. What, I look like a total moron?'

Watching Francis Kingsbury pour another martini, Chelsea felt like seizing the bottle and guzzling himself

CARL HIAASEN

into a Tanqueray coma. The time had come to look
for another job; the fun had leaked out of this one.
A malevolent force, unseen and uncontrollable, had
perverted Chelsea's role from cheery town crier to conniving propagandist. Reflecting on the past weeks, he
realized he should've quit on the day the blue-tongued
voles were stolen, the day innocence was lost.

We are all no longer children, Chelsea thought
sadly. We are potential co-defendants.

'No offense,' Kingsbury was saying, 'but you're just
a flack. I only tell you what I've absolutely got to tell
you. Which is precious damned little.'

'That's the way it should be,' Chelsea said lifelessly.

'Right! Loose dicks sink ships. Or whatever.' Kingsbury slurped at the gin like a thirsty mutt. 'Anyhow,
don't worry about me. I'm taking—well, let's just say,
the necessary precautions. You can be goddamn sure.'

'That's wise of you.'

'Meanwhile, sharpen your pencil. I ordered us more
animals.' Kingsbury wistfully studied his drink. 'Who's
the guy in the Bible, the one with the ark. Was it Moses?'

'Noah,' Chelsea said. Boy, was the old man smashed.

'Yeah, Noah, that's who I feel like. Me and these
fucking critters. Anyhow, we're back in the endangered-
species business, saving the animals. There oughta be
some publicity when they get here. You see to it.'

The woman named Rachel Lark had phoned all the
way from New Zealand. She said she'd done her best
on such short notice, and said Kingsbury would be
pleased when he saw the new attractions for the Rare
Animal Pavilion. I hope so, he'd told her, because we
could damn sure use some good news.

Fearing the worst, Charles Chelsea said, 'What kind of animals are we talking about?'

'Cute is what I ordered. Thirty-seven hundred dollars' worth of cute.' Kingsbury snorted. 'Could be anything. The point is, we've got to rebound, Charlie. We got a fucking void to fill.'

'Right.'

'Speaking of which, we also need another golfer. In case Jake croaks, God forbid.'

Chelsea recoiled at the cold-bloodedness of the assignment. 'It won't look good, sir, not with what happened this morning. It's best if we stick by Jake.'

'Sympathy's all fine and dandy, Charlie, but we got more than golf at stake here. We got waterfront to sell. We got patio homes. We got club memberships. Can Jake Harp—don't get me wrong—but in his present situation can Jake do promotional appearances? TV commercials? Celebrity programs? We don't even know if Jake can still breathe, much less swing a fucking five-iron.'

For once Francis Kingsbury expressed himself in nearly cogent syntax. It must be excellent gin, Chelsea thought.

'I want you to call Nicklaus,' Kingsbury went on. 'Tell him money is no problem.'

'Jack Nicklaus,' the publicity man repeated numbly.

'No, *Irving* Nicklaus. Who the hell do you think! And if you can't get the Bear, try Palmer. And if you can't get Annie, you try Trevino. And if you can't get the Mex, try the Shark. And so on. The bigger the better, but make it quick.'

Knowing it would do no good, Chelsea reminded Kingsbury that he had tried to recruit the top golfing names when he was first planning Falcon Trace, and that they'd all said no. Only Jake Harp had the stomach to work for him.

'I don't care what they said before,' Kingsbury growled, 'you call 'em again. Money is no problem, all right?'

'Again, I'd just like to caution you about how this might appear to people—'

'I need a hotshot golfer, Charlie. The hell do you guys call it—a media personality?' Kingsbury raised one plump fist and let it fall heavily on the desk. 'I can't sell a golf resort when my star golfer's on a goddamn respirator. Don't you understand? Don't you know a goddamn thing about Florida real estate?'

They rode to the airport in edgy silence. Danny Pogue was waiting for Lou to say something. Like it was all *their* fault. Like the people in Queens wanted their money back.

Earlier Bud Schwartz had pulled his partner aside and said, look, they want the dough, we give it back. This is the mob, he said, and we're not playing games with the mob. But it's damned important, Bud Schwartz had said, that Lou and his Mafia people know that we didn't tip off Kingsbury. How the hell he found out about the hit, it don't matter. It wasn't us and we gotta make that clear, okay? Danny Pogue agreed wholeheartedly. Like Bud Schwartz, he didn't want to go through the rest of life having somebody else start his car every morning. Or peeking around corners, watching out for inconspicuous fat guys like Lou.

So when they got to the Delta Airlines terminal,

Danny Pogue shook Lou's hand and said he was very sorry about what had happened. 'Honest to God, we didn't tell nobody.'

'That's the truth,' said Bud Schwartz.

Lou shrugged. 'Probably a wire. Don't sweat it.'

'Thanks,' said Danny Pogue, flushed with relief. He pumped Lou's pudgy arm vigorously. 'Thanks for— well, just thanks is all.'

Lou nodded. His nose and cheeks were splashed pink with raw sunburn. He wore the same herringbone coat and striped shirt that he had when he'd gotten off the airplane. There was still no sign of the gun, but the burglars knew he was carrying it somewhere on his corpulent profile.

Lou said, 'Since I know you're dyin' to ask, what happened was this: the asshole bent over. Don't ask me why, but he bent over just as I pulled the trigger.'

'Bud thought you probably got the two guys mixed up—'

'I didn't get nobody mixed up.' Lou's upper lip curled when he directed this bulletin toward Bud Schwartz. 'The guy leaned over is all. Otherwise he'd be dead right now, trust me.'

Despite his doubts about Lou's marksmanship, Bud Schwartz didn't want him to leave Miami with hard feelings. He didn't want any hit man, even a clumsy one, to be sore at him.

'Could've happened to anybody,' Bud Schwartz said supportively. 'Sounds like one hell of a tough shot from the water, anyway.'

A voice on the intercom announced that the Delta flight to LaGuardia was boarding at Gate 7. Lou said, 'The guy that got hit, I heard he's hanging on.'

'Yeah, some golfer named Harp,' said Danny Pogue. 'Serious but stable.'

'Maybe he'll make it,' Lou said. 'That would be good.'

Bud Schwartz asked what would happen when Lou returned to Queens.

'Have a sitdown with my people. Find out what they want to do next. Then I got this big birthday party for my wife's fortieth. I bought her one a them electric woks—she really likes Jap food, don't ask me why.'

Danny Pogue said, 'Are you in big trouble?'

Lou's chest bounced when he laughed. 'With my wife or the boys? Ask me which is worse.'

He picked up his carry-on and the blue umbrella, and waddled for the gate.

Bud Schwartz waved. 'Sorry it got so screwed up.'

'What the hell,' said Lou, still laughing. 'I got me a nice boat ride outta the deal.'

Joe Winder and Carrie Lanier met Trooper Jim Tile at the Snapper Creek Plaza on the Turnpike extension. They took a booth at the Roy Rogers and ordered burgers and shakes. Winder found the atmosphere more pleasant than it had been at Ocean Reef. Carrie asked Jim Tile if he had phoned Rikers Island.

'Yeah, I called,' the trooper said. 'They thought it was crazy, but they said they'd watch for anything out of the ordinary.'

'Out of the ordinary hardly begins to describe him.'

'New Yorkers,' said Jim Tile, 'think they've cornered the market on psychopaths. They don't know Florida.'

Joe Winder said, 'I don't think he's going to Rikers Island. I think he's still here.'

'I heard about Harp,' said Jim Tile, 'and my opinion is no, it wasn't the governor. I'll put money on it.'

'How can you be so sure?' asked Carrie.

'Because (a) it's not his style, and (b) he wouldn't have missed.'

Winder said, 'Mr. X was the target.'

'Had to be,' agreed Jim Tile. 'Who'd waste a perfectly good bullet on a golfer?'

Carrie speculated that it could have been a disgruntled fan. Joe Winder threw an arm around her and gave her a hug. He'd been in a good mood since trashing Pedro Luz's steroid den.

The trooper was saying Skink might've headed upstate. 'This morning somebody shot up a Greyhound on the interstate outside Orlando. Sixty-seven Junior Realtors on their way to Epcot.'

Panic at Disney World! Winder thought. Kingsbury will come in his pants.

'Nobody was hurt,' Jim Tile said, 'which leads me to believe it was you-know-who.' He pried the plastic cap off his milkshake and spooned out the ice cream. 'Eight rounds into a speeding bus and nobody even gets nicked. That's one hell of a decent shot.'

Carrie said, 'I'm assuming they didn't catch the culprit.'

'Vanished without a trace,' said the trooper. 'If it's him, they'll never even find a footprint. He knows that area of the state very well.'

Winder said it was a long way to go for a man with two fresh gunshot wounds.

Jim Tile shrugged. 'I called Game and Fish. The

panther plane hasn't picked up the radio signal for days.'

'So he's really gone,' Carrie said.

'Or hiding in a bomb shelter.'

'Joe thinks we should go ahead and make a move. He's got a plan all worked out.'

Jim Tile raised a hand. 'Don't tell me, please. I don't want to hear it.'

'Fair enough,' Winder said, 'but I've got to ask a small favor.'

'The answer is no.'

'But it's nothing illegal.'

The trooper used the corner of a paper napkin to polish the lenses of his sunglasses. 'This falls into the general category of pressing your luck. Just because the governor gets away, don't think it's easy. Or even right.'

'Please,' said Carrie, 'just listen.'

'What is it you want me to do?'

'Your job,' Joe Winder replied. 'That's all.'

Later, in the rental boat, Joe Winder said he almost felt sorry for Charles Chelsea. 'Getting your sports celebrity shot with the press watching, that's tough.'

Carrie Lanier agreed that Chelsea was earning his salary. She was at the helm of the outboard, expertly steering a course toward the ocean shore of North Key Largo. A young man named Oscar sat shirtless on the bow, dangling his brown legs and drinking a root beer.

Carrie told Joe he had some strange friends.

'Oscar thinks he owes me a favor, that's all. Years

ago I left his name out of a newspaper article and it wound up saving his life.'

Carrie looked doubtful, but said nothing. Her hair was tied back in a ponytail. She wore amber sunglasses with green Day-Glo frames and a silver one-piece bathing suit. Oscar didn't stare, not even once. His mind was on business, and the soccer game he was missing on television. Most Thursdays he was on his way to Belize, only this morning there'd been a minor problem with Customs, and the flight was canceled. When Joe Winder called him at the warehouse, Oscar felt honor-bound to lend a hand.

'He thinks I cut him a break,' Winder whispered to Carrie, 'but the fact is, I *did* use his name in the story. It just got edited out for lack of space.'

'What was the article about?'

'Gunrunning.'

From the bow, Oscar turned and signaled that they were close enough now. Kneeling on the deck, he opened a canvas duffel and began to arrange odd steel parts on a chamois cloth. The first piece that Carrie saw was a long gray tube.

'Oscar's from Colombia,' Joe Winder explained. 'His brother's in the M-19. They're leftist rebels.'

'Thank you, Professor Kissinger.' Carrie smeared the bridge of her nose with mauve-colored zinc oxide. It was clear from her attitude that she had reservations about this phase of the plan.

She said, 'What makes you think Kingsbury needs another warning? I mean, he's got the mob after him, Joe. Why should he care about a couple of John Deeres?'

'He's a developer. He'll care.' Winder leaned back

and squinted at the sun. 'Keep the pressure on, that's the key.'

Carrie admired the swiftness with which Oscar went about his task. She said to Winder: 'Tell me again what they call that.'

'An RPG. Rocket-propelled grenade.'

'And you're positive no one's going to get hurt?'

'It's lunch hour, Carrie. You heard the whistle.' He took out a pair of waterproof Zeiss binoculars and scanned the shoreline until he found the stand of pigeon plums that Molly McNamara had told him about. The dreaded bulldozers had multiplied from two to five; they were parked in a semicircle, poised for the mission against the plum trees.

'Everybody's on their break,' Winder reported. 'Even the deputies.' At the other end of the boat, Oscar assembled the grenade launcher in well-practiced silence.

Carrie cut the twin Evinrudes and let the currents nudge the boat over the grassy shallows. She took the field glasses and tried to spot the bird nest that Molly had mentioned. She couldn't see anything, the hard-woods were so dense.

'I'm not sure I understand the significance of this gesture,' she said. 'Mockingbirds aren't exactly endan-gered.'

'These ones are.' Winder peeled off his T-shirt and tied it around his forehead like a bandanna. The air stuck to his chest like a hot rag; the temperature on the water was ninety-four degrees, and no breeze. 'You don't approve,' he said to Carrie. 'I can tell.'

'What bothers me is the lack of imagination, Joe.

You could be blowing up bulldozers the rest of your life.'

The words stung, but she was right. Clever this was not, merely loud. 'I'm sorry,' he said, 'but there wasn't time to come up with something more creative. The old lady said they were taking out the plum trees this afternoon, and it looks like she was right.'

Oscar gave the okay sign from the bow. The boat had drifted close enough so they could hear the voices and lunchtime banter of the Falcon Trace construction crew.

'Which dozer you want?' Oscar inquired, raising the weapon to his shoulder.

'Take your pick.'

'Joe, wait!' Carrie handed him the binoculars. 'Over there, check it out.'

Winder beamed when he spotted it. 'Looks like they're pouring the slab for the clubhouse.'

'That's a large cement mixer,' Carrie noted.

'Sure is. A *very* large cement mixer.' Joe Winder snapped his fingers and motioned to Oscar. Spying the new target, the young Colombian smiled broadly and readjusted his aim.

In a low voice Carrie said, 'I take it he's done this sort of thing before.'

'I believe so, yes.'

Oscar grunted something in Spanish, then pulled the trigger. The RPG took out the cement truck quite nicely. An orange gout of flame shot forty feet into the sky, and warm gray gobs of cement rained down on the construction workers as they sprinted for their cars.

'See,' Carrie said. 'A little variety's always nice.'

Joe Winder savored the smoky scent of chaos and wondered what his father would have thought.

We all shine on.

That night Carrie banished him from the bedroom while she practiced her songs for the Jubilee. At first he listened in dreamy amazement at the door; her voice was crystalline, delicate, soothing. After a while Bud Schwartz and Danny Pogue joined him in the hallway, and Carrie's singing seemed to soften their rough convict features. Danny Pogue lowered his eyes and began to hum along; Bud Schwartz lay on the wooden floor with hands behind his head and gazed at the high pine beams. Molly McNamara even unlocked the door to the adjoining bedroom so that Agent Billy Hawkins, gagged but alert, could enjoy the beautiful musical interlude.

Eventually Joe Winder excused himself and slipped downstairs to make a call. He went through three telephone temptresses before they switched him to Nina's line.

'I'm glad it's you,' she said. 'There's something you've got to hear.'

'I'm honestly not in the mood—'

'This is different, Joe. It took three nights to write.'

What could he possibly say? 'Go ahead, Nina.'

'Ready?' She was so excited. He heard the rustle of paper. Then she took a breath and began to read:

'Your hands find me in the night, burrow for my warmth.
Lift me, turn me, move me apart.
The language of blind insistence,

You speak with a slow tongue on my belly,
An eyelash fluttering against my nipple.
This is the moment of raw cries and murmurs when
Nothing matters in the vacuum of passion
But passion itself.'

He wasn't sure if she had finished. It sounded like a big ending, but he wasn't sure.

'Nina?'

'What do you think?'

'It's . . . vivid.'

'Poetry. A brand-new concept in phone sex.'

'Interesting.' God, she's making a career of this.

'Did it arouse you?'

'Definitely,' he said. 'My loins surge in wild tumescence inside my jeans.'

'Stop it, Joe!'

'I'm sorry. Really it's quite good.' And maybe it was. He knew next to nothing about poetry.

'I wanted to try something different,' Nina said, 'something literate. A few of the girls complained— Miriam, of course. She's more comfortable with the old sucky-fucky.'

'Well,' Winder said, 'it's all in the reading.'

'My editor wants to see more.'

'You have an editor?'

'For the syndication deal, Joe. What'd you think of the last part? *Nothing matters in the vacuum of passion but passion itself.*'

He said, ' "Abyss" is better than "vacuum." '

'The abyss of passion! You're right, Joe, that's much better.'

'It's a long way from dry-humping on the Amtrak.'

Nina laughed. He had almost forgotten how wonderful it sounded.

'So how was your hot date with The Voice?'

'It was very enjoyable. He's an exceptional man.'

'What does he do?'

Without skipping a beat: 'He markets General Motors products.'

'Cars? He sells cars! That *is* exceptional.'

Nina said, 'I don't want to talk about this.'

'Buicks? Pontiacs? Oldsmobiles? Or perhaps all three?'

'He is a surprisingly cultured man,' Nina said. 'An educated man. And it's Chevrolets, for your information. The light-truck division.'

'Boy.' Winder felt exhausted. First the poetry, now this. 'Nina, I've got to ask. Does the face match the voice?'

'There's nothing wrong with the way he looks.'

'Say no more.'

'You can be such a prick,' she observed.

'You're right. I'm sorry—again.'

'He wants to marry me.'

'Showing excellent taste,' Winder said. 'He'd be nuts if he didn't.'

There was a brief pause, then Nina asked: 'Are you the one who shot the golfer?'

'Nope. But I don't blame you for wondering.'

'Please don't kill anybody, Joe. I know how strongly you feel about these issues, but please don't murder anyone.'

'I'll try not to.'

'Better sign off,' she said. 'I'm tying up the phone.'

'Hey, I'm a paying customer.'

'You really liked the poem?'

'It was terrific, Nina. I'm very proud.'

He could tell she was pleased. 'Any more suggestions?' she said.

'Well, the line about the nipple.'

'Yes. *An eyelash fluttering against my nipple.*'

'The imagery is nice,' Winder said, 'but it makes it sound like you've got just one. Nipple, I mean.'

'Hmm,' said Nina. 'That's a good point.'

'Otherwise it's great.'

'Thanks, Joe,' she said. 'Thanks for everything.'

THIRTY-ONE

Joe Winder held Carrie in his arms and wondered why the women he loved were always a step or two ahead of him.

'So what are you planning?' he asked.

She stirred but didn't answer. Her cheek felt silky and warm against his chest. When would he ever learn to shut up and enjoy the moment?

'Carrie, I know you're not asleep.'

Her eyes opened. Even in the darkness he could feel the liquid stare. 'You're the only man I've ever been with,' she said, 'who insists on talking afterward.'

'You inspire me, that's all.'

'Aren't you exhausted?' She raised her head. 'Was I hallucinating, or did we just fuck our brains out?'

Winder said, 'I'm nervous as hell. I've been rehearsing it all in my head.'

She told him to stop worrying and go to sleep. 'What's the worst thing that could happen?'

'Jail is a distinct possibility. Death is another.'

Carrie turned on her belly and slid between his legs. Then she propped her elbows on his rib cage, and rested her chin on her hands.

'What are you smiling at?' Winder said.

'It's all going to work out. I've got faith in you.'

'But you're planning something, just the same.'

'Joe, it might be my only chance.'

'At what?'

'Singing. I mean really singing. Am I hurting you?'

'Oh, no, you're light as a feather.'

'You asshole,' she giggled, and began to tickle him ferociously. Winder locked his legs around her thighs and flipped her over in the sheets.

They were kissing when he felt compelled to pull back and say, 'I'm sorry I dragged you into this mess.'

'What mess? And, besides, you're doing the honest thing. Even if it's slightly mad.'

'You're speaking of the major felonies?'

'Of course,' Carrie said. 'But your motives are absolutely pure and unassailable. I'll be cheering for you, Joe.'

'Clinical insanity isn't out of the question,' he said. 'Just thinking about Kingsbury and that damn golf course, I get noises inside my skull.'

'What kind of noises?'

'Hydraulic-type noises. Like the crusher on a garbage truck.'

Carrie looked concerned, and he couldn't blame her. 'It goes back to my old man,' he said.

'Don't think about it so much, Joe.'

'I'd feel better if the governor were here. Just knowing I wasn't the only lunatic—'

'I had a dream about him,' she said quietly. 'I dreamed he broke into prison and killed that guy— what's his name?'

'Mark Chapman,' said Winder. 'Mark David Chapman.'

She heard sadness in the reply, sadness because she

didn't remember the details. 'Joe, I was only fourteen when it happened.'

'You're right.'

'Besides, I've always been lousy with names. Oswald, Sirhan, Hinkley—it's easy to lose track of these idiots.'

'Sure is,' Winder agreed.

Carrie tenderly laced her hands on the back of his neck. 'Everything's going to be fine. And no, you're not crazy. A little zealous is all.'

'It's not a bad plan,' he said.

'Joe, it's a terrific plan.'

'And if all goes well, you'll still have your job.'

'No, I don't think so. I'm not much of a Seminole go-go dancer.'

Now it was his turn to smile. 'I take it there may be some last-minute changes in the musical program.'

'Quite possibly,' Carrie said.

He kissed her softly on the forehead. 'I'll be cheering for you, too.'

'I know you will, Joe.'

As far as Bud Schwartz was concerned, he'd rather be in jail than in a hospital. Practically everyone he ever knew who died—his mother, his brother, his uncles, his first probation officer—had died in hospital beds. In fact, Bud Schwartz couldn't think of a single person who'd come out of a hospital in better shape than when they'd gone in.

'What about babies?' Danny Pogue said.

'Babies don't count.'

'What about your boy? Mike, Jr., wasn't he borned in a hospital?'

'Matter of fact, no. It was the back of a Bronco. And his name is *Bud*, Jr., like I told you.' Bud Schwartz rolled down the window and tried to spit the toothpick from the corner of his mouth. It landed on his arm. 'A hospital's the last place for a sick person to go,' he said.

'You think she'll die there?'

'No. I don't wanna set foot in the place is all.'

'Jesus, you're a cold shit.'

Bud Schwartz was startled by his partner's anger. Out of pure guilt he relented and agreed to go, but only for a few minutes. Danny Pogue seemed satisfied. 'Let's get some roses on the way.'

'Fine. A lovely gesture.'

'Hey, it'll mean a lot to her.'

'Danny, this is the same woman who shot us. And you're talking flowers.'

Molly McNamara had driven herself to Baptist Hospital after experiencing mild chest pains. She had a private room with a gorgeous view of a parking deck.

When he saw her shriveled in the bed, Danny Pogue gulped desperately to suppress the tears. Bud Schwartz also was jarred by the sight—she looked strikingly pallid and frail. And small. He'd never thought of Molly McNamara as a small woman, but that's how she appeared in the hospital: small and caved-in. Maybe because all that glorious white hair was stuffed under a paper cap.

'The flowers are splendid,' she said, lifting the thin plastic tube that fed extra oxygen to her nostrils.

Danny Pogue positioned the vase on the bedstand, next to the telephone. 'American Beauty roses,' he said.

'So I see.'

The burglars stood on opposite sides of the bed. Molly reached out and held their hands.

She said, 'A touch of angina, that's all. I'll be as good as new in a few days.'

Danny Pogue wondered if angina was contagious; it sounded faintly sexual. 'The house is fine,' he said. 'The disposal jammed this morning, but I fixed it myself.'

'A spatula got stuck,' Bud Schwartz added. 'Don't ask how.'

Molly said, 'How is Agent Hawkins?'

'Same as ever.'

'Are you feeding him?'

'Three times a day, just like you told us.'

'Are his spirits improved?'

'Hard to tell,' Bud Schwartz said. 'He don't talk much with all that tape on his face.'

'I heard about the golfer being shot,' said Molly. 'Mr. Kingsbury's had quite a run of bad luck, wouldn't you say?' She asked the question with a trace of a smile. Danny Pogue glanced down at his shoes.

To change the subject, Bud Schwartz asked if there was a cafeteria in the hospital. 'I could sure use a Coke.'

'Make that two,' said Danny Pogue. 'And a lemonade for Molly.'

'Yes, that would hit the spot. Or maybe a ginger ale, something carbonated.' She patted Danny Pogue's hand. Again he looked as if he were about to weep.

In the elevator Bud Schwartz couldn't shake the vision of the old woman sunken in bed. It was all Kingsbury's fault—Molly hadn't felt right since those bastards beat her up at the condo. That one of them had been gunned down later by a baboon was only a partial consolation; the other goon, the one with nine fingertips, was still loose. Joe Winder had said don't worry, they'll all pay—but what did Winder know about the law of the street? He was a writer, for Chrissakes. A goddamn dreamer. Bud Schwartz had agreed to help but he couldn't pretend to share Winder's optimism. As a lifelong criminal, he knew for a fact that the bad guys seldom get what they deserve. More often they just plain get away, even assholes who beat up old ladies.

Bud Schwartz was so preoccupied that he got off on the wrong floor and found himself standing amidst throngs of cooing relatives at the window of the nursery. He couldn't believe the number of newborn babies—it baffled him, left him muttering while others clucked and pointed and sighed. In a world turning to shit, why were so many people still having children? Maybe it was a fad, like CB radios and Cabbage Patch dolls. Or maybe these men and women didn't understand the full implications of reproduction.

More victims, thought Bud Schwartz, the last damn thing we need. He gazed at the rows of sleeping infants, crinkly and squinty-eyed and blissfully innocent, and silently foretold their future. They would grow up to have automobiles and houses and apartments that would all, eventually, be burglarized by lowlifes such as himself.

When Bud Schwartz returned to Molly McNamara's room, he sensed he was interrupting something private. Danny Pogue, who had been talking in a low voice, became silent at the sight of his partner.

Molly thanked Bud Schwartz for the cup of ginger ale. 'Danny's got something to tell you,' she said.

'Yeah?'

'I must admit,' Molly said, 'he left me speechless.'

'So let's hear it already.'

Danny Pogue lifted his chin and thrust out his bony chest. 'I decided to give my share of the money to Molly.'

'Not to me personally,' she interjected. 'To the Mothers of Wilderness.'

'And the Wildlife Rescue Corps!'

'Unofficially, yes,' she said.

'The mob money,' Danny Pogue explained.

Bud Schwartz didn't know whether to laugh or scream. 'Twenty-five grand? You're just givin' it away?'

Molly beamed. 'Isn't that a magnificent gesture?'

'Oh, magnificent,' said Bud Schwartz. Magnificently stupid.

Danny Pogue picked up on his partner's sarcasm and tried to mount a defense. He said, 'It's just somethin' I wanted to do, okay?'

'Fine by me.'

Molly said, 'It automatically makes him a Golden Lifetime Charter Member!'

'It also automatically makes him broke.'

'Come on,' Danny Pogue said, 'it's for a good cause.'

Bud Schwartz's eyes narrowed. 'Don't even think about asking.'

'Danny, he's right,' said Molly. 'It's not fair to pressure a friend.'

Warily Bud Schwartz scanned Molly's bed sheets for any lumps that might reveal the outline of a pistol. He said, 'Look, I wanna go straight. That money's my future.'

Danny Pogue rolled his eyes and snorted. 'Cut the bull—I mean, don't kid yourself. All we're ever gonna be is thieves.'

'Now there's a happy thought. That's what I mean about you and your fucking attitude.'

To Danny Pogue's relief, Molly barely flinched at the profane adjective. She said, 'Bud, I respect your ambitions. I really do.'

But Danny Pogue wasn't finished whining. 'Man, at least can't you spare *some*thing?'

For several moments the only sound was the muted whistle of Molly's oxygen machine. Finally she said, in a voice creaky with fatigue, 'Even a small donation would be appreciated.'

Bud Schwartz ground his molars. 'How does a grand sound? Is that all right?' Christ, he must be insane. One thousand dollars to a bunch of blue-haired bunny huggers!

Molly McNamara smiled kindly. Danny Pogue exuberantly chucked him on the shoulder.

Bud Schwartz said, 'Why don't I feel wonderful about this?'

'You will,' Molly replied, 'someday.'

Among the men hired by Pedro Luz as security officers was Diamond J. Love, Diamond being his given name and the 'J' standing for Jesus. As was true with most of the guards at the Amazing Kingdom of Thrills, Diamond J. Love's personal history was investigated with only enough diligence to determine the absence of outstanding felony warrants. It was a foregone conclusion that Diamond J. Love's career in law enforcement had been derailed by unpleasant circumstances; there was no other logical reason for applying as a private security guard at a theme park.

Initially, Diamond J. Love was apprehensive about his employment chances at the Amazing Kingdom. He knew that Disney World and other family resorts were scrupulous about hiring clean-cut, enthusiastic, All-American types; Diamond J. Love was worried because in all ways he defied the image, but he need not have worried. Nobody from the Amazing Kingdom bothered to check with previous employers, such as the New York City Police Department, to inquire about allegations of bribery, moral turpitude, substance abuse, witness tampering and the unnecessary use of deadly force, to wit, the pistol-whipping of a young man suspected of shoplifting a bag of cheese-flavored Doritos.

Diamond J. Love was elated to be hired for the security force at the Amazing Kingdom, and pleased to find himself surrounded with colleagues of similarly checkered backgrounds. On slow days, when they weren't breaking into the RVs of tourists, they'd sit around and swap stories about the old police days—tales of stacking the civil-service boards to beat a brutality rap; perjuring themselves silly before grand juries; rounding up hookers on phony vice sweeps just to cop a free hummer; switching kilos of baking soda for cocaine in the evidence rooms. Diamond J. Love enjoyed these bull sessions, and he enjoyed his job. For the most part.

The only area of concern was the boss himself, a monster steroid freak whose combustible mood swings had prompted several of his own officers to leave their holsters permanently unsnapped, just in case. Some days Pedro Luz was reasonable and coherent, other days he was a drooling psycho. The news that he had chewed off his own foot only heightened the anxiety level on the security squad; even the potheads were getting jumpy.

Which is why Diamond J. Love did not wish to be late for work on this very important morning, and why he reacted with exceptionally scathing impudence to the mild-mannered inquiry of a black state trooper who had pulled over his car on County Road 905.

'May I see your driver's license, please?'

'Get serious, Uncle Ben.'

From there it went downhill. The trooper was singularly unimpressed by Diamond J. Love's expired NYPD police badge; nor was he particularly understanding on the issue of Diamond J. Love's outdated New York driver's license. Or the fact that, according to some computer, the serial numbers on Diamond J. Love's Camaro matched precisely those of a Camaro stolen eight months earlier in New Smyrna Beach.

'That's bullshit,' suggested Diamond J. Love.

'Please get out of the car,' the trooper said.

At which point Diamond J. Love attempted to speed away, and instead felt himself dragged by the collar through the window and deposited face-first on the macadam. Upon regaining consciousness, Diamond J. Love discovered Plasticuffs cinched painfully to his wrists and ankles. He further was surprised to see that he shared his predicament with several other security guards, who had apparently encountered the highway patrol on the pre-dawn journey to the Amazing Kingdom of Thrills. There sat Ossie Cano, former Seattle robbery detective-turned-fence; William Z. Ames, former Orlando patrolman-turned-pornographer; Neal 'Bart' Bartkowski, former sergeant with the Atlanta police, currently appealing a federal conviction for tax evasion.

'The hell's going on here?' demanded Diamond J. Love.

'Roadblock,' Cano replied.

'A one-man roadblock?'

'I heard him radio for backup.'

'But still,' said Diamond J. Love. 'One guy?'

By sunrise there were nine of them handcuffed or otherwise detained, a row of sullen penguins lined up along County Road 905. Basically it was the Amazing Kingdom's entire security force, except for Pedro Luz and one other guard, who had spent the night at the amusement park.

Trooper Jim Tile was impressed by the accuracy of Joe Winder's intelligence, particularly the make and license numbers of the guards' personal cars—information pilfered by Carrie Lanier from the files of the Personnel Department. Jim Tile was also impressed that not a single one of the guards had a clean record; to a man there arose problems with driver's licenses, expired registration stickers, doctored title certificates or unpaid traffic tickets. Each of the nine attempted to slide out of the road check by flashing outdated police ID— 'badging,' in cop vernacular. Two of the nine had offered Jim Tile a whispered inducement of either cash or narcotics; three others had sealed their fate by making racial remarks. All had been disarmed and handcuffed so swiftly, and with such force, that physical resistance had been impossible.

When the van from the Monroe County Sheriff's Office arrived, the deputy's eyes swept from Jim Tile to the cursing horde of prisoners and back again.

The deputy said, 'Jimmy, you do this all by yourself?'

'One at a time,' the trooper answered. 'A road check, that's all.'

'I know some of these boys.'

'Figured you might.'

'We lookin' at anything serious?'

'We're considering it.'

From the end of the line came an outcry from Diamond J. Love: 'Dwight, you gonna let this nigger get away with it?'

Jim Tile gave no indication of hearing the remark. The deputy named Dwight did, however. 'Damndest thing,' he said in a hearty voice. 'The air-conditioning broke down in the paddy wagon. Just now happened.'

The trooper said, 'What a shame.'

'Gonna be a long trip back to the substation.'

'Probably gets hot as hell inside that van.'

'Like an oven,' Dwight agreed with a wink.

'Fuck you!' shouted Diamond J. Love. 'Fuck the both of you.'

The phone bleeped in Charles Chelsea's apartment at seven-fifteen. It might as well have been a bomb.

'That fucking Pedro, I can't find him!' Who else but Francis X. Kingsbury.

'Have you tried the gym?' Chelsea said foggily.

'I tried everywhere, hell, you name it. And there's no guards! I waited and waited, finally said fuck it and drove myself to work.' He was on the speaker phone, hollering as he stormed around the office.

'The security men never showed up?'

'Wake up, dicklick! I'm alone, *comprende*? No Pedro, no guards, *nada*.'

Dicklick? Charles Chelsea sat up in bed and shook his head like a spaniel. Do I really deserve to be called a dicklick? Is that what I get for all my loyalty?

Kingsbury continued to fulminate: 'So where in the name of Christ Almighty is everybody? Today of all days—is there something you're not telling me, Charlie?'

'I haven't heard a thing, sir. Let me check into it.'

'You do that!' And he was gone.

Chelsea dragged himself to the kitchen and fine-tuned the coffee-maker. In less than two hours, some lucky customer would breach the turnstiles at the Amazing Kingdom of Thrills and be proclaimed the Five-Millionth Visitor. Officially, at least. Chelsea was fairly certain that at least one enterprising journalist would take the time to add up the park's true attendance figures and expose the promotion for the hoax that it was. The scene was set for a historic publicity disaster; already the national newsmagazines and out-of-state papers were snooping around, waiting for poor Jake Harp to expire. In recent days Chelsea's office had been deluged with applications for media credentials from publications that previously had displayed no interest in covering the Amazing Kingdom's Summerfest Jubilee. Chelsea wasn't naive enough to believe that the New York *Daily News* was seriously interested in a feature profile of the engineer who'd designed the Wet Willy water slide; no, their presence was explained by pure rampant bloodlust. The kidnapped mango voles, the dead scientist, the dead Orky, the nearly dead Jake Harp, flaming bulldozers, phony snake invasions, exploding cement trucks—an irresistible convergence of violence, mayhem and mortality!

Charles Chelsea understood that the dispatches soon to be filed from the Amazing Kingdom of Thrills wouldn't be bright or warm or fluffy. They would be dark and ominous and chilling. They would describe a screaming rupture of the civil order, a culture in terminal moral hemorrhage.

And this would almost certainly have a negative effect on tourism. Oh well, Chelsea thought, I gave it my best.

He foraged in the refrigerator, unearthed a stale bagel and began gnawing dauntlessly. Hearing a knock at the door, he assumed that the pathologically impatient Kingsbury had sent a car for him.

'Just a second!' Chelsea called, and went to put on a robe.

When he opened the door, he faced the immutable, bewhiskered grin of Robbie Raccoon.

Who was holding, in his three-fingered polyester paw, a gun.

Which was pointed at Charles Chelsea's throat.

'What's this?' croaked the publicity man.

'Show time,' said Joe Winder.

THIRTY-TWO

The raccoon suit was musty and stifling, but it smelled reassuringly of Carrie's hair and perfume. Even the lint seemed familiar. Through slits in the cheeks Joe Winder was able to see the procession: Bud Schwartz, Danny Pogue and the captive Charles Chelsea, entering the gates of the Amazing Kingdom of Thrills.

To affect Robbie Raccoon's most recognizable mannerisms, Winder took floppy exaggerated steps (the way Carrie had showed him) and jauntily twirled the bushy tail. In spite of the serious circumstances, he felt a bolt of childlike excitement as the amusement park prepared to open for the Summerfest Jubilee. Outside, the trams were delivering waves of eager tourists—the children stampeding rabidly toward the locked turnstiles; the women bravely toting infants and designer baby bags; the men with shoulder-mounted Camcorders aimed at anything that moved. Fruity-colored balloons decorated every lamppost, every shrubbery, every concession; Broadway show tunes blasted through tinny public-address speakers. Mimes and jugglers and musicians rehearsed on street corners while desultory maintenance crews collected cigarette butts, Popsicle sticks and gum wrappers off the pavement. A cowboy from the Wild

Bill Hiccup show tested his six-shooter by firing blanks at Petey Possum's scraggly bottom.

'Show business,' said Joe Winder, 'is my life.' The words echoed inside the plaster animal head.

If the costume had a serious flaw (besides the non-functioning air conditioner), it was a crucial lack of peripheral vision. The slits, located several inches below Robbie Raccoon's large plastic eyes, were much too narrow. Had the openings been wider, Winder would have spotted the fleshy pale hand in time to evade it.

It was the hand of famed TV weatherman Willard Scott, and it dragged Joe Winder in front of a camera belonging to the National Broadcasting Company. Danny Pogue, Bud Schwartz and Charles Chelsea stopped in their tracks: Robbie Raccoon was on the 'Today Show.' *Live.* Willard flung one meaty arm around Winder's shoulders, and the other around a grandmother from Hialeah who said she was 107 years old. The old woman was telling a story about riding Henry Flagler's railroad all the way to Key West.

'A hunnert and seven!' marveled Danny Pogue.

Charles Chelsea shifted uneasily. Bud Schwartz shot him a look. 'What, she's lying?'

Morosely the publicity man confessed. 'She's a complete fake. A ringer. I arranged the whole thing.' The burglars stared as if he were speaking another language. Chelsea lowered his voice: 'I *had* to do it. Willard wanted somebody over a hundred years old, they told me he might not come, otherwise. But I couldn't find anyone over a hundred—ninety-one was the best I could do, and the poor guy was completely spaced. Thought he was Rommel.'

Danny Pogue whispered, 'So who's she?'

'A local actress,' Chelsea said. 'Age thirty-eight. The makeup is remarkable.'

'Christ, this is what you do for a living?' Bud Schwartz turned to his partner. 'And I thought *we* were scumballs.'

To the actress, Willard Scott was saying: 'You're here to win that 300-Z, aren't you, sweetheart? In a few minutes the park opens and the first lucky customer through the gate will be Visitor Number Five Million. They'll get the new sports car and all kinds of great prizes!'

'I'm so excited!' the actress proclaimed.

'You run along now, but be careful getting in line. The folks are getting pretty worked up out there. Good luck, sweetheart!' Then Willard Scott gave the bogus 107-year-old grandmother a slurpy smooch on the ear. As he released his grip on the woman, he tightened his hug on Joe Winder.

And an awakening nation heard the famous weatherman say: 'This ring-tailed rascal is one of the most popular characters here at the Amazing Kingdom of Thrills. Go ahead, tell us your name.'

And in a high squeaky voice, Joe Winder gamely replied: 'Hi, Willard! My name is Robbie Raccoon.'

'You're certainly a big fella, Robbie. Judging by the size of that tummy, I'd say you've been snooping through a few garbage cans!'

To which Robbie Raccoon responded: 'Look who's talking, lard-ass.'

Briefly the smile disappeared from Willard's face, and his eyes searched desperately off-camera for the director. A few feet away, Charles Chelsea tasted bile creeping up his throat. The burglars seemed pleased to be standing so close to a genuine TV star.

A young woman wearing earphones and a jogging suit held up a cue card, and valiantly the weatherman attempted to polish off the segment: 'Well, spirits are obviously running high for the big Summerfest Jubilee, so pack up the family and come down to'—here Willard paused to find his place on the card—'Key Largo, Florida, and enjoy the fun! You can swim with a real dolphin, or go sliding headfirst down the Wet Willy or bust some broncos with Wild Bill Hiccup. And you kids can get your picture taken with all your favorite animal characters, even Robbie Raccoon.'

Obligingly Joe Winder cocked his head and twirled his tail. Willard appeared to regain his jolly demeanor. He prodded at something concealed under one of the fuzzy raccoon arms. 'It looks like our ole pal Robbie's got a surprise for Uncle Willard, am I right?'

From Winder came a strained chirp: ''Fraid not, Mr. Scott.'

'Aw, come on. Whatcha got in that paw?'

'*Nothing.*'

'Let's see it, you little scamp. Is it candy? A toy? Whatcha got there?'

And seventeen million Americans heard Robbie Raccoon say: 'That would be a gun, Willard.'

Chelsea's ankles got rubbery and he began to sway. The burglars each grabbed an elbow.

'My, oh, my,' Willard Scott said with a nervous chuckle. 'It even *looks* like a real gun.'

'Doesn't it, though,' said the giant raccoon.

Please, thought Bud Schwartz, not on national TV. Not with little kids watching.

But before anything terrible could happen, Willard Scott adroitly steered the conversation from firearms to a tropical depression brewing in the eastern Caribbean. Joe Winder was able to slip away when the weatherman launched into a laxative commercial.

On the path to the Cimarron Saloon, Charles Chelsea and the burglars heard howling behind them; a rollicking if muffled cry that emanated from deep inside the globular raccoon head.

'Aaaahhh-ooooooooooo,' Joe Winder sang. 'We're the werewolves of Florida! Aaaahhh-ooooooooooo!'

The smoke from Moe Strickland's cigar hung like a purple shroud in The Catacombs. Uncle Ely's Elves had voted unanimously to boycott the Jubilee, and Uncle Ely would honor their decision.

'The cowboy getups look stupid,' he agreed.

The actor who played the elf Jeremiah, and sometimes Dumpling, lit a joint to counteract the stogie fumes. He declared, 'We're not clowns, we're actors. So fuck Kingsbury.'

'That's right,' said another elf. 'Fuck Mr. X.'

Morale in the troupe had been frightfully low since the newspapers had picked up the phony story about a hepatitis outbreak. Several of the actor-elves had advocated changing the name of the act to escape the stigma. Others wanted to hire a Miami attorney and file a lawsuit.

Moe Strickland said, 'I heard they're auditioning up at Six Flags.'

'Fuck Six Flags,' said Jeremiah-Dumpling elf. 'Probably another damn midget routine.'

'Our options are somewhat limited,' Moe Strickland said, trying to put it as delicately as possible.

'So fuck our options.'

The mood began to simmer after they'd passed the joint around about four times. Moe Strickland eventually stubbed out the cigar and began to enjoy himself. On the street above, a high-school marching band practiced the theme from *2001: A Space Odyssey.* Filtered through six feet of stone, it didn't sound half bad.

One of the actor-elves said, 'Did I mention there's a guy living in our dumpster?'

'You're kidding,' said Moe Strickland.

'No, Uncle Ely, it's true. We met him yesterday.'

'In the dumpster?'

'He fixed it up nice like you wouldn't believe. We gave him a beer.'

Moe Strickland wondered how a homeless person could've found a way into The Catacombs, or why he'd want to stay where it was so musty and humid and bleak.

'A nice guy,' said the actor-elf. 'A real gentleman.'

'We played poker,' added Jeremiah-Dumpling. 'Cleaned his fucking clock.'

'But he was a sport about it. A gentleman, like I said.'

Again Moe Strickland raised the subject of Six Flags. 'Atlanta's a great town,' he said. 'Lots of pretty women.'

'We'll need some new songs.'

'That's okay,' said Moe Strickland. 'Some new songs would be good. We'll have the whole bus ride to work on the arrangements. Luther can bring his guitar.'

'Why not?' said Jeremiah-Dumpling. 'Fuck Kingsbury anyhow.'

'That's the spirit,' Moe Strickland said.

From the end of the tunnel came the sound of boots on brick. A man bellowed furiously.

'Damn,' said one of the actor-elves. He dropped the nub of the joint and ground it to ash under a long, curly-toed, foam-rubber foot.

The boots and the bellowing belonged to a jittery Spence Mooher, who was Pedro Luz's right-hand man. Mooher was agitated because none of the other security guards had shown up for work on this, the busiest day of the summer. Mooher had been up all night patrolling the Amazing Kingdom, and now it looked as if he'd be up all day.

'I smell weed,' he said to Moe Strickland.

In this field Mooher could honestly boast of expertise; he had served six years with the U.S. Drug Enforcement Administration until he was involuntarily relieved of duty. There had been vague accusations of unprofessional conduct in Puerto Rico—something about a missing flash roll, twenty or thirty thousand dollars. As Spence Mooher was quick to point out, no charges were ever filed.

He shared his new boss's affinity for anabolic steroids, but he strongly disapproved of recreational drugs. Steroids hardened the body, but pot and cocaine softened the mind.

'Who's got the weed?' he demanded of Uncle Ely's Elves.

'Lighten up, Spence,' sighed Moe Strickland.

'Why aren't you shitheads up top in rehearsal? Everybody's supposed to be there.'

'Because we're boycotting,' said Jeremiah-Dumpling. 'We're not going to be in the damn show.'

Mooher's mouth twisted. 'Yes, you are,' he said. 'This is the Summerfest Jubilee!'

'I don't care if it's the second coming of Christ,' said Jeremiah-Dumpling. 'We're not performing.'

Moe Strickland added, 'It's a labor action, Spence. Nothing you can do.'

'No?' With one hand Mooher grabbed the veteran character actor by the throat and slammed him against a row of tall lockers. The actor-elves could only cry out helplessly as the muscular security officer banged Uncle Ely's head again and again, until blood began to trickle from his ears. The racket of bone against metal was harrowing, and amplified in the bare tunnel.

Finally Spence Mooher stopped. He held Moe Strickland at arm's length, three feet off the ground; the actor kicked spasmodically.

'Have you reconsidered?' Mooher asked. Moe Strickland's eyelids drooped, but he managed a nod.

A deep voice down the passageway said, 'Let him go.'

Spence Mooher released Uncle Ely and wheeled to face . . . a bum. An extremely tall bum, but a bum nonetheless. It took the security guard a few moments to make a complete appraisal: the damp silver beard, braided on one cheek only; the flowered plastic rain hat pulled taut over the scalp; the broad tan chest wrapped in heavy copper-stained bandages; a red plastic collar around the neck; one dead eye steamed with condensation, the other alive and dark with anger; the mouthful of shiny white teeth.

Here, thought Spence Mooher, was a bum to be reckoned with. He came to this conclusion approximately one second too late, for the man had already seized Mooher's testicles and twisted with such forceful-ness that all strength emptied from Mooher's powerful limbs; quivering, he felt a rush of heat down his legs as he soiled himself. When he tried to talk, a weak croaking noise came out of his mouth.

'Time to go night-night,' said the bum, twisting harder. Spence Mooher fell down unconscious.

With a slapping of many oversized feet, the actor-elves scurried toward the slack figure of Moe Strickland, who was awake but in considerable pain. Jeremiah-Dumpling lifted Moe's bloody head and said, 'This is the guy we told you about. The one in the dumpster.'

Skink bent down and said, 'Pleased to meet you, Uncle Ely. I think your buddies better get you to the vet.'

Charles Chelsea tested the door to Francis X. Kings-bury's office and found it locked. He tapped lightly but received no reply.

'I know he's in there,' Chelsea said.

Danny Pogue said, 'Allow us.' He produced a small screwdriver and easily popped the doorjamb.

'Like ridin' a bicycle,' said Bud Schwartz.

From inside the raccoon costume came a hollow command. The others stood back while Joe Winder opened the door. Upon viewing the scene, he clapped his paws and said: 'Perfect.'

Francis X. Kingsbury was energetically fondling himself in front of a television set. On the screen, a dark young man in a torn soccer jersey was copulating with a wild-haired brunette woman, who was moaning encouragement in Spanish. Other video cassettes were fanned out like a poker hand on the desk.

Kingsbury halted mid-pump and wheeled to confront the intruders. The boxer shorts around his ankles greatly diminished his ability to menace. Today's hairpiece was a silver Kenny Rogers model.

'Get out,' Kingsbury snarled. He fumbled for the remote control and turned off the VCR. He seemed unaware that the Amazing Kingdom's stalwart mascot, Robbie Raccoon, was pointing a loaded semi-automatic at him. Joe Winder tucked the gun under one arm while he unzipped his head and removed it.

'So you're alive,' Kingsbury hissed. 'I had a feeling, goddammit.'

Bud Schwartz laughed and pointed at Kingsbury, who shielded his receding genitals. The burglar said, 'The asshole's wearing golf shoes!'

'For traction,' Joe Winder theorized.

Charles Chelsea looked disgusted. Danny Pogue tossed a package on the desk. 'Here,' he said to Kingsbury, 'even though you tried to kill us.'

'What's this?'

'The files we swiped. Ramex, Gotti, it's all there.'

Kingsbury was confused. Why would they return the files now? Bud Schwartz read his expression and said, 'You were right. It was out of our league.'

Which was baloney. The true reason for returning the files was to ensure that no one would come searching for them later. Like the police or the FBI.

'I suppose you want, what, a great big thank-you or some such goddamn thing.' Francis X. Kingsbury tugged the boxer shorts high on his gelatinous waist.

The indignity of the moment finally had sunk in. 'Get out or I'm calling Security!'

'You've got no Security,' Winder informed him.

'Charlie?'

'I'm afraid that's right, sir. I'll explain later.'

Bud Schwartz said to his partner, 'This is pathetic. Let's go.'

'Wait.' Danny Pogue stepped up to Kingsbury and said: 'Beating up an old lady, what's the matter with you?'

'What the hell do you care.' By now Kingsbury had more or less focused on Joe Winder's gun, so he spoke to Danny Pogue without looking at him. 'That fucking Pedro, he gets carried away. Not a damn thing I can do.'

'She's a sick old woman, for Chrissake.'

'What's your point, Jethro?'

'My point is this,' said Danny Pogue, and ferociously punched Francis Kingsbury on the chin. Kingsbury's golf cleats snagged on the carpet as he toppled.

Surveying the messy scene, Charles Chelsea felt refreshingly detached. He truly didn't care anymore. Outside, a roar of thousands swept the Amazing Kingdom, followed by gay cheers and applause. Chelsea went to the window and parted the blinds. 'What do you know,' he said. 'Our five-millionth customer just walked through the gate.'

With gray hands Kingsbury clutched the corner of the desk and pulled himself to his feet. In this fashion he was also able to depress a concealed alarm button that rang in the Security Office.

But Schwartz said, 'We'll be saying good-bye now.'

'You're welcome to stay,' offered Joe Winder.

'No thanks.' Danny Pogue examined his knuckles for bruises and abrasions. He said, 'Molly's having surgery this afternoon. We promised to be at the hospital.'

'I understand,' Winder said. 'You guys want to take anything?' He motioned with his gun paw around the lavish office. 'The VCR? Some tapes? How about a cellular phone for the car?'

'The phone might be good,' said Danny Pogue. 'What'd you think, Bud? You could call your little boy from the road, wouldn't that be cool?'

'Let's roll,' Bud Schwartz said.

Later they were driving on Card Sound Road, halfway back to the mainland, when Bud Schwartz motioned with a thumb and said: 'Right about here's where it all started, Danny. Me throwin' that damn rat in the convertible.'

'It was a vole,' said Danny Pogue. 'A blue-tongued mango vole. *Microtus mango*. That's the Latin name.'

Bud Schwartz laughed. 'Whatever you say.' There was no denying he was impressed. How many burglars knew Latin?

A few more miles down the road, Danny Pogue again brought up the topic of portable phones. 'If we had us one right now, we could call the hospital and see how she's doin'.'

'You know the problem with cellulars,' said Bud Schwartz.

'The reception?'

'Besides the reception,' Bud Schwartz said. 'The problem with cellulars is, people always steal the damn things.'

'Yeah,' said his partner. 'I hadn't thought about that.'

The emergency buzzer awakens Pedro Luz in the storage room. He sits up and blinks. Blinks at the bare light bulb. Blinks at the pitted walls. Blinks at the empty intravenous bags on the hangers. He thinks, What the hell was it this time? Stanozolol, yeah. He'd pilfered a half-dozen tabs from Spence Mooher's locker. Ground them up with the toe of a boot, stirred it in the bag with the dextrose.

Feeling good. Feeling just fine. The beer sure helped.

Then comes Kingsbury's alarm and it sounds like a dental drill. Better get up now. Better get moving.

Pedro Luz pulls the tubes from his arms and tries to stand. Whoa, hoss! He forgot all about his foot, the fact that it was missing.

He grabs a wooden crutch and steadies himself. Facing the mirror, Pedro notices he's buck naked from the waist down. The image shocks him; his legs are as thick as oaks, but his penis is no larger than a peanut. Hastily he scrambles into the trousers of his guard uniform, the gun belt, one sock, one shoe.

Time to go to work. It's the Summerfest Jubilee and Mr. Kingsbury's in some kind of trouble.

And the damn door won't open.

Pedro can't fucking believe it. Okay, now somebody's either locked the damn thing from the outside, which don't make sense, or maybe welded it shut, which is even crazier. Pedro lowers one shoulder and hits the door like a tackle dummy. *Nada*. Now he's getting pissed. Through the steel he yells for Cano or Spence or Diamond J. Love, and gets no answer. 'Where the hell *is* everybody?' hollers Pedro Luz.

Next logical step is using his skull as a battering ram. Wedging the crutch against the baseboard, he uses it to vault himself headfirst at the door. Amazing thing is, it don't hurt after a while. Tense the neck muscles just before impact and it acts like a spring. Boom, boom, boom. Boing, boing, boing.

No more door! Flattened.

What a fine feeling, to be free again.

The Security Office is empty, which is a mystery. Pedro checks the time cards and sees that none of the other guards have clocked in; something's going on here. Outside, the morning sun burns through a milky August haze, and the park is crawling with customers. There's a middle-aged lady at the security window complaining how somebody swiped her pocketbook off the tram. Behind her is some guy from Wisconsin, red hair and freckles, says he locked his keys in the rental car. And behind him is some bony old man with a shnoz that could cut glass. Claims one of the animals is walking around the park with a gun. Which one? Pedro asks. The possum? The raccoon? We got bunches of animals, says Pedro Luz. And the old guy scratches his big nose and says he don't know the difference from animals. Was Wally Wolverine for all he knows, but it damn sure was a gun in its paw. Sure, says Pedro, whatever you say. Here's a form to fill out. I'll be back in a few minutes.

Between the whiny tourists and all that banging with his head, Pedro's finally waking up. On the floor near the broken door he spots something shiny, and checks it out: a new Master padlock, still fastened to the broken hasp.

Pedro never would've imagined it was the lovely Princess Golden Sun who'd locked him in the storage room with his drugs and beer. He figured it was Spence

Mooher or one of the other security guards, playing a joke.

He could deal with those jerk-offs later. Now it was time to haul ass over to Mr. Kingsbury's office and see what was wrong. For a moment Pedro Luz thought he heard the alarm go off again, but then he realized no, it was just the regular buzzing in his eardrums. Only it seemed to be getting louder.

THIRTY-THREE

'**First things first,**' Joe Winder said. 'Who killed Will Koocher?'

Francis X. Kingsbury was rolling a shiny new Titleist from hand to hand across the top of his desk. The brassy strains of a marching band rose from the street below; the Summerfest Jubilee was in full swing.

'This Koocher,' Kingsbury said, 'he was threatening to go public about the voles. Pangs of conscience, whatever. So what I did, I told that fucking Pedro to go talk sense with the boy. See, it would've been a disaster— and Charlie'll back me up on this—a goddamn mess if it came out the voles were fake. Especially after the stupid things got stolen—talk about embarrassing.'

Winder said, 'So the answer to the question is Pedro. That's who committed the murder.'

Kingsbury smothered his nose with a handkerchief and snuffled like a boar. 'Damn hay fever!' The handkerchief puckered with each breath. 'Far as I'm concerned, Koocher drowned in the Orky tank. Plain and simple. Case closed.'

'But everyone knew the truth.'

'No!' Chelsea protested. 'I swear to God, Joey.'

'Tell me about the blue-tongued mango voles,' said Joe Winder. 'Whose clever idea was that?'

447

From behind the veil of the soggy hanky, Kingsbury said: 'I figured wouldn't it be fantastic if the Amazing Kingdom had an animal we could save. Like Disney tried to do with the dusky sparrow, only I was thinking in terms of a panda bear. People, I've seen this, they go fucking nuts for pandas. Only come to find out it's too hot down here, they'd probably croak in the sun.

'So I call this connection I got, this old friend, and I ask her what's endangered in Florida and she says all the good ones are taken—the panthers and manatees and so forth. She says it'd be better to come up with an animal nobody else had or even knew about. She says we might even get a government grant, which it turns out we did. Two hundred grand!'

Chelsea tried to act appalled; he even made a sound like a gasp. Impatiently, Winder said, 'Charlie, this might come as a shock, but I don't care how much you knew and how much you didn't. For the purposes of settling this matter, you've become superfluous. Now show Mr. Kingsbury what we've prepared.'

From an inside pocket Chelsea withdrew a folded sheet of Amazing Kingdom stationery. He handed it across the desk to Francis X. Kingsbury, who set aside both the handkerchief and the golf ball in order to read.

'It's a press release,' Chelsea said.

'I see what it is. Horseshit is what it is.' Kingsbury scanned it several times, including once from the bottom up. His mouth moved in twitchy circles, like a mule chewing a carrot.

'You ought to consider it,' Winder advised him, 'if you want to stay out of jail.'

'Oh, so now it's blackmail?'

'No, sir, it's the cold fucking hand of fate.'

Nervously Kingsbury fingered the bridge of his nose. 'The hell is your angle, son?'

'You arranged an elaborate scientific fraud for the purposes of profit. An ingenious fraud, to be sure, but a felony nonetheless. Two hundred thousand is just about enough to interest the U.S. Attorney's Office.'

Kingsbury shrugged in mockery. 'Is that, what, like the end of the world?'

'I forgot,' Winder said, 'you're an expert on indictments. Aren't you, Frankie?'

Kingsbury turned color.

'Frankie King,' said Winder. 'That's your real name, in case you don't remember.'

Kingsbury shrank into the chair. Winder turned to Charles Chelsea and said, 'I think somebody's finally in the mood to talk.'

'Can I leave?'

'Certainly, Charlie. And thanks for a terrific job on the publicity release.'

'Yeah, right.'

'I mean it,' Winder said. 'It's seamless.'

Chelsea eyed him warily. 'You're just being sarcastic.'

'No, it was perfect. You've got a definite flair.'

'Thanks, Joe. And I mean it, too.'

The rescue of Francis Kingsbury was further delayed when a disturbance broke out near the front gate of the Amazing Kingdom; a tense and potentially violent dispute over the distribution of prizes, specifically a Nissan 300-Z.

The security-guard uniform is what gave Pedro Luz away. As he crutched toward Kingsbury's office, he was spotted and intercepted by a flying wedge of disgruntled customers. Something about the Summerfest contest being rigged. Pedro Luz insisted he didn't know about any damn contest, but the customers were loud and insistent. They led the security man back to the stage, where a short plump tourist named Rossiter had just been presented the keys to the sleek new sports car. Draped around Mr. Rossiter's neck was a shiny streamer that said: 'OUR FIVE-MILLIONTH SPECIAL GUEST!' In response to questions from a tuxedoed emcee, Mr. Rossiter said he was visiting the Amazing Kingdom with his wife and mother-in-law. He said it was only his second trip to Florida.

Mr. Rossiter gave the car keys to his wife, who squeezed her torso into the driver's seat and happily posed for pictures. Several persons in the crowd began to hiss and boo. Somebody threw a cup of frozen yogurt, which splattered against one of the car's wire wheels.

This was too much for Pedro Luz's jangled, hormone-flooded sensory receptors. He grabbed the microphone from the emcee and said, 'Next person that throws food, I break their fucking spine.'

Instantly a lull came over the mob. Pedro Luz said, 'Now somebody explain what's going on.'

At first no one spoke up, but there was a good bit of whispering about the bloody purple knots on the security chief's forehead. Finally a man in the crowd pointed at the Rossiters and shouted, 'They cheated, that's what!'

Another male voice: 'He cut in line!'

Pedro Luz said, 'Jesus, I can't believe you people.'

He turned to the Rossiters. 'Is it true? Did you cut in line?'

'No, Officer,' Mr. Rossiter answered. 'We got here first, fair and square.'

Mrs. Rossiter popped her head from the car and said, 'They're just a bunch of sore losers.' Mrs. Rossiter's mother, a stubby woman wearing sandals and a Petey Possum T-shirt, said she'd never seen such rude people in all her life.

Pedro Luz didn't know what to do next; for one pleasantly deranged moment, he considered throwing the Rossiters off the stage and claiming the 300-Z for himself. *Daring* anyone to try to take it away from him. Then Charles Chelsea materialized and Pedro Luz gratefully surrendered the microphone. His ears buzzed and his head clanged and all he really wanted to do was limp to the gymnasium and pump some iron.

'Ladies and gentlemen,' Chelsea intoned, 'please settle down.' He looked smooth and confident in a crisp blue oxford shirt and a wine-colored tie. He looked as if he could talk his way out of practically anything.

'I've reviewed the tapes from our security cameras,' Chelsea told the crowd, 'and whether you like it or not, Mr. Rossiter and his family were clearly the first ones through the turnstiles this morning—'

'But he threatened me!' yelled a teenager in the crowd. 'I was here first but he said he'd kill me!'

A middle-aged woman in a straw Orky hat hollered: 'Me, too! And I was ahead of that kid—'

The crowd surged toward the stage until Pedro Luz drew his revolver and aimed it toward the sky. Seeing the gun, the tourists grew quiet and rippled back a few steps.

'Thank you,' Chelsea said to Pedro Luz.

'I got an emergency.'

'You can go now. I'll be fine.'

'You need a gun?'

'No,' said Chelsea, 'but thanks just the same.'

'You got something against fun.'

Francis Kingsbury made it an indictment. 'What, you got something against little children? Little cutey pies having a good time?'

Joe Winder said: 'You can keep the park, Frankie. The park is already built. It's the golf resort that's eighty-sixed, as of today.'

'Oh, ho,' said Kingsbury. 'So you got something against golf?'

'That's the deal. Take it or leave it.'

'You think you can scare me? Hell, I got gangsters shooting at me. Professionals.' Kingsbury cut loose an enormous sneeze, and promptly plugged his nostrils with the handkerchief.

Winder said, 'I was hoping to appeal to the pragmatic side of your nature.'

'Listen, I know how to handle this situation from up North. The way to handle it is, I cut the wop bastards in. The Zubonis, I'm talking about. I cut 'em in on Falcon Trace, you'd be surprised how fast they let bygones be bygones. You watch what good friends we are once I start using Zuboni roofers, Zuboni drywall, Zuboni plumbing.' Kingsbury looked positively triumphant. 'Blackmail, my ass. The fuck are you going to blackmail me with now?'

'I believe you misunderstood the offer,' Joe Winder

said. 'I'm not planning to go to the mob. I'm planning to go to the media.'

Defiantly Kingsbury snatched the hanky from his nose. 'Jesus, you're pissing me off.' He picked up the phone and commanded the operator to connect him with Security. Joe Winder took two steps toward the desk, raised his paw and shot the telephone console to pieces.

Impressed, Kingsbury probed at the tangle of wires and broken plastic. 'Goddamn lunatic,' he said.

Winder sat down and tucked the gun into the furry folds of the costume. 'Think in terms of headlines,' he said. 'Imagine what'll happen when the newspapers find out the Amazing Kingdom of Thrills is run by a Mafia snitch. You'll be famous, Frankie. Wouldn't you love to be interviewed by Connie Chung?'

'Let me just say, fuck you.'

Winder frowned. 'Don't make me shoot up more office equipment. Stop and consider the facts. You obtained the bank notes and financing for Falcon Trace under false pretenses; to wit, using a false name and phony credit references. Ditto on your construction permits. Ditto on your performance bond. Once the money boys find out who you really are, once they read about it on the front page of the *Wall Street Journal*, not only is Falcon Trace dead, you can look forward to spending the rest of your natural life at the courthouse, getting your fat ass sued off. Everybody'll want a piece, Frankie. We're talking cluster-fuck.'

He now had Francis X. Kingsbury's undivided attention. 'And last but not least,' Winder said, 'is the criminal situation. If I'm not mistaken, you're still on probation.'

'Yeah, so?'

'So the terms of probation strictly prohibit consorting with known felons and other unsavory dirtbags. However, a review of your Security Department indicates you're not only consorting with known criminals, you've surrounded yourself with them.'

'This isn't Orlando,' Kingsbury said. 'Down here it's not so easy to get good help. If I was as strict as Disney, I'd have nobody working for me. What, maybe altar boys? Mormons and Brownie Scouts? This is Miami, for Chrissakes, I got a serious recruiting problem here.'

'Nonetheless,' Joe Winder said, 'you've gone out of your way to dredge up extremely primitive life-forms.'

'What's wrong with giving a guy a second chance?' Kingsbury paused for a second, then said, 'I'm the first to admit, hell, Pedro was a bad choice. I didn't know about the damn drugs.' Speaking of Pedro, he thought, where the hell is he?

'What's done is done,' Winder said. He fanned himself with his spare paw, it was wretchedly hot inside the costume. 'Frankie, this is a matter for you and the probation bureau. Between us boys, I wouldn't be surprised if they packed you off to Eglin for six or eight months. You do play tennis, don't you?'

The haughtiness ebbed from Kingsbury's face. Pensively he traced a pudgy finger along the lines of his infamous rodent tattoo. 'Winder, what exactly is your problem?'

'The problem is you're mutilating a fine chunk of island so a bunch of rich people have a warm place to park their butts in the winter. You couldn't have picked a worse location, Frankie, the last green patch of the Keys. You're bulldozing next door to a national wildlife refuge. And offshore, in that magnificent ocean, is the only living coral reef in North America. I believe that's where you intended to flush your toilets—'

'No!' Kingsbury snapped. 'We'll have deep-well sewage injection. High-tech facilities—no runoff, no outfall.'

'Imagine,' Winder mused, 'the shit of millionaires dappling our azure waters.'

Kingsbury reddened and clenched his fists. 'If I go along with this deal, what, it's some major victory for the environment? You think the ghost of Henry Fucking Thoreau is gonna pin a medal or some such goddamn thing on your chest?'

Joe Winder smiled at the thought. 'I've got no illusions,' he said. 'One less golf course is one less golf course. I'll settle for that.'

'The lots, Jesus, they're worth millions. That's what this goddamn piece of paper'll cost me.'

'I'll settle for that, too.'

Kingsbury was still stymied. He glared furiously at Charles Chelsea's final publicity release.

'You'll never understand,' Winder said, 'because you weren't born here. Compared to where you came from, this is always going to look like paradise. Hell, you could wipe out every last bird and butterfly, and it's still better than Toledo in the dead of winter.'

With a dark chuckle, Kingsbury said, 'No kidding.'

'Don't read too much into this operation, Frankie. I'm just sick of asshole carpetbaggers coming down here and fucking up the place. Nothing personal.'

It came out of the blue, Kingsbury saying, 'There was a guy named Jack Winder. Big-time land developer, this goes back a few years, before I was selling water-front. Winder Planned Communities was the company.'

'My father.'

'What?' said Kingsbury. 'Quit whispering.'

'Jack Winder was my father.'

'Then what the hell are you doing? Biting the hand is what I'd call it. Dishonoring the family name.'

'Depends on your point of view.'

Kingsbury sneered. 'I hear this line of bullshit all the time: "We got our slice of sunshine, fine, now it's time to close the borders." Selfish is what you are.'

'Maybe so,' Winder said. 'I'd like to fish that shore-line again, that's for sure. I'd like to see some tarpon out there next spring.'

Dramatically, Francis Kingsbury straightened in the chair. He began talking with his eyes and hands, unmis-takably a sales pitch: 'People come to the Amazing Kingdom, they might like to play some golf. Mommy takes the kids to the theme park, Daddy hits the fair-ways. So what?'

Winder said nothing. Kingsbury began to knead his jowls in exasperation. 'What the hell's so wrong with that picture? Eighteen lousy holes, I just don't see the crime. It's what Disney did. It's what everybody does with prime acreage. This is Florida, for Chrissakes.'

'Not the way it ought to be, Frankie.'

'Then you're living in what they call a dreamworld. This ain't Oz, son, and there's no fairy wizard to make things right again. Down here the brick road's not yellow, it's green. Plain and simple. Case closed.'

But Joe Winder wasn't changing his mind. 'I hope the papers get your name right,' he said.

Bleakly Kingsbury thought of front-page headlines

and multimillion-dollar lawsuits and minimum-security prisons with no driving range. 'All right,' he said to Winder, 'let's talk.'

'You've got my offer. Read the press release, it's all tied up with a pretty ribbon. You shut down Falcon Trace for the noblest of reasons and you're a hero, Frankie. Isn't that what you want?'

'I'd rather have my oceanfront lots.'

Then the door flew open and there, bug-eyed and seething, was Pedro Luz. He aimed a large blue handgun at Joe Winder and grunted something unintelligible.

'Nice of you to put in an appearance,' Kingsbury remarked. His eyes flooded with a mixture of rage and relief. 'This asshole, get him out of my sight! For good this time.'

'Drop the gun,' Pedro Luz told Winder. 'And put on your goddamn head.'

Winder did as he was told. Zipping himself in, he felt cumbersome and helpless and feverishly short of breath.

Kingsbury said, 'He doesn't leave the park alive, you understand?'

'No problem,' said Pedro Luz.

'No *problem*,' mimicked Kingsbury. 'No problem, my ass. This is Mr. Crackerjack Bodyguard, right? Mr. Lightning Response Time.'

For a moment Pedro Luz felt an overwhelming urge to turn the pistol on Francis X. Kingsbury; something told him it would be every bit as satisfying as shooting Joe Winder. Maybe another time, he decided. After payday.

A muted voice inside the raccoon head said: 'This is a big mistake, Frankie.'

Kingsbury laughed mordantly and blew his nose. 'Pedro, it's your last fucking chance. I hope you still got enough brain cells to do this one simple chore.'

'No problem.' With the crutch he roughly shoved Joe Winder toward the door.

'Hey, Pedro.'

'What, Mr. Kingsbury?'

'That's a six-hundred-dollar animal costume. Try not to mess it up.'

THIRTY-FOUR

Carrie Lanier was practicing a song at the mirror as she dressed for the pageant. The door opened behind her, and she saw a flash of orange.

'Hey! We thought you were headed for New York.'

'I seriously considered it.' Skink shut the door with his foot.

'Your friend Officer Tile mentioned Orlando. Somebody shot up a tour bus, he figured it might be you.'

'Another pale imitation, that's all. Where's your boyfriend?'

Carrie described Winder's plan to confront Francis Kingsbury. 'Joe's got all the bases covered.'

Skink shook his head. 'It'll never work.'

'Where have you been, anyway?'

'Down here in the underground, away from all radio beams. I needed a break from that damn plane.'

Carrie moved closer to the mirror and began to put on her makeup. 'What's with the gas cans?' she asked.

Skink carried one in each hand. 'Let's pretend you didn't see these,' he said. 'I just want to make sure you've got a way out of the park.'

'When?'

'Whenever.'

'What about Joe?'

'I expect he's in some trouble,' Skink said. 'I've got a chore to do, then I'll check around.'

'Don't worry, Pedro's locked in the storage room.'

'How? With what?'

When Carrie told him, Skink frowned. 'I guess I'd better get going.'

She said, 'Can you zip me up? There's a little hook at the top.'

Skink set down the gas cans and fastened the back of her gown. He wondered what had happened to the Indian theme.

'When do you go on?' he asked.

'Half an hour.'

'The dress is lovely,' he said, stepping back. 'Half an hour it is.'

'Thanks. Wish me luck.'

'You'll do fine.'

Carrie turned from the mirror. 'Should I wait for Joe?'

'Of course,' said Skink, 'but not too long.'

When they got to the security office, Pedro Luz ordered Joe Winder to remove the raccoon costume and hang it neatly in the uniform closet. Then Pedro Luz dragged Winder into the storage room, clubbed him to the floor and beat him seven or eight times with the crutch—Joe Winder lost count. Every time Pedro Luz struck a blow, he emitted a queer high-pitched peep that sounded like a baby sparrow. When he finally stopped to rest, he was panting heavily and his face shone with damp splotches. Spying from a fetal position on the floor, Joe Winder watched Pedro Luz swallow two handfuls of small orange tablets. Winder assumed these were not muscle relaxants.

'I can kill you with my bare hands,' Pedro Luz said informatively.

Winder sat up, hugging his own chest to prevent pieces of broken ribs from snapping off like dead twigs. He couldn't figure out why Pedro Luz kept a full-length mirror in the storage room.

'It's raining outside,' Pedro Luz said.

'That's what we're waiting for?'

'Yeah. Soon as it stops, I'll take you out and kill you.'

Pedro Luz stripped off his shirt and began to work out with a pair of heavy dumbbells; he couldn't take his eyes off his own glorious biceps. The syncopation of Pedro's breathing and pumping put Joe Winder to sleep. When he awoke much later, still on the floor, he saw that Pedro Luz had put on a fresh uniform. The security man rose unsteadily and reached for the crutch; his hands trembled and his eyelids were mottled and puffy.

'The parade starts soon,' he said. 'Everyone in the park goes to watch—that's when you're gonna break into the ticket office to rip off the cashboxes.'

'And you're going to catch me in the act, and shoot me.'

'Yeah,' Pedro Luz wheezed, 'in the back.'

'Pretty sloppy. The cops'll have plenty of questions.'

'I'm still thinking it through.' His head lolled and he shut his eyes. Joe Winder sprang for the door and regretted it instantly. Pedro Luz was on him like a mad bear; he grabbed Winder at the base of the neck and hurled him backward into the stock shelves.

'And that was one-handed,' Pedro Luz bragged. 'How much do you weigh?'

Winder answered, with a groan, 'One seventy-five.'

The security man beamed. 'Light as a feather. No problem.'

'I'd like to speak with your boss one more time.'

'No way.' Pedro Luz hoisted Winder from a tangle of intravenous tubes and set him down in a bare corner. He said, 'Remember, I still got that gun you were carrying—I figure that's my throwdown. The story is, I had to shoot you because of the gun.'

Winder nodded. 'I'm assuming there'll be no witnesses.'

'Course not. They'll all be at the parade.'

'What about the rain, Pedro? What if the parade's washed out?'

'It's August, asshole. The rain don't last long.' Pedro Luz hammered the heel of his hand against the side of his skull, as if trying to knock a wasp out of his ear. 'God, it's loud in here.'

'I don't mean to nag,' Joe Winder said, 'but you ought to lay off the steroids.'

'Don't start with me!' Pedro Luz cracked the door and poked his head out. 'See, it's stopped already. Just a drizzle.' He gripped Joe Winder by the shoulder. 'Let's go, smartass.'

But Winder could barely walk for the pain. Outside, under a low muddy sky, the tourists rushed excitedly toward Kingsbury Lane, where a band had begun to play. Pedro Luz marched Winder against the flow of yammering, gummy-faced children and their anxious, umbrella-wielding parents. The ticket office was on the other side of the park, a long hike, and Joe Winder had planned to use the time to devise a plan for escape. Instead his thoughts meandered inanely; he noticed, for example, what a high percentage of the Amazing Kingdom's tourists were clinically overweight. Was this a valid cross-section of American society? Or did fat people travel to Florida more frequently than thin people? Three times Winder slowed to ponder the riddle, and three times Pedro Luz thwacked the back of his legs with the dreaded crutch. No one stopped to interfere; most likely they assumed that Winder was a purse snatcher or some other troublemaker being rousted by Security.

Eventually the crowds thinned and the light rain stopped. The two men were alone, crossing the walkway that spanned the dolphin tank. The swim-along attraction had closed early because the trainers were needed at the parade, in case the lion got testy. Joe Winder heard a burst of applause across the amusement park— fireworks blossoming over Kingsbury Lane. The pageant had begun!

Winder thought of Carrie Lanier, and hoped she had the good sense not to come looking for him. He felt Pedro Luz's crutch jab him between the shoulder blades. 'Hold it,' the security man commanded.

A hoary figure appeared at the end of the walkway ahead of them. It was a tall man carrying two red containers.

'Now what?' said Pedro Luz.

Joe Winder's heart sank. Skink didn't see them. He went down two flights of stairs and stacked the gas cans on the back of a Cushman motor cart. He ran back up the steps, disappeared through an unmarked door near the Rare Animal Pavilion and quickly emerged with two more cans of gasoline.

'The Catacombs,' Pedro Luz said, mainly to himself.

Joe Winder heard him unsnap the holster. He turned and told Pedro Luz not to do anything crazy.

'Shut up, smartass.'

As they watched Skink load the second pair of cans onto the Cushman, Winder realized his own mistake: he had tried too hard to be reasonable and civilized and possibly even clever. Such efforts were wasted on men such as Francis X. Kingsbury. Skink had the right idea.

Pedro Luz aimed his .45 and shouted, 'Freeze right there!' Skink stopped at the top of the steps. Pedro Luz ordered him to raise his hands, but Skink acted as if he didn't hear.

'Don't I know you?' Skink said, coming closer.

Pedro Luz found it difficult to look directly at the bearded stranger because one of the man's eyeballs seemed dislodged from the socket. As Skink approached, he gave no indication of recognizing Joe Winder.

'Hello, gentlemen,' he said. Casually he bent to examine the taped stump of Pedro Luz's leg. 'Son, you're dropping more parts than a Ford Pinto.'

Flustered, Pedro Luz fell back on standard hardass-cop colloquy: 'Lemme see some ID.'

Skink reached into the blaze-orange weather suit and came out with a small kitchen jar. He handed it to the security man and said, 'I believe this belongs to you.'

Pedro Luz felt his stomach quake. At the bottom of the jar, drifting in pickle juice, was the tip of his right index finger. It looked like a cube of pink tofu.

'The old woman bit it off,' Skink reminded him, 'while you were beating her up.'

Beautiful, Joe Winder thought. We're both going to die long horrible deaths.

Hoarsely, Pedro Luz said, 'Who the hell are you?'

Skink gestured at the soiled bandages around his chest. 'I'm the one you shot at the trailer!'

All three of them jumped as a Roman candle exploded high over Kingsbury Lane. A band was playing the theme from *2001: A Space Odyssey*. It sounded dreadful.

In the tank below, Dickie the Dolphin rolled twice and shot a light spray of water from his blowhole. A few drops sprinkled the barrel of Pedro Luz's gun, and he wiped it nervously on the front of his trousers. The circuits of his brain were becoming badly overloaded; assimilating new information had become a struggle— the drugs, the finger in the jar, the one-eyed stoner with the gas cans, the fireworks, the god-awful music. It was time to kill these sorry bastards and go to the gym.

'Who first?' he asked. 'Who wants it first?'

Joe Winder saw no evidence of urgency in Skink's demeanor, so he took it upon himself to ram an elbow into the soft declivity beneath Pedro Luz's breastbone. Winder was stunned to see the bodybuilder go down, and idiotically he leapt upon him to finish the job. Winder's punching ability was hampered by the searing pain in his rib cage, and though Pedro Luz was gagging and drooling and gulping to catch his wind, it was a relatively simple exercise to lock his arms around all hundred and seventy-five pounds of Joe Winder and squeeze the breath out of him. The last thing Winder heard, before blacking out, was a splash in the tank below.

He hoped like hell it was the pistol.

Marine biologists debate the relative intelligence of the Atlantic bottle-nosed dolphin, but it is generally accepted that the graceful mammal is extremely smart; that it is able to communicate using sophisticated underwater sonics; that it sometimes appears capable of emotions, including grief and joy. Noting that the dolphin's brain is proportionally larger and more fully developed than that of human beings, some experts contend that the animals are operating in a superior cognitive realm that we simply cannot comprehend.

A more skeptical view (and one endorsed by Joe Winder) is that dolphins probably aren't quite as smart as tourist lore suggests. Otherwise why would they allow themselves to be so easily captured, subjugated, trained and put on public display? It seemed to Winder that somersaulting through hula hoops in exchange for a handful of sardines was not proof of high intellect. Given fins and some Milk-Bones, your average French poodle could master the same feat.

It is certainly true, however, that captive dolphins exhibit distinct and complex personalities. Some are gregarious and easily tamed, while others are aloof and belligerent; some are happy to perform stunts for cheering tourists, while others get ulcers. Because each dolphin is so sensitive and unique, curators must be extremely careful when selecting the animals for commercial aquarium shows.

When it came to jumping hula hoops, Dickie the

Dolphin was competent if unspectacular. The same could be said for his tail-walking, his backward flips and his mastery of the beach ball. While most spectators thought he was a lovable ham, experienced dolphin trainers could see he was just going through the motions. Ever since replacing the deceased Orky as the Amazing Kingdom's aquatic star, Dickie had approached each performance with the same sullen indifference. He took a similar attitude into the swim-along sessions, where he habitually kept a large distance between himself and whatever loud pale humanoid had been suckered into entering the tank.

The exception, of course, was when Dickie the Dolphin got into one of his 'moods.' Then he would frolic and nuzzle and rub eagerly against the swimmer, who inevitably mistook these gestures for honest affection. Dolphin researchers have documented numerous sexual advances upon human beings of both genders, but they cannot agree on the animal's intention in these circumstances. If dolphins truly are second to people on the intelligence scale, then they most certainly would not mistake a bikini-clad legal secretary for a member of their own species. Which raises a more intriguing hypothesis: that captive male dolphins attempt these outrageous liaisons out of mischief, or perhaps even revenge. The truth is locked deep inside the dolphin's large and complicated cerebrum, but the phenomenon has been widely reported.

On the evening of August 6, Dickie the Dolphin was in a state of high agitation as he circled the darkened whale tank at the Amazing Kingdom of Thrills. Perhaps it was the percussion of the nearby fireworks that disrupted the powerful creature's peace, or perhaps it was the effect of a long and lonely confinement. Although the trained seals and pelicans could be entertaining, Dickie the Dolphin probably would have preferred the companionship of a female partner. And he would have had one if Francis X. Kingsbury had not been so cheap. In any event, the solitary dolphin was keeping a sharp and wily eye on the commotion taking place along the walkway above.

At the first splash, Dickie swiftly sounded, tracking a small steel object to the bottom of his tank. He never considered retrieving the item, as there would be no reward for his effort—the buckets of cut fish had been hauled away hours ago. So the dolphin disregarded Pedro Luz's gun, glided slowly to the surface and waited.

The second splash was different.

Pedro Luz was astonished by the strength of the one-eyed man. He took a punch as well as anyone that Pedro Luz had ever assaulted, plus he was quick. Every time Pedro Luz swung and missed, the bearded stranger hit him two or three times in the gut. It was starting to hurt immensely.

Having lost his own gun, Pedro Luz tried to retrieve the spare—Joe Winder's gun—from the pocket of his trousers. Every attempt brought a new flurry of punches from the one-eyed hobo, so Pedro Luz abandoned the plan. With a bellowing lunge, he was able to get a grip on the stranger's collar—an animal collar!—and pull him close. Pedro Luz preferred squeezing to boxing, and was confident he could end the fight (and the big freak's life) with a vigorous hug. That's when somebody grabbed Pedro Luz's hair from behind, and yanked his head back so fiercely that a popping noise came from his neck. Next thing he knew, his pants were off and he was thrashing in the warm water. Above him stood Joe Winder and the stranger, peering over the rail.

Swimming is an exercise that depends more on style than muscle, and Pedro Luz was plainly a terrible swimmer. The throbbing of his truncated leg added pain to ineptitude as he paddled the tank haplessly in search of a ladder. When the massive dolphin rolled beside him in the dark, Pedro Luz cursed and splashed his arms angrily. He was not the least bit afraid of stupid fish; perhaps he was deceived by the dolphin's friendly smile, or misled by childhood memories of the hokey 'Flipper' television series. In any event, Pedro Luz struck out at the creature with the misguided assumption that he could actually hurt it, and that it was too tame and good-natured to retaliate. Pedro's drug-inflamed brain failed to register the fact that Dickie the Dolphin was a more attuned physiological specimen than Pedro Luz himself, and about five hundred pounds larger. When the animal nudged him playfully with its snout, Pedro Luz balled his fists and slugged its silky gray flank.

'Be careful,' Joe Winder advised from the walkway, but Pedro Luz paid no attention. The damn fish would not go away! Using its pectoral flippers almost as arms, it held Pedro Luz in a grasp that was gentle yet firm.

Spitting curses, he kicked the dolphin savagely and pushed away. Stroking clumsily for the wall of the tank, he saw the long sleek form rise beneath him. A fin found Pedro Luz's armpit and spun him roughly. He came up choking, but again the creature tugged him down. Once more Pedro Luz fought his way to the top, and this time Dickie the Dolphin began to nip mischievously—tiny needle-like teeth raking Pedro's neck, his shoulders, his bare thighs. Then the dolphin rolled languidly on its side and gave a soft inquisitive whistle, the same sound Flipper used to make at the end of the TV show when he waved at the camera. Pedro Luz tried not to be afraid, but he couldn't understand what this dolphin was trying to say, or do. The salt water stung his eyes and his throat, and the stump of his leg felt as if it were on fire.

Again Pedro Luz felt cool fins slide under his arms as the dolphin gradually steered him toward the deepest part of the tank. The security man tried to break free, but it did no good. Something else propelled him now—a formidable protuberance that left no doubt as to Dickie the Dolphin's true purpose.

Pedro Luz was awestruck and mortified. The long pale thing loomed from the gray water and touched him—hooking, in fact, around his buttocks. The amphibious prodding brought an unfamiliar plea to Pedro Luz's lips: 'Help!'

Watching events unfold in the tank below, Skink agreed it was an extraordinary scene.

'I told you,' said Joe Winder. 'It's one of Nature's marvels.'

Pedro Luz began to whimper. No regimen of weight training and pharmaceutical enhancement could have prepared him, or any mortal man, for an all-out sexual attack by a healthy bottle-nosed dolphin. Pedro Luz had never felt so helpless, exhausted and inadequate; desperately he punched at the prodigious inquiring tuber, only to be rebuked by a well-placed slap from Dickie's sinewy fluke.

Leaning over the rail, Joe Winder offered more advice: 'Just roll with it. Don't fight him.'

But the futility of resistance was already clear to Pedro Luz, who found himself—for the first time in his adult life—completely out of strength. As he was pulled underwater for the final time, terror gave way to abject humiliation: he was being fucked to death by a damn fish.

THIRTY-FIVE

Nina asked where he was calling from.

'Charlie's office,' Winder said. 'Here's what I'm going to do: I'll leave the phone off the hook all night. That way you can work on your poetry and still make money.'

'Joe, that'll cost him a fortune. It's four bucks a minute.'

'I know the rates, Nina. Don't worry about it.'

'You ready for the latest?'

'Just one verse. Time's running out.'

'Here goes,' she said, and began to recite:

> 'You flooded me with passions
> Hard and lingering.
> You took me down again
> Pumping breathless, biting blind.
> Hot in your bloodrush, I dreamed of more.'

'Wow,' Winder said. Obviously things were going gangbusters between Nina and the light-truck salesman.

'You really like it? Or are you patronizing me again?'

'Nina, you're breaking new ground.'

'Guess what the moron at the phone syndicate wants.

Limericks! Sex limericks, like they publish in *Playboy*. That's his idea of erotic poetry!'

'Stick to your guns,' Winder said.

'You bet I will.'

'The reason I called was to say good-bye.'

'So tonight's the night,' she said. 'Will I be seeing you on the news?'

'I hope not.' He thought: What the hell. 'I met a woman,' he said.

'I'm very happy for you.'

'Aw, Nina, don't say that.'

'I *am*. I think it's great.'

'Christ Almighty, aren't you the least bit jealous?'

'Not really.'

God, she was a pisser. 'Then lie to me,' Winder said. 'Have mercy on my lunatic soul and lie to me. Tell me you're mad with jealousy.'

'You win, Joe. You saw through my act.'

'Was that a giggle I heard?'

'No!' Nina said. The giggle burst into a full-blown laugh. 'I'm dying here. I might just leap off the building, I'm so damn jealous. Who is she? Who is this tramp?'

Now Winder started laughing, too. 'I'd better go,' he said, 'before I say something sensible.'

'Call me, Joe. Whatever happens, I'd love to get a phone call.'

'I know the number by heart,' he said. 'Me and every pervert on the Gold Coast.'

'You go to hell,' Nina teased. 'And be careful, dammit.'

He said good-bye and placed the receiver on Charles Chelsea's desk.

*

Skink mulched a cotton candy and said, 'These are excellent seats.'

'They ought to be.' Joe Winder assumed Francis X. Kingsbury would arrive at any moment; it was his private viewing box, after all—leather swivel chairs, air-conditioning, video monitors, a wet bar. Thirty rows up, overlooking the parade route.

'What will you do when he gets here?' Skink asked.

'I haven't decided. Maybe he'd like to go swimming with Pedro's new friend.'

The grandstand was packed, and Kingsbury Lane was lined five deep with eager spectators. As the history of Florida unfolded in song and skit, Joe Winder imagined that the Stations of the Cross could be similarly adapted and set to music, if the audience would only forgive a few minor revisions. Every float in the Summerfest pageant was greeted with the blind and witless glee displayed by people who have spent way too much money and are determined to have fun. They cheered at the sight of a bootless Ponce de León, an underaged maiden on each arm, wading bawdily into the Fountain of Youth; they roared as the pirate Black Caesar chased a concubine up the mizzenmast while his men plundered a captured galleon; they gasped as the Killer Hurricane of 1926 tore the roof off a settler's cabin and the smock off his brave young wife.

Skink said, 'I never realized cleavage played such an important role in Florida history.' Joe Winder told him to just wait for the break-dancing migrants.

Carrie Lanier gave a cassette of the new music to the driver, and took her place on the last float. The Talent

Manager showed up and demanded to know why she wasn't wearing the Indian costume.

'That wasn't an Indian costume,' Carrie said, 'unless the Seminoles had streetwalkers.'

The Talent Manager, a middle-aged woman with sweeping peroxide hair and ropes of gold jewelry, informed Carrie that a long gown was unsuitable for the Jubilee parade.

'It's ideal for what I'm singing,' Carrie replied.

'And what would that be?'

'That would be none of your business.' She adjusted the microphone, which was clipped into the neck of her dress.

The Talent Manager became angry. 'Paul Revere and the Raiders isn't good enough for you?'

'Go away,' said Carrie.

'And where's our lion?'

'The lion is taking the night off.'

'No, missy,' the Talent lady said, shaking a finger. 'Thousands of people out there are waiting to see Princess Golden Sun ride a wild lion through the Everglades.'

'The lion has a furball. Now get lost.'

'At least put on the wig,' the Talent lady pleaded. 'There's no such thing as a blond Seminole. For the sake of authenticity, put on the damn wig!'

'Toodle-loo,' said Carrie. And the float began to roll.

At first, Sergeant Mark Dyerson thought the telemetry was on the fritz again. How could the panther get back on the island? No signal had been received for days, then suddenly there it was, beep-beep-beep. Number 17. The sneaky bastard was at it again!

Sergeant Dyerson asked the pilot to keep circling beneath the clouds until he got a more precise fix on the transmitter. The greenish darkness of the hammocks and the ocean suddenly was splayed by a vast sparkling corridor of lights—the Amazing Kingdom of Thrills. The plane banked high over a confetti of humanity.

'Damn,' said the ranger. Sharply he tapped the top of the radio receiver. 'This can't be right. Fly me over again.'

But the telemetry signals were identical on the second pass, and the third and the fourth. Sergeant Dyerson peered out the window of the Piper and thought, He's down there. He's inside the goddamn park!

The ranger told the pilot to call Naples. 'I need some backup,' he said, 'and I need the guy with the dogs.'

'Should I say which cat we're after?'

'No, don't,' Sergeant Dyerson said. The top brass of the Game and Fish Department was tired of hearing about Number 17. 'Tell them we've got a panther in trouble,' said Sergeant Dyerson, 'that's all you need to say.'

The pilot reached for the radio. 'What the hell's it doing in the middle of an amusement park?'

'Going crazy,' said the ranger. 'That's all I can figure.'

The break-dancing migrant workers were a sensation with the crowd. Skink covered his face during most of the performance; it was one of the most tasteless spectacles he had ever seen. He asked Joe Winder if he wished to help with the gasoline.

'No, I'm waiting for Kingsbury.'

'What for?'

'To resolve our differences as gentlemen. And possibly pound him into dog chow.'

'Forget Kingsbury,' Skink advised. 'There's your girl.'

Carrie's float appeared at the end of the promenade; a spotlight found her in a black sequined evening gown, posed among ersatz palms and synthetic cypress. She was perfectly dazzling, although the crowd reacted with confused and hesitant applause—they'd been expecting a scantily clad Indian princess astride a snarling wildcat.

Joe Winder tried to wave, but it hurt too much to raise his arms. Carrie didn't see him. She folded her hands across her midriff and began to sing:

> *'Vissi d'arte, vissi d'amore*
> *Non feci mai male ad animal viva!*
> *Con man furtiva*
> *Quante miserie conobbi, aiutai. . . .'*

Winder was dazed, and he was not alone; a restless murmuring swept through the stands and rippled along the promenade.

'Magnificent!' Skink said. His good eye ablaze, he clutched Winder's shoulder: 'Isn't she something!'

'What is that? What's she singing?'

Skink shook him with fierce exuberance. 'My God, man, it's Puccini. It's *Tosca*!'

'I see.' It was a new wrinkle: opera.

And Carrie sang beautifully; what her voice lacked in strength it made up in a flawless liquid clarity. The aria washed sorrowfully across the Amazing Kingdom and, like a chilly rain, changed the mood of the evening.

Skink put his mouth to Winder's ear and whispered: 'This takes place in the second act, where Tosca has just seen her lover tortured by the ruthless police chief and sentenced to death by a firing squad. In her failed effort to save him, Tosca herself becomes a murderess. Her song is a lamentation on life's tragic ironies.'

'I'd never have guessed,' Winder said.

As the float passed the Magic Mansion, Carrie sang:

> *'Nell'ora del dolore*
> *Perchè, perchè, Signore,*
> *Perchè me ne rimuneri così?'*

Skink closed his eyes and swayed. 'Ah, why, dear Lord,' he said. 'Ah, why do you reward your servant so?'

Winder said the audience seemed fidgety and disturbed.

'Disturbed?' Skink was indignant. 'They ought to be distraught. Mournful. They ought to be *weeping*.'

'They're only tourists,' Joe Winder said. 'They've been waiting all afternoon to see a lion.'

'Cretins.'

'Oh, she knew,' Winder said fondly. 'She knew they wouldn't like it one bit.'

Skink grinned. 'Bless her heart.' He began to applaud rambunctiously, 'Bravo! Bravo!' His clapping and shouting caught the attention of spectators in the lower rows, who looked up toward the VIP box with curious annoyance. Carrie spotted both of them in Kingsbury's booth, and waved anxiously. Then she gathered herself and, with a deep breath, began the first verse again.

'What a trouper.' Joe Winder was very proud.

Skink straightened his rain cap and said, 'Go get her.'

'Now?'

'Right now. It's time.' Skink reached out to shake Winder's hand. 'You've got about an hour,' he said.

Winder told him to be careful. 'There's lots of kids out there.'

'Don't you worry.'

'What about Kingsbury?'

Skink said, 'Without the park, he's finished.'

'I intended to make him famous. You should've heard my plan.'

'Some other time,' Skink said. 'Now go. And tell her how great she was. Tell her it was absolutely wonderful. Giacomo would've been proud.'

'*Arrivederci!*' said Joe Winder.

From his third-floor office above Sally's Cimarron Saloon, Francis X. Kingsbury heard the parade go by. Only Princess Golden Sun's dolorous aria brought him to the window, where he parted the blinds to see what in the name of Jesus H. Christ had gone wrong. The disposition of the crowd had changed from festive to impatient. Unfuckingbelievable, thought Kingsbury. It's death, this music. And what's with the evening gown, the Kitty Carlisle number. Where's the buckskin bikini? Where's the tits and ass? The tourists looked ready to bolt.

Carrie hit the final note and held it—held it forever, it seemed to Kingsbury. The girl had great pipes, he had to admit, but it wasn't the time or place for Italian caterwauling. And God, this song, when would it end?

As the float trundled by, Kingsbury was surprised to

see that Princess Golden Sun wasn't singing anymore; in fact, she was drinking from a can of root beer. Yet her final melancholy note still hung in the air!

Or was it something else now?

The fire alarm, for instance.

Kingsbury thought: Please, don't let it be. He tried to call Security but no one answered—that fucking Pedro, he should've been back from his errand hours ago.

Outside, the alarm had tripped a prerecorded message on the public-address system, urging everyone to depart the Amazing Kingdom in a calm and orderly fashion. When Kingsbury peeked out the window again, he saw customers streaming like ants for the exits; the performers and concessionaires ran, as well. Baldy the Eagle ripped off his wings and sprinted from the park at Olympic speed; the animal trainers fled together in a hijacked Cushman, but not before springing the hinge on the lion's cage and shooing the wobbly, tranquilized beast toward the woods.

Kingsbury ran, too. He ran in search of Pedro Luz, the only man who knew how to turn off the fire alarm. Golf spikes clacking on the concrete, Kingsbury jogged from the security office to King Arthur's Food Court to The Catacombs, where he found Spence Mooher limping in mopey addled circles, like a dog who'd been grazed by a speeding bus.

But there was no trace of Pedro, and despair clawed at Kingsbury's gut. People now were pouring out of the park, and taking their money with them. Even if they had wished to stop and purchase one last overpriced souvenir, no one was available to sell it to them.

Chickenshits! Kingsbury raged inwardly. All this panic, and no fire. *Can't you idiots see it's a false alarm?*

Then came the screams.

Kingsbury's throat tightened. He ducked into a photo kiosk and removed the laminated ID card from his belt. Why risk it if the crowd turned surly?

The screaming continued. In a prickly sweat, Kingsbury tracked the disturbance to the whale tank, where something had caught the attention of several families on their way out of the park. They lined the walkway, and excitedly pointed to the water. Assuming the pose of a fellow tourist, Kingsbury nonchalantly joined the others on the rail. He overheard one man tell his wife that there wasn't enough light to use the video camera; she encouraged him to try anyway. A young girl cried and clutched at her mother's leg; her older brother told her to shut up, it's just a plastic dummy.

It wasn't a dummy. It was the partially clothed body of Pedro Luz, facedown in the Orky tank. His muscular buttocks mooned the masses, and indeed it was this sight—not the fact he was dead—that had shocked customers into shrieking.

Francis X. Kingsbury glared spitefully at the corpse. Pedro's bobbing bare ass seemed to mock him—a hairy faceless smile, taunting as it floated by. So this is how it goes, thought Kingsbury. Give a man a second chance, this is how he pays you back.

Suddenly, and without warning, Dickie the Dolphin rocketed twenty feet out of the water and performed a perfect triple-reverse somersault.

The tourists, out of pure dumb reflex, broke into applause.

*

The Amazing Kingdom of Thrills emptied in forty minutes. Two hook-and-ladder rigs arrived from Homestead, followed by a small pumper truck from the main fire station in lower Key Largo. The fire fighters unrolled the hoses and wandered around the park, but found no sign of a fire. They were preparing to leave when three green Jeeps with flashing lights raced into the empty parking lot. The fire fighters weren't sure what to make of the Game and Fish officers; an amusement park seemed an unlikely hideout for gator poachers. Sergeant Mark Dyerson flagged down one of the departing fire trucks and asked the captain if it was safe to take dogs into the area. The captain said sure, be my guest. Almost immediately the hounds struck a scent, and the old tracker turned them loose. The wildlife officers loaded up the dart guns and followed.

Francis Kingsbury happened to be staring out the window when he spotted the lion loping erratically down Kingsbury Lane; a pack of dogs trailed closely, snapping at its tail. The doped-up cat attempted to climb one of the phony palm trees, but fell when its claws pulled loose from the Styrofoam bark. Swatting at the hounds, the cat rose and continued its disoriented escape.

Lunacy, thought Kingsbury.

Someone knocked twice on the office door and came in—a short round man with thin brown hair and small black eyes. A hideous polyester-blend shirt identified him as a valued customer. Pinned diagonally across the man's chest was a wrinkled streamer that said 'OUR FIVE-MILLIONTH SPECIAL GUEST!' In the crook of each arm sat a stuffed toy animal with reddish fur, pipestem whiskers and a merry turquoise tongue.

Vance and Violet Vole.

'For my nieces,' the man explained. 'I got so much free stuff I can hardly fit it in the car.'

Kingsbury smiled stiffly. 'The big winner, right? That's you.'

'Yeah, my wife can't fuckin' believe it.'

'Didn't you hear it, the fire alarm? Everybody else, I mean, off they went.'

'But I didn't see no fire,' the man said. 'No smoke, neither.' He arranged the stuffed animals side by side on Kingsbury's sofa.

The guy's a total yutz, Kingsbury thought. Does he want my autograph or what? Maybe a snapshot with the big cheese.

'What's that you got there?' the man asked. 'By the way, the name's Rossiter.' He nodded toward a plaid travel bag that lay open on Kingsbury's desk. The bag was full of cash, mostly twenties and fifties.

The man said, 'Looks like I wasn't the only one had a lucky day.'

Kingsbury snapped the bag closed. 'I'm very busy, Mr. Rossiter. What's the problem—something with the new car, right? The color doesn't match your wife's eyes or whatever.'

'No, the car's great. I got no complaints about the car.'

'Then what?' Kingsbury said. 'The parade, I bet. That last song, I swear to Christ, I don't know where that shit came from—'

'You kiddin' me? It was beautiful. It was Puccini.'

Kingsbury threw up his hands. 'Whatever. Not to be rude, but what the fuck do you want?'

The man said, 'I got a confession to make. I cheated

483

a little this morning.' He shrugged sheepishly. 'I cut in line so we could be the first ones through the gate. That's how I won the car.'

It figures, thought Kingsbury. Your basic South Florida clientele.

The man said, 'I felt kinda lousy, but what the hell. Opportunity knocks, right? I mean, since I had to be here anyway—'

'Mr. Rossiter, do I look like a priest? All this stuff, I don't need to hear it—'

'Hey, call me Lou,' the man said, 'and I'll call *you* Frankie.' From his Sansibelt slacks he withdrew a .38-caliber pistol with a silencer.

Francis Kingsbury's cheeks went from pink to gray. 'Don't tell me,' he said.

'Yeah,' said Lou, 'can you believe it?'

THIRTY-SIX

Francis X. Kingsbury asked the hit man not to shoot.

'Save your breath,' said Lou.

'But, look, a fantastic new world I built here. A place for little tykes, you saw for yourself—roller coasters and clowns and talking animals. Petey Possum and so forth. I did all this myself.'

'What a guy,' said Lou.

Kingsbury was unaccustomed to such bald sarcasm. 'Maybe I make a little dough off the operation, so what? Look at all the fucking happiness I bring people!'

'I enjoyed myself,' Lou admitted. 'My wife, she's crazy about the Twirling Teacups. She and her mother both. I almost spit up on the damn thing, to be honest, but my wife's got one a them cast-iron stomachs.'

Kingsbury brightened. 'The Twirling Teacups, I designed those myself. The entire ride from scratch.'

'No shit?'

The hit man seemed to soften, and Kingsbury sensed an opening. 'Look, I got an idea about paying back the Zubonis. It's a big construction deal, we're talking millions. They'd be nuts to pass it up—can you make a phone call? Tell 'em it's once in a lifetime.'

Lou said, 'Naw, I don't think so.'

'Florida waterfront—that's all you gotta say. Florida

fucking waterfront, and they'll be on the next plane from Newark, I promise.'

'You're a good salesman,' said the hit man, 'but I got a contract.'

Kingsbury nudged the plaid travel bag across the desk. 'My old lady, she wanted me to go on a trip—Europe, the whole nine yards. I was thinking why not, just for a couple months. She's never been there.'

Lou nodded. 'Now's a good time to go. The crowds aren't so bad.'

'Anyhow, I emptied the cash registers after the parade.' Kingsbury patted the travel bag. 'This is just from ticket sales, not concessions, and still you're talking three hundred and forty thousand. Cash-ola.'

'Yeah? That's some vacation, three hundred forty grand.'

'And it's all yours if you forget about the contract.'

'Hell,' said Lou, 'it's mine if I don't.'

Outside there was a bang, followed by a hot crackling roar. When Kingsbury spun his chair toward the window, his face was bathed in flickering yellow light.

'Lord,' he said.

The Wet Willy was on fire—hundreds of feet of billowed latex, squirming and thrashing like an eel on a griddle. White sparks and flaming bits of rubber hissed into the tropical sky, and came down as incendiary rain upon the Amazing Kingdom of Thrills. Smaller fires began to break out everywhere.

Francis Kingsbury shivered under his hairpiece.

Lou went to the window and watched the Wet Willy burn. 'You know what it looks like?'

'Yes,' Kingsbury said.

'A giant Trojan.'

'I know.'

'It ain't up to code, that's for sure. You must've greased some county inspectors.'

'Another good guess,' Kingsbury said. Why did the alarm cut off? he wondered. Where did all the firemen go?

Lou farted placidly as he walked back to the desk. 'Well, I better get a move on.'

Kingsbury tried to hand him the telephone. 'Please,' he begged, 'call the Zuboni brothers.'

'A deal's a deal,' Lou said, checking the fit of the silencer.

'But you saw for yourself!' Kingsbury cried. 'Another five years, goddamn, I'll be bigger than Disney.'

Lou looked doubtful. 'I wasn't gonna say anything, but what the hell. The car and the prizes are great, don't get me wrong, but the park's got a long ways to go.'

Petulantly, Kingsbury said, 'Fine, let's hear it.'

'It's the bathrooms,' said Lou. 'The fuckin' Port Authority's got cleaner bathrooms.'

'Is that so?'

'Yeah, and it wouldn't hurt to keep an extra roll a toilet paper in the stalls.'

'Is that it? That's your big gripe?'

Lou said, 'People notice them things, they really do.' Then he stepped toward Francis X. Kingsbury and raised the pistol.

Joe Winder led her through the dense hammock, all the way to the ocean's edge. It took nearly an hour because Carrie wore high heels. The gown kept snagging on branches, and the insects were murder.

'I'm down two pints,' she said, scratching at her ankles.

'Take off the shoes. Hurry.' He held her hand and waded into the water.

'Joe!' The gown rose up around her hips; the sequins sparkled like tiny minnows.

'How deep are we going?' she asked.

At first the turtle grass tickled her toes, then it began to sting. Winder kept walking until the water was up to his chest.

'See? No more bugs.'

'You're full of tricks,' Carrie said, clinging to his arm. From the flats it was possible to see the entire curving shore of the island, including the naked gash made by the bulldozers at Falcon Trace. She asked if the trees would ever come back.

'Someday,' Joe Winder said, 'if the bastards leave it alone.'

Stretching toward the horizon was a ribbon of lights from the cars sitting bumper-to-bumper on County Road 905—the exodus of tourists from the Amazing Kingdom. Winder wondered if Skink had waited long enough to make his big move.

He listened for the distant sound of sirens as he moved through the shallows, following the shoreline south. The warm hug of the tide soothed the pain in his chest. He pointed at a pair of spotted leopard rays, pushing twin wakes.

'What else do you see?' Carrie said.

'Turtles. Jellyfish. A pretty girl with no shoes.' He kissed her on the neck.

'How far can we go like this?' she asked.

'Big Pine, Little Torch, all the way to Key West if you want.'

She laughed. 'Joe, that's a hundred miles.' She kicked playfully into the deeper water. 'It feels so good.'

'You sang beautifully tonight. Watch out for the coral.'

When Carrie stood up, the water came to her chin. Blowing bubbles, she said, 'I didn't know you liked opera.'

'I hate opera,' Winder said, 'but you made it wonderful.'

She splashed after him, but he swam away.

They didn't leave the ocean until the road was clear and the island was dark. They agreed it would be best to get out of Monroe County for a while, so they took Card Sound Road toward the mainland. The pavement felt cool under their feet. They wanted to hold hands, but it hampered their ability to defend themselves against the swarming mosquitoes. Every few minutes Winder would stop walking and check the sky for a change in the light. One time he was sure he heard a helicopter.

Carrie said, 'What's your feeling about all this?'

'Meaning Kingsbury and the whole mess.'

'Exactly.'

'There's thousands more where he came from.'

'Oh, brother,' Carrie said. 'I was hoping you'd gotten it all out of your system.'

'Never,' said Winder, 'but I'm open to suggestions.'

'All right, here's one: Orlando.'

'God help us.'

'Now wait a second, Joe. They're shooting commercials

at those new studios up there. I've got my first audition lined up for next week.'

'What kind of commercial?'

'The point is, it's national exposure.'

'Promise me something,' Winder said. 'Promise it's not one of those personal-hygiene products.'

'Fabric softener. The script's not bad, all things considered.'

'And will there be singing?'

'No singing,' Carrie said, picking up the pace. 'They've got newspapers in Orlando, don't they?'

'Oh no, you don't.'

'It'd be good for you, Joe. Write about the important things, whatever pisses you off. Just write *something*. Otherwise you'll make me crazy, and I'll wind up killing you in your sleep.'

The Card Sound Bridge rose steeply ahead. A handful of crabbers and snapper fishermen sleepily tended slack lines. Joe and Carrie took the sidewalk. For some reason she stopped and gave him a long kiss.

Halfway up the rise, she tugged on his hand and told him to turn around.

There it was: the eastern sky aglow, fat clouds roiling unnaturally under a pulsing halo of wild pink and orange. Baleful columns of tarry smoke rose from the Amazing Kingdom of Thrills.

Joe Winder whistled in amazement. 'There's arson,' he said, 'and then there's arson.'

Bud Schwartz and Danny Pogue were surprised to find Molly McNamara wide awake, propped up with a stack of thin hospital pillows. She was brushing her snowy hair and reading the *New Republic* when the burglars arrived.

'Pacemaker,' Molly reported. 'A routine procedure.'

'You look so good,' said Danny Pogue. 'Bud, don't she look good?'

'Hush now,' Molly said. 'Sit down here, the news is coming on. There's a story you'll both find interesting.' Without being asked, Danny Pogue switched the television to Channel 10, Molly's favorite.

Bud Schwartz marveled at the old woman in bed. Days earlier, she had seemed so weak and withered and close to death. Now the gray eyes were as sharp as a hawk's, her cheeks shone, and her voice rang strong with maternal authority.

She said, 'Danny, did you get the bullets?'

'Yes, ma'am.' He handed Molly the yellow box.

'These are .22-longs,' she said. 'I needed shorts. That's what the gun takes.'

Danny Pogue looked lamely toward his partner. Bud Schwartz said, 'Look, we just asked for .22s. The guy didn't say nothin' about long or short.'

'It's all right,' Molly McNamara said. 'I'll pick up a box at the range next week.'

'We don't know diddly about guns,' Danny Pogue reiterated. 'Neither of us do.'

'I know, and I think it's precious.' Molly put on her rose-framed glasses and instructed Bud Schwartz to adjust the volume on the television. A nurse came in to check the dressing on Molly's stitches, but Molly shooed her away. She pointed at the TV and said, 'Look here, boys.'

The news opened with videotape of a colossal raging fire. The scene had been recorded at a great distance, and from a helicopter. When the TV reporter announced what was burning, the burglars simultaneously looked at one another and mouthed the same profane exclamation.

'Yes,' Molly McNamara said rapturously. 'Yes, indeed.'

Danny Pogue felt mixed emotions as he watched the Amazing Kingdom burn. He recalled the gaiety of the promenade, the friendliness of the animal characters, the circus colors and brassy music, the wondrous sensation of being inundated with fun. Then he thought of Francis X. Kingsbury killing off the butterflies and crocodiles, and the conflagration seemed more like justice than tragedy.

Bud Schwartz was equally impressed by the destruction of the theme park—not as a moral lesson, but as a feat of brazen criminality. The torch artist had been swift and thorough; the place was engulfed in roaring, implacable flames, and there was no saving it. The man on TV said he had never witnessed such a fierce, fast-moving blaze. Bud Schwartz felt relieved and lucky and wise.

'And you wanted to stay,' he said to Danny Pogue. 'You wanted to ride the Jungle Jerry again.'

Danny Pogue nodded solemnly and slid the chair close to the television. 'We could be dead,' he murmured.

'Fried,' said his partner. 'Fried clams.'

'Hush now,' Molly said. 'There's no call for melodrama.'

She announced that she wasn't going to ask why they'd gone to the Amazing Kingdom that night. 'I don't like to pry,' she said. 'You're grown men, you've got your own lives.'

Danny Pogue said, 'It wasn't us who torched the place.'

Molly McNamara smiled as if she already knew. 'How's your foot, Danny?'

'It don't hardly hurt at all.'

Then to Bud Schwartz: 'And your hand? Is it better?'

'Gettin' there,' he said, flexing the fingers.

Molly removed her glasses and rested her head against the pillows. 'Nature is a wonder,' she said. 'Such power to renew, or to destroy. It's an awesome paradox.'

'A what?' said Danny Pogue.

Molly told them to think of the fire as a natural purge, a cyclical scouring of the land. Bud Schwartz could hardly keep a straight face. He jerked his chin toward the flickering images on television, and said, 'So maybe it's spontaneous combustion, huh? Maybe a bolt a lightning?'

'Anything's possible,' Molly said with a twinkle. She asked Danny Pogue to switch to the Discovery Channel, which just happened to be showing a documentary about endangered Florida manatees. A mating scene was in progress as Danny Pogue adjusted the color tint.

Not tonight, thought Bud Schwartz, and got up to excuse himself.

Molly said, 'There's a Dodgers game on ESPN. You can watch across the hall in Mr. McMillan's room—he is in what they call a nonresponsive state, so he probably won't mind.'

'Swell,' Bud Schwartz muttered. 'Maybe we'll go halfsies on a keg.'

Danny Pogue heard none of this; he was already glued to the tube. Bud Schwartz pointed at his partner and grinned. 'Look what you done to him.'

Molly McNamara winked. 'Go on now,' she said. 'I think Ojeda's pitching.'

Trooper Jim Tile braked sharply when he saw the three green Jeeps. The wildlife officers had parked in a precise triangle at the intersection of Card Sound Road and County 905.

'We'll be out of the way in a minute,' said Sergeant Mark Dyerson.

The rangers had gathered between the trucks in the center of the makeshift triangle. Jim Tile joined them. He noticed dogs pacing in the back of one of the Jeeps.

'Look at this,' Sergeant Dyerson said.

In the middle of the road, illuminated by headlights, was a battered red collar. Jim Tile crouched to get a closer look.

'Our transmitter,' the ranger explained. Imprinted on the plastic was the name 'Telonics MOD-500.'

'What happened?' Jim Tile asked.

'The cat tore it off. Somehow.'

'That's one tough animal.'

'It's a first,' Sergeant Dyerson said. 'We've never had one that could bust the lock on the buckle.'

Another officer asked, 'What now?' It was the wretched plea of a man being devoured by insects.

'If the cat wants out this bad,' said Sergeant Dyerson, 'I figure we'll let him be.'

From the south came the oscillating whine of a fire truck. Sergeant Dyerson retrieved the broken panther collar and told his men to move the Jeeps off the road. Minutes later, a hook-and-ladder rig barreled past.

Jim Tile mentioned that the theme park was on fire.

'It's breaking my heart,' Sergeant Dyerson said. He handed the trooper a card. 'Keep an eye out. My home number is on the back.'

Jim Tile said, 'All my life, I've never seen a panther.'

'You probably never will,' said the ranger, 'and that's the crime of it.' He tossed the radio collar in the back of the truck and slid behind the wheel.

'Not all the news is bad,' he said. 'Number Nine's got a litter of kittens over in the Fokahatchee.'

'Yeah?' Jim Tile admired the wildlife officer's outlook and dedication. He was sorry his old friend had caused the man so much trouble and confusion. He said, 'So this is all you do—track these animals?'

'It's all I do,' Sergeant Dyerson said.

To Jim Tile it sounded like a fine job, and an honorable one. He liked the notion of spending all day in the deep outdoors, away from the homicidal masses. He wondered how difficult it would be to transfer from the highway patrol to the Game and Fish.

'Don't you worry about this cat,' he told Sergeant Dyerson.

'I worry about all of them.'

'This one'll be all right,' the trooper said. 'You've got my word.'

As soon as he spotted the police car, Joe told Carrie to hike up her gown and run. She followed him down the slope of the bridge and into a mangrove creek.

Breathlessly they clung to the slippery roots; only their heads stayed dry.

'Don't move,' Joe Winder said.

'There's a june bug in your ear.'

'Yes, I'm aware of that.' He quietly dunked his face, and the beetle was swept away by the milky-blue current.

She said, 'May I raise the subject of snakes?'

'We're fine.' He wrapped his free arm around her waist, to hold her steady against the tide. 'You're certainly being a good sport about all this,' he said.

'Will you think about Orlando?'

'Sure.' It was the least he could do.

The metronomic blink of the blue lights grew stronger, and soon tires crunched the loose gravel on the road; the siren died with a tremulous moan.

Winder chinned up on a mangrove root for a better view. He saw a highway patrol cruiser idling at an angle on the side of the road. The headlights dimmed, and the trooper honked three times. They heard a deep voice, and Winder recognized it: Jim Tile.

'We lucked out,' he said to Carrie. 'Come on, that's our ride.' They climbed from the creek and sloshed out of the mangroves. Before reaching the road, they heard another man's voice and the slam of a door.

Then the patrol car started to roll.

Joe Winder sprinted ahead, waving both arms and shouting for the trooper to stop. Jim Tile calmly swerved around him and, by way of a farewell, flicked his brights as he drove past.

Winder clutched his aching rib cage and cursed spiritedly at the speeding police car. Carrie joined him on the centerline, and together they watched the flashing blue lights disappear over the crest of the Card Sound Bridge.

'Everyone's a comedian,' Joe Winder said.

'Didn't you see who was in the back seat?'

'I didn't see a damn thing.'

Carrie laughed. 'Look what he threw out the window.' She held up a gooey stick of insect repellent. The top-secret military formula.

'Do me first,' she said. 'Every square inch.'

EPILOGUE

A team of police divers recovered the body of PEDRO LUZ from the whale tank at the Amazing Kingdom of Thrills. The Monroe County medical examiner ruled drowning as the official cause of death, although the autopsy revealed 'minor bite marks, contusions and chafing of a sexual nature.'

JAKE HARP recovered from his gunshot wound and rejoined the professional golfing circuit, although he never regained championship form. His next best finish was a tie for 37th place at the Buick Open, and subsequently he set a modern PGA record by missing the cut in twenty-two consecutive tournaments. Eventually he retired to the Seniors' Tour, where he collapsed and died of a cerebral hemorrhage on the first hole of a sudden-death play-off with Billy Casper.

With his payoff money from the mob, BUD SCHWARTZ started a private security company that specializes in high-tech burglar-alarm systems for the home, car and office. Bearing a letter of recommendation from Molly McNamara, DANNY POGUE moved to Tanzania, where he is training to be a game warden at the Serengeti National Park.

After Francis X. Kingsbury's murder, AGENT BILLY HAWKINS was docked a week's pay, and given a written reprimand for taking an unauthorized leave of absence. A month later he was transferred to the FBI office in Sioux Falls, South Dakota. He endured one winter before resigning from the Bureau and returning to Florida as an executive consultant to Schwartz International Security Services Ltd.

NINA WHITMAN quit the phone-sex syndicate after three of her poems were published in the *New Yorker*. A later collection of prose and short fiction was praised by Erica Jong as a 'fresh and vigorous reassessment of the female sexual dynamic.' Shortly after receiving the first royalty statement from her publisher, Nina gave up poetry and moved to Westwood, California, where she now writes motion-picture screenplays. Her husband owns the second-largest Chevrolet dealership in Los Angeles County.

The estate of FRANCIS X. KINGSBURY, aka FRANKIE KING, was sued by the Walt Disney Corporation for copyright infringement on the characters of Mickey and Minnie Mouse. The lawsuit was prompted by accounts of a pornographic tattoo on the decedent's left forearm, as described by newspaper reporters attending the open-casket funeral. After deliberating only thirty-one minutes (and reviewing a coroner's photograph of the disputed etching), an Orlando jury awarded the Disney company $1.2 million in actual and punitive damages. PENNY KINGSBURY is appealing the decision.

CHARLES CHELSEA accepted a job as executive vice president of public relations for Monkey Mountain. Four months later, disaster struck when a coked-up podiatrist from Ann Arbor, Michigan, jumped a fence and attempted to leg-wrestle a male chacma baboon. The podiatrist was swiftly killed and dismembered, and the animal park was forced to close. Chelsea retired from the public-relations business, and is now said to be working on a novel with Gothic themes.

At his own request, TROOPER JIM TILE was reassigned to Liberty County in the Florida Panhandle. With only 5.1 persons per square mile, it is the least densely populated region of the state.

DICKIE THE DOLPHIN survived the fire that destroyed the Amazing Kingdom of Thrills, and was temporarily relocated to a holding pen at an oceanfront hotel near Marathon. Seven months later, a bankruptcy judge approved the sale of the frisky mammal to a marine attraction in Hilton Head, South Carolina. No swimming is allowed in Dickie's new tank.

After the Amazing Kingdom closed, UNCLE ELY'S ELVES never worked together again. Veteran character actor MOE STRICKLAND branched into drama, taking minor roles in television soap operas before miraculously landing the part of Big Daddy in a Scranton dinner-theater production of *Cat on a Hot Tin Roof*. A freelance critic for the *Philadelphia Inquirer* described Strickland's performance as 'gutsy and brooding.'

Several weeks after fire swept through Francis X. Kingsbury's theme park, a piano-sized crate from Auckland, New Zealand, was discovered outside the padlocked gate. No one was certain how long the crate had been there, but it was empty by the time a security guard found it; whatever was inside had clawed its way out. Soon residents of the nearby Ocean Reef Club began reporting the disappearance of pet cats and small dogs at a rate of two per week—a mystery that remains unsolved. Meanwhile, Kingsbury's estate received a handwritten invoice from a person calling herself RACHEL LARK. The bill, excluding shipping, amounted to $3,755 for 'miscellaneous wildlife.'

The widow of DR. WILL KOOCHER hired a Miami lawyer and filed a wrongful-death action against the Amazing Kingdom of Thrills, Ramex Global Trust, N.A. and Bermuda Intercontinental Services, Inc. The insurance companies hastily settled the lawsuit out of court for approximately $2.8 million. The gutted ruins of the Amazing Kingdom were razed, and the land was replanted with native trees, including buttonwoods, pigeon plums, torchwoods, brittle palms, tamarinds, gumbo-limbos and mangroves. This restoration was accomplished in spite of rigid opposition from the Monroe County Commission, which had hoped to use the property as a public dump.

The surviving owners of the FALCON TRACE golf resort sold all construction permits and building rights to a consortium of Japanese investors who had never set foot in South Florida. However, the project stalled once again when environmentalists surveying the Key Largo

CARL HIAASEN

site reported the presence of at least two blue-tongued mango voles, previously thought to be extinct. According to an unsigned press release faxed to all major newspapers and wire services, the tiny mammals were spotted at Falcon Trace during a nature hike by MOLLY MCNAMARA and the Mothers of Wilderness, who immediately reported the sighting to the U.S. Department of Interior.

Eventually the Falcon Trace and Amazing Kingdom properties were purchased from bankruptcy by the state of Florida, and became part of a preserve on NORTH KEY LARGO. In the spring of 1991, a *National Geographic* photographer set out to capture on film the last surviving pair of blue-tongued mango voles. After two months in the woods, the photographer contracted mosquito-borne encephalitis and was airlifted to Jackson Memorial Hospital, where he spent three weeks on clear fluids. He never got a glimpse of the shy and nocturnal creatures, although he returned to New York with a cellophane packet of suspect rodent droppings and a pledge to keep searching.

STRIP TEASE

For the amazing Esther Newberg

ONE

On the night of September sixth, the eve of Paul Guber's wedding, his buddies took him to a strip joint near Fort Lauderdale for a bachelor party. The club was called the Eager Beaver, and it was famous county-wide for its gorgeous nude dancers and watered-down rum drinks. By midnight Paul Guber was very drunk and hopelessly infatuated with eight or nine of the strippers. For twenty dollars they would perch on Paul's lap and let him nuzzle their sweet-smelling cleavage; he was the happiest man on the face of the planet.

Paul's friends carried on with rowdy humor, baying witlessly and spritzing champagne at the stage. At first the dancers were annoyed about being sprayed, but eventually they fell into the spirit of the celebration. Slick with Korbel, they formed a laughing chorus line and high-kicked their way through an old Bob Seger tune. Bubbles sparkled innocently in their pubic hair. Paul Guber and his pals cheered themselves hoarse with lust.

At half-past two, a fearsome-looking bouncer announced the last call. While Paul's buddies pooled their cash to pay the exorbitant tab, Paul quietly crawled on stage and attached himself to one of the performers. Too drunk to stand, he balanced on his

knees and threw a passionate hug around the woman's
bare waist. She smiled good-naturedly and kept moving
to the music. Paul hung on like a drowning sailor. He
pressed his cheek to the woman's tan belly and closed
his eyes. The dancer, whose name was Erin, stroked
Paul's hair and told him to go home, sugar, get some
rest before the big day.

A man yelled for Paul to get off the stage, and Paul's
friends assumed it was the bouncer. The club had a
strict rule against touching the dancers for free. Paul
Guber himself heard no warning – he appeared coma-
tose with bliss. His best friend Richard, with whom
Paul shared a cubicle at the brokerage house, produced
a camera and began taking photographs of Paul and
the naked woman. Blackmail, he announced playfully.
Pay up, or I mail these snapshots to your future mother-
in-law! Everyone in the club seemed to be enjoying
themselves. That's why Paul's friends were so shocked
to see a stranger jump on stage and begin beating him
with an empty champagne bottle.

Three, four, five hard blows to the head, and still
Paul Guber would not release the dancer, who was
trying her best to avoid being struck. The bottle-
wielding man was tall and paunchy, and wore an
expensive suit. His hair was silver, although his bushy
mustache was black and crooked. No one in Paul
Guber's bachelor party recognized him.

Raw sucking noises came from the man's throat as
he pounded on the stockbroker's skull. The bouncer got
there just as the champagne bottle shattered. He
grabbed the silver-haired man under the arms and prepared to throw him off the stage in a manner that would
have fractured large bones. But the bouncer alertly

noticed that the silver-haired man had a companion, and the companion had a gun that might or might not be loaded. Having the utmost respect for Colt Industries, the bouncer carefully released the silver-haired man and allowed him to flee the club with his armed friend.

Amazingly, Paul Guber never fell down. The paramedics had to pry his fingers off the dancer's buttocks before hauling him to the hospital. In the emergency room, his worried buddies gulped coffee and cooked up a story to tell Paul's fiancée.

By the time the police arrived, the Eager Beaver lounge was empty. The bouncer, who was mopping blood off the stage, insisted he hadn't seen a thing. The cops clearly were disappointed that the nude women had gone home, and showed little enthusiasm for investigating a drunken assault with no victim present. All that remained of the alleged weapon was a pile of sparkling green shards. The bouncer asked if it was okay to toss them in the dumpster, and the cops said sure.

Paul Guber's wedding was postponed indefinitely. His friends told Paul's bride-to-be that he had been mugged in the parking lot of a synagogue.

In the car, speeding south on Federal Highway, Congressman David Lane Dilbeck rubbed his temples and said: 'Was it a bad one, Erb?'

And Erb Crandall, the congressman's loyal executive assistant and longtime bagman, said: 'One of the worst.'

'I don't know what came over me.'

'You assaulted a man.'

'Democrat or Republican?'

Crandall said, 'I have no earthly idea.'

Congressman Dilbeck gasped when he noticed the pistol on his friend's lap. 'Jesus, Mary and Joseph! Don't tell me.'

Without emotion, Crandall said, 'I had no choice. You were about to be maimed.'

Five minutes passed before the congressman spoke again. 'Erb,' he said, 'I love naked women, I truly do.'

Erb Crandall nodded neutrally. He wondered about the congressman's driver. Dilbeck had assured him that the man understood no English, only French and Creole. Still, Crandall studied the back of the driver's black head and wondered if the man was listening. These days, anyone could be a spy.

'All men have weaknesses,' Dilbeck was saying. 'Mine is of the fleshly nature.' He peeled off the phony mustache. 'Let's have it, Erb. What exactly did I do?'

'You jumped on stage and assaulted a young man.'

Dilbeck winced. 'In what manner?'

'A bottle over the head,' Crandall said. 'Repeatedly.'

'And you didn't stop me! That's your goddamn job, Erb, to get me out of those situations. Keep my name out of the papers.'

Crandall explained that he was in the john when it happened.

'Did I touch the girl?' asked the congressman.

'Not this time.'

In French, Crandall asked the Haitian driver to stop the car and wait. Crandall motioned for Dilbeck to get out. They walked to an empty bus bench and sat down.

The congressman said, 'What's all this nonsense? You can talk freely in front of Pierre.'

4

'We've got a problem.' Crandall steepled his hands. 'I think we should call Moldy.'

Dilbeck said no way, absolutely not.

'Somebody recognized you tonight,' said Crandall. 'Somebody in that strip joint.'

'God.' Dilbeck shut his eyes and pinched the bridge of his nose. 'It's an election year, Erb.'

'Some little twerp, I didn't get the name. He was standing by the back door when we ran out. Some skinny jerk-off with Coke-bottle glasses.'

'What'd he say?'

' "*Attaboy, Davey.*" He was looking right at you.'

'But the mustache—'

'Then he said, "Chivalry ain't dead." ' Crandall looked very grim.

Congressman Dilbeck said, 'Did he seem like the type to stir up trouble?'

It was all Crandall could do to keep from laughing. 'Looks are deceiving, David. I'll be calling Moldy in the morning.'

Back in the car, heading south again, Dilbeck asked about the condition of the man he'd attacked.

'I have no earthly idea,' Crandall said. He would phone the hospital later.

'Did he seem dead?'

'Couldn't tell,' replied Crandall. 'Too much blood.'

'Lord,' said the congressman. 'Lord, I've got to get a grip on this. Erb, let's you and me pray. Give me your hands.' He reached across the seat for Crandall, who shook free of the congressman's clammy fervent paws.

'Knock it off,' Crandall snapped.

'Please, Erb, let's join hands.' Dilbeck flexed his

5

fingers beseechingly. 'Join together and pray with me now.'

'No fucking way,' said the bagman. 'You pray for both of us, David. Pray like hell.'

The next night, Erin was taking off her clothes, getting ready, when she told Shad that she'd checked with the hospital. 'They said he's out of intensive care – the man who got hurt.'

Shad's eyes never looked up from the card table. 'Thank God,' he said. 'Now I can sleep nights.'

'The gun frightened me.' Erin was changing into her show bra. 'He sure didn't look like a bodyguard, did he? The one with the gun?'

Shad was deeply absorbed. Using a surgical hemostat, he was trying to peel the aluminum safety seal from a four-ounce container of low-fat blueberry yogurt. The light was poor in the dressing room, and Shad's eyesight wasn't too sharp. He hunched over the yogurt like a watchmaker.

'I gotta concentrate,' he said gruffly to Erin.

By now she'd seen the dead cockroach, a hefty one even by Florida standards. Legs in the air, the roach lay on the table near Shad's left elbow.

Erin said, 'Let me guess. You've had another brainstorm.'

Shad paused, rolling a cigarette from one side of his mouth to the other. He sucked hard, then blew the smoke to twin plumes from his nostrils.

'The hell does it look like?' he said.

'Fraud,' said Erin. She stepped behind a door and

6

slipped out of her skirt. 'Fraud is what it looks like to me.'

Triumphantly, Shad lifted the foil (intact!) from the yogurt container. Carefully he placed it on the table. Then, with the hemostat, he lifted the dead cockroach by one of its brittle brown legs.

'Isn't that your music?' he said to Erin. 'Van Morrison. You better get your ass out there.'

'In a minute,' Erin said. She put on her G-string, the red one with seahorses. When Erin first bought it, she'd thought the design was paisley. One of the other dancers had noticed that the pattern was actually seahorses. Laughing seahorses.

Erin came out from behind the door. Shad didn't look up.

'Have the police been around?' she asked.

'Nope.' Shad smiled to himself. Cops – they usually got about as far as the front bar and then forgot why they'd come. They'd wander through the Eager Beaver bug-eyed and silly, like little kids at Disney World. Cops were absolute saps when it came to bare titties.

Erin said she'd never seen a man get hit so hard with anything as the bachelor who got clobbered with the champagne bottle. 'It's a miracle there wasn't brain damage,' she said.

Shad took this as criticism of his response time. 'I got up there as quick as I could.' His tone was mildly defensive.

'Don't worry about it,' Erin told him.

'He didn't look the type. Of all the ones to go batshit.'

Erin agreed. The man wielding the Korbel bottle was

7

not your typical strip-show creep. He wore a silk tie and passed out twenties like gumdrops.

Erin checked her stiletto pumps for bloodstains. 'This is a lousy business,' she remarked.

'No shit. Why'd you think I'm sitting here fucking with a dead roach? This little bugger is my ticket out.'

As steady as a surgeon, Shad positioned the cockroach in the low-fat blueberry yogurt. With the beak of the hemostat, he pressed lightly. Slowly the insect sunk beneath the creamy surface, leaving no trace.

Erin said, 'You big crazy dreamer.'

Shad absorbed the sarcasm passively. 'Do you get the *Wall Street Journal*?'

'No.' She wondered where he was heading now.

'According to the *Journal*,' Shad said, 'the Delicato Dairy Company is worth one hundred eighty-two million dollars, on account of Delicato Fruity Low-Fat Yogurt being the fastest-selling brand in the country. The stock's at an all-time high.'

Erin said, 'Shad, they won't fall for this.' She couldn't believe he was trying it again.

'You're late, babe.' Shad jerked a thumb toward the stage. 'Your fans are waiting.'

'I've got time. It's a long number.' Erin slipped into her teddy (which would come off after the first number) and her heels (which would stay on all night).

Shad said, 'That song, how come you like it so much? You don't even got brown eyes.'

'Nobody looks at my eyes,' Erin said. 'It's a good dancing song, don't you think?'

Shad was scrutinizing the yogurt. A hairy copper-colored leg had emerged from the creamy bog. Was it moving? Shad said to Erin: 'You ever see *Deliverance*?

The movie, not the book. That last scene, where the shriveled dead hand comes out from the water? Well, come here and look at this fucking roach.'

'No thanks.' Erin asked if Mr Peepers was in the audience tonight. That was the nickname for one of her regulars, a bony bookish man with odd rectangular eyeglasses. He usually sat at table three.

Shad said, 'What, all of a sudden I'm supposed to take roll?'

'He called and left a message,' Erin said. 'Said he had a big surprise for me, which is just what I need.' She dabbed on some perfume – why, she had no idea. Nobody got close enough to smell it. Unlike the other strippers, Erin refused to do table dances. Ten bucks was ridiculous, she thought, to let some drunk breathe on your knees.

Shad said, 'You want me to, I'll throw his ass out.'

'No, if you could just hang close,' said Erin, 'especially after what happened last night.'

'No sweat.'

'It's probably nothing,' Erin said. Next came the lipstick. The boss preferred candy-apple red but Erin went with a burgundy rose. She'd hear about it from the other dancers, but what the hell.

Shad sat back from the yogurt project and said, 'Hey, come and see. It's just like new!'

'They could put you in jail. It's called product tampering.'

'It's called genius,' Shad said, 'and for your information, I already got a lawyer can't wait to take the case. And a Palm Beach shrink who swears I'm totally fucking traumatized since I opened a yogurt and found this damn cockroach—'

9

Erin laughed. 'Traumatized? You don't even know what that means.'

'Grossed out is what it means. And look here—' Shad lifted the foil seal with the hemostat. 'Perfect! Not even a rip. So the bastards can't say someone broke into the grocery and messed with the carton.'

'Clever,' Erin said. She checked her hair in the mirror. Most of the dancers wore wigs, but Erin felt that a wig slowed her down, limited her moves. Losing a wig was one of the worst things to happen on stage. That, and getting your period.

'How's my bottom?' she asked Shad. 'Is my crack showing?'

'Naw, babe, you're covered.'

'Thanks,' Erin said. 'Catch you later.'

'Go on and laugh. I'm gonna be rich.'

'Nothing would surprise me.' She couldn't help but envy Shad's optimism.

'The way it goes,' he said, 'them really big companies don't go to trial on stuff like this, on account of the negative publicity. They just pay off the plaintiff is what the lawyer told me. Major bucks.'

Erin said, 'The customer's name is Killian. Table three. Let me know if he comes in.' Then she was gone. He could hear the heels clicking on stage, the applause, the gin-fueled hoots.

Shad peered into the container. The roach leg had resubmerged: the surface of the yogurt looked smooth and undisturbed. A masterful job of sabotage! Shad placed the foil seal in a Ziploc bag and closed it by sliding his thumb and forefinger along the seam: evidence. Gingerly he carried the yogurt container to the dancers' refrigerator. He placed it on the second tray, between a six-pack of Diet Sprite and bowl of cottage cheese. Over the Delicato yogurt label he taped a handwritten warning:

'Do Not Eat or Else.'

He reread the note two or three times, decided it wasn't stern enough. He wrote out another and taped it beneath the first: 'Property of Shad.'

Then he went out to the lounge to see if any asses needed kicking. Sure enough, at table eight a pie-eyed Volvo salesman was trying to suck the toes off a cocktail waitress. Effortlessly Shad heaved him out the back door. He dug a Pepsi out of the cooler and took a stool at the bar.

At midnight, the skinny guy with the square glasses came in and staked out his usual chair at table three. Shad strolled over and sat down beside him.

On stage, Erin was grinding her heart out.

She's wrong about one thing, Shad thought. *I* notice her eyes, every night I do. And they're definitely green.

TWO

Malcolm J. Moldowsky did not hesitate to address United States Congressman Dave Dilbeck as 'a card-carrying shithead'.

To which Dilbeck, mindful of Moldowsky's influence and stature, responded: 'I'm sorry, Malcolm.'

Pacing the congressman's office, Moldowsky cast a cold scornful eye on every plaque, every commemorative paperweight, every pitiable tin memento of Dilbeck's long and undistinguished political career.

'I see problems,' said Malcolm Moldowsky. He was a fixer's fixer, although it was not the occupation listed on his income-tax forms.

There's no problem, Dilbeck insisted, none at all. 'We were gone before the police showed up.'

Moldowsky was a short man, distractingly short, but he made up for it by dressing like royalty and slathering himself with expensive cologne. It was easy to be so impressed by Moldy's fabulous wardrobe and exotic aroma that one might overlook his words, which invariably were important.

'Are you listening?' he asked Dave Dilbeck.

'You said there's a problem, I said I don't see any problem.'

Moldowsky's upper lip curled, exposing the small

12

and pointy dentition of a lesser primate. He stepped closer to Dilbeck and said, 'Do de name Gary Hart ring a bell? Fuckups 101 – you need a refresher course?'

'That was different,' the congressman said.

'Indeed. Mr Hart did not send anyone to the emergency room.'

Dilbeck felt the heat of Moldowsky pressing closer – smelled the sharp minty breath and inhaled the imported Italian musk, which was strong enough to gas termites. Dilbeck quickly stood up. He was more at ease speaking to the crown of the man's head, instead of eye to eye. The congressman said, 'It won't happen again, that's for sure.'

'Really?'

The acid in Moldowsky's remark made the congressman nervous. 'I've been doing some soul-searching.'

Moldowsky stepped back so Dilbeck could see his face. 'David, the problem is not in your soul. It's in your goddamn trousers.'

The congressman shook his head solemnly. 'Weakness is spiritual, Malcolm. Only the manifestation is physica—'

'You are so full of shit—'

'Hey, I can conquer this,' Dilbeck said. 'I can control these animal urges, you just watch.'

Moldowsky raised his hands impatiently. 'You and your damn urges. It's an election year, Davey. That's number one. Only a card-carrying shithead would show his face at a nudie joint in an election year. Number two, your man pulls a gun, which happens to be a felony.'

'Malcolm, don't blame Erb.'

'And number three,' Moldowsky went on, 'during the commission of the act, you are recognized by a patron of this fine establishment. Which raises all sorts of possibilities, none of them good.'

'Whoa, whoa, whoa.' Dilbeck wedged his hands to signal time-out, like a football coach. 'Let's not jump to conclusions.'

Malcolm Moldowsky laughed harshly. 'That's my job, Congressman.' Once again he started to pace. 'Why did you hit that man with the bottle? Don't tell me – you got something going with the stripper, right? She's carrying your love child, perhaps?'

Dilbeck said, 'I don't even know her name.'

'But still you felt this uncontrollable impulse to defend her honor, such as it is. I understand, David, I understand perfectly.'

'It's a sickness, that's all. I should never be around naked women.'

All the fight had gone out of the congressman. Moldowsky circled the desk and approached him. In a softer voice: 'You don't need this shit right now. You got the campaign. You got the sugar vote coming up. You got a committee to run.' Moldowsky tried to chuck the congressman on the shoulder but wasn't quite tall enough. He wound up patting him on the elbow. 'I'll take care of this,' he said.

'Thanks, Mmm – Malcolm.' Dilbeck almost slipped and called him Moldy, which is what everyone called Moldowsky behind his back. Fanatically hygienic, Moldowsky hated the nickname.

'One more request,' he said. 'Keep David Jr in your pants until November. As a personal favor to me.'

Dilbeck's cheeks flushed.

'Because,' Moldowsky went on, 'I'd hate to think how your constituents would look upon such behavior – all those senior citizens in those condos, those conservative Cubans down on Eighth Street, those idealist young yupsters on the beach. What would they think if Congressman Davey got busted with a bunch of go-go dancers. How'd you suppose that would play?'

'Poorly,' admitted the congressman. He needed a drink.

'You still an elder in the church?'

'A deacon,' Dilbeck said.

'Is that a fact?' Malcolm Moldowsky wore a savage grin. 'You get the urge to chase pussy, call me. I'll set something up.' He dropped his voice. 'It's an election year, deacon, you gotta be careful. If it's a party you need, we'll bring it to you. That sound like a deal?'

'Deal,' the congressman said. When Moldy had gone, he cranked open a window and gulped for fresh air.

Every few years, the Congress of the United States of America voted generous price supports for a handful of agricultural millionaires in the great state of Florida. The crop that made them millionaires was sugar, the price of which was grossly inflated and guaranteed by the US government. This brazen act of plunder accomplished two things: it kept American growers very wealthy, and it undercut the struggling economies of poor Caribbean nations, which couldn't sell their own bounties of cane to the United States at even half the bogus rate.

For political reasons, the government's payout to the sugar industry was patriotically promoted as aid to the struggling family farmer. True, some of the big sugar companies were family-owned, but the family members themselves seldom touched the soil. The closest most of them got to the actual crop were the cubes that they dropped in their coffee at the Bankers' Club. The scions of sugar growers wouldn't be caught dead in a broiling cane field, where the muck crawled with snakes and insects. Instead the brutal harvest was left to Jamaican and Dominican migrant workers, who were paid shameful wages to swing machetes all day in the sweltering sun.

It had been this way for an eternity, and men like Malcolm Moldowsky lost no sleep over it. His task, one of many, was making sure that Big Sugar's price supports passed Congress with no snags. To make that happen, Moldowsky needed senators and representatives who were sympathetic to the growers. Fortunately, sympathy was still easy to buy in Washington: all it took was campaign contributions.

So Moldowsky could always round up the votes. That was no problem. But the votes didn't do any good unless the sugar bill made it out of committee, and this year the committee of the House was in bitter turmoil over issues having nothing to do with agriculture. No fewer than three formerly pliant congressmen had been stricken with mysterious attacks of conscience, and announced they would vote against the sugar price supports. Ostensibly they were protesting the plight of the migrants and the disastrous pollution of the Everglades, into which the growers regularly dumped billions of gallons of waste water.

Malcolm Moldowsky knew the dissenting congressmen couldn't care less about the wretched cane workers, nor would they mind if the Everglades caught fire and burned to cinders. In truth, the opposition to the sugar bill was retaliation against the chairman of the committee, one David Dilbeck, who had cast the deciding vote that killed a hefty twenty-two-percent pay raise for himself and his distinguished colleagues in the House.

Dilbeck had committed this unforgivable sin by pure accident; he had been drunk, and had simply pushed the wrong lever when the matter of the pay raise was called to the floor. In his pickled condition, it was miraculous that Dilbeck had found the way back to his own desk, let alone connected with the tote machine. The following noon, the bleary congressman turned on the television to see George Will praising him for his courage. Dilbeck had no idea why; he remembered nothing of the night before. When staff members explained what he'd done, he crawled to a wastebasket and spit up.

Rather than admit the truth – that full credit for the deed belonged to the distillers of Barbancourt rum – David Dilbeck went on 'Nightline' and said he was proud of voting the way he did, said it was no time for Congress to go picking the public's pocket. Privately, Dilbeck was furious at himself; he'd needed the extra dough worse than anybody.

And now his fellow politicians were striking back. They knew Dilbeck depended on Big Sugar for his campaign contributions, and they knew Big Sugar relied upon Dave Dilbeck for the price supports. So the House members decided to screw with him in a major way; they aimed to teach him a lesson.

Malcolm J. Moldowsky saw the ugliness unfolding.

It would require all his subterranean talents to save the sugar bill, and he couldn't do it if Dilbeck got caught in a sex scandal. After years of slithering through political gutters, Moldowsky was still amazed at how primevally stupid most politicians could be, on any given night. He hadn't a shred of pity for Congressman Dilbeck, but he would help him anyway.

Millions upon millions of dollars were at stake. Moldy would do whatever had to be done, at whatever the cost.

The other dancers knew something was bothering Erin. It showed in her performance.

'Darrell again,' said Urbana Sprawl, by far the largest and most gorgeous of the dancers. Urbana was Erin's best friend at the Eager Beaver lounge.

'No, it's not Darrell,' Erin said. 'Well, it is and it isn't.'

Darrell Grant was Erin's former husband. They were divorced after five rotten years of marriage and one wonderful child, a daughter. The court battle was protracted and very expensive, so Erin decided to try out as an exotic dancer, which paid better than clerical work. There was nothing exotic about the new job, but it wasn't as sleazy as she had feared. The money just about covered her legal fees.

Then Darrell got cute. He filed a petition charging that Erin was an unfit mother, and invited the divorce judge to come see for himself what the future ex-Mrs Grant did for a living. The judge sat through seven dance numbers and, being a born-again Christian, concluded that Erin's impressionable young daughter was

better off in the custody of her father. That Darrell
Grant was a pillhead, a convict and a dealer in stolen
wheelchairs didn't bother the judge as much as the fact
that Erin took her undies off in public. The judge gave
her a stern lecture on decency and morality, and told her
she could see the child every third weekend, and on
Christmas Eve. Her lawyer was appealing the custody
ruling, and Erin needed dancing money now more than
ever. In the meantime, the divorce judge had become a
regular at the Eager Beaver lounge, sitting in a dim
booth near the Foosball machines. Erin never said a
word to the man, but Shad always made a point of
secretly pissing in the Jack Daniels he served him.

Urbana Sprawl said to Erin: 'Come on, don't make
me beat it out of you.' They were taking off their
makeup, sharing the chipped mirror in the dressing
room.

A customer, Erin admitted. 'Mr Peepers, I call him.
His real name is Killian.'

'Table three,' said another dancer, who was known
as Monique Jr. There were two Moniques dancing at
the club, and neither would change her name. 'I know
the guy,' Monique Jr said. 'Funny glasses, bad necktie,
shitty tipper.'

Urbana Sprawl said to Erin: 'He giving you a
problem?'

'He's missed a couple of nights is all.'

'Wow,' said Monique Jr. 'Call the fucking FBI.'

'You don't understand. It's about my case.' Erin
opened her purse and took out a cocktail napkin, which
was folded into a tiny square. She handed it to Monique
Jr. 'He gave me this the other night. He wanted to talk,

but Shad was sitting right there, so he wrote it down instead.'

Monique Jr read the note silently. Then she passed it to Urbana Sprawl. Mr Killian had printed carefully, in small block letters, with an obvious effort to be neat:

I can help get your daughter back. I ask nothing in return but a kind smile. Also, could you add ZZ Top to your routine? Any song from the first album would be fine. Thank you.

'Men will try anything,' Monique Jr said, skeptically. 'Anything for pussy.'

Erin thought it was worth listening to Killian's pitch. 'What if he's for real?'

Urbana Sprawl folded the note and gave it back. 'Erin, how does he know about Angela?'

'He knows everything.' It was her first experience with a customer who'd gone off the deep end. For three weeks straight Killian had been swooning at table three. 'He says he loves me,' Erin said. 'I haven't encouraged him. I haven't told him anything personal.'

'This happens,' Urbana said. 'Nothing to do but stay cool.'

Erin said he seemed fairly harmless. 'It can't hurt to listen. I'm at the point where I'll try anything.'

Monique Jr said, 'Tell you one thing. The little prick needs to learn how to tip.'

Shad poked his head in the doorway. 'Staff meeting,' he announced, coughing. 'Five minutes, in the office.'

'Beat it,' snapped Urbana Sprawl, who was largely nude. Shad truly didn't notice. Eleven years of strip joints had made him numb to the sight of bare breasts.

An occupational hazard, Shad figured. One more reason to get the hell out, before it was too late.

Erin said, 'Tell Mr Orly we're on the way.'

Shad withdrew, shutting the door. To Erin, he resembled a snapping turtle – his vast knobby head was moist and hairless, and his nose beaked sharply to meet the thin severe line of his lips, forming a lethal-looking overbite. From what Erin could see, Shad also had no eyebrows and no eyelashes.

'Creep,' Monique Jr said.

'He's not so bad.' Erin slipped into a blue terrycloth robe and a pair of sandals. She told the other dancers about Shad's plan for the dead roach.

'Yogurt!' Monique Jr cried. 'God, that's disgusting.'

Urbana Sprawl said, 'I hope it works. I hope he gets a million bucks and goes off to live in Tahiti.'

Dream on, thought Erin. Shad wasn't going anywhere unless Mr Orly told him to go.

Orly's office was done in imitation red velvet. He hated it as much as anyone. The vivid decor had been the choice of the club's previous owner, before he was shot and dumped in the diamond lane of Interstate 95. Orly said the crime had nothing to do with the man's taste for imitation velvet, but rather with his inability to account for gross profits in a timely fashion. Meaning he'd skimmed. The imitation velvet remained on Orly's walls to remind employees that, unless one is very good at it, one does not skim from professional skimmers.

As the dancers assembled before Orly's desk, he became overwhelmed by the commingling of fruity perfumes, and began to sneeze and cough spasmodically.

Shad brought a box of tissues and a can of Dr Pepper. Orly made quite a spectacle of blowing his nose and then examining the tissue, to see what had been expelled. Erin looked at Urbana Sprawl and rolled her eyes. The man was a pig.

'All right,' Orly began. 'Tonight let's talk about the dancing. I been hearing complaints.'

None of the strippers said a word. Orly shrugged, and went on: 'Basically, here's the problem: You girls gotta move more. By that, I mean your asses and also your boobs. I was watching tonight and some of you, I swear, it's like watchin' a corpse rot. Not even a twitch.' Orly paused and popped open the Dr Pepper, which foamed out of the can. When he licked the rim with his tongue, several of the dancers groaned.

Orly glanced up and said, 'Has somebody got a problem? Because if they do, let's hear it.'

Erin raised a hand. 'Mr Orly, the style of our dancing depends on the music.'

Orly motioned with the can. 'Go on.'

Erin said, 'If the songs are fast, we dance fast. If the songs are slow, we dance slow—'

'We been through this before,' he cut in. 'You wanted to pick your own songs, and I says fine on the condition that they're good hot dance songs. But some a this shit, I swear, it's elevator music.'

Urbana Sprawl said, 'Janet Jackson, Madonna – I don't call that elevator music. Paula Abdul? Come on.'

This was the wrong approach with Orly, who didn't know Janet Jackson from Bo Jackson. He put down the soft drink and rubbed the moisture into his palms. 'All I know is, tonight I see a guy sleeping like a baby at table four. *Sleeping!* His face is maybe twelve inches from Sabrina's fur pie, and the guy is fucking snoring. With my own eyes I gotta see this.' Orly sat forward and raised his voice. 'Tell me what kind of a stripper puts a customer to sleep!'

Sabrina, who was combing a chestnut wig on her lap, said nothing. The dancers preferred not to argue with Mr Orly, who was boastful about his connections to organized crime. Besides, some of the women weren't very good on stage, and they knew it. Listless was a charitable way to describe their dancing. Erin tried to help with the routines, but generally the other dancers were not keen on rehearsals.

Orly said, 'Fast, slow or in between – it doesn't matter. The point is to take what God gave you and move it around.' He sneezed suddenly, reached for a tissue and plugged it into both nostrils. He continued speaking, the tissue fluttering with each word: 'Think of it as humping. Humping to music. What counts is not the goddamn speed, it's the motion, for Christ's sake, it's the attitude. I don't pay you girls to bore my customers, understand? A man who's sleeping isn't buying any of my booze, and he sure as hell ain't stuffing any cash in your garters.'

It was Erin who spoke up again. 'Mr Orly, you mentioned attitude. I agree we've got a morale problem here at the club, but I think I know why.'

This got everybody's attention. Even Shad perked up.

'It's the name,' Erin said. 'Eager Beaver – it's a very crude name.'

Orly yanked the tissue out of his nose. Normally he would've fired a woman for such a remark, but Erin brought in lots of business for the club. She was one of the few dancers who could actually dance.

'I like "Eager Beaver," ' Orly said. 'It's catchy and it's clever and it damn near rhymes.'

Erin said it was crude and demeaning. 'And it's bad for morale. It gives the impression we're a bunch of whores, which we're not.'

Orly told her to lighten up. 'It's a tease, darling. We're a strip joint, for Christ's sake, who's gonna pay a seven-dollar cover to watch *nice* girls?'

The man had a point, yet Erin persisted. 'I'm aware of the nature of our business, but it doesn't mean we can't have some pride. When friends and relatives ask where we work, some of us lie about it. Some of us are embarrassed to say the name.'

Orly seemed more amused than offended. He looked at the other dancers and asked, 'This true?'

A few nodded. Orly turned to Shad. 'How about you? You embarrassed to work here?'

'Oh no,' Shad said. 'It's my life's ambition.' He winked at Erin, who tried not to laugh.

Orly rocked back in the chair and folded his hands behind his head. His white shirt was stained the color of varnish at both armpits. 'The name stays,' he announced.

'What about a contest?' Erin suggested. 'To come up with a better one.'

'No!'

Urbana Sprawl said, 'I remember when it was the Pleasure Palace. And before that, the Booby Hatch.'

Monique Jr said, 'And I remember when it was Gentleman's Choice, until the state shut it down for prostitution.'

Orly cringed at the word. 'Well, now it's the Eager

Beaver, and it will stay the Eager Beaver as long as I say so.' He still owed two grand on the new marquee.

'Fine,' said Erin, 'Eager Beaver it stays. Very classy.'

He ignored her. 'The bottom line is, work on your goddamn dancing.' He opened a drawer and pulled out a stack of videotapes. 'This is from a joint in Dallas. Take it home, study how good these girls move. Three, four hundred a night in tips is what they make, and I'm not surprised.'

Shad handed a cassette to each of the dancers.

Urbana Sprawl said, 'Mr Orly, I don't have a VCR.'

'I got one you can rent.'

Erin said, 'Four hundred a night, huh? Maybe it's worth a trip to Dallas. Maybe they've got some openings.'

Again, Orly ignored her. 'One more item,' he said, 'then you can all go home. It's about what happened the other night. The fight on stage.'

Monique Jr said it wasn't much of a fight, just some guy swinging a bottle.

'Whatever,' said Orly. 'You didn't see a damn thing, OK? Anybody asks about it, you go tell Shad.'

Erin was surprised by these instructions. Fights broke out frequently at the Eager Beaver, but Mr Orly seldom took an interest. 'What's going on?' she asked. 'Is it the police?'

'The bottom line is, you don't get paid to answer questions. You get paid to take off your clothes.' He drained the Dr Pepper, burped and tossed the can at Shad, who caught it effortlessly. Orly said, 'Now. We all clear on this?'

The strippers muttered apathetically.

'Good,' said Orly. He started a sneeze, but caught

himself. The dancer named Sabrina shyly raised a hand. Orly told her to make it quick.

She said, 'The guy who was sleeping at table four? That wasn't really my fault, Mr Orly. He was on pills.'

'Darling, I don't care if he was on a fucking respirator. In my club, I want their eyes open. Understand?'

The dancers rose and, in an arresting gust of perfume, bustled out of the office. Orly told Erin to hang around for a minute. When they were alone, he said, 'That guy didn't hurt you the other night, did he?'

'Which guy – the one who grabbed me or the one with the champagne bottle?'

'Either,' Orly said. 'I mean, if you got hurt, let me know. Cuts, bruises, whatever, we'll get you to a doctor. It's on the house.'

On the house? Erin was stunned. She told Orly she was fine.

'Good,' he said, 'but just so you know: it won't happen again. Shad's been spoken to.'

'It wasn't his fault—'

He cut her off with the wave of a hand. 'A bouncer's job is to bounce. I pay that asshole good money.'

Erin stood up to leave.

Orly said, 'One more thing. I wasn't talking about you in here tonight. When it comes to the dancing and all – you're the last girl needs to look at some frigging video. You're one a the best we ever had.'

'Thank you, Mr Orly.'

'The music I don't get. It's awful damn soft but, hey, you make it work. They can't take their eyes off you.'

'Thank you,' she said again.

'Keep it up,' Orly said. 'You need anything, I mean *anything*, lemme know.'

Erin walked out of the office absolutely certain that she was in the middle of trouble.

When she got to the car, the man she called Mr Peepers was waiting.

THREE

When Paul Guber regained consciousness, the first thing he saw at the foot of the hospital bed was a lawyer. He knew without being told; it was a man who could've had no other purpose in a three-piece suit.

'My name is Mordecai,' the lawyer said. Over a vast belly he clutched a thin burgundy valise, brushed leather. 'I'm here to help in any way I can.'

Paul Guber's brainpan sloshed with morphine. He tried to speak but it felt as if he were spitting ash. His field of vision was narrow and electrical around the edges, like a cheap television. A woman came into the picture, her lips moving.

'Darling, how do you feel?'

It was Joyce, his fiancée. Paul Guber saw her reach out and touch a lump in the blanket – his left foot. Paul Guber was pleased to discover that he wasn't paralyzed.

Mordecai said, 'Your friends told me what happened. I was sickened, to be very honest. Such a world we live in.'

Paul Guber blinked rapidly to improve his focus.

'You are lucky to be alive,' confided Mordecai.

Paul wasn't so sure. He wondered what Richard and the others had said to Joyce about the bachelor party.

The appearance of a lawyer in his hospital room caused him to suspect the worst.

He opened his mouth to launch a provisional defense, but Mordecai halted him with a flabby pink palm. 'It would be better if you didn't,' the lawyer said, smiling like a wolf.

By way of introduction, Joyce said, 'Mordecai is my cousin. Uncle Dan's oldest son – you met Uncle Dan. I called him the minute I heard what happened.'

She didn't seem the least bit homicidal. Paul Guber was relieved, but wary.

Mordecai said, 'You probably don't remember much. That's to be expected.'

But Paul remembered everything. Joyce patted his shins under the bedcovers. 'Oh Paul,' she said. 'I can't believe such a thing could happen.'

'In my game,' said Mordecai, 'it's known as gross negligence.'

Paul coughed. It felt like someone had taken a cheese grater to his throat.

'Don't try to speak,' the lawyer advised again. 'You've been beaten severely, resulting in physical and emotional damage. *Permanent* damage, as a result of gross negligence.'

The words came out of a tunnel, but Paul got the general idea. The lawyer was itching to sue somebody. Paul wanted to nip that scheme in the bud – prolonged litigation against a strip joint would please neither his employer nor his future in-laws.

'We're not interested in who did this,' Mordecai was saying. 'We're interested in how it was allowed to happen. Accountability, in other words. We're interested in compensation of a magnitude that no simple street thug could afford.'

Joyce moved to the front of the bed and began stroking Paul's forehead. 'Someone's got to pay for this,' she said quietly.

Mordecai was quick with the follow-through. 'You are not the only aggrieved party, Mr Guber. The cancellation of a wedding is a heart-wrenching event for all concerned. I'm thinking of the bride-to-be.'

'All those engraved invitations,' Joyce elaborated. 'The musicians, the florists, the deposit on the reception hall. The Hyatt's not exactly cheap.'

Paul shut his eyes. Maybe it was all a dream. Maybe there was no naked lady dancing to Van Morrison.

The lawyer said, 'I could scarcely believe it when your friend Richard described the circumstances. Getting mugged on the grounds of a synagogue!'

Paul groaned involuntarily.

'Don't worry, we intend to pursue an action,' Mordecai said. 'You can depend on it.' He raised the briefcase as if it held some secret power.

'Unh—' said Paul, but Joyce pressed two fingers to his lips.

'Rest now,' she whispered. 'We'll come back later.'

'And not a word to anyone,' said Mordecai the lawyer. 'In my game, the best client is a helpless client.'

Paul Guber felt a stab in his arm, and he opened his eyes to see a beautiful nurse injecting him with drugs. He was so grateful he could've kissed her on the lips.

Erin's mother lived in California with her fifth husband. She wrote biweekly letters to Erin – richly detailed accounts of shopping sprees. Always the letters ended with a plea: 'Quit that awful job! Leave that awful place! Come live with us!'

Erin's mother didn't approve of nude dancing as an occupation. Erin didn't approve of marrying men for their money. The two women seldom conversed without argument. Each of Erin's successive stepfathers had offered financial assistance, but Erin wouldn't take a dime. It infuriated her mother. Money was the name of the game, she would say. We girls ought to stick together!

Erin's real father, who was also rich, had died in an automobile accident when she was young. One night he got drunk and drove his Eldorado into a drainage canal. The three young women in the back seat managed to climb out and swim to shore. It was just as well for Erin's father that he did not.

On the way to the funeral, her mother said it was a shame the sonofabitch hadn't lived, so she could've divorced him in a manner consistent with his sins. Over the years, Erin's mother came to be an expert at divorce, and also at widowhood. It was no coincidence that each of Erin's stepfathers was wealthier and more elderly than his predecessor. As Erin grew older, she accepted the fact that her mother was a restless gold digger who would never be happy, never be satisfied. On the other hand, her husbands knew exactly what they were getting, and didn't seem to care. It taught Erin one of life's great lessons: an attractive woman could get whatever she wanted, because men were so laughably weak. They would do *anything* for even the distant promise of sex.

Erin had almost forgotten this precept until her

marriage broke up, and she was left broke and fighting for her daughter. It hit her on the day her divorce lawyer explained what it might cost to gain permanent custody of Angela. Erin was dumbstruck at the figure, which was more money than an office secretary would earn in two or three years. It all depended, said the lawyer, on how big of a prick her ex-husband Darrell intended to be. The biggest, Erin replied.

She knew then that a regular nine-to-five job wouldn't do, that she'd have to find another way. That night she'd gone home and stood at the bedroom mirror and slowly removed her clothes, starting with the blouse. It looked ridiculous. She put on some music, Mitch Ryder and the Detroit Wheels, and tried again. Erin had always been a good dancer, but she'd never seen herself dancing in a full-length mirror, stark naked. Even though she had a good figure, she felt silly. She thought: Who in the world would pay to see this?

The next night Erin went to the Eager Beaver to get a sense of the atmosphere. The place was crowded and the music was very loud. It took about an hour before she relaxed enough to take inventory of both the talent and the clientele. Erin noticed that many of the women were extremely poor dancers who tried to compensate with stage gimmicks. A common move was to wheel around, bend over and show off one's buttocks. Another trick, when hopelessly out of rhythm, was to halt midstep and lick one's own index finger in a salacious way. It spurred the male audience from boredom to wild cheers. Erin watched in amusement as customers lurched toward the stage, whistling and waving beer-soaked currency. How easily amused they are! she thought. There was little difference between this and what her mother did; it was the same game of tease, the same basic equation. Use what you've got to get what you want.

The following morning, Erin drank two cups of black coffee and phoned her mother in San Diego. 'Guess what?' Erin said, and delivered the news in a chirpy tone.

Erin's mother disapproved. She said it was a tawdry way to make a living, even for a few months. She said it was no place to meet high-class guys.

'The money's good,' Erin said, 'and I think I can do it.'

'Not with those tits,' said her mother.

The modest dimensions of Erin's breasts had been an issue for a long time. Erin's mother (who was on her third set of saline implants) believed that surgical enhancement would increase Erin's chances of attracting a good man. She pointed to Darrell Grant as an example of the lowlife trash that was drawn to small-bosomed women. She insisted there was a mathematical corollary between the size of one's boobs and the financial viability of one's suitors.

Erin said she was satisfied with the God-given size of her breasts, and confident that customers would find her sexy.

'Ha!' Erin's mother said. 'You'll see, young lady. You'll see who gets the biggest tips – the girls with the knockers, that's who!'

Erin's mother was wrong. Her daughter was quite a dancer.

*

Erin was startled to meet Jerry Killian in the parking lot of the Eager Beaver lounge. He handed her a bouquet of yellow roses, and a small box containing a diamond lavaliere. Then he told her that he loved her more than life itself.

'Try to get a grip,' Erin said.

'I am lost.'

'Obviously.'

'Lost in love!'

Erin said, 'You don't know me. If you're in love with anything, it's my dancing. And possibly the fact that I was naked at the time.'

Killian's face twisted in pain. 'I would love you as much,' he said, 'if you were a bank teller.'

'Fully clothed?'

'In a potato sack,' he declared.

Erin accepted the roses but gave back the diamond necklace. She unlocked the car and laid the bouquet on the front seat. She felt around on the floorboard for the .32, just in case.

'Erin, I know all about you. Did you read my note?'

'Anybody can go down to the courthouse, Mr Killian. It's all in the files.'

Abruptly Killian dropped to one knee, on the pavement. 'I'm a serious man.'

'Don't do this,' Erin said, wearily.

'I love you. I can fix the custody case.' His voice was burning. 'I can get your child back.'

Stay cool, thought Erin. She was dying to ask him how it would work, how he would do it. 'Mr Killian, get up. You're ruining a perfectly good pair of pants.'

Killian maintained his genuflection. He folded his hands at his breast, as if praying. 'The judge has aspirations for higher office. He has an eye on the federal bench.'

'And I suppose you've got connections.'

Killian glowed. 'One phone call, and he will see your case in a different light.'

'I'll tell you about this judge,' Erin said. 'He comes to the club, sits in the back and doodles with himself while I'm dancing.'

Killian said, 'That's good information. We can use that.'

'Forget it—'

'Please,' he cut in, 'don't underestimate me.'

Erin was thinking, What if he can do this thing? What if he's really got some pull?

'Tell me about your connections. Why should a call from you make a difference?'

Killian said, 'Not from me. From a certain United States congressman.'

Erin took the car keys from her purse and jangled them impatiently.

Killian merrily went on: 'Think about it, Erin. A US congressman asks a favor. Would you dare say no? Not if you had hopes of getting a federal judgeship. Not if you needed some pull in Washington.'

He touched her arm lightly, and she noticed that his fingers were shaking. He said, 'Your little girl – her name is Angela. She belongs with you.'

Erin felt a hitch in her breath. The sound of her daughter's name, coming from this stranger, filled her with sorrow.

'I'm single myself,' Killian said.

'Don't get carried away.'

'You're right, Erin. I'm very sorry.' He stood up,

brushed the dirt from his trousers. 'I've been working on this plan, making progress. Give me another week and you'll have a new court date. And I think you'll find the judge to be much more open-minded about the case.'

He was bowing to kiss her hand when Shad tackled him from the side. It hardly qualified as a scuffle, as there was no resistance from Killian. He seemed to go limp. When his eyeglasses flew off, a dreamy look came to his face.

Erin told Shad not to hurt him.

'Why not?'

Killian was stretched out on the damp asphalt. When he raised his head, pebbles stuck comically to one cheek. 'I'm a man of my word,' he said in a marbly voice.

Shad pointed at him. 'Don't come back, you little dork.'

'Do you speak for the management?' Killian inquired.

Shad placed a size-thirteen shoe on his windpipe.

'Be careful,' Erin said again.

'It's so tempting.'

'But I love her,' Killian croaked. 'I am lost in love.'

Shad shook his head. 'You're pathetic,' he told Killian. 'But you got good taste.'

'Don't underestimate me. I am not without influence.'

Shad looked at Erin, who shrugged.

'Be my wife,' Killian cried.

Shad leaned over and seized him by the collar. 'That's enough a that,' he said.

Erin started the car. Shad didn't let Jerry Killian off the ground until she had gone.

*

The next night, in the dressing room, Monique Sr announced that Carl Perkins was sitting at table seven.

Erin, who was repairing a heel, glanced up and said, 'Carl Perkins the guitarist?'

Monique Sr beamed. 'Is there another?' She regularly spotted celebrities in the audience. Last Tuesday it was William Kunstler, the renowned attorney. A week before, Martin Balsam, the actor.

The sightings were imaginary, but none of the other dancers made an issue of it. Each had a private trick for self-motivation, some inner force that pushed her toward the stage when the music came on. For Monique Sr, the inspiration came from believing that someone famous was in the club, someone who might be impressed by her moves, someone who could whisk her away and change her life for ever. Erin thought it clever of Monique Sr to choose personalities whose names were well known, but whose faces were not exactly national emblems. Carl Perkins, for instance, was a stroke of genius. In the smoky blue shadows of the Eager Beaver, a dozen customers might resemble the legendary musician. It was a bullet-proof fantasy, and Erin admired it.

'Old Carl tipped me forty bucks,' Monique Sr was saying. 'Not that he can't afford it. He only wrote "Blue Suede Shoes".'

'Great song,' said Erin, tapping the new heel in place. Monique Sr was an encyclopedia when it came to rock 'n' roll.

Shad entered the dressing room without knocking. He handed Erin a wrinkled envelope, marked up with red postal ink: her most recent letter to Angela, returned as undeliverable.

Urbana Sprawl said, 'Oh no.'

Erin bitterly crumpled the letter in the palm of her hand. The bastard Darrell had done it again – moved away without telling her. And taken Angie.

'No forwarding address?' Monique Sr asked.

Erin cursed acidly. The man was such a despicable asshole. How had she ever fallen for him?

Shad said, 'Take the night off, babe.'

'I can't.' Erin whipped out her lipstick and hairbrush, and got busy in front of the mirror. 'Dance, dance, dance,' she said, softly to herself.

Monique Sr had fictitious celebrities to motivate her; Erin had Darrell Grant. The divorce judge had ordered him not to go anywhere, but it was like talking to a tomcat. Every time her ex-husband went mobile, Erin saw her legal fees go up another five grand. Finding the bastard, then serving him with new papers, cost a fortune.

'Your lucky night,' Shad told her. He held another envelope; it was crisp and lavender, with familiar block lettering. 'I took the liberty,' he said.

'You opened it?'

'After what happened, yeah. You're damn right.'

Erin said, 'I told you, he's harmless.'

'If he's not,' said Shad, 'he will be.'

Erin read the message twice:

The plan is in motion. Soon my devotion to you will be proven. Still awaiting the smile, and the ZZ Top.

The other dancers clamored to see the note, but Erin tucked it in her purse. 'No, this one's private.'

'One thing – he doesn't listen so good,' Shad said.

He'd warned Mr Peepers that his attentions were unwelcome.

Erin was determined not to get her hopes up. Monique Jr was probably right; Killian was probably trying to get in her pants, nothing more. Maybe the business with the congressman and the judge was hot air. Maybe it wasn't. The question was, How far would Killian go to impress her?

She began brushing her hair, with long even strokes, and listened for her song on the speakers. She was due up next on stage.

Malcolm J. Moldowsky had no qualms about dealing with the owner of a mob strip joint. It was better than dealing with congressmen and senators.

At first, Orly was cagey and snide. He asked why a bigshot congressman's office should give a rat's ass about who hangs out at a nudie joint. But as soon as Moldowsky raised the subject of liquor licenses and the renewal thereof, Orly became a model of friendliness and cooperation. He identified the customer at table three from credit card receipts and then, when the customer returned to the club, Orly phoned promptly with the news. By that time, of course, Moldowsky knew the man's identity. By that time the man had made contact with Congressman David Lane Dilbeck.

Still, Moldowsky was grateful for Orly's information. It was good to know Jerry Killian's movements.

'Nothing happened,' Orly said. 'My help got there first.'

'The young lady wasn't hurt?'

'Not at all. But the bottom line is, I can't have some horny creepoid chasing my best dancer.'

'I understand, Mr Orly.'

'See, I got prettier girls. Longer legs, bigger tits. This one, she ain't even a blonde. But she can dance like I don't know what, and she's built up a good clientele, which is what pays the freight in my business.'

'It won't happen again,' Moldowsky assured him.

'This girl, pass her on the street and you wouldn't look twice. But the moves she's got, I swear to Christ.'

'Natural talent is rare,' Moldowsky said, 'in my line of work, as well.'

'You understand, I can't have guys hanging in the parking lot, waiting for the girls. Some hardass cop shows up and it's loitering for the purpose of solicitation. I been through that before. Like you say, I got a license to think about.'

'Mr Killian's been having some personal problems.'

'Who doesn't,' Orly said. 'It's a fucked-up world, no?'

'Yes, it is.' Again Moldowsky praised Orly for his assistance and discretion. 'If there's anything we can do to repay the favor, please let us know.'

'Just put in a good word,' Orly said.

A good word? For who – the Gambino family? Moldowsky smiled to himself. 'Done,' he said to Orly.

'Also, my brother's got a little trouble with the IRS. Maybe you know somebody over there.'

Nothing's ever simple, Moldowsky thought. 'I can't promise any miracles,' he said. 'But I'll make a few calls.'

Orly thanked him, and added, 'I'm not looking to give this Killian guy any trouble. I'm trying to save him some. My man Shad, he's in a mood to break the fucker in two.'

Moldowsky said, 'Mr Killian won't be back.'

'Whatever.'

Orly didn't ask for details. And Moldowsky had no intention of telling him.

FOUR

Darrell Grant had been living in a suburb called Lauderhill, which offered an exceptionally wide selection of run-down apartments. He'd rented a furnished duplex on a dead-end street where every front lawn, without exception, had an automobile on blocks. Erin wondered if it was a zoning requirement.

In front of Darrell Grant's apartment was a rusted Buick Riviera with a holly tree sprouting from its dashboard. The license plate revealed that the car had been there since 1982, long before Darrell Grant's arrival. Why he hadn't moved it was no great riddle: tow trucks cost money.

The other half of Darrell's grim duplex was occupied by two young Mormon missionaries, who greeted Erin politely as she came up the sidewalk. The missionaries were oiling their bicycles in preparation for another journey among South Florida's sinners. Erin admired their high spirits and fortitude; it was a tough neighborhood for proselytizing.

'Have you seen Mr Grant today?' she asked.

The missionaries said no, Mr Grant hadn't been around in a week or so. Erin went through the motion of knocking on the door. Darrell had taped aluminum foil over the inside windows, so nothing was visible from the front. As Erin headed toward the rear of the duplex, one of the young Mormons warned her to be careful because the yard was full of wheelchair parts.

Erin carefully stepped through an obstacle course of rusting rims, loose spokes, brakes, frames and footrests. She surmised that the wheelchair-stealing business must be doing pretty well for Darrell Grant to abandon so much valuable inventory – that, or the cops were on his back again, forcing a hasty departure.

Typically, Darrell had left the back door of the apartment unlocked. When Erin opened it, she saw that her ex-husband truly was gone. As was his custom, he had stolen everything that wasn't nailed down, plus several items that were. Furniture, carpets, appliances, lamps, plumbing fixtures, ceiling fans, water heater, phone jacks, even the toilet tank was missing. Darrell Grant was nothing if not a master scavenger; he had painstakingly pried the tiles off the kitchen floor. Erin couldn't believe there was a big market for second-hand linoleum, but it was possible that Darrell was ahead of the curve. The commerce of stolen property wasn't immune to recessionary trends.

Darrell had cleaned out every room except one: Angie's bedroom. Erin gasped when she walked in.

The walls were bare except for a dozen old nails and a heart-shaped mirror. The floor was strewn with broken dolls: beheaded Barbies, dismembered Muppets, eviscerated Cabbage Patch Kids. The dolls had something in common: each had been a gift to Angela from Erin.

That was Darrell Grant's way. Weak in the verbal skills, he was inclined to express himself with displays of idiotic violence.

Erin's heart pounded in anger. She envisioned Darrell in their daughter's room, methodically separating the dolls from Angela's other toys, then attacking with a steak knife or pruning shears or God knows what . . . and leaving the mirror up so he could watch his own performance.

No! Erin thought. That wasn't the reason for the mirror. He'd left it for Erin, so she could see herself at the moment of discovery, could see the shock on her own face when she found what he'd done in Angie's bedroom. Could see herself crying.

But she didn't cry.

Touching nothing, she backed out of the room. Then she hurried outside and asked the friendly Mormons if she could borrow a camera.

Darrell Grant's sister lived in a trailer park thirty miles south of Miami. She shared a doublewide with a man who worked nights as a security guard at the Turkey Point nuclear power plant. The guard's name was Alberto Alonso. He greeted Erin warmly at the front door. The fact she was a professional stripper made him absolutely giddy.

'Come in, come in!' Alberto sang out. He opened his arms and attempted a hug; more of a lunge, actually. Erin deftly skirted his grasp.

'Where is Rita?' she asked.

'Out with the cubs,' Alberto said. 'Lupa's new litter – you want to come look? We got an albino.'

'Maybe later,' Erin said. Lupa was the family pet, a fifty-fifty cross between a German shepherd and a wild Mt McKinley timber wolf. At regular intervals, Rita bred Lupa with other wolves. She was able to sell the cubs for three hundred dollars each, sometimes more. It was the newest rage in macho dogs, since pit bulls had gone out of fashion.

'Six babies,' Alberto reported, 'and the only male is albino. You should see the size of his balls!'

Erin said, 'You must be very proud.'

'I'm trying to get the power company interested.'

'In what?'

'Wolf dogs, what else?' Alberto's grin revealed many crooked gaps. Erin didn't know how anyone could invest full confidence in a security guard with so many teeth missing.

'Think about it,' Alberto was saying. 'Packs of wolves patrolling the perimeter. There goes your terrorist threat. There goes your sabotage.'

The screen door opened and Rita charged in. 'Al, how many times I tole you – they ain't no guard dogs. They don't got the disposition for it.'

She wore a housedress, thong slippers, a catcher's mask, and canvas logging gloves that went up to the elbows. The sight of her reminded Erin that none of Darrell's siblings had grown up to be remotely normal or well-adjusted. In the Grant family, procreation had become a game of genetic roulette.

'Hello, Rita,' said Erin.

'Oh. Hi there.' Rita took off the catcher's mask, revealing a nasty track of fresh stitches from the midpoint of her forehead to the bridge of her nose. 'Lupa,' she explained. 'She damn jumpy around those cubs.'

Alberto said, 'Erin, honey, how about a drink?'

'Water would be fine.'

'No, I mean a *drink*.'

Rita said, 'Make that two.'

'Just water,' Erin said. 'I can't stay long.'

Alberto was plainly disappointed. He shuffled to the refrigerator and began grappling with an ice tray. Rita tugged off the logging gloves and said, 'Well, this is quite a surprise.'

Erin said, 'It's about Darrell. He's gone again.'

'Now don't get all worked up.'

'You know where he is?'

'No, ma'am, I do not.' Rita lowered herself onto a black Naugahyde sofa, which hissed beneath her weight. She said, 'You still workin' at that tittie place?'

Rita wasn't going to be easy; playing dumb was her life's work. Alberto was the weaker link.

'I hear the money is good,' Rita remarked. 'But it damn well ought to be.'

Erin said, 'When's the last time you talked to your brother?'

'Lord, I'm sure I don't remember.'

Alberto reappeared with water for Erin and a bourbon for Rita, both served in Fred Flintstone jelly jars. Out of the blue, Alberto said, 'What about private parties? Some of the boys at the plant were asking. They were talking about getting a banquet room at the Ramada.'

'I don't do private parties,' Erin told him. 'I dance at the club. That's it.'

'What about the other girls?'

'You'd have to ask them, Alberto.'

Rita said, 'He's been up to your place. What's the name again?'

'The Eager Beaver,' said Alberto, helpfully.

Rita furrowed her brow. 'I thought it was the Flesh Farm.'

Alberto said. 'No, that's another one.'

'Well, anyhoo, he's seen you dance.'

'Really?' Erin didn't like the idea of Alberto tiptoeing into the club, sneaking a peek. She could picture him giving a full report to the guys down at Turkey Point. It was pathetic, really. Erin was the closest thing to a celebrity that Alberto would ever know.

'I hope it was a good show,' she said sweetly. 'I hope you got your money's worth.'

'Gawd.' Rita lit a cigarette. 'It's all he talked about for weeks after. You'd think he ain't never seen pubic hairs before.'

Alberto Alonso reddened, finally. Erin said, 'You should've told me you were coming. I would've sent some champagne to the table.'

'Are you kidding? Pink champagne?'

A howling commotion erupted in the backyard. Rita grabbed the catcher's mask and hurried out the screen door.

'Careful now!' Alberto shouted after her.

Erin motioned him to sit down. 'We don't get to visit much anymore,' she said.

'Well, the divorce and all.'

'Doesn't mean we can't still be friends,' Erin said.

'I'd like that,' said Alberto. He scooted the chair closer. 'Friends it is. You and me!' His breathing had become audibly heavy, and his eyebrows looked moist.

Erin didn't often see men sweating from their eyebrows. 'There's two sides to every story,' she went on. 'Darrell had his faults.'

'Now that's a fact. He is no saint.'

From outside, they heard Rita shouting curses at the wolf dog. Then came a chilling feral scream.

'Damn,' Alberto said. 'Another cat, I'll bet.'

Erin lightly touched his knee. 'I need to find Darrell. It's very important.'

'He moved away, Erin.'

'I know that.'

'Don't worry, honey.' Alberto flopped a fat moist hand upon hers. Clumsily he tried to intertwine fingers, but Erin pulled away.

'Where is he, Alberto?'

'Rita would kill me.'

'It's my daughter we're talking about.'

Alberto nervously glanced toward the screen door. 'Look, he calls here a couple, three times a week. Needing money, per the usual. But I'm not sure where he's at.' Alberto attempted another hand-holding, but Erin shook him off.

'Anything would be a help,' she said. 'State, county, whatever. I'll settle for an area code.'

Alberto said, 'Rita's the one he talks to, not me. Darrell never told me anything about anything. He don't trust law enforcement, period.'

It was a reach for Alberto Alonso to classify himself as law enforcement, but Erin let it slide. Alberto's job applications had been rejected by every municipal police department in the southeastern United States. Though he had the heart of a lawman, he did not have the acceptable psychological profile. 'Squirrelly' was the term most commonly heard when Alberto's file came up for consideration.

He told Erin: 'Don't worry, I'm sure Angie's fine.'

'She's not fine, Alberto. She's with that fuckhead ex-husband of mine.'

Alberto was shocked into silence. Outside, the chaos in the backyard abated suddenly. Rita poked her head in the screen door. 'Where's the damn shovel?'

Alberto said, 'I thought it was with the rakes.'

'Well, it ain't!' The door slammed.

Erin asked Alberto for some aspirin.

'You got a headache?'

'A killer,' she said.

'Poor thing.' He stood up and cupped her face in his hands. 'You feel hot, honey.'

'Alberto, it's not a fever. It's a headache.'

'I'll get you some Bayers. Be right back.' He went to the bathroom and began searching the cabinet. 'I got Advil!' he called out. 'Tylenols. Anacins. Excedrin PMs. You prefer tablets or them new gel-caps?'

Alberto returned to the living room with an armful of pills, powders and capsules. Rita was there, settling into the Naugahyde, sucking fiercely on a cigarette. Erin was gone.

'Well, well.' Rita's voice cut like a blade. 'If it ain't Marcus Welby.'

Erin was fully aware that the theft of US mail was a federal offense, punishable by fines, imprisonment or both. She was also aware that in the Southern District of Florida, the United States Attorney spent exactly zero man-hours in pursuit of mail thieves, as the government's time was consumed by the prosecution of drug dealers, gunrunners, deposed foreign dictators, savings-

and-loan executives, corrupt local politicians and crooked cops of all ranks.

The workings of the federal justice system were well known to Erin because her previous job, before becoming a nude dancer, was typing and filing intelligence reports for the Federal Bureau of Investigation. Erin was efficient, precise and perceptive. In some ways she was sharper than the FBI agent to whom she reported. Although his filing system was flawless, his street instincts were shaky. Erin liked him and tried to help, but the agent was young, inexperienced and hopelessly Midwestern in his approach; South Florida ate him alive.

When Erin was dismissed from her job, the agent (whose name was Cleary) was more distraught than she was. He tried everything within bounds of the Bureau's turgid hierarchy to reverse the decision, but it was no use. Erin had been reclassified as a security risk after her husband had been charged with the fourth felony of his life: the grand theft of eleven wheelchairs from the Sunshine Groves Retirement Village. It didn't matter that Erin was separated from Darrell Grant at the time – he'd phoned her from jail, and that was that. Phoned her at work, the moron! Told her to hurry and ditch the Camaro and for God's sake don't let the cops look in the trunk. Darrell Grant, yelling these instructions, forgetting that most phone calls out of the Broward County Jail (and all phone calls into the FBI building) were automatically recorded.

Erin herself was never suspected of complicity, for on both audio tapes her words to Darrell Grant were clear.

'You asshole. Where's my daughter?'

Although she didn't want to leave the job, Erin wasn't bitter. She understood the problem. Nobody should be married to a career criminal, but it was especially important for employees of the FBI. Agent Cleary was crestfallen, and wrote a glowing letter of reference, To Whom It May Concern, on official FBI stationery. For him that was quite a daring gesture. As it turned out, the letter was not needed when Erin applied for work at the Eager Beaver lounge. 'Show me your boobs,' Mr Orly had said. 'Fine. When can you start?' Erin didn't have the heart to tell Agent Cleary of her new occupation.

Ironically, the felony charge against Darrell Grant was dropped, as he'd agreed to become a secret informant for the sheriff's department. His first task was ratting out three of his scumdog thief friends; for this, Darrell was rewarded with a pristine new past, courtesy of the DELETE button on the sheriff's crime computer. The vaporizing of Darrell's prior record was egregiously illegal but not without precedent; if questioned, Darrell's handlers could always claim it was an accident. Crime computers were famous for spontaneous erasures.

In the subsequent battle for custody of Angela, Erin found herself fighting not just Darrell Grant, model citizen, but the detectives who so foolishly believed that he was working on their behalf. 'Whenever a new court date was set, the detectives conveniently arranged for Darrell Grant to be out of town on an undercover assignment. Affidavits attesting to the urgency of the mission were available by the handful. On the rare occasions when Darrell actually showed his face in court, not a soul came forward who would swear to his felonious exploits. The file room had been purged as neatly as the computer's memory. On the issue of Darrell Grant's criminal character, the judge was left only with Erin's word, which he coolly rejected.

Broke and discouraged, Erin refused to give up. She planned to pursue Darrell Grant through the legal system for as long and as far as necessary. Angela was in peril not because Darrell was abusive, but because he was unfailingly careless. It was only a matter of time before something bad happened to him, and then the real nightmare would begin. Then Erin's daughter would be delivered into the custody of the great state of Florida, which was not known for its attentiveness toward children.

Angie would never be a foster child. Erin wouldn't let it happen. To save the girl, she would do anything, including stealing Rita Grant's mail off the kitchen counter.

Erin put on a Jimmy Buffett tape, lay down on the bed and went through Rita's letters. She wore cutoff jeans and a baggy Hawaiian shirt and wraparound shades, electric blue. Her hair was in a ponytail, tucked under a pink cotton baseball cap. Her bare feet bounced to the music, and she was feeling better about her prospects.

Most of the stolen mail was worthless to Erin's private investigation – the electric bill, a Penthouse subscription reminder, a homesick letter from yet another wayward sibling (Darrell's youngest brother, feigning insanity at the state hospital in Chattahoochee), and a membership notice from the National Rifle Association, to which both Rita and Alberto had hopefully applied.

Only one item was of interest to Erin: the telephone

bill. FBI training wasn't necessary to scan the long-distance entries and pinpoint Darrell Grant's location. He hadn't run far: Erin counted seven collect phone calls from a number in Deerfield Beach. It made perfect sense. Deerfield Beach was overwhelmingly populated by retirees. Where you had retirees, you had wheelchairs.

Erin turned down the stereo and picked up the phone. Her hand trembled as she dialed – not from nerves, but from anger. It rang six times before he answered. Erin used her old-lady voice. She said she was calling from the St Vitus Society, collecting donations for the homeless.

Darrell Grant said: 'Donations of what?'

'Anything you can spare. Food, clothing, medical equipment.'

'Like wheelchairs?' Darrell Grant asked.

Erin listened for the sound of a child in the background. She heard only a television, tuned to a talk show.

Darrell Grant said: 'Hello? You mean like wheelchairs?'

'Actually, we've got plenty of wheelchairs and gurneys. But any other medical equipment would be most appreciated.'

'That's too bad,' said Darrell Grant. 'I got some used wheelchairs in pretty good shape.'

Erin resisted the urge to scream something terrible into the phone. Still using the old-lady voice, she said, 'Well, we've just received a shipment of brand-new ones donated by the hospital district. But thank you anyway.'

'Yeah? What kind?'

'I really couldn't say. Can I put you down for some canned goods or bedding?'

'Sure,' Darrell Grant said. 'Better yet, I'll haul the stuff over there myself. Gimme your address. And spell the name a that saint again, would you?'

Erin smiled. What a champ.

FIVE

Moldowsky didn't know that Jerry Killian was crazy drooling mad with love. Not that it mattered; blackmail was blackmail.

'Where's Dilbeck?' Killian demanded.

'I'm here as the congressman's personal representative.' Malcolm Moldowsky took out a monogrammed notebook. From an inside pocket came a gold fountain pen. 'All right, let's have the terms.'

'Not so quick.'

They were seated on the top deck of the *Jungle Queen*, a gaudy ersatz paddlewheeler that motored up and down the Intracoastal Waterway in Fort Lauderdale. It was Killian's idea to meet there, safely surrounded by yammering tourists and conventioneers.

He said, 'I specifically asked to meet the congressman.'

Moldowsky sighed a patient sigh. 'Mr Dilbeck is very busy. This morning he's touring Little Haiti. This afternoon he will dedicate a domino park in Little Havana. This evening he'll be speaking to the Democratic Sons and Daughters of Nicaragua in Exile.'

Killian whistled derisively. Malcolm Moldowsky said, 'It's an election year, my friend.'

'He has nothing to fear from me.'

'He's a busy man is all I'm saying.'

Killian folded his arms. 'So he sends a guy who smells like a Bangkok bidet.'

'You're referring to my cologne?'

'No offense. I'm a Brut man myself.'

Moldowsky doodled placidly on the notepad. 'No offense taken.'

'He's an excitable boy, your congressman. Beat the living Jesus out of that schmo in the dance club.' Killian awaited an explanation, but Moldowsky continued to draw, saying nothing.

'He's got a problem around the ladies,' Killian went on. 'I think he needs help, before word gets out.'

Moldowsky said, 'May we get down to business?'

'The only reason I mention it is I'm concerned. He could hurt somebody, or get hurt. They're tough places, those dance bars.'

'I'll pass that along. Can we begin now?'

Point by point, Killian explained his demands. There were only two. Moldowsky listened impassively and took notes. When the blackmailer finished, Moldowsky looked up and said, 'This is completely outrageous.'

The *Jungle Queen* blew four long whistles. The captain was trying to get the attention of a bridgetender.

Killian said, 'Which part is outrageous?'

'The money, of course. A million dollars!'

'Forget the money. What about the other part?'

Moldowsky eyed him. 'Forget the money?'

'Sure. I was just busting your balls.' Killian gave a hearty laugh. He signaled a waiter for two more beers.

Moldowsky said, 'Just so I've got this clear: You don't want any money. Not a dime.'

Killian removed his thick eyeglasses and held them

to the sunlight, inspecting for smudges. He said, 'For a guy who dresses so sharp, you're thick as a brick. No, Mr Personal Representative, I don't want money. All I want him to do is fix a simple court case.'

'Keep your voice down.'

'*Grant* versus *Grant*.'

'Yes, I got it the first time,' Moldowsky said. 'A custody matter. What's your interest in the case?'

'None of your business,' Killian replied. 'And if you pursue that line of inquiry, I will go instantly to the police and report what I saw at the Eager Beaver. Headlines are certain to follow.'

Finally the drawbridge opened to let the *Jungle Queen* pass, and the tourists broke into silly tourist applause. A waiter appeared with beers. Moldowsky and Killian drank in silence until the merriment subsided on deck.

'This is a great boat ride,' Killian said brightly. 'They've got one like this down in Miami, right?'

'In Biscayne Bay. A tour of celebrity homes.' Moldowsky remained polite even though he'd decided that Jerry Killian was a flake. Flakes could still cause trouble.

'Like who? Which celebrities?' Killian asked.

'The Bee Gees.'

'Which Bee Gees?'

'The whole damn bunch. They've all got mansions on the water.'

'Is Madonna's house on the tour?'

'Undoubtedly,' Moldowsky said, with a sigh. He steered the conversation back to blackmail. 'What makes you think Congressman Dilbeck can influence a local divorce judge? I mean, even if he wanted to.'

'Easy. The divorce judge is sick of being a divorce

judge. He wants to move up in the world, namely a seat on the federal bench. For that he needs political connections.'

Moldowsky frowned. 'But it's the Senate that confirms—'

'I know that!' Killian angrily gripped the edge of the table. 'I *know*, you pompous fuck. I know it's the Senate that confirms. But a letter from a congressman would be helpful, would it not? It might carry weight with certain senators on the Judiciary Committee, correct?'

'Sure,' Moldowsky said. 'You're right.' His eyes were on Killian's ratty necktie, which was soaking in his beer mug. Killian noticed and removed it quickly. If he was embarrassed, he didn't let it show.

'The judge would be impressed to hear from a United States congressperson. That's the point, that's what we're talking about, Mr Personal Representative – not influence so much as the appearance thereof. Who cares if this hayseed ever makes it to the federal bench? We want him to think he can. We want him to think Dilbeck has the clout to make or break. And I've got a feeling you're just the sneaky little maggot to deliver that message.'

Sometimes Malcolm Moldowsky regretted his own coolness. After so many years as a political fixer, he'd lost the capacity to be personally insulted; virtually nothing provoked him. In his line of work, emotions were risky. They distorted the senses, led to grave miscalculations and foolhardy impulses. Naturally it would've been fun to punch Jerry Killian so hard that he puked up blood, but it also would've been counter-productive. The man was motivated by forces deeper and more urgent than greed, and that made him dangerous indeed.

So Moldowsky said: 'I'll see what I can do.'

'I thought you would.'

'In the meantime, you can't go back to that strip club.' Moldowsky closed his notebook and capped his pen. 'If you show your face in the place, the deal's off. Got it?'

'Fair enough,' Killian said. 'I can handle that.' But his heart ached at the thought.

Suing a synagogue was challenging under the best of circumstances. Mordecai was having difficulty finding guidance. His law books were barren of precedents. Enthusiasm was equally hard to come by. When he told his mother of the case, she slapped him across the face with an oven mitt. It was her way of reminding him that two of his uncles were Orthodox rabbis.

Mordecai's plan for the Paul Guber case was further hindered by the victim's own friends, who couldn't recall the name or location of the synagogue at which the savage attack had occurred. The young men blamed their confusion on darkness, the late hour and alcohol, but Mordecai knew better. Collective amnesia was a sure sign of conspiracy. He considered asking Paul Guber for the true details of the incident, but that would've required Paul to open his mouth and speak, thus ruining a key plank of Mordecai's legal strategy. He wanted the jury to behold a stockbroker rendered mute and helpless by violent trauma. A stockbroker who could still work the phones wasn't nearly so pitiable a plaintiff. Mordecai's plan called for poor Mr Guber to remain silent.

The lawyer decided to try visual aids. He got a map of Broward County and attached it to a tall easel. With colored pins he marked the location of every synagogue from Tamarac to Hallandale. Mordecai's idea was to assemble Paul Guber and his buddies in front of the map; either it would jog their memories, or help them agree on a plausible story. Synagogues in the most affluent neighborhoods were denoted by shiny green pins – Mordecai's subtle way of suggesting a suitably prosperous defendant.

The map was brought to Paul Guber's hospital room, and his friends gathered on each side of the bed. Mordecai stood back and waited. The men squinted at the map. They mumbled. They pointed. They rubbed their chins in feigned concentration. It was a dreadful scene. After an hour, Mordecai ordered them all to go home and think about it.

Outside the hospital room, Paul's fiancée said, 'What does it mean?'

'It means I'm losing interest,' the lawyer replied.

Back at the office, Mordecai's secretary seemed relieved to see him, which was unusual. She took him to the conference room, where a new client was waiting. It took all of Mordecai's courage to shake the man's hand.

'I'm Shad,' the man said. 'We talked on the phone.'

The man was broad, bumpy and hairless. He wore a tank top, parachute pants and black Western boots. He had the grip of a wrestler.

Mordecai's secretary vanished. The lawyer took a seat at the table and motioned for Shad to do the same.

'You got a fridge?' Shad said.

'Pardon?'

Shad opened a brown grocery sack and took out the Ziploc pouch containing the undamaged foil seal; this he held up, dramatically, for Mordecai to see. Then Shad reached in the sack and removed the container of Delicato Fruity Low-Fat Yogurt. 'Blueberry,' he announced, removing the Glad Wrap.

'Ah yes,' said Mordecai. 'You're the one with the insect.'

'Roach,' Shad said, firmly. He pushed the yogurt across the table. Mordecai examined it tentatively, finding nothing.

'It's in here?' He peered at the flawless creaminess.

'You bet,' Shad said. 'We're talking jumbo.'

Mordecai lifted the wax carton up to the light. 'I wish I could see it.'

Shad offered him a spoon and said, 'Happy hunting.'

The lawyer hesitated. 'First we should get some pictures.' He buzzed the secretary and told her to bring the camera. Moments later, she buzzed back to report it was out of film.

Shad said, 'Hope you got a fridge.'

'Well, of course.'

'And I'd like a receipt.'

Mordecai was offended. 'You don't trust me?'

'Not yet,' said Shad.

'Don't worry. We'll have a contract.'

'Still, I'd like a receipt. That's my future there.' He pointed at the yogurt carton. 'That's my retirement.'

Mordecai explained the customary arrangement in such cases. When he got to the part about the contingency fee, he saw Shad stiffen.

'Forty percent? That's what you get?'

'It's standard, Mr Shad. You can check around.'

'Forty motherfucking percent!'

'Most attorneys quote similar rates.'

'Is that so?' Shad lowered his head and leaned across the table. 'I had a guy took a rat case for thirty-three, plus expenses.'

'Well,' said Mordecai, unsettled, 'my forty includes all costs.' He didn't want to hear about the other case, but he needed to know. 'When you say rat . . .'

'Baby Norway.' With his hands Shad indicated the size. 'About yea long. It was up at the Beef N' Reef in Wilton Manors. I open the steak sauce and there she comes, bingo, a rat! Lying there on my Rib-eye Special. Talk about traumatized.'

The image made Mordecai pause. 'And you filed suit?'

'Yeah, but something happened. The other side . . . I really don't know. They sued me back, believe it or not, and my lawyer said I was better off to forget the whole thing.' Shad spoke of the experience bitterly. 'I never paid the bastard a nickel,' he added pointedly. 'That was the deal.'

'It's the usual contingency contract.' Mordecai felt better now, back in familiar territory. 'Suing a big corporation isn't easy. It's hard work. Expensive, too.'

'On the phone you said they'd settle.'

'They probably will, Mr Shad, but not without a fight. That's where I'll earn my forty percent – if we win.'

Mordecai wasn't displaying the fiery optimism that Shad would have liked. He wondered if he'd made the right choice in attorneys. 'How long does yogurt stay good?' he asked.

The lawyer said he didn't know.

'You better find out.' Shad held up the carton. 'When this shit starts to turn, watch out, Mother. The stink is so bad it peels wallpaper.'

Mordecai said, 'We'll freeze it if necessary.'

'It ain't lunch,' said Shad, 'it's evidence. So don't go fucking up the chain of custody.'

'Certainly not.' Mordecai thought: Chain of custody? What's the story on this guy?

Shad said, 'Tell me about your ace shrink.'

'A good man. I've used him on other cases. You should start seeing him as soon as possible, and as often as possible.'

'And who pays for that?'

Mordecai smiled paternally. 'Don't you worry. Eventually the Delicato company will take care of all expenses. In the meantime, we need to build up a detailed medical record.'

Shad said, 'I never been to a shrink. I got a feeling I won't like it.'

'It's important to document your pain and suffering. It will help determine the final damages.'

'The money, you mean.'

'Exactly. The court needs to know the ordeal you've been through. You might even consider quitting your job.'

'Can't do that,' Shad said flatly.

'Lost income would greatly enhance a jury award. How about taking a leave of absence?'

Shad said no, he couldn't quit work. Mordecai

backed off. They could discuss it another time. 'What kind of job do you have?' he asked.

'I'm in the entertainment business,' Shad said.

'Really?' Mordecai couldn't imagine it. 'Are you a . . . performer?' He was thinking: Circus.

Shad shook his head. 'Security. I provide security.'

'May I ask where?'

'At a bottomless joint.'

Mordecai took a deep breath. He imagined jurors would do the same. He imagined how it would be in court, watching helplessly as the sympathy drained from their eyes. Mordecai felt very sorry for himself; it had been such a crummy day. First the Paul Guber debacle and now this. Why didn't he ever snare the choice plaintiffs – the adorable little kids, the winsome young widows, the sad but plucky pensioners?

Not me, thought Mordecai. I get a bouncer from a tittie bar. Not a normal-looking bouncer either; some hairless pop-eyed 'Star Trek' reject.

The man named Shad said, 'The hell's the matter? If your heart's not in it, just say so.' He probed the yogurt with the spoon. 'I want you to see this.'

'Not necessary,' the lawyer protested. 'I believe you.'

Mordecai kicked with both feet, rolling the chair back from the conference table. He got up just as Shad struck paydirt.

'Ha!'

'My God,' said Mordecai.

'Did I tell you? Is that a fucking roach or what?'

The prehistoric pest filled the spoon. Shad raised it to the level of Mordecai's eyes. The lawyer gaped in revulsion. Wings askew, the dead cockroach knelt in a creamy blue puddle. Its yogurt-flecked antennae drooped lifelessly.

Shad was very proud. 'Well?'

'Put it back,' the lawyer rasped.

'Just think,' Shad said, 'sittin' down to breakfast and—'

'No!'

'Makes you want to gag, don't it?'

'Yes,' Mordecai whispered. For balance he clutched the corner of the table. 'Put it away now, please.'

Shad carefully dropped the insect into the yogurt and stirred gently. Soon the crispy corpse disappeared from view. 'There,' he said. 'Now, where's that fridge?'

'I'll get Beverly to show you.' The lawyer mopped his jowls with a handkerchief.

'Does this mean we got a deal?'

'It does,' said Mordecai.

Times were tough, and a roach was a roach.

SIX

Monique Sr announced that Alan Greenspan was drinking a beer at table fourteen.

Orly clapped his fat hands together. 'See! Another reason you gotta work.' He didn't want Erin to take the night off. 'Famous comedian in the audience, you shouldn't miss the chance.'

'Alan Greenspan,' Erin said pleasantly, 'is an economist.'

'That's the one.' Monique Sr stuck by her claim. 'Check him out yourself. Corona from the bottle, no lime.'

'Not to mention it's Tuesday,' Orly carped. 'Tuesday being oil wrestling. Only one of our busiest nights.'

'I don't wrestle,' Erin reminded him. 'Not in oil, not in custard, not in mud. No wrestling for me.'

Nude oil wrestling was a tradition at the Eager Beaver, but Erin declined to participate. In her view, professional dancers shouldn't roll around in a wet tub with shirtless, semi-tumescent drunks. As a secondary issue, Erin didn't like the looks of the oil. Orly was vague about the brand; one day he'd say it was Wesson, another day he'd swear it was Mazola. Erin had a hunch it was neither. Once a health inspector showed up for an on-site bacterial census. Amazingly, not a single living microbe was found in the wrestling vat. The mystery was explained later the same evening, when the health inspector returned with four of his civil service buddies. They shared a front-row table and all the Amaretto they could drink, courtesy of Mr Orly.

'Tuesday is a big night,' Orly was saying. 'Bottom line is, we need all our best dancers.'

'Please, Mr Orly. It's personal.'

'Tell me.'

'I'm meeting my ex-husband,' Erin said, 'to discuss future custody arrangements for our daughter.'

Here Urbana Sprawl interjected her opinion of Darrell Grant, describing him so vividly that Mr Orly immediately offered to have him killed.

Erin said, 'That's not necessary.'

'Beat up? Crippled? You gives the word.' Orly pantomimed dialing a telephone. 'That's how easy it is when you know the right people.'

'Thanks, but I can handle it myself.' Erin played along with Mr Orly's Mafia routine as a matter of politeness. He looked about as Sicilian as David Letterman.

Urbana Sprawl urged Orly to give Erin the night off for the sake of her lost little daughter. Orly wasn't the least bit moved. He said, 'Promise me this is really a domestic-type deal. Promise you're not sneaking down the street for an audition.'

'Oh right,' said Erin. 'My lifelong dream is to work for those freaks.'

Mr Orly was paranoid about losing his best strippers to the Flesh Farm, which recruited aggressively with signing bonuses. The owners recently introduced Friction Dancing Night to compete with Nude Oil Wrestling

Night at the Eager Beaver. Friction dancing was not so much dancing as it was rubbing, vigorously, against the frontal surfaces of fully clothed customers. It was demonstrably more erotic than oil wrestling, and not nearly as messy. Orly was definitely feeling the pressure.

'Tell me the truth,' he said to Erin.

'I told you the truth. I'm meeting my ex-husband.' She picked up her purse to indicate the conversation was over. 'If you don't believe me, ask Shad. He's coming along.'

'My Shad?' Orly's eyebrows twitched with concern.

'As a favor to me,' Erin explained. 'There could be trouble.'

'Then be damn careful.'

'I will.'

'Because good bouncers are hard to find,' Orly said. 'Harder than dancers, believe it or not.'

Erin first met Darrell Grant at Broward General Hospital, where her mother was recuperating from an operation in which her navel had been cosmetically inverted. Erin's mother had paid a plastic surgeon $1,500 to transform her 'outie' bellybutton to an 'innie'. Erin was unaware that such a procedure was available, but her mother assured her that all the big-name fashion models had it done.

Erin was standing at her mother's bed, admiring the surgeon's work, when Darrell Grant appeared with fresh linens and a clean bedpan. He worked as an orderly at the hospital and, as Erin later learned, it was there he acquired his taste for narcotics and his aptitude for boosting wheelchairs. In appearance, though,

Darrell seemed anything but a criminal. Erin was still naïve enough to believe that all crooks had bad teeth, greasy hair and jailhouse tattoos. She assumed that cleancut, good-looking men possessed the same natural advantage as cleancut, good-looking women: the world treated you better, and consequently there was no reason for unwholesome behavior.

And Darrell Grant was uncommonly handsome, with a lean face and bright mischievous eyes. He took her to the hospital cafeteria and charmed her with a hastily fabricated story of his life. The centerpiece of the yarn was an authentic Bronze Star, which Darrell Grant kept in the breast pocket of his hospital garb. He told Erin he'd won it for killing a Cuban sniper during the invasion of Grenada. Erin chose not to question Darrell's tale, knowing the Pentagon had given out about a hundred thousand medals in appreciation for making the tiny spice island safe once again for Holiday Inns. Much later in their relationship Erin would learn that Darrell had actually acquired the Bronze Star, along with two cases of Michelob, in the burglary of an American Legion post.

They dated for six months, to the horror of Erin's mother. She had steered a long line of doctors, lawyers and accountants in her daughter's direction, and Erin had found them all too serious and self-absorbed. Some of them were old enough to be her father. Darrell Grant was impulsive, full of tricks, and he made her laugh. At the time, that seemed important. Erin's decision to marry him was sudden and cataclysmic, and it had the desired effect of freeing her from the clutches of her mother.

The sociopathic side of Darrell Grant didn't surface

for about eighteen months, until he abandoned all pretense of honest labor and devoted himself full time to larceny. To explain the odd hours and fluctuating income, he told Erin he was selling medical equipment. Darrell's boyish wit and warmth evaporated dramatically under the icy twin spells of amphetamines and methaqualone; he was either a dervish or a zombie, depending on the chemical cycle. Newly pregnant, Erin didn't want to bail out of the marriage without giving Darrell Grant a chance to reform. The thought of divorce was almost as daunting as the thought of her mother's shrill I-told-you-so.

When he learned that Erin was expecting a child, Darrell vowed to change his ways. He got off the pills, removed all stolen property from the garage and took a job selling rustproofing at a Chrysler dealership. He was a new man, for about a month. One Thursday, Erin returned home from work and found Darrell in the living room, chiseling the serial numbers off a pediatric wheelchair. Confronted, he broke into a rage and slapped Erin twice across the face. The amusement ended abruptly when Erin punched him in the larynx, pushed him to the floor and whacked him in the testicles with a mop handle. It was Darrell's first glimpse of his wife's temper, and it made an impression. From then on he never laid a finger on her; instead, he vented his feelings by destroying things that she valued – artworks, furniture, photo albums, her favorite clothes. By the time Angela was born, the marriage was irretrievably pulverized.

Erin didn't torment herself with remorse. She'd gotten conned, and learned a lesson. Now it was time to concentrate on getting Angela back.

Waiting in the car with Shad, Erin outlined the latest plan.

'So it's a trap,' he said.

'Exactly.'

'He won't be bringing no wheelchairs for the poor.'

'No,' said Erin, 'he'll be looking to steal some.'

Shad spit something out the window. 'And you were married to this asswipe?'

'We all make mistakes.'

'Don't you hate it,' Shad said, 'when love turns around and bites you like a damn rattlesnake? It happens, by God. Happens every day.'

Erin showed him the photographs of the mangled dolls in Angie's bedroom. 'Christ almighty,' he said.

'My daughter is the one I'm concerned about. That's what this is all about.'

Shad said nothing for several minutes. Then he asked Erin if she was satisfied with her lawyer. 'I'm not so sure about mine,' he added. 'He needs some firing up.'

Erin said, 'My lawyer's all right. It's the system that's so frustrating.'

'Tell me about it.' Shad was glad to chat with Erin about these matters; he felt they were warriors on the same battlefield. 'If there's such a thing as true justice,' he said, 'you'll get your little girl, and I'll get rich off my dead roach.'

'That would be nice,' Erin said quietly.

The car was in the farthest, darkest corner of a parking lot attached to a strip shopping mall in Oakland Park. The address Erin had given Darrell Grant belonged to a bankrupt video store, located at the other end of the plaza. A few movie posters remained in the window; from the car, Erin could make out the blown-up likeness of Arnold Schwarzenegger in sunglasses.

Shad said, 'How do you know he's coming tonight?'

'Because I told him they ship the wheelchairs every Wednesday morning. He'll be looking to load up on inventory.'

'Any particular model?'

'He favors Everest-and-Jennings,' Erin said. 'Rolls and Theradynes are good, too.'

Shad was intrigued. He'd assumed all wheelchairs were pretty much the same. 'Rolls as in Royce?'

Erin said no, it was a different company. Shad asked why her ex-husband didn't steal cars like everybody else.

'Because he couldn't hotwire a goddamn toaster,' said Erin. 'Cars are too complicated for Darrell Grant.'

Shad spit out the window again. He seemed to be aiming at a particular curbstone. 'You want me to – do what exactly? When he gets here, I mean.'

Erin said, 'Let's play it by ear.'

'I could break something. Maybe start with a finger.' Shad wiggled one of his pinkies. 'Depends how serious you are.'

'I just want to talk with the man.' Erin leaned against the headrest and closed her eyes. She thought about the young bachelor beaten senseless on stage at the Eager Beaver – was he still in the hospital? She remembered the rabid expression on the face of his attacker, the wheezy primal grunts as he swung the champagne bottle.

Erin thought: Is it me? Do I bring that out in men?

Then here's Orly, now Shad, offering to maim her ex-husband. A casual favor, like jumping the car battery or hooking up the stereo.

'The ulna is a good one,' Shad was saying. He tapped Erin's forearm to show her the spot. 'A crowbar right about there, we'll have his attention.'

Erin sat up. 'Can I ask you something? Do I seem the type of woman to be impressed by violence?'

He grunted non-committally.

'I'm serious, Shad. Is that your opinion of me?'

He cocked his huge head and stared at her curiously. In the darkness he resembled a shaved bear. 'It's what I know best, that's all – kicking ass. On account of my job.'

'Then it's not me?'

'Ha! No, it ain't you.'

'Because I am *not* impressed by that sort of thing.'

'Is that why there's a gun under the seat?'

Erin couldn't think of a sharp retort.

Shad grinned. 'It's all right, babe. You're entitled.'

'I've never used it,' she told him.

'But you might.' Shad folded his arms. 'All I'm saying is, violence can be helpful. Sometimes it's the best way to make your point.'

'Not with Darrell.' Erin's ex-husband would cherish an injury. What better proof that she was hanging out with a rotten crowd, and was unfit to care for Angela! Darrell, the conniving bastard, would milk a broken limb for all it was worth. He'd wear the cast until the plaster rotted off his arm.

'Your call,' Shad said.

'I just want to talk with the man.'

'Fine.'

But deep inside, Erin briefly savored a vision of Shad pounding Darrell Grant into dogmeat. She probably should've been ashamed by the feeling, but she wasn't.

Especially when she thought of what he'd done to Angie's dolls.

At midnight Shad went looking for a Coke machine. Erin put on a Buffett tape and turned the volume low. She liked the Caribbean songs the best. Her imagination set sail, and before long she was dreaming of pearly beaches and secluded harbors. She was barefoot in the surf, wiggling her toes into the sand.

When she opened her eyes, her shoes were gone. Both doors on the old Fairlane had been opened. When she got out of the car, she stepped on something plastic, which cracked into sharp pieces. The Buffett cassette on the pavement.

Erin froze. 'Shad?'

A hand grabbed her by the hair, twisting hard, jerked her head back so that all she saw was sky. She felt something sharp against her throat.

'You still snore like a pig.' It was Darrell Grant.

Erin shook uncontrollably. It was embarrassing to let him see her so afraid.

He said, 'I can't believe you tried to set me up. I can't fucking believe it.'

'What?' Erin didn't recognize the pitch of her own voice.

Darrell Grant slapped a hand across her mouth, told her to shut the hell up. They both heard the footsteps. 'Your boyfriend,' Darrell whispered. 'This'll be choice.'

Shad came out of the shadows with a Diet Coke in

one hand and an unopened can of Canada Dry in the other. He put both cans down as soon as he saw the long knife at Erin's neck. Darrell Grant told him not to try anything stupid. Shad's expression remained invisible in the darkness.

'I got an idea,' Darrell said. He told Shad to lie on his belly or else get a bucket to catch Erin's blood. Shad nodded and got down on the ground. Darrell Grant released Erin and immediately pounced on the bouncer, digging his knees into the other man's enormous shoulder blades. Laughing, Darrell managed to cinch Shad's thick wrists with a pair of flexible plastic handcuffs.

'Knock it off,' Erin said, still shaky.

With both hands Darrell Grant poised the dagger at the crest of Shad's bare skull; the smooth flesh dimpled under the pressure of the blade.

Again Erin told him to stop, and again her ex-husband cackled. He rolled the knife handle back and forth in his palms, so that the point twirled against Shad's skin. Erin saw the first drop of blood, blackish in the dim light.

'That hurt?' Darrell Grant asked.

'Nope,' Shad replied, truthfully. He felt little in the way of physical pain. The doctors didn't seem to know why.

Erin said, 'Since when do you carry a knife?'

'Since when do you hang out with ugly bald-headed Amazons?' Darrell Grant got up and whipped the dagger like a sword through the air. He was batty on speed. 'I suppose it's just a coincidence that you're here in this very parking lot tonight? *En garde!*' He slashed a Z in the air. 'What, you think I'm blind? I saw your car from three blocks away, Erin. Jesus, you'd make a great spy. Maybe next time you can set off fireworks.'

She said, 'You're such an asshole.'

Darrell Grant grinned crookedly. 'Is that how they speak at the St Vitus Society? That *was* you on the phone, right? Talking about all those brand-new wheelchairs.'

'You've lost your mind.'

'Then explain this!' Accusingly, he pointed the dagger at the Fairlane. 'And this!' He poked Shad with the toe of a tan cowboy boot. 'You fucking set me up!'

Erin said: 'Darrell, I'm keeping a list: assault with a deadly weapon, false imprisonment, burglary, possession of narcotics—'

'Shut up,' he snapped. 'What'm I supposed to believe, that you and Igor stopped here to make out? I know you're lonely, Erin, but this is ridiculous. I seen handsomer iguanas.'

She thought of the gun in the car, gauged the steps back to the driver's side. Then she pushed the idea from her mind. Shooting Darrell would mean she'd never see Angie again. The judge would make sure of it.

'Junior?' It was Shad, speaking from the side of his mouth. He had no choice, being face down on the asphalt. 'Junior, listen up. The lady and I work together. She was giving me a lift home when this piece a shit excuse for a Ford overheated. We pulled in to let the radiator cool, and that's it. That's the whole story.'

Darrell Grant dropped to his haunches and tweaked Shad's nose. 'Well, I'll be damned. It talks.'

Wonder drugs, thought Erin. 'What's with your hair?' she asked. Darrell flared at her caustic tone. For a man whose profession was stealing from invalids, he was surprisingly vain about his appearance.

He said, 'I lightened it a touch. So?'

'And the stubble,' Erin said. 'Come here, let's see.'

'No way.' He stood up, sullenly.

'Is this your Don Johnson period?'

'Shut up, Erin.'

She was trying to take his mind off Shad and further mischief with the knife. 'I'll bet you got yourself a white linen Armani to go with the hair.'

Darrell Grant said, 'Fuck you.' When he put the dagger in his belt, Erin felt slightly better about the situation. She hoped he was downgearing for a simple argument.

Then he stood on Shad's head with the heels of his cowboy boots.

'Get off!' Erin cried.

'Make me.'

'Darrell, stop!'

Shad made no sounds. Erin wasn't sure if he was still conscious.

'I like it up here,' Darrell Grant chirped. He balanced on Shad's skull as if it were a cypress stump.

'Don't,' Erin pleaded.

'What's it worth to you? How about a twenty?'

Erin looked at Shad's face under the boots. His eyes were closed but his jaw was set.

'Twenty bucks,' Darrell Grant repeated. 'Hurry, hurry.'

He had tossed Erin's purse under the car. She had to crawl for it. Darrell Grant leered as he watched her down on all fours. 'I like that,' he said. 'Brings back memories.'

Mechanically Erin fumbled in the purse for her cash. She found a twenty-dollar bill and handed it to her ex-husband. He sniffed it as if it were cognac. 'Amazing,' he said. 'All you gotta do is flash your twat and men throw money. Isn't it a great country, Erin? Aren't you proud to be an American?'

At that moment, the only person she hated more than Darrell Grant was herself, for marrying him. 'Get off the man,' she said coldly. Darrell hopped from Shad's head.

'Where's Angie?'

'Safe and sound,' said Darrell Grant. 'If you're a good mummy, I'll let her call on Christmas Day.'

'We're going back to court.' Erin's voice trembled. 'You've already violated the judge's order.'

'Back to court!' Darrell Grant's hooting filled the night. 'Back to court! I love it.'

'What's happened to you, Darrell?' She really wanted to know. He was worse than she'd ever seen him.

He yanked the knife from his belt and bent over Shad. For a moment Erin feared that he would slit Shad's throat. She had an image of herself hanging on Darrell's back, digging her fingernails into his eye sockets.

'Don't do it,' she said.

'Do what?'

Using the dagger as a pen, Darrell playfully etched the letter G into the crown of Shad's naked scalp. Blood trickled down his head and puddled in the folds of muscle at the base of his neck. Erin felt woozy and chilled. Shad remained silent, although his eyes had opened.

'There.' Darrell Grant stood back and admired his work.

Erin said, 'What does that prove?'

'We're not going back to court.'

'You're wrong, Darrell.'

'I won, sweetheart. All the marbles, remember?'

'What'd you do with my shoes?'

Again came the hooting laughter. 'Wake up, little Dorothy,' he said. 'You're not in Kansas any more!'

Darrell Grant circled Erin's car, puncturing each tire with a thrust of the knife. Then he kicked each of the soda cans and sauntered off across the parking lot. As he disappeared in the darkness, Erin could hear him singing, 'Somewhere Over the Rainbow'.

At her feet, Shad rolled over and blinked up at the stars.

'Nice guy,' he said. 'Too bad it didn't work out for you two.'

SEVEN

The next night, Erin danced to ZZ Top.

Her record store didn't stock the band's first album, so she bought one of the newer releases. Kevin, the club's disc jockey, was pleased with the hard guitar and fast bass beat. Her regular customers didn't seem to mind the change of pace.

The one she called Mr Peepers was not in the audience. Erin feared that Shad had scared him away from the Eager Beaver for ever. Either that, or he'd given up the hustle.

So much for love.

Against her better judgment, Jerry Killian had become a reed of hope for Erin in her battle for Angela. Dealing with Darrell Grant was impossible, but maybe Killian could get to the judge. Maybe political pressure was the way to go. Erin needed to know more about Killian's connection, the congressman.

His name, for starters.

She danced out of the spotlights long enough to shield her eyes and scout the back rows. The judge was in his customary booth near the Foosball machines. Monique Sr was on the tabletop, bouncing up a storm. The judge watched droopy-eyed and inert. Erin figured his hands were busy under the table.

After the set, Mr Orly came to the dressing room and announced that he approved of the new music. 'Faster the better,' he said.

Urbana Sprawl said ZZ Top was hazardous to her health. 'My tits are killing me.'

'Hey,' Orly said, 'we put up with your rap crap. Ice Puke or whatever.'

'Ice Cube!'

'Bottom line is, you can tolerate eight minutes of hard rock.'

'Instant stretch marks,' Urbana complained.

Erin said, 'I'll find some slower cuts.'

'Don't!' Orly protested. 'Fast is good. Everybody sweats, everybody drinks.'

'And everybody tips,' said Monique Sr, waving a fifty. The other dancers whistled.

'Case closed,' said Orly, and he was gone.

When the shift was over, Erin scrubbed off her makeup and dressed quickly. Urbana asked what was the hurry.

'I've got an errand.'

'Three in the morning?'

'Meeting somebody.'

'Tell me it's not Darrell.' Urbana and the other dancers knew about the harrowing incident at Erin's car. They'd seen the dagger cuts on Shad's bald head.

'Don't worry,' Erin said. 'It's only Jerry Killian.' She zipped her jeans and stepped into a pair of sandals.

'Mr Peepers?' Monique Jr said. 'Why?'

'To talk.'

'Bad idea,' said Monique Sr.

'Not many good ones at three in the morning.' Erin

checked herself in the mirror. 'Desperate times call for desperate measures.'

'Be patient,' Urbana Sprawl advised. 'He'll be back. Especially you keep playing his songs.'

'I can't wait,' Erin said.

'How you gonna find him?'

'He's found.'

Urbana Sprawl smiled. 'The phone book!'

'Nope,' said Erin. 'Unlisted, unpublished.'

'Then how'd you find him?'

'Research,' Erin explained, enigmatically. Erin couldn't tell them the truth. One phone call had sent Agent Cleary to the computer keyboard. He was glad to help, and asked few questions; he still felt bad about her dismissal.

Monique Jr told Erin that it was crazy to call on Mr Peepers in the middle of the night. 'He could be a psycho slasher for all you know.'

'Oh, I believe he's harmless.'

'That's what they said about Ted Bundy.'

'Thank you,' said Erin, gathering her purse and dancing clothes, 'for the peace of mind.'

Without much effort, Urbana Sprawl blocked the door. 'Give him till the weekend,' she said.

Erin felt a wave of fatigue. She was losing the energy to argue. Her friends were right: it was craziness.

'Patience,' Urbana said.

'Until the weekend,' Erin promised. 'If you can stand the new music that long.'

Monique Jr said the ZZ Top was dynamite. She said she'd never dance to rap again. She wanted a white top hat and tails as a costume for 'Sharp-Dressed Man'.

Frowning, Urbana hoisted a titanic breast in each

hand. 'Try jumping around with *these* suckers and you'd be in traction. So screw your ZZ and gimme that slow Cube.'

Erin was sympathetic. She couldn't imagine going through life with a bosom so large. None of the dancers doubted the rumor that Urbana had once smothered a man on a convertible sofa. It was completely plausible.

'See you tomorrow,' Erin told her friends.

'You headed home?' Monique Sr asked. 'Be honest.'

'Home,' Erin said.

Shad followed in his own car, just to make sure.

Moldowsky found the congressman in a state of massage. A redheaded woman in a gold tank suit straddled his back, chopping at his pale shoulder blades. The woman had very long fingernails for a masseuse.

'Say hi to Eve.' Dilbeck's words thrummed comically with each chop.

'Hello, Eve,' Moldowsky said. 'We need a moment of privacy. Do you mind?'

Eve said that was perfectly fine. She spoke with a light British accent.

'Go hop in the shower,' Dilbeck told her. 'I'll be there in a flash.'

When she was out of the room, Moldowsky said, 'David, where is your wife?'

'Shopping, I think.'

'You think?'

'Yes, shopping. I told Pierre to drive slow.'

Moldowsky said, 'You are a hopeless shithead.'

Dilbeck sat up and covered himself with the towel.

'What'd I do now, Malcolm? Hell, you're acting like my mother.'

They heard the faucets turn in the shower down the hall.

Moldowsky motioned with his chin. 'Is she a hooker?'

'I don't know yet,' said the congressman. 'And even if she is, so what? She's got no earthly idea who I am, Malcolm. She just moved here from London.'

'Beautiful. Hands across the water.'

'What's the matter with you?'

'The sugar bill, Davey. Your colleagues are playing it tough, and my clients are deeply concerned. They want to know if they've got their money on the wrong horse.'

'Relax. I'm entertaining young Christopher tonight.'

Relax? Moldowsky thought. The moron has a prostitute in the tub, an assault victim in the hospital and a blackmailer who's ready to call the newspapers. 'Did you speak with the judge?' he asked.

Dilbeck nodded. 'Yes, we had lunch.'

'Well?'

'He was grateful for my interest in his career. He does, as you say, have his heart on the federal bench.' Dilbeck stood up and adjusted the towel. He looked longingly down the hall, toward the gentle sounds of the shower.

Moldowsky said, 'And what about *Grant* versus *Grant*?'

'Oh, we talked it over.' Dilbeck began to move around the room, trying to get upwind of Moldy's cologne. 'The judge is deeply religious,' Dilbeck said, 'or at least he pretends to be.'

'Born again, I suppose.'

'Several times. He feels strongly that he made the correct decision in the custody case. He seems to have a personal interest in the situation.'

'True enough,' Moldowsky said.

'He said the mother is a harlot. Is that right, Malcolm?'

'I haven't the faintest idea.'

'There's something you're not telling me.'

'There's lots I don't tell you, David.'

'I've got a soft spot when it comes to harlots.'

'Don't even think about it.' Moldowsky wasn't giving Dilbeck anything. The less he knew, the better. 'So what's the punch line? What did the judge say?'

'He doesn't need me, Malcolm. He plays golf with a fucking senator.'

Moldowsky cursed dispiritedly.

' – a senator on the Judiciary Committee. The next time there's an opening in our district, the judge has got it locked. He doesn't need us, is what I'm saying.'

'So he won't fix the case,' Moldowsky said, 'even as a favor.'

' "The woman is a tramp and a sinner. She is unfit to raise a child." Those are his words, Malcolm. Plus he quotes the Bible.'

'This is bad news.'

'Yes,' Dilbeck said. 'It was not a productive lunch.'

Moldowsky ground his knuckles together in agitation. 'Would he go for a bribe? Straight cash?'

'It's against his principles,' David Dilbeck said. 'But he's amenable to a free blowjob.'

A pulse became visible in Moldowsky's neck. 'Let's

see if I understand: only if the lady goes down on the judge does she get custody of her child—'

'He says he'll consider it. That's all. "Brownie points" is the way he put it.'

'David, I'll say this. You're one terrific negotiator. They needed you at the fucking SALT talks.' Moldowsky began to pace and rant, 'Who is this jizzbag judge? Bible quotes – from what, the Book of Dick?'

'Hey,' the congressman said, 'we're talking one lousy blowjob.'

Moldowsky cornered David Dilbeck and seized him by the arms. 'Killian won't go for it. The mother won't go for it. Hell, Davey, I got no morals whatsoever and *I* wouldn't go for it. It's the worst goddamn thing I ever heard.'

The vapors from Moldy's cologne made the congressman's eyes water. 'The judge won't take cash, Malcolm. I tried.'

'That's a disgrace.'

'Not even for his campaign,' Dilbeck said. 'I offered to funnel it through a PAC but he said no. See, that's the main reason he's angling for a federal gig, so he won't have to run for office any more. He has a very shitty opinion of politicians.'

The plumbing emitted a metallic screech as the shower stopped. Dilbeck turned sharply at the noise. His expression was a familiar glaze of sexual distraction.

'You're hopeless,' Moldowsky grumbled.

'What?' Dilbeck licked his lower lip.

'I said you're hopeless. Go check on your friend. I'll let myself out.'

'Thanks, Malcolm.'

'And stay out of trouble tonight.'

'Of course,' said the congressman. 'Erb will be there.'

'Fine,' said Moldowsky. Erb Crandall was good, but he was only one man. On some nights Dilbeck needed double-teaming.

As Moldowsky stalked down the hall, the bathroom door flung open and he was enveloped in a cloud of sweet-smelling steam. Eve stood there, sleek and wet and flushed in the cheeks. If Moldowsky was the least bit dazzled, it didn't show. He courteously stepped to the side and motioned for her to pass.

'You've got soap on your ears,' he said.

Less than two hours later, Congressman David Lane Dilbeck was a portrait of male contentment and relaxation. He smiled, he blew smoke rings, he tapped his shoes, he hummed to the music. A fresh rum-and-Coke appeared inches from his fingers, further improving his mood. Sitting to his right was Erb Crandall, who was huddled anxiously over an orange juice. Every so often he glanced toward the door in anticipation of a raid. Sitting to the congressman's left, a man named Christopher Rojo folded a fifty-dollar bill into an airplane and sailed it toward the stage, where a woman danced cautiously with a nine-foot Burmese python. The reptile's jaws were secured with Scotch tape, and someone had painted a bottlebrush mustache on its snout. Erb Crandall figured it was some kind of Hitler joke.

'This is so wonderful,' said Dilbeck. 'Isn't she something, Erb? How about that damn snake!'

'Yeah,' Crandall said, 'what a life.'

The woman, whose stage name was Lorelei, had

arranged the python in an intriguing way. The tail followed the crease of her bare buttocks downward through her legs, curling out to the crotch.

'That's a well-trained animal,' the congressman observed.

Christopher Rojo was similarly impressed. He was making a new paper airplane with a one hundred-dollar bill. Rojo was a wealthy young man with few ambitions and plenty of spare time. His family owned a large sugarcane operation on the southern shore of Lake Okeechobee. Christopher had never been to the farm, but he'd seen photographs. The cane fields looked like a stinking hellhole; he was astounded at the fortune they produced. There was so much money that one couldn't possibly spend it all. Heaven knows he was trying.

'Here, Davey,' he said. 'Your turn.'

Dilbeck took the paper airplane and tossed it toward the python dancer. It landed between her feet. She gave the men a slow wink, and scissored elegantly into a split. Picking up the money, she pretended to show it to the snake. Dilbeck laughed and laughed. Lorelei sprung to her feet, waved once and disappeared offstage. The set was over.

Erb Crandall sagged with relief. Maybe they'd get through the evening without incident.

Rojo said to Dilbeck: 'What's your bet?'

The congressman sipped his rum thoughtfully. 'Thirty-eight B,' he said. 'Nature's own.'

'And I,' said Rojo, waving more cash, 'say she's thirty-six inches of plastic fantastic.' He smoothed a fifty on the table. David Dilbeck did the same. They turned toward Crandall, who signaled himself out of the wager. They'd been at it all night, every time a new dancer came on stage. There were two parts to the bet: the size of the breasts, and whether or not they were surgically enhanced. Rojo was getting creamed, and Crandall wasn't surprised. The congressman had an unfailing eye for the female form; it was his life's passion, graft being a close second.

Rojo rose drunkenly and called for a man named Ling. Soon a small Oriental in a black tuxedo and a Yankees cap appeared at the table. He didn't look like the co-owner of a strip joint, but he was.

'Mr Ling!' Rojo said, opening his arms. 'Give us the scoop on Python Lady.'

'Her name is Lorelei,' said Dilbeck. 'Have some respect.'

Rojo sat down. Dilbeck pointed at the cash. 'Mr Ling, you see what's at stake.'

Ling nodded tolerantly. 'You want the knocker report?'

'Indeed we do.'

'Miss Lorelei is a thirty-eight B.'

'Ha!' Dilbeck crowed.

He grabbed for the money but Christopher Rojo caught his arm. 'Implants!' the young man hissed. 'Tell him, Mr Ling. Tell him it's implants, and we halve the bet.'

'No, sir,' Ling said. 'Lorelei is all Lorelei.'

'*Mierda*,' said Rojo.

The congressman gloated as he scooped up the cash.

Ling said, 'Only the best at Flesh Farm. Only the finest.'

'Top of the line,' agreed Dilbeck.

'Where else you see a snake so big?' Ling bragged. 'Snake like that could eat a pony.'

'So could Lorelei, I'll bet.' Dilbeck chuckled at his own incredible wit. It wasn't a light breezy chuckle, though. It was deep and ominous. Erb Crandall went on full alert.

He said, 'Davey, it's getting late.'

'Nonsense.' The congressman lit a cigarette. 'Mr Ling, I would like to meet the python princess.'

'Me, too,' said Christopher Rojo.

Ling shrugged. 'With or without the snake?'

'Without,' Dilbeck said. 'Tell her I've got one of my own.'

Rojo busted a gut. Erb Crandall shifted uneasily. This wasn't a smart idea, not at all. He said, 'Come on, Davey, you've got a speech in the morning.'

The congressman postured idiotically. 'Four score and seven years ago, our foreskins brought forth a new nation . . .'

Crandall didn't smile. Dilbeck said, 'All right, Erb, who the hell is it?'

'Chamber of Commerce.'

'Shit.' Dilbeck slapped Rojo's shoulder. 'Chris, you've never seen such stiffs. The Chamber of Cadavers is more like it.'

'Still,' said Crandall, 'it's for seven-thirty sharp.'

'We'll get him there,' Rojo promised.

'So,' said Ling, mildly impatient, 'you want a friction dance or what?'

The congressman spread his arms. 'Sounds enchanting, Brother Ling. Go fetch what's-her-face.'

'Miss Lorelei?'

'Absolutely.'

Crandall edged closer to Dilbeck and spoke sternly into his right ear. Dilbeck shook his head back and forth, keeping the drink to his lips the whole time. 'One little frictionating *lambada*,' he said with a slurp. 'What harm could it do?'

'Yeah,' said Rojo. 'Let the poor man have some fun.'

It was useless to object. Crandall removed all loose bottles and other potential weapons from the table. Then he made a slow pass through the club to see if he recognized anyone. He wasn't worried about the press, because reporters didn't make enough money to hang out in places like the Flesh Farm. Republicans were what Erb Crandall feared – all it took was one, spying from the shadows, and the Hon. David Lane Dilbeck was cooked. The crummy wig and dark glasses only made him more conspicuous; the chauffeur's cap, borrowed from the taciturn Pierre, was at least three sizes too small. To keep it from falling off, Dilbeck had pinned it to his wig; every time the cap moved, the hair moved with it. Not even Christopher Rojo seemed to notice. That was one good thing about Dilbeck's little problem; customers in nudie joints didn't spend much time scrutinizing each other. The dancers got all the attention.

Tonight the club was scarcely half full, and Crandall spotted no one from the wonderful world of politics. When he returned to the table, the congressman's chair was empty. Rojo pointed to the rear of the club, where a row of gilded booths lined one wall. The booths were reserved for friction dancing and other private interludes.

'I slipped him two hundred,' Rojo said. 'He wanted three but I made it two.'

'Two's plenty.' Crandall sat down and checked his wristwatch. He'd give it ten minutes.

Rojo said, 'I'm tired, man.' He reached into his coat and took out a tiny foil packet. 'You want some blow?'

Erb Crandall felt exhausted. 'That's brilliant, Chris. What a nifty idea. May I?' He unfolded the foil and examined the powder. Rojo smiled encouragingly. Crandall smiled back. Then he hawked up a glob and spit all over Christopher Rojo's dope.

'Jesus!' Rojo cried.

Crandall pushed the foil across the table. 'Get rid of it,' he said, 'on your way out the door.'

'You crazy mother!'

'Chris, listen. You're not gone in thirty seconds, I'll tell your old man about this. First thing *mañana*.'

Rojo saw the family trust fund evaporating before his eyes. He hastily wrapped the spit-soaked cocaine in a monogrammed handkerchief. 'There,' he said to Crandall. 'You happy now?'

'I said get lost.'

'But what about my turn?'

Crandall didn't understand the whining.

'With the snake lady, Erb. I'm next after Davey!'

'Take a rain check,' Crandall told him. He got up to search for the congressman.

Nothing took David Dilbeck's mind off his troubles like friction dancing. The sugar vote, the re-election campaign, the wife, the blackmail – who cared? He was alone with the python princess. They were swaying to imaginary Johnny Mathis tunes. The congressman had his hands on Lorelei's bottom. She was rubbing her delightfully natural protuberances against his middle-aged flab. Her voice sounded sweet and sincere. Her hair smelled like orchids. Dilbeck was getting hard. Life was good.

When he tried to unsnap Lorelei's top, she blocked the move.

'That's a no-no,' she whispered.

'What!'

'It's the law, baby.'

'Don't worry about it,' he said.

'Look, if you want to slow dance, I can't be naked. That's the law. I'm naked, you can't touch me anywhere.'

Dilbeck had a passing knowledge of the county obscenity ordinances.

Lorelei said, 'I'm sorry, baby.' She moved her hips against him in sinuous rhythm. 'That's not so bad, is it?' She had him pinned against the door to the booth.

'I've got an idea,' Dilbeck said.

'Yeah?'

'What if you get half naked? Then I can touch the part that's not.'

'Nice try,' Lorelei said, 'but it's all or nothing.'

So they continued dancing until Dilbeck felt himself poking her through his pants. In a low voice, he said, 'And what are we going to do about *him*?'

'Admire it,' Lorelei said, 'but that's all.'

Dilbeck gazed at his groin forlornly.

'Look,' she told him, 'you could be a cop for all I know.'

He whipped off the cap and the hairpiece, and presented his true self to the python lady. 'I'm not a policeman. I'm a United States congressman.'

93

'Yeah, and I'm Gloria Steinem.'

Dilbeck sensed from Lorelei's demeanor that the friction dance would soon be finished.

'How much time do we have?' he asked.

'About forty-five seconds, baby.'

David Dilbeck hurriedly unbuttoned his shirt, dropped to the floor and lay on his back. Lorelei studied him guardedly.

'Dance on me,' he said.

'How much?'

'Two hundred bucks.'

'Heels or bare feet?'

'One of each,' said the congressman, shutting his eyes.

Carefully, Lorelei stepped on his chest. 'What's that scar?'

'Double bypass,' Dilbeck replied with a grunt. 'Don't worry, I'm good as new. Now dance, please.'

'Jesus,' mumbled the python woman.

'Oh yeah. Good girl.'

'Let me know if it hurts.'

'I'll let you know if it doesn't,' said the congressman. Lorelei had difficulty keeping her balance, as Dilbeck's topography was spongy and uneven.

'You're a wonderful talent,' Dilbeck said, groaning pleasurably under the weight. His hands crept spiderlike toward his crotch.

'Oh, no you don't.' Lorelei stepped hard on his wrists. 'That's not allowed.'

'Stop, mommy.'

'You wanna play with yourself, go home and do it.'

David Dilbeck cried out once. Next came a series of wet suckling noises. Then he began to thrash epileptically beneath the astonished dancer; legs kicking stiffly, mad-dog eyes rolling back and forth.

Lorelei was afraid to take her feet off the man's arms. Inwardly she berated herself for not demanding payment up front; if the jerk croaked, she'd have to go through his pockets.

Dilbeck began to buck as if jolted by a hot wire. To keep from falling, Lorelei braced both arms against the walls of the booth. The door flew open and a stranger took her under the arms. He carried her out and asked if she was hurt. She said she'd left a shoe inside. The man said she probably wouldn't want it back, all things considered. He handed her three hundred dollars.

'Thanks,' Lorelei said. 'Will he be OK?'

'Don't you worry.'

The dancer's hands were shaking as she folded the money. 'You know what he told me? He told me he was a congressman.'

Erb Crandall laughed. 'Some guys,' he said, 'will try anything.' He dug into his pocket for another hundred-dollar bill.

EIGHT

The next day, Malcolm Moldowsky made the call. The meeting was set at a bowling alley on Sunrise Boulevard. 'Grab any lane you can,' the man said. 'It's League Night.'

Moldowsky's feet were so small he had to rent women's shoes. He got a nine-pound ball and tried to clean the germy holes with his monogrammed handkerchief. He willed himself to not think about those who had fingered the ball before him.

He bowled alone for an hour until the man showed up. He was as big as a wine keg, and wore a brown UPS shirt. He scanned Moldowsky's scores and said, 'Not bad.'

'I cheated,' Moldy said, tossing a gutter ball. He had knocked down maybe forty pins in all. On the score pad he had given himself a 164.

The man put on his bowling shoes and bowled strike–spare–strike. 'You picked a good lane,' he said to Moldowsky.

A waitress came by and the man waved her away. Moldowsky handed him a thick brown envelope. 'It's all there,' he told him. 'The tickets, too. Check for yourself.'

'Nuh-uh,' said the bowler. 'I don't care what's inside. I'm just the delivery boy.'

He rolled a snapping curve that left the seven-ten combination. 'Are you a gambling man?' he asked Moldowsky. 'Wait, that's a dumb question. Of course you're a gambling man. Otherwise you wouldn't be involved.'

'Good thinking.'

'Five bucks says I make this split.'

'Sure,' said Moldy. 'Five it is.' His lack of interest would've been obvious to a three-year-old.

The big man made it look easy, nicking the seven-pin just enough to kick across and take out the ten. 'That's the toughest split in bowling,' he said. 'Did you know that?'

'Amazing,' said Moldowsky with a yawn. He gave the man five ones. 'Ask your people to move as quickly as possible. We're up against a deadline.'

'I don't know what the hell you're talking about,' the man said, 'but I'll be happy to pass it along. Your turn, sport.'

Unhappily, Moldowsky positioned himself at the head of the lane. He made three tiny, stiff steps and heaved the ball down the alley. Somehow he got a strike.

'Pure luck,' Moldy admitted.

'The best kind,' said the man in the UPS shirt. 'You go on home now, OK? Everything's under control.'

A single piece of rotten news affirmed the leaden sense of futility that had burdened Mordecai every day since his graduation from law school, 207th in a class of 212.

The setback was especially cruel, coming at a rare moment of optimism. A lawyer from the Delicato Dairy

Company had arrived at Mordecai's office to discuss a possible settlement in the case of the roach-tainted blueberry yogurt. For Mordecai, the company's willingness to negotiate (without the customary exchange of nasty correspondence) was a glorious surprise. An out-of-court agreement would have spared him long hours of excruciating preparation for a trial; it would also have saved him from exposing a jury to the sight of his client, Shad the bouncer.

The informality of the meeting had sent Mordecai's hopes soaring. The attorney from the Delicato Dairy Company had been civil, sensible and not given to bluster. He was keenly aware of the public-relations consequences of a high-profile insect trial. The central concern was television: in Florida, TV cameras are allowed in court. The two men agreed that color videotape of a cockroach being plucked from a Delicato container could have a negative impact on consumer confidence. The extent of damage, sales-wise, would depend on how many major markets picked up the satellite feed from the courtroom. The attorney's eagerness to avoid such a risk was obvious by the size of his initial offer – a settlement in 'the mid-six figures'. Mordecai struggled to mask his elation.

Of course, the Delicato attorney requested to see Shad's roach. Just a formality, he assured Mordecai. The attorney had brought a 35 millimeter camera to document the contamination. Photographs would be important, he explained, should his clients challenge the wisdom of settling. A brief slide show in the boardroom would turn them around.

Mordecai was impressed by the attorney's thoroughness. He could see how product liability might be an attractive field of practice, if one could avoid the courthouse.

He wished Beverly were there to share the triumph, but she was out with one of her three-day migraines. Mordecai was using a temp named Rachel, whose unflagging bubbliness compensated for her lack of shorthand skills and slothful pace at the typewriter. Mordecai called Rachel into his office and told her to fetch the blueberry yogurt from the refrigerator. The smile left her face instantly, and Mordecai knew.

'I'll get some more,' she said quickly, 'on my lunch hour.'

Mordecai found no words to express his dismay. The Delicato attorney politely excused himself to use the telephone in the other room.

'Oh Rachel,' said Mordecai, abjectly.

'I'll buy the variety pack. Eight kinds of tropical fruit.'

'Rachel!'

'Yes, sir?'

'What possessed you?'

'I was hungry.'

'Did you not notice that the carton was open?'

'I thought it was Bev's. I didn't want it to sit there and go sour.'

'Rachel,' said Mordecai. 'You don't understand.'

'I'm very, very sorry.' She began to weep.

'Shut up,' Mordecai said. 'Shut up this instant.' When he thought of Shad, the flesh on his neck got damp. How would he tell him? What bloody havoc would ensue? Mordecai also mourned his own financial loss: forty percent of zero was zero. His vast stomach pitched.

'I didn't know it was yours,' Rachel slobbered. 'I didn't know you liked yogurt.'

'I hate yogurt. It gives me the runs.'

The secretary's remorse clouded with confusion. 'Then why are you so upset?'

'Because you swallowed my evidence.' Mordecai spoke in an odd singsong voice. 'So how was it, Rachel?'

'The yogurt?'

'Yes, the yogurt. A little chunky, perhaps?'

'Now that you mention it.' She sounded worried. 'Are you going to fire me?'

'Oh, worse than that,' said Mordecai. 'Please sit down.'

'What are you going to do?'

'Something that will give me great pleasure. I'm going to tell you exactly what you ate.'

Visitation day.

Erin waited under cloudy skies at Holiday Park. She chose a bench near the public tennis courts where Chris Evert had learned to play. Today it was a doubles match among French Canadian tourists. They had the whitest skin and the bluest veins that Erin had ever seen.

Darrell Grant always kept Erin waiting because it gave him a feeling of power, knowing how she lived for these afternoons. Today he arrived forty-five minutes late, pushing Angela in a wheelchair.

'Momma, look what we got at the hospital!'

Erin lifted her daughter to the sidewalk and told Darrell Grant to get lost.

'How's your butt-ugly boyfriend?' he said.

'Momma's got a boyfriend?' asked Angela.

'No, baby, I don't.'

Erin was furious that Darrell was using Angie in his wheelchair heists. If he were caught, the consequences would be terrible – the state authorities would take the little girl for good. Erin felt perfectly entitled to scream at Darrell and tell him what a reckless idiot he was, but she didn't want to spoil her brief time with Angela.

Darrell Grant said, 'I see you got new tires.'

Erin ignored him. She checked her daughter's dress and socks and underpants, to make sure they were clean. For a sociopath, Darrell was good about doing the laundry.

'Take care of my pretty little partner,' he said, and pushed the empty wheelchair back to his van, where he waited. On visitation days, he never let Erin and Angela out of his sight. Given an opportunity, Erin surely would try to run away with the girl. Darrell knew it for a fact.

Erin held her daughter's hand and they began to walk.

'How are you, baby?'

'Just OK.'

'Are you making new friends?'

'I spent Friday at Aunt Rita's. She's got a real wolf!'

Terrific, thought Erin. Crazy Rita and her cuddly carnivores. 'Stay away from the wolf, Angela. They can be mean sometimes.'

'She said I can have one of the babies, Momma.'

'No, we'll get you a real puppy—'

'But Daddy said no. He said maybe a bird.'

'A bird?' Erin said. Just what every four-year-old wants.

'A talking one,' Angie said. 'Like Big Bird, only littler.'

'Would you like that?'

'He said we can call it Humpy. Is that a good name?'

'No,' said Erin. 'Not really.'

They walked the perimeter of the park. Darrell Grant followed slowly in his van. Erin fixed a picnic under the trees. She and Angela ate peanut butter sandwiches and sang songs from 'The Electric Company'. A gray squirrel appeared and they fed it Cheese Doodles.

At ten minutes to three, Darrell began honking the horn. When Erin didn't react, he leaned on it annoyingly. The blare drowned the gentle sounds of the park. The Canadians stopped playing tennis and began cursing at Darrell Grant in French.

'For God's sake,' said Erin.

'Is Daddy making that noise?'

'I'm afraid so.' Erin gave her daughter a hug and a kiss. She smelled Darrell's goddamn cigarettes in the girl's hair.

'Momma, I forgot to tell you.'

'What, honey?'

'I lost all my dolls.'

'I'm so sorry.'

'When we moved. Daddy said he couldn't find them.'

'I'll get you some new ones,' Erin promised. She would never reveal to Angela what her father had done. Such a thing could not be explained.

'I love you, Angie.'

'Love you, too, Momma. Can I tell Daddy about the new dolls?'

'Let's keep it a surprise.'

*

From Agent Cleary, Erin had learned the following basic information about Jerry Killian: he was five-foot-nine, 140 pounds, 48 years old and divorced. He worked as a videotape editor at the local CBS affiliate. He was a registered Democrat. He drove a 1988 Chevrolet Caprice. He purchased his eyeglasses from a discount optician. He subscribed to *Newsweek, Harper's, The New Yorker, Rolling Stone, Consumer Reports* and *Hustler.* His ex-wife recently opened a macramé shop in a suburb of Atlanta, and he co-signed the loan. They had two daughters at Georgia State University. He owned season tickets to the Miami Dolphins. He rented every movie that Debra Winger ever made. He carried a $3,000 credit limit on his Visa card. In the fall he went trout fishing in western Montana, and always rented a compact car. In his entire life he had never been arrested for anything.

And he lived in Apartment 317 at 4566 Green Duck Parkway, Fort Lauderdale, Florida.

Erin phoned ahead. Killian was flabbergasted to hear her voice. He put on a coat and a tie to meet her at the door.

'In my purse,' said Erin, 'is a loaded gun.'

'So be it.'

'I'm here on business only.'

'Understood,' Killian said.

She had expected his apartment to be tidy, and it was. The place smelled of Lemon Pledge. They sat in opposing chairs at an oval-shaped dining table.

'I just wanted to thank you,' she said. 'That music you suggested is great for stage dancing.'

Killian glowed. 'You tried it? I'm so pleased.'

'You should come by the club to see. I told Shad it's fine if you do.'

'Really?' He looked wistful. 'Maybe later down the road.'

'Why later? Why not now?'

'The deal is cooking. Part of the agreement is for me to steer clear of the Eager Beaver.' Killian paused. 'It's the hardest thing I've ever done. I miss you so much.'

Here we go, Erin thought. Get the hose.

She said, 'May I call you Jerry?'

'I'd be in heaven if you did—'

'Jerry, look. I need to know more about this so-called deal. It's my life we're talking about. My little girl.'

'Naturally you don't trust me.'

'I don't *know* you.'

'Erin,' he said, 'I would do nothing to put you or your daughter in jeopardy. My devotion is complete and enduring and pure. I am consumed by it, day and night. I am lost in love.'

Erin's heart didn't flutter even slightly. She said, 'Jerry, who is this congressman?'

'His district is elsewhere. You wouldn't know his name.'

'Try me. I read the newspapers.'

'The name is unimportant,' Killian said. 'The key fact is, he's got a serious problem with the ladies. I'd feel uncomfortable going into details.'

'Oh please.'

'I'm a gentleman. That's how I was raised.'

'And I'm a stripper, Jerry. Once I had a customer eat the G-string off the crack of my ass – chew it up, swallow it, wash it down with Southern Comfort. Then he burped the elastic.'

Killian's ears turned red.

'The point is,' Erin said, 'nothing a man does can shock me. I have an ex-husband who carves his initials into other people's scalps. Is your congressman that much fun?'

'I'm not protecting him,' Jerry Killian said. 'I'm protecting you.'

'In case there's trouble?'

Killian got up and said, 'Come with me.'

Erin followed him through the apartment. The purse was tucked tightly under her left arm, so she could feel the gun through the fabric. Killian opened the door to a small guest bedroom, which he had converted to a private hall of fame. The walls were decorated with publicity pictures of local nude dancers. Interestingly, the photographs were all standard head-and-shoulder shots; one could have shown them to a kindergarten without fear of corruption. Erin's publicity photo was framed in wood and centered prominently in the pantheon. It was illuminated by its own brass lamp.

Scanning his collection, Killian said, 'Nothing is more beautiful than a woman's smile.'

'Oh really,' said Erin. 'That's why you come to the Eager Beaver – for our smiles?'

'It's the portal to true love and serenity. Without a smile, what's the rest of it? Just boobs and a patch of hair.'

'Jerry?'

'Yes.'

'You're giving me the creeps.'

'Well, Erin, I'm lost. I admit it.'

'You know all these girls?'

'I knew them. Befriended them. And whenever I

could, I helped them.' He pointed to a platinum blonde with a sharp nose and spiky greased eyelashes. 'Allison had a substance problem. I got her into a very fine program, and today she's clean.'

Erin asked if she was still dancing.

'No, she's not.' Killian stepped close to the photograph, contemplating each detail as if it were a Monet. 'A week after she got out of treatment, she married a tree surgeon and moved to Tallahassee. I never even got a postcard.' He turned to Erin and brightened. 'But that's all right! I ask for nothing.'

'Except a smile.'

'When it's from the heart.'

Erin turned off the light and directed Killian back to the living room. She sat beside him on a deacon's bench, and spoke to him as if he were a small boy.

'This is not a game,' she said.

'I heard they call me Mr Peepers.'

'We all like you, Jerry. It's an affectionate nickname.'

'I do have a frail and bookish appearance.'

'Scholarly is the way I'd describe it.'

'Don't be fooled, Erin. I can play hardball.'

She took both his hands – a standard move, to keep them from wandering. 'Exactly what've you got on the congressman?'

Killian said he couldn't tell her. He pulled one hand free and made a zipping motion across his lips.

'It must be good,' Erin coaxed, 'to make him lean on a judge.'

'I can't discuss it,' Killian repeated. 'It's man's work.'

Erin sighed and relaxed her grip. 'Here's my problem, Jerry. Do I believe your story? Do I get my hopes up for nothing? The whole thing with Angie and Darrell has been a nightmare.'

'I understand,' he said. 'I read through the files at the courthouse. That's how I got the judge's name.'

'If I knew more, maybe I could help set this up.'

'It's set up just fine,' said Killian.

He wouldn't budge. Usually a soft hand-holding would do the trick, but not this time. Erin rose and said, 'All right, Jerry. How long will it take?'

'I'm expecting a phone call this afternoon.'

'Congressmen work on Sundays?'

'They do when their careers are at stake.'

Erin stood at the door, searching for a humane way to say what had to be said. 'If this works out, if I get Angela back . . . well, I can't give you anything, Jerry. You should know that.'

'By anything, you mean—'

'You know what I mean,' Erin said. 'I'll be eternally grateful for your kindness. That's the most I can promise.'

'Do I look crushed?'

'Slightly.'

'Well, who wouldn't be?' He chuckled softly. 'I bet you'll quit the club, too.'

'Absolutely. Once I get Angie back, I'm gone.'

'Then there's one thing you can do for me.' He went to the stereo and picked through a stack of CDs. 'Just a second,' he called to Erin. 'Please!'

Soon the apartment filled with heavy rock – 'She's Got Legs', by ZZ Top. Erin gave Killian a look of mock disapproval.

'Let me guess,' she said.

'Do you mind?'

'Just one dance,' Erin said. Urbana would've wrung her neck.

The first time she went on stage at the club, Erin vomited before and after the performance. Urbana Sprawl took her aside: 'It's like wing-walking, OK? You're fine, long as you don't look down.' Monique Jr hugged her and whispered: 'It's a slumber party, hon. That's how come we're in our nighties.' And Monique Sr said: 'Quit crying, for God's sake. Bobby Knight is at table nine!'

It had taken Erin a week to find a method that worked. Whenever she froze and found herself asking why – why am I doing this! – she thought of Angie. Once on stage, the trick was to dream herself away with the music. That's why she was so picky about the selections: the songs had to mean something. If things felt right, the awful anxiety would melt away and Erin would become wondrously detached from the surroundings. She'd forget she was jumping around in her birthday suit before a roomful of drunks. In Erin's fantasy, the men in the audience were cheering the high kicks and fluid turns, and not the shape of her ass.

Smiling was a struggle at first, because Erin wasn't particularly ecstatic about the work. Moreover, she'd noticed that many of the customers didn't smile, either. Instead they watched with studious and impassive expressions, like judges at a cattle auction. Again, Urbana had offered valuable counsel: 'A nice smile beats forty-inch jugs any day!'

So Erin made herself smile, and the money got better. The men came forward and folded ten-dollar bills into

her garters or the elastic of her G-string. Many customers were nervous about standing so close, and
plainly terrified of touching a foreign thigh. Erin was
constantly reminded of the ridiculous power of sex:
routine female nakedness reduced some men to stam-
mering, clammy-fingered fools. For the bolder clientele,
Shad's spooky presence discouraged groping and crude
solicitation.

Erin had conquered her shyness in about a month.
Unlike some of the dancers, she would never be totally
comfortable on stage. There was a small thrill to the
tease, but no hot rush from the cheers and whistles
of strangers. By contrast, the two Moniques loved the
boisterous attention, because it made them feel like
glamorous stars. The wilder the audience, the wilder
their performance. Erin didn't play to the crowd. The
music was her master, and also her escape. When Van
Morrison sang, Erin *was* dancing in the moonlight.

But that was in the club, not in a customer's
apartment.

Still, she wasn't afraid. Mr Peepers obviously was
helpless in her presence; he would have inserted his
tongue in a light socket if she'd told him to. Erin further
neutralized the man by asking about the sepia portrait
of a curly-haired woman, gazing up at them from the
credenza. It was, as Erin had surmised, Jerry's dear
departed mother. Erin felt safer under the late Mrs Killian's watchful eye.

Killian cleared the oval table and helped Erin climb
up. She handed him her sandals and her purse. By then
Killian had already forgotten about the gun, the congressman, the blackmail, what day it was ...

The wood was slick and cool under Erin's feet. She

danced for four minutes and never even removed her sweater. Killian was dazzled. 'Splendid,' he said over and over, to himself.

As the song ended, he tucked something into the back pocket of Erin's jeans. It wasn't a tip.

At the door she gave him a sisterly peck on the cheek. Killian jumped at the moment of contact. He said, 'If I have good news, you'll see me outside the club.'

'Be careful,' said Erin, although she wasn't seriously concerned. The worst that could happen was that the congressman would tell Killian to blow off.

He waved fondly from the doorstep as Erin walked to her car. She waved back and gave him one of her best smiles. She had decided that he was basically a good person.

When Erin got home, she took the note from her pocket and unfolded it on the kitchen counter. It said:

Thank you for saving my soul.

That night, Erin worked a double shift at the Eager Beaver in the hopes that Jerry Killian would show up. He didn't. The following morning, she phoned his apartment and got no answer. When she tried the TV station, the news director told her that Mr Killian had gone on vacation. He was expected back in two weeks.

At the club, Erin switched back to her familiar dancing routines – Clapton, Credence Clearwater, the Allman Brothers. Soon she got lost in the blues guitar, and the world seemed like a better place, even though it wasn't.

She never saw Jerry Killian again.

NINE

On the evening of September sixteenth, at a tavern called the Lozeau Lounge in western Montana, the Skyler brothers drank six beers apiece, threw darts at a stuffed elk and argued over the cosmic meaning of a Randy Travis song.

Then they headed for home, which was a valley in the Bitterroot Mountains. Johnny Skyler drove because brother Faron's license had been suspended four times and revoked twice permanently. That was no small achievement in the great and free state of Montana, where driving and drinking are regarded as inalienable rights.

Johnny Skyler followed the dirt road toward the Clark Fork River and the one-lane steel bridge that would carry them to their respective wives and children, waiting in identical doublewide trailers that had been purchased for twenty percent off at a spring trade show in Spokane. The money that the Skyler brothers saved on the mobile homes had been put to good use: a large satellite dish was wired to the earth on a flat clearing between the two doublewides. A parabolic eyesore among the regal vectors of Douglas firs and Ponderosa pines, the TV dish was still the finest investment that Johnny and Faron had ever made: Wrestlemania!

Japanese game shows! One night, flipping channels, they'd stumbled onto a guy talking with real Playboy bunnies! The interviewer was so tan that the Skylers speculated he might be an Indian, except he talked too fast and laughed too loud. Around the man's neck hung a gold medallion as thick as a goose turd. Johnny and Faron couldn't get over it.

No doubt about it: satellite TV preserved the Skyler family units. In the long bleak stretch of winter, it was all that kept the men from going mad with boredom. In the summer, it entertained the wives and kids so that Faron and Johnny could stay out extra late: crack open another Rolling Rock, kick back, watch the sun drop down over the mountaintops.

On this night, though, a storm was rolling in hard from Idaho. There would be no sunset, just an ominous and sudden darkening. Bruised clouds stacked up over the Bitterroots, and a cool wind chased down the river. It rattled the tin price sign that hung over the gas pump outside the Lozeau Lounge. Inside, Johnny Skyler reared back and heaved one more dart at the taxidermied elk, yanked his brother off the bar stool and said they'd better get on home, while they could still see the way.

The dirt road fed straight downhill to the old steel span across the river. Fat raindrops began to slap against the Bronco, dimpling the chalky brown dust on the tinted windshield. Mindful of the strong wind, Johnny Skyler took it slowly. First gear. High beams. Both hands on the wheel. Approaching the bridge, he was careful to line up the truck's wheels on the twin wooden planks, already slickened by the drizzle.

Halfway across, Faron Skyler said, 'Hold up.'

His brother braked the truck to a stop, idling.

'Out there,' Faron said.

'On the river?'

'Yeah. I seen a raft.'

'No way,' said Johnny Skyler. He lowered the window. It was too dark to see anything on the Clark Fork.

His brother said, 'Wait for the lightning.'

Up the valley it came, an ultraviolet burst that illuminated the river for a fraction of a second. In that blink of a moment, Johnny Skyler spotted the raft, twenty yards downstream from the bridge.

'There – against the gravel bar,' Faron said.

'Yeah, I saw it.'

'Did you see the guy?'

'No.' Johnny dimmed the headlights and squinted into the thickening night. The rain was coming down pretty good, soaking the sleeve of his left arm. Johnny spit hard, and the wind hurled it back in his face.

Another rip of lightning, high and far away. A purple strobe brightened the valley, then it was dark again. But the scene was stamped in Johnny's eyes: a red raft, oars askew, gliding sideways along a narrow gravel spit that briefly split the river in two. The man in the raft had his back to the bridge. He wore an olive vest and an updowner-style cap, either of which marked him definitively as an out-of-towner. His arms were straight at his sides. A fishing rod lay across his lap.

'Crazy bastard,' said Faron Skyler.

'Think he needs help?'

'Hell, yes, he needs help. He needs his damn head examined. Crazy bastard trout fiend.'

Johnny wasn't sure what to do next, wasn't sure what could be done. As the sizzling electrified maw of

113

the storm boiled down on them, a steel bridge seemed not such a smart place to be. Thunder had begun to shake the struts.

'He better get off the water,' Johnny Skyler remarked, staring at the place where the rafter had last appeared in a blast of light. Johnny briefly considered the logistics of a rescue, then pushed the notion out of his head. Here the banks of the Clark Fork were rocky and steep, and of course the Skyler brothers were full of beer. Disaster was the word that came to Johnny's mind.

He cupped his hands to his mouth and shouted against the wind: 'Hey out there!'

Faron said, 'Forget it, man. He can't hear you.'

Johnny tried again: 'Hey you!'

Another flash, another glimpse of the raft, slipping farther downstream. The fisherman appeared not to have heard the shouts. The rod still lay across the man's lap; the oar handles remained unattended – one pointing upriver and the other pointing the opposite way.

'There's one crazy bastard,' Faron reiterated.

'Somethin' ain't right.'

Lightning exploded nearby, and the brothers covered their heads. They heard the crash of a lodgepole pine, breaking in three pieces.

'Time to go,' Faron said. 'Would you agree?'

Johnny Skyler had a bad feeling in his gut. He gazed down the Clark Fork, waiting for more lightning, for one more look at the lunatic trout fiend.

'He'll be all right, Johnny. The river slicks out for the next mile. A blind dog could make it to shore.'

'I suppose.' Johnny had never seen a raft on this leg of the Clark Fork so late in the evening. The next takeout was twelve miles downriver. And who the hell goes fishing at night in a thunderstorm?

'Would you please fucking step on it?' Faron Skyler was saying. 'I don't feel like gettin' barbecued up here on this damn bridge. Besides, we're missing the ballgame.'

Ever since Denver had gotten a major-league franchise, Faron had become a baseball fanatic. His brother could take it or leave it. Football was something else. With the dish they could even pull in the Argonauts.

'It's nine-thirty,' Johnny Skyler noted. 'Game's almost over.'

'Well, shit.'

'Faron, I can't see him no more.'

'Maybe he turned the big bend.'

'Not without rowing he didn't. Not unless he's got an Evinrude on that raft.'

Faron said, 'All he's got to do is hang on, he'll be OK. Now let's go.'

'Just a minute.' The rain came down in sheets, thrumming on the roof of the Bronco. Johnny finally rolled up the window but he didn't take his eyes off the water.

Sky crackled and the river became a pink mirror. This time the brothers had no difficulty spotting the small red raft, turning in the slow current as it floated downstream.

'Oh my Lord,' Johnny Skyler said.

Faron grabbed the dashboard with both hands. 'Crazy goddamn bastard,' he said.

The raft was empty. The man was gone.

The Skylers hopped from the truck and ran for the river.

*

The rain stopped two hours later. By then the Mineral County Sheriff's Office had arrived with a motorboat and a bona fide scuba diver. The US Forestry Service had promised to send four rangers and a helicopter, providing the weather didn't act up again. A few residents turned out with rafts, rowboats and waterproof flashlights. The small riverside campground at Forest Grove served as headquarters for the search, which by local standards was heroic and exhaustive.

By dawn, the raft had been found, wedged sideways under a piling of the I-90 bridge, due west of Lozeau. The oars had been lost, and the raft contained no clues to the identity of the missing angler. An empty can of Colt 45 and a crumpled Snickers wrapper were the only evidence of a human passenger.

The search for the body lasted eighteen hours, and proved fruitless. A reporter from the *Missoulian* arrived at Forest Grove and interviewed the Skyler brothers, who gave a richly embroidered account of what they'd seen on the river during the thunderstorm. Then they posed for pictures next to the Forestry Service helicopter. For the next several days the brothers faithfully watched C-Span on the satellite dish, but saw no mention of the Clark Fork rescue effort or their role in it. Fame embraced the Skylers in more modest ways; it was years before they had to pay for their own beers at the Lozeau Lounge.

The children of Al García's second wife called him Al, and that was fine. 'Dad' was out of the question. The kids already had a dad, who was in prison because of Al García.

That was how García had met his second wife –
while arresting her husband for a drug murder. There
were no hard feelings. Six months after the trial, she
filed for divorce and married Al.

From hash dealer to homicide detective, García had
told her, you're moving up in the world. Not by much,
Donna had said. Quick on the draw, that was Donna.
The children were all right, too: a boy and a girl, ages
eight and nine, or nine and ten – García had trouble
remembering. Overall he was very fond of the kids, and
didn't feel the least bit guilty about the circumstances.

The first time the boy asked when his real dad was
getting out of jail, Al García took the small hand and
said: 'Never, Andy.' When the boy asked why, García
said: 'Because your daddy shot a man between the eyes.'
Andy appreciated the seriousness of the situation. His
sister, Lynne, who was either a year older or a year
younger said maybe her dad had a good reason for
shooting the other guy. A hundred thousand reasons,
Al García had said, but none good enough. Just then
Donna had come storming in from the kitchen and
ordered them all to hush up, or else.

When it came time for their first family vacation,
Donna chose western Montana because she and the
kids had never seen mountains. It sounded fine to Al
García. He made a few calls and found out that
Montana, for all its Wild West lore, was a safe and
tranquil place; there were traffic intersections in Dade
County with higher murder rates.

Donna arranged to rent a small log house on the
Clark Fork River, about sixty miles outside of Missoula.
García was no outdoorsman, but a cabin on the water
seemed like a splendid idea. He promised Andy and

Lynne he would help them catch a big rainbow trout and they could fry it up for supper. He promised Donna he wouldn't talk about his job and wouldn't call Miami, not even once, to check on his open cases.

In fourteen years as a homicide detective, Sgt Al García had personally investigated 1,092 murders. It was his curse to remember every one; the oddest details, too. 'Rescue 911' playing on the television while they chalked the body. The counterfeit Rolex worn by the victim. The smell of burned biscuits in the kitchen. A photograph in the hall, the dead man whooping it up at Disney World. Al García hated the unfailing thoroughness of his memory; it made him an excellent detective but a deeply troubled person.

Montana turned out to be better than he had expected; wide-open and friendly, with a few exceptions. A desk clerk at the motel in Missoula shot him a hard look when she saw the name on the credit card. Being a García from Miami wasn't easy these days. Some people automatically assumed you had six kilos in the trunk and a loaded Uzi under the front seat.

The next day, when they got to the log house on the river, Al García nearly forgot where he'd come from and what he did for a living. Standing on the wooden deck, he thought the river valley was the most peaceful place he'd ever seen. He drank the piney air, closed his eyes and easily lost himself in the silence of the surrounding woods. The first day, Andy spotted two deer. The second night, Lynne found a small bleached skull from a dead skunk; she wanted to take it home to Florida, but Donna said no, give it a decent burial in the garden.

On the third day, Andy came running up the bank

so fast that García thought a bear was chasing him. The boy was shouting: 'Al, you better come! You better come fast!'

García told him to slow down, take a breather. Andy grabbed his arm and tugged hard. 'Come on. Down to the river.'

'What is it, son?'

'A floater!' Andy exclaimed..

García felt a sour knotting in his gut. Living with a homicide cop had given Donna's youngsters a gruesome vocabulary. They knew all about trunk jobs, John Does, Juan Does, gunshots, accidentals and naturals.

And floaters, of course.

García followed the boy down the hill to the river's edge. The detective waded into the water, skating his tennis shoes across the gravel bottom. The body floated face-up, tangled in a shallow brushpile. The face was violet and bloated, the eyes springing out in a cartoonish way.

'Is he dead, Al?' Andy stood on the bank; he folded his small arms across his chest, looking very serious. 'He's dead, isn't he?'

'Extremely,' García said.

'I told you!'

The dead man wore heavy rubber trousers and an olive vest with many small pockets. García unzipped the one over the left breast, and removed a wallet. The wallet held three one hundred-dollar bills, a half-dozen traveler's checks and a laminated driver's license with familiar colors.

García said, 'Goddammit to hell.'

The boy shouted, 'Who is he, Al?'

'Go tell your mother to call the police.'

The boy ran off. The dead man's face stared up googly-eyed from the hissing river.

'You're a prick,' Al García said to the corpse. 'You're a prick for spoiling my vacation.'

He looked again at the dead man's license and cursed acidly. The sonofabitch was from Fort Lauderdale, Florida.

Why? García wondered. Why won't they let me be?

TEN

Shad was intrigued by the psychiatrist's eyebrows, lush and multi-hued.

'Those real?' he asked.

'Please,' said the doctor, recoiling. 'No touching.'

It was Shad's first visit to a shrink – Mordecai's man. His name was Vibbs, Palm Beach sharpie and plaintiff's best friend. A laminated diploma from Yale University hung on one wall. Shad was more interested in a jar of hard candy on the doctor's desk. He filled his cheeks and began to chew.

'Tell me about the roach,' Dr Vibbs said.

'Big fucker.' The words crackled out of Shad's mouth.

'Did it upset you?'

Shad's laugh exposed a wet maw of peppermints and butterscotch. 'Upset? Hell, I'm traumatized. Write that down.'

Dr Vibbs was rattled by Shad's hairless, hulking presence. Most of Mordecai's referrals had nothing wrong with them; this one was different. When the hairless man bent to pick up a candy wrapper, the psychiatrist noticed a 'G' carved into his scalp. He assumed that Shad had done it to himself.

Vibbs probed with caution. 'I need to ask some personal questions – it's standard for these evaluations.'

'Evaluate away,' said Shad. 'I told you I was fucking traumatized. What more do you want?'

'Are you having bad dreams?'

'Nope.'

'Not even about the roach? Try to remember.'

'Ah,' Shad said. He was catching on. 'Now that you mention it, I been havin' fearsome nightmares.'

'That's understandable,' said the psychiatrist, scribbling up a storm. 'Tell me about them.'

'I get chased down Sunrise Boulevard by a giant cockroach with yogurt dripping from its eyeball sockets.'

'I see,' the psychiatrist said. He scarcely glanced up from his notes. Shad took this as a signal to try harder.

'Yeah, so this monster roach is chasin' me back and forth, drooling and growling like a thousand tigers. The fucker's as big as a tanker truck. Plus it's got a dead baby in its teeth.'

'I see.'

'And when it gets real close ... it turns into my mom!'

'Good,' said Dr Vibbs, without emotion. 'So tell me more about your mother.'

'Eh?'

'Please. I'm interested in your relationship with your mother.'

'You are?' An odd light flickered in Shad's eyes. He dragged Dr Vibbs out of the chair and put him face down on the floor. Then he took a handsome pair of wood-handled scissors and sliced the psychiatrist's clothing from neck to buttocks. On the desk Shad found a rotating tray of rubber stamps. He selected a red one that said NO INSURANCE, and stamped it all over Dr

Vibbs's naked torso. It was quite some time before Shad ran out of ink. Meanwhile, sad puppy noises rose from the doctor's throat.

'What a phony,' Shad complained. He tossed the stamp on the desk and grabbed a handful of hard candies, for the road.

'You're disturbed!' Vibbs cried.

'I ain't disturbed. The word is fucking traumatized. You should've wrote it down.'

'Go away,' said Vibbs.

Shad stood over him. 'Not until you spell it.'

'What?'

'Come on, wigpicker. *Trau-ma-tized.* I'll even spot you the goddamn T.'

In a shaky but defiant voice, the psychiatrist spelled the word perfectly.

'Proud of you,' Shad said, stepping across him. 'And forget that business about my mom. I don't know what got into me.'

To quell employee unrest at the Eager Beaver, it was Orly's custom to pound on the desk and invoke the Mafia. He would brag of lifelong bonds with Angelo Bruno, Nicky Scarfo, Fat Tony Salerno and other famous gangsters whose names he'd clipped from crime magazines. He would talk of blood oaths, and the certain death awaiting those who violated them. Orly's performance usually had the desired effect of stanching demands for pay raises, health benefits or the slightest improvement in work conditions at the club. In truth, he had no connections whatsoever to organized crime. The mob wasn't interested in the Eager Beaver because strip joints got too much heat from police. Orly heard this first-hand from the only genuine Mafioso he'd ever met, a loan shark on trial for breaking the thumbs of a delinquent Chrysler salesman. Orly had gone to court as personal research, to learn how the mob actually operated. During a recess he approached the loan shark and struck up a friendly conversation. When Orly asked if the loan shark knew anyone in the market for a nude dance club, the man frowned and said no fucking way, there's too much heat. Now video arcades, the mob guy said, that's a whole other deal. A video arcade would be very attractive, investment-wise. Orly was disappointed, but out of politeness he hung around to hear the verdict. Not guilty, it turned out. The jurors (among them, several recent purchasers of Chrysler products) were visibly unmoved by the victim's tale of woe. Orly noticed a few of them smiling as the salesman described his hands being placed in the doorjamb of a steel-blue New Yorker sedan. All that muscle over a six hundred-dollar debt! Orly was impressed. He clung to his dream that someday the Mafia would make him a partner.

For now, though, the illusion would have to suffice. Orly faced a roomful of disgruntled dancers. As usual, Erin spoke for the group.

'Item Number One,' she began. 'The air conditioning.'

Orly scowled. 'So what about it?'

'It's way too cold,' said Erin.

Urbana Sprawl spoke up. 'Thermostat's on sixty-eight degrees. That's awful cool.'

Orly turned to Shad, who stood expressionless in a corner. 'You chilly?'

'No,' said Shad, 'but I don't feel much in the way of hot and cold.'

'Well,' Orly said, 'I'm quite comfy at sixty-eight.'

Because you're a reptile, Erin thought. She said, 'You're wearing a cardigan, Mr Orly. We, on the other hand, are freezing our bare butts.'

Orly rubbed his palms together. 'The cold makes you look sexier. Makes those nipples good and hard. Customers go for that, am I right?'

The room got tense. Erin said to Orly, 'Congratulations. You've hit a new low.'

'Watch it,' he warned. 'You just watch how you talk.'

Monique Jr, normally timid, said: 'I don't believe it – that's why you made it so cold? So we'd get hard?'

'Nipples,' Orly declared, 'are a mighty important part of this enterprise.'

In the corner, Shad muffled a laugh.

Erin said, 'Turn up the thermostat, or we don't dance.'

'I'll pretend I didn't hear that,' said Orly.

Erin picked up a ballpoint pen and wrote on the blotter: 72 DEGREES OR NO DANCING!

Orly said, 'I'll pretend I didn't see that.' He was waiting for Erin to back down. So were the other dancers. Orly adopted a menacing tone: 'Insubordination can be dangerous, young lady. Remember what happened to poor Gonzalo.'

Poor Gonzalo was the Eager Beaver's previous owner, whose bullet-riddled corpse had been dumped on the interstate – punishment, Orly claimed, for filching from the coin boxes on the Foosball machines.

'Bottom line is, Fat Tony likes things to run smooth,' Orly said.

Erin suspected that Fat Tony and the Mafia had nothing to do with Gonzalo's death. More likely, it was a dispute between Gonzalo and one of his many PCP suppliers.

'Tell you what,' said Erin. 'Why don't you ask Fat Tony to stop by the club tonight?'

Orly was dumbstruck. He rocked precariously in his roost.

'I want him to strip down,' Erin said. 'See if he doesn't freeze his saggy old Mafia tits.'

The other dancers murmured in amazement. What had gotten into this girl?

'Well?' Erin said. 'Give the man a call.'

Orly looked whipped. 'You're on very thin ice,' he said weakly.

Erin smiled. 'I bet it's warm and cozy down at the Flesh Farm.'

'Oh Christ,' said Orly. 'Don't even think about it.'

She turned to the other dancers. 'Show of hands?' One by one, the women joined up.

'No!' cried Orly. 'You stay away from those fucking Lings!'

'Then turn up the damn thermostat,' said Urbana Sprawl, freshly emboldened. 'Fat Tony don't want his dancers out sick with a chest cold.'

The two Moniques began to giggle. Shad turned toward the imitation red velvet wall, to hide his grin. He knew there was no Fat Tony and no mob connection. The principal investors in the Eager Beaver were a group of relatively harmless orthopedic surgeons from Lowell, Massachusetts.

A reluctant Orly said he'd raise the temperature in

the main lounge to seventy degrees. Erin held out for seventy-one.

'All right,' Orly agreed, 'but I want to see some rock-hard cherries. I mean it!'

Erin proceeded with Item Two on the agenda. 'We've been kicking around some ideas for a new name.'

'Forget it,' Orly sniffed. 'I already said no.'

'Something classy.'

'You want classy? Teach these fucking bimbos how to dance. *Then* maybe we'll talk about a classy name. For now, the Eager Beaver is perfect.'

'Candy Rockers,' Erin said. 'Sexy but not crude. What do you think?'

'I think,' Orly said, 'that I give these girls a video from only the hottest joint in Dallas, right? All they gotta do is pop it in the VCR and watch the mother-fucking tape. I mean, a chimpanzee could pick up some a these steps—'

'It takes time,' said Erin.

'Like hell.' Orly pointed at Sabrina, who was absorbed in polishing her toenails. 'You watch that tape?'

Sabrina bowed her head and said no.

'Case closed.' Orly slammed his hand on the arm of the chair. 'Case closed. We'll switch to a classy name when I see some classy dancing.'

Urbana Sprawl waved. 'Mr Orly, I looked at that video. I believe those Dallas girls were high on crack.'

'Oh, is *that* it?' Orly laid on the sarcasm.

'Candy Rockers,' Erin said again. 'Think about it, OK?'

Someone knocked quietly on the door. Orly

motioned to Shad, who went to the back of the office and positioned himself strategically at the doorway.

'Who's there?' he asked.

A thick voice on the other side said: 'Police.'

Shad looked to his boss for instructions.

'Shit,' Orly said. 'What now?' His face turned the color of spackle.

Erin wasn't sure what to make of Sgt Al García. She didn't know if he was a good policeman or a lousy policeman, but she knew he'd never make it in the FBI. He was not an assiduous note-taker.

However, other factors worked in his favor. Eleven whole minutes had passed and Al García hadn't yet propositioned her, or even asked if she was married. That set him apart from most cops who dropped by the Eager Beaver.

He sat across from Erin in a back booth. Orly, citing phony flu symptoms, had slithered out the front exit. Shad was at the bar, haggling with a wholesaler over two cases of Haitian rum. On stage, Urbana Sprawl danced to a dirty rap song.

Erin wore a lace teddy, a white G-string and high heels – not ideal attire for a police interview. García smoked a cigar and paid no attention to the perfumed surroundings. He handed Erin a Xeroxed copy of a Florida driver's license. When she saw the photograph of Jerry Killian, she knew she was looking at a dead man. García had already told her.

'Exactly what happened?' Her mouth had gone dry and her eardrums buzzed faintly.

'Drowned,' the detective said. 'Your picture is hanging in his apartment.'

'Mine and a dozen others.'

'I found a stack of cocktail napkins on the bedstand. Did you know about that? Eager Beaver cocktail napkins.'

With extreme firmness, Erin said: 'I never saw his bedroom.'

'He wrote notes on these damn napkins. Notes to himself, notes to his kids, notes to you.' García paused. 'Is the smoke bothering you?'

'No,' said Erin, 'it's my all-time favorite aroma. That and gum turpentine.'

Without apologizing, the detective extinguished the cigar.

'Tell me what happened,' Erin said. It was still sinking in – Mr Peepers was dead. This was too much. 'I want to know everything,' she said.

'What happened is, your friend floated up deceased in the Clark Fork River and spoiled my trout fishing. You ever been there – the Clark Fork?' García reached in his jacket and took out an envelope of family snapshots. He found one photo showing the river and the mountains and he handed it to Erin. 'Mineral County, Montana. Beautiful country, no?'

Erin agreed. In the foreground of the photograph was an attractive woman and two children. They looked perfectly normal, Al García's family.

'Not many homicides in Mineral County,' the detective was saying. 'The coroner takes one look at Mr Tourist, all dressed up in his L.L. Beans, and says Accidental Drowning. Being the hardass ill-mannered big-city Cuban that I am, I politely request to peek inside Mr Tourist's chest. The coroner, nice guy, says sure. Unzips 'em right on the spot.'

Erin's low-cal lunch did a slow somersault in her stomach. She asked García what was found inside Jerry Killian.

'Not much.' García held his dead cigar poised, like a paintbrush. 'A little water in the lungs. That's to be expected. But when a man drowns in a lake or a river, he also tends to suck up grass, bugs, sand – you'd be surprised. One night we got a floater off Key Biscayne, had a baby queen angelfish in his bronchioles!'

Al García spoke loudly to be heard over the dance music. 'You don't look so hot. Want me to come back some other time?'

'Could you get to the punch line,' Erin said, impatiently. 'In ten minutes it's my set.'

'Sure,' said García. 'Here's the deal. The Clark Fork was full of bugs and leaves – dip a bucket in the river and you'd see what I mean. But the water in Killian's body was amazingly clean.'

'Tap water,' Erin said.

'You're a smart girl.'

'So somebody killed him?'

'Probably in a bathtub,' García said, 'if I had to guess.'

'Can we go outside?' Erin asked.

'Only if you let me smoke.'

Shad followed them to the parking lot. Erin motioned him to go away. Al García acted as if he didn't care one way or the other. He lit his cigar and leaned up against his car, an unmarked blue Caprice.

Erin said, 'You're serious about Jerry being murdered?'

'His ex says he went fishing out West every year. This time was different in one respect: when he got there, he never took out a fishing license. That's damn strange.' García turned away and blew smoke into the darkness. 'Two local boys saw him going downriver on a raft, alone in a rainstorm.'

'Alive?'

'I doubt it. You got any ideas, Mrs Grant?'

Erin said, 'Let me think on it. Things are complicated.' Maternal instinct told her to avoid the subject of Angela, and Jerry Killian's promise. It was possible that García already knew.

'For the record,' he said, 'you didn't kill him, did you?'

Erin laughed in bitter astonishment. 'No, sir. I didn't love him, I didn't sleep with him, and I most definitely didn't kill him.'

'I believe you,' García said. 'But I'm a sucker for high heels.'

He gave her his card. She studied it curiously. 'This says Dade County.'

'Yeah, that's a problem. We're in Broward, aren't we?' García rolled the stogie back and forth in his mouth. 'Montana's a long way off, Mrs Grant. It may take me a while to drum up local interest.'

'But technically it's not your jurisdiction.'

'That's right,' he said, agreeably. 'I'm meddling, pure and simple.'

'Why?' Erin asked.

'Because my boy is the one who found him.' García took out his car keys. 'You got children, you'll understand.'

'Is he all right – your son?'

'Sure. He just wants to know what happened, and I'd prefer to tell him the truth. Anyway, floaters happen to be right up my alley, I'm proud to say.'

Al García's voice trailed off. He looked tired and preoccupied and ten years older than he probably was. Erin fought back an urge to tell him everything.

'I'd like to help,' she said, 'but I doubt if I can. Mr Killian was a customer, that's all. I hardly knew the man.'

García flicked the cigar. It landed with a hiss in a puddle.

After he got in the car, Erin motioned him to roll down the window. She stepped up to the door and said, 'If it's not an official investigation, how'd you get inside his apartment?'

'All I did was ask the super.' García winked. 'A badge is a badge.' He started the car. 'Get back inside,' he told Erin, 'before you catch cold.'

'Will there be a service?' she asked.

'For Killian? Not for a while. The coroner promised he won't sign the papers for a week or so, until I check around.'

'So where's Jerry's body?'

'In a freezer in downtown Missoula,' García said. 'Him and two tons of dead elk.'

Cousin Joyce wasn't the very last person in the world that Mordecai wanted to see, but she was high on the list.

'Disaster,' she said, dropping a stack of color slides on his desk. 'I found these in Paul's underwear drawer.'

'And how is Paul?' asked Mordecai.

'Feeling better,' Joyce said. 'Temporarily.'

'Any luck locating the phantom synagogue?'

'There was no synagogue,' she said. 'Look at the slides, Mordecai.'

They were the photographs taken by Paul Guber's friend at the ill-fated bachelor party. The lawyer went through the slides methodically, holding each one up to a goosenecked lamp.

Joyce sat down and began to sniffle. 'That's the man I wanted to marry.'

As Mordecai peered at the pictures, he longed for a projector and a screen. The women were happy-looking, gorgeous and nude. The lawyer pitied Paul Guber, for there was no mistaking his youthful face, buried serenely in the bare loins of a brunette. The effect was to give him a curly goatee.

'Obviously alcohol was involved,' Mordecai said. 'Too much alcohol.'

'Don't make excuses. I want you to sue the bastard.'

'For what? You're not married yet.'

'Some lawyer,' she said, blowing her nose.

'What's this?' Mordecai was examining the last slide, which differed in content from the others. In it, a paunchy silver-haired man loomed over the still-kneeling Paul Guber. With both hands the stranger was raising a green bottle over his head, as if swinging an ax. His face was twisted with rage. Behind the stranger was the figure of a larger man lunging with outstretched arms, trying to stop the attack.

'Dynamite,' Mordecai said. He took a magnifying glass from the top drawer and hunched over the slide.

'I'm so glad you're amused,' said Joyce. 'My future is in shambles, but thank God you're enjoying yourself.'

'Joyce?'

'What?'

'Shut up, please.'

The sniffling stopped. His cousin's expression turned cold and spiteful.

Mordecai glowed as he looked up from the pictures. 'I *know* these guys!'

'Who? What are you smiling about?'

'Joyce, go home immediately. Take care of your fiancé.'

'I can't. He's playing golf.'

'No!' Mordecai exclaimed. 'He can't possibly be playing golf. He's a very sick man. He's got cluster migraines. Blackouts. Double vision. Go find him, Joyce. Tend to him.'

The lawyer hustled her toward the door. 'I'll be out to see you tomorrow. We've much to talk about.'

Joyce balked. 'And what about me? I'm expected to forget what I saw on those pictures? My fiancé, the man I planned to marry, licking at the belly of some sleazy whore. I'm supposed to put that awful image out of my mind!'

'If you're smart, yes,' the lawyer said, 'because we've still got one hell of a case.'

'Suing a nudie bar?'

'Don't be silly.' Mordecai held his cousin by the shoulders. 'First rule of torts: always go after the deepest pockets – in this case, the fellow who assaulted Paul.'

'So who is he?' Joyce demanded.

'We'll discuss it later.'

'A celebrity?' She was hoping for a movie star. 'Let's see that picture again.'

'Later,' said Mordecai, aiming her toward the door.

'He's got money? You're absolutely sure?'

'Oh, I'm certain he can get it,' the lawyer said. 'I'm as certain as I can be.'

Mordecai thought: Finally it pays to be a Democrat!

ELEVEN

Midnight found Congressman Dilbeck and Christopher Rojo in high spirits at the Flesh Farm. They were celebrating Dilbeck's good news, as related by Malcolm Moldowsky via Erb Crandall: the blackmail threat was vanquished! The elated congressman sought no details, and none were offered. Moldy was a magician, his tricks meant to be secret and mystical. Dilbeck and Rojo drank a toast to the greasy little ratfucker, then turned their attentions toward the dance stage. Soon the blue haze filled with paper airplanes made from US currency. By closing time, Dilbeck and Rojo were fast friends with two of the Flesh Farm dancers.

Dawn found the foursome eighty miles away, on a levee on the southeastern shore of Lake Okeechobee. Wearing only knee socks and jockey shorts, Chris Rojo was orating the history of sugar cultivation and Congressman Dilbeck's role in it. The dancers complained of being chewed by fire ants, and retreated on four-inch heels to the air-conditioned comfort of the limousine, where Pierre prepared Bloody Marys.

Rojo paced the dike and chattered nonstop, a typically brilliant cocaine monologue. 'Two hundred thousand acres of muck, glorious muck,' he said. 'Sweet sugarcane, far as the eye can see . . .'

Dilbeck's gin-clouded retinas barely saw past the laces of his shoes. The first rays of sunlight warmed his bare shoulders and ignited an itchy prickle of insect tracks. Dilbeck rocked from one leg to the other, as if he'd spent the night on a very small boat. 'I may puke,' he announced to Rojo.

It was the young millionaire's first visit to the fields where his family fortune was sown. He raised lean brown arms to the sky and cried: 'Twenty-three cents a pound!' The bleating caused Dilbeck to wince. 'Twenty-three cents!' Rojo yowled again. 'Thank you, *Tio Sam*! Thank you, Davey.'

Twenty-three cents per pound was the average wholesale price of the sugar grown by Christopher Rojo's family corporation. The inflated figure was set by the United States Congress and monitored by the Commodity Credit Corporation, an arm of the Department of Agriculture. Rojo had good reason to be thankful: cane sugar from the Caribbean sold for only twelve cents per pound on the world market. Strict import quotas kept most foreign sugar out of America, thus allowing the Rojos to maintain their fixed price and, thus, their grossly excessive lifestyle. Whenever the import quotas came under attack from international trade groups, Congress charged to the rescue. Dilbeck was one of Big Sugar's best friends, and Chris Rojo never missed an opportunity to demonstrate his gratitude. Now, standing on the levee, he locked the congressman in a ferociously sloppy embrace.

Dilbeck felt himself teetering, and pulled free. 'I don't feel so good. Where are the girls?'

'Who knows,' said Rojo. 'Relax, my friend. There will always be girls.'

The congressman squinted into the sun. 'Did we get laid last night?'

'I haven't a clue.'

'Me neither,' Dilbeck said. 'I'm assuming we did.'

'For a thousand dollars, I certainly hope so.'

Dilbeck grimaced at the sum. 'That's what you paid?'

'Five hundred each. So what?' Chris Rojo's voice was dry and high-pitched. 'It's nothing to me,' he said. 'Just money.'

Dilbeck felt his body heat rise with the sun. He touched the back of his neck and found it damp. He wondered what had happened to his shirt. He hoped that one of Mr Ling's dancers had chewed it off in a sexual frenzy.

Rojo said, 'It's a crazy world, Davey. I give some girl five hundred bucks just to go for a ride, OK? The poor fucks who cut this cane' – he waved toward the fields – 'that's three weeks' pay.'

'Are you serious?' Dilbeck said.

'This is some country, my friend. Now I must find my pants.'

By the time they returned to the limousine, Christopher Rojo had come down hard from the coke, and David Dilbeck wobbled on the brink of heatstroke. Pierre held the door as the two men tumbled into the backseat. The dancers were asleep, a bright tangle of blonde, lace and Spandex. Dilbeck's shirt and Rojo's trousers lay crumpled on the floor of the car. The congressman dug a handful of ice from the portable refrigerator and packed it to his forehead.

'It's so fucking hot,' he said.

Chris Rojo grunted. 'Florida, man.'

In the driver's seat, mute Pierre turned to receive directions.

'Civilization,' Rojo commanded. 'And step on it.'

Dilbeck watched the flat brown acres fly by at ninety miles an hour, tall stalks of cane stretching to the horizon. He couldn't believe that human beings worked in such suffocating heat from dawn to dusk. He'd heard it was bad but, Christ Almighty, he'd never imagined it like this.

'How much do you pay them?' he asked Rojo.

'The girls? I told you, Davey – five each.'

'No, I mean the migrants.'

'Oh, that.' Rojo was struggling to fit his legs into the wrinkled trousers. 'My father says it's up to thirty dollars a day. All depends if the foreman's in a good mood. But when you subtract room and board, booze and smokes – who knows? And medical care isn't cheap, either.'

'Jesus,' said the congressman.

'Hey, they keep coming back. Compared to Santo Domingo, this is fucking Club Med.'

'How long do they work?'

'Until it's done,' Rojo said. 'My father says a good hand cuts a ton of cane every hour. You believe that? A whole goddamn ton – amazing what a man can do when he's properly motivated.'

David Dilbeck turned from the window and closed his eyes. It made him dizzy and sick, just thinking about it.

The judge was startled when Erin sat down at the table.

She said, 'You remember me? The unfit mother.'

The judge stiffly drained his Jack Daniels. 'I was hoping this was a social visit,' he said.

Erin fought to steady herself. She'd had two martinis during her break – a rare indulgence while performing. The problem was Jerry Killian being dead. Even peripheral involvement with a murder could ruin her chance of getting Angie back. In his lovestruck quest to help, Killian might've provoked the wrong people. How far had he taken his screwball scheme? Had he actually tried extortion on a US congressman? Erin needed to know more, before she told Al García about her own supporting role. The judge was her strongest lead, and also the riskiest.

Erin feinted in the obvious direction. 'I'd like you to hear my side of the case.'

'I already have,' the judge said, 'in court.'

A waitress brought a fresh drink, which the judge eyed longingly but did not sip. Erin wondered if Shad had defiled it in the usual way.

'Thanks to you,' she said, 'my daughter is in the custody of an incorrigible felon.'

'The record reflected no such thing.'

'The record was sanitized, Your Honor. Darrell Grant is a paid informant for the sheriff's office, and you know it. They purged his rap sheet.'

Fidgeting in a dark booth, the judge wasn't nearly as imposing as he was in the courtroom. Here at the Eager Beaver, he was just another horny old fart with impossible fantasies.

Erin said, 'My ex-husband deals in stolen wheelchairs. He's made an accomplice of our daughter.'

The judge told her that he based his opinion on the known facts of the case; that's the law. 'But it's also true that a decision can be reversed.' He twirled the ice cubes counterclockwise in the bourbon. 'Are you going to dance on my table?'

'I don't do that.'

'The others do.'

'Not I,' said Erin.

'Then perhaps something else?' The judge clutched his glass with both hands, as if it were a sacred chalice. His voice took on a sly tone: 'I mentioned one particular idea to your friend.'

'Which friend was that?'

'Your "special" friend.'

Naturally, Erin thought. 'I've got lots of special friends,' she said, 'with lots of special ideas.'

The judge pursed his wormy lips and said: 'You're playing games.' He fumbled under the table as if scratching himself, but brought forth a Bible. 'I come here often to pray for sinners like you.'

'Oh, that's a good one.'

'I keep the Good Book on my lap at all times.'

'I'll bet,' Erin said. 'Levitating?'

'Fighting the devil on his own turf.'

'Whatever,' she said.

'Good versus evil, evil versus good. It's an eternal struggle.' The judge found a dry corner of the cocktail table and placed the Bible there. Then he treated himself to a noisy gulp of bourbon. On stage, the two Moniques danced as gunslingers: fringed boots, stetsons, holsters and a silver star on each bare breast. The judge was briefly transported.

'Time to get ready,' Erin said, slipping out of the booth.

The judge snapped to attention. 'Does this mean the answer is no?'

'What did my special friend say my answer would be?'

'Mr Dilbeck wasn't sure.'

Finally, Erin thought: Jerry's congressman.

'We talked about your custody case,' the judge said. 'I suggested an oral settlement. Didn't he tell you?'

Oral settlement. How incredibly clever! A regular Noel Coward, this one. 'Your Honor,' Erin said, 'I don't know anyone named Dilbeck. And whatever you suggested to him, I promise that my answer would be no.'

The judge seemed more perplexed than humiliated. 'All right,' he said, stirring the ice, 'but perhaps we could pray together some fine Sunday morning.'

The lawyer, grinning like an imbecile, was waiting at the door. 'Come in, come in, come in!'

Shad distrusted joviality. 'I heard you the first time. What's the news from Delicato Dairy?'

Mordecai led him to the conference room. 'Coffee, Mr Shad?'

'Answers, Mr Mordecai.'

From his waistband Shad pulled a Black & Decker cordless drill with a $1/4$-inch steel bit. Without a word he began to cut numerous holes in Mordecai's favorite Matisse print. 'The new pointillism,' Shad explained to the stupefied lawyer.

Soon the painting fell off the wall, exposing an identical pattern of fresh holes in the plaster. Mordecai's secretary pounded urgently on the door and Shad instructed her to go away. Mordecai dropped to his knees and began begging for mercy. He'd been rehearsing ever since Dr Vibbs had phoned, weepy on Nembutals. His session with Shad had gone quite badly.

'Don't kill me,' Mordecai pleaded. 'I'll do anything.'

Shad tucked the drill under his arm. 'Start at the beginning, fuckhead.'

The lawyer's story came out in whimpers: The yogurt had been stored securely in the office refrigerator. One day Beverly was out sick. The temp helped herself, never asked . . . ate the whole damn thing, roach and all. You believe that dumb twat?

Shad's amphibian eyes closed slowly, and remained that way for a long time. He was thinking that he should have left the warning note on the yogurt carton.

The lawyer's knees ached, but he was too frightened to move. Beverly rapped on the door again, and this time Mordecai was startled to hear his own voice telling her to relax, everything's OK.

Just another narcoleptic sociopath in need of legal advice.

'You all right?' the lawyer asked Shad.

The hairless giant opened his eyes. His face showed nothing. From a breast pocket he scooped a handful of crispy dead insects – cockroaches, grasshoppers, june bugs, Japanese beetles, even a scorpion – which he organized on the table for Mordecai's inspection.

'This time,' Shad said, 'no fuckups.'

The lawyer rose to his feet. He circled the table slowly, pretending to admire Shad's collection.

'We should discuss this,' Mordecai said.

'Nothing to discuss, partner. Send your girl off to the supermarket. Fruit flavors only.'

'You don't understand—'

'And tell her to check the date on the cartons. I ain't stickin' my pinkies in expired yogurt. No way.' Shad sat back and waited for Mordecai to get rolling.

The lawyer said, 'But this is fraud. I could be disbarred.'

'You could be dis*membered*,' said Shad, 'if you don't move your fat ass.'

Mordecai felt the blood rush from his legs. Soon he lost all feeling below the waist. His throat tightened. 'I . . . have . . . another plan.'

'Sure you do.'

'I . . . d-d-do!'

With a single punch to the shoulder, Shad knocked the lawyer down. Mordecai wailed. Shad told him to shut up, don't be such a pussy. Mordecai wailed louder.

Shad stood over him, taking aim. All he said was: 'Pitiful.' Then he dropped the dead scorpion into Mordecai's open mouth. Instantly the lawyer stopped crying, in order to gag.

'There's more where that came from,' Shad said.

Suddenly Mordecai's secretary came through the door. It was a half-hearted charge. For a weapon Beverly had chosen a cheap gold-plated letter opener, which crumpled like foil against Shad's massive rib cage. He calmly disarmed the woman, and directed her to fetch a glass of water for the boss.

Later, after Mordecai had regurgitated the scorpion and everyone had settled down, Beverly confirmed the lawyer's version of what had happened to Shad's evidentiary cockroach: the temp had scarfed it down.

'Mmmmm,' Shad said, 'I smell malpractice.' He arranged the other dead insects in military formation on the table.

Mordecai said, 'Please. It was an accident.'

'That fucking roach was my retirement. Understand?'

'You want to retire a rich man, Mr Shad, then listen to my offer.' Mordecai signaled for his secretary to leave the room. 'Please pay attention,' he said to Shad.

Shad held a grasshopper and a Japanese beetle delicately in between the thumb and forefinger of each hand. He was making the dead bugs dance a little jig on the table. 'Go ahead,' he told the lawyer. 'I'm perfectly tuned in.'

Mordecai unveiled the color slide from Paul Guber's bachelor party. 'Take a look.'

'What is it?'

'Here. Hold it by the corner.'

Shad put the insects back in formation, and turned his scrutiny to the slide. He held it to the lamp, and squinted with one eye at the stamp-size image.

He said, 'Well, lookie there.'

'Do you know where that photo was taken?'

'Sure. At the club.'

'And who's in the picture?'

'Me and Erin and a couple asshole drunks.'

'Erin would be the stripper?'

Shad's head turned slowly. 'She would be a dancer. The best.'

His voice was murderous. Mordecai thought: Good Christ, now I've insulted the monster's girlfriend. Can anything else possibly go wrong?

The lawyer hesitantly moved on: 'The young man's name is Paul Guber. He's my client.'

'Then God help him.'

'The older man, the one swinging the wine bottle – do you recognize him?'

Shad glanced at the picture again. 'Nope. And it's a champagne bottle. Korbel, I would guess.'

'The man's name is David Dilbeck. Do you follow politics, Mr Shad?'

'Do I *look* like I follow politics?'

'Mr Dilbeck is a United States congressman.'

Shad thought about that as he studied the slide once more. He said, 'Man's put himself in one helluva posture. I'm guessing you're gonna sue his ass.'

'It may come to that,' Mordecai said. 'However, I'm hoping the matter can be settled privately, in a reasonable atmosphere.'

' "However?" ' Shad disapproved of snooty verbiage. He pinched one of Mordecai's plump cheeks and said: 'I liked you better with the scorpion in your gullet.'

'Quit!' the lawyer cried out.

Shad released him. 'So how do I fit in? And no more shrinks. I've had it with phonies.'

Mordecai rubbed the sting from his face. 'You saw everything, Mr Shad, the entire assault. When Dilbeck's people learn I've got an eye-witness, they will – pardon the expression – shit a brick.'

'Tell me,' Shad said. 'How much money can a lousy congressman have?'

'Trust me. The lousier they are, the more they have.' Mordecai eased himself out of Shad's lunging range. 'The thing to remember, always, is that we're not after Dilbeck. The serious money is with the men who own his soul.'

Shad was toying with his dead insects again. 'I should try this on a chessboard,' he remarked.

'Please,' said Mordecai. 'Trust me. I know about

146

Dilbeck – both of us were Mondale delegates back in
'84.'

Shad said, 'I may just cry.'

'We're talking millions of dollars!'

The man appeared to be serious. Shad postponed his
decision to stomp the shit out of him.

'Millions,' Mordecai repeated, huskily. 'The people
who own David Dilbeck, the people who'd do *anything*
to keep him in office – they're some of the richest bastards in Florida. They've got money to burn.'

'In that case,' Shad said, 'let's burn some.'

TWELVE

Orly hired a new dancer whose stage name was Marvela. She was a tall strawberry blonde with a lovely figure, and she knew how to move. On her first night working the birdcage, she doubled Erin in tips.

Later, over a tub of vanilla Häagen-Dazs, Urbana Sprawl told Erin that it was about time she had some competition.

'An off night,' Erin muttered. She had danced poorly, with a smile so forced and insincere that only the drunkest customers wouldn't have noticed. 'My concentration's shot,' she said.

'You wanna talk about it?'

'Mr Peepers is dead.'

Urbana whispered, 'Oh my Lord.'

'Possibly murdered.'

'Sweet Jesus.'

Until now, Erin had told no one the true reason for Sgt Al García's visit to the Eager Beaver. The other dancers had assumed that the topic was Erin's ex-husband, in whom many police agencies had expressed interest.

Urbana Sprawl begged for the details of Jerry Killian's death.

'It's a long story,' Erin said, 'and I think I'm in the

middle.' She reached back and locked the dressing room door. 'Apparently somebody drowned the little guy.'

'Because of you?'

'Indirectly.'

'Then you'd better hide, girl. Come stay with me and Roy.' Urbana's boyfriend, Roy, was a mechanic for an outlaw motorcycle gang. He and Urbana specialized in unexpected house guests. Erin said thanks, anyway.

'I was you, I'd be on the first plane out.'

'Not without Angela. And first I need more money.' Her options were limited, and all were expensive.

Urbana suggested table dances and private parties. 'You're the only one who won't.'

'It may come to that.'

'There's other ways, too,' Urbana said, gravely. 'I know you wouldn't, but some girls do. It's all according to what you need, and how bad.'

Erin patted her friend's hand and told her not to worry. 'I'll rob Jiffy Marts before I'll turn tricks. Urbana, would you tell Mr Orly I'm knocking off early tonight?'

Erin was too tired to scrub her makeup or take off the dancing clothes. Over the red teddy and G-string, she put on gray sweats and a baggy T-shirt. She tied her hair in a loose ponytail, folded the tip money in her purse and put her pumps in a Penney's bag. She looked at the hollow-eyed face in the mirror and said, 'What a hot number I am.'

'Anything I can do to help,' Urbana said, 'you name it.'

'Break Marvela's legs?'

'Go home now, honey. Get some sleep.'

'Sleep? What's that?' Erin said goodbye and unlocked

the dressing room door. Monique Sr was in the dim hallway, struggling to repair a broken garter.

'Of all nights,' she said. 'John Chancellor's at table eleven.'

'Yeah?' Erin said. 'I'm a Brokaw fan, myself.'

Erin went home and fixed herself a martini. She put Tom Petty full blast on the tape deck and took off her clothes. Lying on the bed, she contemplated familiar gaunt faces on the wall – posters of legendary rock stars, including a few who were still alive. The posters were a gift from one of Erin's ardent customers, a concert promoter. He was so eager to impress her that he once forged Peter Frampton's autograph on a compact disc. It was beyond pathetic.

Erin's apartment was decorated minimally because it was a temporary stop. She refused to invest in anything that wasn't plastic and portable and couldn't be moved in one day by a woman laboring alone. Even the sound system, Erin's only extravagance, broke down into four lightweight boxes.

Nothing connected her soul to the place, not even memories. The three men who'd been in the bedroom were as forgettable as the discount decor. One of them hadn't gotten his pants off before Erin told him to get lost. She'd been watching '60 Minutes', her favorite TV program, when the young visitor remarked that he didn't like the show because 'there was too much talking.' Erin ordered him to button his trousers and hit the bricks. Never again would she date a baseball player – at least, nothing below Triple A.

She bunched a pillow under her head. Acidly she thought: Quite a life I've made for myself!

The telephone looked red-hot on the bedstand; so many possibilities. Call Mom and borrow money for more lawyers? Perhaps when Biscayne Bay freezes over.

Call García and spill everything? Erin doubted the detective would be moved to tears by a recounting of her domestic problems. He would, however, be greatly intrigued by the weird details of Jerry Killian's blackmail plot. A homicide with political connections would be a welcome break from the drudgery of domestics and drug murders.

Maybe that was the phone call to make, Erin thought. Get it over with.

She changed her mind and put the empty martini glass on the floor. Jimi Hendrix loomed over the headboard, tonguing his left-handed Stratocaster. Dead at twenty-seven. Erin thought: Not me, buster.

She took the telephone off the bedstand and balanced it on her tummy. She punched a number in Deerfield Beach and closed her eyes, thinking *please, please, please*.

Angela answered on the third ring.

'Baby?'

'Momma?'

'It's me. Did I wake you?'

'Where are you, Momma?'

'Is your father there? Talk softly if he is.'

'Can you come see us? Every day we go for rides in the hospital.'

'Which hospital, baby?'

'Different ones. Daddy dresses up like Doctor Shaw.'

'Oh God,' Erin said.

'Then he puts me in a wheelchair and pushes real fast. Can you come see us? We go real fast – you can push, too.'

'Angela, listen to me.'

'I think I gotta go. Love you, Momma.'

'Angela—'

Long silence. Somebody breathing. Then a wet cough.

'Angie?'

Darrell Grant laughed, high-pitched and juiced by speed. 'I gotta get this number changed.'

Erin said, 'You are one dumb shit. If you get caught using that little girl—'

'Hell, I won't get caught. It's a dream setup, didn't she tell you? I stole a doctor's jacket, a real stethoscope, the works. Man, I look so legit! Fact, I'm thinking seriously about trying some gynecology on the side—'

'Darrell, they'll take her away! The HRS will take her away from both of us. For ever.'

'Lord, you *do* worry. I already told you, I won't get caught. The setup is, I dress Angie in pajamas so she looks like a real patient. Her Cookie Monster pajamas, remember? The ones with the little feetsies in the bottom—'

'You asshole.'

'Now, don't be judgmental. You, who flashes her tits for a living. Don't fucking judge me, sweetcakes—'

Erin hurled the phone to the floor. She was too mad to cry, too upset to sleep. She pulled on a sweatshirt and blue jeans, and grabbed car keys off the dresser.

*

Special Agent Tom Cleary wore a burgundy bathrobe and brown floppy bedroom slippers. To Erin, he looked practically adorable. She'd never seen him rumpled and ungroomed. Sleep had sculpted his sandy hair into a sharp peak, like the crest of a cardinal.

'Coffee?' he croaked.

They sat in the kitchen and spoke in low tones while Cleary's wife heated a bottle for the baby, who was yowling upstairs. It was the couple's fourth child in six years and the stress of fecundity was taking a toll. When Erin apologized for the lateness of the hour, Mrs Cleary said it was no problem. No problem at all! She was about to explode with artificial politeness. The moment she went upstairs, her husband sagged with relief.

'I need some help,' Erin said, leaning forward.

'Darrell again?'

'Naturally.' She told him about her ex-husband becoming a police informant, about the expensive court fight, about Darrell Grant's wheelchair scam with Angela as a human prop—

'Back up,' the agent interjected. 'He's got custody? That doesn't seem possible.'

Erin's throat felt chalky. 'The judge says I'm an unfit mother. How 'bout them apples?'

Cleary was incredulous. 'Unfit?' The word came out in a horrified whisper, as if he spoke of a dreaded disease. 'What in the world ... Erin, did something happen?'

She thought: I can't tell him about the job. The Eager Beaver he would never understand.

'It's a long story,' she said.

'Darrell got to the judge?'

'Well, something did.'

The coffee was ready. Cleary poured. Upstairs, the baby finally stopped crying. Erin said, 'Tom, he's turning my daughter into a gypsy.'

The FBI man nodded soberly. 'The problem is, we can't stretch jurisdiction.' She started to say something but Cleary cut her off. 'Let me finish, Erin. Your divorce, that's a civil matter, totally out of our scope. But if you've got proof the judge is corrupt, then maybe we can do business—'

'I don't have proof,' Erin said sharply. 'I thought that was your department.'

Cleary's eyes flashed but he continued: 'The wheel-chair racket – now I agree it's despicable. But basically you're talking grand larceny, which the Bureau won't touch.'

'But the locals have Darrell on the damn payroll!'

'Listen,' Cleary said, 'if I tried to run this one past my supervisor – well, there's no chance in hell. He'd throw it right back in my face.'

The agent was rueful but unwavering. Erin felt whipped. 'A phone call from you and the cops would drop him like a rock,' she said. 'One lousy phone call, Tom.'

'I don't work that way. Rules are rules.'

'But you helped me before.'

'I ran a name. That's easy, Erin.' Cleary took off his glasses and kneaded his temples. 'What I cannot do,' he said wearily, 'is open a federal case on your ex-husband. I'm very sorry.'

'Me, too,' Erin mumbled into her coffee cup.

The agent asked if the information about Jerry Killian had been helpful. Oh yes, Erin said, very helpful. She thanked him for the coffee and rose quickly to leave, but not before Cleary asked: 'How does he fit into all this? Killian, I mean.'

'Another long story,' Erin said. Cleary would panic if he knew Jerry Killian was dead. Automatically he would connect the murder to his own leak of the computer check. Next he'd feel compelled to confess the breach of regulations. Several cubic yards of paperwork would accumulate before an actual field investigation of Killian's drowning began. Meanwhile, Tom Cleary most certainly would be transferred to the FBI equivalent of Siberia, where his wife would ponder a future of frigid winters and limited day-care possibilities. Eventually the Bureau might sort out the facts of Killian's death and exonerate the exiled Cleary. By that time, though, Darrell Grant could be safely in Tasmania, or anywhere, with Angela.

Erin had no time to wait for the FBI. And she wanted Agent Tom Cleary in Miami, in case she needed him.

As he walked her to the door, Cleary asked where she was working.

'A dive,' Erin replied, 'tending bar.' Not an unmanageable lie. The same one she told her grandparents.

Cleary said. 'Which dive?'

'You don't know the place, Tom. It's definitely not in your jurisdiction.'

The agent accepted the sarcasm impassively. He said he hated to think of her slinging drinks. Erin said the money wasn't bad.

Cleary, his voice heavy with guilt: 'On this Darrell thing, I wish I could bend the rules, but I can't. I simply can't.'

'I understand, Tom.' Erin checked discreetly for the

wife, then pecked him on the cheek. 'Thanks, anyway,' she said.

When she got home, Mexican championship boxing was on ESPN. The face of one fighter was purple and pulped, blood trickling from what appeared to be three nostrils. The other boxer aimed meticulous jabs at the man's fractured nose, until the bleeding got so bad that the referee lost his footing on the slippery canvas.

At one time in her life, Erin couldn't have comprehended how a human being could inflict such misery on an opponent he scarcely knew. Now, thinking of her ex-husband, Erin began to understand the boxer's drive: a simple transfer of aggression, from real life to the ring.

By morning, she had cooled off. She did one hundred sit-ups, reassembled the telephone and tried another phone call. This, too, was a long shot.

Erb Crandall noticed something new in the front hallway of Malcolm J. Moldowsky's penthouse. It was a color portrait of John Mitchell, former attorney general and convicted felon.

'A dear friend and mentor,' Moldy explained. 'Savagely maligned, long before your time. An American tragedy.'

'I know all about him, Malcolm.'

'Political genius,' said Moldowsky. 'Misplaced loyalty was his fatal flaw. He took the fall for Nixon.'

'Who didn't?' Erb Crandall had been in college during the Watergate hearings. He remembered John Mitchell as a surly old dog who couldn't lie his way out of a paper bag.

'The ultimate insider,' Moldy said, aglow. He stroked the frame of the portrait in a tender manner that worried Crandall.

'Don't you have a hero?' Moldowsky asked.

'Nope.'

'That's very cynical, Erb.'

'People with heroes usually believe in something. How about you?'

Moldy thought about it while he poured two cognacs. He handed one to Crandall and said, 'I believe in influence for the sake of influence.'

'Pushing buttons.'

'It's a kick – wouldn't you agree?'

Crandall said, 'To be honest, some days it sucks.'

'You're still in the trenches, Erb. Be patient.'

'You mean someday I could end up like . . . *him*?' He pointed at John Mitchell's toady visage. 'Gee, Malcolm, I can hardly wait.'

'You are one cynical fuck.'

They sat in Moldowsky's plush living room, which featured a panoramic vista of the Atlantic Ocean. Distant lights of freighters and cruise ships winked at them from the Gulf Stream. Crandall was soothed by the view and warmed by the cognac.

Moldowsky asked for an update on the re-election campaign. He was pleased to hear that David Dilbeck's Republican opponent, a right-wing appliance dealer, had raised only sixty thousand dollars to date. The hapless yutz was spending most of his days fending off the press, and trying to explain two long-ago convictions for mail fraud back in Little Rock, Arkansas. Moldy himself had unearthed the obscure rap sheet, and passed it along to a friendly Miami columnist.

On the home front, Erb Crandall reported that every living Rojo, including scores of far-flung cousins, had dutifully sent cashier's checks for the maximum allowable contribution to the Re-elect Dave Dilbeck Committee. Additional thousands of dollars were pouring in from supposedly ordinary citizens wishing to support the congressman's exemplary work. Cross-checking those contributors' names with voter rolls, or even with the telephone book, would have been useless. The names belonged to Caribbean farm workers, imported by the sugar industry to work the cane fields. It was Moldowsky's inspired idea to use the untraceable migrants as a cover for illegal Rojo donations.

'Davey still doesn't know,' Crandall said.

'Don't tell him,' said Moldy.

'He thinks he's adored by the masses.'

'Encourage that notion, Erb. We like a candidate with confidence.'

'Oh, he's confident,' Crandall said. 'He's so goddamn confident I can't control him.' He handed Moldy the congressman's most recent tab from the Flesh Farm. Mr Ling had boldly tacked on forty bucks for 'replacement of damaged pasties'.

'And where were *you*?' Moldowsky demanded of Crandall.

'He went out the back door, Malcolm. Chris Rojo sent the car.'

'I said, where were you?'

'Asleep in the living room.'

'Nice work.'

'Fuck off,' Crandall said. 'Tonight *you* can tuck him in. That I'd pay to see.'

Moldowsky was disturbed to hear that Dilbeck was

up to his old licentious tricks. Obviously the idiot had learned nothing from the Eager Beaver episode.

Erb Crandall said, 'Can we put something in his food? I was thinking saltpeter.'

'Yeah? I was thinking thorazine.' Moldowsky was astounded by the congressman's stupidity. Didn't he realize how close he'd come to disaster? Jerry Killian was gone, but there would be other Killians, other dangerous blackmailers, if Dilbeck didn't steer clear of the tittie bars.

'There's something else,' Crandall said.

Moldowsky loosened his necktie vigorously, as if escaping a noose.

'Let me guess: he's gone and knocked up a cheerleader. Make that an underaged cheerleader. Catholic girls' school?'

'You told me to keep you posted in the weirdo department.'

'So post me, Erb. Before I die of fucking suspense.'

Crandall popped a cough drop into his mouth. 'The congressman got an unusual phone call this morning.'

'Here, or in the Washington office?'

'Washington. One of the secretaries took the message.' As he spoke, Erb Crandall clacked the lozenge from cheek to cheek. He said, 'It was a woman calling.'

'There's a shocker.'

'Said she was a friend of Jerry Killian.'

'You're shitting me.' Moldy's jaw hung. 'Erb, this better be a joke.'

'You see me laughing?'

'What else?' Moldowsky barked. 'What else did she say?'

'That's it, Malcolm. She didn't leave a name or a

159

number. Very polite, according to the secretary. Said she'd call back another time, when the congressman was available.'

Moldowsky ran his fingernails raggedly through his hair – that's how Crandall knew he was upset. Impeccable grooming was one of Moldy's trademarks.

'Did you tell Davey?' he asked.

'Of course not.'

'Which secretary took the call?'

'The older one – Beth Ann. Don't worry, she doesn't know a thing. The name Killian meant zero to her.' Crandall noisily chewed the cough drop and washed it down with cognac. 'Malcolm, it's about time you filled me in.'

'Be glad I haven't.'

'But you said it was taken care of.'

Moldowsky stared out to sea. 'I thought it was.'

At the moment his pager beeped, Sgt Al García was sitting on a meat freezer, chewing gum, filling out paperwork. Inside the freezer were Ira and Stephanie Fishman, ages eighty-one and seventy-seven, folded up like patio furniture. They had passed away within two days of each other in the month of July during the first full year of Gerald Ford's presidency. Daughter Audrey, their only child, had placed the dead Fishmans in a Sears industrial-size deep freeze, which she'd purchased especially for that purpose. Between them, Ira and Stephanie Fishman had been collecting about $1,700 a month in Social Security, disability and veteran's benefits. Being chronically unemployed and without prospects, Audrey felt no urgency to inform the government or anyone else that her parents had died. Friends assumed that the couple had grown tired of the hot weather and moved back to Long Island. No one but Audrey knew that Ira and Stephanie lay perfectly preserved beneath three dozen Swanson frozen dinners, mostly Salisbury steaks. The Social Security checks kept coming, and for all these years Audrey cashed them.

Her secret was safe until this day. She got up early and took the church bus to Seminole bingo, as usual. At about noon, a young outlaw named Johnnie Wilkinson broke a bedroom window and entered the Fishman residence in search of cash, handguns, credit cards and stereo equipment. Curiosity (or perhaps hunger) attracted Johnnie Wilkinson to the big freezer, and his subsequent screams were heard by a passing postal carrier. Audrey returned to find the small house swarming with cops. She was immediately taken into custody, but detectives were unsure what charges should be filed.

Days would pass before the Fishmans defrosted enough for a proper autopsy, although it appeared to García that they'd died of natural causes. Florida had no specific law against freezing one's own dead relatives, but Audrey had committed numerous misdemeanors by failing to report her parents' deaths, and by storing the bodies in a residentially zoned neighborhood. As for her Social Security flimflam, that was a federal crime. Al García had no jurisdiction, or interest. He was rather pleased when his pager went off.

Erin met him at a Denny's on Biscayne Boulevard. They took the farthest booth from the frozen pie display. When García attempted to light a cigar, Erin plucked it from his mouth and doused it in a cup of coffee.

'Unnecessary,' the detective groused.

'Get out your notebook,' she said.

Al García smiled. 'Good old FBI training.'

'You know about that?'

'I'm not as slow as I look.' A waitress appeared, and García ordered a burger and fries. Erin asked for a salad.

She said, 'What else do you know?'

'You went through a blonde phase.'

Erin laughed. 'God. Not my driver's license!'

'You look better as a brunette.' Al García took out the notebook. He clenched the cap of his pen in his teeth, to compensate for the missing cigar. He said, 'All I got really is the basics. Height, weight, marital status. Big fat zilch on the FCIC, which is good. Oh yeah, you're overextended about a hundred bucks on your Visa card. Boy, do I know *that* drill.'

'I'm impressed,' Erin said.

'Don't be.'

'You know about Darrell?'

'He's a hard one to miss. But let's hear about the late Mr Killian.'

The more Erin talked, the better she felt. García acted as if he believed every word, although she wondered if it was part of the routine. The detective was non-threatening to a fault. He made notes in sloppy cop shorthand, careful not to let the transcribing interfere with the eating of his hamburger. Predictably, he perked up when he heard that Killian had boasted of a pipeline to a congressman. 'I got the name from the judge,' Erin

said. She watched as the detective printed the word
DILBECK in neat block letters in his notebook.

She added: 'Whatever Jerry tried, I'm praying that it
isn't what got him killed.'

'Love can be a dangerous item,' García said.

'I didn't stop him because – OK, I figured there was
an outside chance to get my daughter back. I know it
sounds a little crazy.'

'Not to me,' said García. 'I read the divorce.'

'Wonderful,' Erin said. The file was a trove of slander.
Darrell Grant had invented lurid lies about her sexual
appetite, and bribed two of his pals to corroborate the
fiction. Then there were the cutting words of the judge
himself, pontificating on Erin's unfitness for motherhood. She looked hard at García. 'I wouldn't hurt my
daughter for the world.'

'I know you wouldn't.'

Erin went for the salad with a vengeance. It tasted
like wet napkins.

'What I meant,' García said, 'is it doesn't sound so
crazy, your going along with Mr Killian's scheme. Your
ex-husband is a shitbird, if I can be blunt. He's got no
business raising the girl. It's Angela, right?'

'What he told the judge, the stuff in the files—'

'Forget about it,' García said.

'It's lies.'

'I said don't worry. How about some Key lime pie?'

Erin had a piece. Al García ate two. Then he
unwrapped a fresh cigar, holding it safely out of Erin's
reach. 'Please,' he said, 'I beg of you.' She found herself
smiling. As García clipped off the butt, Erin picked up
his lighter and flicked it open. She reached across the
table and lit the cigar.

'They shipped the body back from Montana,' García said, puffing out the words. 'Back to Atlanta, I should say. Killian's ex-wife wants to bury him up there.'

'What about the murder investigation?'

'They don't like that word out in Mineral County. *Murder*, I mean. *Unclassified* was the best they could do. The coroner says he'll reopen the case if I turn up something new. Something besides a few drops of tap water in the lungs.'

'You'll keep at it?'

'In my spare time, sure.' García leaned back in a pose of total relaxation. He asked Erin if anything unusual had happened at the Eager Beaver lately. 'Think hard,' he said.

'Things stay quiet. We've got a pretty large floor manager.'

'No incidents? No bad fights?'

Erin mentioned the lunatic drunk with the champagne bottle. 'He sent a young man to the hospital,' she said. 'I'm sure there's a record.'

'So where was your bigshot "floor manager"?'

'He couldn't do much. They had a gun on him.'

'Don't stop now,' García said.

'It wasn't the guy swinging the bottle. It was his bodyguard who had the gun.'

'You get lots of bodyguards in the Eager Beaver?'

'No shots were fired,' Erin said. 'The whole thing was over in five minutes.'

'And you didn't recognize this particular drunk.'

'I had another one attached to my thigh. The guy with the Korbel came out of nowhere.'

García leaned forward. 'Did you see his face? Would you know him if you saw him again?'

'Maybe.' Erin paused. 'Shad got a better look than I did.'

'The bouncer?'

'Don't ever call him that. "Floor Manager" is the title.'

García said, 'I need to chat with him.'

Erin was skeptical. 'He's the strong, silent type.' She chose not to burden García with Shad's opinion of cops.

'I'll come by the club some night,' the detective said. 'You make the introductions and we'll play it by ear. All he can do is say no.'

Wrong, thought Erin. That's not all he can do.

García asked if Jerry Killian had been in the audience on the night of the champagne-bottle attack. Erin didn't remember; she said she'd check with the other dancers.

'This is probably a dumb question,' Al García said, 'but it'll save me some time: Was anybody arrested?'

Erin giggled. She couldn't help it.

'I'll take that as a no,' said the detective. He signaled for the check.

Erin said that there was something else he should know. 'Today I called the congressman's office. I told them I was a close friend of Jerry Killian.'

'Cute,' García said. 'I'm guessing he didn't take the call.'

'Right.'

'And I'm praying you didn't leave your name.'

'Right,' Erin said. 'Want me to try again?'

'Please don't.' García slid out of the booth and went to pay the bill. Erin waited by the front door, then followed him out. A light summery rain was falling. The palm trees along the boulevard looked droopy and anemic.

García stood beneath the Denny's awning and jotted on a piece of paper. He gave it to Erin and said, 'My home number. Guard it with your life.'

Erin put the number in her purse. 'Does your wife know what you're working on?'

'Don't worry about it. You call anytime.' He shielded his cigar from the rain and walked Erin to her car. 'Donna'll understand. Trust me.'

Erin said, 'I'll bet she had a Darrell, too.'

'A world-class Darrell. Makes yours look like an altar boy.'

'What happened?'

'First, I put his ass in jail,' García said, 'then I married his wife.'

'Now that's style,' said Erin.

'Yup. That's what Donna says, too.'

THIRTEEN

On the morning of September twenty-fifth, a breezy autumn day, Jerry Killian was laid to rest at Decatur Memorial Gardens, a few miles outside Atlanta. Burial followed a small ceremony attended by Killian's ex-wife, his daughters and nine friends from the television station in Florida. All who came to the funeral were secretly photographed by a man concealed forty-five yards away in a vale of young Georgia pines. The man wore the drab overalls of a gravedigger, but he worked for Malcolm J. Moldowsky. He used a Leica 35 millimeter camera with a long lens and a motordrive, and bracketed the exposures just to be safe. By midafternoon, six strips of black-and-white negatives were sitting on Moldowsky's desk in Miami. Every person in every frame had been identified; none seemingly could have connected the late Mr Killian to Congressman David Lane Dilbeck.

Moldy was convinced that the woman who'd phoned Dilbeck's office was not present at the funeral. Who was she – a mistress? A secret partner in the blackmail scheme? Finding her wouldn't be easy. Had Killian worked any place but a TV station, Moldowsky could've sent a discreet private investigator to chat up his pals and colleagues. In this case it was too risky.

Press people tended to be cranky and suspicious, and a visit from a PI would only stir things up. The safest strategy was to wait. Maybe the mystery woman would call again, maybe she wouldn't.

Either way, Malcolm J. Moldowsky couldn't relax. It was like having a cobra loose in the house. Eventually you're bound to step on it. The only question was: when?

Darrell Grant was loading wheelchairs when Merkin and Picatta arrived, unannounced. The Broward robbery detectives got out of the unmarked car and walked slowly around the U-Haul three times. Finally one of them asked Darrell Grant what the fuck he was doing.

'Business,' he said.

'You steal these?' Merkin asked.

'Of course not.' Darrell Grant was twitchy and freckled with sweat.

Picatta said, 'What's the substance of the day, tiger?'

'Folger's,' Darrell Grant said, rolling an Everest-and-Jennings up the ramp. 'You wanna move please so I can finish here? Please?' He was worrying about something Erin had said – about what might happen to Angie if he got popped again.

Picatta and Merkin were exchanging cop-style glances, which increased Darrell Grant's nervousness. He ran a long bungie cord through the spokes of the stolen wheelchairs, and hooked it to a ring on the wall of the U-Haul; that way, they wouldn't roll all over creation every time he took a corner.

Picatta said, 'What about your van?'

'What about it?'

'Why rent the truck, is what I mean.'

'Van's too small,' Darrell Grant said. 'That should be obvious.'

'Yeah,' said Merkin. 'This broken wheelchair business is going gangbusters. Pretty soon you'll be franchising.'

Picatta laughed. Darrell Grant locked up the U-Haul and sat down on the bumper.

'Ain't like stealin' cars,' Picatta said. 'Cars got a VIN number you can check.'

'And registration,' said his partner.

'And a license tag, too,' Picatta said. 'That's the beauty of wheelchairs. They're pretty much untraceable.'

Darrell Grant took out the dagger and began cleaning his fingernails, wiping the blade on his jeans. The cops couldn't believe the balls on this guy.

'You think I stole these?' Darrell said. 'Let me put it another way: Do you want the honest-to-God truth? If I did steal these goddamn chairs, would you guys really want to know?'

'No,' Merkin said. 'We wouldn't.'

'Then stop these bullshit head games, OK?'

Picatta said, 'Funny, we were about to make the same request of you.'

Darrell Grant looked up, feigning innocence.

'You gave us a grand total of three tips this month.' Picatta paused. 'Three red-hot leads. You ready for the box score, tiger? No hits, no runs, nobody left on base.'

Darrell tapped the knife on his kneecap. 'You know how it goes,' he said. 'Win some, lose some.'

'You,' Merkin said, 'are a fucking fountain of wisdom.'

The detectives ran through a list of Darrell's bum tips: An alleged coke peddler turned out to be dealing uncut grams of Tide laundry detergent. An alleged big-time bank robber turned out to be a teenager who vandalized (but seldom penetrated) suburban ATM machines. And a ring of allegedly sophisticated foreign-car thieves turned out to be a trio of hapless hubcap boosters.

'Bad luck streak,' said Darrell Grant, pondering his sneakers.

Picatta crouched down to eye level. 'Look at me, handsome, I'm speaking to you.'

'I got lousy information, that's all.'

'We stuck our necks out for you, tiger.'

'And I appreciate it—'

'Not once, but twice we stuck our necks out. Where's your little girl?'

Darrell Grant went rigid. The knife fell out of his hand. 'None a your goddamn business,' he said.

Merkin grabbed him roughly by the forelock. 'Blondie, lemme 'splain de facts o' life. Everything you do is our business: What you drive, what you eat, where you sleep, what you steal or don't steal. Whether you wipe your ass with your left hand or your right hand. It's all our business.'

'She's in the day care,' Darrell Grant said. 'She's fine.' He knocked Merkin's hand away and smoothed his hair. When he bent down to pick up the knife. Picatta kicked it away.

'We could always call that judge.'

'Fuck the both of you,' said Darrell Grant.

'Then give us some cases,' Merkin said. '*Good* cases.'

'Which means,' Picatta said, 'you need to be out on

the street, with those pretty blue eyes wide open. Lay off the wheelchairs, tiger.'

'And the dope,' Merkin added. 'Think of it like this: What if that judge suddenly hauls you in to drop urine? You want to keep custody of that little girl, you better clean up.'

'Speed freaks make lousy parents,' Picatta said. 'That's a well-known fact.'

Darrell Grant stood up. 'Thank you, Dr Spock.' Sullenly he picked up the dagger and climbed into the cab of the U-Haul. 'I'll be in touch,' he said.

As the truck pulled away, Merkin frowned. 'You hate to see that – so much bitterness in such a young man.'

'What'd you expect from a career asshole.'

'Yeah,' Merkin said, 'but he's *our* asshole.'

Shad was short-tempered and withdrawn. Undoubtedly it was the job – the drunks, the unpredictable girls, Orly, the whole damn shooting match. Now Kevin, the disc jockey, was on a Hammer spree: twenty solid minutes of the most annoying music Shad had ever heard. Finally he couldn't stand it. He vaulted into the booth, knocked Kevin aside and tore the compact disc from the CD player. The Eager Beaver was plunged into silence – the dancers stopped moving, mid-thrust. Customers murmured worriedly. A Peruvian tourist, anticipating a raid, bolted for the door; from his abandoned tabletop came a curse of self-pity from Monique Jr. The fleeing Peruvian had been trimming her garter with twenty-dollar bills.

Shad chewed up the Hammer CD like a big shiny wafer, never feeling the sharp pieces cut his tongue and gums. He spit the whole bloody mess on Kevin's mike stand, and commanded him to play Bob Seger or die. Watching from the rear of the club, Orly silently retreated to his imitation red velvet sanctuary.

Erin waited about an hour for Shad to settle down. When she approached him he was sitting alone in the corner booth, reading a large-print edition of Kafka's 'The Metamorphosis'.

'Good book?' she asked.

Shad looked up. 'I'm startin' to feel sorry for cockroaches.'

'I've been meaning to ask,' Erin said. 'How's the lawsuit?'

Shad shook his head glumly. 'On to other projects, babe.'

'Like what?'

How Shad had fretted over this moment: Should he include Erin in Mordecai's scheme? She was Shad's friend, or the closest he had to one. Wouldn't she be surprised to learn that the drunken lunatic with the champagne bottle was a congressman! It was almost worth telling her, just to see that beautiful smile.

On the other hand, a potentially mountainous sum of money was at stake. The more participants in Mordecai's shakedown enterprise, the smaller everyone's cut. There were times, Shad reasoned, when financial exigencies overshadowed friendship.

'I'm sworn to secrecy,' he said. 'Nothing personal.'

'Is there a yogurt angle?'

He laughed, loosening up. 'No yogurt, no fucking insects.'

Erin inquired about the scalp wound. Shad lowered his head to show her how Darrell Grant's dagger mark was healing. 'The scar's fading,' he said. 'I'm a little disappointed.'

For the fiftieth time, Erin apologized for what happened.

'Forget it,' Shad said. 'I imagine we'll meet again, me and your ex.'

'Not if I can help it,' said Erin. She had a fleeting image of Darrell Grant being loaded into an ambulance.

The new dancer, Marvela, came out on the main stage. With both hands she seized one of the gold poles, straightened her long legs and leaned back at a languorous slant. She began tossing her head like a mop, around and around in time to the music. The men in the front row crowed enthusiastically.

'What do you think?' Erin asked Shad. 'Is it the boobs or the hair?'

'Hair, definitely.'

'Supposedly she cleared four hundred the other night.'

'Oh yeah?' Shad made a mental note to speak with this upstart Marvela; she'd only tipped him out five bucks. 'You're still the best,' he told Erin.

'I don't know. She can really dance.'

'Not like you.' He went back to his Kafka.

Erin knew she should've been up dancing, making a few bucks, but it felt good to take a break. She was comfortable sitting in the dark booth with Shad.

'I've got a small problem,' she told him.

'What'sa matter?' He glanced up from the book.

'I need you to talk to somebody.'

'Who?'

'He's all right. I think he can help me.'

'I said, who?'

When Erin told him it was a cop, Shad snorted. 'You got more than a small problem.'

'Well, yes. It's a homicide detective.'

'Christ Almighty.'

'It's not as bad as it sounds.' But when Erin related what had happened to Mr Peepers, it sounded bad indeed. Shad didn't understand why anyone would bother to kill the little guy, and he didn't honestly care. He was more worried about Erin.

'Aren't you due for a vacation?' he said. 'I recommend Mars.'

'The detective wants to know about that night a few weeks ago, when the guy pulled a gun on you.'

'I don't remember. Sorry.'

'Come on,' Erin said, pinching his arm. 'It'll help with Angela. Everything's connected.'

'How?' Shad asked. 'Your daughter's involved – how'd you manage that?' He couldn't believe Erin had dug herself into such a mess.

'Shhh,' she said.

Monique Jr approached the booth and said Mr Orly wanted to speak with Shad. She said Kevin was demanding an apology. Shad said he'd be glad to apologize as soon as Kevin displayed a trace of good taste in music. Monique Jr cheerlessly agreed to take that message back to Mr Orly.

After she was gone, Shad turned to Erin and said the floor manager's job was getting to him. 'I definitely need a new career.'

'Me, too,' Erin said. 'A job where I could wear underpants again.'

Shad put his hands on his head and squeezed lightly, as if testing a cantaloupe for ripeness. He squinted hard, then blinked repeatedly. 'I ain't noticing ordinary things anymore, that's what's got me worried. For instance, it just now hit me that your boobs are hangin' out.'

Erin covered up. 'Jeez, I'm sorry. I was in the middle of a set—'

'Point is, I should've picked up on that. Don't you agree?'

'But you see so much of it—'

'Exactly! Too much of it. I need to get out.' Shad pointed at the book on the cocktail table. 'The guy in this story, he turns into a motherfucking centipede. Wakes up one morning and bingo, he's a bug. Sounds asinine but it sure makes you think. People change overnight, they're not careful.'

Erin said, 'Maybe *you* need the vacation.'

'Yeah, maybe so.' Shad drummed his fists softly on the table. 'OK, I'll talk to your damn detective. But as I mentioned, my memory ain't so hot.'

Erin leaned over and kissed his vast forehead.

Shad said, 'Hey, that's a new G-string.'

'Sure is.'

'Very snazzy.'

'Look here. Velcro instead of snaps.' Erin demonstrated how it worked.

'I'll be damned.' Shad studied the plastic patch thoughtfully. 'Whoever dreamed that up, he probably made a bundle.'

'*She* probably made a bundle.'

Shad shrugged. 'One thing's for sure, we're in the wrong end a this business.'

'Amen,' said Erin.

*

When David Dilbeck heard the latest fund-raising figures, he told Erb Crandall to summon the limousine. It was time to celebrate! Crandall said absolutely not, tonight we stay home.

'Erb,' said the congressman, 'look at the day I had. *Three* goddamn anti-Castro rallies. Fidel is a tyrant. Fidel is a bum. Fidel is a monster—'

'Every politician's got to sing that tune.'

'It's tiresome, Erb. A man needs to unwind.'

'Out of the question, Davey.'

'I've bought a new wig—'

'Forget it.'

'We'll sit way in the back, Erb. No friction dancing, on God's word. Call the Lings and get us a table.'

Crandall offered an alternate plan. The congressman looked intrigued.

'Where's Pamela?' Crandall inquired.

'In Virginia. One of the Kennedys is having a benefit for some disease. I'm not sure which one.'

'Which Kennedy?'

'No, which disease,' Dilbeck said. 'Some kind of anemia.'

'But Pamela definitely won't be home tonight?'

'Not until Sunday.'

'So it's safe to have visitors.'

The congressman beamed. 'The more, the merrier.'

At half-past nine, the dancers from the Flesh Farm arrived. They brought their own music. Erb Crandall directed the two women toward a teak coffee table in the den. Dilbeck appeared in a loose white robe and sat cross-legged on the floor. He asked Crandall to fetch a bottle of Korbel from the refrigerator. The dancers expressed concern about damaging the fine wood, so

Dilbeck encouraged them to remove their high heels and go barefoot. Erb Crandall returned with the champagne. He poured three glasses, iced the bottle and left the room. He pulled a chair into the hallway, and positioned himself near the doorway of the den. The music throbbed through the walls, unbearably monotonous. After about an hour, Erb Crandall went to Pamela Dilbeck's medicine cabinet in search of migraine relief. He lucked into a bottle of Darvons, and swallowed two with a glass of bitter orange juice from the kitchen.

When he got back to his post, the dance music seemed louder than ever. Crandall noticed that the door of the den was ajar. Before he could peek inside, one of the dancers emerged from a bathroom across the hall. In one hand she carried a curly black wig, in the other a damp towel. She seemed in a hurry.

'Everything OK?' Crandall asked.

'Peachy,' the dancer said. 'I hope you know CPR.'

In the den, there was no sign of the second dancer. The congressman lay unconscious next to the teak coffee table. His robe was open, exposing pink belly lard and silk paisley boxer shorts. Erb Crandall knelt down and placed a hand on David Dilbeck's chest, which rose and fell rapidly.

'Heart attack,' Crandall speculated.

'Wrong,' said the wigless dancer. She told Crandall what had happened.

He said, 'Jesus Christ. Where'd she hit him?'

'Between the eyes.'

'With what?'

'Right cross.'

'Her fist?' Erb Crandall found this amazing. He

carefully examined Dilbeck's pallid face. A nasty blue knot was rising between the congressman's eyebrows. In the center of the bruise was a microscopic indentation, perfectly rectangular.

'She's wearing a ring,' Crandall observed.

'Aquamarine,' the wigless dancer said. 'Her birth-stone.'

Erb Crandall placed a pillow under Dilbeck's head, and fashioned the damp towel around his neck. The dancer offered to call 911, but Crandall said no.

'Where's your partner?' he asked.

'Out in the car. She's scared shitless.'

Dilbeck stirred slightly, emitting a gerbil-like squeak. Crandall put his lips near the congressman's ear, and said: 'Davey, wake up!' Dilbeck grew quiet again. Crandall went to the desk and found the number of Dilbeck's private physician. He dialed rigidly, leaving an emergency message with the service.

The wigless dancer said, 'Better get him to a hospital.'

'Sure,' Erb Crandall said, caustically. Show up at Mt Sinai and tomorrow it's all over the papers.

CONGRESSMAN INJURED BY MYSTERY BLOW TO HEAD
Aides Mum Over Late-Night Incident –
Dilbeck Re-election Campaign on Hold.

Crandall gazed at the coldcocked candidate with alternating fury and panic. Whether Dilbeck lived or died, Malcolm Moldowsky would be enraged – and the blame would again fall on Crandall. It wasn't fair. Short of house arrest, it seemed impossible to control Dilbeck's carnal appetites.

'He looks bad,' said the dancer, now dressed in street clothes. 'What if he croaks?'

'Then the country loses another great leader. How much do we owe you?'

'Mr Ling said five each.'

Erb Crandall got two thousand cash from an envelope locked in the usual place, the bottom-right drawer of Dilbeck's desk. Crandall gave the money to the wigless dancer and said: 'You weren't here tonight, you never saw me, you never saw him. Same goes for the other girl, OK? You don't know this man.'

'But I *don't* know this man. I really don't.'

'God bless you,' Erb Crandall said.

'He shouldn't have done what he did. No matter who he is.'

'For that, we're truly sorry. If you count the money, I think you'll see how sorry we are.'

Something moved on the floor: the congressman's right leg, kicking out at unseen demon dogs.

The wigless dancer put the money away, strapped the purse over her shoulder. She said, 'There's no call for what he did. Everything was going fine, a nice little party. I don't know what got into him.'

'Beats me,' Crandall said. Where was the doctor?

'Maybe he should lay off the champagne.'

'Yeah, that's it. The champagne.'

The dancer stepped closer for a final look at the bruise between Dilbeck's eyebrows. 'Damn,' she said. 'That's a big stone she's wearing.'

'Goodbye,' said Erb Crandall.

'Can we take the limo back to Lauderdale?'

'Sure,' he said. 'Take the limo. Have a ball.'

FOURTEEN

Paul Guber wasn't gushing enthusiasm about Mordecai's plan. 'I want no part of it,' he said.

The lawyer clucked disapprovingly. 'This is a rare opportunity.'

'I heard you before. The answer is no.'

Joyce, sitting with her fiancé, prodded forcefully. 'It's our future we're talking about, Paul. We'll be set for life.'

From the young man's bleak expression, it was plain he didn't wish to be set for a life with Joyce. Mordecai sensed his gossamer skein unraveling and acted swiftly to save it.

'Come,' he said to the troubled couple. 'Let's go for a ride.'

An hour later, they were in a northbound Lincoln on a two-lane truck route known as Bloody 27. Mordecai maintained a steady monologue to mask his nervousness on the highway. Joyce had forgotten what a terrible driver her cousin was; poor vision, sluggish reflexes, and limited range of motion behind the wheel due to excessive girth. Paul Guber was a basket case by the time they reached Clewiston. Mordecai parked the car with a jolt and extricated himself from the front seat.

'Where are we?' Paul asked.

'Sugar mill,' said the lawyer. 'Ever seen one?'

The mill was a sprawling collection of irregular barns, smokestacks and warehouses. Harvest season was weeks away, so the millworks were quiet except for the clatter of pneumatic wrenches; groups of shirtless mechanics worked on tractors, flatbeds and migrant buses. A flaking blue-and-white sign, planted by the road, said ROJO FARMS. In smaller letters:

Division of Sweetheart Sugar Corp.

'Well,' Mordecai said. 'Shall we request a tour?'

'We shall not,' Paul said. Joyce concurred, fearing that offensive agricultural aromas might taint the fabric of her imported blouse.

The lawyer sagged heavily against the fender of the car. 'Fine,' he said. 'As you wish.'

Joyce crossed her arms impatiently. 'It's sticky out here. Can you get to the point?'

Mordecai sighed like a tortoise. 'The purpose of this field trip was to illustrate the financial dimensions of your case. The Rojo family' – nodding toward the sign – 'is worth approximately $400 million.'

'Hmmmm,' Joyce said.

'Conservatively.'

'We aren't suing the Rojos,' Paul Guber noted.

'True,' the lawyer said, 'but we're suing their favorite congressman, the fellow who makes all this wealth possible. Are you beginning to understand? Sugar money.'

'Look, I got clobbered in a strip joint. That's all.'

'The short view,' Mordecai scolded.

'I'm damn lucky my boss hasn't found out. If this thing goes to court, I'm out of a job.'

'Paul, you won't need a job,' the lawyer said. 'You'll need a Brink's truck. Tell him, Joyce.'

The sting of the bachelor-party photos had apparently abated, for Joyce wholeheartedly supported her cousin's scheme. 'Mordecai swears it'll never get to trial. Remember, darling, this is an election year.'

'Which means,' the lawyer cut in, 'the settlement will be timely, substantial and extremely secret. The congressman, too, has much to lose.'

'Paul Guber replied with a skeptical grunt.

'We're talking two, three million dollars,' Mordecai said. 'That's a handsome nest egg for two young newlyweds.' He chose not to mention Shad's role in the enterprise, or his percentage.

Paul kicked idly at pebbles while a big jet passed overhead, drowning the conversation. When it was quiet again, he turned to Joyce and Mordecai. 'The answer is still no,' he said.

'Sleep on it,' the lawyer advised. He winked instructively at Joyce. 'You two should discuss it alone.'

Paul said he didn't need to sleep on it, didn't need to discuss it: he flatly refused to sue anybody. 'What happened just happened. There's no permanent damage – heck, my insurance covered the hospital bills.' He broke into a series of jumping jacks, causing Joyce to gasp in concern.

'See?' said Paul breathless. 'I'll be back at the brokerage house next week.'

In exasperation, Mordecai slapped a fleshy hand on the hood of the Lincoln. 'There's a legal term for your condition,' he told Paul. 'It's called "diminished capacity". Which means the injury to your head is affecting your judgment.'

Joyce nodded. 'He hasn't been sleeping well.'

Paul Guber stopped jumping and let his arms fall slack. 'You two are incredible,' he said, panting. Joyce's glare failed to intimidate him. 'It must run in the family,' he said, 'this conniving.'

'Is that what you call it?' Joyce's voice was taut.

Mordecai moved between them. 'Come now. Let's have a nice peaceful ride home.'

Joyce insisted on driving. Mordecai wedged into the Lincoln beside her. Paul Guber rode in the backseat alone; he fell asleep before they got to the I-595 interchange. His snores brought a mirthless chuckle from Mordecai.

'Young Paul is being foolish,' he said.

'Tell me about it.'

'This is such an opportunity,' the lawyer said. 'Such a rare, rare opportunity.'

Joyce glanced back at her snoozing husband-to-be. It was not a look of pure, unconditional love.

She said, 'I was thinking . . .'

'Go on.'

'Do we need him? I mean, when all is said and done . . .' She pretended to concentrate on the highway. 'Supposing they agree to a settlement right off the bat – then you wouldn't even need to file court papers, is that right?'

'Correct. A few phone calls, a few meetings, a cashier's check made out to a trust account – that's the simplest way, for all concerned.'

Joyce lowered her voice. 'So . . . do we really need him?'

The lawyer fingered the multiple clefts of his chin and pondered the innocent snores of his client. 'That's a good question,' he told his cousin. 'A very good question.'

When Erin arrived at the Eager Beaver, she saw a crew of workmen on the roof, dismantling the fluorescent sign. Orly and Shad stood in the parking lot, deep in discussion. As Erin got out of the car, Orly waved for her to join them.

'Well, you get your wish,' he said.

'You're changing the name?'

'Got to,' Shad said. He seemed to be enjoying himself.

Orly told Erin not to get a swelled head. The decision had nothing to do with the dancers' complaints; it was strictly a legal matter.

'Don't tell me,' said Erin. 'There's another strip joint with the same awful name.'

'Not a strip joint,' Orly said, 'a chainsaw.'

Shad bit his lower lip, trying not to laugh. Erin was on the verge of exploding. With a straight face, she said, 'Mr Orly, I've never heard of Eager Beaver Chainsaws.'

He sneered. 'Me, neither. Apparently they're very big in New England, like I give a shit.'

Shad said, 'They sent a registered letter. Threatened to sue.'

'You believe that?' Orly threw his hands in the air. 'They said I'm hurting their corporate image, on account of using the name to promote sex and nudity. Fucking asshole lawyers!'

A liquor truck pulled in, and Shad excused himself to check the shipment. Up on the roof, the last plastic vestige of BEAVER fell to a workman's wrench. Orly winced at the sight, as he still had three remaining payments on the lettering.

'How,' he mused, 'can you slander a fucking garden tool?'

Erin said she was impressed that the Eager Beaver Chainsaw Company had heard about Orly's club, so far away. Orly said it was reported by a vacationing chainsaw salesman. 'Supposedly he just drove by and noticed the name.'

'Oh sure,' Erin said. 'He just drove by.'

'Anyway, my asshole lawyers talked to their asshole lawyers and the upshot is, it's easier to switch the goddamn sign than go to court.'

Erin couldn't resist a Mafia dig. 'I never imagined the mob would be scared off by a lawsuit.'

'Scared's got nothing to do with it,' Orly grumped. She'd nailed him good this time. 'Little Nicky, guys like him, they don't like publicity. Case like this could wind up on the front page.'

'I hadn't thought of that.'

'So their attitude is screw it, just change the name.'

'The end of an era,' Erin said, with mock wistfulness.

'You know me. I'd love to fight the bastards!'

'But they could drag it out for years,' she said. 'It's best to be practical.'

Orly rubbed his nose fiercely, as if trying to dislodge a bumblebee. 'Anyone tells you it's a free country, they're full a shit. That's all I can say.' He trudged toward the entrance of the lounge. Erin stayed at his side. She asked him if he'd given any thought to a new name.

'Yeah, as a matter of fact. And I don't want to hear boo about it, OK?'

'Let's have it,' said Erin.

Orly shuffled into the club. Erin wasn't offended that he didn't hold the door. The man was a pig. He couldn't help it. In the office, he went directly to the refrigerator and got a cold Dr Pepper. The thought of offering one to Erin never crossed his mind.

'Tell me the new name,' she said.

'You'll be a big girl? No whining?'

'No whining.'

'All right,' Orly said, slurping his soda. ' "Tickled Pink." How about that?'

'You're joking.'

'I think it's fine.' Orly smacked his lips. 'Feminine. Funny. I like it.'

'It's dreadful,' Erin said. She got up to leave.

'Now don't go making trouble out there—'

'Tickled Pink?'

'Hey, this ain't the Christian Science Reading Room, it's a tittie bar. I got a product to sell.'

Erin said, 'You're the boss.'

'Sometimes I think you forget what you do for a living, which is take off your clothes for money. Or maybe it's just you prefer to forget.' Orly rocked back and forth behind the desk. 'It's only a name, honey. Doesn't change the merchandise.'

Erin didn't back down. She wanted to keep Orly on the defensive.

He said: 'Both Moniques love "Tickled Pink". They said it sounds like the name of a French boutique.'

'No,' said Erin, 'it sounds like a gynecologist's yacht.'

Orly slammed the soda can on his desk. 'That's all in your head!' he snapped. 'I can't help it you got a filthy mind.'

As Erin walked down the hall, she heard Orly shouting: 'Hell, it's classier than "Flesh Farm"! It's classier than those fucking Lings!'

Sgt Al García spent the morning at a rockpit on the outskirts of Hialeah. He was searching for Francisco Goyo's head. Goyo was a gun dealer who'd been kidnapped on Key Biscayne, murdered in Carol City and dismembered in Homestead. Body parts were turning up from one end of Dade County to the other. Al García had put hundreds of bitter miles on the Caprice, collecting Francisco Goyo's hands, feet, torso and limbs. García hated dismemberments because the paperwork multiplied in direct proportion to the number of body parts; it took hours to write up a simple severed thumb. Naturally, the Goyo case had spawned an office pool. To win, one had to match a particular component of Francisco Goyo with the date of discovery. When an anonymous caller reported a possible floating head in Hialeah, a detective named Jimbo Fletcher let out a jubilant roar – if the head was that of the murdered gun dealer, Fletcher stood to make sixty-five bucks. As much as García disliked Fletcher, he found himself hoping that the floating head did belong to the late Señor Goyo. García wanted the case to be over. He had a suspect and a motive; what he needed was a semi-assembled corpse.

While the police divers probed the milky depths of the rockpit, García walked the shoreline. It was so windy that he couldn't light a cigar. Sand from the mountainous limerock dredgings whipped across the wide water, stinging the detective's eyes. Trudging

through the chalky dirt, García turned his thoughts
to Jerry Killian, and the nearly impossible obstacles to
solving that murder. Jurisdiction was a tangle, and it
depended on where Killian had died. If he was killed at
his apartment, the case belonged to the Fort Lauderdale
police. If he was murdered near the river in Montana,
the investigation fell to authorities in Mineral County.
And if Killian was abducted from Florida to Montana
against his will, the FBI should get a piece of the action.

García himself had no jurisdiction whatsoever, no
legitimate excuse for pursuing the case except one:
nobody else seemed interested. The detective was
nagged by an old-fashioned belief that no one should
get away with murder so easily. He also wanted to
punish the creeps who ruined his family's vacation. The
possible involvement of a bigshot politician added
urgency to the quest. In fact, García had become so
fascinated with the Killian case that he was tempted to
take extended sick leave from his Dade County homicide duties. He resented every minute wasted on
mundane murder chores, such as bagging fragments of
Francisco Goyo. Here was a common shitbird felon
with a five-page rap sheet. The world was enriched by
his sudden passing. Why, García wondered, am I out
here hunting for the man's head? The cosmic purpose
eluded him.

At noon, one of the police divers surfaced with
a splash. As he paddled to shore, he held an object
high out of the water. The object was the shape of a
large coconut. Assuming the worst, García retrieved
the voluminous Goyo paperwork from the trunk of
the Caprice. Returning to the shore, he found the divers

gathered around the severed head of a large brindle hog. The hog was wearing a baseball cap: Atlanta Braves.

'Fletcher'll be pissed,' García said.

The divers debated the significance of the find. Animal sacrifice was common among worshipers of Santería, a black magic popular in parts of South Florida. Chickens, goats, turtles and other creatures were slaughtered to appease specific gods; depending on the ceremony, it wasn't unusual to find these grisly offerings in public places. The baseball cap was a riddle, though; none of the cops knew what to make of it. Was the hog beheaded as a curse on the Atlanta Braves, or as a tribute? For guidance the divers turned to Al García. As the senior Cuban, he was presumed most knowledgeable in matters of the occult.

'It's not a religious sacrifice,' García said, winging it. 'It's a family pet.'

'No way,' scoffed the diver who'd found the head.

'Didn't you ever watch "Green Acres"? They had a helluva pig.'

The diver said, 'Come off it, Al. What kind of people kill their own pet?'

'Hey, *chico*, we're in a recession. All bets are off.' On that somber note, García departed the rockpit. Instead of driving back to the station, he took the turnpike north toward Broward County. On the way, he stopped at a toll plaza, phoned Donna and told her he'd probably be late for dinner.

'What's up?' she asked.

'The usual,' García said. 'Murder. Topless babes. Nude oil wrestling.'

'You poor thing.'

'See you around nine.'

'Good,' Donna said. 'I expect to be regaled.'

Shad was everything that García had expected, and more. The man's musculature was enormous, but typical for his line of work. The detective was more impressed by the cumulative balefulness of Shad's presence – gleaming smooth pate, ferocious overbite, engorged but expressionless eyes. The man's age was impossible to guess. He was not a freak so much as a living dinosaur, slow-blinking and fearless. When he spoke, the voice was low but the tone was hard. When he smiled, which was seldom, he showed no teeth.

Still, Erin Grant seemed to trust him. From this García concluded that, for all his brutishness, Shad was a gentleman toward the dancers. It was a hopeful sign.

They'd found a relatively clean booth near a dance cage. Erin asked Kevin to drop the volume a couple notches so that García wouldn't have to holler over the music. The detective spread several black-and-white photographs on the table. Without prompting, Erin immediately identified the drunk with the champagne bottle.

Except he had a mustache,' she said, pointing.

García looked positively delighted. 'Know who that is? That's our famous Congressman Dilbeck!'

Staring at the picture, Erin thought: Perfect. This is just my luck. 'But he was a maniac,' she said. 'A drunken nut case.'

The detective nodded enthusiastically. 'Is it making sense yet? Your little pal Jerry witnesses the assault, recognizes Dilbeck on stage and immediately grasps the wonderful possibilities. Yet of all the blackmail options available, he chooses the most unselfish of all: arranging for you to get your child back. Or so he thought.'

Erin couldn't take her eyes off Dilbeck's photograph – the starched smile, the smug eyes. He had not looked so dignified while bashing Paul Guber's skull. 'Sonofabitch,' she said.

Al García awaited Shad's confirmation of the lecherous drunk's identity. None came. 'Ring a bell?' he asked.

'Nope,' Shad replied. He would need to consult with Mordecai as soon as possible. Police involvement could screw up the lawyer's plan, and seriously interfere with Shad's retirement.

García selected a picture of Erb Crandall. 'How about him?'

Shad's brow crinkled. 'I'm not sure.'

'I am,' Erin said. 'That's the one who had the gun.'

'Very possible,' García said. 'Mr Crandall is licensed to carry a concealed weapon. Him and seventy-five thousand other upstanding Floridians.'

Shad asked if Crandall was a professional bodyguard. García said his official title was Executive Assistant to Representative Dilbeck. 'Meaning babysitter,' the detective added, tapping a finger on Crandall's unsmiling face. 'Bagman, too, according to the rumors. But that's of little interest to us.'

García quizzed Erin about the other photographs – assorted aides and cronies of David Dilbeck – but none looked familiar.

'So here's our scenario,' García said, steepling his hands. 'Ms Grant has positively identified Congressman Dilbeck and Mr Crandall as being in the Eager Beaver on the night of September sixth. She's also identified the congressman as the man who jumped on stage and assaulted another customer. The attack ended when Mr Crandall displayed a handgun and escorted Mr Dilbeck out of the club. Is that correct?'

'Right,' Erin said. She shot a suspicious glance at Shad, who shifted uneasily. It bothered him to hold out on Erin. If she and the cop only knew about Mordecai's incriminating photo!

García said, 'It's all right, Mr Shad. If you don't remember, you don't remember. Think on it is all I'm asking.'

'I see assholes every night. They start to look the same.'

'Christ, I know exactly what you mean. Erin, can I have a Diet Coke?'

'She ain't a waitress,' Shad said.

'I'm sorry, you're right. I'll get it myself—'

García started to rise, but Erin motioned him down. 'I've got to dress, anyway. I'll bring three on my way back.'

As Erin headed for the dressing room, Shad began sliding out of the booth. Al García grabbed his elbow and told him to sit tight. He wasn't sure if Shad was stunned or amused by the command.

The detective leaned close. 'Listen, Mr Floor Manager, I don't know your angle, why your memory suddenly is so shitty. That's your business and you sure don't owe me a goddamn thing. But I know you care about that pretty lady, am I right?'

Shad's huge neck throbbed, all veins.

'Here's the deal,' García said. 'She got herself tangled in a blackmail. Not her fault – just some love-crazed customer trying to play hero, trying to get the lady's daughter back from her ex. You're familiar with Mr Darrell Grant, no?'

Shad nodded, barely.

'Ha! Your recall's improving every second.' García let out a grand laugh. 'Anyway, the idea was to put the arm on the congressman, make him pull a string with the divorce judge. The lady gets her little girl, the customer gets to be Sir Galahad. Except somebody whacks him first, which is why I'm sittin' here.'

'You're saying Erin's in trouble.'

'Could be,' the detective said. 'It's an election year, which is no time for a sex scandal. They might figure, hell, who's gonna miss a dead stripper?'

'She ain't a stripper. She dances.'

'Point is, you don't want her to die. Me neither. She's a nice person, works hard, loves her kid, et cetera. So if anything important shakes loose inside that incredible bulbous noggin of yours, gimme a ring.' García stacked the photographs and slipped them into his coat. He said, 'In case you didn't notice, I need all the fuckin' help I can get.'

Shad's expression was stone, but his gut was churning. A keen judge of cops, he knew this one was no bullshitter. Erin might be in real danger, and over what – politics? The woman was a dancer, for God's sake. All she wanted out of life was her daughter.

Insanity is what it was. A world gone mad. Shad felt a strange fever in his breast.

García stood up and laid a five-dollar bill on the table. 'Have my soda,' he said. 'You look thirsty.'

FIFTEEN

Congressman Dilbeck was revived by the sharp tang of
Malcolm Moldowsky's cologne. He sat up coughing in
spasms. At the foot of the bed stood Moldy and Erb
Crandall, appearing dour and unsympathetic.

Moldowsky's greeting confirmed the mood. 'Good
morning, shit-for-brains.'

'Hello, Malcolm.'

'Erb told me about your evening.'

'I'm sorry, Malcolm. I got swept away.'

'Know what we need to do? We need to teach you to
masturbate creatively. Then maybe you wouldn't bother
women.'

Crandall said, 'Those blow-up dolls might do the
trick. We'll order him an assortment, all shapes and
colors.'

Dilbeck felt dizzy. Slowly he lowered his pounding
head to the pillows. He was relieved to see that he
was in his own bedroom, not a hospital. From this he
concluded, perhaps prematurely, that his injury wasn't
so serious. Touching the bruise, he moaned melodramatically; the knot was huge.

He said, 'Don't I need a doctor?'

'Been here and gone,' Crandall reported. 'You're a
very lucky man – no concussion, no brain damage.'

'As if we could tell,' Moldy said.

The congressman pleaded for them to lay off, his head was killing him.

'But you've got a fund-raiser tonight, David.'

'No way, Malcolm. Look at me. *Look at me!*'

Moldowsky moved to Dilbeck's side and hovered gravely, like a dentist. 'Under no circumstances will you miss this function, understand? The marquee is Bradley, Kerry and Moynihan, who don't wish to be stood up. More important, we've got six potential sugar votes coming down from the Hill.'

'Those fellows, they're still pissed about the pay raise—'

'Extremely pissed,' said Moldowsky. 'That's why we're flying them first class. That's why we've got Dom and fresh citrus waiting in their suites. It's suck-up time, Davey. Everyone's counting on you to make things right again.'

'What's that supposed to mean?'

'It means the senior Rojos called, among others.'

Overwhelmed by Moldowsky's musk, Dilbeck began to sneeze violently. Moldy backpedaled, shielding his mouth and nose from flying germs. When the congressman regained normal respiration, he announced that he wouldn't be seen in public looking as pitiable as he did.

Erb Crandall said, 'It's not the public, David, it's thousand-dollar-a-plate suckers. Tell them whatever you want. Tell them you got hit with a fucking golf ball.'

'We're locking out the media,' Moldy added. 'Feel free to lie your ass off.'

David Dilbeck grimaced as he fingered the bruise.

'What about X-rays?' he asked. 'How can they be sure about concussions if they didn't take X-rays?'

'The doctor checked your ears,' Crandall explained, 'for fresh blood.'

'Jesus, Mary and Joseph!'

Dilbeck's whining grated on Moldowsky's nerves. 'We'll ice your fucking head, all right? Spend the day on your back, and by tonight the swelling's gone.'

'Exactly,' Crandall said. 'You'll be as dashing as ever.'

'Stop making light of the situation.'

Moldowsky twisted the cap off a pill bottle and tapped out two orange tablets. He instructed Dilbeck to swallow them for his headache: 'Erb told me what happened. In my view, you're lucky that girl didn't stomp on your balls.'

As usual, the congressman remembered almost nothing of the incident. He asked, 'What was her name?'

'Jeanne Kirkpatrick,' said Erb Crandall. 'A very hot number.'

'Seriously, I can't recall a damn thing. Her name. What she looked like. Was she blonde or redheaded, Lord, it's all a blank.'

'Keep it that way,' Moldy said. He closed the drapes to darken the room. 'Get some rest. You've got a big night.'

'Malcolm?'

'What is it, Dave?'

'This is the last time, I swear to God. I'm cured.'

'I'd love to believe you, I dearly would.'

'On my mother's grave, Malcolm. Never again. Never! I hurt so damn bad.'

Moldowsky said goodbye and left the room. His aroma, however, lingered like an industrial smog.

Crandall packed a towel with ice cubes and placed it on the congressman's forehead.

'Erb, you believe me?' Dilbeck asked. 'It's out of my system for good.'

'Sure it is,' said Crandall. 'I'll be in the hall if you need me. Try to sleep.'

As David Dilbeck slept, psychedelic visions flashed and popped behind twitching eyelids. Eventually, jumbled starbursts gave way to soothing scenes. The congressman dreamed of a lovely dancer with rich brown hair and small round breasts and a smile that could stop an executioner's heart.

When Dilbeck awoke, the ice in the towel was melted and the pillowcase was soaked against his cheek. His breathing was hot and irregular, but his head no longer throbbed. He bolted upright, energized by the knowledge that the woman dancing in his sleep was real, that he couldn't have dreamed such a smile.

He had seen that dancer somewhere: a radiant moment, buried deep in submemory by a drunken blackout.

Yes, he'd seen her. And she most definitely smiled.

'What did she mean?' In a sing-song tone, the congressman addressed silent walls. 'Who is this lovely?' He shook off the sheets and hopped from the bed. The room rolled under his legs. He stumbled to the bathroom and flipped on the lights. Anxiously he examined both ears for signs of blood, but found nothing but clotted wax.

'Who is she?' he cried to the mirror. 'What does she want with me?'

*

After less than a week, Marvela quit the club and defected to the Flesh Farm. The enticement was a $500 signing bonus, Mondays off and a new wardrobe. Orly was livid. To all who would listen, he declared that the Ling brothers henceforth were dead men – gator bait, orchid fertilizer, breakfast sausage, D-E-A-D. Orly said he was calling Staten Island and arranging a murder contract. Nobody stole his dancers and got away with it!

The next day, he installed a wind machine among the footlights on the main stage. He said it was part of a new campaign to make the Tickled Pink a classier joint – new name, new spiffy image. Erin and the other dancers suspected that Orly was upgrading mainly to compete with the hated Lings.

The wind machine was a hooded electric fan, aimed at an angle to blow and swirl the dancers' hair. The desired effect was an untamed, sultry look. 'I got the idea from Stevie Nicks videos,' Orly told Erin. 'You go on and try.'

She danced a short set in front of the wind machine. The air hitting her face made her blink continually. She didn't feel particularly sexy.

Afterwards, Orly said, 'It's your hair.'

'Oh, here we go.'

'Just listen for once. Would it kill you to grow it down past the shoulders? Or at least get a perm?' He knew better than to suggest a dye job.

Erin said, 'Stevie's got her look, I've got mine.'

'I also bought smoke cannisters and a neon blue strobe.'

'You're really trying,' Erin said, 'and we all

appreciate it.' Now if he'd only eighty-six the damn oil wrestling.

Orly opened a box of the new cocktail napkins – pink, naturally. 'Notice anything?' he said. 'Lookie. No tits. No snatch.'

The club's previous napkins had featured drawings of saucy nudes in feathered hats and spiked heels. Erin favored the plain pink. 'These are elegant,' she said, 'relatively speaking.'

Orly was pleased. 'It occurred to me, why overdo it with the tits and so forth? No sense staring at poon on a napkin when the real McCoy is wiggling right in front of your nose.'

'Good thinking,' Erin said. Orly was hopeless, but at least he was making an effort. In fact, the long-haired dancers and those with lush wigs did seem to enjoy performing in front of the wind machine. Only Urbana Sprawl declined to use it, complaining that the fan aggravated her allergy to dust mites. She said there was no tactful way for a naked person to cope with a runny nose, especially while dancing. Orly grudgingly agreed.

Discussion of the new wind machine continued all evening in the dressing room. Most of the dancers considered it a worthwhile investment; it was heartening to see Orly spend on capital improvements. Preliminary feedback from customers was positive, too, judging from the tips. For club regulars, windblown hair was an exotic diversion from leaden footwork and half-hearted pelvic thrusts.

'Speaking of customers,' Erin said, 'remember Mr Peepers?'

The two Moniques said they did. Erin asked if they recalled seeing him on the night of the champagne-bottle attack. Monique Jr said yes, she was giving him a private dance at table three when the fighting broke out. She remembered it well because Jerry Killian had scurried to the main stage to see the commotion, leaving her unpaid and dancing on an empty table.

'I was pissed,' Monique Jr said, 'but he came back later and gave me a whole ten dollars.' She rolled her eyes in disdain.

'Did he say anything?' Erin asked.

'He said I had bold nipples, whatever the hell that means.'

'No, did he talk about what he saw – the fight?'

'He asked did I know the guy with the bottle, and I says no. Then he asked do I know what chivalry is, and I said sure I know what chivalry is. "Well," he goes, "you'll be glad to know it's not dead." And I said great, glad to hear it. Then he started on again about my nipples.'

Urbana Sprawl was impressed by the junior Monique's detailed recollection of a three-week-old conversation; most dancers ignored the idle babble of customers.

'I always remember the shitty tippers,' Monique Jr explained, 'just like I remember the good ones.'

Erin fluffed her hair, touched up her lipstick and headed for a three-dance set in the cage. Kevin cued up one of her favorite Allman Brothers cuts, and Erin blew him a kiss. Long songs were bad for business, but occasionally she needed one to help her disconnect from the routine, drift away with the music.

Tonight she used the time to think about murder. The facts seemed to fit Sgt Al García's scenario: Killian was in the audience when the horny congressman sailed

off the deep end. The little guy probably recognized
Dilbeck, ratty mustache and all, and hatched the idea
for a blackmail.

And days later he was killed . . .

Erin was so absorbed that she didn't spot the customer right away. He stood below the cage, staring at
her bottom, waiting for her to spin in his direction.
Finally he called Erin's name, and she danced up to the
bars. He reached up and folded some money in her
garter. It was a fifty-dollar bill. Erin smiled and crossed
her arms over her breasts, teasingly lovestruck. Later
she sat down at his table to say thanks, a strip-joint
ritual when a customer gives an exceptional tip. A
three- or four-minute visit was considered sufficient; any
longer took precious time off the dancer's clock. Chatty
friendliness inevitably gave way to salesmanship, and
experienced strippers were masters of the blend. A good
table dancer could work the same customer for a half-
dozen private numbers between performance sets. That
was how most of them made their money; Erin was the
only one who got by on stage tips alone.

This big tipper was in his mid-fifties, and dressed like
a senior loan officer. He was sipping a Jack Daniels too
carefully, and hadn't bothered to loosen his necktie.
Obviously he had plans for the evening. When Erin
thanked him for the money, he reached for her hand:
'If that's how much I'll pay just to look, imagine how
much I'll pay to touch.'

Another smoothie, Erin thought. She tried to pull
away, but the man wouldn't let go. She said, 'Obviously
this is your first time here.'

'How'd you know?'

'I'm guessing the Midwest – Chicago, Minneapolis?'

'St Paul,' the man said. 'You're pretty good, Honey Pie.'

'Honey Pie? That's the best you can do?' Erin wasn't in the mood for dumb banter. It had been many months since she'd been groped by an out-of-town creep – Sweetie Pants, he'd called her. That one was from Syracuse: the hairiest arms she'd seen outside a zoo.

'Please let go,' she said to St Paul.

'Dance for me.'

'I did.'

'Not here. I've got a room on the beach.' His grip was dry and firm. 'A room with a sauna.'

'No, thank you.'

'For two thousand dollars?'

'I'm not worth it, believe me.' Erin dug her fingernails into the soft underside of the man's wrist. He yelled angrily and let go. As she pushed back from the table, the man's leg shot out and kicked her chair. Erin went over backward.

The customer's laughter died with an epiglottal peep. Erin rose to see the man's face pinched in the crook of Shad's arm. The face was bloody and full of deep remorse. Shad was punching in his usual calm and methodical way, but in his expression Erin saw genuine rage, which was rare.

'That's enough,' she told him.

Shad let the man fall, face down. The customer rolled onto his back and blubbered something about a lawsuit.

'Really?' Shad said. 'You wanna call your wife? I'll bring the phone.' He nudged sharply with a boot. 'Well?'

Ten minutes later, the man from St Paul was strapped in his rented black Thunderbird. He adjusted the rearview mirror to check the condition of his nose and lips, which were swollen to the size of wax party gags.

Shad propped himself on the door of the car. 'Don't ever come back,' he advised.

'I meant no harm.'

'She look like a hooker?' Shad's barren orb filled the window. 'Answer me, bud. Did the lady look like a whore?'

The man from St Paul was shaking. 'I'm really sorry.'

Shad called Erin to the car and told the man to apologize again, which he did with all his heart.

Erin said, 'You should learn some respect.'

'I'm so sorry. I swear to God.'

Shad said, 'What kinda place you think this is? Does it look like a whorehouse?' The man shook his head tensely.

'This is a classy operation,' Erin chimed in. 'Surely you noticed the napkins.'

The man from St Paul drove swiftly into the Florida night. Erin put an arm around Shad's waist. 'You're in a lousy mood tonight,' she said. 'What's the matter?'

'I'm just worried about you is all.'

'Why?'

'There's bad people in the world, that's why.'

She laughed. 'But you're here to protect me.'

'Right,' Shad said. First thing tomorrow he would go see Mordecai and tell him the deal was off. The stakes had gotten too damn high.

Down the street came the wail of sirens. Soon a police cruiser raced past the Tickled Pink; then an ambulance, two more police cars, another rescue truck. Shad and Erin walked to the curb to see if there was a traffic accident. Moments later they were joined by Orly, bubbling with mirth.

'There *is* a God!' he said.

'Now what?' Erin asked.

'Just listen.'

As if on cue, the sirens began winding down, one at a time. The flashing lights had converged a half-dozen blocks away, on the opposite side of the highway.

'Must be some wreck,' Shad said.

Orly giggled. 'Ain't no wreck. It's the Flesh Farm!'

'What'd you do?' Shad asked. 'Did you pull something?'

'Wasn't me, it was Marvela. She just called, bawling her pretty eyeballs out.' Orly was jubilant. 'She wants her old job back. Haw!'

Shad said, 'Something bad happened.'

Orly grinned. 'Yeah, very bad. Guy dropped dead at the table.'

Erin thought: Poor Marvela.

'And not just any guy,' Orly said. 'A goddamn judge.'

Erin heard herself say: 'Which judge?'

'Who cares? A dead judge is a dead judge. Those fucking Lings, I hope they're pissing razor blades . . .'

Erin started down the road toward the winking blues and reds. Orly called her name but she kept walking. Traffic slowed and a few drivers honked salaciously. Erin clicked along in her tall heels, sequined G-string and black lace bra, aiming for the flashing lights, walking faster, telling herself: maybe, maybe, oh maybe Mr Orly is right.

Maybe there is a God.

*

The judge considered Marvela a sleek and delicious archangel. She was the only one at Orly's club who flirted properly. The other dancers were detached, perfunctory, even chilly; some refused to perform for him at all. The judge suspected that Erin had poisoned the others against him – they probably despised him for separating their friend from her only child. How unfair! The justification was there in the Bible, plain as day, but none of the dancers wanted to hear him explain it, no matter how heavily he tipped. Everybody had a gift, the judge would say. Everybody had a special purpose on this earth. Motherhood was one, he would say, dancing naked was another.

Being new, Marvela wasn't aware that the judge had been unofficially ostracized. She gave him some terrific table dances, and in a matter of days he was infatuated. When she quit Orly's club, the judge eagerly followed her to the Flesh Farm and the brave new world of friction dancing.

The distance between the clubs was half a mile, but the drive seemed to take for ever. The judge found a parking spot far from the streetlights to avoid being recognized by a passing motorist. Discretion was extremely important until he was confirmed for the federal bench. After that, he was free to recreate as he pleased; to his knowledge, no one had ever been impeached for patronizing a tittie bar.

As the judge turned off the ignition, his heart hammered against birdlike ribs. He felt light-headed, but attributed the feeling to raw excitement. Before entering the steamy house of Ling, he recited a silent prayer, thanking God in advance for the blessings he was about to receive. To be able to lay hands on the beautiful Marvela, to feel her rub those velvet loins against him – these would be fantasies come true!

Sadly for the judge, they did not. Anticipation killed him moments before friction was to begin. He died with his tongue on the table, the Bible balanced on his knees. One hand was fastened to his crotch like the claw of a lobster; it remained attached throughout vigorous rescue maneuvers, including cardiopulmonary massage.

Death had taken the form of a massive cerebral hemorrhage: a significant part of the judge's brain had more or less exploded when the prancing Marvela had draped her *bustier* across the crown of his head. A quick-thinking bouncer had removed the garment before paramedics showed up.

Considering the traffic, their response time was outstanding. The frantic Lings had no opportunity to move the corpse off the premises; all they could do was whimper at the mayhem. Within moments of the first policeman's appearance, the Flesh Farm emptied as if there were a toxic gas leak. The bartenders and dancers were the last to flee.

When Erin arrived, she saw an old man stretched out on the floor. He was surrounded by young medical technicians in blue jumpsuits. One of them knelt beside the lifeless form, thumping the man's chest in perfect time to Janet Jackson's 'Rhythm Nation', which was playing on the club speakers. The Lings stayed well back from the scene, yammering about bad publicity, loss of revenue and a possible visit from state beverage agents.

Erin casually walked up and positioned herself between paramedics. Lifesaving efforts were winding down, along with the music. The man on the floor was plainly deceased. Erin leaned over to examine the face; he looked like the right judge, but she wasn't certain. 'Can you take off the oxygen mask?' she asked.

One of the paramedics, smitten by Erin's attire, cheerfully obliged. He asked if she knew the victim.

'In passing,' she replied.

Marvela, who had changed into street clothes, was being interviewed by two uniformed officers and a detective. She chain-smoked furiously, tapping her ashes into a beer stein. Erin sat at the bar and waited for the cops to finish. Shad came in and joined her. He said, 'You oughta see the helicopter outside.'

'Waste of fuel,' said Erin. 'He's dead as a flounder.'

'It's not from the hospital. It's from Channel 7.'

'No kidding?' Erin laughed darkly. 'Shad, I'm enjoying this. I hate to admit it, but I am.'

'Well, the guy was a prick.'

'And such a hypocrite.'

'Maybe now you can get your girl back.'

Erin said, 'That's what I'm thinking. It's awful, I know, under the circumstances—'

'Forget it. The man was puke.' Shad reached behind the Lings' well-stocked bar and got two glasses. He unhooked the fountain gun and squirted each of them a Coke. Erin watched the paramedics place the dead judge on a stretcher, strapping him under a brown woolen blanket.

'My lawyer,' she said, 'will be amazed.'

'So will your ex.' Shad's lips cracked into a cold smile. 'I'd love to be there when you tell him.'

'I doubt if I'll get that pleasure,' Erin said.

When the police were done with Marvela, she came to the bar and sat with Erin. 'I never even touched him,' she confided, her voice raw with disbelief. The weeping began, and Erin gave her a hug. She didn't know Marvela well, but she could appreciate the trauma of seeing a customer keel over.

Shad hopped the bar and fixed a Dewar's for Marvela, who continued sobbing intermittently. She said she didn't know what happened – she'd barely gotten her top off. 'I can't believe he fucking died. *Died!* I wasn't even down on his lap—'

'That's enough,' Erin told her. 'It wasn't your fault.' She stroked Marvela's hair, which smelled like Marlboros and mousse. Marvela's tears dripped freely on Erin's bare shoulder.

'Look at it another way,' Shad said. 'The man died staring at pussy. There's worse ways to go.'

Marvela was not consoled. She drained her drink and fumbled for another cigarette. 'I should've stuck to straight modeling. Swimwear and teddies, that's it.'

Shad held out a lighter and said, 'For Christ's sake.'

'It's all my fault. He's dead because of me!'

'Hush,' Erin told her. 'You were only doing your job.'

SIXTEEN

Rita and Alberto Alonso agreed to keep Angela while Darrell Grant drove a load of stolen wheelchairs to St Augustine. Alberto was fond of the girl, but Rita preferred the company of canines; Lupa's pups were getting big and frisky. Darrell Grant told his sister to keep Angie inside the trailer, away from the damn wolves. Rita asked where was the kid's toys, and Darrell said there wasn't room in the van for no toys. Alberto said don't worry, there's plenty around here for a girl to play with. He brought out a bag of golf balls and dumped them on the floor. Angela amused herself as best she could.

Alberto slept all day while Rita spent much of the time in the yard with the animals. Angela was fascinated by her aunt's eccentric appearance – catcher's mask, cigarette, logger mitts, baggy housedress. The little girl sat for hours at the window, watching Rita work with her high-strung pets. Once, alone in the trailer, Angela picked up the phone and dialed her mother's number, which she had memorized. There was no answer, but Angela let it ring for twenty-five minutes. Rita came inside and pitched a fit. She snatched the telephone and placed it on top of the refrigerator, out of the little girl's reach.

Darrell Grant was glad to leave town, even for a short time. Free of parental responsibility, he no longer had to be discreet about gobbling speed, upon which he was increasingly reliant. The drugs gave him the nerve to steal, and the guile to lie about it. They also helped him cope with Merkin and Picatta, who hassled him relentlessly. The detectives were vicious nags, always after hot tips. Darrell didn't mind snitching on other criminals, especially since the alternative was prison, but sometimes there simply was nothing to snitch. Merkin and Picatta didn't seem to understand that many crooks were chronically lazy; weeks, even months might pass between crime sprees. Yet the detectives were always demanding fresh stats and warm bodies. If there were no serious felonies afoot, they expected Darrell Grant to hit the streets and get the ball rolling.

The trouble was, Darrell didn't have time to hang out with dirtbags. Dealing wheelchairs was a full-time gig. The St Augustine run, for instance, promised to net three grand – a nursing home was waiting, COD. Then Merkin and Picatta called, harping at him to go see some Cuban bartender in frigging Hallandale who might or might not be dealing kilos. Darrell Grant needed to think fast, and that's where the speed saved his ass. It helped him remember the name of Tommy Tinker, the heroin man. Darrell knew how much the cops in South Florida loved a scag case. Not only was it a refreshing change of pace from crackheads, it was a guaranteed commendation, usually officer-of-the-month. So Darrell pitched Tommy Tinker as the Number One Heroin Dealer east of I-95, and told

Merkin and Picatta exactly where on Sunrise Boulevard they could find him.

'Grams or ounces?' Picatta asked.

'Ounces,' Darrell Grant said quickly, 'but he don't sell to white guys. Otherwise I'd be happy to make the score.'

And off went the two detectives in search of a black snitch, while Darrell made tracks for St Augustine. He was passing the Vero Beach city limits when his brain decelerated just enough to remember that Tommy Tinker had been fatally firebombed in New Orleans back in 1987. Darrell Grant experienced a brief flush of panic, but at no time considered turning back or making a call. He popped three more beauties, and stepped on the pedal. Soon the van was racing as fast as his heart, and life seemed fine.

The congressman rallied in time for the gala fund-raiser. He was able to dress without assistance, shave with a dull blade and comb his own hair. Tan makeup camouflaged the bruise, which had shrunken to a greenish marble in the center of his brow.

Erb Crandall drove him to the hotel, and hung near his side throughout the evening. The dinner was well attended and the speeches flattering. The most effusive testimonial came from Senator Moynihan, who'd never met David Dilbeck and was therefore unencumbered by sour memories.

After dessert, Dilbeck himself rose to the podium and managed to speak for eleven minutes without repeating himself. He was careful to lavish absurd praise on colleagues whose votes were crucial to renewing the price

supports for domestic sugar. Dilbeck inwardly prayed
that his remarks would begin to thaw the ill feelings –
after all, how often did such small-timers get compared
to the Roosevelts and Kennedys! Erb Crandall said the
other congressmen seemed genuinely moved. Dilbeck
hoped so, since he'd practically gagged on the compli-
ments he'd dished out.

Later he pinballed from table to table, thanking the
paying guests for their generosity. Normally Dilbeck
adored being the center of attention, but tonight the
limelight was excruciating; the vision in his left eye
was blurry, and both ears pounded with an invisible
orchestra of steel drums. He sustained himself by silently repeating Erb's mantra: each handshake is worth
one thousand dollars.

At a far table, the congressman was greeted by a
rotund fellow with flushed cheeks and jumpy rodent
eyes. The man was dressed for a funeral. He said he
was a lawyer, and introduced a stern female companion
as his cousin. Dilbeck noticed a slight family
resemblance.

'Remember me?' said the lawyer.

'Well, you certainly look familiar,' Dilbeck lied.

'San Francisco. The Mondale Express.'

'Of course, of course.' Dilbeck didn't have the faintest recollection; he'd spent much of the convention on
a barstool at Carol Doda's topless revue. 'I saw Fritz
about three weeks ago,' Dilbeck improvised. 'He looks
absolutely fantastic.'

The lawyer invited the congressman to sit for a few
minutes, but Dilbeck said no thanks, they've got me on
a tight schedule. That's when the lawyer handed him
the photograph.

'For your album,' he said.

'Jesus, Mary and Joseph!' said the congressman.

Dilbeck cupped his bad eye and gazed at the color print of his drunken self, swinging a bottle at a stranger's head. Dilbeck had no distinct memory of the raunchy scene, except for the woman on the stage. It was the dancer in his dream – by God, she was real! The congressman experienced a tingle that was grossly inappropriate for the moment.

The lawyer said, 'We had the photo enlarged from a slide, which I'm keeping in a very safe place.' He paused, running a finger along his upper lip. 'If I may say so, sir, you look better without the mustache.'

Dilbeck smiled anemically. Erb Crandall, craning over the congressman's shoulder, was comforted not to see his own likeness in the background of the photograph. He wondered, though, if there were other pictures in sequence – pictures of him pointing the gun, for example. Jesus, what a lousy night that was.

'It's peculiar,' Dilbeck said, 'how I don't remember this.'

'But it's you, isn't it?' The lawyer gloated.

Crandall curtly demanded to see identification. Mordecai handed him a business card and said, 'I'm sure you're curious about Joyce's interest. The fellow being assaulted is her betrothed.'

Crandall put his lips to Dilbeck's ear. 'Don't say another word.'

'It's all right, Erb. I honestly don't remember.'

The lawyer went on: 'You're probably wondering about the young man's condition. Unfortunately, the news is not good. He suffered grievous injuries in this attack.'

Dilbeck slumped. 'What can I say? I'm terribly sorry.'

'Shut up,' Crandall hissed.

Joyce spoke up. 'Sorry is fine and dandy, but my Paul will never be the same.'

'Severe head trauma,' the lawyer added. 'That's a champagne bottle you've got there. Korbel, if I'm not mistaken.'

The congressman gave the photograph to Crandall and said, 'You were there, Erb. What the hell happened?'

From the corner of his eye, Crandall spotted a ragged line of well-wishers, including several prominent Rojos, moving across the ballroom toward David Lane Dilbeck. Crandall deftly concealed the dangerous photo in his tuxedo jacket, and told Mordecai to meet him upstairs in the hospitality suite.

The lawyer said, 'Good, we were hoping for some privacy.'

'Fifteen minutes,' Crandall said. Then he rushed off to find Malcolm J. Moldowsky.

Strength fading, David Dilbeck managed to finish his rounds – shaking hands, feigning recognition, chuckling at lame jokes, bowing at banal flattery . . . and thinking only of the sleek dancer whose honor he'd so nobly defended that night at the Eager Beaver. Did she think of him, too?

Joyce paced the lobby while Mordecai met Moldowsky alone, in the hospitality suite. There were no formalities. The lawyer stated his demands; Moldowsky took a few notes. The photograph, creased by Crandall's tuxedo, lay on the coffee table between them.

'Extortion,' Moldy said, thoughtfully.

'In my game, it's called negotiating a settlement. Do you suppose I'm joking about filing a civil action? The picture speaks for itself, Mr Moldowsky.'

'I disapprove of shakedowns.'

Mordecai shrugged. 'Other attorneys would've sued first, then offered to settle. Of course a lawsuit instantly puts the matter in the public eye. Considering Mr Dilbeck's position, I assumed he wished to avoid the publicity.'

'Thanks for being so damn considerate.' Moldowsky got up and fixed himself a drink. His eyes flickered toward the incriminating photo of the Honorable David Lane Dilbeck – homicidal, out-of-control, crazed by lust. It would make quite a splash on the front pages of the newspapers.

The lawyer said, 'I'll understand if you need some time. It must be quite a shock.'

'Not really,' Moldy said. 'The man's name is Paul Jonathan Guber. He spent five days at Broward General with cuts, bruises and a mild concussion. He's doing just fine now, but I guess that's beside the point. Right?'

Mordecai was stunned into a momentary silence. After a few seconds, he said, 'Am I to assume that you called the hospital out of concern for my client's health?'

Malcolm Moldowsky tapped his polished fingernails on the side of his glass. 'We look out for the congressman,' he said. Erb Crandall had been keeping tabs on young Mr Guber since the night of the assault.

'I'm impressed,' said Mordecai. 'However, your interest in my client's medical condition could be perceived as an acknowledgment of responsibility. A jury might be curious to know why Mr Dilbeck never volun- tarily came forward. So might the State Attorney.'

Moldy was amused. 'Who do you think you're dealing with?'

'That's what I came to find out. I was hoping for a civilized discussion.' Mordecai rose and smoothed the wrinkles from his suit. 'I'll be at the courthouse first thing in the morning. Prepare the congressman for the worst.'

Moldowsky said, 'Sit down, hotshot.'

'No, sir. I've said my piece.'

'Three million is too high.'

'Really?' Now it was Mordecai's turn to be amused. 'Do you know what Sweetheart Sugar grossed last year?'

Moldy made a sucking noise through his front teeth. In slow motion he placed his glass on the table. The lawyer remained smug. He wished that Joyce could see him in action, cutting the nuts off the big boys.

Moldowsky said, 'You know a man named Jerry Killian?'

The lawyer said he'd never heard of him. Moldy could tell he was being truthful. Leave it to Dilbeck to get blackmailed twice for the same fuckup – three times, if you counted the mystery woman who phoned his Washington office.

'I need to know who else is involved.'

Mordecai said, 'My clients are Joyce and Paul.' He didn't mention that Paul Guber, having disassociated himself from the scheme, would never be told about the money. Nor did Mordecai reveal that a modest slice of the settlement would be shared with a violent bouncer named Shad.

'The check,' the lawyer said, 'should be made out to my firm's trust account.'

'A check?' Malcolm Moldowsky laughed harshly.

'Surely you don't intend to pay in cash.'

'No. Wire transfer.'

'From Overseas?'

'Nassau,' Moldy said. 'Possibly the Caymans. Is that a problem?'

'Not as long as it's US dollars.' The lawyer fancied himself the portrait of slick.

Moldowsky said, 'Three million won't fly. Try two-point-five.'

'You're playing games, Mr Moldowsky. We both know the price of sugar, and how it stays so high.'

'Don't push your luck, hotshot. According to my information, Paul Guber is completely recovered.'

'Never know about the human brain,' Mordecai mused. 'One day the man could be fine. The next day it's intensive care.'

'Oh, you're a pistol.'

'The prospect of a trial would be most stressful for the young man and his bride-to-be. I'd recommend some long-term counselling.'

Moldy flicked a hand in the air. 'Cut the bullshit. I'll talk to some people and get back with you.'

'Of course.'

'In the meantime, have a chat with Joyce. Explain the importance of confidentiality.'

'Don't worry,' Mordecai said, 'she's a smart lady.'

And soon to be a rich one.

*

The Rojos' boat was called the *Sweetheart Deal*. It was ninety feet long, made in the Netherlands. All three staterooms had wet bars and Dolby sound.

The yacht was docked at Turnberry Isle, on the Intracoastal Waterway. By the time Moldowsky arrived, it was almost two in the morning. The elder Rojos, Joaquin and Willie, offered a cup of Cuban coffee to their guest. Moldy didn't need it; he was wide awake. Two young women were taking a bubble bath in the jacuzzi. Christopher was passed out on the carpet, next to a spotted ocelot in an emerald-studded collar. The wild cat groomed its paws and rumbled.

The Rojos led Moldowsky upstairs to a small sitting room on the captain's deck. Willie asked about David Dilbeck.

'I didn't invite him,' Moldy said, 'for his own protection.'

'Tell us the problem, Malcolm.'

He kept it simple: The congressman had gotten himself into an unsavory situation. A compromising photograph had been taken. Now a lawyer had come forward, demanding three million dollars.

The Rojos were deeply concerned, and conferred quietly in Spanish. Moldowsky noticed that the brothers wore matching robes with the name of the boat stitched over the left breast. One of Joaquin's earlobes was white with dried soap bubbles.

Moldy said, 'The options are limited.'

'Three million dollars,' said Willie, 'is not possible.'

'I'm sure he'll settle for two.'

Joaquin Rojo whispered a curse. The timing of the lawsuit threat couldn't be worse – Dilbeck should hustle the sugar legislation out of committee immediately, so that the full House of Representatives could vote on it before the November election.

Impossible, Moldowsky said. 'Those jerks couldn't pass a kidney stone right now. Everybody's home campaigning.' Besides, he added, the Speaker didn't want the bill on the floor so soon – too controversial. Ralph Nader had gone on 'Nightline', making a stink about subsidies for Big Agriculture. The tobacco and rice lobbies panicked, which caused their stooges in Congress to do the same. A House vote now would be dicey; the smart thing to do was to wait. Which meant the Rojos were forced to rely on David Dilbeck for several more months – and they needed him squeaky clean.

Willie asked, 'How bad is the photograph?'

'Fatal,' said Moldy.

'*Mierda*. Let's pay the goddamn money.'

'No!' Joaquin said. 'I will not be blackmailed.'

'Do we have a choice?' Willie turned to Moldowsky. 'Well, Malcolm?'

Without mentioning Jerry Killian by name, Moldy confided that a similar problem had arisen a few weeks earlier. 'I handled it myself. But this one is more complicated.'

'Because of the photograph?'

'And the fact it's a lawyer.'

Willie Rojo nodded. 'That's what worries me, too. Let's just pay the bastard and forget it.'

His brother rose, shaking a pale fist. 'No, Wilberto. You want to pay, do it with your own children's inheritance. I'm out!'

Spanish erupted again, and this time the brothers' voices escalated in argument. Moldowsky picked up a word here and there. Finally, Joaquin Rojo sat down.

'Malcolm,' he said, 'how much do you know about cane farming?'

Moldowsky shrugged and said he didn't know much.

'We plant in muck,' Joaquin said. 'Mostly sawgrass muck, sometimes custard apple. They call it black gold because it produces such rich sugar. A farmer might get ten good seasons out of a field, then the tonnage starts to drop. Why? Because with each crop, the layer of muck shrinks.' He dramatized with a thumb and fore-finger. 'Eventually the soil isn't deep enough for cane, and the land becomes useless. Underneath is solid limestone.'

Willie said, 'When the muck is gone, Malcolm, it's gone for ever. Our people are telling us five, maybe six more seasons.'

'Then what?'

Joaquin turned up his hands. 'Rock mining. Condo-miniums. Golf resorts. That's not important right now.'

'Later, yes,' said his brother. 'But for now, our busi-ness is sugarcane. We need these last few years to be good ones.'

'A legacy,' Moldowsky agreed.

'Please make Mr Dilbeck's problem go away.'

'I assume you're not paying off the lawyer.'

'My brother and I have decided against it.'

The emerald-collared ocelot trotted up the steps and crouched at Willie Rojo's slippered feet. The old man dug into the folds of his monogrammed robe and pro-duced a gooey chicken drumstick. The brothers watched fondly as the animal devoured the piece, bone and all. The crunching bothered Malcolm J. Moldowsky, who was not much of a cat person.

Joaquin yawned and announced it was time for bed. 'Call us when it's done,' he told Moldowsky.

'This'll still be expensive.'

Willie Rojo giggled as he let the ocelot lick chicken grease off his fingers. 'How expensive?' he asked. 'Not three million dollars, I'm sure.'

'Not even close,' Moldy said; 'but there's a certain risk.'

'Not to us, I hope.'

'No, gentlemen. Not to you.'

Darrell Grant sold the wheelchairs for $3,200 cash and drove straight from St Augustine to Daytona Beach. There he purchased an assortment of colorful pills, and picked up two prostitutes on the boardwalk. Later, when they thought he was asleep, the hookers let their pimp enter Darrell's motel room and pick through his belongings. Darrell waited a suitable interval, then slipped his hand under the pillow where he kept the dagger. With a ghoulish screech, he sprung from the bed and stabbed the pimp in the fleshy part of a thigh. While the man wriggled on the floor, the hookers straddled him and frantically tried to stanch the bleeding. Darrell Grant calmly yanked the sheet from the bed and sliced it into long strips. Then he tied up the thrashing pimp and the two hookers, and stuffed dirty socks in their mouths. The women didn't struggle, as they had gotten a close-up glimpse of Darrell Grant's microdot pupils.

As he worked on the pimp, Darrell hummed a tune from *The Jungle Book*, which Angela had on video cassette. Gaily, he lathered the man's curly black hair and shaved him bald. Then he took the dagger and cut a perfect capital G on the scalp. The pimp moaned and grunted into the filthy gag. Blood trickled in twin rivulets down both sides of his head. The women watched silently, fearing they were next.

Darrell Grant said: 'Now I'm going to teach you people a lesson.'

He got his keys and ran to the van. Two minutes later he returned, carrying an electric staple gun that he'd stolen from a construction site in Boca Raton. At the sight of the stapler, one of the hookers began to sob. Darrell Grant walked over to the pimp and untied one of his arms.

Still panting, he said, 'Were you going to rob me?'

The pimp shook his head violently.

'Liar, liar, pants on fire,' Darrell sang.

He plugged the staple gun into a wall outlet, and said, 'Next time you want money, ask polite.' He grabbed the pimp's hand and stapled a one-dollar bill to the palm. He held the trigger down a long time – ping ping ping – until the staple gun was empty. The pimp's eyelids fluttered and he lolled unconscious. The women shivered with fright.

Suddenly Darrell Grant felt spent. He stretched on the bed and dialed Rita's house. She growled at him for phoning so late, three-goddamn-thirty in the morning.

Her brother apologized and said, 'Listen, I might take a few extra days up here. That OK?'

'Suit yourself. Erin's coming tomorrow.'

'What?'

'Visitation day,' Rita said.

'No!'

'That's what she told us.'

'Jesus, Rita, did you tell her Angie was there? How the hell did she know?'

'I can't help it your daughter knows how to use the phone. And she climbs, too, like a little monkey.'

'Angie called her?' Darrell Grant pounded a fist on the bare mattress. 'Goddamn, I can't believe you let this happen.' He was too overmedicated to concentrate on two crisis situations simultaneously. He didn't notice that one of the tied-up hookers had managed to twist an arm free, and was working covertly on the other knots.

Darrell choked the telephone receiver and cried: 'Don't let that cunt in the house, you understand?'

'It's visitation day!' Rita repeated.

'It ain't fucking visitation day!'

'Then *you* come back and deal with it. I got wolves to train.'

'Lord Christ.'

'Another thing, it was on the news – what's the judge that got your divorce?'

Darrell Grant told her the name.

'Yep, Alberto said it was him. He's dead, Darrell.'

'Now hold up—'

'It was on the TV,' Rita said. 'He died last night at a nudie joint.'

Darrell Grant rested his cheek on the foul-smelling mattress. It was definitely time for more pills.

On the other end of the line, Rita was telling the story. 'His family said he went there to preach gospel at the naked girls. You believe that shit? They found a Bible on his lap – it was all on the television.'

'I'll be home by morning,' Darrell Grant said thickly.

'What about Erin?' Rita asked. There was no answer

from Daytona Beach. 'Darrell? Whoa hey, little brother, wake up!'

But he was out cold, sapped on the skull by a hooker swinging a staple gun. They made off with the cash, the drugs, the dagger, and of course the van. They did not take Darrell Grant's dirty socks, which were the first things he tasted when he regained consciousness four hours later.

SEVENTEEN

On the morning of September twenty-eighth, Sgt Al García drove through a light drizzle to the Flightpath Motel, two hundred yards due west of the main commercial runway of Fort Lauderdale–Hollywood International Airport. The motel manager, an amiable Greek named Miklos, led the detective to Room 233. As Miklos fit the key in the door, García said, 'I bet the carpet is brown.'

'How you know that?'

'It came to me in a dream,' García said. Miklos opened the door and pointed gleefully at the carpet, which was a cocoa-brown shag.

The detective said, 'Sometimes I scare myself.' The Mineral County coroner had found three brown carpet fibers under Jerry Killian's left thumbnail.

'What else you dream?' Miklos asked.

'A man named Killian was murdered in this room.'

'Oh no,' Miklos said. 'Don't tell me.' He said the maid found Killian's checkbook beneath the bed.

'He probably threw it there on purpose,' García said, 'so the bad guys wouldn't get it.' People did weird things on the verge of dying.

Miklos said, 'I send it back right away, next day.'

'You did the right thing.'

'Who called the police?'

'Nobody,' Al García said. 'I opened Mr Killian's mail. There was the checkbook, and your note.'

Miklos frowned. 'Is that OK? To open his letters?'

'Oh sure. I'm an officer of the law.' García got on his knees and crawled under the bed. His fingers probed the ratty shag in search of other clues. All he found was a petrified pizza crust and a nickel. García got up and brushed the fuzz off his trousers.

Miklos said, 'Since I work here, seven people die. It is very sad. Seven in seven months.'

'Guests?'

'Yes, sir. Drugs, guns, stabs, problems with the heart. The police come many times. Always we are replacing carpets and sheets.'

'Maybe it's the location,' García said, his voice rising over the roar of an incoming jet. The place was ideal for customers wishing not to be overheard. He took out a photograph of Jerry Killian.

'I never see him before,' Miklos said. 'You say this man was a murder?'

'Yeah. In the tub is my guess.'

'The bathrooms we clean three times a week.'

'Wow,' García said. 'Your Lysol bill must be outta sight. Can I have a look?'

Miklos sat on the bed and waited. He heard the detective fiddling with the faucets in the bathtub. 'Mr Miklos, what happened to the hot-water knob?'

'Somebody broke.'

'How?'

'I dunno. Maybe two weeks ago.'

The detective came out, drying his hands on a towel. Another jet howled overhead. García said, 'Looks like somebody kicked that fixture right off the wall.' The drowning Jerry Killian had put up a pretty good fight.

Miklos said, 'You say murder but the maid didn't find no dead body.'

'That's because the killer drove the dead body to Montana and dumped it in a river.'

'Why?'

'To mess up my vacation,' Al García said. 'Can I see the guest register?'

Miklos took him back to the office, which wasn't much larger than the bathroom. Killian's name did not appear on the check-in sheets; García would've been shocked if it had. He made notes on everyone who'd rented Room 233 during the previous two weeks. One name showed up five times.

'He's a local,' Miklos said.

'Local what?'

'Businessman. He entertains.'

'Oh,' said García. 'You mean he's a pimp.'

Miklos squirmed. 'Boy, I dunno.'

The detective asked if any of the other guests in 233 had made an impression. Miklos said yes, one man checked in with a bag of live gerbils and a video camera.

'And you find that unusual?' García smiled. 'Go on.'

'Another night was three Jamaicans. I tell them there's only one bed but they say it's OK, *mon*. Three big guys in that room – you saw how small it is.'

García tapped the guest register. Miklos found the name: 'John Riley'. Conveniently generic. The address was a post-office box in Belle Glade, of all places. Lake Okeechobee.

'Big strong guys,' Miklos reported. 'They check out before midnight.'

'Paid cash, I'm sure.'

'We don't see many credit cards,' Miklos said.

'Remember what they were driving? Was there anybody else in the car?'

'Boy, I dunno.'

'What else?' García asked. 'You said they stood out.'

'They all have scars. Very bad scars.'

'On the face?'

'Legs.'

'Do tell,' García said.

'They were in short pants. Red, green, I dunno, but was very bright colors.'

'Gym shorts,' the detective said.

'That's how I saw the scars.' He reached down and patted his shins. 'All down here.'

'You've been a big help, Mr Miklos.'

The friendly motel manager offered to show Al García the other rooms where guests occasionally died. The detective said no thanks, maybe another time.

'So maybe it was Jamaicans who killed the man who lost his checkbook.'

'It's a thought,' García said.

Miklos winked. 'Maybe your dreams will tell you who did it.'

The detective laughed. 'I deserve that.'

The motel manager accompanied him to the car. Miklos said he'd applied to be night clerk at a Ramada near the beach. He said the waiting list was two pages long.

'But I got more experience than most.'

'You're not kidding,' García said. 'Good luck with that job.'

'Thank you,' said Miklos. 'Good luck with your murder.'

Erin got to the trailer park at seven. Rita was already out in the backyard, yelling at the wolf dogs. It was Alberto Alonso who opened the front door. He'd just returned from the nuclear plant, and still wore his gabardine security-guard uniform. Erin was shocked that he was allowed to carry a gun.

'Coffee?' Alberto said. He unbuckled his holster and casually hung it over the back of a chair. Erin felt sick to her stomach; she had a flashing image of her daughter picking up Alberto's pistol, thinking it was a toy.

'Where's Angela?' she said tensely.

'Asleep, I think.'

Erin checked both bedrooms, which were empty. She returned to the kitchen, where Alberto was tending the coffee maker.

'Where is my daughter?' Erin said.

'Better touch base with Rita.'

'No, I want an answer from you.' She felt her arms shaking with anger. 'Alberto, it's visitation day.'

He poured a cup of coffee at the dinette. 'I remember last time you stopped over. Took off without even saying so long.'

Erin said, 'I didn't feel so well.'

'Rita sure was pissed about the mail.'

'I sent it all back.'

Alberto Alonso eyed her over the rim of the coffee cup. 'You look good in blue jeans,' he said. 'How's the job? I hear they changed the name of the place.'

Erin felt short of breath. What had these two cretins

done with her daughter? She said, 'OK, I'll go ask Sheena of the Jungle.'

'Hold on there.' Alberto snickered nervously. 'Maybe we can work something out, just the two of us.'

They heard Rita shouting curses outside. It sounded as if she was being dragged through the shrubbery. 'Lupa don't take to the leash,' Alberto explained.

Erin steadied herself; outmaneuvering Alberto shouldn't be hard. He moved to a window and peeked through the blinds. 'Rita's got her hands full,' he reported in a furtive voice. He jostled back to the kitchen, and swept the dishes and silver off the table.

'How about a little show?' he whispered to Erin. 'Just like you do at the club, only private.'

She thought of that final night, dancing on the table at Jerry Killian's apartment – he'd been so sweet and shy about it. Alberto Alonso was a different story.

He said, 'One little number, OK. Then I'll show you where Angie's at.' He sat on a stool, and excitedly motioned for Erin to climb on the dinette.

'Music would be helpful,' she said.

'Just pretend,' said Alberto. 'Rita hears the stereo, she'll want to know what's up.'

Erin wasn't sure she could dance just then, with or without her songs; all she could think about was finding Angela. Darrell Grant must've called and warned Rita to hide the child. If he knew that the judge was dead, then surely he knew Erin's plan. That he would disregard an emergency injunction, or any court order, was a foregone conclusion. The man would skip the country before surrendering custody of his daughter. To Darrell, it wasn't an issue of rightful parenthood, it was competition – a game of keep-away, with Angela as the prize.

Erin knew she had to strike fast, before her ex-husband got back to town.

Stepping up on the table, she almost bumped her head on the drop-ceiling of the trailer. She began humming 'Brown-eyed Girl', slowly moving her hips, waiting for Alberto's inevitable grope.

'Faster,' he said.

Erin put on her stage smile. As she danced, her sneakers skated on the Formica. After a minute or so, she started to hear the music, clear and tender, in her head. Alberto's coffee-stained leer seemed far away and harmless. She didn't flinch when he clamped his hands around her ankles.

'Go faster,' he said again.

Erin thought: Everything will be all right. Softly she sang the first verse.

'Not too loud,' said Alberto, glancing toward the screen door.

'It's such a great song,' Erin said, to no one.

Alberto dropped his voice. 'How about some titties?'

Erin raised her eyebrows.

'Just a peek,' he said. 'Maybe take off your top.'

Still smiling, Erin undid the top two buttons. Then she said, 'You do the rest, OK?'

A blissful glow came to Alberto Alonso's face. He rose off the stool and reached for her, his fingers wriggling like night crawlers. Erin knew that Alberto would never locate, much less master, the tiny buttons of her blouse; in such extreme states of desire, men tended to lose their fine-motor skills. Alberto's paws ultimately settled upon Erin's chest, and began to massage in rhythmic circles. His coarse touch gave her an ugly chill, but Erin kept dancing like a pro. Alberto's groans intensified with the pace of his fondling; the tip of his tongue emerged between his teeth, a sluglike sentinel of arousal.

Erin's next move was to tousle Alberto's hair, which was more than he could stand. He got a clumsy grip on her breasts and tried to pull her down, toward his waiting mouth. It presented Erin with an irresistible target. She brought her right knee up, majorette-style, high and hard against the point of Alberto's unshaven chin. The crack was like a rifle shot.

Suddenly Alberto lay flat on his back, gargling blood. Erin stood over him. The stage smile was gone. Her blouse was fully buttoned. In one hand she held the coffee pot; Alberto could see steam curling off the sides.

'I intend to pour this on your balls,' Erin said.

Alberto attempted to speak, but the words came out in bubbles.

'I'm not sure this'll kill you,' Erin said, taking aim, 'but you'll wish it had.'

A squeal rose from Alberto: 'Neth doe! She neth doe!'

'Next door?'

He nodded hysterically. Erin put down the coffee pot and dashed out of the trailer. Alberto began gagging on the severed chunk of his tongue. Rita burst in the screen door; at her heels stood Lupa, ears pricked.

'Aiyeeee!' cried Alberto, shielding himself with both arms. But the wolf dog had already picked up the primal scent of the freshly wounded.

Erin held Angela's hand the whole way back to Fort Lauderdale.

'What's wrong?' the girl asked.

'I'm just glad to see you, baby.' It had been fourteen months since she and her daughter had been alone, without Darrell Grant hovering nearby – the worst year of Erin's life. She wondered what had been lost.

Angela said, 'Mrs Bickel has an aquarium. She let me feed her eels.'

Mrs Bickel was the elderly next-door neighbor of Rita and Alberto Alonso. She had been microwaving glazed donuts for Angela's breakfast when Erin arrived to collect her daughter.

'I didn't notice an aquarium,' Erin said.

'It's in the bedroom near the TV. The eels are green and they ate all her pretty fish.'

'I see,' said Erin. It sounded like Mrs Bickel fit perfectly in the demographic strata of the trailer park.

Angela said, 'Are we going to your house now?'

'We sure are. *Our* house.'

'For all day?'

'Better than that,' Erin said.

Angela looked worried. Erin's heart sank at the thought that her daughter might rather be with Darrell, or Rita, or the old lady with the eels. It was Erin's most dreadful nightmare, a year's worth of nightmares. Now she felt paralyzed, afraid to say something that might prompt a lacerating burst of candor from Angie. *I want Daddy!* Erin couldn't have endured it.

The little girl broke the silence with one word: 'Pajamas.'

She was wearing her favorites, starring Big Bird and the Cookie Monster. 'But they're dirty,' Angela said. She pinched a sleeve to show her mother. 'All my clothes are at Daddy's. And what about clean underpants!'

Erin said, 'We're going to buy you some new clothes.'

'Good!'

'You like to shop?'

'I don't know. Daddy only takes me to hospitals.'

'Right. To ride in the wheelchairs.' Erin thought: How will I ever explain that man to his daughter? At what age is a child capable of understanding that her father is irredeemable scum?

Angela said, 'One time I saw a boy riding a wheelchair.'

'At a hospital?'

'Yep. Daddy said the little boy was very sick, so we couldn't race.'

'Your daddy was right,' said Erin.

'When they put the boy back in his room, Daddy got the wheelchair and took it home.'

'Oh?'

'To fix it,' Angela said proudly. 'It needed a new brake.'

'Is that what Daddy said?'

'And new wheels. Wasn't that nice of him?'

Erin sighed. 'Angie, I'm glad you called last night.'

'Me too.'

To Mordecai, the term 'blackmail' was a melodramatic way to describe what he was doing to Congressman David Lane Dilbeck. Playing hardball is what it was. Strip away the tedious formalities of a lawsuit and the essence was no different: give me money – or else. In or out of court, the seminal element of negotiation was the threat. It was an art, the core of Mordecai's chosen livelihood.

Man falls in supermarket, hires attorney; super-market settles for six figures. Happens all the time and nobody calls it blackmail. Here an innocent man gets mauled by a drunken congressman, hires an attorney – and they're calling it a shakedown! Mordecai was amused by the double standard.

The attack on Paul Guber was vicious and indefensible; any personal-injury lawyer would've jumped at the case. Of course, most lawyers wouldn't have arranged a secret settlement against their client's wishes, or devised to keep the bulk of the money for themselves. It wasn't Mordecai's proudest moment as a member of the Bar, but these days a fellow did what he must. In fifteen years of practice, youthful fantasies of immense personal wealth had evaporated in disappointment. The Delicato cockroach fiasco was a prime example of his recurring foul luck. Now, the horny congressman loomed as Mordecai's first realistic chance at collecting a seven-figure lump. He proceeded on the assumption that it would be his only shot.

In the early 1970s, Mordecai was among the hundreds of idealistic young law-school graduates who rushed to South Florida with the dream of defending drug smugglers for astronomical cash fees. He'd even studied Castilian Spanish in anticipation of his Colombian clientele! But Mordecai arrived in Miami to discover a depressingly small number of imprisoned South American drug barons; defense lawyers seemed to outnumber the defendants. An attorney of modest talents stood little chance of landing a billionaire narco-trafficker as a client; Mordecai was lucky to get the occasional mule or offloader. Before long, he moved to Fort Lauderdale and opened a personal-injury practice.

The strategy had seemed sound: Broward County was growing much faster than Dade County, and most of the new arrivals were elderly. The elderly tended to fall down more often than younger people, Mordecai noticed, and their injuries usually were more complicated. Better still, there was an inexhaustible supply of old folks, thousands upon thousands, with more on the way each winter. Condos sprouted from the beach to the edge of the Everglades – high-rise bank vaults, in Mordecai's view.

He set up shop and made plans to become absurdly rich. It didn't happen. Mordecai's income was respectable but not profane. He got by on minor negligence cases, insurance litigation and probate, which he hated. He told his secretary that they could both retire to Bermuda if his clients spent half as much time falling down as they did drawing up new wills.

Still, Mordecai was in no position to be picky. South Florida was swarming with young lawyers who prowled the courthouses in a feral hunger, scrabbling like jackals for the tiniest morsel. Competition in all specialties was savage because there wasn't enough work to go around. Desperation was manifested in an epidemic of oily late-night advertising. Once the exclusive province of negligence lawyers, television now attracted all fields of the profession: immigration, divorce, adoption, even traffic violations. One of Mordecai's former classmates had become famous touting himself as 'Doctor D.U.I.' It was survival of the slickest.

Mordecai refused to make a commercial, as it involved the unpalatable prospect of trimming down for the cameras. His mother nagged doggedly – she was dying to see her son on television! – but Mordecai held firm against it. Maybe that had been a mistake. Maybe his career would've taken a loftier trajectory had he chosen the glitter of self-promotion. Then again, what was worse: shaking down a sleazy politician, or putting drunk drivers back on the road?

'I've got to live with myself,' he confided to Joyce.

'You did the right thing,' she said.

They were going to see Malcolm J. Moldowsky, who had called first thing that morning. Moldowsky said there was good news; he wanted to meet both of them in an hour. Mordecai told Beverly to reschedule his morning appointments, and euphorically thundered from the office. Crossing the lobby, a flash caught the lawyer's attention – a ray of sun, glinting off Shad's enormous head. The bouncer was waiting tight-lipped at the west elevator. Mordecai nearly stumbled: What did the lunatic want today? Had he somehow gotten wind that a deal was imminent? The lawyer slipped unseen through the easternmost exit.

When he picked up Joyce, she said, 'You're excited. Let me drive.'

'No, I'll be fine.'

Joyce warned him about the wet roads and checked the fit of her seatbelt. 'Are you sure you got this right?'

'House of Pancakes. That's what he said.'

'In Davie? Why so far?'

'I don't know, Joyce, but that's what the man said.' Mordecai's voice was tight. 'Do you seriously think I wouldn't write it down – something this important?' He pulled the note from his pocket and thrust it toward her.

'Eyes on the road,' she said. Then, skimming her

cousin's scribble: 'All right, so it says Pancake House. We'll see.'

Mordecai was silent for several miles while Joyce searched for a radio station that suited her taste. Mordecai wondered why Moldowsky had requested her presence at the meeting.

'Joyce, I'm going to ask a favor. When we get there, let me do the talking.'

'You don't have to get nasty.'

'Now listen—'

'Besides, it was my idea. Cutting Paul out.'

Mordecai took a deep breath. 'So it was.'

'Maybe, I'm not so stupid then?'

'I didn't say you were stupid. It's a delicate situation, that's all. These are serious people, and we both need to be mindful of what we say.'

Joyce flipped the visor and examined her makeup in the vanity mirror. 'I'm a serious person, too,' she said. 'Slow down, there's the exit.'

They pulled off the interstate at Davie Road and quickly spotted the International House of Pancakes. In his excitement, Mordecai mistakenly parked the Lincoln in a handicapped zone. Before he could back out, a man in blue tapped on the windshield. Mordecai rolled down the window.

'I work for Mr Moldowsky,' said the man. The blue was a bowling shirt. 'He's waiting at the country club.'

'Who are you?' the lawyer asked.

'Messenger,' the man replied. 'Part-time. You want to see an ID?'

Mordecai shrugged and said, 'Hop in.'

The man told Mordecai to take Orange Drive west to Flamingo Road. 'How far?' asked the lawyer.

'Not far.'

Joyce wore a cocky smirk. She reached across and poked her cousin in the arm. 'I told you,' she said. 'House of Pancakes! I knew that couldn't possibly be right.'

'Enough,' said Mordecai.

Joyce turned to the stranger in the backseat. 'What's the name of the country club? Is it Brook Run or Pine Abbey?'

The man hesitated, but not long enough for Joyce to notice. 'Brook Run,' he said.

'I hear it's just lovely.'

'Yeah,' the man said. 'That's what I hear, too.'

'Do they have a brunch?'

Mordecai said, 'Joyce, for God's sake.'

The man in the bowling shirt sat forward. 'Yeah, they got a helluva brunch,' he said. 'Slow down and make the next turn.'

EIGHTEEN

Erin moved out of her apartment on the same day that she snatched Angela. She found a place in a suburban development called Inverarry, where Jackie Gleason once lived in a luxury mansion with a billiard room. Erin was in a bind, so she took what was available – a two-bedroom town house that was too expensive. The security deposit was a thousand dollars plus first and last month's rent. She paid in cash and signed the lease under her maiden name. She and Angela relocated the entire household by themselves in three trips. The only casualty was the Jimi Hendrix poster, which ripped when Erin removed it from the wall.

The next day, she withdrew another two thousand dollars from her savings account, drove to her lawyer's office and gave him the money – which (by his secretary's tabulation) reduced Erin's outstanding balance from eleven thousand dollars to nine thousand dollars. That afternoon, the lawyer asked the new judge in Erin's divorce case to remove Angela from Darrell Grant's custody because he had dumped the child with dangerously unreliable relatives. Alberto's pistol and Rita's wolves figured prominently in the judge's decision. Neither Darrell nor his attorney showed up to argue. The judge ordered a full hearing on the case in four weeks. He was curious to know more about Erin's occupation.

The other dancers congratulated Erin and doted on Angela in the dressing room of the Tickled Pink. They took turns playing with the little girl until she dozed off on the floor. Erin wasn't happy about the arrangement; the club was no place for a child. The new judge would take a dim view.

Dancers with children customarily worked the day shift so they could be home at night. Erin couldn't afford to work days because the money was lousy, and she was now nearly broke – the apartment, the lawyer, Angie's new wardrobe.

'The shoes are adorable,' said Urbana Sprawl, fingering the tiny Reeboks. 'Where'd you find these?' She spoke in a whisper, trying not to wake the girl.

Erin said, 'I'm doing tables tonight. So don't fall off the stage when you see me.'

'Damn, you *must* be tapped.' Urbana knew how Erin hated table dances. 'But you'll make money,' she told her. 'Real good money.'

'First one that touches me—'

'No, girl. You call Shad. That's what he's there for.' Urbana removed her top and studied her breasts critically in the mirror. 'Mosquito got me on the left one,' she reported.

Erin said you could hardly see it.

'Hardly ain't good enough.' Urbana found a jar of dark makeup and touched up the bite. 'Don't you worry,' she told Erin. 'Everybody does tables. Fact, you're the only one I ever knew who didn't. That's how fine a dancer you are. Most girls'd starve to death on stage tips.'

'Well, now I'm dancing for two,' Erin said.

Monique Sr came in and announced that Keith Richards was sitting at table five. 'I told Kevin to play some Stones,' she said excitedly. 'Next set, I'm gonna knock his socks off.'

'Keith Richards,' Erin said, failing to conceal her amusement.

'What – you don't believe me?'

Urbana asked what he was drinking.

'Black Jack and water.'

'Then it ain't Keith. What he drinks is Rebel Yell, straight up.' Urbana was an encyclopedia of trivia when it came to the Rolling Stones.

Monique Sr looked crestfallen. Erin, feeling guilty, said: 'Hey, maybe he switched labels.'

'It's *him*,' Monique Sr insisted. 'Come see for yourself.'

Erin said, 'We believe you.'

'No, we don't,' said Urbana. 'Anyway, what's the difference? The Stones don't use dancers. What could he do for us, even if it was really him?'

Monique Sr started to tell Urbana to go fuck herself, but then she spotted Angie, sleeping. She would not swear in the presence of a child.

'Now, say it was Rod Stewart,' Urbana went on, 'then we got us some possibilities. He uses dancers in all his videos. That's when you got my attention, when Rod the Bod takes table five.'

Erin cut in: 'Monique, you want us to come look?'

'Keith would be thrilled,' she said icily.

'Let's go then.' Erin opened the door and there stood Orly, looking gassy and dour. Monique Sr curtly excused herself and hurried back to the lounge.

Orly trudged in and closed the door. He glared at Angela, curled on the carpet. 'I could lose my license,' he said to Erin. 'Tell me that's not a minor on the premises. Tell me it's a midget stripper in tennis shoes. Otherwise I lose my fucking liquor license.'

Erin apologized for bringing Angie to the club. She told Orly it was a family emergency.

'Shit,' he muttered, and sagged down in a folding chair.

Urbana Sprawl said: 'Don't you wake that child, Mr Orly.'

'Don't worry,' Erin said. 'She doesn't sleep, she hibernates.'

Overcome by cosmetic fragrances, Orly immediately fell victim to an allergy attack. He stifled his sloppy sneezes as best he could.

'Hush,' Urbana said. 'You ain't even supposed to be in the dressing room. Or did you forget?'

'Forgive me,' Orly said. 'See, I couldn't control myself. It's been at least ten minutes since I seen your fat ass naked, so I snuck back here to cop a peek. You don't mind if I whack off now, do you?'

Erin said, 'God, you're in a lousy mood.'

'Damn right.' Orly grabbed a handful of tissues from a box on the vanity. 'The Ling brothers are doing standing-room, on account of that old judge croaking in their club. They got so much business, they're takin' reservations. *Reservations*, at a goddamn tittie bar!'

Erin said, 'The TV news is what did it. You can't buy that kind of publicity.'

Orly began to fulminate obscenely, then caught himself. He glanced irritably at the sleeping girl. In a bitter rasp: 'We're talking about a dead body, a stiff –

just about the worst thing you can imagine. And people are lined up around the block to see where it happened. I don't understand human nature, I honestly don't.'

Urbana's eyes were full of mischief. She said, 'Let's keep our fingers crossed. Maybe somebody famous will die here, too.'

'Not the way these girls dance,' said Orly. 'The only thing my customers might die of is sheer goddamn boredom.'

'That's enough,' Erin said sharply. 'I mean it.'

Urbana hustled off to do a set in the cage. Orly shrunk deeper in the folding chair, which pinched his torso like an oversize clothespin. 'Even Marvela's cashing in,' he complained.

'She's overcome her grief, has she?'

'The Lings got her name in big letters on the marquee: come see the pussy that killed the judge!'

'Is that what it says?'

'I'm paraphrasing,' Orly admitted. 'Bottom line, my business is down fifteen percent.'

Bracing for the worst, Erin said, 'So what do you want from us?'

'Reconsider friction dancing.'

'Absolutely not. We took a vote, Mr Orly.'

'Yeah, yeah.' He dismissed the idea with a brusque wave. 'Then how about this: creamed corn.'

Erin said nothing. She wanted him to choke out every depraved detail, with no help or encouragement. She wanted him to be as uncomfortable as possible.

'Instead of Wesson oil,' he said. 'What do you think?'

Erin's face gave nothing away; she didn't even blink. Orly's hands fidgeted on his belly like two fat crabs.

'Wrestling!' he blurted. 'For God's sake, that's what

I'm talking about. Creamed corn instead of oil. There's a place in West Palm where it started. First the guys climb in and wrestle the girls. I'm thinking twenty bucks a pop.'

Finally Erin spoke. 'Just so I understand. You want me to jump into a puddle of creamed vegetables and roll around nude with a bunch of drunk slobs.'

'Not nude. Topless.' Orly gnawed off a hangnail and spit it on the floor. 'Health department won't go for nude. Not with food products.'

'What happened to classy?' Erin demanded. 'New name, new image – what happened to that?'

'Those fucking Lings is what happened to that.' Orly looked despondent. His words carried a tinge of genuine shame. 'You want the truth, I'm hurting. I need a goddamn gimmick, Erin. This creamed corn thing is what they call camp. I'm told the yuppies are suckers for it.'

She said, 'So it's come to this.'

'I can't force you to do it.'

'No shit,' she said. 'With a shotgun you couldn't force me to do it.'

Orly straightened and put on his businessman's face. 'What's the part that gripes you – is it the wrestling or the corn itself? Because something else occurred to me.'

'I can hardly wait,' Erin said.

'How about this? Forget the creamed corn—'

'Bravo.'

'Consider pasta.' Orly's eyebrows danced. 'You mention class, well, there you are. What's classier than pasta?'

'Pasta wrestling?' Erin was tumbling through space.

'Egg noodles, linguini, take your pick.'

'I've got to undress now, Mr Orly. Could I have some privacy please?'

When he stood up, the chair fell off his ass with a clatter. Angie stirred but did not awaken.

'Think about it,' Orly told Erin. 'Like I say, it's a smash in West Palm.'

In the mirror she watched him go out the door. 'What happened to just plain dancing?' she said.

Sabrina came in to keep an eye on Angie while Erin performed. 'I heard you're doing tables tonight,' Sabrina said, combing a jet-black wig. 'It's not so bad.'

'Unless they grab you,' said Erin.

'They won't grab tonight. Shad's in one of his moods.' Sabrina's hairbrush hit a snag and the wig jumped off her lap. 'Damn,' she said.

Erin fastened her G-string and checked her butt in the mirror, to make sure the strap was lined up. She said, 'The thing is, I need the money.'

'You'll do good,' Sabrina said. 'Just be careful not to fall.'

Kevin was playing 'Honky Tonk Woman' when Erin went on stage. The song brightened her mood nearly as much as the sight of Monique Sr dancing wildly on the table of a man who actually looked like Mr Keith Richards, if you used your imagination.

Which is all that was keeping Erin sane.

Visions of Valium tablets danced in Beverly's head. The phones were beeping off the hook, the mail had piled up, and that horrid bald man was reading *National Geographic* in the waiting room, for the second straight day – the same man she'd tried to stab with a letter opener! Seeing him again was awkward; in sixteen years as a legal secretary, she'd never assaulted a client. Half in terror, Beverly had offered a meek apology.

For what? the bald man said. He'd already forgotten about it. Beverly felt more afraid of him than ever.

'I do need to see the boss,' Shad had said.

'You just missed him.'

That was yesterday. The lawyer had rushed to a meeting and failed to return. He hadn't even phoned in for messages. Today, Beverly's exasperation was turning into concern: Mordecai could not be found. So far he'd skipped four office consultations, two depositions and an important hearing in Circuit Court. The court hearing was significant because it involved the awarding of attorney's fees, an occasion that Mordecai never missed.

Beverly was mystified. Now a bank officer was on the line, seeking to verify the number on Mordecai's client trust account. The officer recited the account number and Beverly told him it was correct. 'All deposits usually go through me,' she said.

The bank officer said it wasn't a deposit, it was a withdrawal. A substantial withdrawal. He said Mordecai had called with instructions to close out the account immediately.

Beverly didn't like the sound of that one bit. Another line lighted up – Paul Guber, mildly worried. He hadn't heard from his fiancée in two days. It was unlike Joyce not to pester him hourly. Did Mordecai happen to know where she was?

Poor Beverly had no answers. Now Shad loomed in front of her desk. Today he wore camo fatigues. 'This is getting ridiculous,' he said.

'I know, I know,' the secretary agreed. 'I can't imagine where he's gone.'

Shad said, 'Let me check around.' He stepped past her and opened the door to Mordecai's office. Afraid to protest, Beverly followed.

'Did you turn all these lights on?' Shad asked.

The secretary said no, the lights were on when she got there. 'He might've worked late last night,' she said. The phones resumed beeping, but she didn't pick up. She was determined not to let Shad out of her sight.

He circled the desk, touching nothing. 'Someone's been through this.'

'How can you tell?'

'It's too damn neat,' Shad said. A man working late hours would leave some clutter, but Mordecai's desk was abnormally tidy, not a pencil out of place. Even the trash can looked as if it had been vacuumed.

Shad asked if there was a drop safe. Beverly said no – Mordecai kept all sensitive files in a lock box at a bank.

'How many keys?' Shad asked.

'Two, I think.'

'Where are they?'

'I don't know,' said Beverly. 'He won't tell me.'

'This is good,' Shad said.

'He won't even tell me which bank.'

'Figures.'

Beverly speculated that maybe the janitors had left the lights on. That might explain why the place was so orderly.

Shad shook his head. The place had been gone over by pros. 'I seem to remember a Rolodex.'

Beverly scanned Mordecai's desk. 'A locked Rolodex, yes. He kept it by the telephone.'

'Well, somebody got it,' Shad said. Damn, this was shitty news.

'Shall I call the police?'

'Suit yourself,' he said. 'My guess is, they'll be calling *you.*'

A man followed Erin home from work. It was three in the morning and the streets were empty. The man was careful to keep a distance of three or four blocks between his car and Erin's smoky old Fairlane. He did a good job, because Erin never suspected that she was being tailed.

She parked beneath a streetlight and led Angela across the lot toward the town house. The man parked not far away, turned on the car radio and napped until dawn. He kept watch on the apartment until ten in the morning. When Erin didn't reappear, the man drove away.

This happened two days in a row. On the third morning, Erin came out of the town house carrying a basket of laundry, Angela scampering close behind. Together they got in the Fairlane and went to a laundromat off Oakland Park Boulevard. Again the man followed, parking at a video store directly across the street. Through binoculars he watched Erin loading the washing machines. An hour later, he watched her loading the dryers. After she was done, the man didn't tail her back to the apartment. Instead he hurried on foot across the street to the laundromat. He was thinking: This is the sickest thing I've ever done . . .

The congressman had been adamant.

'Erb,' he'd said, waving the photograph of the stripper, 'I want her.'

'No, you don't,' Erb Crandall said.

'I've never felt like this before.'

'Yes, you have.'

'I want her in all the wondrous ways that a man can want a woman.'

'Give me a fucking break,' said Erb Crandall.

'If you don't help me find her, I'll do it myself.'

'After the election.'

David Dilbeck said, 'I can't wait that long. I'm under a spell, Erb. I am . . . driven.'

'Sorry,' Crandall said, 'I've got my orders.'

They were riding first class on a Delta flight from Miami to Dulles; a one-day quickie. Somebody was giving a bullshit party for Tip O'Neill. Dilbeck paced the aisle, clutching the incriminating photograph to his breast. He simply would not shut up and sit down.

'Did you see the picture? Did you see what she looks like?'

'Very attractive,' Erb Crandall said.

'I want you to find her and offer her a job on my staff.'

'Have some breakfast,' said Crandall. Other passengers were starting to murmur. The next time Dilbeck came within range, Crandall grabbed the Eager Beaver photo and stuffed it inside a flight magazine, which he placed in his briefcase.

Soon Dilbeck tired. He sat down and said, 'Erb, I won't get through the campaign without her. She haunts my dreams.'

'Really. You know who haunts *my* dreams? Malcolm J. Moldowsky.'

'I need to learn everything about her. Everything.'

'We don't even know her name,' Crandall lied.

'Find out, dammit. Find out everything.' Dilbeck's eyes were on fire. 'Erb, she's not like the others.'

'Yeah, I can tell from the picture. For a minute I thought it was Julie Andrews, dancing in the Alps. Except she was naked with some guy's face between her legs.'

The congressman seized Erb Crandall's arm and said, 'God, I am hopelessly possessed.'

You're half right, thought Crandall. The hopeless part. 'Eat your omelet,' he told David Dilbeck.

'After the election, you said?'

'Right.'

'Maybe I can endure it, Erb. Maybe I could get by if I had something of hers. Something to cherish!'

'Keep your voice down,' Crandall said. 'I'll see what I can do.'

The congressman tugged his arm again. 'No, not like the others. No panties or garters or bra cups.'

'What then?'

He couldn't believe it when Dilbeck told him. 'You are deeply warped,' Crandall said.

'Now, what harm could it do? Seriously, Erb.'

So Crandall found himself in a laundromat, surreptitiously scraping the lint from the filter of a dryer. Not just any lint – the lint from the beautiful nude dancer's personal laundry. Crandall wrapped the sheath of pink fuzz in a handkerchief. He saw a customer peeking over a stack of folded linens, and flashed a phony FBI badge that he kept handy for odd occasions.

When Crandall returned to the house, the congressman met him in the foyer. Dilbeck's hair was freshly combed and his cheeks shone. He received the lint gratefully, in cupped hands. 'My God,' he said. 'You did it.' Then he disappeared into the master bathroom for a long time.

Erb Crandall locked the front door, went to the den, and lay down on a sofa. He turned on a game show and got drunk on gin. He closed his eyes and tried to remember when politics was fun.

NINETEEN

Shad called Sgt Al García and said it was time to talk. García picked him up at noon and took the new interstate west, out of the city. Shad wondered where they were headed. He told the detective about Mordecai's plan to shake down the congressman. García wanted to hear about the photograph.

'Who's in it, besides Dilbeck?'

'The guy he's whaling on,' Shad said, 'then me and Erin.'

'Where's the original?'

'It's a color slide. The lawyer's got it, probably in a bank box but I don't know where. Not even the secretary knows.'

García asked about Mordecai. How had Shad met him? What was he like? Shad recounted everything, starting with the cockroach scam. The detective chuckled at the business about the temp eating Shad's yogurt, but otherwise listened seriously. He said: 'So it's your guess the lawyer braced Dilbeck with a copy of the picture.'

'That's the way he laid it out.'

'And he promised you a cut of the payoff?'

'Yeah. Because I was a prime witness.'

'And because he screwed up your roach case.'

'Royal,' said Shad, spitting out the window.

'Now he's missing and you're finally worried. You think maybe the same thing happened to your lawyer that happened to poor Jerry Killian. And you're thinking you might be next.'

Shad said, 'It's not me I'm worried about.'

'Me neither, Cueball. It's your stripper friend.'

'Dancer friend.'

'Right. She's a nice lady.'

Shad blinked straight ahead. 'She got her daughter back. That ups the stakes.'

'I see your point.'

They came to a tangle of converging highways. García bore north on US 27. On both sides was a rolling horizon of water and sawgrass.

'The hell are we going?' Shad asked.

'Beautiful downtown Belle Glade. How about a cigar?'

Shad said sure. Al García was pleased. They both lit up and the car filled with smoke. The detective rolled down the windows.

'Good?' he asked.

'All right,' Shad said.

'Hey, *chico*, you inhaling?'

'Yeah. I like it.'

'Damn,' García said. 'That doesn't burn like hell?'

Shad said he didn't feel a thing. 'I got what they call a high threshold.'

They rode about ten miles working on their cigars, not saying a word. Eventually García asked what it was like to work at a nude dance club.

Shad puffed out a heavy grunt. 'After a while, you don't notice.'

'Come on.'

'Really. I'm to the point where I get excited when they put their clothes *on*. That's what happens after too long.'

García said, 'I know guys would kill for your job.'

'They can have it. Being around naked women all day is bad for your outlook. After a while it's just tits and ass and nothin' special. Like if you worked an assembly line making Ferraris – before long, they're just cars and that's all. You understand?'

'Everything gets boring.'

'Damn right,' Shad said, teething the cigar, 'and when pussy gets boring, it's time for a career move.'

'I know exactly how you feel.' Al García jerked a thumb over one shoulder. 'Guess what I got in the trunk? An Igloo cooler. And guess what's in the cooler? A human head.'

Shad violently expelled the cigar out the window. He wiped his mouth on the sleeve of his camo jacket.

'No joke,' García said. 'Property of one Francisco Goyo, deceased. I can't begin to tell you how much gas I've wasted on the case. The fat prick got dumped in a dozen different zip codes.'

'Why,' Shad asked, 'do you got his head in an Igloo?'

'So it won't stink up the car.'

'That ain't what I mean.'

The detective said that a windsurfer on Key Biscayne had found the gruesome item by accident that morning. 'I gotta drop it by the morgue on the way home. They got a Frigidaire full of Señor Goyo.'

'Goddamn,' Shad said, gravely.

'But I know what you mean about boring. Same old

255

shit, day in day out.' García flicked the ash from his cigar. 'You want to trade jobs?'

'Goddamn,' Shad said again.

García drove directly to the Belle Glade post office. He asked Shad to wait in the car so as not to terrify bystanders. At the desk, García showed his police badge and asked about the box number given by the three mysterious Jamaicans at the Flightpath Motel. The clerk, a handsome woman with thick gray hair, said the box indeed belonged to a Mr John Riley, but that Mr Riley had not picked up his mail in six months. There was an excellent reason.

'He's passed on,' the clerk said.

'I'm very sorry.'

'Then you're in the minority.'

García said, 'Who could tell me about it?'

'Anybody,' the clerk replied. 'Riley was a crew boss at Rojo Farms. He was shortin' his cutters and they all knowed it. One morning he got runned over by a migrant bus.' The clerk paused. 'It was a accident, accordin' to the state patrol.'

'But maybe not,' García said.

'Misself, I lean toward a act of God. Riley was a bad man. Bad things happen to bad men.'

'And this was six months ago?'

'At least. And they still curse his name, the cutters do.'

'Anybody curse it more than others?'

The clerk said, 'I don't follow.'

'Did any of the men have a special reason to hate Riley, besides the money he was stealing?'

The clerk was greatly amused. 'What other reason would they need?' She began sorting the mail, arranging it in neat stacks. Many of the envelopes bore scriggly printing and foreign stamps; Belle Glade was a migrant town. The clerk said, 'Sounds like you're after somebody in particular.'

'Don't laugh,' García said. 'It's three Jamaicans.'

'Oh my.'

'I asked you not to laugh.'

'But his whole crew was Jamaicans.'

'I figured,' García said. 'And they all hated him, right?'

'Worse than a snake.'

Back in the car, García asked Shad if he wanted to ride over to Clewiston and see a sugar mill. Shad said he had no earthly interest.

'It'll help make sense of all this,' García said.

'Save your gas and tell me about it on the way back to Lauderdale.'

'Why the hurry?'

Shad's neck inflated. 'Because there's a goddamn Cuban head in the trunk!'

'Señor Goyo was Panamanian.'

'Jesus!' said Shad.

A marsh rabbit appeared in the middle of the road. Al García weaved around it without braking. 'This congressman,' he said, 'his balls belong to the sugar companies. They need him up in Washington, to keep things right. So when dorky little Killian threatens a blackmail, the sugar people's people get nervous. You with me?'

Shad pointed ahead and said, 'Speed trap.'

García said, 'For Christ's sake, I'm a cop. Remember?' He blinked his dashboard light at the state trooper as they flew by. 'You aren't even listening,' he said to Shad.

'Yeah, I am. Sugar money.'

'Killian makes his demand, which is so weird it probably freaks out Dilbeck's people. Fix a custody case? they're thinking. Lean on a judge? We're dealing with a crackpot, they're thinking. So somebody – not Dilbeck, but somebody close – makes a phone call.'

'And so long, crackpot.'

'Right. Three cane cutters show up and snatch Killian, probably out of his apartment.'

'How do you know they're cane cutters?'

'Scars, man. They've got the scars on their legs. Cutters are always whacking themselves by accident with those damn machetes; even the good ones do it. Anyway, they haul Killian to a cheap motel and – as a sick joke – register in the name of a dead boss man. The motel is where they drown him. Then they put him on ice—'

'Don't tell me,' Shad said. 'Another fucking Igloo.'

'Not likely,' said García, steering with one hand, waving the dead cigar stub with the other. 'Anyway, they ice him down and drive straight to Missoula, Montana. Or maybe they use the Rojo corporate jet, who knows—'

Shad said, 'Why Montana?'

'That's where Killian vacations. See, it was set up to look like a fishing accident.'

Finally Shad cracked a smile. His colossal white dome bobbed as García heard him swallow a laugh.

'What is it?'

'Man,' Shad said, 'three Jamaicans cruising through Montana.'

'Yeah, I know.'

'Holy Christ. Is that a riot? Jamaican cowpokes.'

'They had nerve,' Al García said. 'Whoever it was.'

'You'll never get 'em.'

'You're right.'

'Never in a million years.'

'I'm quite sure,' García said, 'they're already back in Kingston. Or dead.'

The temperature light on the dashboard flashed red, so he steered the Caprice to the shoulder of the road. He opened the hood and checked the hose fittings, which seemed tight. There was no sign of a leak from the radiator. 'Wires,' the detective muttered, and slammed the hood.

Shad was gone from the car. Al García found him forty yards away, three rows deep in a field of tall cane.

'So this is it,' Shad said. A fat blue horsefly gorged on his gleaming scalp. The fly was so big it looked like a tattoo.

García snapped off a stalk of cane and sniffed it. 'What a deal these bastards get. All the water they want for practically nothing. Imported slave labor for the harvest. Then they get to sell the crop at jacked-up prices, courtesy of the US Congress. And when they're all done, they're allowed to dump the stink straight into the Everglades.'

Shad was impressed. 'Land of opportunity,' he said, probing the black muck with the tow of his boot.

'Millions and millions of dollars,' García said. 'Killian had no idea what he was dealing with. Same goes for your ace attorney.'

They got back in the car. Shad declined the offer of

another cigar. The horsefly remained attached to his head. García reached over and brushed it away.

Five miles later, Shad said, 'So where's your jurisdiction on this deal? I don't see a Miami connection.'

The detective smiled ruefully. 'Dilbeck's congressional district is in Dade County. That's the best I can do.'

'Pitiful,' Shad remarked.

'Nobody else is much interested. I can't just let a homicide slide.'

'Other words, you're doing this off the clock.'

'That's why I need your help,' García said.

'Think they'll come after Erin?'

'I think they'll come after everyone in that photograph, if necessary. I think they won't even hesitate.'

Shad turned to look out the window. They were out of farm country now. The Everglades shimmered west to the horizon. 'She's got her little girl back.'

'So you said.'

'I guess that don't count.'

'Not with these people.' García stopped at a fishing camp to buy another bag of ice for Francisco Goyo's severed head. Shad frowned when he heard the trunk pop open, the cubes pouring out of the plastic. He hoped García wouldn't try to show him the damn thing. Some cops got off on shit like that.

When they were back on the road, Shad told the detective that he'd done some state time.

'Oh, I know. Manslaughter.'

'Manslaughter *two*,' Shad said.

'That was the plea. The crime was manslaughter.' García saw that the temperature light had come on again. He thumped the dashboard with a fist, and the light went out. 'God bless General Motors,' he said.

Shad asked if he knew about the agg assaults, too. García said sure.

'My boss, Mr Orly, he'd hit the fucking roof,' Shad said. 'Hiring a felon and all. He could lose his license.'

García kept his eyes on the road. 'Don't worry about your boss,' he said. 'I needed to know. He doesn't.'

'I appreciate that.'

'Here's another thing: I'd prefer not to be informed if you've got a piece, OK? Because if I see it, then I gotta do something. Like arrest your ass, OK? That's the law, felons can't carry a gun. So don't feel obliged to take it out and play, because then we got a problem.'

Shad said, 'I'm with you. Let's talk about Erin.'

'Yeah.' The detective drummed his fingers on the steering wheel. 'We gotta figure something out.'

'Shouldn't be hard,' said Shad. 'With my good looks and your brains.'

Malcolm J. Moldowsky prowled the penthouse restlessly. The ocean view did not soothe him, nor did the fine cognac. He was a resentful man, deeply resentful that a person of his stature should be forced to worry.

Moldy was at the top of his game: insidiously powerful, obscenely wealthy and largely untouchable. Up until now. Lately his hard-earned arrogance had lost some of its starch. He was feeling vulnerable, even shaky. Others were to blame. Free-floating incompetence threatened to destroy an artifice that Moldowsky had spent years constructing. He knew how his hero, John Mitchell, must've felt when those idiots bungled a simple burglary. A life's work destroyed by unspeakable stupidities.

In protecting David Dilbeck's career, Moldowsky had breached a realm far beyond the mere peddling of influence. Committing illegal acts was nothing new. It was the nature of the recent felonies that concerned Moldy: a superb white-collar criminal, he'd been forced out of his element. Diverting election funds was a breeze. Unlawfully compensating an elected official was child's play. Falsifying campaign finance reports was a routine chore.

But this! Goddamn that Dilbeck.

For the first time in many years, Moldowsky was second-guessing himself. He hated the feeling because he hated all forms of introspection. In Moldy's line of work, a man's worst enemy was a functioning conscience. He poured another cognac and resumed his idle pacing through the apartment. Passing a mirror, Moldowsky saw that he'd skipped a belt loop in the back of his pants. Also, he had misbuttoned the cuff of his left sleeve. God, was he rattled!

It was the sudden death of the divorce judge that did it. The judge who couldn't be persuaded to help a congressman and fix a lousy custody case. The judge who didn't need a favor because he was already coasting on his merry way to the federal bench.

Jerry Killian was killed because the judge wouldn't budge. Moldowsky had seen no other solution; eliminating the blackmailer removed the threat to David Dilbeck. It was simple, logical, expedient – but had it really been necessary? Moldowsky was annoyed at himself for fretting about it. The Killian decision made perfect sense at the time. Who could've predicted that the judge would obligingly croak?

Moldy was a man who appreciated cruel irony. Normally he would've been amused by the seedy circumstances under which the pious little shit had expired – his brain detonating in a sea of bare breasts. The TV crews swarming the Flesh Farm had left little to the imagination.

Yet the only thing that had entered Moldowsky's mind was an unfamiliar stab of doubt: Maybe I acted too precipitously. If I'd stalled Killian, jerked him around for a couple weeks, then the judge would've solved both our problems by dying. *Grant* v. *Grant* automatically would've been reassigned, and Killian would've backed away from David Dilbeck.

Oh well, Moldy thought. What's done is done. The three Jamaican cane cutters have gone home. Next month there would be a terrible truck accident near Montego Bay; no survivors. And the flight logs for the Rojos' *Gulfstream II* would show a trip to Aspen, not Missoula. Push came to shove, the FAA would back him up with tower tapes. The daughter of a deputy assistant administrator owed her job to Malcolm J. Moldowsky . . .

The phone beeped twice and Moldy picked it up. He stood at the broad window and gazed across the Atlantic. Under cloudy skies, the water was foamy-gray and unalluring. Just over the horizon, in Nassau, was the man on the other end of the phone call. He was a banker who'd been educated in London, but whose speech had retained its soothing island cadence. He told Moldowsky that the wire transfer had been completed.

'What shall we do with the balance?'

'It's entirely up to you,' Moldowsky said.

'We can put it in trust,' the banker suggested.

'Hell, you can keep it, for all I care. Buy yourself a new Hatteras.'

The banker chuckled nervously. 'Certainly, Mr Mordecai left some instructions.'

'As a matter of fact, he didn't.'

'But, sir, the account is in excess of eighty thousand dollars. I'm sure he expects the money to be properly invested.' The banker paused. 'Is there a problem I should know about?'

'Not that you should know about, no. A trust is fine, Mr Cartwright.'

'Unless he needs frequent access.'

'No,' Moldy said. 'That's one thing he definitely won't need.'

He thanked Cartwright and hung up. Immediately the phone rang again. It was the lobby – Erb Crandall was coming up for a visit. Moldowsky took out another glass, just in case the bagman was in a mood to unwind. He wasn't. He said he was ready to quit David Dilbeck's campaign.

Moldy said, 'Now slow down, Erb.'

Crandall stood rigid, arms folded. 'I've been telling you he's a time bomb. Well, the fuse is finally lit.'

Moldowsky was glad he'd had the foresight to start drinking early. 'What's he done?' he asked.

Crandall told him about the clandestine lint mission to the laundromat.

'Lord,' Moldy said. 'That *is* bad.'

'It's only the beginning, Malcolm. He wants more.'

'More what?'

'He's crazy for this stripper. The one in the picture.'

Moldowsky squinted. 'So he wants more lint?'

'Not just lint.'

He described the congressman's current fantasy. Malcolm Moldowsky rocked on his heels, the brandy boiling up in his throat.

'He's off the deep end,' Moldy said hoarsely. 'Completely insane.'

'Thank you, Dr Freud.' Erb Crandall went to the bar and got an ice-cold can of ginger ale, which he rolled back and forth across his throbbing forehead. He slumped in an armchair, his back to the ocean. 'What now Malcolm?'

'The girl,' Moldowsky said. 'Obviously.'

Urbana Sprawl was right about the money. Erin made an extra ninety bucks on her first night of table dancing. Shad stayed close, and nobody touched her. Still, she hated it. The tables at the club were so small that the dancers couldn't move their feet without kicking the customer's drink in his lap. The performance itself wasn't dancing so much as wiggling in place, which was fine for the girls with large breasts – gravity did all the work. But Erin's strong suit was choreography, and there simply was no room to show off. On the tables she was just another stripper, bouncing up and down for tips.

Another drawback was the music. The dancer on the main stage got to pick the songs, which was only fair, but it meant that the table dancers never knew what was coming next. Most of Kevin's play list was disco, techno, fusion, dance-club, hip-hop and rap, all of which Erin detested. There was no heart to any of it, and pretending otherwise was an ordeal. She smiled so intractably that her facial muscles soon became numb; toward the end of the shift, she looked in the mirrored walls and saw a rictus grin, earnest but unsexy. The tabletop customers never noticed, since their eyes were riveted on her crotch.

On the second night, Erin made two hundred and ten dollars on the tables; the third night, one-eighty-five. On the fourth night, the homicide detective showed up. He and Shad sat down and began to talk. Erin watched curiously from table five, where she was dancing against her better judgment to an extremely long number by Paula Abdul – or, as Mr Orly called her, Kareem Abdul Paula. Erin was eager to finish the dance so she could find out why Al García had come to the club. As the song thumped to an end, the customer reached up and folded a bill into Erin's garter. She thanked him as he helped her step off the table. While reattaching her G-string, Erin saw that the man had given her a hundred-dollar bill. She thanked him again, this time with the standard hug and peck reserved for overly generous customers.

'How about another one?' the man said. He was a handsome young Latin, doing his smoothest Jimmy Smits. His clothes were expensive and his hair was raked back and there were knobs of gold on both hands. He wasn't yet drunk enough to present a problem, so Erin said sure and got back on the table. Shad and García were still hunched in conversation at the bar – she hoped they'd be there for a while. A smart dancer didn't walk away from a heavy tipper, not when she still owed her lawyer nine grand.

Erin did five table dances for the young Latin, and

he gave her a hundred each time. She was excited about the money, but also suspicious. The guy wanted something else. Had to.

Eventually it came her turn to dance on the main stage. Kevin put on a cut by the Black Crowes, which woke up the whole joint. The song was fast and nasty, and Erin loved it – she kicked and whirled and double-clutched, working out lots of unspent energy. At the bar, Shad sat alone; Al García was on the pay phone near the front door, with his back to the stage. Oblivious, Erin thought, thoroughly unmoved by my spirited performance. It was funny.

The young Latin customer came to the footlights and waved Erin over. He slipped two hundred dollars in her garter. When Erin leaned down to thank him, he put a hand on her shoulder and whispered something.

Shad tensed, watching Erin's expression. He was ready to move fast, if the creep made a grab. Erin seemed puzzled, but not upset, by the young man's words. When she moved back to the middle of the stage, her smile looked solid and her eyes were calm. She even took a languid, Stevie Nicks-style twirl in front of the wind machine. Shad held steady.

After the set, Erin returned to the young Latin's table. Shad didn't see her stand up for another dance. Before long, the Latin man rose and left the club. Erin appeared at the bar and said: 'I would like a martini.'

Shad asked what was wrong.

'Nothing,' Erin replied. 'Show business.'

'Quite a fan there.' It was Al García. He sat down on the other side of Erin. 'You know who that was?'

'Said his name was Chris.'

'Christopher Rojo,' the detective said. 'Of the sugar Rojos.'

Erin said, 'That would explain all the money. But it doesn't explain this.' She spun on the stool, and swung her right leg across Shad's lap.

'Where's your shoe?' he asked.

'Young Christopher just purchased it,' Erin said, 'for one thousand dollars.'

The bouncer's vast brow crinkled in astonishment. Erin herself was in a mild daze. The money was a godsend, but it wasn't the career of her dreams – selling used footwear to wealthy perverts.

'A fucking shoe,' Shad muttered. 'What for?'

Erin covered her face. 'I don't want to think about it.'

'Love,' said Al García. 'Ain't it grand?'

TWENTY

Merkin cupped the receiver and asked Picatta if they should accept a collect call from Darrell Grant.

Picatta said, loudly, 'I don't know a Darrell Grant. How about you?'

'Never heard of him.'

'Where's he calling from?'

'The Martin County jail,' Merkin said. He grinned and held the phone away from his ear. Darrell could be heard, pleading with the long-distance operator to put him through.

Picatta leaned close to the receiver and boomed: 'The only Darrell Grant I know is a lying cocksucker who's getting his probation yanked the second he's back in Broward County!'

Merkin said, 'Is that the same misfortunate Darrell Grant that's about to lose custody of his kid, due to his felony records suddenly showing up on the courthouse computer after being lost all those years?'

'The damnedest thing,' said Picatta, 'after all those years. That new judge was real surprised, is what I heard.'

On the other end, Darrell Grant fell silent. The long-distance operator, an angel of patience, again asked if Detective Merkin would accept the call.

'No, ma'am,' he said. 'You tell Mr Grant if he needs to chat, he should phone up Mr Thomas Tinker, that so-called big-time heroin dealer he told us about. The switchboard at the graveyard will patch you right through. Goodbye now.'

Merkin hung up. The operator clicked off. Darrell Grant glumly handed the telephone to the patrolman, who put it back on the jailhouse wall.

'They're playin' a joke,' Darrell Grant said.

'Didn't sound like a joke.' The patrolman pulled Darrell's arms behind him and snapped on the handcuffs.

'You're makin' a big-time mistake. I work for those boys.'

'Really? They told you to come all the way up here and steal Miss Brillstein's wheelchair?'

The cop marched Darrell Grant to the holding cell. He said someone from the Public Defender's Office would stop by later to discuss a plea.

Darrell Grant found an empty place on a steel cot, between two sleeping drunks. 'You let me know when Merkin calls back,' he told the patrolman.

'In your dreams.'

'I work for the goddamn Broward County Sheriff!'

'Maybe once upon a time,' the cop said, disappearing.

Darrell Grant rocked miserably on the cot, grinding his molars, picking his cuticles, tapping his feet. Was Merkin bluffing, or had they really cut him loose? Worse, had they given his rap sheet to Erin's lawyer? Darrell couldn't believe the detectives could be such bastards. He had to get back to Lauderdale and see what's what. Meanwhile, he needed something to clear the brain and settle the nerves. He asked the other prisoners where he could score some crack. They were not particularly helpful.

A burly redhead with twin cobra tattoos stepped forward. 'Hey, beach boy. True you stole a wheelchair off a cripple?'

'I didn't know she was a cripple,' Darrell said. 'I thought she was just old.'

The Palm Lake Rest Home – he'd cased it pretty carefully, considering he was still foggy from when the hooker had clobbered him . . .

Noon sharp. There's the cute Filipino nurse wheeling Miss Elaine Brillstein down the driveway toward the van. Nurse chatting as she pushes Miss Brillstein, who squints into the sunlight and clutches a fuzzy white sweater across her lap. '*Scuze me, ladies.* Who's that? says Miss Brillstein, squinting harder. *Excuse me, y'all need a hand?* Well, all right, says Miss Brillstein, thank you very much. *I'll get the door.* Hold my sweater, please. *Here, let me help with that.* My, what a nice young man.

Soon as Miss Brillstein's up in the van – the nurse half in, half out, wrestling with the old lady's seat belt – Darrell Grant hijacks the wheelchair and off he runs. Two blocks later, the brake switch drops a bolt and Darrell goes ass-over-teakettle in the middle of a school zone. There's a black-and-white parked on the median, clocking speeders. Darrell Grant can't fucking believe his lousy luck.

From the redheaded prisoner with the snakes on his arms: 'The cop said the old lady had polio.'

Darrell Grant's eyes felt raw and swollen. He

experienced an urge to sleep. 'I thought polio was extinct,' he said.

The redhead moved closer. 'My aunt's got polio.'

'Yeah?' said Darrell. 'Is her name Brillstein?'

'No, it ain't.'

'Then mind your own goddamn business.' Without his drugs, Darrell often got pissed at the whole universe.

The redhead said, 'I bet you'd look good in a wheelchair.'

'Not as good as you,' said Darrell Grant, 'with a two-foot donkey schlong up your ass.'

Later, when he awoke in the county hospital and saw that they hadn't bothered to cuff him to the gurney, Darrell Grant congratulated himself for such a bold and brilliant plan.

In South Florida, the disappearance of a lawyer was seldom front-page news. It happened often enough, usually coinciding with the theft of a client's money. The man from the Florida Bar used the term 'misappropriation' when he described the scenario to Beverly.

'How much?' the secretary asked.

'Approximately eighty-five thousand dollars.'

'No way,' she said. 'I can't believe it.'

'Then what do you think happened? Where is he?'

'Maybe he was kidnapped.' Beverly told him that burglars had gone through Mordecai's office one night – even the Rolodex had been stolen! The man from the Florida Bar asked if she'd called the police. Beverly admitted that she hadn't.

'Because you were afraid,' the man said, 'that the clues would point toward Mordecai himself.'

'I kept hoping he'd show up.'

The man from the Florida Bar was sympathetic, but firm. 'The trust account was emptied on his direct instructions. The assets were transferred out of the country three days ago.'

'Yes,' she said glumly. 'The bank called.'

The man from the Florida Bar sat before an open briefcase at Mordecai's desk. The law office was closed – temporarily, according to a note on the front door. Beverly wasn't optimistic. She let the answering service take all the angry calls.

The man from the Bar asked, 'Do you know the number-one cause of disbarment in Florida?'

'Moral turpitude?'

'Good guess, but no. Misuse of client trust funds. Some lawyers simply cannot resist.'

Beverly was in the high-backed chair where Mordecai's clients normally sat. She tolerated the arrangement only because she was curious about what the Bar might know of her boss's whereabouts.

The man said, 'Did he have many elderly clients?'

'Not enough,' Beverly said. 'Why?'

'It's part of the pattern. Older clients tend to be conservative with their money. They put it somewhere and let it sit. Years and years might go by.'

Beverly said, 'Like in their lawyer's trust account.'

The man from the Florida Bar nodded. 'Meanwhile the balance keeps growing. Some lawyers dip in, call it borrowing. Some even go through the motions of trying to pay it back. Others just flat out grab it all.'

Beverly didn't particularly like Mordecai, and had no illusions about his sterling character. But she'd never pegged him as the sort to skip town with clients' money.

He seemed more of a small-time chiseler and cutter of corners. Embezzlement seemed too ambitious for Mordecai.

The man from the Florida Bar said, 'Who knows what triggers the impulse. A financial setback, gambling problems, a secret love affair. Which brings us to the obvious question—'

'We were *not* involved,' Beverly cut in. 'Give me a little credit, please.'

'Looks aren't everything. Even a physically . . .' – the man groped for the right word – '*daunting* fellow can have his charms.'

'Not Mordecai,' Beverly said. 'Believe me.'

'Tell me: How did he feel about his cousin?'

The secretary acted confused. 'Which cousin – Joyce?'

'Yes. We believe they're together. Did he ever discuss an attachment?'

'Joyce and Mordecai!' It was so twisted that Beverly almost hoped it was true. Joyce was an avaricious bitch, always angling for the big score. Maybe she'd romanced Mordecai into the swindle. No man was immune to seduction, but Mordecai (who hadn't dated in years) was exceptionally vulnerable. Beverly imagined the two cousins entwined, and it made her shiver.

The man from the Florida Bar said: 'Joyce's fiancé doesn't think much of the theory but, I must tell you, stranger things have happened.'

'Maybe it wasn't a love affair,' Beverly said. 'Maybe it was a straight business deal.'

The man from the Bar folded his hands across his chest. 'What would he need her for? Mordecai alone had access to the trust account. He didn't require an accomplice.'

'No, I suppose not.'

'In many of these cases, these sudden disappearances, the lawyer brings a woman along on the adventure. Frequently, it's his own secretary.'

'Well, I'm still here,' Beverly said sourly. 'And he owes me two weeks' pay.'

'Could be worse. You could be one of those clients.'

'Is that who called you? Was it a client?' The investigator's arrival at the law office had surprised Beverly. The Florida Bar was not renowned for swift and aggressive pursuit of errant members.

The man said, 'We received a tip. That's all I can say.' He gave her a business card with an 800 number in Orlando. 'If you should hear from him, please encourage him to return swiftly and make restitution. The longer he's gone, the worse it will be.'

Beverly felt more abandoned than ever. 'What do I tell everyone about the office being closed? What should I put on the door?'

The man from the Florida Bar shut his briefcase and crisply snapped the brass locks. 'We recommend "Death in the family." Most clients won't press the issue.'

They moved from the lounge to Orly's office: Orly, Al García, Shad, and Erin. Angela was in the dressing room with one of the fully clothed Moniques.

García had Orly in a sweat. 'I want to know more about the phone calls.'

'Me, too,' said Erin.

'Some guy, I don't know.' Orly was slurping a Dr
Pepper. 'He's asking about a certain customer—'

'Jerry Killian.'

'Yeah, so big deal. There was a fight on stage and
this Killian is in the audience, like I give two shits. Man
calls and I tell him what he wants—'

'How'd you know Killian's name?'

'Credit card slips,' Orly said. 'Anyway, this guy who
calls, he says to keep him posted if the customer shows
up again.'

Al García said, 'Why'd you agree?'

'Because I got a license to consider, and this guy
says he can give me problems. Says he works for a
congressman. So . . . a few nights later, Killian shows
up again. This time he's outside, hanging around Erin's
car. You remember?'

Shad and Erin nodded together.

'See,' Orly continued, 'I can't have customers hassling
my dancers. The guy on the phone says he'll make sure
it doesn't happen again. That's it. End of story. I don't
hear from him anymore, until today.'

García had a notebook in his hand, but he wasn't
writing much. 'Why won't you tell me the man's name?'

'Because you don't understand. The nature of my
business, I don't need any grief. I got a liquor license to
protect.'

Erin told Orly that Jerry Killian had been murdered.

'Shit,' Orly said, sucking air. He looked at García.
'Is that why you're here?'

'What a sharpie you are. Now give me the damn
name.'

Orly looked cornered. 'Maybe I should check with
my lawyer. Maybe you should come back tomorrow.'

García said, 'If I have to come back tomorrow, I'm bringing beverage agents. You follow? We'll board the place up, *chico*.'

'Screw you.' Orly was feeling worn out and reckless.

Shad stirred. 'Mr Orly, you better listen. This is no bullshit.'

Al García tapped a ballpoint pen on his knee. 'The deal is, Erin's life is in danger. I've advised her to get out of town, but there's a complication.'

The new judge had forbidden Erin from taking Angela out of Florida. 'As long as I'm stuck here, I might as well work,' she said, 'considering I'm broke.'

Orly's puzzlement deepened. 'Who'd want to kill *you*? I mean, besides your ex.'

Someone knocked sharply on the door. Before Orly could respond, Sabrina burst in. She wore a thin sleeveless T-shirt and pink bikini bottoms. She was splattered with yellowy goop that Erin despondently recognized as creamed corn. Random kernels clotted Sabrina's platinum wig, which she clutched in one fist.

'I can't do this!' she cried.

'Later,' Orly said. 'We got a meeting here.'

'But it got up my nose—'

'Later, I said.'

The dancer ran out. A brief silence followed. Finally Orly said, 'Erin's the best of the bunch.'

'So you wouldn't want anything to happen to her,' García said.

'No, I sure wouldn't.'

Erin said she was deeply touched. Orly scratched at a scab on his arm. 'Plus your little girl. That's a factor.'

'You're all heart,' the detective said.

'The guy's name is Moldowsky. And don't ask me to spell it. Melvin or some damn thing.'

García said, 'Excellent. What did he want today?'

Orly jerked a thumb toward Erin. 'He asked about her. What kind of person she is. Has she got a drug problem. Is there a boyfriend.'

Erin felt a bolt of fear. She'd never heard of this person.

'Another thing,' said Orly. 'He knows about the kid. Knows there's a problem with your ex-husband. The guy, he knows lots.'

'He mentioned Angie?' Erin's voice cracked. She sat forward, balling her fists. 'What did you say?'

'Not a damn thing,' he said. 'I swear, I told him zippo.' Erin's glare was scalding. Orly angrily jabbed a finger in the air. 'You tell her, Shad. Tell her how I handled it.'

Shad backed up Orly's version. 'I was there when the asshole called. Mr Orly didn't give him shit.'

'OK,' Erin said, leaning back. 'I'm sorry.'

'He's a heavy hitter,' said Orly. 'He dropped a few names to get my attention. Otherwise I'd say fuck off.' His piggy eyes narrowed on García. 'I lose my license and there's hell to pay. Bottom line, there's some serious people I answer to.'

'Don't worry, Mr Orly. You cooperate and every-thing'll turn out just beautiful.'

'Cooperate?' Orly sprayed the word. 'Sweet Christ Almighty, what more you want? I gave up the goddamn name.'

'Yeah, you did,' García said. 'If only there was a phone number to go with it.'

Orly adopted the impatient pose of a man with better

things to do. 'Yeah, Moldowsky left a number. I got it here somewheres.' He pawed halfheartedly at the clutter on his desk.

The detective said, 'Excellent. I want you to call him.'

Orly frowned. 'What the hell for? I'm not callin' nobody.'

'Come on,' said Al García. 'Let's find that number.'

Shad winked at Erin, as if to say: This part might be fun.

García stayed at the club until closing time. He waited in the parking lot until Erin came out with Angie. The detective tried to make friends, but the little girl was tired and cranky. She climbed in the backseat of the Fairlane and lay down. García said it was a lousy arrangement, letting Angie stay at the club.

Erin said, 'Sorry you disapprove.' She was in no mood for a male lecture. 'The other girls are terrific with her. And, no, she's not allowed in the dance lounge to see what her bimbo mom does for a living.'

'Easy now,' García said. 'I'm not talking about the atmosphere, I'm talking about the child's safety.'

He held the door while Erin got in the car. She turned the key and revved the engine noisily. 'I want her near me at all times,' she said, 'as long as Darrell's out there.'

From the backseat: 'Momma, can we go home now?'

García lowered his voice to a whisper. 'Think about it. If someone's after you, where's the first place they're gonna come? Right here. Say the shit hits the fan – you want that little girl asleep in the dressing room?'

'Fine,' Erin said. 'Then you find me a kindergarten that's open at three in the morning.' She slipped the car in gear. 'Besides, what's there to worry about? We got you and Shad to protect us.'

Erin drove away fast, burning rubber on the corner. Very childish, she thought, but wonderful therapy. She gunned it all the way home.

When Al García arrived at the town house, twenty minutes later, Erin and Angela were still sitting in the Fairlane. Erin's face was taut as she stared at the front of the apartment. When the detective approached the car, he saw a small pistol on the dash. In the backseat, Angela was as still as a porcelain doll.

García asked Erin to put the gun away. She pointed at the second-story window and said, 'The bedroom light's on.'

'You didn't leave it that way?'

'No lights,' Erin said. She'd shut off everything before leaving for work. It was an old habit; the electric bills were murder.

They watched the window for signs of a shadow. Nothing moved behind the half-drawn drapes.

'Give me the key,' García said.

'It's probably open.'

'And the gun, please.'

Erin gave him the keys and the .32. 'The safety's on,' she said.

'Thanks. If things break loose, lean on the horn.'

The front door was locked. The detective opened it softly and went inside. For several interminable moments, nothing happened; it was as if Al García had been swallowed up in the darkness. Erin scanned the windows and braced for the sound of a muffled gunshot, but all she heard was Angela's gentle breathing in the backseat. Eventually the other windows lit up, one by one, as García moved from room to room. When he reappeared at the front door, he waved for Erin to come in.

The place looked untouched. The detective accompanied her and Angela through the kitchen, the living room, up the stairs to the bedrooms. Nothing seemed to be missing.

So I made a mistake, Erin thought. I left the damn light on.

'This is all your stuff?' García asked.

'Angie and I travel light.' It felt strange to have the detective in her bedroom. Erin caught him smiling at the rock posters on the wall.

She said, 'I'm saving for a Van Gogh.'

'No, I like it.'

Angela ran down the hall and returned with a crayon drawing. 'I drew this myself,' she said, thrusting it at García.

'What a pretty dog.'

'No, that's a wolf. Aunt Rita's.' Angela traced the outline with a finger. 'See the bushy tail? And here's the baby wolves under the tree.'

'Right,' said the detective. 'Wolves.'

Erin took the drawing from his hands. She said, 'That's Darrell's side of the family. I need some aspirin.'

The bathroom was the last place she expected to find signs of an intruder. At first she didn't notice. She got a bottle of Advils from the medicine chest and swallowed three. Standing at the sink, looking in the mirror, Erin sensed something was out of place. She turned and saw what it was.

'God,' she said. A prickle went down the back of her neck.

García walked in. Erin told him to look at the shower curtain, which was pulled open along the length of the bathtub.

'You didn't leave it that way?'

'Never,' Erin said.

Angie squeezed between the grown-ups' legs and said: 'Because of mildew.'

'That's right,' said her mother. 'It mildews if you leave it bunched up that way.'

García smiled. 'Every day I learn something new.'

Erin gave Angie a glass of chocolate milk and put her to bed. Then she and the detective went through the medicine chest, the cabinets, the vanity. They found nothing missing or even disturbed, yet Erin was sure that someone had been there.

Inside her house.

Not Darrell Grant, either. He wouldn't have come and gone without leaving tracks. His ego couldn't abide an anonymous entry. No, Darrell would've mangled something intimate and left it on display.

Erin sat on the edge of the tub and fingered the shower curtain, as if it held the clue.

'Weird,' García said. 'Not your average burglar.'

'I can't afford to pack up and move again. I just can't.'

García leaned against the bathroom sink. He was dying for a cigar. 'I wonder what he wanted,' he said.

Erin said she was too tired to keep looking.

'One more try,' the detective said. 'I got an idea that might help. Tell me everything you do to get ready for work.'

'Please,' said Erin.

'I'm serious. Everybody's got a routine when they get up in the morning. Tell me yours.'

'I'd say the high point is flossing my teeth.'

'Whatever. Walk me through it.'

Erin agreed, out of pure exhaustion. 'Well, first I shower, do my hair, shave my legs. Then I touch up my nails . . . Wait a second.' She was looking at the window sill where she kept her bath articles.

'God, this is sick. Now I know what's missing.' She stood up, shaking. 'Angela can't stay here,' she said, 'not another single night!'

The detective put an arm around her. 'Tell me what they took.'

'You won't believe it,' Erin whispered. '*I* don't believe it.'

TWENTY-ONE

The congressman lay flat on the bed. He wore a black cowboy hat, a white towel around his waist and a pair of green lizardskin boots. The surgical scar on his breastbone pulsed like a worm in the ultraviolet light.

Erb Crandall said: 'What've you done here?'

'Created a mood.' David Dilbeck opened his eyes. 'Did you get what I wanted?'

'Yeah, I got it. Where's the wife?'

'Ethiopia, courtesy of UNICEF. Then Paris and probably Milan. Do you like the black lights?'

'Brings back memories.'

'Pierre found them at a head shop in the Grove. Let me see what you've got, Erb.'

Crandall stepped tentatively through the purple glow. He said. 'Geez, look at you.'

Using handkerchiefs, the congressman had tied one arm and both feet to the bedposts. Above the boots, his pale shins gleamed, as if shellacked.

'Vaseline,' Dilbeck explained. 'First I warmed it in the microwave – it's best to use the sauce setting.' Erb Crandall's disgusted expression prompted Dilbeck to add: 'This is what happens when you won't let me go out and play.'

'David,' Crandall said, 'tell me you've been drinking.'

'Not a drop, my friend.'

So he was insane, Crandall thought; downhill from downhill. He wondered what the chairman of the Florida Democratic Party would say if he could see the senior congressman at this moment.

Dilbeck thrust out his free arm. 'Come on. I've been waiting all night.'

'Crandall dropped it – the thing he had stolen from the stripper's apartment – in Dilbeck's open palm. The congressman squirmed on the bed as he examined the illicit treasure; a pink disposable razor.

'Now, this is the genuine article?'

'From her very bathroom,' Crandall said, listlessly.

Dilbeck twirled it between his fingers. With an edge of excitement, he said. 'I bet she used it this morning.'

'I wouldn't know.'

'I can see the little hairs!'

'Be careful, Davey.' With any luck, the dumb shit would slice his own wrists.

Dilbeck's chest rose and fell heavily. 'Erb, do you like Garth Brooks?'

'Is that who you're supposed to be?'

Dilbeck smiled dreamily. 'My boots are *full* of Vaseline.'

Well, thought Crandall, enough's enough. He took one of the burglar tools from his pocket – a small screwdriver – and put the blade to Dilbeck's neck. The congressman seemed surprised, but not particularly afraid.

Crandall pressed firmly and said, 'I'd be doing us both a tremendous favor.'

'Erb, please. This is harmless sport.'

'You're a sick puppy.'

Dilbeck said, 'Stop that right now.'

'This isn't why I went into politics, David – to pimp and steal for a perverted old fuck like you. Believe it or not, I once had ideals.'

Crandall was romanticizing; he was not a man of ideals so much as a man of instinct. He had been drawn to politics by the sweet scent of opportunity. The bitter backlash from Watergate had guaranteed a landslide for the Democrats, so that's when Crandall invested his loyalty. The choice was not between good and evil, but between winning and losing. Occasionally, Erb Crandall was compelled to question the wisdom of his allegiance, but never had it been so tested as it was now.

'Know what?' he said to the prone and bound congressman. 'Even that jizzbag Nixon wouldn't have pulled something like this.'

'Maybe he'd have been a better President if he had.' Dilbeck arched his silvery eyebrows. 'Ever think of that?'

Dispiritedly, Crandall put the screwdriver away.

'That's a good boy,' David Dilbeck said.

'Moldy's coming in an hour. If I killed you, there wouldn't be time to clean up the mess.'

Dilbeck studied the plastic razor from all angles, as if it were a rare gem. 'What's her name?'

'Erin,' Crandall said.

'That's beautiful. Irish, obviously. Erin what?'

'Never mind.'

'Come on, Erb. I won't try to find her, I promise.'

Crandall walked to the door. 'I need a drink. By the way, you look absolutely fucking ridiculous.'

The congressman paid no attention. 'Erb, one more small favor.'

'Let me guess. You want me to tie your other arm to the bed.'

Dilbeck cackled. 'You better not!'

'What then?'

He wiggled the pink razor in the air. 'Shave me, Erb. Shave me all over.'

Crandall glared loathsomely as he stalked from the room.

David Lane Dilbeck was the only son of Chuck 'The Straw' Dilbeck, once the foremost pumper of septic tanks in Dade, Broward and Monroe counties. In the early boom days of South Florida, before sewers were available, nearly every family relied on a septic tank buried in the backyard. The massively squat cylinders were vital components of the average household, and a frequent source of whispered anxiety. A septic-tank backup was the secret nightmare of every rural husband, as dreaded as a hurricane or a heart attack. Cleaning clogs was a vile business, and only a few hardy entrepreneurs had the will to compete.

The Dilbeck name was widely known in the solid-waste industry, and its prominence endured long after most South Florida septic tanks had rusted out. Young David never spent a day pumping sewage (he insisted it gave him a rash), but early on he recognized the value of having a notable father. In 1956, at the age of twenty-four, he boldly announced his candidacy for the Hialeah city council. Many of the town's citizens were lifelong customers of Chuck Dilbeck, and were glad to support his son's ambitions. Speedy response was critical in a septic-tank crisis, so it was important to stay on The

Straw's good side. Hundreds of local septic-tank owners enthusiastically volunteered to help in young David's first political campaign, which he won handily.

Even by Florida standards, Hialeah was – and remains – egregiously corrupt. For council members, the easiest graft was the fixing of zoning cases in exchange for cash, real estate and other valuables. David Dilbeck was fortunate to be in Hialeah during the salad years, when there was still plenty of land to be carved up and paved. He spent four fruitful terms listening, learning and successfully avoiding indictment. He excelled at negotiating bribes, and carried the skill with him when he went to Tallahassee as a junior member of the state senate.

The atmosphere in Florida's capital was different, and the pace of life was faster. Corruption was a sociable affair, rich with tradition; the stakes were higher, as well. Because of occasional scrutiny by pesky news reporters, it was unwise for legislators to be seen drooling openly on the laps of private lobbyists. David Dilbeck worked hard to polish his rough edges. He learned to dress and talk and drink like a country gentleman. The senate was loaded with self-cultured rednecks, and most were unabashedly crooked. But the pecking order was rigid, and newcomers who ignored protocol paid dearly for the mistake. Dilbeck adapted smoothly, and was soon studying at the knees of some of Florida's most prolific thieves. He was rewarded in the usual ways.

It was in Tallahassee where he first learned that some women were attracted to politicians and would actually have sex with them. Dilbeck gained this pleasant knowledge episodically, and with each conquest he became more obsessed. He'd always anticipated that public service would make him wealthy, but he never dreamed that it would get him laid. For eight years, Dilbeck wallowed promiscuously and then – in fine Southern tradition – married a phosphate tycoon's gorgeous, semi-virginal daughter, who seldom consented to sleep with him. Pamela Randle Dilbeck was more interested in new fashions and social causes. Her husband encouraged her to travel often.

By the mid-1970s, Dilbeck's career had stalled in the halls of state government, where he had authored exactly two pieces of legislation. Neither could be described as landmark. One of the bills made it illegal for sporting-goods stores to sell machine-gun clips to minors on Sunday. The measure passed narrowly, despite staunch opposition from the National Rifle Association. Dilbeck's only other achievement was a joint resolution naming the Okaloosa dwarf salamander as Florida's official state amphibian; a special limited-edition license plate was made available to the motoring public for thirty-five dollars, plus tax. The salamander tag was designed by a vivacious art instructor from Florida State University, who was paid $40,000 from the general revenue fund, and who also happened to be screwing a certain senator on Thursday afternoons.

Dilbeck's big break was the passing, at age eighty-two, of Congressman Wade L. Sheets of South Miami. The venerable old Democrat had been mortally ill for the better part of three terms, and was rarely seen on Capitol Hill. Those close to Sheets sadly reported that his numerous health problems were complicated by fast-advancing senility; toward the end, he refused to wear pants and demanded to be addressed as 'Captain

Lindbergh.' By the time Sheets died, a score of local politicians had positioned themselves to make a run for his seat in the House of Representatives. Among the hopefuls was David Lane Dilbeck.

At Sheets's funeral, Dilbeck delivered a eulogy that was uncharacteristically graceful, bringing fond laughter and tears from the huge assembly of mourners. The emotional speech was even more remarkable, considering that Dilbeck had met Wade Sheets only twice in his life and on both occasions the ailing congressman appeared not to be conscious. Dilbeck's remarkable panegyric (written by an eager young staffer named Crandall) borrowed heavily from old John F. Kennedy scripts, which had borrowed heavily from everybody else. No one in the hushed church picked up on the plagiarisms. The other candidates for the dead Sheets's seat also presented eulogies, but none were as moving or as memorable. The others knew they were sunk when all the TV stations led the news with a video snip of David Dilbeck in the pulpit. That single maudlin oratory ensured his selection as Wade Sheets's successor. Hands down, Dilbeck had given the best damn sound bite at the funeral.

He was thrilled to travel all the way to Washington; the farther one got from one's constituents, the harder it was for them to keep an eye on you. Again, Dilbeck modified his style of larceny to fit local custom. Outright cash-in-a-bag bribery was rare on Capitol Hill; special-interest groups were more subtle and sophisticated. A compliant congressman might receive four skybox seats to a Redskins game in exchange for a key vote. Such arrangements were virtually impossible to trace, much less prosecute. Another quick way to a politician's heart was by exorbitant campaign donations; in this manner, David Dilbeck was seduced by the powerful sugar lobby. Other industries found him equally receptive to their attentions. For two decades he was content to coast along as a well-lubricated lackey. He weathered several stiff Republican challenges and numerous negative news stories, but always managed to get re-elected. Those who owned Dilbeck's soul remained silent because they were satisfied with his favors. Consequently, he was never threatened by a scandal.

Until now.

'Good evening, deacon.'

'Hello, Malcolm.' The congressman shrank in Moldowsky's presence. Erb Crandall could be handled, but Moldy was something else. The man held no loyalties beyond the contractual.

He said, 'Where's the cowboy suit, Davey?'

'So Erb told you.' Dilbeck had ditched the boots and the cowboy hat for a maroon jogging suit. He stood casually in the den, sipping an iced tea.

'Erb is concerned,' Moldowsky said. 'Frankly, so am I.'

As always, Dilbeck found himself admiring Moldy's elegance. He wore a gorgeous dove-colored Italian suit with an indigo necktie. Tonight's cologne was particularly memorable; Moldowsky smelled like an orange grove.

'David,' he said, pacing, 'I hear talk of Vaseline.'

'I'm trying to cope—'

' – and laundry lint. Is this possible?' Moldy's fulsome pucker suggested that he was about to spit on the carpet.

'Malcolm, I wish I could explain. These are forces rising up in me, animal urges . . . and it's simply a matter of coping.'

'Sit down,' Moldy barked. No taller than a jockey, he hated staring up at the person he was berating. 'Sit, goddammit.'

Dilbeck did as he was ordered. Moldowsky moved slowly around the den, occasionally pausing to scowl at the photographs and laminated press clippings that hung on the wall. Without glancing at Dilbeck, he said, 'Erb found a lady's shoe in your desk. Where did that come from?'

'Chris bought it for me.'

'From this stripper?'

'Yes, Malcolm.' Dilbeck took a gulp of tea. 'These little things – they help me get by. It's harmless sport.'

Moldy felt a jolt of desperation. Insanity was one thing he could not fix, spin, twist or obscure. And David Dilbeck was plainly nuts.

'What did Erb do with the shoe?' the congressman demanded. 'He didn't throw it away, did he?'

Unbelievable, thought Moldowsky. He's like a damn junkie.

'My inclination,' Moldy said, 'is to haul your ass back to Washington and lock you in my apartment until the sugar vote. Unfortunately, we've got a campaign to worry about. It would be poor form for you to vanish.'

'I suppose,' Dilbeck said, absently.

'David, you do understand what's at stake?'

'Of course.'

'What if I brought in a woman, to be here just for you – for when you got in these moods. Maybe two women . . .'

Dilbeck thanked Moldowsky for the offer but said it wouldn't solve the problem. 'Love has swept me away,' he said.

'Love?' Moldy laughed acerbically.

'It's frightening, Malcolm. Haven't you ever felt so passionately about someone?'

'Never,' Moldowsky said, truthfully. He stuck to call girls. They spoke his language.

'Don't worry, it'll be all right,' Dilbeck told him. 'I'll make it to the election just fine.' He rested his glass on the arm of the chair. 'Erb says Flickman wants a debate. I'm ready.'

'Ignore the little fuck,' advised Moldowsky.

Eloy Flickman was Dilbeck's hapless opponent in the congressional race. Under ordinary circumstances, a debate might've been productive, since ideologically Flickman stood slightly to the right of Attila the Hun. Among his campaign promises: televised executions of drug dealers, free sterilization of welfare mothers and a US military invasion of Cuba. Even the state GOP was leery, providing the shrill appliance salesman with only nominal support.

Dilbeck said, 'I could destroy him, Malcolm.'

'Why bother? He's destroying himself.'

'I worry about that Cuban thing. It's loony enough to catch on.'

'No debate!' Moldowsky said. He stopped pacing and planted himself in front of Dilbeck's face. 'Davey, we've got a more pressing matter – this goddamn stripper you're so taken with.'

The congressman bowed his head. 'What can I say? I'm no longer in control of my impulses.'

In Malcolm Moldowsky's grand vision of the future,

David Dilbeck already was a goner. The day the sugar bill moved out of committee, he was finished. A stiff. Moldy and the Rojos would get him dumped from the chairmanship. Other congressmen would be elated to assume Dilbeck's special role; surely not all of them were so conspicuously deranged. In the meantime, Moldowsky had formed a plan. It was not without risk.

'I'll make you a deal,' he told Dilbeck. 'First you've got to promise: no more collecting her laundry lint and razors and her goddamn shoes. Is that understood?'

'All right. But what do I get?' The congressman sounded skeptical.

'A date.'

Dilbeck rose slowly, eyes widening. 'God, you're serious.'

'Her boss called me tonight. He said she might be up for it, if the price is nice.'

'When?' Dilbeck's voice jumped. 'You mean, right now?'

Incredible, Moldowsky thought. He's about to come in his pants. 'Tie a knot in it,' he told the congressman.

'A date, you said.'

'I'm working out the details.'

Dilbeck showed no curiosity about Moldy's relationship with the owner of the nudie bar. He held Moldowsky by the shoulders. 'If you can arrange this, honest to God—'

Moldy brushed Dilbeck's hands away. 'Then you'd behave until the election? This crazy shit'll stop?'

'On my father's grave, Malcolm.'

'Very funny.'

The Straw – a showman to the end – had been buried

in a silk-lined septic tank. Moldowsky thought: His lunatic son should have so much class.

Dilbeck rubbed his damp palms on the knees of his jogging suit. 'Malcolm, are we talking about a *date* date, or the other kind?'

'Meaning, do you get to screw the girl? That's between you and her. Hell, I can't do everything—'

'You're right, you're right—'

' – I can't get it hard and put it in for you. Some things you've gotta do for yourself.'

The congressman was on a cloud. 'My friend, you've got no idea what this would mean to me.' He raised his glass to Moldowsky. 'Another coup, Malcolm.'

'Try miracle,' Moldy said. 'A fucking miracle.'

'Your specialty!'

'Oh yeah,' Moldowsky mumbled. Rep. David Dilbeck had no inkling of the drastic steps that had already been taken to save his worthless hide.

By the 1970s, the once-dazzling underwater reefs of Miami and Fort Lauderdale were dead, poisoned by raw sewage dumped into the ocean from the toilets of swank waterfront hotels. Submerged pipes carried the filth a few hundred yards offshore, so beachgoers wouldn't see the billowing brown spumes. It was assumed that even the most dogged tourist might think twice about snorkeling in a torrent of shit.

Decades of rancid outfall eventually killed the delicate corals and drove the glittering fish away. The reefs became gray escarpments, barren and manifestly untropical. Drift-boat captains and dive-shop operators complained of losing customers to the Florida Keys and the Bahamas, where the water was still clear enough to see one's hand in front of one's face. A few South Florida coastal cities took modest measures to reduce the off-shore pollution, but the reefs failed to regenerate; once dead, coral tends to stay that way.

Biologists theorized that it was possible to attract fish without real coral, and thus was born the concept of 'artificial reefs', which was neither as exotic nor as high-tech as it sounded. Artificial reefs were created by sinking old ships; once nestled on the bottom, the ghost hulks attracted schools of baitfish which in turn attracted barracudas, jack crevalles, sharks, groupers and snappers. The drift boats and scuba captains were happy, as they no longer had to travel forty miles to find an actual fish to show their customers.

From a public-relations standpoint, the artificial reef program was a grand success – a sort of living junkyard of the deep. For once, human practices of waste disposal could be passed off legitimately as a benefit to the environment. Every few months another derelict freighter would be towed offshore and blown up with dynamite. Local TV stations swarmed the event, as it gave them an opportunity to use their expensive helicopters for something other than traffic reports. Predictably, the highly publicized demolitions became a regular South Florida tourist attraction, attended by hundreds of boaters who cheered wildly as the rusty vessels exploded and disappeared under the waves.

On the morning of October second, an eighty-six-foot Guatemalan banana boat called the *Princess Pia* was towed from Port Everglades to a pre-selected site off the Fort Lauderdale coast. The *Princess Pia* had been salvaged meticulously from the inside out: gone were the melted twin diesels, the corroded navigational gear, the radio electronics, the bilge pumps, the ropes, the hoses, the pipes, the fixtures, the hatch covers, the windshield, even the anchor – every item of value had been stripped from the boat. What remained essentially was a bare hull, degreased to minimize the purple slick that inevitably would form when the *Pia* went down.

The preparation of the ship had taken nearly a month, and was supervised by a Coast Guard inspector, a Broward County environmental engineer and an agent from the US Customs Service, which had seized the vessel fourteen months earlier. Once the Customs agent was satisfied that the *Princess Pia* had no more hidden cargo compartments and carried no more hidden hashish, he signed off on the project. The Coast Guard inspector and the county environmental expert walked through the old heap one last time on the evening of October first. Much later, both men would testify that, except for the explosives, the *Pia* was empty that night; specifically, the aft hold was bare.

A single guard, hired by the demolition company, was posted at the ship's mooring to prevent the dynamite from being stolen from the hull. The guard kept watch dutifully until approximately three in the morning, when a group of friendly stevedores invited him aboard a Japanese lumber barge to play cards and watch pornographic videotapes. In all, the *Princess Pia* was unguarded for at least three and possibly five hours, depending on whose testimony one believed.

This much was undisputed: At dawn the next day, two tugs hauled the *Pia* out to sea on a falling tide. Three Florida Marine Patrol boats and a Coast Guard cruiser led the way, positioning themselves between the celebratory armada and the dynamite-laden freighter. The site for the new artificial reef was only three miles offshore, but it took a full hour for the *Princess Pia* to get there. The ocean was choppy, with northeast winds kicking to twenty knots; the tug captains kept a cautious pace.

By 9 a.m., the *Pia* was tethered in place, bow facing into the breeze. The police boats raced in widening arcs, clearing a buffer zone. At precisely 10 a.m., a radio signal detonated twin explosions in the ship's hull and stern. Tall blasts of dirty smoke rose from each end, and the ship listed dramatically starboard. She sunk in nine minutes flat. Boaters clapped and howled and sounded air horns.

Nobody suspected that there was a 1991 Lincoln Continental chained to the beams of the aft cargo hold. Nobody knew, until much later, what was in it.

TWENTY-TWO

The wrestling pit was in the back room, which had its own stage and a small horseshoe bar. Erin was dancing tables while Urbana Sprawl wrestled members of a bachelor party in ninety gallons of Green Giant niblets. The bachelor of honor was a young mortgage banker with many pallid, out-of-shape companions. They stood no chance against Urbana, who played rough and employed her formidable cleavage to maximum advantage. She specialized in pinning opponents without using her arms.

Erin remained baffled by the success of the nude wrestling exhibitions, which had become a red-hot fad in upscale strip joints. There was nothing erotic about grappling with a topless woman in a vat of cold vegetables, although the sodden realization came too late for most customers. By the time the bell rang, few were able to climb from the ring without assistance. The young bankers appeared especially whipped after their sessions with Urbana Sprawl.

Working table to table, Erin paid little attention to the comic slaughter in the wrestling pit. She was thinking about politics, which suddenly had touched her life in a dramatic way. Erin couldn't remember the last time she'd stood in a voting booth. Campaigns bored her. Every politician wore the same horseshit smile and gave the same horseshit speech. Erin was amazed that anyone would believe a word. She recalled being stricken by severe intestinal cramps while trying to watch the Bush–Dukakis debates.

Agent Cleary, bless his buttoned-down heart, used to scold her for being so cynical. On election day he'd lecture the office staff, telling them that democracy is futile without 'an informed and participatory electorate'. He'd say that people get exactly the kind of government they deserve, and those who won't vote have no grounds to complain. He was right, Erin thought. This is what I get for not paying attention. Thieves like David Lane Dilbeck couldn't get elected dogcatcher without the gross apathy of the masses.

And this is my punishment, Erin thought. I've got to date the asshole.

Al García had laid out the situation in his maddeningly laconic way. Erin, who was seldom shocked at the depth of human sordidness, found herself stunned by what she heard: Jerry Killian had been murdered over *sugar*. The lovestruck little nerd was killed because he'd threatened the career of a crooked congressman. According to García, the congressman's principal contribution to the governing of the republic was to direct jillions of dollars in aid to the sugar cartels. Poor Mr Peepers jeopardized that arrangement, so he was swatted as dead as a fly.

García said he wanted to catch the killers before they came looking for Erin. She said that was an excellent idea, and agreed to help in any way possible. Self-preservation was the main motivation; guilt was another. Erin couldn't forget that it was her sexy dancing that had fatally infatuated Jerry Killian.

Men were so helpless, she thought, so easily charmed. Monique Jr was right: they'd do anything for it. Anything.

That's what Erin's mother didn't understand about yuppie strip clubs; it wasn't the women who were being used and degraded, it was the men. Her mother thought these places were meat markets, and indeed they were, the meat being the customers. Experienced dancers always kept one eye on the front door, scouting for the next mark. If you knew your stuff, you could work a guy all night and get every last dollar out of his wallet. You didn't have to blow him or screw him or even act like you might. A girlish smile, a sisterly hug, a few minutes of private conversation – Urbana Sprawl said it was the easiest money in the world, if you could get past being naked.

Because men were so easily charmed. That was a fact.

But Erin was apprehensive about the congressman. He wouldn't be shy and polite like Killian and the other regulars. No, Dilbeck would be pushy and crude and probably kinky. Al García warned her to be prepared.

'You think he's the one who took my razor?'

'Ask him,' García had said.

Fear wasn't the worst part for Erin; the worst part was sending Angela away. It was the sensible move, because certainly Angie couldn't stay in the new apartment – couldn't stay anywhere near her mother – until the danger was over. Erin felt terrible about it. She didn't like being alone again. She dreaded the silent afternoons, the dinners for one. Angie was safe, and at least Darrell Grant wouldn't find her. But still . . .

'Hey, babes.'

A hand clamped on Erin's leg. She snapped back to reality – Urbana rolling in the creamed corn, Aerosmith blaring on the speakers, her own bra and G-string in a lacey mound between the Michelob bottles at her feet. Three young bankers sat at the table, trying to appear cool and unimpressed. The drunkest of them kept snapping Erin's garter, where the cash tips were folded. She asked him to stop but he didn't. She brushed his hand off her leg and spun a circle on the table, making evasion part of the dance; when she stopped spinning, the banker's hand returned, crawling like a mantis up her thigh. Erin looked across the room for Shad, but couldn't see him.

'That's enough,' she told the banker.

The next thing she felt was his tongue. He was licking vertically from ankle to knee, long, sloppy Popsicle licks.

Erin snatched the man's hair and lifted his head. 'You behave,' she said sharply.

But he wouldn't.

That morning, a small item had appeared on page 6-D of the Fort Lauderdale *Sun Sentinel*, under the headline: BAR TO PROBE MISSING LAWYER. The four-paragraph story said the Florida Bar was investigating whether a lawyer named Mordecai had looted his client trust account and fled the country. The article said the man had not been seen for several days, and was believed to have flown to the Bahamas with an unnamed female companion.

Sgt Al García clipped the story and put it with his homicide paperwork in his briefcase. Then he drove to a street corner in Liberty City, where two crack dealers had done the planet a tremendous favor by killing each other in a pre-dawn shootout. Witnesses were as scarce as mourners, but García took out his notebook and went to work.

Another man who clipped the *Sun Sentinel* item was Erb Crandall, sitting in the lobby of the Sunshine Fidelity Savings Bank on Galt Ocean Mile. Crandall was about to commit a minor crime for major stakes. He was about to forge a false name on a vault-room ledger, and use a stolen key to open a stranger's safe-deposit box. Crandall was searching for a Kodak color slide that Malcolm Moldowsky urgently sought to possess. The slide was the original photograph of Congressman David Lane Dilbeck assaulting Paul Guber with a champagne bottle on the stage of the Eager Beaver lounge. Erb Crandall's plan to obtain the incriminating picture began smoothly in the vault room. He signed a well-practiced version of Mordecai's name to the ledger, and handed the key to the clerk. The clerk pulled the steel box from the wall and unlocked it. He led Erb Crandall to a windowless cubicle and left him alone.

When Crandall opened the lid, he found no Kodak slide. Mordecai's box had been cleaned out. In the bottom, face up, lay only a business card:

> Sgt Alberto García
> Metropolitan Dade County Police
> Homicide Division (305) 471–1900

Erb Crandall's fingers were shaking as he carried the safe-deposit box to the clerk's desk. It was all he could do not to run from the bank.

That evening, over dinner, Sgt Al García took out the news clipping and read it again. He was impressed that anyone would go to the trouble of framing a lawyer who most likely was dead. The trust account ruse was very nifty.

Andy asked: 'Al, did you catch 'em yet? The guys who killed that man in the river?'

'Not yet,' García said. The boy talked about the floater all the time; it was the highlight of the family vacation.

'Any suspects?'

'No, Andy. It's a tough one.'

Donna said: 'That's enough, both of you. Remember our rule.'

The rule was: no talk of dead bodies at supper. Al's work was to be discussed only after the dishes were cleared.

'Sorry Mom,' Andy said.

Lynne, the little girl, asked if they could go to Sea World next summer. She wanted to see some turtles and sharks. Andy said he'd rather go back to Montana and hunt for clues.

Donna chased the children from the table and brought her husband a pot of coffee. He said, 'Look what I've gotten you all into.'

'It's all right. She seems like a nice person.'

'Of course she's a nice person. Next question: How come she's working at a nudie bar? Right?'

Donna shrugged. 'It's no great mystery. Have a slice of pie.'

García was intrigued. 'Could you do that – take off your clothes in front of all those drunken strangers?'

'If I had to,' Donna said. 'For the kids.'

'Jesus, there's only about a million other jobs. The girl's not stupid. She can type seventy words a minute.'

'You said she owes her lawyer.'

'Yeah,' García said. 'Who doesn't?'

'So maybe she wants a nest egg. Where's the crime in that?'

'You're right, sweetheart.'

'I like her.'

'Me, too,' he said. 'But it's the job that's got her into so much damn trouble.'

'No, honey, it's the men.' Donna cut a piece of apple pie and put it on a plate. 'So what does she look like, Al?'

'You saw her.' He teased with a long pause. 'Oh, you mean with her clothes off? Tell you the truth, I didn't notice.'

Donna smiled. 'You are a pitiful liar. Eat your dessert.'

The phone rang. Donna didn't bother to get up. Only cops called at dinner time. García went in the kitchen to take it. He looked grim when he came back.

'That was the Broward sheriff's office,' he said.

'They still don't want the case?'

'I knew they wouldn't.' García sat down heavily. 'Hell, I can't even get that cowpoke coroner to say Killian's death was a homicide. Meanwhile I got no weapons, no witnesses and no suspects.' He took a large bite of pie. 'I don't blame BSO for taking a pass.' Another huge bite. 'Least they were decent about it. I mean, they didn't laugh too hard.'

Donna said, 'Slow down. You'll choke to death.'

'It's good pie.'

'Not *that* good. Now tell me what else is wrong.'

'I end up on a speaker phone with two brain-dead detectives. See, the girl's ex was a CI for Broward Robbery.' García didn't need to translate police jargon for Donna. She'd learned plenty from her first husband, the dope dealer.

'The ex is still an informant?'

García, chewing mechanically: 'Nope, they cut him loose after he got busted for grand theft up the coast.'

Donna shook her head. 'I don't get it. If the ex got arrested, isn't that good news for Erin?'

'Oh, great news,' García said, wiping his mouth, 'if they'd managed to keep the bastard in jail.'

'You're kidding.'

'Nope, he escaped. From a county hospital! Stole a wheelchair and rolled out the fucking door!'

Donna told her husband to keep his voice down. 'We've got company,' she reminded him. 'Where's your cigar?'

'Wait, there's more.' García slashed the air with both hands. 'The girl's ex-husband – the kid's father – he's not only mean, he's not only violent, he's got a frigging drug problem. Isn't that a hoot!'

Andy dashed into the dining room and asked what Al was hollering about.

'Work,' Donna said. 'What else.'

Andy clambered up on García's lap. 'Maybe you need another vacation.'

Donna turned away, smothering a laugh. 'So everybody's a smart-ass,' García said, tickling the boy until he howled.

*

Shad was at the bar in the main lounge. He was distracted by a management problem.

Orly had connived to hire Lorelei, the fabulous python princess, away from the Ling brothers. Tonight was to be her first stage performance at the Tickled Pink, but she'd arrived in puffy-eyed hysterics. Orly could not decipher the problem, and delivered the distraught dancer to Shad, who was on break, reading a large-type edition of *The Plague* by Albert Camus. The book made Shad feel slightly better about living in South Florida.

He was interrupted by Lorelei's convulsive sobs. Her snake was missing, and she suspected the vengeful Lings of abduction. When Orly was informed, he ordered Shad to find another snake for his new star. Shad noted there were no all-night reptile stores in the neighborhood. Unfortunately, Lorelei refused to dance without Bubba, which is what she called her nine-foot Burmese python.

'She says they're a team,' Shad reported. 'She says the snake is trained.'

Orly crumpled an empty can of Dr Pepper and lobbed it grenade-style behind the bar. 'First, there's no such thing as a trained snake, OK? And Item B, did you see the fucking marquee? LORELEI in great big letters – I got customers drove all the way from Miami. Tell her she's got ten minutes to get her boobs on stage.'

Shad glanced toward the hallway, where the weeping python princess now huddled in grief. 'She'll need more than ten minutes,' he said. 'She looks like hell.'

Orly cursed and hacked and massaged his nostrils. 'You don't know anyone with a goddamn snake?'

'Not a big snake,' Shad said. 'I know some guys who breed diamondbacks.'

'Sweet Christ Almighty.'

'They're not much good for dancing.'

'OK,' said Orly. 'Here's what you do. Go see those fucking Lings. Find out how much they want for the girl's python.'

'Bubba is the name.'

'Whatever. Offer five hundred.'

Shad said the Lings likely would tell him to fuck off and die. 'They hate your guts,' he told Orly.

'No, this is business. Now hurry it up.'

Shad put the book by Camus behind the bar, under the popcorn platters. Then he drove up to the Flesh Farm, where the Ling brothers kept him waiting an hour – a nervy move. Shad passed the time drinking Virgin Marys and surveying the dance talent in case Orly demanded a scouting report. Shad's ominous bald presence quickly thinned the audience and further irritated the Lings. Shad finally got his meeting, but the brothers reacted to the python proposition more biliously than anticipated.

He returned to find the Tickled Pink in an uproar. Erin seemed to be in the thick of it. Paramedics were fitting a neck brace on a pale and dazed young man. The victim was encircled by a dozen equally wan companions with corn kernels stuck in their hair. From a distance it looked as if they'd been bombed by sparrows. The men shouted high-pitched questions at the paramedics, over the jack-hammer music. As a protective measure, Urbana Sprawl had stationed her insurmountable breasts between Erin and Orly, who was red-faced and raving.

'Damn,' said Shad, and waded into the chaos.

Later, in the office, Orly blustered about liability and lawsuits and his liquor license.

'You aren't listening,' Erin said. 'The man touched me.'

Urbana Sprawl, showered and fully dressed, spoke out in support of her friend: 'I saw the whole thing, Mr Orly. He got what he deserved.'

Orly snorted. 'A sprained neck. Is that what he deserved? A trip to the hospital, for copping a feel!'

'He touched me,' Erin said, 'between my legs.'

'Aw, he was drunk.'

Erin turned to Urbana. 'This is why I hate table dances.'

Orly said, 'You could've crippled the guy, kickin' him in the head like that.'

'And what's she supposed to do?' Urbana said. 'Give him a nice friendly finger fuck?'

Orly flinched, turning his head. 'Christ, that's enough. No more a that talk.'

'So it's OK for Shad to beat a customer's ass, but not us. Is that the deal?'

'I said, that's enough.'

'Urbana's right,' Erin said. 'It's not fair.'

'Screw fair,' said Orly, puffing his cheeks. 'Shad's job is keeping the peace. Your job is to dance. That's the bottom line.'

Standing by the office door, Shad reluctantly

abandoned his silence. 'I got sent up the street,' he said. 'Otherwise it wouldn't have happened.'

Orly gave a corrosive laugh. 'Wonderful. Now it's all my fault. Well, fuck the whole bunch a you.'

Urbana was livid. She leaned her double-wide bosom across his desk and shook a Day-Glo fingernail in his face. 'Nobody touches me 'less I wanna be touched, especially down there. I don't care who it is or how shitfaced they are or how much money they got, I won't stand for it. That little shit's lucky to get out with a sprained neck, because if it was me, I'd rip his damn balls off with my bare hands, just like this—'

Orly gaped as Urbana simulated her technique, snatching imaginary testicles off an imaginary oaf.

' – and don't think I can't!'

Then she was gone. Nobody moved for several moments.

Orly said: 'That girl gives big tits a bad name.'

Erin stood up. 'Well, I'm through for the night.'

'Now wait a second—'

'No. I'm going to visit my daughter.'

After Erin left, Shad came to her defense. He told Orly that Erin had many good reasons to be jumpy – the custody case, the burglary of the apartment, and now a congressman in hot pursuit. 'It's a bad time for her right now. That's how come she blew up tonight.'

Orly wiped his neck with a soiled handkerchief. 'You and me are the only ones in this joint that don't get PMS, and sometimes I'm not too sure about you.'

'It's the music,' Shad said. 'It makes my head hurt.'

'Talk to Kevin.'

'Kevin says talk to you.'

Orly said, 'I don't know rap from reggae. You know

my secret? I don't even listen.' He twisted an invisible knob at his right earlobe. 'Just turn it off. I don't hear a damn thing.' He asked how it went with the Lings.

'Lousy,' Shad said.

'They don't have the girl's snake?'

'Yeah, they got it. They just won't ransom it.'

Orly raised his palms. 'Why the fuck not? Business is business.'

'Mainly because they hate your guts.'

'Because of me hiring Lorelei?'

'Because of everything,' Shad replied.

'So the answer is no. It took you two damn hours to get a simple N-O from those jerkoff Japs. Meanwhile I got a crazed stripper doing a Chuck Norris routine on my customers—'

'The answer wasn't only no,' Shad said. 'It was this, too.' He placed an oblong package on Orly's desk. 'The Ling brothers wanted you to have it.'

Orly eyed the crude parcel wrapped in Flesh Farm cocktail napkins and bound with masking tape. 'What the hell is it?' he asked Shad.

'About twelve inches of dead Bubba.'

Orly yelped and pushed away from the desk, away from the unopened package. 'Did I tell you they were animals? Did I? Jesus, what else did they say, those goddamn Lings?'

'They said there's plenty more where that came from.'

TWENTY-THREE

On the morning of October third, under a hard blue sky, Perry Crispin and Willa Oakley Crispin went down to the beach.

The attractive young couple spread out towels from their suite at the Breakers Hotel, and lay side by side in the bleached sand. They took turns smearing number 29 sunblock all over each other: Perry spelled out 'I Luv You!!!' on his wife's tummy. Willa drew an oily heart on the small of her husband's prodigiously freckled back.

A strong breeze put a salty tang in the air, and made the waves bite raggedly against the shore. The Crispins planned a brief swim later, when they were sweaty. They wore matching black Ray-Bans and pink terrycloth tennis visors. They smiled and whispered and touched each other frequently, as is the habit of newlyweds. Willa and Perry were from large, wealthy families in Connecticut, so the wedding had been suitably extravagant. Palm Beach was the first leg of a four-week honeymoon that would take them to Freeport, St Bart's and finally Cozumel. The sun was high and bright, and the Crispins glistened on their towels. They were unabashedly romantic, totally relaxed and not at all apprehensive about their future together. Substantial trust funds awaited both of them.

By noon, Willa's adorable nose had turned pink. Perry noted it with alarm; his father was a limited partner in four dermatology clinics, and skin cancer had been a recurrent topic at family gatherings. From an early age, Perry showed an eagle eye for discolored moles and suspicious lesions. He told his bride that it was time to get out of the UV rays.

'I came to get a tan,' she protested.

'Darling, we've got four whole weeks.'

As they crossed the beach toward the hotel, the Crispins were followed by a slender blond man in dirty jeans and cowboy boots. Perry and Willa didn't notice the stranger – they were engrossed in discussing the poor quality of the sunblock ointment, and the possibility of trying zinc oxide instead, at least on their noses.

The man behind them said, 'Scuze me, folks.'

Perry and Willa turned. The man wasn't dressed for Palm Beach. His blue eyes were bloodshot and jumpy. His hair was matted on one side, as if slept on.

'You got a car?' he said.

Willa looked frightened. Perry sized up the stranger and took a small step forward. The man displayed a rusty steak knife and said, 'Don't make me ask twice.'

The Crispins led Darrell Grant to their rental car, a candy-apple Thunderbird. Darrell Grant said he approved. He took the keys from Perry and ordered the couple to hop in the backseat.

'Why?' Willa asked.

'Till we get across the bridge,' Darrell said.

The Intracoastal Waterway separated the town of Palm Beach from West Palm Beach. Two more disparate worlds would be hard to find; West Palm was for normal humans, Palm Beach for the eccentric rich. The cops on the island were notorious rousters of unwanted visitors – blacks, Hispanics, and anyone not wearing Polo. If you worked in one of the mansions, fine. Otherwise, get your ass over the bridge. Darrell Grant figured he might need the Crispins to talk him out of a Palm Beach traffic stop.

'You got a purse?' he asked Willa.

The newlyweds squeezed each other's hands. Perry was relieved to see that Willa had left her two-carat diamond wedding band in the hotel room. He hoped she'd done the same with the traveler's checks.

'Halloo?' Darrell Grant said.

'Yes, I've got my purse.'

'Thatta girl.'

'All I carry is forty dollars.'

Darrell snorted. 'How about you, sport?'

'Credit cards is all I've got,' Perry said.

'Figures.' Darrell barreled through a red light on Worth Avenue. He liked the way the T-bird handled. 'All right, honey, gimme the cash. And your medicines, too.'

Willa looked confounded. Her husband motioned gravely at her purse. She took out two twenties and nervously extended them over the headrest, as if feeding a bear at the zoo.

'I don't have any pills,' she told Darrell Grant. 'Except my birth control.'

'That'll do fine.' He grabbed the money with his steering hand. The other hand held the steak knife, running the stained blade through the stubble on his jawline.

From the backseat, Willa said: 'I'm sorry but you can't take my pills.'

'Oh yeah?' Darrell was heartily amused.

'You'll get sick,' said Willa. 'They're not made for men.'

'Sick?'

'They're made of hormones!'

'No shit,' Darrell Grant said. 'So, like, I might grow knockers. Is that what you mean? Or maybe even a love muffin.'

'No, I didn't—'

'Be a good girl and hand over the fucking pills.' Darrell's arm came down and speared the rusty knife into the white upholstery. He ripped a long sibilant gash in the stiff vinyl.

Perry Crispin said: 'Willa, give the man what he wants.'

'No.'

'My God,' said her husband. 'Don't be foolish.'

'Fine, Perry. And what're we supposed to do for the next four weeks – hold hands?' Willa protected the purse with both arms. 'Our pharmacy is in Westport, remember?'

Perry Crispin said: 'I'm not believing this.'

'What – you want me to get pregnant?'

In the front seat, Darrell Grant was humming the theme from *The Sound of Music*, which was his sister Rita's favorite movie of all time. Or maybe that was *Mary Poppins*, he always got the two mixed up. 'Which is the one with Dick Van Dyke?' he asked. 'Did I get it right?'

The Crispins had no clue what he was talking about. A dope fiend, jabbering. Willa leaned forward to plead her case. 'Please, don't take the birth-control pills. It's our honeymoon.'

Ahead was one of the drawbridges leading to West Palm. Finally, thought Darrell, I can dump these brainless puppies. He goosed the accelerator.

'My sister's a nurse,' Willa was saying. 'These pills are very strong. They *will* make you sick.'

Ahead, the crossing gates swung down and a tinny bell rang. The bridge began to rise. Darrell Grant cursed vehemently and hit the brakes.

Perry Crispin's feeble voice: 'It's just a sailboat going through. It shouldn't take long.'

Darrell Grant whirled in the driver's seat. He thrust a calloused palm at Willa and said: 'The pills.'

She shook her head adamantly. Her husband was dumbstruck.

Darrell said, 'Listen, you silly cunt. I ain't gonna eat the damn things, I'm gonna sell 'em. You understand? I'm gonna go across this bridge and scam me some stoners who don't know birth control from LSD. Get it?'

Tears appeared in Willa's eyes. She blinked downheartedly at her husband. 'Perry, he called me a cunt.'

Perry Crispin felt horrible. He felt he should attack the crazed dope fiend in defense of his wife's honor. On the other hand, he was crippled with terror. He expected his bladder to fail at any second.

'Don't you worry,' he told Willa. 'We'll get more pills.'

'How? My prescription is in Westport.' Despair fogged her voice.

'FedEx, darling. Now do as the man says.'

The drawbridge began to go down, one side at a

time. Darrell Grant announced that he would count to five, then hack out Willa's heart and make Perry eat it on a hoagie for lunch. Willa immediately opened the purse and gave the madman her pills. Darrell drove across the bridge and parked at a Mini-Mart. He took Perry Crispin's Ray-Bans and also the hot pink tennis visor. Then he told the couple to get their sorry butts out of the car.

The pavement scorched the soles of the Crispins' bare feet, and they hopped like palsied flamingos to a triangular patch of shade. Darrell Grant adjusted the side mirror of the Thunderbird so he could admire the fit of his new sunglasses. The Crispins watched morosely, waiting for the criminal to drive away. Willa remained very angry. 'Thank you very much,' she called out acidly, 'for ruining our honeymoon.'

Darrell Grant scowled and revved the engine. 'You people ever heard of rubbers? It's a new thing, sport. Fits right on your dick.'

'Perry won't use them.' Willa's tone was reproachful. Perry Crispin turned away.

'Figures,' Darrell said. He waved tootle-oo with the steak knife before speeding off. It took two hours to find a junkie bent enough to buy birth-control pills and believe they were Belgian Dilaudids. Darrell only got thirty bucks from the scam but, added to Willa Crispin's forty, it was enough to gas up the T-bird and score some reds. He had a good buzz on by the time he made the interstate, which carried him south in blazing pursuit of his precious little girl and her worthless mother.

*

The Rojos were in Santo Domingo, so Malcolm Moldowsky was given use of the yacht. Erb Crandall dropped off the congressman at nine sharp, and went directly to a dockside bar to drink alone. He had already delivered the bad news about the lawyer's safe-deposit box. Moldy had taken the homicide detective's card delicately, like a butterfly, between two fingers. 'This changes things,' he'd said, turning the card back and forth, as if marveling at a hologram. 'I guess it's time for Plan B.' Erb Crandall didn't ask for an explanation. The time had come to forsake party loyalty and begin thinking of one's own situation, and of covering one's own ass. Crandall was grateful that Moldy didn't ask him to stay for the meeting on the yacht.

When David Dilbeck stepped into the master state-room, the first thing he saw was The Photograph from the Eager Beaver. Moldowsky had tacked it on the wall, over the wet bar.

'A reminder,' he said, pouring Dilbeck a drink.

The congressman's eyes riveted on Erin's face. 'Isn't she something,' he said, breathlessly.

Moldy said, 'Don't look at her, David. Look at yourself.'

'It was a bad night.'

'You don't say.' He shoved a tumbler into Dilbeck's gut. 'Sit down and have a drink.'

The congressman obeyed. 'Ginger ale? That's precious, Malcolm.'

Moldowsky climbed into a canvas director's chair. He wore rubber-soled deck shoes, pressed white slacks and a navy pullover. It was one of the few times Dilbeck had seen him in casual clothes.

'I want you sober,' Moldy began. 'I want you to

remember every goddamn word I say. Whatever arrangement you and this girl reach, that's fine. But you're to talk to her, David. There are certain things we need to know.'

'Good Lord, she's not a spy. She's only a stripper—'

'Bring her here tomorrow night,' Moldowsky said. 'It'll be safe.'

'Safe from what?'

'From blackmailers, David.' Moldy pointed up at the photograph. Again Dilbeck's gaze settled on Erin, shielding herself from the bottle attack.

'What if she doesn't like me?' Dilbeck asked.

Moldowsky cracked an ice cube in his molars. 'She'll love you, trust me. Two thousand dollars buys serious love.'

'And what do I get for that?'

'Two hours of dancing.'

'That's all?'

'It's a start.'

David Dilbeck sipped at the ginger ale, which tasted flat. 'I want sexy music, champagne, candles, the whole nine yards—'

Moldy said it was all arranged. He went through a series of questions that Dilbeck was to ask the nude dancer. Dilbeck said no way, it would spoil the mood.

'Come on,' said Moldowsky. 'You're the slickest son-ofabitch I ever saw. Go easy. Be cool.'

The congressman was reluctant. 'Malcolm, I do not wish to scare her off. This may be my only shot.' Once more his eyes wandered to the grainy photograph on the wall. 'Fantastic,' he whispered, to no one.

Moldy shot to his feet and tore the picture down. He charged up to David Dilbeck's chair and confronted him, nose to chin. 'You *will* do this,' he growled at the congressman. 'There are things we need to know. It's *essential*, David' – spraying the word *essential* – 'considering what's happened the last month.'

Moldowsky's breath smelled like bourbon and peppermint mouthwash. The mixture clashed fiercely with his cologne. Dilbeck turned away and huffed for fresh air. The yacht rocked gently on the wake of a passing speedboat.

'You will do this,' Moldy repeated in the congressman's ear.

'But I don't understand—'

Moldowsky whirled away. He snatched his glass of bourbon off the bar and took a slug. He noticed a small rectangular outline in the fabric of his pocket – the homicide detective's card, taken from the lawyer's safe-deposit box. Moldy said, 'People are trying to harm you, David. We need to be sure she's not one of them.'

Dilbeck shook his head. 'You're completely paranoid.'

'Humor me.'

'But she's just a stripper.'

Malcolm Moldowsky grabbed Dilbeck's shirt. 'Fannie Fox,' he said, 'was "just a stripper." Donna Rice was just a model-slash-actress. Elizabeth Ray was just a secretary who couldn't type. Gennifer Flowers was just a country singer. Don't you get it? Ask Chuck Robb. Or that horny idiot Hart. Teddy Kennedy, for pity's sake. They'll all tell you the same: in politics, stealing is trouble but pussy is lethal.'

Moldy released his grip. Exhausted, he wilted on a bar stool. 'Those who ignore history,' he said, 'are doomed to get their nuts cut.'

David Dilbeck said, 'All right. I'll talk to the girl.'

'Thank you.'

'I'm smarter than those others.'

Moldowsky could scarcely contain himself.

'I'm also stronger,' Dilbeck added.

'Yeah,' said Moldy. 'A rock, that's what you are. A regular Rock of Gibraltar.'

The congressman sidled to the bar and disposed of the ginger ale. Keeping his back to Moldowsky, he poured himself a very sturdy rum-and-Coke. 'Malcolm,' the congressman said, 'is it possible she would let me shave her?'

Moldowsky fell to his knees and gagged spectacularly on the Rojos' carpet.

Al García heard music in Erin's apartment. He knocked loudly and rang the bell. When he got no answer, he took out the key she had given him and let himself in. On the bed Erin lay motionless, a pillow wrapped like a helmet around her head. She wore pink panties and a matching bra, and appeared to be breathing just fine. Half a pitcher of martinis perspired on the nightstand, and the stereo was cranked up full blast. García turned it down.

Erin's voice, muffled: 'What d'you think you're doing?'

The detective sat on the edge of the bed. 'We need to talk.'

'Orly won't let me dance to Jackson Browne any more.'

'How come?'

'Or Van Morrison. He says it's too slow. He says I'm pissing off the girls on the tables.'

'Erin, how you doin' on gin?'

'That's the first time you called me Erin.' Her face peeked out of the pillow. 'By the way, I want my gun back.'

'It's in the dresser,' García said.

'Loaded?'

'Yes, ma'am.'

'Good. What time is it?'

'Noon.' García tried to cover her with a sheet. Erin kicked it off and gave a gravelly laugh.

'Don't tell me you're embarrassed,' she said.

The detective reddened. Erin reminded him that he'd seen her nude several times at the club.

'That's different,' he said.

'Oh?' Erin unsnapped her bra and lobbed it at him. It landed on his right shoulder. Then she squirmed out of her panties and tossed them on the floor. 'There you are,' she said, spreading her arms.

The detective stared at his shoes. 'Let me take a wild guess here. You're upset about meeting the congressman.'

'Upset is a good word for it. Nervous, disgusted, terrified, and pretty much all alone. The only thing in the world I care about, I can't have—'

'Angela's doing great,' Al García said. 'You'll be together soon.' He took the bra off his shoulder and folded it on the bed.

Erin enfolded herself listlessly in the bedsheets. She looked too worn for her age. 'Some guy grabbed me last night.'

'Christ.'

'I came unglued. Nothing in particular.'

'Did you kill him?'

'Nah.'

'So what's the big deal?' The detective pulled a cigar from his shirt. He put it in his mouth but didn't light it.

Erin stared at the ceiling. 'I had a dream about the other man in that picture, the one who's hugging me on his knees. I had a dream they killed him, too, just like Mr Peepers.'

García told her not to worry. 'His name is Paul Guber and he's safe and sound. He went to New York for a few weeks.'

'At your suggestion?' Erin poked him playfully with a toe.

'His firm's got an office on Wall Street. It seemed like a good time for a visit.'

She said, 'You take care of everyone, don't you?'

The detective shook his head unhappily. He told Erin about Darrell Grant's ludicrous escape from the Martin County authorities. She received the news more passively than he expected; then again, she'd had the benefit of several martinis.

'Darrell,' she declared, 'is off the fucking rails.'

'Is he crazy enough to show up at the club?'

'Possibly.' Erin rolled on her belly. 'I can sure pick 'em, huh?'

García left the room to make a phone call. When he returned, Erin had put on a white T-shirt and jeans. She stood at the mirror, brushing her hair. The martini pitcher was empty.

'I poured it out,' she said. shooting him a sharp look. 'I'm not as bombed as you think.'

They went to a Friday's and ordered cheeseburgers.

García had a beer. Erin drank coffee. They were conducting a perfectly amiable conversation until the detective asked if she had a boyfriend.

She said, 'Shit, don't do this.'

'What?'

'You know what.'

García chewed thoughtfully. 'My interest is purely professional. I need to cover all the angles.'

'You're not trying to ask me out?'

'Nope.' He raised his right hand, cheeseburger and all. 'I swear to God.'

'You sure?'

'For Christ's sake, Erin, I took you to meet my wife.'

She apologized, sheepishly. She felt like the queen bitch of all time. 'It's not that I've got such a red-hot opinion of myself—'

'I understand,' García said, 'believe me.'

'It's the damn job.' She was so accustomed to being propositioned that she was automatically suspicious of any man who didn't try. It made for a relentlessly cynical view of the opposite sex. Having Darrell Grant in one's past contributed to Erin's attitude.

She said, 'The answer is no, there's no boyfriend. But you knew that, right?'

'Just a hunch.'

'At the end of the night, I don't have much energy left for men. Or much interest, for that matter.'

'Occupational hazard,' said García, attacking a pile of french fries. 'Is there any man you trust completely?'

'Don't laugh,' Erin said. 'I trust Shad.'

Al García grinned. 'Me, too.'

After lunch, he drove out to the ocean. Erin said that she wanted to stand in the sunshine and bleach out the gin. The detective parked at Bahia Mar, and they walked across the overpass to the beach. García wished he'd taken off his coat and tie; people were giving him odd looks.

Erin walked down far enough to get her toes wet. The detective stopped a few feet from the waves. He lit the cigar and blew the smoke over his right shoulder, safely downwind from Erin.

She said, 'You think I'm a whore?'

'Don't be ridiculous.'

Erin stepped back from the water. 'But you wouldn't want your daughter doing what I do.'

'My daughter,' said García, 'is not leaving the house until she's thirty years old.'

Erin smiled. 'Angie is fascinated by Mommy's costumes.'

The detective said, 'The time comes, she'll understand.'

Erin stretched. The sun felt glorious on her face and arms. She said, 'I tell myself it's just dancing.'

'And I tell myself I'm an ace crime fighter. So what?'

Erin had an urge to jump in the ocean. She got a running start and dove in. She swam fifty yards and stopped. Floating on her back, she blinked the salty sting from her eyes. The swells lifted the T-shirt, billowing around her breasts. Seagulls kited above the surf and cawed raucously. Silver mullet jumped and skittered toward deeper water. She heard the whoosh of a windsurfer and a lewd whistle from the teenager riding the board. Erin serenely flipped him the finger.

When she waded from the water, Al García offered his coat. Erin thought: How can you not like this guy? She said, 'I guess you don't go for the wet look.'

CARL HIAASEN

'Please.' He cloaked the jacket around her shoulders. 'Be kind to a shy old fart.'

In the parking lot, García searched the Caprice for a clean towel. Erin spotted the Igloo cooler and said she hoped there was a cold six-pack inside. The detective said the ice chest was for human body parts, not refreshments.

'Yum,' said Erin. She picked up a clear bag of blue hospital masks. 'I bet you looky snazzy in one of these.'

García said they came in handy. He tossed her a striped beach towel that belonged to Donna.

Erin said, 'I'll ask you what you've been dying to ask me: How in the world can you do it?'

'Do what?'

'Your job. Dead bodies day after day – I couldn't take it.'

The detective said, 'Hey, it's a growth industry. The state could sell fucking bonds.'

On the drive home, they talked about Erin's date with the congressman. She had plenty of questions. Would he be alone? How long did she need to stay? What should she do if he went crazy again? Some of García's answers were more comforting than others.

The detective's car phone beeped. He spoke for less than a minute and hung up, frowning.

Erin said, 'Duty calls.'

'Trunk job,' García muttered. 'Miami International.'

'That's ninety minutes away.'

'No hurry. The guy's been there since Labor Day.' He said the stink wasn't so bad if you dabbed Old Spice inside your hospital mask, before popping the trunk. To Erin, it was the stuff of nightmares.

Back at the apartment, she waited by the front door

326

while Al García checked for signs of intruders. He came back out and told her it was safe. He didn't tell her that he'd emptied her bottle of Beefeater's down the bathtub drain.

At the door, the detective told her to think some more about meeting David Dilbeck alone. If she wanted to change her mind, he'd understand. It was a risky deal.

'I won't change my mind,' she said.

'Then be ready for the worst. For two grand, he'll want more than a peek.'

'Oh, he'll definitely get more than a peek,' Erin said. 'Just one thing: Can I bring my own music?'

Al García said sure, absolutely.

TWENTY-FOUR

Orly asked Shad where he got the scorpion. Shad said he bought it off a guy at Dania jai-alai.

'Dead or alive?'

'Alive,' Shad said.

Orly leaned in for a closer look. 'Is it sick or what?'

Shad said, 'No, I drowned it.'

'How?'

'Johnnie Walker.'

Orly laughed, sucking air through his teeth. 'Red or black?'

'Red,' Shad said. He used his tweezers to lift the dead scorpion from the jar.

'Big fucker,' Orly observed. 'So the idea is to make it look like the company's fault?'

'Sure.' Shad placed the dead scorpion in an eight-ounce carton of cottage cheese. He spooned curds over the soggy corpse except for the stinger, which he purposely left exposed.

Orly said, 'And they'll pay off? The company, I mean.'

'Wouldn't you?' Shad placed the lid on the container and pressed firmly on the edges. He hadn't yet decided whether to sue the cottage-cheese manufacturer or the national supermarket chain that carried the product.

'The guy who sold you the scorpion, is he the same one that sold you the snake?'

'No,' Shad said.

'Because Lorelei ain't thrilled with the snake.'

'I heard.'

On short notice, Shad had located a half-blind boa constrictor for two hundred bucks. The seven-foot reptile was mean, restless and extremely difficult to handle on the dance floor. Even with its mouth taped, the boa intimidated Lorelei.

'She's scared to hang it around her neck,' Orly said.

'So tell her don't hang it on her neck.'

'Then where? She's buck naked, man.'

Shad gave a shrug. 'You wanted a new snake. I got one.'

'It peed on her,' said Orly.

'I heard.'

'Now she's threatening to quit on me. Go back to the Flesh Farm.'

Shad said, 'What the hell, Mr Orly. Snakes pee.' It felt like a chainsaw was cropping the top of his skull. He placed the cottage cheese in the refrigerator and wrote a note in block letters warning the dancers not to touch it. Orly watched quietly, his back to the mirror. Monique Jr limped into the dressing room with a broken heel, which Shad fixed with Crazy Glue. A new hire named Danielle dashed in for a cosmetic emergency; a sharp-eyed customer had spotted the incision marks from her recent surgery. While the dancer lifted her round new breasts, Shad applied Maybelline powder to the scars.

When they were alone again, Orly said: 'The Lings don't know who they're dealin' with.'

'I sure told them.'

'About Fat Tony? Nicky Scarfo?'

'The works,' Shad said. 'They don't particularly give a shit. By the way, Fat Tony croaked. The Lings saw it in *The Herald*.'

Orly planted his elbows on the vanity. 'America's going down the shitter, that's my theory. Why? Because these goddamn foreigners don't respect our national institutions – not Detroit, not Wall Street, not even the Mafia.'

Shad didn't like the direction of the conversation. Soon Orly would ask him to sabotage the Flesh Farm; the subject had arisen often.

'I'd like to help,' Shad said, 'but I can't.'

'What's the big deal?'

'I just can't.' He was hesitant to tell Mr Orly about his rap sheet, as the liquor commission frowned on the practice of hiring convicted felons. 'Call up North,' Shad said. 'Get a real torch artist.' Of course the phone call would never be made; Orly didn't know a soul in the mob.

The club owner picked up a hairbrush and tapped a beat on the dressing table. 'Those Lings,' he said. 'I can't believe they'd hack up a perfectly good snake.'

Shad said they were definitely making a statement.

'They broke the girl's heart,' Orly said. 'Hey, see if there's a cold drink in the fridge.'

Shad found him a cream soda.

'I was thinking,' said Orly, lapping the rim of the can. 'Remember when the business was mainly bikers? Back when we were The Booby Hatch and The Pleasure Palace? Biker girls, biker clientele, biker fights. Those days you knew the rules.'

'It was a pit,' Shad said, unsentimentally.

'Yeah, but we knew what was what. The strippers hooked. The customers dealt dope. Everybody carried a knife or a piece.'

Shad said, 'The good old days. I might just cry.'

'Bottom line, yes, it was a dive. Yes, it was a sewer. But there was a logical fucking order to things.' Orly took a gulp of soda, sloshed it around both cheeks and swallowed. 'Those days I never had to worry about crooks like the Lings. Competition? There wasn't none. DJs. Play lists. Wind machines. Trained fucking pythons, forget it! Back then, the girls couldn't dance worth a lick, and I'll also say they were in no danger of getting hired off by *Playboy*. You remember Thin Lizzie?'

Shad couldn't help but chuckle. Lizzie was a biker dancer who stood five-foot-four, weighed a hundred and seventy-seven pounds and had a stock car tattooed on her back. Who could forget? A red-and-blue Dodge, Number 43. King Richard Petty hisself.

'Remember?' Orly said, glowing. 'So maybe she did suck off half of Fort Lauderdale in my parking lot. The lady was no trouble to me. No trouble at all. I tell her to dance fast, she danced fast. I tell her to dance slow, she goes slow. That was long before this wrestling thing caught on, but lemme say – if I'd told Lizzie to wrestle in transmission fluid, she'd by God wrestle. The girl was a trouper and she understood the rules.'

Shad opened a bottle of Bayer aspirins and chewed up five. Orly offered a swig of cream soda, which Shad declined.

'Now look how the business is changed,' Orly went on. 'My dancers are practically unionized, thanks to your friend Erin. They pick their own songs, pick their own hours. Meanwhile my liability premiums are tripled on account of all the bankers and lawyers and CPAs hanging out at the joint. Every time there's a fight I nearly have a fucking coronary, wondering which yuppie asshole's gonna sue me next.'

Shad said, 'One thing about the bikers. They don't sue.'

'Damn right.'

'On the other hand, you're makin' real good money now. We're selling four, five times the booze.'

Orly crumpled the soda can and pinged it off the wall. 'Prosperity,' he said, 'ain't all it's cracked up to be.'

Shad was disillusioned, too, but for other reasons. He knew better than to share his innermost feelings with the boss.

Orly said, 'I had a chance to get into a Taco Bell franchise up in Orlando. Fifteen minutes from fucking Disney World – did I tell you? This was October last year.'

'You told me,' Shad said. Orly's wife had vetoed the deal because Mexican food aggravated her colon.

'So there goes my best chance to get out,' Orly said, 'all because Lily gets the runs from *fajitas*.'

'She'd rather have you runnin' a strip joint?'

'It's crazy, I know, but she's never said a word.' Orly lowered his voice. 'Between you and me and the four walls, I'm so tired of naked poon I can't stand it. It's been years since I had a serious boner, I swear to God.'

Shad agreed it was a draining job. Lord, didn't he know!

Orly said, 'I'll ask straight up. What happens you

hit it big on this scorpion deal? Say the cottage-cheese company comes through with a couple hundred grand. I guess I'll be needing a new bouncer.'

'Maybe. Maybe not. I like you all right, Mr Orly.'

'Hey, you could even buy a piece of this joint. We could be goddamn partners!'

'To be honest,' Shad said, 'I don't like you that much.'

'Whatever. That's OK, too.'

In eleven years it was the longest conversation that the two men had ever had. Orly was plainly overwrought about something. Shad asked what had happened to put him in such a mood.

'Not a damn thing,' he snapped.

'Moldowsky called again, right? About Erin.'

'On top of everything else, yeah.' Orly became subdued. 'He's looking for a picture of this horny congressman. A picture from right here at the club. I'm sure you wouldn't know anything about that.'

'Nope,' said Shad. 'What else?'

'He had a message for Erin.' Orly pulled a shred of paper from his damp breast pocket and gave it to Shad. 'Ten o'clock tomorrow night down at Turnberry. Here's the name of the yacht.'

Shad struggled to decipher Orly's scribble; his sweat had made the ink run. '*Sweetheart* something,' Shad said. He didn't like the idea of Erin meeting Dilbeck on a boat.

Orly said, 'So I suppose she's gonna screw this guy.'

'Why?'

''Cause he's a politician, for God's sake.'

Shad said, 'You know her better than that.'

'A United States congressman, you're telling me it's

just a private dance party? No sex is what you're telling me?'

'I'd be very surprised.'

Orly did a poor job of masking his disappointment. Shad did an equally poor job of masking his anger; the stare he leveled at Orly was harrowing.

'Fuck the liquor license,' he said.

Orly stiffened. 'But the guy's busting my balls.'

'Then *you* sleep with him.'

'Take it easy, take it easy.' Nervously Orly chucked Shad on the forearm. 'See, this is what I mean. This is my exact point. In the old days we never worried about evil shit like this. Rednecks, bikers and whores – that was the tittie business. Now look out there, you see beepers and cell phones at every fucking table. Blow-dried dorks in designer suspenders, honest to Christ! The parking lot's full of Beemers and Blazers but, shit, I can't sleep nights. No, you keep your fucking upscale clientele.'

'And politicians,' Shad said. The impulse to choke Mr Orly had ebbed slightly.

'Bikers are better customers,' said Orly. 'I swear to God, Shad, I'd rather have a barful of bikers than one shitfaced congressman. The fights we could handle, remember? Hell, I'd take a stabbing every night over evil shit like this. Some guy I never met, busting my balls about the license.'

In five minutes Urbana Sprawl was due to wrestle in a vat of cooked linguini. Shad planned to supervise. He stood up and said, 'What's done is done. We'll fix things right.'

'How?'

'Don't worry about it, Mr Orly.'

They walked through the main lounge together. Rap music pounded pneumatically from the walls. On stage, Lorelei was struggling with the new snake, which had coiled itself the full length of her right leg. Even the most drunken customers realized it was not part of the act.

Orly cupped a hand to Shad's ear and shouted: 'Maybe I'll put a sign at the door: No politicians allowed! Ax murderers and perverts welcome, but no goddamn politicians!'

Shad faked a smile. He was grumpy enough to bite the head off a kitten.

'Give me bikers any day,' Orly was saying. 'No more congressmen in my joint . . .'

On stage, Lorelei gimped stoically out of the spotlight. She yelled something about her leg turning blue.

Shad thought: I've got to get out soon. Before I do some damage.

Malcolm J. Moldowsky knew that the congressman couldn't be blackmailed by a geek bouncer with a felony rap sheet. More problematic was the younger stockbroker, Paul Guber, but he had abruptly left town. It was the third person in the scandalous bachelor-party photograph who most worried Moldy: the stripper.

If so inclined, Erin Grant could singlehandedly destroy the congressman's fragile reputation. Which is precisely why Moldowsky had arranged for the two of them to meet.

Moldy spent the morning of October fourth in a high-level strategy session, by himself. He neither needed nor sought the counsel of others. Silence bred clarity of thinking, and solitude restored one's perspective. It was important to set aside his personal contempt for David Dilbeck and concentrate on the mission for which he was being paid. Many fires burned out of control. It was time to focus.

He needed ammunition, but there wasn't much in Erin's past. The custody file was loaded with juicy accusations, but Moldowsky was skeptical of the ex-husband's veracity; Darrell Grant came off as a despicable creep. No sense opening that particular can of worms.

Moldy decided to treat Mrs Grant very gently indeed. Look but don't touch, he'd warned the congressman. Do nothing to frighten or anger this woman. If she says no, don't argue. If all else fails, try to make friends.

If only Dilbeck could be trusted to stick to the script. The subject of the deceased Jerry Killian was to be avoided. Subtle inquiries were to be made about the stripper's daughter. If Mrs Grant complained about the custody litigation, Dilbeck was to offer his assistance. *I know the new judge quite well* – something mild like that, not pushy or boastful. If Mrs Grant brought up Dilbeck's bloody outburst at the Eager Beaver, the congressman was to appear remorseful but offer nothing. Moldowsky drilled him on these points. He tried to keep things simple because he knew Dilbeck's brain would be fogged with lust. Precautions had been taken to protect the stripper from lewd assault, but risk was unavoidable. The congressman was coming apart. It was a race against time.

Malcolm Moldowsky studied his reflection in the bay window. He liked what he saw – a portrait of elegant confidence under stress. Even at home, Moldy was rarely comfortable wearing anything but a coat and tie. He'd read that Nixon was the same way, but so what? Casual attire impeded Moldy's genius; he simply didn't feel powerful in a tank top and a pair of wrinkled Dockers. On this morning he wore a three-piece charcoal suit, tailored in Paris. The necktie was burgundy with a gray diagonal stripe.

Moldowsky sat at the cherry desk in his den. The phone rang often, but he let the machine answer. He made notes on a legal pad. He wrote: 'What does she want?' Then he jotted a list of possible scenarios, from worst to best.

Worst: The stripper could sink the congressman. She could do it on her own, or at an enemy's behest. She wouldn't necessarily need the photograph, either; an afternoon press conference would do nicely. The revelation would be an instant catastrophe. If it didn't cost Dilbeck the election, it certainly would imperil the sugar subsidies. The Rojos stood to lose millions. Malcolm Moldowsky would do anything to prevent such a calamity. He had painstakingly mended Dilbeck's political fences, and the committee vote was all but nailed down. The single remaining hurdle was a Republican named Tooley from northern Alabama who claimed to be a born-again Christian and railed tirelessly against R-rated movies, all forms of rock music, and the annual *Sports Illustrated* swimsuit edition. Moldowsky happened to know that Congressman Tooley was a syphilitic old fraud, but it didn't matter. The sonofabitch would repudiate David Dilbeck immediately if a seedy sex scandal came to light. Tooley wouldn't vote in the same column as a philandering pagan – not for farm subsidies or any other damn fool thing. If Dilbeck was exposed, the sugar vote would be in grave jeopardy.

At the bottom of Moldy's list was his dream scenario: What if the stripper let the whole thing slide? Maybe she had no hard feelings about the champagne-bottle attack, no interest in blackmailing the hot-blooded congressman, no secret doubts about Jerry Killian's death. Perhaps she just wanted to be left alone to dance her heart out.

Not likely, Moldowsky thought. The woman surely needed money, and surely understood how deeply she could wound David Dilbeck by opening her mouth. Moldowsky guessed that Erin Grant's silence was available for purchase. He figured she'd be content to accept a large sum and leave town quietly with her little girl. That would be fine. A payoff carried its own risks, but arranging a permanent disappearance was no longer viable. Not with a homicide cop hovering in the shadows.

Moldy was vexed by Al García. How did his card turn up in the lawyer's safe-deposit box? Was the detective looking into Mordecai's disappearance? Moldy made a note to check with the Florida Bar. It was he, after all, who had tipped investigators to the missing lawyer's trust-fund 'scheme'.

There were more riddles: Why would a Dade County homicide cop be snooping around Fort Lauderdale? Was García investigating Jerry Killian's death, too? More important, was it he who removed the Kodak slide from Mordecai's safe box?

Experience had taught Malcolm Moldowsky to brace for the worst. Assume García was hot on the trail. Assume he'd gotten wind of the blackmail plots. Assume he suspected foul play in the death of Killian and the disappearance of Mordecai . . .

Let him assume his fool head off, Moldowsky thought.

There's no proof, no evidence, no thread linking these unfortunate coincidences to the congressman. Homicides? A lonely bachelor has a fishing accident in Montana, a slimy lawyer skips town with embezzled accounts. What homicides? What the hell was García doing? Moldy wondered if the detective was playing a little game of his own – maybe the business card was left as bait. If so, the only smart move was to ignore the bastard. Play it cool.

Moldowsky's problem was a pathological lack of restraint. He owned a huge ego, a short temper and no patience. He was unaccustomed to doing nothing. He had so many connections and so much sway that his reflex was to grab the phone and ream some ass. That's what fixers did, they spotted trouble coming and headed it off. But an influence-peddler was only as good as his information, and Moldy didn't know jack about this pushy Cuban cop. It gnawed at him all morning. Two, three phone calls would do the trick . . . but why panic? He'd been so thorough, so careful – a mistake was flatly impossible, ridiculous even. Señor Detective García didn't have squat. Nobody could've put it together so fast.

Yet Moldy found himself eyeing the telephone. Buffed nails tapped restlessly on the cherrywood. He needed to know more. His hand shot across the desk toward the Rolodex. His fingers tripped lightly through familiar index cards. It was an astounding trove of sources. Names and numbers, numbers and names. And they each owed Malcolm J. Moldowsky a favor.

It was like a drug, this power he had.

TWENTY-FIVE

The two goons guarding the Rojo yacht were dazzled by Erin's arrival. She wore blood-red lipstick, gold hoop earrings, a white miniskirt, fuck-me pumps and a sleeveless salmon blouse. She looked great, she smelled great. A walking fantasy. The hired goons envied David Lane Dilbeck.

'You're Mrs Grant?'

'No,' Erin said. 'I'm Tipper Gore.'

'Who's your friend? He's not invited.'

Shad emerged from the shadow. The goons shifted uneasily in their shiny black suits. They clenched their fists and swelled their chests, but the stripper's bodyguard seemed unimpressed. He was as broad as a meat locker, and wore a red beret that barely covered the crown of his lumpy bald dome. His mouth was a cruel-looking beak. He blinked with bulging eel eyes. He had a .38 tucked in his belt, and a South American kinkajou on his left shoulder. The kinkajou was eating a candy bar.

'Relax,' Shad told the goons. 'He's on a leash.'

'Who the hell are you?'

Erin said, 'He's a Guardian Angel. Can't you tell?'

'Get lost,' said one of the goons.

Erin took Shad's hand. 'He goes, I go,' she said.

The goons stepped away and conferred briefly. One

of them disappeared into the yacht. He returned with a decision: 'OK, Mr Guardian Angel, you can stay out here with us. But your monkey goes back to the zoo.'

Shad said, 'It ain't a monkey.' The kinkajou chittered through a mouthful of nougats. When Shad stroked its neck, the animal turned and bit him on the wrist. The goons jumped but Shad showed no reaction. He wiped the blood on his camouflage trousers and said, 'I got him off a guy at jai-alai. He loves chocolate.'

'Crazy fuck,' muttered one of the goons.

Two couples came strolling down the dock in the moonlight. The men wore white dinner jackets and the women, both blondes, wore shiny evening gowns. They drank Rum Runners and laughed. The women were impressed by the tall fishing boats and gleaming yachts, and the men seemed to be expert mariners. They were much older than their dates. When they reached the slip where the *Sweetheart Deal* was moored, conversation stopped. The men eyed Erin, who smiled tolerantly. On deck the pinheaded Rojo goons stood shoulder to shoulder, steroid bookends. Shad adjusted the angle of his red beret.

One of the blondes: 'Say, can I pet your monkey?'

'It ain't a monkey. It's a kinkajou.'

'Oh, I love kinkajous.'

'Then what the hell. Pet away.'

One of the dinner jackets: 'He doesn't bite, does he?'

Shad looked insulted. 'No, sir, he doesn't.'

'See you later,' Erin said. She slipped between the two goons and opened the cabin door.

*

Al García's boss in Homicide was Lt William Bowman, who once played linebacker for the University of Florida. Billy Bowman hated cigars and was eleven years younger than García, but García didn't mind because Bowman was a decent cop, for an Anglo. Most of the time, he left García alone.

On the night that Erin was to dance for the congressman, Bllly Bowman called García into the office. There was the traditional discussion of the wretchedness of the Miami Dolphins offense, followed by a cursory inquiry about the late Francisco Goyo.

'We found everything,' García told Bowman, 'except four toes and a buttock.'

'Nice work.'

'Billy?'

'Yeah.'

'Why am I here?'

Bowman cracked his knuckles. 'Is that a cosmic question? Such as: What's the point of it all? What is God's grand plan?'

García, grumbling: 'No, *chico*, I mean why the fuck am I *here*? In your office. Shooting the shit for no apparent reason.'

'How about closing that door.'

García extended a leg and kicked the door shut.

Bowman said, 'I got an interesting phone call from the chief, who had an interesting call from one of the county commissioners.'

'Do tell,' said García.

'Are you working a case with Broward?'

'Several, Billy.'

'A missing lawyer?'

'This is fascinating,' García said. 'Let's have some coffee.'

Over the next half-hour, he told Lt Billy Bowman the whole story, beginning with the floater in Montana. Bowman was a good listener and he asked sharp questions. When García finished, the lieutenant said he was very impressed. 'You got 'em to drill a lock box without a court order.'

García said, 'I knew a girl at the bank, she's a vice-president now. We set a little trap.'

Billy Bowman winced. 'I didn't hear that.'

'Whoever opened the lawyer's safe box found my card. And whoever found my card got on the phone.'

'Which is exactly what you wanted.'

Al García was generous about handing out his business cards during murder investigations. Frequently he'd give one to a prime suspect, just to gauge the reaction.

'So,' said the lieutenant, 'under whose ass did you light this particular fire?'

'If I had to guess,' García said, 'it's Malcolm Moldowsky.'

Bowman said he'd never heard of the guy. García told him he wasn't supposed to. Political fixers were like vampires, the way they avoided daylight.

'This is how it went: Moldowsky calls the commissioner, who probably owes him a big favor. Maybe several big favors, who knows? So the commissioner calls the chief and says who's this guy García, why's he mucking around up in Broward? The last thing Metro needs is some jurisdictional beef with BSO.'

'Believe it or not,' Bowman said, 'the commissioner was almost clever about it. He claims to be a dear friend of the missing lawyer. Says they met at a Dukakis fund-raiser and he can't believe – what's the dickhead's name?'

'Mordecai.'

'Yeah. The commissioner can't believe Mordecai would take off to the islands with embezzled money.'

García laughed. 'That's very slick, making it personal. Like he was upset about his pal and that's all.'

'Right. And anything we could tell him would be greatly appreciated – and very confidential, of course.'

Bowman took a call on the speaker phone while García poured the last coffee. A uniformed road officer had shot a burglar after a chase down the Palmetto Expressway. Bowman took notes and said he was on the way. He hung up swearing because the dead burglar was a drag queen, which meant that the local TV stations would go wild. The lieutenant said, 'My whole career, I never shot a guy in a strapless cocktail dress. How about you?'

'The world's changing, William.' García lifted a salute with the coffee cup.

Billy Bowman swung his size-thirteen Reeboks up on the desk. 'About this lawyer – you figure he's dead, too?'

'Most likely,' García said.

'And dumped, like the other guy.'

'Yeah, but who knows where.'

'The Everglades is perfect,' Billy Bowman said. 'Why go all the way to Bumfuck, Montana, when you got the Everglades in your own backyard? Hell, a dead body decomposes faster here than anywhere else in the country. That's a known fact, Al.'

'Don't tell me they've done a study.'

345

'Seriously. Miami's got the fastest rot-rate, because of the heat.'

'Really?' García mused. 'I thought it was the humidity.'

'The point is, Montana makes no sense.'

'It does if your victim's supposed to be on vacation. Killian was a trout fisherman, remember? This shitbird lawyer, who knows where they put him? The nearest landfill, probably.'

The lieutenant said nothing for several moments. Then: 'Al, you can't just go out and bust a fucking congressman.'

'I'm aware of that.'

'Unless you catch him in the act. Preferably on video-tape, with the pope and Mary Tyler Moore as eyewitnesses.'

'Bill, I'm aware of that.'

'Where's the Kodak slide? I'm curious is all.'

García let the question hang. Bowman was a smart guy; it wouldn't take him long to see the problem. About eleven seconds, in fact.

'You're right,' he told García. 'I don't want to know.'

'Tell the chief there's no missing-lawyer case with Broward.'

'You were just checking out a tip.'

'Right,' García said. 'Dry hole.'

'Sorry we couldn't be more help.'

'Yeah,' García said. 'We're very sorry.'

'And this'll go straight back to Moldowsky?'

'You can bet on it.'

'Then what happens, Al? Can we look forward to an actual arrest in our lifetime?'

García rubbed his chin. 'Frankly, I got shit for evidence. But I got some beautiful theories.'

Bowman liked Al García because he was an excellent detective with no ambition to be anything more. Bowman himself wished to be chief some day, and cops such as García often made him look brilliant. Consequently, he wanted García to be happy and productive, not bored or burned out. Al enjoyed challenges, and the lieutenant usually tried to oblige. But this . . .

'Where's our jurisdiction?' Bowman asked.

'It's iffy,' García admitted. 'Dilbeck lives in Dade County. So does Moldowsky.'

'But the crimes took place elsewhere, right?' Bowman cracked his knuckles again. 'Al, would you hate my guts if I said you're on your own?'

'You'd be crazy not to. Maybe I'll take some sick days.'

'But, as your friend, let me also say I'd love to see you pull this off.'

'It's a long shot, Billy.'

'Yeah, but I got a personal stake here. I voted for the dumb bastard.'

'No shit?' Al García couldn't believe that Bowman was a registered Democrat.

The lieutenant pulled his feet off the desk. 'I remember what you told me a long time ago—'

'The world is a sewer and we're all dodging shit.'

'Very uplifting, Al. I'm surprised Hallmark hasn't bought up the copyright.'

'Words to live by,' García said.

'You know what's sad? I'm beginning to think you're right. I'm beginning to think there's no hope.'

'Of course there's no hope,' García said, 'but don't let it get you down.'

'I'm pissed, Al. I voted for the asshole.'

'Here's what you do: First thing tomorrow, sign up for some range time. Check out an Uzi, one of the fully automatics, and go nuts for about an hour. Shoot the living shit outta the place. You'll feel a thousand percent better.'

Billy Bowman said it sounded like a good idea. He tossed a notebook and a Pearlcorder in his briefcase. 'Well, I better get a move on.'

'Good luck with the drag-queen burglar.'

'Thanks, Al. Good luck with the degenerate congressman.'

David Lane Dilbeck greeted Erin timidly. He wore a blue blazer, a white shirt, pleated camel trousers and expensive cordovan loafers; no socks. His silver hair had a grooved look, as if it had been combed about twenty times in the past hour. Additionally, the congressman reeked of Aramis.

Erin was accustomed to overdoses of cologne, but she wasn't sure if she could hack the comical distraction of a turtleneck.

She said, 'This is a gorgeous boat.'

'Belongs to a friend,' Dilbeck said. 'I use it any time I please.'

'For this?'

Dilbeck stammered in the negative.

'What's that on the stereo?' Erin asked.

'Dean Martin. Music for lovers.'

He's serious, Erin thought. That *is* Dean Martin. 'Well, it's pretty,' she said, 'but I brought my own.'

'Fine.' Dilbeck sounded disappointed. 'It's your show.'

Erin had never spoken with an actual United States congressman. She expected a smoother presentation, an air of self-assurance if not downright conceit. But David Dilbeck struck her as just another jittery old lech.

'Let's try this.' Erin handed him a cassette. 'I put it together myself.' She went to the head and changed to a dance outfit. It wasn't easy; the bathroom was fiendishly small. Erin wriggled into a white teddy. Underneath she wore a lace brassiere and a matching G-string. She was betting that Dilbeck would go for the honeymoon look.

When she came out, ZZ Top was playing on the Rojos' sound system. She balanced the bass and cranked up the volume a couple of notches. The stage was a captain's table that had been moved to the center of the room. The congressman sunk into a canvas director's chair. He crossed his ankles and entwined his hands. A silver champagne bucket sat at his right elbow.

Erin stepped on the table and tested it for traction. As she began to dance, she felt vaguely claustrophobic; the yacht's salon had a low roof, and the paneled walls had no mirrors. Erin never performed without mirrors, and now she was uncomfortable. Mirrors helped her concentrate on the footwork, helped her detach from the stares.

Dilbeck's chin bobbed a half-beat behind the music; he was trying his damnedest to look like a rocker. Erin removed her top and dropped it on his lap. He gazed reverently at the undergarment, his mouth parted. He breathed a low growl. When he raised his eyes, Erin flashed her million-dollar smile. She unsnapped the G-string and slipped it down around the garter. The congressman's neck went limp, and his body swayed.

Scary, Erin thought. A genuine sexual trance. She felt she was witnessing a rare phenomenon, like a total eclipse.

'She's Got Legs' faded into 'Brown-Eyed Girl', which blended into 'Under My Thumb'. With each song the dance tempo slowed, and so did the congressman's pulse. His eyes rolled and his jaw fell open, exposing a fortune in capped teeth. A large man, he seemed to shrink visibly as the music played – a marionette cut loose from its strings. Performing for a catatonic was lonely. Erin missed Orly's mirrors.

When the set ended, David Dilbeck snapped upright and began to clap. Erin was startled at his rapid recovery. The congressman folded two hundred-dollar bills in her garter and offered to pour the champagne. She put on the white teddy and turned off the tape deck. Dilbeck had a chair waiting.

He said, 'You are positively amazing.'

'So are you.'

'The most incredible blue eyes!'

'They're green,' Erin said, 'but thanks, anyway.'

Dilbeck handed her a glass and made a toast to new friendships. 'Do you remember me?' he asked. 'The last time we met, I wore a mustache.' Already he'd deviated from Moldowsky's script.

Erin said, 'How could I forget. You nearly bashed me in the skull.'

'I'm so sorry.'

'What in the world came over you?'

Dilbeck looked away. 'Truly I don't remember. It was

inexcusable.' He tossed back the champagne. 'I hope you can forgive me.' It was, he thought, a cunning way to elicit Erin's frame of mind. If she let the subject drop, she probably wasn't planning to shake him down.

'Come on,' she said, 'how about another number?'

The congressman relaxed. 'Wonderful,' he said, peeling off his blazer.

By the fourth set, he was helpless, exhausted and bombed. Erin had done some of the best dancing of her life. Dilbeck sat cross-legged on the floor of the salon. He'd kicked off his loafers and unbuttoned his shirt. Erin perched topless on the edge of the captain's table. Dilbeck clutched at her knee but she nudged his hand away.

'I love you,' he said. 'Desperately I do.'

'I love you, too, sweetie.'

'Be my girlfriend.'

'Your what?'

'How would . . .' His eyes fluttered. 'How would you like an apartment on the Intracoastal? And a car – what'd you think of the new Lexus? You can quit your job and live like a queen.'

'You're kidding. All that, just for being your girlfriend?'

'Whatever you want.'

'Wow.' Erin saw an opportunity to have some fun. 'Davey, can I ask a question?'

'Anything, darling.'

'I wouldn't have to screw you, would I?'

Dilbeck squinted in puzzlement. 'Well now,' he said, working his lips like a plowhorse.

'What I mean,' said Erin, 'is you wouldn't expect sex in exchange for your kindness. I can tell you're not that kind of person.'

The congressman chuckled wretchedly. He groped for the champagne bottle and took a swig.

Erin let her foot brush against Dilbeck's leg. 'You wouldn't believe some men,' she said. 'They're such pigs. They give you a sports car, they expect at least a hand job. Sometimes two!'

'Huh,' said Dilbeck. 'Imagine that.'

Erin gave a convincing sigh of disgust. 'Some guys,' she said. 'I swear to God.'

'But I love you.'

'I'm sure you do, Davey. But I couldn't accept an apartment or anything else. It wouldn't be right.'

'Please. I want your life to be wonderful.'

The congressman watched sorrowfully as Erin put on her bra top. She liked the rush on nights like this, when the dancing was so good. The feeling of control was indescribable. More important, a plan – a wondrously reckless plan – was taking shape.

'What is it you do in Washington?' she asked Dilbeck. 'Give me a job description.'

Dilbeck took several moments to reassemble his thoughts. 'Mainly I help people. My constituents.' He paused theatrically. 'You may not know this, but I once tried to help you.'

'Really.'

'Yes, ma'am. With regards to your daughter.'

Erin stiffened. She said, 'I didn't know.'

'Oh yes, oh yes. I spoke to a certain judge. He wouldn't listen to reason.'

'My divorce judge?'

'The old man, yes. A difficult fellow, God rest his soul.'

Erin said, 'Why did you do that? How'd you know

about my case?' She tried to sound curious and not accusatory. This was the important part, and Al García would want every detail. Was Dilbeck drunk enough to blab about Jerry Killian?

Apparently not. He said, 'A little birdie told me about your case.'

Erin coaxed but he wouldn't budge.

'I was glad to try,' the congressman said. 'I have great compassion for working mothers.'

'Thank you. I had no idea.'

He slid closer to the table. 'I know the new judge, as well.'

Erin said she was impressed that a man as important as Dilbeck would take an interest in her family problems.

'That's my job,' he said. 'Helping people.' One of the congressman's hands came to rest on Erin's thigh. She gave him three, maybe four seconds of thrill before flicking it away.

She said, 'The case is working out fine. My daughter's with me now.'

'I'm glad to hear it. But, remember, if you need anything—'

'Aren't you a sweetheart.'

'Anything at all—'

'Hey, Davey?'

'What is it?'

'Did you steal the razor out of my bathroom?'

David Dilbeck turned gray. Moldy hadn't prepared him for this. He said, 'God help me, I did.'

'You're a sick puppy.'

'That's what Erb says.'

'Who's Erb?'

353

'Erb Crandall. He works for me.'

Erin said, 'Why'd you take the razor?'

The congressman's jowls quavered. He appeared on the verge of tears. 'That's how much I love you,' he said. 'I took some lint, too.'

'Lint.'

'From your laundry. I'm awfully sorry.'

Erin stood on the table and put her hands on her hips. Dilbeck was sprawled in a wrinkled heap on the wooden floor.

'Davey, I don't mean to pry. But what did you do with my laundry lint?'

'I'm afraid I made love to it.'

The room began to whirl. 'Come closer,' Erin told him.

Dilbeck gripped the corners of the captain's table and pulled himself to his knees.

Erin said, 'Shut your eyes.'

'Oh God.' The congressman's dreams ran wild.

Erin removed one of her shoes and, with all her strength, hammered the four-inch heel into the bones of David Dilbeck's right hand. So much for García's instruction to remain calm.

Dilbeck didn't scream so much as whinny. Erin snatched a handful of oily silver hair.

'Davey, if you ever come into my apartment again, *ever*, I'll shoot you. Is that understood?'

Through his agony the congressman whispered: 'But I love you so much!'

'I know you do, sweetheart.'

*

The two goons asked Shad if he was really a Guardian Angel. He said yes, but he moonlighted nights at a nudie joint. The goons wanted to know all about it. Shad said the music was terrible and the pay sucked.

'Who cares,' said one of the goons. 'Think of all the pussy.'

Shad said, 'Pussy don't pay the rent.' He plucked an ice cube from his glass and gave it to the kinkajou. The animal snarled as it chewed.

The other goon, who had tiny crumpled-looking ears, asked Shad if he had to pay the dancers for sex. 'Or do you get it free? What's the deal?'

Shad said, 'They pay *me*.'

'Aw, bullshit.'

'It's in my contract.'

The first goon said, 'Yeah, right.'

'Any girl I want.'

Shad transferred the kinkajou from one shoulder to the other. His shirt was sticky with blood, from the animal digging its claws. The crumple-eared goon grimaced when he saw the mess. He and his partner had given Shad and his strange pet a wide berth on the yacht's aft deck. Shad knew that the men feared the kinkajou more than they feared him. That was the plan.

The first goon said, 'So, like, you get to watch all the auditions?'

'Watch, my ass. I do the hiring.'

'Man! So you get to see everything.'

'Everything,' Shad said with a sly smile.

'And you been at it how long?'

'Ten, eleven years.'

'Think of all the titties you've seen.'

'Thousands,' said Shad. 'It boggles the fucking mind.'

He couldn't believe what morons they were, these hired guards.

The first one said: 'When you do the auditions, what do you go by? Is it just size? Reason I ask, once I was with this girl who had gigantic boobs but they didn't look so hot when she took off her top. Know what I mean?'

Shad said, 'We got very high standards.'

The crumple-eared goon asked: 'You ever audition anyone famous? I mean, before they got famous.'

'Oh sure,' said Shad, thinking fast. These dolts would believe anything. 'Kim Basinger danced at the club for a while. So did Meryl Streep, only back then she used a different name.'

'No shit?'

'Chesty LeFrance. That's what she went by.'

The first goon said, 'Kim Basinger, sure. But Meryl Streep, man, she ain't exactly stacked.'

'Not now she isn't,' Shad said. 'You should've seen her before the operation. Awesome.'

The kinkajou climbed down his arm and hopped to the deck. Shad gave a sharp tug on the leash. The animal growled and rolled on its back.

'How about that,' said the goon with the bad ears.

Shad said, 'Yeah, I got him trained good.' Truthfully, he wasn't crazy about the kinkajou. He was glad the two hours were almost over, so he could return the animal.

'How about you boys,' Shad said. 'You like this gig?'

The first goon said he'd rather be down below, doing what the old man was doing. The second goon said yeah, the worst part of the job was trying to stay awake. Shad asked how much the old man paid.

'We don't work for the old man. We work for the Rojos.'

'Who's that?'

'Rojo Farms,' said the crumple-eared goon. 'We get two hundred a day.'

'Damn,' Shad said.

'And mostly we just hang out.'

The first goon said, 'They call us drivers but that's bullshit. We're security. The Rojos do lots of entertaining, and we keep an eye on the guests . . . speaking of which.' He motioned to his partner, who stepped to the salon door and listened.

'Music's stopped,' he reported. 'Sounds like they're just talking.'

Shad said, 'So who's the old man in there – some bigshot?'

'Friend of the family.'

The kinkajou began pacing restlessly, tangling the leash around Shad's legs. The Rojo goons were amused by the bald man's efforts to extricate himself. In frustration Shad let go. The kinkajou ambled to a corner and sat down, licking its paws.

One of the goons said, 'I never heard of a stripper with a bodyguard.'

Shad said a woman can't be too careful these days.

The one with the deformed ears motioned toward Shad's gun. 'Is that a .38?'

'Special,' Shad said.

'That's what I want, too. How long before your license came through?'

'I didn't bother with a license. See, I got a slight history.'

'That's rough,' said the goon.

'Fucking computers.' Shad emptied his glass over the rail.

'But still they let you in the Guardian Angels?'

'No problem. I had references.' Shad pointed at his head. 'Plus I already had the hat.'

Erin came out the door. She looked tired but unmolested.

'All set?' Shad said.

'Fine and dandy.'

He held her arm as she stepped from the yacht to the dock.

'Nice night,' she said, smiling up at the teardrop moon.

'Very pleasant,' Shad agreed. He waved goodbye to the halfwit goons.

'Wait,' said the one with the normal ears. 'Don't forget your monkey!'

Al García met them at a bagel joint near the jai-alai fronton in Dania. Erin and Shad were late because Shad couldn't find the guy who'd rented him the kinkajou. After twenty minutes of circling the block, he pulled off the road, opened the door and put the animal out. Shad threw a bag of Snickers bars from the car and drove away. When he walked into the bagel joint, a waitress noticed the bloodied shirt and offered to call 911. She assumed that Shad had been stabbed.

García was waiting at a table near the rear of the restaurant. He was mouthing the nub of a very old cigar. He asked Erin how it went with the congressman.

'Piece of cake.' She gave a slightly edited account.

The congressman's lint confession was the highlight. Even Shad was astounded.

'That's some honor,' he said.

García asked Erin if Dilbeck tried anything weird while she was dancing. She said no, just the usual hopeful groping. She left out the part about smashing his hand.

'So what's your impression?' the detective asked.

'One, Davey's not too bright. Two, he probably doesn't know exactly what happened to Jerry Killian.'

García concurred. 'He doesn't have the nerve to do it himself, and the people who did are smart enough not to tell him.'

'In other words,' Shad said, 'we're wasting our goddamn time.'

The waitress brought a platter of bagels and a pot of coffee. Shad took off his shirt and asked the awestruck waitress to please throw it in the garbage. As they ate, Al García peppered Erin with questions.

'Did he say whose yacht it was?'

'A friend,' Erin said. 'That's all he'd tell me.'

García smiled. 'Remember the Cuban kid who paid a thousand bucks for your shoe? His family owns the *Sweetheart Deal*.'

'The sugar people?'

'Yeah. They got Dilbeck's balls in a vault somewhere.'

Erin drummed her nails on the table. 'So the kid bought my shoe as a present for Davey.'

'A nice gesture,' Shad remarked. 'Fetish-of-the-month.'

García said, 'Are either of you history buffs? Me, I love American history.' He leaned forward, dropping his voice. 'I'm trying to imagine what Thomas Paine would think of a congressman who has sex with old shoes and laundry lint.'

Erin agreed that the republic was doomed. She said Tasmania was looking pretty good as an alternate homeland.

Al García asked if David Dilbeck had mentioned the crucial photograph. Erin said he'd barely talked about that night at the Eager Beaver, except to apologize.'

'What about Angela?'

'He offered to help with the new judge,' Erin said. 'That's the only time I was nervous. He seemed a little too interested.'

Shad got up to call the club and make sure no disasters had occurred in his absence. Orly got on the line and bitched about him taking the night off. A British sailor had almost choked to death in the pasta pit – Monique Sr saved him with a modified Heimlich.

'Sorry I missed it,' Shad said. Orly hung up.

Shad returned to the table and said he'd better go, Mr Orly was pissed. García offered Erin a ride home.

In the car, she said: 'So tell me.'

'What?'

'You're humming, Al. You never hum. What happened?'

'Progress!' The detective waggled the cigar nub. 'A very nice lady at the Missoula Holiday Inn remembers three Jamaicans getting a room and ordering a half-dozen rib-eye steaks sent up. This happened a few weeks back. Apparently not a multitude of Jamaicans cruise through Montana this time of year. Anyhow, the nice lady punched their bill up on the computer and read me the charges.'

'And?'

'There was a twenty-two-minute phone call,' García said, cigar bobbing, 'to a certain residence in Miami, Florida.'

Erin said, 'Dilbeck?'

'God, how I wish,' said García. 'No, darling. It was Malcolm Moldowsky – the congressman's fairy godfather. The guy who keeps hassling your boss.'

So there was no doubt about it, Erin thought. They'd murdered Mr Peepers.

'I'll never prove it,' García said, 'but I can sure raise some hell. Did Davey Boy happen to mention Moldowsky's name? Between hard-ons, I mean.'

'He talked about a guy named Crandall.'

'But no Moldowsky?'

'Not tonight,' Erin said. 'I'll try again next time.'

The detective's foot came off the accelerator. 'Did I miss something?'

'I'm dancing for Davey again.'

'Like hell—'

Erin cut him off. 'He tipped me a thousand bucks, Al. That's three grand I walked with. A couple more nights like this, my lawyer's paid off and I've got cash in the bank.'

'Too risky.'

'He's harmless. Trust me, he's a little boy.'

She didn't tell the detective what she had in mind, because he couldn't help. In fact, he probably would've stopped her from going through with it. Likewise, Shad would be an unsuitable accomplice; too impulsive, too volatile. If things got hot, he'd wind up in the back of a squad car. Maybe Erin would, too. She couldn't take the chance.

'Where,' García asked, archly, 'is the next rendezvous?'

Erin shrugged. 'It's entirely up to him.'

'Oh, for God's sake.'

They rode in prickly silence for several miles before she said, 'Al, tell me what's wrong.'

'Nothing.' He spit the spent cigar out the window. 'I think you liked it. Am I right?'

'It was easy tonight. I like it when it's easy.'

He slapped the steering wheel with both hands. 'Christ, it's not a game. I pulled your dead pal out of the river, remember?'

She thought: He wasn't there tonight. He didn't see for himself. Dilbeck was completely helpless.

García warned her that it was bound to get hinky. He said she was pressing her luck, seeing the congressman again. She told him he didn't understand.

'Sure I understand,' he said. 'It's not about the money, is it?'

'Not entirely.' Erin's eyes flashed.

'It's about power. Pure and simple.'

'Al,' she said, 'you've been watching too much "Oprah."'

TWENTY-SIX

The next day, Erin took her daughter to see *101 Dalmatians* at a mall in South Miami. After the movie, they stopped at an ice cream shop, where Erin ordered two scoops of chocolate pistachio for both of them.

Angela, licking a cone: 'Can we get a dog someday?'

'Sure,' said Erin.

'Not like Aunt Rita's, either.'

'How about a Dalmatian? Just like in the movie.'

Angela said, 'No, I want a Great Dane. But not one that bites, OK?'

'Then we'll get a puppy. We'll train it together.'

'What about Daddy?'

Erin crunched hard on a pistachio. 'Good question,' she said.

'He doesn't like dogs. He likes birds.'

'I remember,' Erin said. 'The dog'll be yours and mine.'

Angela wore a thoughtful expression. 'Is Daddy in trouble?'

'Yes, baby, I'm afraid so.'

'Are you in trouble, too?'

'No, Angie, I'm doing just fine.'

Later they walked around Burdine's and looked at the clothes. Erin bought her daughter two dresses, two overalls and a pair of white Nike sneakers with pink slashes.

Angela said, 'Momma, it's not my birthday.'

'I know, honey.'

'What's the matter?'

'Nothing's the matter,' Erin said. 'I love you, that's all.'

'I love you, too, Momma. But don't cry.'

'I'm not crying. It's my allergies.'

Angela looked doubtful. She said, 'Allergies make you sneeze, not cry.'

'For your information, little lady, there are many different types of allergies.'

They held hands, strolling the mall. Coming toward them, a handsome Latin man pushed a girl in a small wheelchair. The girl was pale with jet-black hair, done in braids. She wore a steel brace on one of her legs.

Quickly Erin tugged her daughter toward the doorway of a toy shop. 'Remember all those Barbie dolls you lost—'

'But, Momma—'

'Let's pick out some new ones.'

'But, Momma, look!' Angie had spotted the wheelchair going by. 'It's an Everest-and-Jennings.'

Great, thought Erin. He even taught her the names.

Angela said, 'That's like Daddy does, pushing me. Only why are they going so slow?'

'Because that little girl is hurt. It's not safe for her to go fast.'

'Maybe when she's all better?'

'Yes, baby. When she's all better.'

Erin considered explaining to her daughter the saddest of truths – that some sick people never get better. It would've been a convenient segue back to the subject of Angela's father, and why Angela could never be with him again.

But Erin let it slide. The child was only four years old; she had a whole lifetime to learn about sadness. Today was for Dalmatians, ice cream and new dolls. At the toy store, Erin bought two new Barbies, plus swimsuits and evening gowns. She said no to the fur stoles, but Angie didn't make a fuss.

In the car, she asked, 'Momma, when can I go home?'

'It won't be long.' Erin prayed that Angie meant 'home' with her, not Darrell Grant. 'You mean the new apartment, right?'

Angela nodded excitedly. 'I liked the stairs. That was fun.' She paused. 'Where will Daddy go?'

Erin thought: What do I tell her – Daddy's off to prison? No, *prison* is a scary word. How about: A special place for grown-ups who get in trouble. Or better: A big building that looks just like a hospital, except for the barbed wire. Again, Erin chose to dodge the topic of Darrell's fate.

'He'll be taken care of,' she said.

'Does he have another girlfriend?'

'I don't know.' The question caught Erin by surprise.

''Cause I don't want him to be lonely.'

'He won't be lonely, baby. I promise.' Erin had a depressing vision of Angela as a young woman, loyally visiting her father on weekends at Raiford. Darrell undoubtedly would try to recruit her in the smuggling of cigarettes and pills.

'Where are we going now?' Angie asked.

'Victoria's Secret.'

'What's that?'

'That's where Mommy buys her outfits for work.'

'Your waitress clothes?'

'Right,' Erin said, with a sigh. 'My waitress clothes.'

It was nearly five o'clock when they got back to Miami. Erin didn't want to say goodbye, but she only had one hour to drive back to the club, and the traffic northbound was hell.

Angela kissed her on the nose and pinched her chin; it was a game they played.

'Momma, thank you for the new Barbies.'

'Remember to be nice, and share.'

'I promise.' Angie hopped out of the car, carefully clutching the shopping bag that contained her dolls. She stood on the sidewalk and waved.

'You run on inside,' Erin said. She blew a kiss and tapped the tip of her nose. As Angela started toward the house, Erin slowly drove away. Halfway down the block, she glanced in the rearview and saw her daughter running after the car. Erin braked hard, making the tires squeal.

'Momma!' Angela was on tiptoes at the window. Her cheeks were pink, and she was out of breath. She hugged the bag of dolls to her chest.

Erin said, 'What is it, baby?'

'I'm scared.'

'Of what?' She opened the car door and Angela clambered onto her lap. Erin turned to see if someone else was on the street, someone who might have frightened the girl. She saw nothing.

'Angie, what's the matter? What are you scared of?'

'Please don't get in trouble like Daddy.'

'Oh, honey. Is that it?'

'Please!'

'Don't worry,' Erin said, holding her daughter to her breast. 'Don't you worry about me.'

Darrell Grant phoned his sister from the Wal-Mart and said, 'Where's the nearest water from your place?'

Rita said, 'Don't tell me you got a boat.'

'A car,' Darrell said, 'but I need to dump it.'

'Not in the water.'

'Yeah, in the water.'

'A brand-new car?'

'Lord Christ, Rita, can't you just answer a simple question?'

Darrell Grant ditched the stolen Thunderbird in a drainage canal at Turkey Point, where Alberto Alonso worked. Then he hitchhiked to the trailer park and enjoyed one of Rita's peanut butter-and-plantain sandwiches.

She said, 'They's been cops calling, all hours. Alberto says you must've fucked up.'

'You got any Gatorade? The green kind?' Darrell asked.

'It ain't cold.'

'That'll do.'

Rita poured him a tall glass. 'We lost a pup to an eagle.'

'No shit,' said Darrell. 'A real eagle?'

Rita said it damn sure looked like an eagle when it swooped into the backyard. 'Also, your wife kicked the Christmas out of Al. Then Lupa got after him, too . . .'

Darrell Grant waved the sandwich and said, 'Hold up now—'

'He's up to the Veterans' Hospital this afternoon. His tongue's all infected.'

'Goddamn, Rita, you don't mind if I finish my lunch.' Darrell puffed his cheeks to dramatize his urge to vomit.

Rita apologized. Then she said: 'You can't stay here.'

'I know.'

'The cops, they drive by all the time.'

Darrell said, 'I need to borrow your car.'

'The axle's broke.'

'What about that Pontiac across the way?'

'Mrs Gomez,' Rita said. 'We ain't speakin' on account of the wolves got her Siamese.'

Darrell said his idea was to steal the Pontiac, not borrow it. Rita asked since when did he know how to hotwire a car.

'I don't,' Darrell Grant said. 'But I surely know how to use a key.'

From the backyard came a raw chorus of yowls. Rita scooped up her catcher's mask and hurried out through the screen door. Darrell darted to the bathroom and explored the medicine chest; it was cluttered with gauze, adhesive tape and antiseptic ointments. Quickly he spied a bottle of codeine Tylenols, prescribed for the recently mangled Alberto Alonso. Darrell emptied the pills into a front pocket of his jeans.

He was fixing another sandwich when Rita returned. She said, 'So what's the plan, little brother?'

'Well, listen,' he said, wiping his mouth. 'I intend to collect my beautiful daughter and get the hell pronto out of Florida. How's that sound?'

'Start a new life.'

'Exactly.'

'Because you're too smart for this shit.'

'I know it, Rita. I sure do know it.'

She always said her brother should've been an actor, he was so handsome. She could easily picture him on one of her soaps – maybe a charming young drifter on 'All My Children'.

'What about your wife?' she asked.

Darrell Grant laughed caustically. 'Erin will be very lucky,' he said, 'if I don't hurt her before I go.'

Rita poured more Gatorade. This time she tossed in a handful of ice cubes. 'Raising a child by yourself, I don't know.'

Her brother shot her a cold look. 'What's your point?'

'I'm just sayin' it might be easier by yourself. To get a fresh start and all.'

'I'm a super father, Rita.'

'Who said you wasn't?'

'And, besides, Angie and I are partners.'

'That's the part I don't like,' Rita said. 'Usin' that little girl the way you do.'

Darrell said, 'Hey, she has a ball with it. Just ask her if Daddy shows her a fun time.'

'Lord, I'm sure. Stealin' wheelchairs.'

'Hey, you should hear how she laughs when we're rollin' down the halls. The way her hair flies all back, looks just like silk. Nurses wave and say, "See that pretty little angel!" ' He smiled. 'And out the door we go.'

Rita said, 'You're too good for that, Darrell. That's gypsy shit.'

'Well, it works,' said Darrell Grant, 'whatever the fuck it is. Now – where you figure old Mrs Gomez keeps her keys?'

*

The morning after Erin danced on the yacht, David Lane Dilbeck gave one of the most magnificent performances of his political career. It began with a rally in Little Haiti, where the congressman excoriated the US Immigration Service for its heartless treatment of black Caribbean refugees. He declared that America owed its strength and heritage to courageous boat people, and that the Founding Fathers would be shame-stricken to see us now rebuff the neediest and most desperate. The only awkwardness arose when Dilbeck, speaking in fractured Creole, badly mistranslated the Emma Lazarus inscription from the Statue of Liberty ('Give me your oxen, your seedless guavas, your broken truck radiators . . .'). Though perplexed, the Haitian crowd remained enthusiastic.

Next the congressman raced to an American Legion barbecue, where he recounted the Battle of Inchon so vividly that many of the rapt veterans assumed that he'd seen action in Korea. He had not, for an undescended testicle had kept David Dilbeck out of the army. The congressman told his story with chin held high. His voice cracked as he poignantly described a young man's private heartbreak, denied a chance to fight for his nation. Leaving the enlistment center on that sad autumn day in 1951, Dilbeck said, he had vowed to overcome his handicap and serve America as devotedly as any man with two normally descended testicles. Patriotic fervor led him first to municipal government, then to Congress! Let me keep my dream, David Dilbeck boomed. Let me serve again! Cheers rose from the vets, who put down their spareribs and waved, with sticky fingers, dozens of miniature American flags. The congressman placed a bandaged hand over his heart and led the Legion crowd in 'The Star-Spangled Banner'.

The final stop was the Sunset Bay condominium, and here Dilbeck hit his peak – lucid, heartfelt and damn near eloquent. Erb Crandall was flabbergasted. He called Malcolm Moldowsky from a phone booth outside the rec room, where the congressman was addressing three hundred retirees.

'Malcolm, it's unbelievable,' Crandall said. 'He's got 'em in tears.'

'The Israel thing?'

'Yeah, but he shitcanned the script. It's all off the top of his head.'

'Oh Jesus,' Moldy said. 'You see any reporters?'

'Just Channel 10, but it's all right. He's a major hit, Malcolm. They're bawling all over their bagels.'

Moldowsky tried to envision the scene. 'Erb, I want an honest answer. Does David know anything at all about the Mideast?'

'He's weak on the geography,' Crandall conceded, 'but he's gangbusters on the Palestinian question. I counted four standing ovations.'

Moldowsky clicked his teeth. 'And he looks OK?'

'Like a million bucks. The best part, Eloy Flickman showed up for an ambush debate. That's how come the TV crew was here.'

'Sneaky bastard.'

'Davey tore him apart,' Crandall said. 'It was fantastic. Flickman took off like a scalded chihuahua.'

'Is that right?' On Crandall's end, in the background, Moldowsky heard a wave of fresh applause. It seemed too good to be true. He thought: What happened last night between Dilbeck and the stripper? She must've screwed him silly.

Moldowsky wanted a full debriefing. 'Put David on the line.'

'He's on a roll, Malcolm. He's into his Holocaust material.'

'I'll wait.'

Six minutes and two ovations later, the congressman got on the phone.

Moldowsky said, 'So tell me about your hot date.'

'A delight,' said Dilbeck, short of breath.

'No shakedowns? I want the truth. What about the photograph?'

'The subject never came up. She was a perfect lady.'

'And you were the perfect gentleman.'

'A monk, Malcolm. By the way, I'll need the yacht again in a few days. Erin's coming back to dance.'

'Why?'

'Because she enjoyed herself.' The congressman's tone was defensive. 'She's very fond of me, Malcolm. Oh, and I'll need more cash.'

'David, I want my people there.'

'That won't be necessary—' A gaggle of crowlike voices drowned Dilbeck's words. 'Malcolm, I've got to sign some autographs. Talk to Erb, OK?'

Moldy fidgeted until Crandall's voice came on the line: 'Malcolm, you should see. They got him in a yarmulke!'

'Stick close for a few days.'

'No, I'm afraid not.' From now on, Crandall was steering clear of Dilbeck's glandular adventures. 'I'm going to Atlantic City.'

'Like hell,' Moldy said.

'Malcolm, let me explain something. I don't work for you, I work for David. And David thinks it's terrific if I take a few days off and fly to Atlantic City.'

'That's because David's got big plans.'

'Well,' said Erb Crandall, 'I got front-row seats to see Cher.'

'Really? I hope your plane hits a fucking mountain.'

'Thanks, Malcolm. I'll be sure to send a postcard.'

'Could you at least find out when he's meeting the girl? Or is that too much to ask?'

'I'll see what I can do,' Crandall said. 'Whatever happened last night, Davey's a new man on the stump. He sparkles, Malcolm.'

'I suppose that's good.' Sparkles?

'Kennedy-esque, according to the Hadassah ladies.'

'Very funny.'

'Gee,' Crandall chided, 'we thought you'd be pleased.'

'The man is ill. You know it, I know it.'

'He carries her shoe in his briefcase.'

'And you're off to the fucking casinos.'

'Malcolm?'

'What?'

'I'll miss you.'

Erb Crandall reached the parking lot just as the congressman's limousine pulled out. Crandall waved pleasantly. Pierre, the driver, tipped his cap in reply. David Lane Dilbeck remained invisible behind tinted windows.

A nasty canker bloomed on Orly's lower lip. Erin couldn't look at him, even though they were deep in

argument. She scanned the imitation red velvet walls
while Orly told her no fucking way could she take
Saturday night off.

'That's twice this week!'

Erin said, 'I can count.'

'The answer is no fucking way. I'm thinking maybe
you got another gig.'

'I do,' she said. 'Congressman Dilbeck.'

'Shit.' Orly had no choice but to back down. He
didn't want to piss off a congressman, and he definitely didn't want more heat from that ballbuster
Moldowsky.

'I'll work a double on Monday,' Erin promised.

'Bet your ass.' Orly picked pensively at the cold sore.
'I'm curious,' he said. 'What's he like?'

'Nothing special.'

'Big tipper?'

'Fair,' Erin said. She knew where Mr Orly was
headed. 'I didn't sleep with him,' she said. 'You can ask
Shad.'

'I already did.'

'And what did he say?'

'He said you just danced.'

'Don't act so surprised.'

Orly shrugged one chubby shoulder. 'He's a bigshot.
Those guys usually want the full treatment.'

Erin's arms began to itch. It happened whenever she
sat too long in Orly's office.

He said: 'Lorelei's got phlebitis. She's flying home to
Dallas.'

'I'm sorry,' Erin said.

'It was that fucking snake, squeezing on her legs.'

Bravely Erin sneaked a glance at Orly's face. He

looked downcast and subdued. Of course the canker didn't help. She nearly felt sorry for him.

'How was the yacht?' he asked.

'Fine, except there's no mirrors. I'm dancing blind.'

Orly said, 'I'll need Shad here at the club. For the noodle wrestling – last night some guy nearly cacked.'

'I'll be fine by myself,' Erin said. 'Look, I know it's still early but why don't I get started on my sets?'

Orly said great, but no slow stuff. 'Not to beat a dead horse, but I'm serious. You can't strip to fucking Jackson Browne.'

'Congressman Dilbeck would disagree.' Erin stood up and pushed the chair away. 'Here's the part he liked best.'

Singing now: ' "Down on the boulevard, they take it hard." ' Dancing in baggy jeans and sneakers. A kick-boxing move – punch, punch, right leg out, then spin. ' "They look at life with such dis-regard." ' Punch, kick, kick and split.

When she finished, Orly whistled and said, 'Damn.'

'I told you.'

'That's Jackson Browne?'

'The table dancers,' said Erin, 'don't know what they're missing.'

Urbana Sprawl said that there was a guy jerking his weenie in a green Pontiac. Shad went to the doorway and scanned the cars in the lot. The green Pontiac was parked far away, near the road; Shad could make out a silhouette behind the wheel. He went behind the bar to fetch his tire iron, but then Orly called him over to break up a fight between two men at the Foosball table.

Men in suspenders! Orly bellowed. By the time Shad got out to the Pontiac, it was empty. He decided to prowl around.

Darrell Grant already had broken into the club through the fire door. He was sitting in the dressing room when Monique Sr arrived to freshen her makeup. She gave him a radiant smile and said, 'Are you Kiefer Sutherland?'

'That's me.' Darrell was cooked on codeine and Halcions and some unidentified lemon-yellow capsules that he'd purchased from a newspaper vendor on Dixie Highway. Darrell's eyelids hung half-mast and his tongue stuck to his teeth. He said, 'I'm looking for Missus Erin Grant. She works here in a nude capacity.'

Monique Sr told him to put the knife away. Darrell Grant was unaware that he was holding it.

'You lost some weight,' Monique Sr said, 'since your last movie. My name is Monique.' When she held out her hand, Darrell flicked it with the blade. The dancer cried out and pulled away. A stripe of blood appeared on her fingers.

'Hush up,' Darrell said. He grabbed her arm and yanked her into his lap. Monique Sr told him to stop and balled her fist, to stanch the bleeding.

Darrell Grant rubbed the stubble of his beard on the nape of the dancer's neck. He bounced her on his knees and said, 'Here's a news flash, sweetie. I ain't Keith O'Sutherland.'

'I kind of figured.'

He cut the strap of her bra top, which dropped to the carpet. In the mirror, Monique Sr studied the man's slack leer and fogged eyes. She felt him getting hard beneath her.

'Let me go,' she said. 'I'll find Erin.'

'What's the hurry.' He'd spotted the wad of bills in her black garter. 'How much you got there?'

'I don't know. Maybe a hundred.'

'Excellent.' He slid the flat side of the knife down Monique Sr's leg, under the elastic of the garter. He twisted his wrist and the garter broke. The cash fell in a clump. It landed in one of her bra cups.

Darrell Grant said, 'Pick it up.'

As she bent over, he said, 'Those are some tits you got.'

'Please let me go.'

He propped the steak knife behind his right ear, like a pencil. Then he reached around Monique Sr and slapped a hand on each breast. 'I would estimate,' he said, 'these are about three times bigger than my ex-wife's.'

Monique Sr said, 'Shit. Now I know who you are.'

She threw an elbow that caught Darrell Grant flush in the right temple. No pain registered in the lifeless blue eyes. He locked both arms around the dancer's rib cage and squeezed. He gave a grunt that started low in the throat, then rose to a musical hum.

Monique Sr, who'd taken eight years of piano, recognized the note as a high C-sharp. She was equally startled by the man's strength, and watched herself go pale in the mirror. The walls pulsed as the man's eerie humming filled her head. Within moments she passed out.

When she regained consciousness, Monique Sr heard Darrell Grant say: 'Wake up, Little Dorothy.' She felt the man's kneecaps bouncing her bottom and realized that he still held her on his lap. She opened her eyes and saw, in the mirror, that he'd cut off her G-string.

She said, 'You want a screw, get it over with.'

Darrell squirmed beneath her. 'I'd like to, but I sorta lost momentum.'

'Then let me go. I was due in the cage ten minutes ago.'

'Just hold up,' he said. 'Maybe if I squeeze them titties again.'

'Nope,' said Monique Sr. 'You're done for the night. I can feel it.'

'Shut up!'

'It's not your fault, sweetheart. It's the drugs.'

Darrell Grant fumbled one-handed at his fly. There was no point. 'Look what you did,' he whined.

'Wasn't me.'

He traced the point of the blade along her bikini lines. 'How about a tattoo down there? Be the first on your block.'

Monique Sr said, 'Please don't cut on me again.' A dancer with scars didn't get much work – not at the good clubs, anyway.

When Darrell stung her with the knife, she promised to do whatever he wanted. 'Thatta girlie,' he said.

The door opened and Erin came in. It took a few seconds to absorb the scene: Her ex-husband sitting in the makeup chair, Monique Sr trembling on his lap, the glint of steel against her tanned belly.

Darrell Grant giggled. 'This is perfect. Shut the damn door and pull up a seat.'

Erin could see he was wrecked. She regretted leaving the pistol at home.

He said, 'I'm gonna give this lady the ride of her life, and you're gonna watch.'

'Hot damn,' said Erin. She sat down and winked at Monique Sr, who was not reassured. She raised her hand to show Erin the blood.

Darrell Grant said, 'We're gonna give you a peep show.'

'Anytime you're ready,' Erin said, crossing her legs.

Darrell's tipsy smile disappeared and his lips pursed in childlike concentration. He commanded Monique Sr to touch him. She said she was. He told her to *grab* him, then.

'I am,' she said.

'I don't feel a damn thing.'

'That makes two of us,' Monique Sr said.

Erin folded her arms. 'I'm waiting, Mr Sex Machine.'

Darrell Grant squinted and strained and bared his teeth.

Erin said, 'Maybe you need a laxative.'

Monique Sr caught herself laughing. Darrell's muscles – legs, arms, neck – went limp in defeat. 'Goddamn you,' he said to Erin.

'Fine. Now let Monique go, and we'll discuss the problem like grown-ups.'

'Not until you take me to Angie.'

Erin said, 'You better talk to the judge.' She couldn't resist: the exact line he'd used on her so many, many times.

He touched the knife to Monique Sr's neck. Teardrops and runny mascara streaked the dancer's cheeks. Erin knew it was important to keep her ex-husband confused and off guard. Any sign of weakness would embolden him.

She said, 'Monique, I apologize. Darrell makes a shitty first impression.'

'He cut my goddamn hand!' the dancer cried, displaying the wound again. 'It's not funny, Erin. Give him what he wants.'

'I want my daughter,' Darrell Grant snarled.

'Well,' said Erin, 'I don't have her any more.'

Darrell took the news poorly. He shoved Monique Sr to the floor and lunged wildly at Erin. The swiftness of his fury caught her by surprise. She tried to raise her legs to push him away, but he was already on top. The chair collapsed, and they went down simultaneously. Darrell Grant dug his knees into Erin's chest. He screamed and cursed until he was breathless. She lost track of how many times he called her a dirty rotten cunt.

She was worried about the knife: where was it? Darrell's arms hung at his side. Pinned flat on the floor, Erin couldn't see her ex-husband's hands, couldn't raise her head to try.

Darrell Grant, panting: 'I want Angie back tonight.'

'You're crushing me,' Erin said.

Monique Sr must have gotten out, because the door was ajar and the dressing room flooded with dance music from the lounge: something brassy by Gloria Estefan. Not an ideal tune to die by, Erin thought.

'Who's got her?' Darrell said.

Erin, wheezing: 'I'll take you there.'

His right arm came up with the rusty steak knife. He held it by the tip of the blade, between his thumb and forefinger.

Darrell Grant, weepy, slurring: 'I lost my baby girl.'

'That's not true,' Erin said.

'All because of you.'

'Darrell, it's not too late.'

He turned the knife in his fingers, closed his palm around the handle. 'Don't you understand? I escaped from jail. That means I got no future to speak of.'

Erin said, 'Everyone fucks up occasionally.'

'My plan was me and Angie hittin' the road. Not any more. Is that a fair statement?'

One of his eyelids had closed. Erin prayed that it would affect his accuracy with the knife. 'If you kill me,' she said, 'you'll never see her again.'

'And if I don't kill you,' he said, 'I'll hate myself for not tryin'.'

Erin had always believed that her ex-husband was incapable of homicide, except by accident. Now, watching Darrell Grant fondle the cheap cutlery, she realized she might've misjudged him. What if he stabbed her? Erin thought, ludicrously, of how disappointed her mother would be. When one's only daughter is hacked to death wearing a sequined bra top and a G-string – well, there's really no way to explain it to one's friends at the orchid club.

'Darrell,' Erin began.

'Shut your eyes. I can't manage if you're lookin' at me.'

But Erin wouldn't close her eyes. She scorched him with a glare. 'I won't let you do this to Angela.'

'Hush up,' he cried. 'Who's got the knife, huh?'

'I *won't* let you.'

'Shut your goddamn green eyes!'

'Why?' Erin said. 'They remind you of somebody?'

'Oh, Lord Christ.' He raised the knife with both hands.

Erin said, 'Put it down, Darrell.' A breathless whisper.

'No way.'

'Darrell, please. For Angie's sake.'

'I said, shut your eyes.'

'Drop the fucking knife!' A man's voice at the door. Erin felt Darrell Grant go rigid. He cocked his head, waiting. He did not drop the fucking knife.

'Junior,' said the voice, Shad's voice. 'I'm counting to three.'

Erin watched her ex-husband mouthing to himself: One Mississippi, two Mississippi . . . and then a branch snapped. That's what it sounded like.

Darrell flew off Erin as if launched by a spring. A plangent wailing now accompanied the melodies of Gloria Estefan. Erin sat up, covering her breasts with her hands. There was Shad with his tire iron, Mr Orly clutching a can of Dr Pepper, and Darrell Grant screaming.

Darrell – his arm hanging crooked and splintered at the elbow, a blond spike of a bone poking through the gray skin, dripping darkness down the front of his jeans.

Shad said, 'Junior, you count too slow.' He whipped off the beret and bowed his shiny dome in Darrell Grant's direction. 'You remember carving this punkin? I'll bet you do.'

'Take him outside,' Orly muttered, and disappeared down the hall.

Erin got to her feet, wobbling. The faces in the mirror were a blur. She pointed at the reflection that most closely resembled her ex-husband. 'Darrell,' she said. 'I knew you couldn't do it.' Then: 'God, I don't feel so good.'

Shad caught her in one arm as she sagged. The whimpering Darrell Grant somehow lurched to his feet and stumbled from the dressing room. Shad placed Erin on a small divan and tucked a musty pillow under her head.

'I'll be right back,' he told her. 'Junior forgot his knife.'

TWENTY-SEVEN

Shad searched the property but he couldn't find Darrell. He stalked next door and checked the fried-chicken joint, and then the restrooms of the video arcade down the street. When he returned to the Tickled Pink, the Pontiac was gone. The asshole had escaped again.

Erin was surprisingly calm. She borrowed Orly's phone and dialed the Martin County Sheriff's Office to report the sighting of her fugitive ex-husband. She described his gruesome injury, and hinted that Darrell might soon surface at a local emergency room. The cop on the other end was no Al García. He took the information haltingly, and asked numerous vague questions. Erin had to spell her name three times because he kept asking her if it was 'Aaron – like the baseball player.'

When she got off the phone, Orly said, 'We got a policy against husbands and boyfriends at this club.'

'Darrell is neither,' Erin said, 'and I didn't invite him.'

'He crazy enough to come back?'

'That's hard to say, Mr Orly. The police are after him.'

'Lovely. Maybe we'll have a shootout in the pasta pit.'

Shad said, 'The boy's in no shape to fight. I busted his ulna to smithereens.'

Orly frowned. 'His what?'

Erin announced that she was going home to take a hot shower. Shad got the .38 Special and followed in his car. There was no sign of a lurking green Pontiac. He parked by Erin's apartment until the lights went out. Then he circled the complex four times and drove back to the club. Orly was waiting at the front bar.

'Those fucking Lings,' he fumed, 'they're trying to steal Urbana. A thousand bucks they offered her!'

Shad said nothing. He had a feeling there was more.

Orly, dropping his voice: 'Plus they ratted me to the Health Department.'

'You mean Beverage.'

'No, Health.' Orly unfolded a yellow paper and smoothed it violently with the heels of his hands. He pushed it down the bar toward Shad. 'Read it,' he said.

The complaint charged Orly with using 'contaminated food products in a manner that poses a direct and compelling threat to the public safety.' Shad assumed it referred to the topless pasta wrestling.

Orly said, 'It's a damn lie.'

'I know,' Shad said. 'The stuff is always fresh. I check the packaging dates myself.'

'That's exactly what I told the little creep.'

'And?'

'He claims he got a sample of bad vermicelli from the wrestling pit – I forgot when, last Tuesday or something. It says right there on the paper. He put it in a jar and hauled it to some goddamn lab in Miami.'

Three types of nasty-sounding bacteria – *Escherichia coli, Shigella dysenteriae* and *Staphylococcus* – were listed on the health inspector's complaint. 'This is bullshit,' Shad said. 'We been set up.'

'Keep reading,' Orly told him.

'Hey, what's this about orifices?'

The report stated: 'During the so-called wrestling matches, several male customers were observed attempting to insert said contaminated food product into the mouths and other body orifices of the female performers.'

Shad pushed the paper back at Orly. 'It doesn't happen every night. Guys get drunk, you know how it goes.'

Orly turned away from the bar. 'They make it sound so disgusting. Bottom line, it's just fucking noodles.'

The two men sat wordlessly. Sabrina was on the main stage, Monique Jr was in the cage and a new girl named Suzette was dancing tables in the front row. Suzette's claim to fame was a cameo in a recent George Michael video. Orly said she had played a nun in bicycle pants.

Every song Kevin put on was by Prince or Madonna or Marky Mark; the severity of Shad's headache made him wonder if the music had caused his brain to swell. He removed the beret and balanced a bag of ice cubes on his twitching scalp.

'Where's Urbana?' he asked.

Orly said she went to the Flesh Farm to negotiate with the Lings. 'So much for loyalty.' He paused. 'They got a wind machine over there? Because Urbana won't dance near a wind machine.'

'That's right,' Shad said.

'What'm I saying? A grand is a grand.'

Shad told him not to worry. 'She won't do friction. Not for a million bucks.'

'You ever think,' said Orly, 'that maybe they don't want her for friction?'

Shad signaled the bartender to bring the boss a fresh Dr Pepper. Orly continued: 'The Ling brothers aren't stupid. They know a liability potential when they see one. With those tits, she could kill a man easy.' He tongued the rim of the soda can. 'Here's my theory: They're getting out of friction dancing and aiming upscale. They're trying to buy some class, you know? Be respectable like us.'

'Respectable,' Shad said. Mr Orly could be very amusing at times. Shad adjusted the ice bag to fit the contour of his skull. 'You sure it was them who ratted?'

'Who else? They're still pissed about the snake dancer, what's-her-name.'

Kevin approached the bar and buoyantly asked for a Perrier. His expression darkened when he felt Shad's glare. Quickly the disc jockey backed away. Shad lunged for him, but missed. Kevin scurried back to the sound booth.

Orly was saying: 'That damn health inspector, he went through the whole joint. I mean brick by brick.'

'Yeah?'

'The thing is, I panicked slightly. I dumped your cottage cheese in the toilet.'

Shad shut his eyes. 'Damn,' he said.

'I had to,' said Orly. 'The guy was relentless. He finds that goddamn scorpion and then what? Already he's threatening to shut us down.'

'So you flushed it.'

'Get yourself another one. Send me the bill.'

Shad was downhearted. 'I'm fucking jinxed. That's all.'

Orly motioned for the bouncer to follow him outside. Shad couldn't have been more pleased. The traffic noise was a Brahms lullaby compared to the mindless shit that Kevin was blasting on the sound system.

In the parking lot, Orly selected a Volvo sedan and centered himself heavily on the hood. 'So – what do we do about these Lings? I'm open to ideas.'

Shad said, 'My brain hurts.'

'You're the only one I can trust.'

'I ain't no arsonist, Mr Orly. I can't light a fuckin' barbecue.'

'Well, then, let's you and me think.'

A charcoal Acura pulled in and parked near the front awning. Urbana Sprawl got out. She was dressed for a Palm Beach cancer ball. Orly and Shad had never seen her in such sumptuous clothes.

'So, how'd it go?' Orly's voice was tight.

The dancer said, 'I'm here, right? So let it drop.'

Shad glanced at Orly. 'I told you.'

With a squeak, Orly slid his butt off the hood. 'Wait a minute, girl. You turned down a thousand dollars to stay here and work for me?'

'Don't be a dick,' Urbana said, irritably.

Shad squeezed her hand. 'You don't have to talk about it.'

'He wanted to play "windshield wiper" with my boobs.'

'Who?' Orly said.

'Ling. He tried to pull down my straps and—'

'Which Ling?' asked Shad.

'The little one. I broke two nails on his face.' Urbana displayed her damaged manicure. 'I wouldn't work for those bastards in a zillion years.' She slipped between Orly and Shad and hurried into the club.

Orly said, 'One of us should've got the door.'

Shad gazed down the street, toward the distant winking neon of the Flesh Farm. 'Mr Orly,' he said, 'which Ling is the little one?'

'Does it matter now?'

'Nope. It truly doesn't.'

The *Princess Pia* began attracting fish the day it settled in seventy-nine feet of water off Fort Lauderdale beach. Dive-boat captains such as Abe Cochran scouted the junked freighter regularly, particularly on those mornings when they were low on fuel and energy, and didn't wish to travel far from port. Where in the Atlantic they took their customers depended on the customers themselves. Well-traveled scuba divers wouldn't settle for exploring such an obvious tourist scam as a newly sunken banana boat. Tourists, however, were suckers for it. They were delighted merely to be blowing bubbles, and vastly enthralled by any fleeting glimpse of marine life. Many of them didn't know a queen angelfish from a sturgeon, leaving Captain Abe Cochran free to embellish the underwater sights.

On the morning of October sixth, Kate Esposito and her boyfriend climbed aboard Abe Cochran's thirty-five-foot charter boat, the *Alimony III*. They were joined by four young travel agents who were visiting Fort Lauderdale for a convention. Abe Cochran recognized the group for what it was, and set a true course for the wreck of the *Princess Pia*. The seas were calm, and the anchor held on the first drop. The travel agents were badly hung over, so Abe Cochran handed out snorkels and instructed them to swim close to the stern, where he could keep an eye on them. This left Kate Esposito and her boyfriend to dive the freighter alone.

Kate had learned to scuba dive as a teenager in a YWCA swimming pool in Boston, but her lifelong dream was to visit the tropics. She was greatly anticipating her first moray eel; her boyfriend had purchased an inexpensive underwater camera for the occasion.

As they tumbled backward off Abe Cochran's boat, Kate Esposito noticed that the water was murkier than she expected. 'Gin-clear' is what the tourist brochures had advertised, but Kate could barely see ten feet in front of her face. Her disappointment ebbed as she approached the wreck of the *Princess Pia*, which lay unbroken on its starboard side. To Kate, it seemed as awesome and eerie as the *Titanic*. Together she and her boyfriend swam the length of the bare freighter. Clouds of small aqua-striped fish swam in and out of the dynamite gashes, and once a pair of leopard rays winged gracefully out of the wheel-house. Each sighting brought bubbles of excitement from Kate and her boyfriend, who attempted to snap pictures of every sea creature they encountered.

Kate was the better diver, and it was she who decided to investigate the interior of the hull. She knew, from documentaries on the Discovery Channel, that moray eels preferred dark and remote crevices; perhaps one had taken up residence inside the scuttled *Princess Pia*. Kate tapped on her boyfriend's tank and signaled her intentions. He waved lamely and handed her the camera. Through the dive mask, Kate's eyes flickered in annoyance. Alone she swam through an open hatch cover on the aft deck. Her boyfriend watched the orange flippers disappear into the ship. He checked his wristwatch: ten minutes, then he was going after her.

Milky shafts of pale light broke the darkness of the cargo hold. Kate Esposito moved slowly, feeling her way. The surface of the metal was smooth and unencrusted because the wreck was so new. Seaweed hung in cinnamon tendrils from the braces, and schools of small fish were abundant, shards of glitter in the fuzzy penumbra. As Kate worked her way deeper into the hold, the water felt cooler and heavier against her legs. A saucer-shaped object shone against the freighter's dull iron skin. Kate reached for the shining disc, knowing that it couldn't be anything precious or valuable, but still not expecting a wire-spoked hubcap. Laughing into her regulator, she let the hubcap fall from her hands.

A long gray form took shape in front of her. Swimming closer, Kate Esposito discerned sharp angles of chrome and glass – a car, chained to the spine of the hull! Not a clunker, either, but a late-model American sedan.

Very weird, Kate thought. On a fender panel, she located a plastic nameplate: Lincoln Continental. Why would someone sink a brand-new Lincoln? Maybe it was a gag, she thought, a publicity stunt by one of the radio stations. With one finger, she wrote her first name in the algae film growing on the puckered vinyl roof. Then she snapped a picture of it for her boyfriend.

Except for a cracked driver's window, the Continental was in remarkably good shape. Even the bumper sticker was intact: HAVE YOU HUGGED YOUR LAWYER TODAY?

Kate Esposito saw that the trunk of the car was

slightly ajar: *Now there's an ideal place for a moray eel.* From a mesh dive-bag she retrieved a handful of frozen pilchards, which Abe Cochran had given her to feed the marine life, such as it was. Kate picked up one of the stiff minnows and dangled it gingerly above the crack of the Lincoln's trunk. No sinewy green eel emerged to gobble it. After a minute or so, the pilchard came apart in her fingers. Kate got another one and tried again, wiggling the dead fish as enticement. Nothing moved for it.

No one home, Kate thought. With the toe of a flipper she nudged the lid of the car trunk. It opened in slow motion.

Kate Esposito's boyfriend was trying to catch a baby sea turtle when Kate rifled out of the freighter's hatch and kicked frenetically for the surface. Kate's boyfriend followed the trail of bubbles to Abe Cochran's boat, where Kate had crawled up on the teak dive platform. Now she was on all fours, coughing up breakfast. The travel agents, treading water near the bow, warbled excitedly through their snorkels.

Abe Cochran laconically ordered all hands into the boat. Kate's boyfriend yanked off his mask and asked her what she'd seen inside the *Princess Pia*.

'Crabs,' she sobbed, 'eating a dead lawyer.'

It took the Broward sheriff's divers four hours to recover the bodies of Mordecai and his cousin Joyce. Preserving an underwater crime scene proved too much of a challenge, especially when a school of aggressive lemon sharks arrived. The Lincoln Continental was left for another day.

At noon the TV news reported the discovery of two bodies inside the wreck of the *Princess Pia*. Captain Abe Cochran refused to talk with reporters, and emphasized his reluctance by hoisting a scuba tank to bludgeon a Channel 7 cameraman. Kate Esposito's boyfriend was more voluble. In a live dockside interview, he graphically recounted Kate's discovery of the dead lawyer in the new Lincoln. Sgt Al García, who had a television in his office, immediately phoned a friend at the Broward Medical Examiner's Office and asked permission to sit in on the autopsy. The doctor said sure – there wouldn't be much of a crowd, considering the unpleasantly advanced condition of the deceased.

García, who stopped first at Mordecai's bank, was the last to arrive at the coroner's office in Hollywood. The luckless contingent assigned to the postmortem included two forensic pathologists, three Broward sheriff's detectives and a pair of first-year medical students from the University of Miami. The Florida Bar had declined to send a representative.

Before entering the autopsy room, García stubbed out his cigar and sprinkled the traditional Old Spice cologne inside his disposable surgical mask. The body bag containing Mordecai was the first to be unzipped, and the crabs had been thorough. The skull was practically picked clean, making it easier for pathologists to track the three small-caliber bullet holes. The Broward detectives made notes, and pointed here and there with yellow No. 2 pencils. No one glanced up when the nauseated medical students bolted out the door.

The doctors labored to cut away the dead lawyer's sodden pin-striped suit. García edged up to the table and asked if he could check the pockets. The doctors shrugged and kept cutting.

García held his breath while he pretended to search Mordecai's suit. One of the Broward detectives grumpily asked what the hell he was looking for.

'This,' said Al García. He held up a small key.

Malcolm J. Moldowsky missed the noon news on TV because he was having lunch with two jittery state senators and an overconfident New York bond underwriter. Moldy also missed the six o'clock news; this time he was in the bathroom, grooming himself for an important dinner with the governor. Lately the state of Florida had been pestering operators of phosphate mines about dumping their radioactive sludge into the public groundwater. The phosphate industry regarded as subversive the idea of cleansing its own waste and burying it safely. Malcolm Moldowsky had been hired at a six-figure fee to plead the cause with his old pal, the governor, so that the regulatory climate at the mines might return to normal.

Moldy always dressed by meticulous routine, beginning with his socks. Then came the underwear, shirt, cuff links, necktie, pants and finally the shoes. It was not uncommon for him to spend twenty minutes working a Windsor knot to perfection, and it was at this critical stage that someone knocked on the front door. Moldowsky was irritated, and puzzled, by the interruption; the guard in the lobby was supposed to buzz when a visitor arrived. Moldy strode bare-legged to the door, where he was met by a stocky Cuban with a thick mustache, a damp cigar and a cellular phone under one arm.

'Yes?' Moldowsky made it a demand.

Al García flashed his badge and strolled in. He grinned at the portrait of John Mitchell. 'Either you got a great sense of humor,' he said to Moldy, 'or you're one of the sickest fuckers I ever met.'

Moldowsky said, 'I didn't catch the name.'

García told him.

Moldy felt himself pucker. 'And you're with?'

'Metro Homicide.'

'Is there trouble in the building?'

'I'm sure there is,' García said, 'but that's not why I'm here. How about putting on some pants?'

Malcolm J. Moldowsky nodded coldly, disappeared into the bedroom and robotically finished dressing. He came out brushing the lint from his wool-blend jacket. His mind swarmed with a hundred possibilities, none of them good. He had gambled too recklessly, leaning on the county commissioner; putting the heat on Sgt Al García had backfired.

Moldowsky said, 'I'm meeting the governor for dinner, so I'm in a bit of a hurry.'

'Me, too,' said García. 'I'm going bowling with Ivana Trump.'

The detective's mocking stare was too much. Moldy found a chair. He told himself to shut up, be careful, pay attention!

García said, 'You know a lawyer named Mordecai?'

'No, I don't.'

'He got murdered. Hey, I know what you're thinking and you might be right. Maybe it was a public service.

Maybe we should give the killer a medal. A dead lawyer is a dead lawyer, right?'

Moldowsky said nothing. His throat felt like he'd been swallowing razor blades.

'Without going into gory details,' García said, 'here's the scenario. In the dead lawyer's pocket they find a key to a safe-deposit box up in Lauderdale. And in the safe box they find a Rolodex card with your name and phone number—'

'That's impossible,' said Moldowsky, thinking: *You sneaky prick*. 'Sergeant, I never met this man.'

'I think you're lying, Malcolm, but that's for another day. Don't you want to hear what else they found in the bank box?'

'It doesn't concern me.' Moldy didn't recognize his own voice.

'They found a Kodak slide.' Al García paused to measure Moldowsky's reaction, a flurry of blinks. García said, 'The picture was taken at a nude dance club. Features a certain well-known congressman.'

Moldowsky stoically pretended to know nothing about it. He was afraid to look in the wall mirror; he suspected that his upper lip was moist and curling.

García took out a notebook and uncapped a Bic pen. 'This dead lawyer, you sure he didn't try to blackmail you? He and a woman named Joyce Mizner.'

Moldy stood up and shot his cuffs. 'Sergeant, I'm running very late. Come by the office tomorrow.'

The detective, fishing merrily, cast out a name that Erin had picked up from the congressman: 'You know a guy named Erb Crandall?'

'Of course,' Moldowsky said. His facial muscles were cramping, from trying to appear calm.

'Where do you know him from?' the detective asked.

'From politics. We can talk about this tomorrow.'

'You bet.' García slapped the notebook shut and crammed it crookedly into his coat. He took out a piece of paper and ran his finger down a column of numbers. Then he picked up his cellular phone and dialed.

The telephone on Malcolm Moldowsky's desk began to ring. He stared at it rigidly, hatefully.

Al García said, 'Answer it.'

Moldy didn't move. 'I'm not fond of games.'

The phone kept ringing. 'It's for you,' Garcia said.

'What's your point?'

García turned the cellular off. Moldowsky's phone fell silent. García smiled; he felt like Columbo. 'You got a non-pub number,' he said.

'Of course I do,' said Moldy. 'But you're a police officer. All you need to do is call Southern Bell.'

'That's not how I got it.' García showed the paper to Moldowsky. It was a copy of the itemized bill from the Holiday Inn in Missoula, where the killers had stayed after they dumped the late Jerry Killian into the Clark Fork River.

García said, 'Somebody in Room 212 called here that night. Talked for quite a while.'

'I recall no such conversation.' Moldy's cheeks were on fire. He had assumed the Jamaicans had dialed on a credit card, not direct from the room. *Direct!*

'Maybe you want to contact your lawyer,' García said.

Moldowsky laughed harshly and said don't be ridiculous.

'Your choice,' said the detective. 'One more question, *chico*. Where can I find David Dilbeck tonight?'

Moldowsky said he had no idea.

'Really? I'm told he doesn't wipe his ass without your permission.'

Moldy's composure finally shattered. He bellowed and stomped around the apartment and pounded on the credenza and vowed that Al García would be writing parking tickets for the rest of his miserable career.

'So,' García said, 'you're a man of some influence.'

'Goddamn right.'

'And I've insulted you?'

'Worse than that, Sergeant.'

'Then please accept my sincere apology.' García rose. 'I'll find the congressman on my own.' He straightened Moldowsky's necktie and told him he looked like a million bucks. 'But that cologne of yours could gag a maggot,' he said. 'Personally, I go for the domestic stuff.'

The moment the detective was gone, Malcolm Moldowsky lurched to the desk and seized the phone – the tool of all his genius, the instrument of his betrayal. He was comforted by its feel, the familiar way it fit in his palm, but he was uncertain of his next play. Whom could he call to fix this terrible trouble? Who would have the power to cover it up?

Nobody, Moldy decided gravely. The lawyer's body had been found, and so had the dreaded photograph from the Eager Beaver. The bank box had been opened, emptied, then opened again and salted with evidence – the Rolodex card was a cute touch. At least this prick García had a sense of irony . . .

Moldowsky's gaze fell on the portrait of the great one, John Newton Mitchell – the hooded eyes, the jowly arrogant smirk. What would *he* do, the canny old toad?

Stonewall the bastards. Naturally. Admit nothing, deny everything. It would have worked, too. Watergate would have dried up and blown away like a chicken turd, if only . . . if only Nixon, that paranoid gnome, had listened.

Sweet Jesus, thought Moldowsky. I've got to find David before that goddamn Cuban does.

He dialed the congressman's private line. It rang twice before the machine picked up. Moldy left a curt message but gave no instructions, as it would only confuse David Dilbeck. Next Moldy tried to locate Erb Crandall in Atlantic City, but none of the big hotels showed him on the register. Either Erb was staying in a dive, or lying about his destination.

Moldowsky felt a cold, crushing weight on his heart. He hung up the telephone and groped for his car keys.

When was Dilbeck meeting the stripper? Was tonight the night?

TWENTY-EIGHT

Erin stopped at the club with a present for Monique Sr. It was a sheer silk blouse from Neiman's.

'Sorry about the other night,' Erin said. 'Darrell is Darrell. It's a hopeless situation.'

Monique Sr liked the blouse. She buttoned it over a Day-Glo dance bra. 'Oh, Erin, it's beautiful.'

'That's not for work. That's for somebody special.'

'Special? I wish.' She twirled in front of the mirror, first one way, then another. 'Guess who's ringside at the pit? Garrick Utley.'

Erin said, 'You can't wrestle. Not with your hand cut up.'

'I'm wearing pink evening gloves till it's healed. Mr Orly says I look like Mamie Van Doren.' Monique Sr told Erin about Urbana Sprawl's dispiriting encounter with the Ling brothers.

Erin said, 'Pitiful. I always heard they were gropers.'

There was more unsettling gossip from the dressing room. Once more, Orly surreptitiously had lowered the thermostat to sixty-eight degrees, to promote nipple erections on stage. Also, the multi-wigged Sabrina had been offered three thousand dollars to make a porn film on South Beach.

'She's gonna do it,' Monique Sr said.

'Where is she?'

'The cage.' Monique Sr took off the blouse and put it on a hanger. 'You're too dressed,' she said to Erin. 'I'll go out and tell her you're here.'

Sabrina was her usual sweet-tempered self. She felt a kinship with Erin because both of them had smallish breasts and felonious ex-husbands.

Erin said, 'Tell me about this so-called movie.'

'They said I've got to screw two guys in a hot tub and that's all.'

'Why are you doing this?'

Sabrina seemed puzzled by the question. 'They're paying me,' she said.

'You need money, I'll give it to you.'

The dancer's eyes widened in amusement. 'Three grand? Come on.'

'Whatever you want.'

'Erin, you don't understand. I can't take any more of this wrestling shit. The pasta is just as gross as the creamed corn.'

'But once you do porn—'

'Hey, you don't know what it's like up there. Drunks trying to cram cold niblets up your crack – Jesus, you ought to try it some time.' It was one of the few times Erin had seen Sabrina angry.

'I'll talk to Orly. We'll put a stop to it.'

'Look, the movie can't be worse than wrestling.'

'You ever seen one?'

Sabrina admitted that she hadn't.

'Well, I have,' Erin said. 'When I worked at the FBI, they seized a truckload of tapes at the airport. The agents had a private screening one night in the basement.'

Sabrina's curiosity was earnest. 'What's it like? Are they really so bad?'

'You know what a cum shot is?'

Sabrina said she did not. Erin explained.

'Yukky.' Sabrina reddened. 'The director didn't tell me.'

'I'll bet he didn't.'

'Let me think about this.'

'Take your time,' Erin said.

Sabrina freshened her lipstick and returned to the lounge. Urbana Sprawl came to the dressing room and showed Erin her broken fingernails. She said, 'Men are the scum of the earth.'

'As a general rule,' Erin agreed.

'I think you like that Cuban cop.'

'He's solidly married.'

'Another heartbreaker.'

'His wife's taking care of my daughter,' Erin said. 'She's terrific, too.'

'And here you sit on a Saturday night.'

'Oh, I've got big plans,' Erin said. 'Tonight I dance for the congressman.'

'Mercy,' said Urbana. 'Just answer me why.'

Erin yawned and stretched her arms over her head. 'Because it's my civic duty.'

Rita patiently cleansed her brother's wound.

'I can't do much with this fracture,' she declared.

'Don't even try.'

'What's the goo on your shirt?'

'Mozzarella,' Darrell Grant said. 'Don't ask.'

Rita created a splint for his broken left arm. She used

an Ace bandage, hurricane tape and Alberto Alonso's nine-iron. The blade of the golf club stuck out the same end as Darrell Grant's fingers.

'All set,' Rita told him, biting off the last piece of tape. 'Now get a move on before Alberto comes home.'

Darrell's skin was the colour of oatmeal, and his breathing was rapid. 'I could use some morphine,' he said.

'We don't have no morphine. How's about Nuprin?'

'Lord Christ.'

'They say it's better than Tylenols.'

'Rita, I swear to God—'

'All right, how's about this? I got some special pills for Lupa. The vet gave me a bottle for when she had the puppies.'

Darrell Grant looked hopeful. 'Dog morphine?'

'Yeah, I guess.'

She found the bottle and tried to decipher the name of the drug. Neither she nor her brother had heard of it.

'It says two capsules every six hours.'

'That's if you're a fucking poodle,' Darrell said. 'Gimme four and a cold Busch.'

Afterward he vomited for twenty-five minutes. Rita kept daubing his chin and telling him to hurry – Alberto was on the way home from the nuclear plant. Darrell said he was in no shape to travel. Rita assisted him down the front steps and showed him where to hide, in the crawl space under the mobile home.

'Where'd you park the Pontiac?' she asked. 'In case Mrs Gomez puts her glasses on.'

'Down behind the Circle K.' Darrell Grant shimmied beneath the doublewide. He dragged the splinted arm like a chunk of lumber; the blade of the nine-iron made a groove in the dirt.

Ritz said, 'I'll bring a blanket.'

'What about the damn wolves?'

'Don't you worry. They den on the lee side, strictly.'

'Rita, I can't stay down here!'

A car rolled into the driveway. Rita put her fingers to her lips, then she was gone.

Darrell Grant heard Alberto Alonso's voice, the crunch of gravel under his work boots, the screen door slamming . . .

Trapped! Darrell thought. He turned his head slowly, left then right, to assess conditions in the bunker. He wondered about the chances of Rita's trailer falling off the foundation and crushing him like a bug. Unlikely, he decided; the thing was practically brand new, replacing the one that Rita and Alberto had lost to the hurricane. Darrell Grant pressed his good arm against the aluminum – it seemed as sturdy as a mobile home could be. Yet he felt edgy in his underground refuge. The air was as cool as a tomb and smelled sharply of rodents. Still, it was better than spending another night in a dumpster behind the Pizza Hut.

The pain in his mangled arm was piercing and unremittent; chills racked his other limbs. His whole life, Rita always told him how smart and handsome and fortunate he was. 'You can do anything you want in this world,' she'd say. 'You got the looks and the vocabulary.' In retrospect, Darrell Grant realized that marrying Erin had been the high point, the main window of opportunity. If ever he was going to turn things around, she was his big chance. Hell, he'd struggled to please her, too. He'd tried the conventional life: sobriety, monogamy, a day job, the whole ball of wax. It simply wasn't meant to be. He was chronically ill-suited for the responsibilities that come with lawful behavior. Erin didn't even try to understand. When the marriage broke up, Rita was disappointed. Darrell explained: 'I need a girl that's more of a short-range thinker. Like myself.'

Now, in the short range, Darrell Grant focused on a pair of problems: stopping the flaming agony in his arm, and snatching Angie away from his ex-wife.

After supper, Rita came out and peeked under the trailer. She was ready for an outing with the wolf-dogs – catcher's mask, logger's mitts, the frayed housedress. Darrell noticed that she'd added plastic shin guards to the uniform.

'I brought some fried chicken,' Rita said. 'Extra crispy.'

She placed a cold drumstick in his mouth. Darrell tore off a huge bite and spit the bone. He said, 'Is it Mrs Gomez that's got the cancer?'

'No, her husband. He passed in August.'

'I bet she's still got his pills.'

'Darrell, no!'

'In the bathroom cabinet, I'll bet.' He lifted his head. 'Rita, I'm damn near crazy from the pain. Please?'

'You already stole the poor woman's car.'

'But her husband's croaked, right? So what's the sense of letting good medicine go to waste? Tell me, Rita.'

'I dunno what all to look for.'

'Demerol, Dilaudids, codeine – shit, bring me everything with the old man's name on it.'

'But then you gotta go,' Rita persisted, 'before the damn cops come by again.'

'That's a promise,' said Darrell Grant.

There was something else he needed, but he couldn't ask his sister because she'd never agree. Never in a month of Sundays.

But that's all right, Darrell thought, because I know where it is. I know exactly where Alberto keeps it – the same place as every other macho meathead in Miami.

In the glove box of his car. Fully loaded.

Canceling the dinner engagement was easy. In fact, a less distracted Malcolm J. Moldowsky would have noticed the edge of relief in the governor's voice. Stomach problems? he'd said. That's too bad, Malcolm. Give me a ring when you're feeling better. When he hung up, the governor had turned to an aide and said: 'Let's pray it's a tumor.'

As he drove toward the towers of Turnberry Isle, Moldowsky's mind was preoccupied with thoughts contrived to stave off panic. The cop had nothing, really, but a Kodak slide and a motel bill.

The phone call from Missoula could be explained. Moldy would claim he had houseguests that night. Lots of long-distance calls in and out. It wouldn't be difficult to find someone who would say (for a price): *Yes, come to think of it, so-and-so's boyfriend's foster uncle called from Montana. Drunk as a skunk, yakking his fool head off . . . what was his name again?*

The photograph from the tittie bar was something else. Clearly, that goddamn García knew the story behind it. Malcolm Moldowsky gripped the steering wheel ferociously, zigzagging through the traffic. A ghastly scene played over and over in his head . . .

The congressman, wearing only cowboy boots and boxer shorts, downcast and bleary on the bow of the yacht.

The Cuban cop, puffing maliciously on his cigar, circling like a starved panther, waving the Kodak slide, firing brutal questions faster than David Lane Dilbeck could possibly invent credible answers.

Dilbeck – tremulous, wilting, caving in. Yes, Sergeant, that's me in the picture. Me with the champagne bottle. Please understand, I'm not well. I need help controlling my animal urges. Ask the lady, go ahead. I never meant to harm a soul . . .

Moldy drove faster. For consolation he clutched at the fact that Dilbeck had no knowledge of what had happened to the blackmailers, Killian and the lawyer. The congressman didn't know what drastic steps had been taken to shield him from scandal. This prick García could interrogate him all day long and come up empty. There were many crimes to which a badgered David Dilbeck might legitimately confess, but murder wasn't one of them.

Traffic came to a stop at the Golden Glades cloverleaf, where a truck hauling limerock had jackknifed on a ramp. Moldowsky cursed, snarled, raked his polished fingernails on the dashboard. He couldn't understand García's interest in a drowned fisherman and a murdered lawyer. The cases belonged in Broward County, not Dade. What did he want? What was he after? The way the crazy bastard had come at him, with no pretense of respect or civility. Taunting him, fucking with him – like it was personal.

The cars inched along in maddening spurts. As therapy, Moldowsky jammed both fists on the horn. In the station wagon ahead of him, a frizzy-haired young woman flipped him the finger. The man on the passenger side held a MAC-10 out the window as a hint for Moldy to be patient and shut the fuck up.

For diversion Moldowsky tried the radio, and found a call-in program where the guest happened to be Eloy Flickman, Dilbeck's Republican opponent in the congressional race. Moldy was soothed by what he heard. Flickman now was advocating mandatory tubal ligations for all single mothers applying for food stamps. To another caller, Flickman submitted that Cuba's nascent tourist industry was luring too many European visitors away from Miami, and that only a direct nuclear strike on Havana would remove the burgeoning economic threat. Moldy thought: Wonderful! The man's a certifiable loon. Dilbeck's a lock to win re-election, as long as nothing breaks loose in the headlines.

The traffic jam slowly started to unclog. Malcolm Moldowsky switched to a classical music station, and tried to relax. Tonight's mission was uncomplicated: remove the congressman from the Rojos' yacht, and far away from all naked women.

If the detective got there first, well . . . Maybe a bribe was in order. Maybe that's all García wanted.

Moldy hoped so; it would make life so much easier.

When darkness fell, Darrell Grant snatched the gun from Alberto's car and crawled back under the mobile home. Later Rita showed up with three prescription bottles belonging to the late Rogelio Gomez. Darrell Grant poured the pills into the palm of his good hand, and ate three of everything. An hour later, the whole world was a blur, but Darrell felt marvelous. The pain in his arm was gone, along with much of his short-term memory. Rita had to remind him where he'd hidden the stolen Pontiac.

Once he located the turnpike, Darrell Grant drove northbound at a geriatric pace. His vision and reflexes were abominable. Rita's splint proved sturdy but cumbersome: the nine-iron got in the way of Darrell's driving. He had to hang it out the window of the car, as if permanently signaling for a left turn. Since it was Dade County, no one paid the slightest attention.

The trip to Fort Lauderdale took ninety minutes. Darrell Grant spent most of it in the draft of a slow-moving Pentecostal church bus. Miraculously, he spotted the Commercial Boulevard exit in time to steer off. He stopped at a fast-food restaurant next door to the Tickled Pink, and parked obliviously in the drive-through lane. Roused by a surly assistant manager, Darrell Grant found a new spot. This one offered a clear view of Orly's strip joint; Erin's shitheap Fairlane was parked near the front awning between a Porsche and a Cadillac.

Like she was somebody special, Darrell thought.

He broke out laughing. Everything seemed hilarious tonight; the sight of a dead opossum on the highway had made him giggle all the way from Okeechobee Road to Miramar. These were absolutely top-notch drugs. 'God bless you, Señor Gomez!' he said, saluting the heavens with his nine-iron.

Before long, a limousine appeared at Orly's night-club. Darrell Grant thought his eyes were playing tricks.

The driver, a black man wearing a cap, got out of the limo and opened one of the doors. In the Pontiac,

Darrell leaned forward and tried to squint the blur from his eyes. He was hoping to catch sight of a celebrity. Rock stars were known to hang out at nudie bars; Darrell had seen a video once on MTV.

But it was his ex-wife who walked out of the club toward the limo. She wore blue jeans, a baggy white T-shirt and sandals. She carried a shoulder bag and a shoebox. It looked like she was heading home early. She was alone, too. No trace of Angela.

Darrell Grant was astounded when she got into the limousine.

'The cunt,' he said, turning the key in the Pontiac. Who the fuck does she think she is? Who?

Then he started to laugh again.

When the limousine pulled out of the club, the Pontiac was close behind.

TWENTY-NINE

Shad went to Sears and purchased two jumbo outdoor garbage buckets with clip-on lids. Then he drove to a snake farm near the Tamiami Airport, west of Miami. The man who owned the snake farm called himself Jungle Juan. He told Shad that most of his reptile stock had been wiped out by the hurricane. His insurance company still hadn't paid off.

'They say I padded the claim,' complained Jungle Juan, 'but I had papers on every damn snake. Certified papers!'

'Like they do for dogs,' Shad said.

'*Exactamente.*'

'And they all got killed in the storm?'

'Hard to say.' Jungle Juan thoughtfully fingered his diamond ear stud. 'They was mostly just gone from sight. I'll assume some escapes, I'll assume some mortalities.'

Shad tried to strike a hopeful note. He said, 'Snakes are tough customers.'

'Some are, some ain't. One old diamondback, the wind picked him up and snapped him like a bullwhip. I seen this myself.'

Shad said, 'But the rats and mice made out OK.'

'By and large, yessir. How many you need?'

411

'A hundred ought to do it. Rats only.'

Jungle Juan said, 'Now, these ain't white. These are semi-wild Norways.'

'Perfect.'

The cage was eight feet long and four feet high. It was fashioned of plywood and chicken wire. Inside was an undulating mass of vermin, two and three deep. Anticipating food, the rats swarmed noisily toward the cage door when Jungle Juan approached. Deftly he bare-handed the squealing animals, and dropped them one by one into the jumbo garbage pails.

Shad watched impassively. He had no particular aversion to rodents. 'Looks like you got a surplus,' he remarked.

Jungle Juan snorted. 'Rats up the ass, and no snakes to eat 'em. There's your hundred.' He slapped the lids on the garbage cans and said, 'Thank God there's a shipment of boas due Monday. I expect they'll be hungry.'

Shad said, 'We had a dancer that tried a boa.'

'How big?'

'The snake? Seven feet.'

Jungle Juan said, 'Your ball pythons are better for entertainment purposes. They don't bite so damn much.'

Shad asked how much he owed. Jungle Juan said fifty bucks.

'Man, that's cheap.' Shad handed him the cash.

'Hurricane discount,' Jungle Juan explained. 'I gotta move these buggers before they fuck me into Chapter 11. Every day they's a dozen new litters and what happens is, I swear, they start to consume one another.'

He and Shad carried the garbage buckets out to

Shad's car. The sound of many rat paws could be heard, scratching feverishly against the heavy plastic. As they loaded the animals into the backseat, Jungle Juan inquired about the dancer with the boa constrictor. Shad told him that she'd taken ill and gone home to Texas.

'What about the snake?' asked Jungle Juan, shrewdly.

'I got him in a stockroom at the club.'

'Healthy?'

'A little farsighted, but otherwise OK.'

'Well, I could sure use him,' Jungle Juan said, 'if you ever wanted to sell.'

'Not just yet,' said Shad.

When he returned to the club, Mr Orly asked to see the rats. Shad let him peek in one of the pails.

'Goddamn,' said Orly, crinkling his face.

'We all set?'

'Yep,' Orly said. 'I just wish I could be there to see it. Those fucking Lings.' He laughed venomously. 'I'd love to get the whole thing on video!'

Shad asked about Erin. Orly said she'd left to meet that goddamn horny no-good congressman.

'Where?' Shad asked.

'I'm assuming the boat. Who cares?'

Shad called Al García's office and left a message. Then he went into the stockroom and emerged with a large dirty pillowcase, knotted at the neck. Orly wished him good luck.

'You come right back,' he told the bouncer. 'It's gonna get busy as hell around here.'

'How long since she took off?'

'Erin? Half-hour, tops.' Orly studied him warily. 'Don't you worry about her. You just get your ass back here, OK?'

Shad circled the Flesh Farm until he spotted the health inspector's car, a gray Dodge Aries with yellow state plates. Monique Jr had been recruited to make the phone call, because no man could resist her helpless little-girl voice. *'The rats, they're everywhere!'* she'd exclaimed. *'They're biting me, they're biting me!'* The health department had kept its promise to send someone right over. The inspectors, Shad knew, trampled each other for such an assignment.

Shad parked the car, threw a ladder against the side of the building and hauled the jumbo garbage pails to the roof. The air-conditioning vents rose like squat chimneys at each end of the building. Shad pried off the rusty grids and poured the rats into the duct system. The little guys seemed grateful to be free.

The Lings were hunkered in the office, dodging the health inspector. They had ordered one of the table dancers to get him drunk and compromised. Then they would talk.

Shad barged in and caught the two brothers by surprise.

'What's in the bag?' asked the one wearing a black tuxedo and a Yankees cap. Shad knew him as the Flesh Farm's floor manager. He sat on a torn Naugahyde sofa that was the color of ox blood. Behind the desk was the other Ling, who wore a gray pullover and two ropey gold chains on his neck. He, too, inquired about the contents of the pillowcase.

'Stand up,' Shad said.

Both Lings displayed the identical annoying mannerism of laughing through their teeth, hissing on the inhale. Shad took out the .38 Special and shot three ragged holes in a family portrait on the wall. One of the bullets sensationally disfigured the likeness of the Lings' paternal grandmother; the brothers seemed horrified.

'Bingo,' Shad said. 'Who's next?'

The Lings stood up quickly. Shad arranged them back-to-back in the center of the floor.

One of them said, 'You gone shoot us?'

'Nope,' Shad answered, 'I'm gonna measure you. Take off the damn cap.'

He quickly determined that the tuxedoed Ling was at least two inches taller than the gold-chained Ling. 'You're the one,' Shad said to the shorter brother, 'who grabbed my friend's tits.'

The smaller Ling frowned in vexation. Urbana's fingernail tracks were plainly visible on one cheek. Somebody knocked on the door, and Shad concealed the gun in his belt.

A frantic voice of indistinct gender. 'Mr Ling, come quick! Come now!' A woman's scream cut through the dance music. The brothers glanced at one another in alarm. Shad ordered the one in the tuxedo to go check on the trouble.

The larger Ling said, 'Maybe we should call police.'

'Try an exterminator,' Shad advised.

With both hands the larger brother fitted the Yankees cap tightly on his head, the visor practically touching his nose. Wordlessly he slipped out of the office. Shad locked the door and shoved the smaller Ling into a swivel chair.

'This no business of yours,' the brother protested. 'It's that boss you got. Mister Hotshit Mafia Man.'

Shad twisted Ling's wrist to check the time on the phony Rolex. It was getting late.

Ling pulled his arm away. 'Fat Tony, my ass,' he said, spitting unintentionally. 'Orly must think we stupid, huh? They got Mafia in Japan, too. Plenty fucking Mafia!'

Shad untied the knot in the pillowcase. He felt serene and contented – a rare moment of moral clarity.

Ling said, 'I didn't grab nobody's titties.'

Shad opened the pillowcase and angled it toward the overhead light, so he could see down into the corners. 'I feel good about this,' he said, to no one.

Ling noticed the sinuated movement in the bottom of Shad's sack. He could see the shape of heavy, muscular coils shifting against the fabric.

'You better not!' he shouted.

Shad commanded Ling to stand up and drop his jeans. Ling refused. Shad drew the pistol and poked the barrel in the man's navel. The brother set his jaw and said, 'I rather be shot dead. Make it quick, too.'

Shad thought: What an actor, this guy.

Ling regarded the pillowcase anxiously. 'You sick man,' he said to Shad.

'Really? You're the ones cut poor Bubba to pieces.'

The brother scowled in confusion. 'Bubba?'

Shad clubbed him in the temple with the butt of the .38. Ling fell briefly unconscious. He awoke naked, hot and discomfited. Shad had hung him from the office door, securing his wrists to the coat hook.

The smaller Ling cursed and writhed, his heels and elbows banging against the wood. From the hallway outside came the sounds of mounting chaos. Stretched on the Naugahyde sofa, Shad tended to the liberated

boa constrictor; before leaving town, Lorelei had neglected to remove the tape from the snake's mouth.

'What you doing?' Ling demanded.

Shad said, 'This old boy's half-starved.' He piled the
reptile on the floor, beneath the dangling and helpless
Ling. As the tan-and-brown mass unraveled itself, the
brother's upper lip curled in fear. The boa, being naturally arboreal, searched for something to climb. In the
absence of a tree, it chose Ling's bare leg. The more
vigorously the brother kicked, the tighter the snake
drew its coils.

'You know what?' said Shad. 'Your schlong looks
just like a hamster.'

After a short contemplation, Ling issued a series of
high-pitched screams. The boa's tongue feathered
against his quaking skin. He cried: 'It's gone bite my
wee-wee!'

Shad thought it was very funny. 'Your what? Is that
what it's called in Japan?'

'Get it off me, goddammit.'

The snake continued its ominous ascent.

'You were very rude,' Shad said, 'to grab my friend's
boobs the other night.'

'I'm s-s-sorry. I couldn't help it.' Ling had lapsed into
a pathetic whine. 'Some girls don't mind,' he said.

'Oh, I doubt that seriously.' Shad wondered how
long the coat hook would hold fast under the brother's
weight.

Ling struggled to make himself motionless. Fighting,
he feared, would agitate the creature. 'Please,' he whispered morosely, 'get it off me. I'll do anything you
want.'

Shad yawned. He removed his beret and brushed the

lint off the crown. The boa's tongue flicked in and out. It had drawn a vague bead on Ling's shriveling organ.

'Oh-oh,' said Shad. The poor thing *was* starved.

Ling went slack on the door. He let out an involuntary whimper. 'It's gone eat me,' he asserted. The boa's clouded eyes followed every tremble and sway of Ling's luckless member.

Shad said, 'You act like an animal, you get treated like one. Remember that.'

'I s-s-said I sorry.'

Shad smirked bitterly. 'Sorry is the word for it.'

The snake's head rose in a fluid arc, as if levitated by hydraulics. Its creamy neck banded to muscle in the shape of an S.

'Get ready,' Shad warned.

'Oh my God!'

'Don't be such a pussy. It ain't even poisonous.'

'But my wee-wee!'

The boa's strike was too rapid for the human eye. Ling felt the needle sting of teeth before his mind registered the image of the snake's open jaws, lashing. He passed out mid-scream.

When the brother regained consciousness, he found himself face down on the moldy shag carpet. There was no sign of Shad or the farsighted boa constrictor. When Ling rolled over, the effort ignited a burst of pain between his legs. He allowed one hand to explore the jeopardized zone. The brother sighed gratefully: he was punctured but intact, and fully attached.

In exhausted relief, Ling closed his eyes. 'Sick man,' he said. 'Very sick man.'

A faint noise in the ceiling caught his attention. He opened his eyes just in time to see a fat brown rat jump from the air-conditioning vent. It landed, with a perturbed squeak, squarely on Ling's sad and astonished face.

Some of the Flesh Farm's customers were so drunk that the infestation didn't bother them. The performers and waitresses, however, reacted more intelligently: they fled. All friction dancing ceased. The larger Ling armed his two bouncers with aluminum softball bats and directed a violent but ineffective counterattack. The rodents proved quick-footed and elusive. As if by destiny, one vaulted from the Michelob display to befoul the health inspector's whiskey sour.

Shad watched from a bar stool. He thought things went pretty well. As sabotage, it wasn't exceptionally clever, but Mr Orly couldn't expect miracles on short notice. Orly, after all, had wanted to torch the place! A four-alarm blaze might have been more satisfying, visually, but it wouldn't have put the Ling brothers out of business. They'd have simply rebuilt with the insurance money, and probably upgraded – new marquees, new decor, a new sound system. Orly didn't like that prospect one bit, and endorsed the impromptu rat plague as an alternative. Rodent publicity would be fatal to the Flesh Farm.

The TV crews beat the police by five minutes. Onstage, a beautiful nude Brazilian was on her knees, hammering at a lump of lifeless fur. The weapon was a standard high-heeled shoe. With each blow, the dancer's breasts swung back and forth in tandem, like church bells. Shad wondered how the TV people would edit the tape to make it presentable for the eleven o'clock news.

He went to the parking lot to watch the squad cars arrive. He stopped counting at nine. A busload of orphans could plunge off a bridge and you wouldn't see so many cops. Shad smiled cynically. Nothing brought out the cavalry like strippers in distress.

One of the dancers, a petite brunette, recognized Shad in the gathering crowd. She said, 'You work down the street.'

'Until tonight.'

'I auditioned there about two months ago. When it was the Eager Beaver.'

Shad said he remembered, although he didn't. The dancer put on a long pink sweatshirt to cover her diaphanous stage costume. Shad found her extremely attractive. He had come to adore women in clothes.

The brunette noticed the pillowcase. 'Whatcha got there?'

'A boa constrictor,' Shad said. 'Want it?'

'For what?'

'For your act.'

The brunette said no thanks. One snake dancer in town was plenty.

'But Lorelei's gone,' Shad told her. 'It's wide-open territory.'

'I don't know. I'm not crazy about snakes.'

'Who the hell is?' He handed her the boa in the pillowcase. 'Think about it,' he said. 'Work up a routine.'

He returned to the Tickled Pink and told Orly that the rats were a huge hit. Orly said he figured as much; the place was filling with customers spooked from the

Flesh Farm. Orly wanted to know if Urbana's honor had been avenged, and Shad told him the story of the smaller Ling. Orly laughed so hard that he blew cream soda out of his nose.

'Those fuckers,' he gurgled, 'are finished!'

'Congratulations,' Shad said, turning away.

Orly told him to go check on table four. 'It's a bunch of coked-up roofers. One of 'em brought a goddamn dildo.'

Shad said, 'I need to go see about Erin.'

'Like hell. You're on the floor tonight.'

'No, Mr Orly. I've pretty much had it.' He jumped the bar, punched open the cash register and removed sixty-four dollars. 'Yesterday's pay,' said Shad, fanning the cash. 'What I did tonight, that's for free.' He found the Camus paperback and wedged it into his waistband.

Orly said, 'Hell, don't quit on me.'

'It's time.'

'The fuck does that mean? *It's time.*' Orly blocked Shad's path. 'You want a raise? Is this your way of hitting me up?'

Shad gripped him by the soft meat of the shoulders. 'I'm suffocating,' he said, 'in this world.'

'Get serious,' said Orly, pulling free. 'Wall-to-wall pussy, and you're suffocating? 'Scuze me if I don't break down and cry.'

'It's not your fault, Mr Orly. I seen too much.'

Orly suggested a vacation. He told Shad to take a week off, fly to the islands, get laid repeatedly. Shad shook his head. 'A week won't do it,' he said.

'Then make it ten days.'

'You don't understand, Mr Orly. I gotta get out completely. I've lost my sense of wonderment.'

'Oh, for Chrissake,' Orly said. He led Shad to a quiet corner, away from the dance floor. 'When you were a little boy, what'd you want to be when you grew up? I mean, was your life plan to break heads in a nudie joint?'

Shad said, 'I wanted to play for the Forty-niners.'

'Right! And what happened?'

'I got fucking busted in the ninth grade.'

Orly rolled his eyes. 'Point is, almost nobody gets where they want in this life. Everybody's dream takes a beating. Me, I wanted to be an obstetrician.' He waved a pudgy pale hand at the strobe-lit scene behind him. 'This is as close as I got. You follow? It's called facing reality.'

Shad was sidetracked by the laughable notion of Mr Orly aspiring to a medical career. It was one of the most spectacular lies he'd heard in a long time.

'There's different kinds of reality,' he told Orly. 'I want the mystery back in mine.'

'Fuck mystery. Let's talk loyalty. When I hired you, hell, you still had eyebrows. That's how long ago.'

Shad was unmoved by the sentimentality. He could not recall a single Christmas bonus.

Orly said, 'Like it or not, this is God's plan for you. This is what you're cut out for—'

'You should've been a preacher,' Shad said, 'on TV.'

'If it's the scorpion thing, I said I was sorry. Bottom line, I freaked when the inspector showed up.'

Shad said it was no big deal.

'Then what the fuck else can I say?'

'Just *adios*,' said Shad.

Orly's chest sagged in defeat. He shook Shad's enormous hand and said, 'I suppose you got prospects.'

'Nope, but I got some interesting ideas.' Shad said goodbye. Orly watched, dejectedly, as the huge pearly orb floated above the crowd, toward the door.

Urbana Sprawl hopped off a table and intercepted Shad with a tender hug. 'My hero,' she purred.

'That's me, babe.' Shad took the red beret from his pocket and arranged it at a sly angle on Urbana's head. 'Is Erin at the yacht?' he asked.

'Dancing her pretty heart out.'

'What the hell's she up to?' Shad was forced to holler over a rap number that Kevin had sadistically cranked to ninety decibels.

Urban, shouting in his ear. 'I think she's out to do some damage!'

The music seemed to affect Shad's focus and equilibrium; each bass beat fell like a sledge on his brainpan. He wondered how many bullets would be required to take out the wall speakers.

'Onward and upward,' he said to Urbana Sprawl, and elbowed his way out of the lounge.

The penthouse condominium of Malcolm J. Moldowsky was twenty minutes by automobile from the two-bedroom tract house owned by Jesse James Braden and his wife. It might as well have been a whole other universe, as far as Al García was concerned.

The murder of Jesse James Braden was precipitated by two connected events. At exactly 5:10 p.m. on the sixth of October, Jesse James Braden spilled a shaker of Bloody Marys on the freshly laundered upholstery of his

wife's Toyota Camry. That was the first event. At exactly
5:11 p.m., Jesse James Braden laughed uproariously at
what he'd done. That was the second event.

At exactly 5:12 p.m., the wife of Jesse James Braden
dragged him from the Toyota and shot him fatally in
the genitals.

Neighbors were divided on the question of whether
Mrs Braden had been excessive in her reaction. Witnesses agreed that Jesse had been a prodigious sinner
and often conducted himself in a manner that invited
homicide. The shooting itself was not so much at issue
as Mrs Braden's selection of anatomical targets. The
men in the crowd, sober and otherwise, felt that the
mere spilling of an alcoholic beverage – and subsequent
insensitive laughter – failed to justify three bullets
through the penis. The women of the neighborhood,
however, asserted that the decedent got exactly what he
deserved – a just punishment for years of piggish
whoring, drunken violence and general bad behavior.
Jesse James Braden, they said, did not respect his wife
or her personal belongings.

Into this boisterous debate waded Al García at precisely 6:47 p.m. He didn't want to be there; he wanted
to be setting an ambush for a genuine United States
congressman – flashing the badge, barking out the
Miranda, scaring the piss out of the bastard. He had a
gut feeling that the guy would fall apart, start blab-
bering. García had been looking forward to the
moment.

Instead, the detective stood on a front lawn no different from a million other front lawns, except that
the man who had mowed it was lying agape in the
bromeliads, with his pecker shot off. The paramedics

said Jesse James Braden bled out in three minutes flat. It's like a fire hose, they said, the way it leaks.

García hoped to finish the interviews in an hour, since the witnesses concurred on every detail except the precise final utterance of Jesse James Braden – a brief but vituperative tirade. His wife, now safely handcuffed, insisted on showing García the tomato-juice stains on the seat of her car. She demanded that the police photographer get a picture, so that the judge could see what that worthless Jesse had done. When Al García inquired about the murder weapon, Mrs Braden led him indoors to the kitchen. She had placed the pistol in the refrigerator with her dead husband's booze.

The detective's work proceeded smoothly until Jesse's grief-stricken brother arrived at the crime scene and opened fire with a 16-gauge shotgun. Francis Scott Braden missed Jesse's wife by twenty feet, but he grazed a patrolman and blew the rear window out of Al García's unmarked Caprice. The chaotic interruption meant two hours of extra paperwork for García, who again was reminded how much he hated domestic homicides. It wasn't detective work – it was purely janitorial.

García didn't receive Shad's message until he was back in the car, rolling on the interstate, the air whipping through the busted window, scattering his police papers. He drove the Caprice as fast as it would go, cursing the Saturday night traffic because he was missing the big show: Erin, dancing up a storm.

THIRTY

Erin fixed a drink from the mini-bar in the back of the limousine. She wondered about the dream she'd had the night before: making love to a man in an orchard of coconut palms. The man looked vaguely like Al García. In the dream it was daytime, the lemon sun arcing high and scorching. The man was nude but Erin wore a black dress, cut high to the neck. She remembered getting on top, telling the man to hush now, relax. She remembered her knees stinging on the rough bed of dry fronds. In the dream there was music, too; Linda Ronstadt, singing 'Carmelita'. It was magical. Erin couldn't remember coming, but she did recall rolling over, gently pulling the man along as if he weighed no more than a child. He lay his head on her breasts and closed his eyes, and mysteriously he no longer resembled Al García. Now it was someone new, a stranger, but Erin didn't push him away. She let him rest. In the dream, she was still aroused. A sea breeze whisked through the orchard, and the porcelain sky filled with bright tropical birds – macaws, cockatoos, parrots, cardinals and flamingos. Erin remembered kissing the man's forehead to wake him, so he could see the flaming colors dip and scatter overhead. The man stirred and murmured in Spanish, but didn't open his eyes. In the

426

dream, the radiant migration seemed to last all morning. Finally Erin spotted her daughter running barefoot, in and out of the mop-topped trees. Angela was wide-eyed and intent, laughing as she followed the kaleidoscopic train of birds. Erin slipped from beneath the sleeping stranger and ran through the palm orchard after her daughter. In the dream, the bald trunks of the palms stooped and swayed malevolently to obstruct her path. Angie's laughter grew unfamiliar and distant. Erin remembered stopping, breathless, and turning her face to the sun – the sky was empty, the birds had vanished. She had awakened in a hot sweat.

Now, in the limousine, the Beefeater's provided no insight to the dream's meaning. It did, however, fortify Erin for an evening with David Dilbeck. She was impelled by the certainty that the congressman would escape implication in Jerry Killian's murder, that he was out of Al García's reach. The idea of the arrogant old drooler going scot-free was unacceptable, so Erin had made up her mind to destroy him. Dilbeck wouldn't be harmed, crippled or killed – just destroyed. It seemed the least she could do, and it had to be done alone. Women's work.

She finished the martini and began dressing for the congressman. She hooked on a lace bra top and a matching G-string, the one with the red seahorses. Her shoes, too, were candy-apple red. A wine-colored minidress completed the package. Around her neck she hung two long strands of imitation pearls. As Erin dressed, she noticed the Haitian driver, Pierre, watching her in the rearview mirror. Erin stuck her tongue at him.

'I'm sorry,' he said, and looked away instantly.

Erin scooted forward to one of the jump seats. She put a hand on the driver's shoulder. 'You speak English?'

'At times,' he said.

Erin poured him a cola from the mini-bar. Pierre accepted it graciously.

'Is there a phone in this car?' she asked.

The driver nodded at a cellular receiver under the dashboard. Erin turned on the vanity light and opened her purse. She wrote something on a piece of paper and handed it to Pierre. Without reading it, he placed the note in his breast pocket.

'That's a phone number,' she told him. 'Things may get strange tonight. Say, at eleven sharp.'

Pierre said, 'It will not be the first time.'

'I'll understand if you can't help me,' Erin told him. 'But I need to know now, before I get started.'

'You overestimate my sense of loyalty.'

'A job is a job,' Erin said. 'I wouldn't want to jeopardize your situation.'

The guard booth of Turnberry Isle came into view. Pierre flashed the headlights and coasted toward the gate. Without turning, he said to Erin, 'But a phone call could come from anywhere, couldn't it?'

She smiled. 'You're a decent guy, Pierre.'

'*Oui*,' he said, touching the brim of his cap.

Congressman David Lane Dilbeck glistened with excitement, and a light application of petroleum jelly. He put on the Garth Brooks getup, shined his boots, dabbed on some designer-cowboy cologne, tweezered the stray hairs out of his nose . . .

The dancer had phoned that morning with an

intriguing request. A bit frightening, really. Not all men would've agreed to it.

But Dilbeck instantly consented because he felt an incipient carnal connection with the woman. Something was sparking between them, a promise of lust. The first time, she'd acted so tough, all business – hands off, buster, and so forth. But as the night had worn on, Dilbeck had detected a softening of attitude, traces of affection. The signs were subtle, to be sure; she had, after all, mortared his hand with one of her spiked heels.

Yet even that made sense later, when he took the dancer's phone call. Perhaps pain was a necessary ingredient of her love. The prospect excited Dilbeck; he felt adventuresome and bold. The congressman had frequently heard of such wild women. Now was his chance to tame one and possess her.

He arrived at Turnberry shortly after dusk. He brought, in addition to the item Erin requested, two magnums of Korbel champagne, three dozen red roses, a gold bracelet and a shopping bag of assorted compact discs: Smithereens, Pearl Jam, Toad the Wet Sprocket, Boyz II Men, REM, Wilson Phillips. Dilbeck had no inkling about the nature of the music, nor did he care. He had dispatched an eager young assistant to load up at Peaches, in the hopes that one or more of the selections might prove to be a dancing favorite of Erin's. If crass gift-giving failed, he would endeavour to dazzle her with gossip from inside the Washington Beltway.

That first night on the yacht, it had seemed to Dilbeck that Erin was stubbornly unimpressed by his title. Most of the women who slept with him did so mainly because he was a member of the House of Representatives, and therefore he qualified (marginally) as a power fuck. Erin, however, treated him as just another horny rich guy. She displayed no interest in his position or his grossly embellished achievements, and resisted every conversation that might have led to Washington name-dropping. The relationship could not blossom, Dilbeck decided, until the woman was properly enlightened about his importance. In anticipation, he'd been polishing some of his most trusty cocktail-party yarns. Also, for purposes of documentation, he brought photographs.

Erin came aboard the *Sweetheart Deal* at about eight-fifteen. Entering the salon, she again felt claustrophobic, incarcerated. 'Where's Frick and Frack?' she asked.

'Who?'

'The guards.'

'Grand Bahama,' the congressman said, 'with the Rojos.' The sight of the minidress caused another mild spasm beneath the scar of his double-bypass.

Erin complimented Dilbeck's country-western outfit. 'Dwight Yoakam?' she guessed.

'Garth Brooks, actually.'

'Well, it certainly flatters you.' Erin was pleased at how sincere she sounded. The man looked absurd. And what was that peculiar sheen to his skin?

Dilbeck handed her the gifts. He said, 'I brought some pictures, as well.'

'Of what?' She wasn't in the mood for porn.

'Pictures of me,' said the congressman, 'on the job.'

'Really?' said Erin, swallowing a yawn.

She thanked him politely for the roses and the bracelet, but Dilbeck thought she wore the expression of one who had received such things before, in the course of commerce. She picked through the stack of CDs and rejected all but the Smithereens. As before, she'd brought her own songs for dancing. In honour of Jerry Killian, she again put on ZZ Top.

The congressman said, with an air of masculine accomplishment: 'It took some doing, but I found what you were looking for.'

Erin squeezed his arm. 'Sweetie, I knew you would.'

Her touch made him shiver pleasantly. For a moment, Dilbeck regarded the arm-squeeze as significant, a preliminary to full body contact. Then he realized that Erin was only using him as a brace, to steady her ascent to the captain's table. In a flash she was out of the minidress. The pearls remained.

'What's the hurry?' Dilbeck said. 'I thought we might chat for a while.'

Erin started dancing. Off came the red bra.

'Jesus,' murmured the congressman.

'Sit back, cowboy,' Erin told him. 'Enjoy.'

Malcolm J. Moldowsky approached the docks casually, as if out for an evening stroll. He removed his necktie to look more like a yachtsman.

Twice he walked past the *Sweetheart Deal*. There was no sign of the Cuban detective. Moldy boarded quietly. He heard thumping from inside: drums, heavy guitar licks. The congressman's tastes leaned toward crooners, so Moldowsky knew that David Dilbeck wasn't alone. The show had begun: Erin Grant was there.

Moldy congratulated himself for beating García to the yacht. He put his ear to the door, but heard no human noises mixed with the rock music. He took it as an encouraging sign; silence was always preferable to the sounds of a struggle.

He had this hands on the doorknob when a shadow passed across the deck. Malcom Moldowsky wheeled to see a man balanced on the transom, backlit by the docklights. The man rocked from one leg to the other, in time to the muffled backbeat.

'What do you want?' Moldowsky said.

The man hopped down and stepped toward him. 'I want my daughter,' he said.

Moldowsky smiled with forced patience; the man was too young to be the dancer's father. Moldy said, 'There's been some mistake. Your daughter's not here.'

'Then I might as well shoot you,' the man said.

At the sight of the pistol, Moldowsky raised his hands high. The intruder seemed crazed and displaced. The knees of his jeans were filthy, and his oily blond hair was matted to one side. The eyes were foggy and moist. A golf club was strapped imposingly to a crudely bandaged arm. Moldy figured the man was a hurricane victim, made homeless and insane. They were still out there, addled wanderers, dredging for pieces of scattered lives.

'She's not here,' Moldowsky said, 'your little girl.'

Darrell Grant armed the pistol and squinted one eye. 'Say goodnight, Shorty.'

Moldowsky let out a gasp and covered his face. Expecting to die, his blackening thoughts turned egotistically to the aftermath. Slain on a yacht with a drunken congressman and a stripper – that's the headline! What photo would they choose to accompany the story? A studio portrait, Moldy hoped, not crime-scene gore.

And how would he be described in the press coverage – political consultant? Power broker? Fixer? Jesus, and the quotes. There'd be no shortage of grief-stricken testimonials, all fulsomely insincere. Moldy assumed he would soil himself, dying. What a laugh the cruel bastards would get from *that*. The dapper Malcolm Moldowsky, pissing in his Perry Ellis.

In bitter dread, he waited for the flat crack of the gunshot. Nothing happened.

The problem was Darrell Grant's unfamiliarity with firearms. He didn't like guns, never carried one, never even fired one. Now, steadying himself on the deck of the yacht, he couldn't find the damn trigger. His finger probed intently but was obstructed by a disc of hard plastic. Darrell Grant held the pistol in the light and scrutinized the impenetrable device.

'Fuck me,' he said.

It was a lock. Darrell couldn't believe the rotten luck. The goofy Alberto had to be one of the few citizens in all Dade County with the brains to buy a trigger lock. The advertised purpose of such devices was to prevent dirtbag thieves like Darrell Grant from using a stolen handgun against the innocent citizenry. Darrell, however, suspected that Alberto Alonso harboured other concerns, such as Rita shooting him in his sleep.

In any event, the locked pistol was about as lethal as a doorstop. Darrell Grant hurled it over the wheelhouse, into the Intracoastal Waterway. 'Un-fucking-believable,' he said, with a dry giggle.

Malcolm Moldowsky peeked through his fingers when he heard the splash. The gun was gone. Why? Moldy didn't care. The action confirmed his assessment that the intruder was deranged.

'Out of my way,' Darrell Grant said. He gestured with the blade of the golf club, which protruded from the makeshift splint.

Moldowsky feigned concern. 'You really banged up that arm.'

'Gee, I hadn't noticed.' Darrell Grant hoisted the jerry-rigged limb and poked Malcolm Moldowsky in the belly. 'Double compound fracture,' Darrell said, 'but you know what? I had hangnails hurt worse.'

'Let me drive you to a doctor.'

Darrell Grant lowered his voice and spoke very slowly, as if giving street directions to a foreign tourist: 'Get . . . the . . . fuck . . . out . . . of . . . my . . . way. *Por favor?*'

Moldy flattened himself against the cabin door. ZZ Top pounded up and down the bumps of his spine. 'I can't let you in,' he said to the stranger. It was imperative that the public, lunatics included, remain unaware of the congressman's runaway debauchery.

'But my daughter,' Darrell said, thickly.

'I told you, she's not here. You've made a mistake.'

Darrell's face broke into a crooked smile. 'Hey, I followed her mother, OK? All the way from the tittie bar. And I saw her walk on this boat not fifteen minutes ago. Now some asshole midget's gonna tell me I made a mistake?'

Beautiful, thought Moldowsky. The stripper's ex-husband. Tonight of all nights.

He said, 'Let's go up to the restaurant. I should buy you a drink.'

'A drink?' Darrell Grant threw back his head and yowled at the stars. 'Man, I don't need a drink. I'm full a drugs, OK? I mean *tanked*. Best fucking drugs known to mankind!'

'Fine,' Moldowsky said, tensing.

'These pills are so damn good,' Darrell said, 'I came out here searching for pain. Understand? I'm here to go one-on-one with pain, because I *cannot* be hurt. It ain't humanly possible. I had a railroad spike, I'd give it to you this very minute—'

'Settle down,' Moldy said.

'— and I'd make you hammer that fucking railroad spike straight into my skull, say about here –' Darrell Grant touched the centre of his forehead '– and you know what? I wouldn't feel a damn thing, that's the quality of narcotics I'm talkin' about.'

'Please,' Moldowsky said, 'keep your voice down.'

'I never killed a midget before.'

'Let's discuss this.'

'No, sir, you just move your tiny little ass outta the way. I'm here to fetch my daughter.'

'For the last time,' Moldy said, 'she's not on this boat.'

Darrell Grant grabbed him by the sleeve. 'You're right about one thing, Shorty. It's the last fucking time.' He hurled Malcolm Moldowsky to the deck and stepped on his chest.

Moldy wriggled impotently but did not scream. Ludicrously, he still believed it was possible to avoid a public scene. It wouldn't do to attract a nosy crowd to the Rojos' yacht – not with David Dilbeck inside, doing God knows what to a naked dancer. Fearing a repeat of the Eager Beaver debacle, Moldowsky sought to placate the intruder with promises.

435

'If you let me up,' he told the crazed ex-husband, 'I can help you find your girl.'

'Weeee-heeeee!' exclaimed Darrell Grant.

'I've got,' Moldy panted, 'all kinds of connections.'

The first blow was not a punch but a chip shot. Moldy felt his nose explode. Through the mush he saw the ex-husband, poised in a one-armed backswing. This time the blade of the club caught Malcolm Moldowsky flush in the throat. Madly he gulped for a breath.

'Fore!' Darrell said.

Moldowsky shut his eyes. This was worse than being shot; the newspapers would have a field day.

He clawed uselessly at the madman's legs. The next two swings dislocated Moldy's lower jaw. His cheeks filled with warm blood, spit and broken orthodonture. Even if he'd decided to cry for help, he couldn't. His face was a divot.

God, he thought, what a sorry way to die.

Is it a nine-iron or a wedge? Those fuckers in the press would make a point to find out. Oh, definitely.

The congressman offered Erin a job as his executive secretary in Washington.

'What would I do?' she asked, twirling her pearls.

'Keep my spirits up,' said David Dilbeck. 'Forty-five grand a year, plus major medical.' He cradled the champagne bottle like a doll.

Looking down from the captain's table, Erin said, 'You're so cute.' She tapped a foot on his shoulder, teasing. Dilbeck tried to kiss it. Erin reminded herself to stay alert; the dirty old geezer was halfway gone.

He said, 'Is it time for the jungle toy?'

'Not just yet. You like this song?'

'Yes, ma'am.' The congressman's head lolled, and the cowboy hat fell to the floor. He picked it up and replaced it.

Erin said, 'It's called "Whipping Post".'

Dilbeck perked up. 'Is that right?'

'By the Allman Brothers.'

'Well, I've been such a naughty boy,' he said, 'I believe I could use a whipping.'

Erin continued dancing. Apparently there would be no sexual catatonics tonight; Davey was fully conscious, primed for action.

He said, 'Wouldn't you care to whip me? I'm a bad, bad boy.'

'It's just a song, sweetie.'

'But I love you so much.'

'Of course you do.'

'Here, let me prove it.' He shoved the champagne bottle into the ice bucket, and began fumbling with the buttons of his jeans.

Erin spun away, shaking her ass to the blues rhythm. She thought: Off we go!

The congressman said, 'Look here.'

She turned back, smiling the 500-watt smile. 'It's adorable,' she said.

He stood up, wobbly, and wiggled the limp thing in his hand. 'Please touch it,' he said.

'I'm a dancer, sweetie, not a urologist.' Erin kicked him lightly in the sternum, and he sagged back into the canvas chair.

He said, 'God, I've had too much to drink. Did I give you your money?'

'You sure did.'

'And did I show you my pictures?'

'Put your little friend away,' she said.

'Then you'll look at my pictures?'

Erin said sure. She needed a break, anyway. While David Dilbeck tucked himself in, she stepped off the table and put on her dress. She turned down the stereo, poured a ginger ale over ice and pulled up a chair. She made sure her purse was within arm's reach.

Dilbeck opened a photo album across his lap. He tapped at an eight-by-ten picture of himself with a corpulent white-haired man. 'Know who that is?'

'Tip O'Neill,' said Erin.

Dilbeck was astounded. 'You *are* something special.'

'Former Speaker of the House.'

'Right!'

'So what do I win,' Erin said, 'a dinette set?'

Beaming, the congressman said, 'Tip and I are very close.'

'I can see that. It looks like you're scratching his balls.'

Dilbeck flushed. 'Please! We were at a prayer breakfast.'

Erin reached over and flipped the page. The next photograph had been taken outside the White House: Dilbeck with an arm around General Colin Powell. The general wore an expression that suggested recent taxidermy.

'This was during the Gulf War,' said Dilbeck, matter-of-factly. 'Colin and the President invited certain members of Congress for a briefing. Classified, of course.'

Erin asked if they'd given out balloons. Dilbeck

nearly lost his temper. 'Darling,' he said, 'you should have some respect.' His tone had turned chilly.

'I'm sorry, Davey.'

Rapidly he flipped through the album, jabbing at significant memories. 'See here: Bill Bradley, Chris Dodd . . . and there's Al D'Amato – we were on a fact-finder together in Riyadh. This one is me and Newt Gingrich – remind me to tell you my Gingrich story.'

Erin said, 'I hope that's just cheese dip on his tie.'

'You listen,' Dilbeck said, lecturing with a champagne slur, 'these are important goddamn people. *I'm* an important person.' He slapped the album shut and raised it with both hands, as if it were a holy tablet. 'These are the men who run this nation,' he said, 'the men who control the fate of the world!'

Erin tried not to laugh. The poor schlub truly believed himself to be a pillar of state.

The congressman said, 'It's difficult to describe the raw power. It's intoxifying, darling. Completely addictive. If you came with me to Washington, you'd feel it immediately. You would also understand its seductions.'

Erin said she didn't mean to poke fun. Dilbeck laid the album on the table, and placed a hand upon it. Again he said, 'These are important men.'

'Chuck Norris?'

'That was a charity benefit in Georgetown—'

'Come on, Davey—'

'For polio or something.'

'I know, but—'

'Look, Erin, it's a matter of appreciating who I am. It's a matter of respect.'

'Davey, you know whose picture I'd really like to see? Malcolm Moldowsky. Is he in your album?'

Dilbeck's jaw tightened. 'No, he's not.' Then, suspiciously: 'Do you know Moldy?' Was it possible? Had the little ratfucker been holding out on him? Hurriedly Dilbeck reframed the question: '*How* do you know Moldy?'

'By reputation only,' Erin said with a wink.

The congressman, more perplexed than ever, cursed in a shaky drunken voice: 'Stop, goddammit! Stop making fun and show some goddamn respect.'

'Respect?' Erin smiled. 'Aren't you the same gentleman who had sex with my laundry lint?'

'Let's change the subject.'

She took him by the wrists and guided his slack hands to her breasts. Dilbeck seemed wary and apprehensive, as if anticipating an electric shock.

Erin wouldn't let him pull away. She said, 'Thrilling, huh? Two pleasant handfuls of fat.'

'Jesus—'

'That's your basic human breast, Davey. Ninety-eight percent fat, with a cherry on top. What's the big attraction?'

He yanked away, clenching his fists to his gut.

'Thousands of dollars,' Erin said, 'just for a peek and a jiggle. It baffles me, sweetie.'

'That's enough.' The congressman was gray, despondent. 'You're killing me. You're killing the whole evening. Is that the plan?'

Erin said, 'I'm curious, that's all.' She told herself to settle down, hold her temper.

Dilbeck was saying, 'I struggle with fleshly temptations. All men do.'

'You have a wife, Davey.'

He lunged for the champagne bucket. 'Congratulations,' he snapped. 'The night is officially ruined.'

Erin put on her favorite Van Morrison tape. She stripped off the dress, got on the captain's table and began to dance again – this time, slowly. Soon David Dilbeck and his afflicted moans faded from her consciousness. The songs washed over her soul. She felt euphoric and energized. Every move was perfect – every kick, every fluid turn, every thrust of the hip. She took the pearls in her teeth and closed her eyes, imagining moonlight.

Outside on the deck, something made a sharp noise. Erin blocked it out of her mind. She was far away, dancing on a sugary beach in the islands. Above the dune was a palm orchard, and the only sound was a soft chorus of wild birds.

Darrell Grant couldn't recall the last time he'd seen his ex-wife without clothes. He was pretty sure it had been in the bathroom – she, washing her hair in the shower; he, covertly looting the medicine cabinet for Darvons. Long fucking time ago, Darrell thought. He'd forgotten what a nice body she had. A little puny up top but, God, what great legs! Swaying in the doorway of the cabin, crutching with the nine-iron, he felt an intriguing tingle in his groin. Amazing, really, considering the high-octane pharmaceuticals he'd ingested. The male plumbing was truly an engineering marvel.

Inside the yacht was an old man wearing stiff new jeans, a striped shirt and a black ten-gallon hat. He looked shitfaced or sick, possibly both. Darrell Grant

walked into the salon and sat next to the old cowboy.
With his unbroken arm, he waved mischievously at his
former spouse, up on the table. Darrell felt himself
hardening. He leaned forward and said, 'Hey, you're
pretty damn good. Let's have a look at that sweet little
pussy!'

The sight of her ex-husband hit Erin like a blast of
frigid air. She thought Shad had run Darrell off for good,
but here he was, fucking things up again. Amazing. His
presence greatly enhanced the potential for fiasco. Erin
kept dancing and stared straight through him while she
weighed her next move.

Darrell Grant felt a leafy hand at his shoulder. It was
the old cowboy, pulling himself up in the chair. He put
his lips to Darrell's ear and said, 'You know who I am?'

The man's breath made Darrell grimace. 'Ever heard
of Listerine?'

'I'm in love with this lady,' the congressman confided.

'You poor old fuck.'

'And my boots, they're full of Vaseline.'

'I loved her once, too,' said Darrell Grant, 'but all
she did was cut me down.'

Dilbeck looked sympathetic. Darrell said, 'Call it a
basic clash of philosophies. She can be hell on your self-
esteem.'

'A hard one,' the congressman agreed, 'but still I'm
swept away.'

He said there was plenty of club soda in the liquor
cabinet, in case Darrell Grant wanted to work on those
bloodstains in his shirt. Darrell said no thanks. His
shattered bones had begun to throb; whaling on the
well-dressed midget hadn't helped. Darrell feared that
the late Señor Gomez's painkillers were finally wearing

off. He tapped out a half-dozen more, tossed them into his cheeks and guzzled lukewarm champagne until his eyes watered.

The congressman said, 'I've got some Extra-Strength Tylenols.'

'Lord Christ.'

The Van Morrison tape ended. Erin kept going. She started singing 'Carmelita', to herself. The song was almost too slow for table dancing.

Darrell Grant attempted to hook her ankles with the nine-iron. 'Where's Angie?' he demanded. Erin eluded him.

Dilbeck said, 'Let her finish. This is so beautiful.'

'Yeah, it's a fucking ballet.' Darrell Grant grubbed in his pockets. 'Hey, beautiful, this is for you!'

He lurched halfway out of the chair, and slipped something under the elastic of Erin's lace garter. It was a nickel. Erin stopped singing and dancing. She removed the coin and held it in the palm of one hand. The two men waited to see what she would do next.

Erin was smiling in a private way as she stepped off the table, still smiling as she got dressed.

The congressman said, 'I suppose we're done for the night.'

Darrell pounded the nine-iron sharply on the table. 'Erin, I want my daughter. No more goddamn games.'

'It's over,' she said, adjusting the pearls.

'Fuck the courts,' Darrell declared. 'Angie and me are headed to Arizona. Retirement Capital of North America!'

Erin opened her handbag and dropped the nickel inside. Then she took out the .32.

'Let's go for a drive,' she said.

Darrell Grant cursed under his breath. The congressman felt a subtle contraction in his chest.

Some Saturday night, Erin thought. Me and the two men in my life. Aren't I a lucky girl.

THIRTY-ONE

Predictably, Shad was detained at the guard booth outside Turnberry Isle. The security men remembered his earlier visit with the monkey creature on his neck; tonight they said his name appeared on no guest lists. Shad averted an unpleasant argument by producing coupons for free rum drinks and nude pasta wrestling at Orly's club; the security men couldn't have been more appreciative. Sgt Al García arrived as they were waving Shad through the gate. The detective flashed his badge and coasted into the compound. He parked next to Shad, and the two men hurried together to the *Sweetheart Deal*.

The first thing they noticed was the blood on the deck. In the salon, García inspected the empty champagne bottles, the congressman's photo album, and a pile of compact discs, still in their wrappings. Shad thumbed through a stack of cassettes left on the stereo cabinet.

'These are hers,' he said.

They searched the staterooms and found no bodies, no other signs of violence. Erin and the congressman were gone.

'*Mierda*,' said Al García. He went out to the deck and examined the brownish splatters. Apparently the victim had been dragged, then lifted off the deck. García felt a shudder of nausea; it wasn't the sight of the blood, but the thought of whose it might be. Shad was on the dangerous edge of cold rage. He gripped the rail and stared hauntedly into the tea-colored water. His pinkish skull glistened with perspiration, and he hissed ominously when he inhaled.

García said, 'Don't assume too much.'

A rumble came from Shad. 'Yeah. What's a little blood.'

The detective stepped across to the dock. On his knees: 'There's more here. Know what that means?'

'He didn't dump her over the side. So what?'

A fifty-three-foot Hatteras convertible was moored next to the Rojos' yacht. García wanted to check it out. Shad located a flashlight on the bridge of the *Sweetheart Deal*. They boarded the fishing boat together and found more freckles of blood in the cockpit, near the fighting chairs. There was also the smudge of a partial footprint: the rounded heel of a man's boot.

Morosely, Shad said, 'That's our boy.'

'Maybe, maybe not.' Al García pointed at the fishbox. 'You want me to do the honors?'

'If you don't mind.' Shad looked away.

The detective unfastened the latches and threw open the lid.

Buoyant with relief, he said: 'Surprise, surprise!'

Shad turned to see. 'Who the hell is that?'

'One of the most powerful men in Florida.'

'Not any more.'

'No,' Al García said. 'He be deceased.'

Malcolm J. Moldowsky had fit easily into the fishbox, which he shared with three glassy-eyed bonitos.

The aroma of the dead fish failed to overpower Moldy's imported cologne.

'I don't get it,' Shad said.

'The bonitos probably are shark bait for tomorrow,' García speculated. 'Mr Moldowsky is a late addition to the buffet.'

Shad leaned in for a closer look. 'This is the famous Melvin Moldowsky?'

'Malcolm,' García said, 'in the past tense.'

'Nice threads.'

'Feel better now?'

'About a million percent,' said Shad. 'Who did it?'

García shook his head. 'Maybe Dilbeck went batshit.'

'Don't say that.'

They were worried about Erin. Whoever had bludgeoned Moldowsky owned a monstrous temper. Shad frowned at the mutilated corpse. 'I guess you gotta call somebody.'

'Not right this minute.' Al García closed the fishbox. 'He'll keep.'

They returned to the *Sweetheart Deal* and searched the salon more carefully. Based on the volume of champagne consumed, García calculated that the congressman was too drunk to drive. 'He's got the limo,' Shad said. 'The girls saw it at the club.'

'So the question,' said the detective, 'is where are they now.'

The clue was in the head, where Erin had written in lipstick on the narrow mirror: BELLE GLADE. Shad growled profanely while García fished a gold bracelet from the toilet. Watching the jewelry drip, he said, 'She's got a temper, doesn't she? A simple "no thanks" would've done the trick.'

As they hustled to the cars, Shad asked García to radio ahead for help. García told him he'd been watching too much TV. 'First off, that's Palm Beach County, which is way out of my territory. Second, what do I tell 'em, *chico*?' Facetiously he rehearsed the phone call: 'See, guys, there's this stripper who's been abducted by this congressman who's taking her to fucking Belle Glade, of all places, in a goddamn stretch Cadillac. Yes, I said "congressman". Yes, Belle Glade. Why? Well, we ain't too sure. But we'd appreciate six or seven marked units, if you can spare 'em . . .'

'Fuck it,' Shad muttered.

'As much as cops love strippers, they hate politicians,' García said. 'They hear it's Dilbeck, they'll all be oh-six. Off duty and unavailable.'

'So we're the whole damn cavalry.'

'Mind if I drive?'

'Sure,' Shad said, 'you're the one with the siren.'

Darrell Grant had never ridden in a limousine. He was enjoying it so thoroughly that the circumstances seemed irrelevant. He accepted the fact that his former wife was holding him at gunpoint.

Darrell said to Dilbeck: 'This your car?'

The congressman nodded. 'It's made available for my use.'

'What do you do? What's your gig?'

'I'm a member of the House of Representatives.'

'Which means . . .?'

'I represent the people of South Florida in Congress. And yourself?'

'I steal wheelchairs,' Darrell Grant replied.

Dilbeck glanced plaintively toward Erin, who sat on the bench seat across from the two men. The congressman's roses lay next to her. She held the gun steady in her right hand.

'Darrell and I were married for a time. What else can I say?' Erin felt an inexplicable calm, heightened by the cool soft ride.

Dilbeck asked Darrell Grant what happened to his arm. He said Erin's motherfucking boyfriend broke it with a motherfucking crowbar. Then: 'Hey, driver, does the TV work?'

In a wounded tone, Dilbeck whispered to Erin: 'What boyfriend?'

Erin iced him with a glare. Pathetic, she thought, both of them. She nonchalantly reached under her minidress to unfasten the G-string and the scalloped dance top. She stuffed them in the shoulder bag. Still holding the gun, she gymnastically attempted to put on a plain cotton bra and white panties. It was a crucial detail; Erin didn't want to be found dressed as a stripper. As she changed underclothes, the congressman watched inquisitively.

With an oily trace of a smile: 'Why the white?'

'For you, baby,' she said.

Darrell Grant braced his sloshing head against the window. They were on the interstate, racing away from the downtown skyline. The snaky scroll of lines on the pavement, the stream of headlights made him woozy. 'I'm seriously loaded,' he remarked.

Erin said to the congressman: 'My ex-husband has a drug problem, in case you were curious.'

'I wish you'd put the gun away,' Dilbeck told her.

'You're not listening, are you?'

Darrell Grant, sleepily: 'I never saw you dance before. That was damn good.'

'Aw, shucks,' Erin said.

'Sorry about that business with the nickel.'

'I'd almost forgotten,' she said, 'your scathing wit.'

Darrell Grant basked in the limousine's spaciousness. 'I could get used to this,' he said, stretching his legs. 'Climate-controlled comfort. Yessir!'

David Dilbeck, speaking as if Darrell couldn't hear him: 'That fracture looks bad, Erin. He should see a doctor.'

'Rita's the one who done up my arm,' Darrell said, hoisting it in pride. 'My big sister.'

'She cares about you,' Erin told him. 'She's the only one left.'

'No, Angie cares for me. Angie loves her daddy.'

'She finds you entertaining,' said Erin. 'There's a difference.'

'She loves me!'

Erin dropped the subject. Maybe Darrell was right. She didn't want to think about it now.

The congressman said, 'How much longer till we get there? I have to relieve myself.'

Erin ignored him. Her ex-husband said, 'I killed a guy tonight.'

'Really?'

'On the boat back there.'

'Any particular reason?'

'I'm trying to remember.'

Erin assumed that he had hallucinated the incident. Darrell Grant said, 'It didn't feel the way I thought it would. Killing a guy.'

'You fell for the hype,' Erin said, 'as usual.' She wondered what to do with him. He was screwing up her plans for the congressman.

'I'm serious about Angie,' he said.

'You kidding? You're headed for prison, Darrell.'

'Nope, Arizona. Wheelchair Capital of North America!'

'Crazy bastard.'

'And I'm taking our daughter.'

'I'll shoot you first,' Erin warned.

David Dilbeck abruptly began sobbing and groping for the door handle. He settled down when Erin jammed the .32 into the hollow of his cheek.

Darrell Grant said, 'Since when do you carry a piece? Jesus, I hate guns.'

'My prostate is acting up,' the congressman announced.

'Quit whining,' Erin snapped. 'Both of you.'

Darrell scratched his shin with the head of the nine-iron. 'At least tell us where the hell we're headed. Hey, driver, you speakee American?'

Pierre gave no reaction.

'I'll tell you where we're going,' Erin said. 'We're going to see our congressman in action.'

By early October, the sugarcane near Lake Okeechobee is green, bushy and ten feet tall. The bottomland is the flattest part of Florida; from a passing car, the fields seem to reach and define all horizons. Within a month, nearly two thousand Caribbean migrants arrive to start the cutting, and the mills run twenty-four hours a day. In early October, though, machines do much of the harvesting. An improbable crablike contraption called a cutter-windrower downs the cane and piles it in rows. More machines then retrieve the harvest for transportation to the company mills, where the sugar is made.

Congressman David Lane Dilbeck didn't give much thought to the science or mechanics of cane farming. It was enough that the Rojos were nice people, well-bred and so generous. The mountainous campaign donations were important, of course, but Dilbeck would have traded his congressional vote for just the occasional use of that gorgeous yacht. He also valued the social company of young Christopher, who shared his tastes in bawdy entertainment and never failed to pick up the tab. For David Dilbeck, the attention of wealthy, powerful people was a flattering fringe benefit of the job.

The congressman saw no injustice in the price supports that had made multimillionaires of the Rojos. The grain, dairy and tobacco interests had soaked taxpayers for years by melodramatically invoking the plight of the 'family farmer'. Why not sugar, too? Similarly, Dilbeck lost no sleep over the damage done to the agricultural economies of impoverished Caribbean nations, virtually shut out of the rigged US sugar market. Nor did the congressman agonize over the far-reaching impact of cane growers flushing billions of gallons of waste into the Everglades. Dilbeck didn't understand what all the fuss was about. In truth, he didn't much care for the Everglades; it was torpid, swampy, crawling with bugs. Once, campaigning at a Miccosukee village, the congressman consented to an airboat ride because Erb Crandall saw it as a sensational photo opportunity. The airboat ran out of fuel on the Shark River, and Dilbeck spent two wretched hours picking blood-swollen mosquitoes out of his ears.

'And I've seen prettier water,' he told Erin, 'in a pig trough.'

She was giving him a hard time about whoring for the Rojos. 'Where do you think our drinking water comes from?' She pointed through the window of the limousine. 'Out there, Davey. And your pals are pissing fertilizer into it.'

Darrell Grant was bored silly. He repeatedly sought to engage Pierre in conversation, with no success. The highway narrowed to two unlit lanes that Darrell recognized as US 27. Blackness engulfed the limousine; the only trace of the city was a fuzzy sulfurous glow, far to the east. Darrell couldn't figure out where Erin was taking them, or why. The geezer in the cowboy getup remained a riddle. Was this a rich new boyfriend? The idea of Erin as a gold digger engaged him – like mother, like daughter? Anything was possible.

Darrell struggled to hatch a plan, but the drugs interfered with his concentration. What he really wanted to do was sleep for about six months.

It was half-past ten when they arrived in Belle Glade ('Her Soil Is Her Future,' proclaimed a welcome sign). Pierre turned off the main highway and drove slowly through an empty migrant camp. David Dilbeck was alarmed by what he saw. He told Pierre to step on the gas before desperadoes swarmed from the slum and trashed the limo. 'It's a leaser,' he explained to Erin.

'Don't tell me you've never been out here.'

453

'What's your point?' the congressman groused. The warm embrace of the Korbel had dissipated into a staggering migraine.

Pierre got back on the highway and drove until the town gave way to more green cane fields. Erin asked him to pull over.

'He doesn't understand English,' Dilbeck said, impatiently.

'Is that so?'

Pierre steered off the pavement and stopped on the shoulder of the road. He left the engine running.

'Out we go,' Erin said, brightly. 'And, Davey, don't forget our jungle toy.'

Dilbeck peered into the night suspiciously.

Before harvest, sugarcane is burned to consume the leafy tops, which are useless, and to drive the animals from the fields. In the heart of the season, smoke roils off the stalks in prodigious columns that sometimes block out the sky. Tonight, though, was crystalline – washed with constellations that one never saw in the city. A waning yellow moon hung low.

Pierre got out and opened the back door of the limo. The congressman emerged first, holding a slender brown package. He was followed by Darrell Grant, unsteadily; the protruding nine-iron dinged noisily off a rear fender panel. The last to emerge from the car was Erin, stepping gingerly in her heels. Pierre gave her a small flashlight to go with the pistol.

Darrell Grant complained of a gassy stomach. 'Let me stay here and crash.'

'Sure. In the trunk.' Erin motioned with the gun. 'Pierre, prepare Mr Grant's *boudoir*.'

The Haitian driver obliged. He popped the trunk and moved the spare tire, making room.

'The trunk?' Darrell Grant slapped the congressman on the back. 'Didn't I tell you she's fucking murder on the ego?'

David Dilbeck looked worried. 'Erin, I've got a heart condition.'

'Who doesn't? Darrell, get in the damn trunk.' She shined the flashlight in his eyes.

'You gonna shoot me?' He gave a dopey laugh. 'Somehow I don't think so.'

Erin told him to lie down and take a nap.

Darrell Grant, slouching against the fender of the limousine: 'One thing I been dying to ask: How do you do it? I mean shakin' your poon at strangers.' He jabbed the congressman contemptuously with the golf club. 'Sick old fucks like him, I don't see how you do it.'

'The music takes over. That's all.'

'You mean it's an act? I ain't so sure about that.'

'Men are easily dazzled.'

An urgent moan from David Dilbeck: 'I have to pee.'

Erin waved the flashlight toward the cane rows. 'So pee,' she said. Dilbeck waddled off, clawing at the buttons of his jeans.

Darrell Grant snorted drunkenly. 'I never thought of you as a stripper. It's actually funny as hell.'

Erin said, 'You emptied the savings account. I had a lawyer to pay.'

'Plus you figured out the hustle at these nudie joints, am I right? You mess their hair, play with their necktie, tell 'em how good they smell.'

'Maybe that's why they call it a tease.'

'God, you're a cold one.'

The congressman could be heard irrigating the sugar-cane. From over his shoulder, he called: 'I truly *do* love her!'

'Pity-ful,' Darrell said.

Erin smiled. 'I rest my case.'

'Know what I think? I think you get off on it.'

'Darrell, you're just *full* of theories tonight.' Was this a sermon, she wondered, from a wheelchair thief? 'Get in the trunk,' she told him, 'you like the damn car so much.'

He ignored her. 'I ain't givin' up on Angie. Just so you know: I'll track the both of you to hell and back.' He brushed past her and headed into the cane fields.

'Darrell, stop.' She raised the .32 in one hand, the flashlight in the other.

Her ex-husband turned. The beam of light caught him grinning. 'You won't kill me. Not the father of your only child!'

Erin was considering it. She pictured him hacking up Angie's dolls, and her gun arm stiffened. 'You told the judge I was an unfit mother. Is that what you believe?'

'It was lawyer talk, for Chrissakes. You always take shit so personally.' Beseechingly he spread his arms, the shaft of the nine-iron glinting. 'Hell, you were a good mother. Same as I was a good daddy. It was lawyers talkin', that's all.'

At that moment Erin knew she wouldn't fire. She didn't need to; the sorry bastard was already finished. Broke, strung out, maimed, running from the law – Darrell Grant was history. Killing him would be redundant.

'Come back,' she told him. 'I've got plans for you.'

'You mean "plans" as in jail? No thanks, cutie pie.'
He gave a cocky wave and resumed his getaway.

Erin remembered what Shad advised her about the
gun: when in doubt, shoot at something, *anything*.

She fired twice at the ground near Darrell Grant's
boots. The crack of the shots was absorbed by the
thickets of high cane. She heard her ex-husband yell
the word *cunt*. When she aimed the flashlight where
he'd been standing, he was gone, crashing like a deer
through the crops. She panned the beam in a slow circle
until it landed on the congressman, nervously buttoning
his fly. He waded from the tall grass and asked, 'Are
you all right?'

The gun felt hot in Erin's fist. She thought, Goddamn
that Darrell. Maybe he'll step on a rattler.

She wheeled on David Dilbeck. 'Take off your
clothes,' she told him.

'I knew it. You're going to make me dance.'

Erin said, 'You wish.'

After cane is cut and stacked, a machine scoops the
stalks, thins the excess vegetation and dumps the load
into a field wagon. When the wagons become full, a
mechanical belt feeds the cane into long steel-mesh
trailers attached to truck cabs. Each bin holds twenty
tons and dumps from the side. The trailers are parked
at intervals along the farm roads bordering the Okeechobee sugar fields.

At first Darrell Grant thought he had come upon
the fence of a medium-security prison, a nightmare of
ironies. Weaving closer, pawing at the darkness as if it

were fog, he saw that the mesh edifice actually was the side of a long truck rig. Using a jumbo tire as a foothold, Darrell began to climb.

The cane trailer offered dual enticements: it looked like a safe place to hide from a homicidal ex-spouse and also a fine place to nap. It was important for Darrell to lie down soon, before he fell. The cancer pills had blown his circuit breakers; he accepted the likelihood that he'd guessed wrong on the dosages, seriously misjudged his tolerance. Oh well.

After scaling the mesh, he flopped into the damp sheaths of smoky cane and burrowed like a worm; he felt clever, invisible and safe. Had he been sober, he might have anticipated the destination of the truck and the disposition of its contents.

Once loaded at the fields, the trailers are driven to the mill and emptied on conveyors. The first stage of processing is the shredding of the cane, which is accomplished by many rows of gleaming, turbine-driven knives. The fiber then is mashed beneath five hundred tons of pressure. In this way the essential liquids are removed. Evaporators convert the purified cane juice into a syrup, which is heated carefully until it forms a mixture of sweet molasses and crystals. Separation is achieved using a high-speed centrifuge.

Usually it takes half a ton of cane to produce a hundred pounds of raw sugar. However, both weight and purity can be markedly affected by the introduction of foreign substances, such as human body parts.

Darrell Grant had medicated himself too heavily and concealed himself too well. He was deep in a junkie nod at dawn, when the cane trailer in which he'd hidden began rolling toward the sugar mill. Darrell did not awaken, at least not in a meaningful way. No cries, shrieks or moans halted the sugar-milling process; rather, it was the nine-iron strapped to Darrell Grant's arm that jammed the turbine-driven blades and brought the boys from Quality Control scurrying toward the shredders.

The mill shut down for three hours while local police collected and bagged the remains. The Palm Beach Sheriff later issued a press release saying that a vagrant had died in a freak milling accident at Rojo Farms. Authorities appealed to the public for help in identifying the victim, who was described as a white male, early 30s, with blond hair. No composite sketch of the man was provided, as the shredder left precious little for the police artist to work from. The press release said that the victim wore jeans and boots, and was possibly a golf enthusiast. The Sweetheart Sugar Corporation was reported to be cooperating fully in the case.

At the mill, a memo went up assuring employees that the unfortunate mishap had not compromised the superb quality of the company's product. In private, however, workers anxiously wondered exactly how much of the dead vagrant had ended up in the day's tonnage. The consensus was that one drop of blood, one lousy pubic hair, one microscopic sliver of a wart was too much.

Distasteful rumors spread wildly, and many workers stopped putting sugar in their coffee and tea. Rojo Farms, like most cane processors, maintained a long-standing rule against the use of artificial sweeteners by employees on company property. Violation was regarded as an act of disloyalty – the agribusiness equivalent of a Chrysler salesman buying himself a Toyota.

However, within days after Darrell Grant's gruesome death, a clandestine network of body carriers began smuggling packets of Sweet 'n Low into the Rojo company cafeteria. An internal investigation failed to identify the culprits or shut down the pipeline. To avoid the publicity of a labor confrontation, mill management quietly dropped the matter and rescinded its sugar-only policy. The Rojos themselves were never told.

THIRTY-TWO

Shad punched the dashboard, hard.

'Enough!' said Al García. 'Christ, have a smoke.'

'Some fucking heroes we are.'

García was doing ninety-four on the interstate. Shad's slick dome whimsically reflected the blue strobe of the dashboard light. The highway wind howled through the shotgun-shattered window. Shad spit scornfully into the night.

'Easy,' García said. 'Hey, I gave up on being a hero a long time ago. Sometimes the best you can do is set things in motion.' The detective puffed expansively on a fresh cigar. 'That's why I put my card in the dead lawyer's bank box. I had a hunch it would motivate Mr Moldowsky toward foolish behavior.'

Shad said, 'This ain't a game. You said yourself.'

'Still, there's plays to be made. We made ours.'

'And look what happened. Erin gets snatched.'

'Don't underestimate the lady.' The detective lowered the window and tapped out an inch of dead ash. 'You notice anything odd about the writing on that mirror? Besides it was lipstick?'

Shad hunched sullenly. He occupied himself with devising a suitable fate for the congressman. He thought in terms of muriatic acid and gaping facial wounds.

'Here's what jumped out at me,' García went on. 'The words on the mirror weren't printed in block letters, they were done in cursive. The style was beautiful, no? So tell me, *chico*, who writes perfect longhand when they got a gun to their head and they're about to be kidnapped? Nobody, that's who.'

Shad's naked eyebrows crinkled in concentration. In the shadows, his silky pink orb suggested the head of a 250-pound newborn. 'You're saying she planned it all?'

García said, 'It's possible, yeah.'

'No way did she whack that guy in the fishbox.'

'I agree.' The detective's expression was obscured by a swirling shroud of blue smoke. 'Still, she had a game plan.'

Shad remembered what Urbana Sprawl had said: that Erin was out to do some damage.

'In these situations,' the detective said, 'I ask myself who's holding the high cards? And it's definitely Erin, not Dilbeck. Here's this arrogant old fart who thinks he's God's gift to pussy, but all he wants in the whole wide world is the love of this one gorgeous dancer. I mean, he'd be in heaven if this girl just *smiled* in the general direction of his dick. You follow?'

Shad plucked a cigar from Al García's shirt pocket. He tore off the wrapper with his teeth.

García chuckled. 'All that champagne, I'll bet old Davey couldn't get it up with a block-and-tackle tonight. And Erin, she's got thirty IQ points on him, easy.'

Shad said, 'Men get crazy over her. I seen it before.'

'Dilbeck's not your typical rapist, he's too full of himself.'

'He don't need to be typical,' said Shad, biting the nub off the stogie. 'He just needs the idea to take hold.'

García said nothing for several miles. The traffic thinned as they headed west.

Shad mumbled, 'Belle Glade, shit. *Where* in Belle Glade?' He turned toward García. 'I suppose you got some ideas.'

'What I said before about setting things in motion – see, people have this concept of justice. They talk about "the system", meaning cops, judges, juries and prisons. If only the system worked, they say, there wouldn't be a crime problem! The streets would be safe, the bad guys would be locked up for life!'

Shad gave a desolate laugh. He pulled the lighter from the dented dash and fired up the cigar. He said, 'Look at Erin's crazy fucker of an ex-husband. That's how terrific the system works.'

'Exactly,' García said, chopping the air with his hand. 'Darrell Grant was a snitch for the cops. Good guys putting bad guys on the payroll, in the name of almighty justice. Your average taxpayer can't understand. See, "the system" is a game and that's all. Guy like Moldowsky, I can't touch him. Same goes for the congressman. So what I do then, I try and set things in motion. Make the shit fly and see where it sticks.'

'Because you got no case,' Shad said.

'None whatsoever. But it doesn't mean there can't be justice.'

'Man, you're a dreamer.'

'Maybe so,' said Al García, 'but I'm sure Moldowsky arranged the murders of Jerry Killian and that sleazoid lawyer and the lawyer's cousin. And I'm also sure I couldn't put the case together in a trillion years.' He arched a shaggy black eyebrow. 'But this much I also know: Tonight I open a stinking fishbox and find Mr Malcolm J. Moldowsky permanently expired. Fate, irony, call it whatever. Least now I got something to tell my boy.'

'Your boy?' Shad said.

'He's the one that found the body in the river.'

Shad grunted somberly.

'Least I can tell him it's over,' said García. 'For once the bad guy got what he deserved.'

Shad said, 'I ain't ready to celebrate. I want to see Erin alive.' He took a loud, noxious drag on the cigar. 'You better hope you didn't set the wrong damn thing in motion.'

'Yeah,' the detective said quietly. 'There's always that chance.'

Shad settled in for the ride. He felt better, kicking around the possibility that Erin was on top of the situation.

'Just promise me one thing,' he said to Al García. 'Promise you ain't got another human head in the Igloo.' He jerked a thumb toward the trunk of the Caprice.

García grinned. 'The night is young,' he said.

The congressman stripped to his boxer shorts and cowboy boots. Erin's flashlight played up and down his gelatinous physique. She was mildly embarrassed for him, but the feeling passed quickly.

'What now?' Dilbeck said, swatting at the bugs.

'Time for you-know-what.'

'Ah.' His tone changed. Excitedly he unwrapped the brown package. He held the machete with both hands,

the blade flat across his palms, to show Erin. 'Willie
Rojo loaned it to me. It hangs on the wall of his private
study.'

'Very tasteful,' she said.

The congressman ran a finger along the squared-off
blade. With a coy smile: 'I think I understand what
you're after.'

'Doubtful,' Erin muttered.

'You're into games,' Dilbeck said, hopefully.

'Oh, please.'

'Role playing—'

'No, sweetie.'

'You're the master, I'm the slave!'

Erin thought: The creep is really getting turned on.

Dilbeck said, 'So how does it work, your little game?'

'Here's how it works: I want you to cut some sugar.'

He chuckled anxiously. 'But I don't know how.'

'Oh, give it a try,' Erin said. 'For me.'

'I'd feel much better if you put the gun away.'

'Soon,' she said. 'That's a promise.'

With the flashlight she directed the congressman to
a row of maturing cane. He stepped forward and swung
the machete sidearm. The stalks shook but didn't fall.

Erin said, 'You do better with a champagne bottle.'

David Dilbeck snorted. 'Just watch,' he said, and
began whaling. Each blow brought a high-pitched grunt
that reminded Erin of Monica Seles, the tennis star. The
congressman's reaping technique needed improvement,
too; the cane wasn't being cut so much as pulverized.
Erin kept the flashlight aimed at the crop row, so
Dilbeck could see what he was hacking. She didn't want
him to harvest his own toes by accident.

After less than a minute, the congressman stopped.

His face was flushed, his chest heaved and the blotched flab of his belly was sprinkled with sweat. The boxer shorts had slipped below his waist, exposing the crack of his marbled buttocks. He was panting like a toothless old lion.

Erin said, 'Sweetie, don't quit yet. You're giving new meaning to the term "public servant".'

Dilbeck bent at the waist, sucking to catch his breath. Momentarily he said, 'You've still got your dress on.'

'I certainly do.'

'Fine, fine.' He wiped his palms on his underwear. 'How much more till we can play?'

'I was thinking at least a ton.'

'Very funny—'

'A migrant,' Erin said, 'cuts eight tons a day.'

'Eight tons,' the congressman murmured. That's what Chris Rojo had told him, too. It seemed absolutely impossible.

'One cutter, all by himself,' said Erin. 'I read up on cane farming so we could have a meaningful discussion.' She kicked off her high heels. 'I figured you knew all there was to know about sugar, considering the Rojos own your ass.'

'That's a damn lie.' Dilbeck stiffened.

Erin put the flashlight on him – he was pissed, all right. It wasn't easy to look indignant in boxer shorts. She said, 'Guess what the Rojos pay their cutters.'

'I couldn't care less,' the congressman snapped. 'It's better than starving to death in the *barrios* of Kingston.'

'So that's it – a humanitarian enterprise!' Erin dabbed an imaginary tear. 'Please forgive me, Congressman, I misunderstood. Here I assumed your pals were just greedy businessmen, taking advantage of poor desperate souls. Now I find out they're saints!' She motioned with the gun. 'Keep cutting, sweetheart. And by the way, Jamaica doesn't have *barrios*. They're called slums. You're getting your Third World cultures mixed up again.'

Reinvigorated by anger, Dilbeck went at the sugar cane like a dervish. Between grunts: 'Who are you to lecture me!'

'Merely a constituent,' Erin said. She reminded him that his drinking buddy, young Señor Rojo, had given her a thousand dollars for one of her shoes. 'But I guess he can afford it,' she remarked, 'considering what he pays the migrants.'

The congressman paused in his cutting: 'That's a very simplistic view, young lady. Very simplistic.'

'Davey, when does your committee vote on the sugar subsidies? I wonder what the Rojos would do if you didn't show up.'

Dilbeck couldn't understand how an evening that had started with such promise had deteriorated to this: a stripper with a pistol, in the middle of fucking nowhere – and him, up to his sweaty aching balls in sugarcane. Ruefully he concluded that wild cowboy sex was no longer on the agenda; more harrowing scenarios began to streel through his imagination. All this talk of slave labor, the Rojos, the House committee vote . . . why would a woman speak of such things?

He swung at the cane until his arm was numb. He dropped to his knees, braced himself upright with the machete.

'Good work,' said Erin. 'Only nineteen hundred pounds to go.' She wondered what her mother, the cruising opportunist, might make of this scene. David

Dilbeck was the sort that Mom would view as a matrimonial prize – wealthy, prominent and presentable, when properly attired.

He said, 'What is it you really want?'

Erin crouched beside him. 'You remember a man named Jerry Killian.'

Dilbeck nodded guardedly. 'He's the one who tried to blackmail me. That's when I spoke to the judge about, uh, "reconsidering" your custody case.'

'And what happened, Davey?'

'Judge said no deal. Got on his high horse.'

'And what about Killian?'

'Was he a boyfriend of yours?' The congressman spoke hesitantly. 'I don't know what happened. Malcolm said it was taken care of. We never heard from the man again.'

'That's because he was murdered.'

Dilbeck fell forward to his hands and knees. 'My God,' he said. 'Is that true? It can't be.'

'Oh, it's true.' Erin stood up. 'All because of you, because of the Rojos' – waving the handgun – 'because of all this sugar out here.' She watched him struggle to a sitting position. 'A man's dead, Davey, all because you're a crook.'

The congressman looked ashen and haggard. He told Erin to get the damn light out of his eyes. 'Nineteen years,' he said, hoarsely. 'Nineteen years I've served in Washington, DC. Don't you dare belittle me.'

Erin said, 'A man is dead.'

'Go look up my record, young lady. I've voted for every civil rights bill that's come through Congress. The vital issues of our time – Social Security, equal-opportunity housing, lower cable TV rates – go look up my votes. And farmers, yes, you're damn right. I support the family farmer and I'm not ashamed to say so!'

Erin sighed inwardly. Dilbeck was parroting a boilerplate campaign speech.

'– and who singlehandedly blocked the last congressional pay raise? Me! I cast the deciding vote. You don't think that took courage?'

Hastily Erin moved to derail the monologue. She said, 'I phoned your office once myself.'

Dilbeck paused. 'In Washington? Why?'

'To ask about Jerry Killian. You were busy.'

The congressman said, 'If I'd known—'

'What did the Rojos do for you? Parties, girls, boat rides – what else? Las Vegas? The occasional vacation to the islands?' Erin circled him. 'I think you're a man who can't say no to anything that's free.'

Dilbeck dragged a forearm across his brow. 'My father,' he said with well-practiced reverence, 'was an ordinary working man with ordinary dreams. Know what he did for a living? He pumped septic tanks!'

Erin said, 'We could sure use him now.' She walked back to the limousine to double-check a detail with Pierre. She returned carrying a martini in a plastic glass.

'Bless you,' the congressman said, slurping like a hound.

She unzipped the minidress, tugged it down to her heels and kicked it away. A pleasant confusion returned to David Dilbeck's face; sunken eyes flickering with hope. In a simple white bra the dancer looked virginal, scrumptious. The congressman felt a familiar tremor of lust. The woman was an angel in the night.

'You are diabolical,' he murmured. 'I truly love you.'

'Do you have,' she asked, 'the foggiest clue what's happening here?'

Dilbeck shook his head placidly. 'It's all in the hands of the Lord.'

'Oh brother.'

He discarded the empty glass and said, 'I'm a deacon in the church!'

'Yeah, and I'm the singing nun. Stand up, Davey.'

Raising himself proved to be a long-term project, the congressman top-heavy with exhaustion. Using the machete as a crutch, he eventually levered himself erect, arms slack, while Erin made a final inspection with the flashlight. Sprouting from the silly boots were knobbly blue-veined legs, still slick with Vaseline. The light moved up his body: red and wrinkled knees, the droopy boxers, the pendulous gray belly, the engorged surgical scar, the expectant patrician face and the silvery hair, now a ragged thatch garnished with flecks of jet muck and diced cane.

Erith said, 'You are a sight.'

She guessed the time as between eleven and eleven-thirty. Now or never, she thought. She threw the flashlight as far as she could into the tall cane, where it landed without a sound. Then she did the same with the gun.

I must be nuts.

Dilbeck said, 'Well, well.'

In the yellow moonglow, Erin could see his widening smile.

'So I was right about you,' he said.

I must be crazy.

'David,' she said, 'do you want to talk, or dance?'

'Friction?'

I must be totally insane.

'Whatever you like, sweetheart.' Somewhere in the night, Jackson Browne began to sing.

Where the hell are they?

Seventeen minutes away, on a two-lane road skirting the Loxahatchee wildlife preserve, three cars sped northwest toward the town of Belle Glade. Each of the cars was a slate-gray, late-model Ford. Each was driven by a clean-cut man in a dark suit. There were six in all – two in each sedan – and an attractive dark-haired woman with a young girl. The men all carried guns in shoulder holsters under their suit jackets. The little girl held two Barbie dolls, one blonde and one brunette. The woman sat next to the small girl in the back of the third sedan. She told the girl not to worry, everything was going to be all right.

Angela Grant said she wasn't worried one bit.

Sgt Al García was stuck behind a slow-moving station wagon that was plastered with upbeat religious slogans. The driver either failed to see the flashing blue light in the mirror, or was unfamiliar with its purpose. García wondered why people with JESUS stickers on their bumper always drove twenty miles per hour under the speed limit. If God was *my* co-pilot, he thought, I'd be doing a hundred and twenty.

Shad was sucking the cigar and telling sad tales of lost opportunity – the roach in the yoghurt, the scorpion in the cottage cheese. 'It was all worked out,' he lamented. 'It was fucking golden.'

García said, 'That sounds a lot like fraud.'

'Shit. You got a soft spot for insurance companies?'

García mashed the accelerator and passed the Christian station wagon on the shoulder. A few minutes later, the unmarked Caprice rolled into the modest commercial district of Belle Glade. The detective turned off the dashboard light and slowed down, scouting for the congressman's limousine. He expected it to stand out dramatically.

Shad continued to describe the art of concealing an adult cockroach in a refrigerated dairy product. The secret, he confided to García, was a good pair of tweezers.

The detective, ever eager for insight to the criminal mind, asked: 'What about the roach itself? Anything special?'

'The fresher the better,' Shad advised.

Just then, a convoy of three gray Fords whipped past in the opposite direction. 'So that's the deal!' said García, digging the Caprice into a grinding U-turn. Smart girl, he thought. Gotta give her credit.

Shad said, 'Who the hell are they?' For purchase, he planted both hands on the dashboard. 'Lemme ask something,' he said, cigar bobbing with the bumps. 'Suppose you were an ex-con and you happened to be packin' a piece right now.'

Al García said, 'I believe I'd toss it.'

'Yeah?' Shad rolled down the window. 'Close your eyes,' he told the detective.

Erin said, 'Relax, sweetie.'

'How can I?'

She pressed lightly against him, swaying, dreaming that she was with someone else. She tried to remember the last time she'd been held by a man, in a way that meant something.

'Now I get it,' the congressman said. 'You're trying to kill me. You're trying to give me a damn heart attack.'

Erin said, 'Don't be ridiculous. I could give you a heart attack anytime I choose.'

Damp arms enfolded her waist. One hand still gripped the machete.

'Careful,' Erin whispered.

David Dilbeck said, 'We could go away together in a few weeks. We could take the yacht.'

'Sounds interesting.'

'I could make you happy,' he said. 'After the election, you could come with me to Washington.'

'I don't think so, sweetheart.'

Dilbeck, playing sugar daddy: 'You'd like it there. The shopping is phenomenal.'

Erin resisted the urge to bite. 'Tell me about that night at the club,' she said, 'the night you attacked the young man.'

The congressman said, uneasily, 'I remember so little of it.' He tightened his hold. 'I was overcome, dazed, powerless – normally I'm not a violent person. I think that's obvious.'

'You frightened me,' Erin said. The seconds ticked away so slowly. Gazing into the rows of cane, she thought of Darrell Grant, wondered if he was planning a counterstrike. What would he do if he saw the congressman molesting her? Applaud, probably.

Dilbeck said, 'Malcolm tells me the young fellow is just fine, the one who got hurt with the bottle.'

'You didn't even send a fruit basket.'

'How could I?' The congressman stopped dancing and took her by the elbows. 'You still don't understand, do you? The position I hold is significant and sensitive and powerful. It's an election year, darling.'

'You nearly killed a man,' Erin said.

'Look, I do not wish to be remembered in the same snickering breath with Wilbur Mills and Gary Hart and the rest. Can't you appreciate my situation?' He hugged her fiercely to his sticky chest. 'It's an unforgiving world we live in, angel.'

How right you are, she thought. 'Davey, please don't put your hands in my panties.' The blade of the machete was cool against her thigh.

He said, 'Well ... I'm waiting for the friction.'

'This is it.'

'No, dear, this is slow dancing.'

'Sorry,' said Erin, maintaining the sway.

'I didn't come all this way for a dry hump.'

'Davey, you're so romantic.'

'Don't be like this!' Again Dilbeck's arms locked around her. Clumsily he began to grind his pelvis against her belly. 'There! What about that?' he demanded.

'Stop it,' Erin said, inaudibly. The moist hairs of Dilbeck's chest felt like moss against her cheek. In a way, she was grateful for the darkness, so she wouldn't have to see every awful detail, if things went wrong.

'I'm tired of this game,' the congressman declared. Abruptly he embarked on his own convulsive rendition of an erotic dance – jerking, jumping, his greased flab slapping against Erin's body. She felt the bra peel up, the plastic pearls indent her breasts. With both hands she held her panties in place, thinking: So much for being in control.

David Dilbeck's haphazard thrusting lifted Erin's toes off the ground. Beating on his shoulders proved futile, so she tried a scream.

The congressman displayed no alarm; rather, her panic seemed to please him. 'Finally,' he said, 'you're beginning to understand.' He grabbed the pearl necklaces and began to twist them into a noose. Gradually they came tight on Erin's throat.

She screamed again – not her best effort – and again until it hurt. Finally the strands snapped and the pearls scattered down her breasts, falling into the cane like tiny hailstones.

THIRTY-THREE

While waiting, Pierre leaned against the door of the Cadillac limousine. He plugged his fingers in his ears because, at the young woman's instruction, the stereo was full blast. The song was something about lawyers in love. Pierre didn't understand, suspected he never would.

When he spotted the oncoming cars, he reached into the limo and shut off the music. Gravel dust swirled as three gray sedans braked to a stop in a triangle. The headlights sliced up the night, moths whirling like confetti in the hot white beams.

Pierre slapped his hands on his head, crumpling the chauffeur's cap. He counted six men in dark suits, like pallbearers. They drew guns as they emerged from the sedans. The tallest one, who had neat sandy hair and tortoiseshell glasses, approached Pierre and asked if he was the man who called.

'M-pa konprann,' Pierre said, repeating it twice in a chatter intended to convey incomprehension. It worked temporarily.

The armed strangers held a short huddle in which it was determined that none of them spoke Creole. The sandy-haired man took Pierre firmly by the collar.

'Where is she?' he asked, formidably. 'You know who I mean.'

His hands still fastened to the cap, Pierre pointed urgently with an elbow. At that moment a scream broke the stillness, followed by more. The sandy-haired man and three others disappeared into the cane rows. Pierre was impressed by how fast they could run, dressed as they were for a funeral.

The congressman frictioned himself into a trance. His eyelids drooped half-staff, and the sallow folds of his throat quivered when he moaned. Yet his grip on Erin was cast-iron. He pushed her deeper into the fields, the stalks leaning and shaking with the surge. Erin fought to keep her footing, because she certainly didn't want to go down. Dilbeck was a large man; once he got on top, there would be little to do but grit her teeth, close her eyes, ride with the music . . .

She attempted another scream, but only a faint cry came out. She was suffocating on the man's acrid heat, his foul panting, the rankness of his sweat. A stubby but determined stiffness poked at her from his boxer shorts.

'Baa-aby,' he whimpered for the hundredth time.

Erin attempted a death grab for the congressman's testicles. Not knowing there was only one, she came up empty-handed. Dilbeck tightened his hug and toppled slowly, like a rotted oak, taking Erin with him. Falling, she reflected on what a bad idea the machete had been – clever, sure, but not terribly smart. Because now she stood a fair chance of being speared by the damn thing when they hit the ground.

Fortunately it was the congressman who landed first, Erin bouncing on top. The impact roused Dilbeck from his reverie. He began smooching the crown of her head, murmuring about how sexy she smelled. The white bra remained bunched above her breasts, her cheek flattened against his ribs. She no longer heard the music from the limousine. Maybe the cane was too deep; maybe it had swallowed her screams as well.

Then she thought: Will they ever find me out here?

Suddenly, brutally, the congressman bucked her off. She landed hard on her neck and shoulders. The damp muck gave her a chill. Dilbeck crawled on top, awkwardly, subdued her with dead weight. Erin felt the blade of the machete sliding flat up her hip, sawing the elastic of her panties.

Fumbling at himself with the other hand, Dilbeck was saying: 'Now *this* is true love.'

Erin turned and pressed her lips softly to his chest.

'Oh, that's it,' he said.

Then her tongue, teasing –

'Heaven,' said the congressman.

– exploring, until she tasted the tracks of the scar –

'Circles,' he said. 'Do circles.'

– biting down with all her strength, tearing at him like a cat until he pushed away, keening, groping feebly at the ragged wet hole in his chest . . .

Erin got up spitting blood, meat and hair. 'True love,' she said, wiping her mouth violently. 'So how was it?'

Incredulous, Dilbeck struggled to his feet. 'You little b-b-bitch.'

'Fair enough.' Erin covered herself with her arms. 'You owe me a new pair of undies,' she said.

In the violet darkness, amid the broken matted cane,

the congressman somehow relocated Willie Rojo's machete.

'Oh, don't be ridiculous,' Erin told him.

Dilbeck's breath came in hydraulic gasps. With both hands he raised the blade. 'You tried to chew my heart out,' he said, coiling for the swing.

Erin turned and dashed barefoot through the fields. She imagined Dilbeck suddenly imbued with Olympian swiftness, crashing the cane in his boots; imagined spiders, worms, moccasins, vermin writhing underfoot; imagined Darrell hiding in the tall grass, awaiting revenge. But she ran on, imagining a cool deep pool in which she would dive, wash herself clean, then vanish like an otter. She imagined Angela, waiting with her dolls on the shore, and ran harder.

Straight into the arms of a familiar sandy-haired man.

Special Agent Thomas Cleary.

The congressman said: 'I can explain.'

The three men ordered him to drop the weapon and raise his hands. They had already identified themselves, definitively, as FBI. David Dilbeck was positively relieved.

'Do you know who I am?' he asked, blinking into the sharp cones of light. He tossed the machete away; it landed upright, twanging in the black marl. 'Gentlemen, please,' he said, 'I can explain.'

The FBI trained its agents in many tasks, but memorizing the faces of all 535 members of Congress was not one of them. Moreover, Dilbeck's closest friends and colleagues might not have recognized him in baggy boxer shorts and boots; radish-eyed, shirtless, semi-erect, his trademark silver mane dirty and spiked. An agent's flashlight lingered on the congressman's grisly bite wound, scabbing in the scraggly opposum fur of his chest. Standing nearly nude in a farm field, Dilbeck looked nothing like the distinguished fellow on his campaign billboards. To the agents, he looked very much like a common degenerate, captured mid-rape.

'Thank God you're here,' the congressman said warmly. He thought he was being rescued. Wasn't that the FBI's job?

An agent informed him of his right to remain silent.

'Jesus, Mary and Joseph,' Dilbeck hissed. 'Don't you know who I am?' He told them, repeating it vehemently as they put him in handcuffs.

The FBI men remained polite, firm and unflappable, even when Dilbeck addressed them as junior Nazi brown-shirts.

'Sir, is this yours?' One of the agents had come upon the black cowboy hat. He propped it on Dilbeck's head.

'That's backward,' the congressman groused.

'Naw,' said the agent. 'It looks good. Who are you s'posed to be – George Strait? Dwight Yoakam?'

'Nobody!' Dilbeck barked. 'For God's sake!'

The FBI men bandaged his bleeding wound, gave him four aspirins for the pain and locked him in one of the sedans. Squinting out the window, Dilbeck was engulfed in bewilderment. The gathering commotion revealed more FBI agents, his driver Pierre, a dark-haired woman, a small girl in pajamas being hoisted on the shoulders of an enormous bald Cro-Magnon. At one point a gruff-looking Cuban lowered his face to the glass and grinned, blue smoke seeping from between his teeth.

It's a goddamn circus! the congressman thought.

He ached for a telephone so he could call Moldy. Straighten out this whole damn mess.

Al García kissed his wife and said, 'Fancy meeting you here.'

'They came for Angie,' Donna explained. 'I wouldn't let them take her alone – Al, what's going on?'

García knew that his wife had busted the agents' balls, phoning downtown to verify the IDs. Boy, they hated that. He asked Donna about Andy and Lynne.

'They're at your mother's, and don't change the subject. Tell me what's happening out here.'

'Chaos, near as I can tell.' García introduced his wife to Shad, who'd been galloping through the cane rows with Angela whooping on his shoulders.

'Where's Momma?' the girl wanted to know.

'She'll be here soon,' García said, hoping it was true. The Feebs, as usual, were saying nothing. They eye-balled his sergeant's badge, the same as they'd eyeballed the shot-up Caprice, with minimal curiosity and zero tolerance.

Shad remarked on their snotty attitude. 'Why'd she call *them*?' He kept his voice low. 'The hell they got that you don't?'

'Jurisdiction,' García said. His feelings weren't hurt too badly; by calling the FBI, Erin had saved him a ton of paperwork.

Shad lowered Angie to the ground so that she could retrieve her dolls. He strolled to one of the gray sedans and scrutinized the face at the window: a disheveled old lech in a backward rodeo hat. David Dilbeck wore the agitated look of a stray dog being hauled to the pound.

'Pervie,' Shad muttered. He remembered the asshole from that night at Orly's club.

'Have some respect.' It was García, standing next to him. 'The man is a United States congressman!'

'Un-fucking-believable,' said Shad. Maybe it was time to get a voter's card.

They stood together in the sugarcane. Agent Cleary wrapped Erin in his suit jacket. He looked anxious and a little embarrassed. It rattled him, seeing her this way.

'Where's Angie?' Erin asked. 'Didn't you bring her?'

Cleary nodded, wiped the condensation from the lenses of his eye-glasses. 'I'm not sure why. I'm not sure what we've got here.'

'A kidnapping, more or less.' Erin gave an abridged account of the evening. She was tempted to tell all she knew about the congressman, starting with the Eager Beaver, but there was no point. Cleary was a linear thinker, not a dreamy conspiracist. He wanted overt acts and provable crimes.

In a tight voice he said, 'So you're a dancer.'

'Until tonight,' said Erin. 'Lawyers are expensive, Tom. I told you before, Darrell was running me in circles. By the way, he's out here somewhere' – sweeping an arm toward the fields – 'my darling ex-husband.'

At the mention of Darrell Grant, the agent's expression darkened. Erin knew that Cleary felt rotten about not helping with the Darrell problem on the night she'd come to his house. Rules were rules. Now here they were, out in the sugar fields.

Cleary said, blankly, 'Seems you've had quite a time.'

His well-ordered brain was downshifting, trying to find traction in the mayhem. He struggled briefly with the image of his wholesome ex-secretary dancing naked on tables. Then out came the notebook, and the questions: Did Mr Dilbeck rape you? 'No.' Did he assault you? 'Yes.' Did he attempt penetration? 'Sort of.' Did he have a weapon? 'Yep.' Did he threaten you? 'Definitely.' Did he expose himself? 'Tried.'

The agent scribbled and ruminated simultaneously. 'I'm still not entirely comfortable with our authority here.' Scribble, scribble. 'He didn't take you across the state line, so technically we've got a gray area.' More scribbling. 'On the other hand, he did use a weapon so that's a possibility.'

Erin impatiently snatched the ballpoint pen. 'Tom, the man is a congressman. That's your damn jurisdiction.'

'Yes,' said Cleary. No getting around it.

'You look pale,' she said, 'or maybe it's the moonlight.'

The pallor was genuine. Tom Cleary had become nauseated, anticipating the fallout – the daily inquiries from Justice, the not-so-subtle pressure for investigatory details, the maddeningly accurate media leaks. It was a field agent's nightmare, a sex case against a prominent politician. Cleary envisioned paperwork as high as the Washington Monument, and the turning point of a once-promising career. 'I need the whole story,' he told Erin dourly, 'if you expect us to prosecute.'

Laughing, she touched his arm. 'Tom, I definitely don't expect you to prosecute.'

'Then what?' Anger came to his voice. 'This isn't a lark, Erin. We're talking about a member of the House of Representatives.'

'The sleazy old shit tried to boink me.'

When Cleary closed the notebook, Erin returned the pen. She said, 'The man is sick.'

'You want your name all over the newspapers?'

'Not particularly,' she conceded. Not before the final custody hearing.

'Then we're stuck, aren't we?'

She told him to quit thinking like an FBI man, think like a guy who's running for office. Cleary puffed his cheeks and pretended to gag.

Erin said, 'You don't have to arrest him, Tom. Just explain the facts of life.'

They talked for a few minutes, then started back toward the cars. 'I've still got loads of questions,' Cleary complained.

'There's a guy you need to talk to. A detective.' She took the agent's hand, leading him between the cane rows. 'Hasn't Angie gotten tall?'

'She's beautiful,' Cleary said. 'Has her mom's pretty green eyes.' Moments later, quietly: 'Did the bastard hurt you?'

'No, Tom, I'm fine.'

The roadside scene was like a drug raid: the sweep of lights, the bustle of armed men, the broken gargle of police radios. Cleary had pulled out all the stops. Erin was touched, and told him so. She didn't recognize the other agents, but made a point of thanking each one. They were unfailingly courteous, and tried not to be obvious when peeking at her breasts beneath the loose-fitting jacket.

When Angela spotted Erin, she thrust her dolls at Shad and ran, darting through the legs of the FBI men. Erin scooped her up, tweaked her chin and kissed the top of her nose. Angela, giggling, did the same to her mother.

Sgt Al García watched, a relaxed spectator on the hood of the Caprice. He was out of cigars so he'd resorted to bubble gum. Donna was retrieving two beers from the mini-bar in David Dilbeck's limousine. Erin walked up, bouncing Angela in her arms. The detective said she certainly had a flair for the dramatic.

'Now don't be mad,' Erin said.

'Who the hell's mad?'

'Al, I didn't want to get you in trouble. Shad, either.'

'Whatever,' García said, chiding. 'I'm just grateful for the invitation. This is more fun than Wrestlemania.' He pointed at the doughy figure hunched in the government sedan. 'So that's your guy. Congressman Romeo.'

Dilbeck rapped his cuffed wrists against the glass, beckoning Erin. She waved airily over one shoulder.

'Will you speak to Agent Cleary?' she asked García.

'A genuine FBI man! I would be greatly honored.' García offered Angela a stick of grape-flavored gum.

Erin said, 'I think there's a way to pull this off.'

'I think you're absolutely right.'

Shad lumbered to the car, holding the Barbie dolls like two sticks of dynamite. 'You owe me,' he said to Erin, who couldn't help but laugh.

He took her aside and told her about finding

Malcolm Moldowsky dead in the fishbox. Erin was stunned. In a whisper she recounted Darrell Grant's mad narco-escapade. Shad generously offered to hunt him down and beat him into puppy chow. Erin said no thanks, she and Angie were out of danger for now.

'We're taking a vacation, starting tonight.'

'You deserve it,' Shad said, thinking how much he would miss her.

David Lane Dilbeck, believing himself a master of supple oratory, assumed that he could talk his way out of the trouble. To bolster his credibility, he audaciously scoffed at the suggestion that he call a lawyer. So the FBI agents perched him on the bumper of the car and gathered in a tribal semicircle to listen. Cleary allowed Al García to join them.

The detective was tickled by the spectacle – the moon, the crickets, the rustling cane fields. 'All we need is a campfire,' he whispered to Cleary, 'and some marshmallows.'

Dilbeck told quite a story. The agents took notes by penlight. García pitied their secretaries.

When the congressman was finished, Cleary said: 'Let's get this straight: You are the victim here, not the perpetrator.'

'Absolutely, yes, abducted at gunpoint.'

'Hmmm,' Cleary said. Al García thought the moment called for a stronger response, something along the lines of hooting and derision.

David Dilbeck said, 'She's been after me for weeks.'

'So you're alone on the yacht,' said Cleary, 'working

on a campaign speech, when all of a sudden this crazed woman breaks in and attempts to seduce you.'

'Forcefully,' Dilbeck added, 'and when I rebuffed her, she became enraged.'

'And for this attempted seduction she wore a nine-dollar cotton bra from Kmart?'

'No, she wore red. Lace cups. P-p-paisley G-string! Later she changed all into white, when we were in the car.'

Agent Cleary realigned his glasses. 'So we're to believe that Ms Grant kidnapped you for sexual purposes. Is that a fair summary?'

'She was infatuated,' said the congressman. 'Certainly you've heard of such sad cases.'

García piped in: 'Politicians have groupies, too? I thought it was just rock stars and homicide cops.'

Cleary, keeping order: 'Mr Dilbeck, explain the injury to your chest.'

'She bit me,' he said, 'like a wild animal!'

The agent asked Dilbeck who might verify that he was being stalked by a nude dancer. 'One person,' he replied. 'His name is Malcolm J. Moldowsky. He'll confirm every detail.'

'Unlikely,' said García.

'What do you mean?' the congressman bleated.

García turned to Cleary. 'May I tell him? Please?'

'Yeah, go ahead.'

'Tell me what?' Dilbeck demanded.

'Your friend Malcolm,' said the detective, 'he sleeps with the fishies.'

The congressman slumped sideways off the bumper. The agents dutifully rushed forward to pick him up out of the dirt.

Cleary sighed, frowning at Al García. 'Was that really necessary?'

The two men sat alone in the Caprice. García balanced a bottle of beer on one knee. He jangled the gold bracelet in the congressman's face.

'You lose this?'

Dilbeck turned away coldly. He said, 'I've changed my mind about contacting a lawyer.'

'Too late.' García popped his gum. It didn't taste too bad with Beck's dark. He coiled the bracelet in the palm of his hand. 'You're cooked,' he told Dilbeck.

'Now listen—'

'Just shut up,' suggested the detective, 'and try to comprehend what's happened here. The FBI gets an anonymous call about a kidnapping in progress. The alleged suspect is a US congressman. The alleged victim is a former employee of the Bureau. You with me?'

'Erin worked for them?'

'Ain't it a hoot. Anyhow, the agents arrive to find the suspect – that's you – stripped to his skivvies and armed with a machete. You're chasing the alleged victim across farmland belonging to Joaquin and Wilberto Rojo. Subsequent investigation will reveal that the weapon used in the assault also belongs to this prominent and influential family. Congressman, I want you to imagine all this on the front page of the *Miami Herald*.'

Dilbeck rocked sideways, tugging absently on his lower lip. Al García wondered if he was lapsing into autism.

'Now if I'm you,' the detective said, 'I'm trying to

guess how my version of the story is going to play with the Rojos and also the voting public – namely, that I was kidnapped by a nympho stripper. Remember there's no gun, no evidence, not a single witness to back you up. Even your driver says the lady is telling the truth.'

'Impossible,' Dilbeck said, thickly. 'He speaks no English.'

García smiled. 'Your driver is a modest guy. He's got a degree in hotel management from FIU. Didn't he tell you?'

The congressman stopped rocking. He wrapped both arms around his head, as if bracing for incoming mortars. 'There was another man on the yacht,' he said, a dry rasp. 'Durrell something.'

'You mean Mr Darrell Grant, currently a fugitive on several violent felonies.' García spoke from behind a fat purple bubble. 'I were you, I wouldn't count on a junkie for my alibi.'

'But what about this!' David Dilbeck slapped at his bandaged chest. 'I've been viciously attacked – any damn fool can see.' He clawed at the tape and gauze until the bloody crater was exposed. 'Look!' he said. 'My goddamn nipple is gone! I mean *gone*.'

Al García said, 'I hate to be negative, *chico*, but that's your basic defensive bite wound. Man's got a woman pinned, what else can she do?'

The congressman gathered up the mangled bandage and, half-wittedly, attempted to replace it.

'Prosecutors love bite wounds,' García elaborated. 'One time we had a victim chomp some guy's pecker half off. That's how we caught him, too – turned up in the ER at Jackson, said it was a freak gardening accident. Anyhow, we got forensics to match the punctures in the guy's schlong with the bite pattern of the victim's teeth. The jury was out maybe thirty seconds.'

Bereft, Dilbeck stared at his mutilation as if branded. 'What will happen now? The campaign and all.'

García said, 'It was up to me, I'd throw your fat ass in jail. Lucky for you, it ain't.' He took the empty beer bottle and slid from the car. Erin Grant got in. She crossed her legs and adjusted Agent Cleary's suit jacket to make sure her breasts weren't showing; she wanted Dilbeck undistracted.

'David,' she said, 'what a mess you're in.'

The congressman pulled back like a scalded snail, huddling against the opposite door. His voice cracked with reproach: 'You even called me "sweetie".'

'Maybe I call everyone "sweetie".'

He shouted: 'I don't love you any more!'

'Oh yes you do.'

After a few moments of silence, Dilbeck offered a squirmy apology for his coarse behavior. He inquired whether Erin intended to press charges.

'That's Plan B,' she said.

'And Plan A?'

'You go home tonight,' she told him, 'and have yourself a heart attack.'

The congressman sneered. 'That's not the slightest bit funny.'

'A mild one,' Erin proposed, 'requiring weeks of bed rest, bland dieting and seclusion.'

'In other words, tank the election.'

'Davey, I'm trying to cut you a break. Now if you'd prefer Plan B, that's fine. Have you ever been on "Hard Copy"?'

The last of Dilbeck's hope drained away. 'A heart attack, for God's sake. Is there more?'

'Sweetie, of course there's more.' Erin reached up and turned the congressman's cowboy hat, so it wasn't backward on his head.

Breakfast, predawn. A truckstop on old Route 441, jammed with semis, dump trucks, dairy tankers, pickups, flatbeds hauling farm equipment. The place smelled like a diesel fart.

Shad, Donna García and her detective husband sat three abreast in the front of the unmarked Caprice. Donna nursed a black coffee, Shad inhaled his seventh glazed donut and Al García attacked spicy pork sausages with the hope of scouring multiple layers of grape, beer and stale cigar from his palate.

'Disney World,' the detective mused, munching steadfastly.

'I think it's sweet,' said his wife, 'though I'm not sure about the driver.'

Shad said don't worry, the driver's cool.

Pierre was gassing up the limousine at the high-test pump. He felt the weight of the gold bracelet in the left pocket of his trousers; a gift for your wife, the cop had said. Very strange, Pierre thought. The whole evening.

Angela was curled asleep in the jump seat. Erin had changed into her jeans, T-shirt and sandals; her hair was tied in a ponytail. She stood at the door of the limo and chatted with Cleary, the FBI man, finishing his notes. He looked haggard, rumpled, eager to leave. It pleased García to see another lawman labor in that familiar hollow-eyed condition, particularly a Feeb.

Donna asked, 'Where are the others?'

'They escorted the congressman home,' her husband said. 'He wasn't feeling so great.'

Shad interrupted his donutfest to complain that Dilbeck was getting off easy. 'I vote for jail,' he said, 'or a bullet in the brain. That's what the sonofabitch deserves.'

García disagreed good-naturedly. 'For politicians, some fates are worse than death. Erin came up with a beaut, no?'

Donna said that Angela was excited about the Disney World trip. 'Her favorite ride is the teacups. She says it's fun to get dizzy.' Donna paused. 'On the way here, she asked about her father.'

García said that Darrell Grant remained at large in the cane. 'He'll come out when they burn the fields. Him and the rest of the critters.'

Shad, his cheeks stuffed bulbously: 'Any luck, he'll sleep through the goddamn fire.'

Donna told him to stop, don't take another bite. She lifted a half-crescent of donut from his hand. 'This is so gross,' she said. 'A darn bug!'

Shad snatched it away, flipped on the dome light and examined the find. His hopeful expression faded.

'It's awful damn small,' he observed, doubtfully. He extracted the culprit from a dry crumb of donut – a centipede with a shiny, cocoa-colored carapace. It drew into a protective ball at Shad's touch.

'Long shot,' García remarked. 'You'll need a jury of total suckers.'

'Yeah?' Shad placed the bug on the tip of his pinkie and held it near the light bulb.

'It was me,' said García, 'I'd wait for another jumbo cockroach.'

Donna, annoyed: 'What in the world are you talking about?'

'Dreams,' said Shad. 'Nothing important.' He flicked the centipede out the window and inserted the remainder of the donut in his glaze-crusted lips.

Agent Cleary had trundled his notes to a pay phone, where he was deeply absorbed in official conversation. Pierre backed the Cadillac away from the gas pumps. Erin Grant stuck her head out the window and gave a high-spirited wave. Shad and Donna waved back; Al García pantomimed operatic applause.

'Great smile,' he said, as the limo drove away.

'She looks sixteen,' said Shad, 'I swear.'

García eased the Caprice up to the gas pumps to top off the tank before the long drive home. He had one leg out the door when the car shuddered violently. He heard the tinkle of taillights breaking, and said, 'Aw, shit.'

A tractor-trailer had crunched the rear of the unmarked police car. The driver stood sheepishly over García's crimped bumper. Damage to the Caprice was minor, but the detective was not consoled: another lengthy accident report would be required, in triplicate. Witnesses interviewed. Tedious diagrams sketched. Polaroids snapped for the insurance company and Risk Management. Hours of useless department bullshit.

'Congratulations,' he told the trucker. 'You just hit a cop.'

'Sorry.' The man was a wiry redhead with twitchy Dexedrine eyes. 'I never saw you guys.'

'That was my guess, too,' García said. He popped

the trunk of the Caprice to search for the proper goddamn forms. Donna and Shad got out to see what had happened.

After circling the rig, Shad said, 'Hey, Al. Guess what.'

'What?' García was bent over, rummaging fiercely.

'My neck hurts,' said Shad.

Pad in hand, García slammed the trunk lid. He said, 'You don't *have* a fucking neck.'

The bouncer gave a crafty wink, nodded slightly toward the trailer. 'No kidding, man, I'm in serious pain.'

Donna stood on tiptoes to scout the injury. 'Show me where it hurts.'

'Everywhere,' Shad said, with a theatrical grimace.

Gingerly Donna rubbed the taut slopes between his skull and shoulders. She said, 'Come back to the car. You'd better sit down.'

'Yeah,' Shad agreed, 'I'm pretty damn traumatized.'

The worried truck driver excused himself, creeping off to improve his blood readings with black coffee. Al García walked back to the tractor-rig for a close look. Soon Donna heard him laughing, although she couldn't imagine why; hearty laughter that boomed raw and carefree. Other truckers began to stare, irritated by the disruption of their early morning routine. García sounded daffy and stoned.

Donna found him holding the trailer, his fingers hooked in the steel mesh. He was shaking hysterically. The bin was full of sugarcane. A blue-and-white sign bolted to the side said: ROJO FARMS.

Donna said, 'Now I get it.'

'Well, go ahead,' said her husband, wheezing. 'Call Mr Shad an ambulance.'

'Really, Al.'

'Sweet justice,' the detective said. He wiped his eyes, tried to compose himself, act like a grown-up. Then he felt the laughter rising again like a grand tide. It was one fine moment.

EPILOGUE

Three weeks before the election, DAVID LANE DILBECK was reported to have suffered a minor heart attack while reading in bed. Although missing the remainder of the campaign, he pulled fifty-two percent of the vote and easily won re-election to the House of Representatives. The following day, he stunned political supporters by resigning his seat, citing chronic health problems. The congressman's chiropractor, cardiologist and urologist issued an unusual joint statement endorsing his decision to retire.

Dilbeck's opponent, ELOY FLICKMAN, gave up politics and became a right-wing radio commentator in South Florida. Within months he was leading the daytime Arbitrons, touting himself as 'the weight-watcher's Rush Limbaugh.' One day after signing a contract with the Liberty Radio Network, Flickman was accidentally killed while picketing an abortion clinic during a live remote broadcast. The driver of the death car lost control when one of her seven children got his sneakers tangled in the steering wheel.

In January, the agricultural committee formerly chaired by Congressman Dilbeck approved a bill renewing multimillion-dollar subsidies for US sugar growers. The measure passed the House 271–150 after a brief floor debate. Speaking eloquently in its favor was REP. BO TOOLEY, the Republican from northern Alabama, who had never before sailed on a yacht as long or luxurious as the *Sweetheart Deal*, and was delighted that its short-wave radio picked up all his favorite Bible stations.

Shortly after its mysterious rat infestation, the FLESH FARM was shut down for multiple health-code violations. Two weeks later, the building burned to the ground. The LING brothers claimed that the blaze started when a dancer's trained snake became entwined in the electric wiring. Indicted later for insurance fraud, the Lings fled to western Canada and opened a chain of massage parlors with a hockey motif.

The remains of DARRELL GRANT were identified from a single fingertip. Three days later, the SWEETHEART SUGAR CORPORATION discreetly notified wholesalers that it was recalling all granulated sugar milled between October 6th and October 9th, due to 'possible rodent contamination during processing'.

After interviewing PAUL GUBER and other clients, the Florida Bar issued a harsh public reprimand of ATTORNEY JONATHAN PETER MORDECAI for 'gross ethical misconduct'. The effect of the discipline was minimal, since Mordecai was dead and no longer practicing law. Paul Guber quit his brokerage firm and entered rabbinical college in Chicago. He never spoke of his brief engagement to the late JOYCE MIZNER, or of his ill-fated bachelor party at the EAGER BEAVER lounge.

ERB CRANDALL did not return to Florida. Instead he settled in Atlantic City, accepting a job as the top political aide to a popular but recklessly overextended city councilman. The following summer, after collecting a large cash bribe on behalf of his boss, Crandall was accosted by three muggers demanding the paper bag he was carrying. His dead body – the shredded sack clutched loyally in one fist – was found by German tourists beneath the legendary boardwalk. The city council promptly named a street in Crandall's memory.

The group of orthopedic surgeons who owned the TICKLED PINK sold the nightclub to a group of dentists, who chose a saucy new name (Bare Essentials II) and bold new management (Johnny 'Three Toes' Spladiano). Mr Spladiano's first three business decisions were to fire ORLY, add valet parking, and enlarge the wrestling pit. Considering himself more fortunate than his predecessor, Orly closed out a modest IRA account and moved to Pensacola, where he and his wife opened a topless oyster bar called Eat Me Raw.

URBANA SPRAWL continued to dance at Bare Essentials II until the day Mr Spladiano replaced creamed corn with sardines in the wrestling arena. She is now pre-med at Emory University in Atlanta. SABRINA left dancing and worked briefly in adult films before landing the role of Lucette, the perky Parisian spokesmodel for Thigh Diver exercise equipment. The two Moniques also retired from nude dancing, each marrying one of her customers. MONIQUE JR, whose real name was Loretta Brickman, wed a seventy-four-year-old wholesale diamond broker who had outlived three previous wives. MONIQUE SR, whose actual name was Frances Cabrera, married a middle-aged pottery instructor who was, in her adoring eyes, a dead ringer for Keith Richards.

The man known as SHAD, whose real name was Gerard L. Shaddick, sued Rojo Farms, Rojo Trucking and the Sweetheart Sugar Corporation for injuries allegedly sustained when the loaded cane trailer rear-ended Sgt Al García's police car. In the lawsuit, Shad complained of neck pain, migraines, blurred vision, vertigo, sexual dysfunction and chronic anxiety. The case was settled out of court for $2.3 million. Shortly afterward, Shad purchased a split-level condominium in Telluride, Colorado, and became engaged to his physical therapist, a recent emigrant from Norway.

RITA GRANT also sued Rojo Farms, seeking $5 million compensation for the accidental mulching of her brother, Darrell. The lawsuit was swiftly abandoned when Rita was forced to flee Dade County with Lupa, her beloved wolf hybrid. Animal-control officers had ordered her to surrender the animal after it jumped a nine-foot wall at the Metrozoo and brought down a full-grown African springbok.

The murder of MALCOLM J. MOLDOWSKY remains unsolved. In the days following his death, news stories described the crime scene in gruesome detail, revealing that the murder weapon was a nine-iron made by MacGregor. A local columnist characterized Moldy as a ruthless and shady political fixer who had finally crossed the wrong person. Moldy's eulogist, Congressman Bo

Tooley, angrily denounced the story as a 'damnable lie' – a quote lovingly borrowed from Moldowsky's Watergate idol, John Mitchell. The funeral was brief and sparsely attended. From his sickbed, David Dilbeck sent profound regrets.

CHRISTOPHER ROJO was arrested during a late-night disturbance at the Kennedy compound in Palm Beach. Witnesses claimed that he attempted to demonstrate his oil-wrestling prowess upon Maria Shriver, Daryl Hannah and other female guests. Threatened with the loss of several trust funds, Christopher voluntarily entered a facility for treatment of drug and alcohol abuse. There he met his future wife, a copy editor at *Vanity Fair*.

The elder ROJOS remain prominent in Florida's sugar industry, while secretly optioning vast tracts of cane acreage for future development as condominiums and golf resorts. A few days before Congress voted new price supports for sugar growers, Wilberto and Joaquin Rojo announced the funding of two full scholarships at Georgia State University. The student recipients were KATHERINE and AUDREY KILLIAN, whose father had recently perished in a rafting accident in Montana.

PIERRE ST BAPTISTE resigned from Gold Coach Limousines to become catering manager of a new Sheraton in Key West. In the evenings he teaches English to the children of Haitian exiles.

A Broward County judge awarded ERIN GRANT permanent custody of her daughter, ANGELA. They moved to Orlando, where Erin took a night dancing job as Cinderella's eldest stepsister in Disney World's famous Main Street Parade. During the day she works as a data-entry specialist for the local office of the FBI. Her application to the academy at Quantico is currently under review.